I0612591

HYPERBOREA

⊶ SHATTERED SOUL ⊷

by

E.M. Zolotor

Zolotor Publishing

Text Copyright © 2024 by Ethan Zolotor.
Illustration Copyright © 2024 by Ethan Zolotor.
Published by Zolotor Publishing.

Paperback ISBN: 978-1-7338072-8-9
Hardack ISBN: 978-1-7338072-9-6

Written by E.M. Zolotor

Chapter Art (Title; 2; 16; 19; 20) by E.M. Zolotor

Cover Art and Chapter Art by Rodrigo Rizo 2023

Written and Illustrated by E.M. Zolotor

Cover Art by Rodrigo Rizo 2023

All rights reserved. No part of this publication may be reproduced, distributed or transmitted in any form or by any means, or stored in a database or retrieval system, without the prior written permission of the publisher.

Disclaimer: The material in this book is intended only for those aged 11 and older.

www.hyperboreabooks.com

CONTENTS

ALSO BY E.M. ZOLOTOR

Severed Legacy
Hyperborea Book One

Traitor's Path
Hyperborea Book Two

HYPERBOREA

— SHATTERED SOUL —

PROLOGUE

VISIONS AND POSSESSION

"They say that if you listen closely enough, you may hear the whispers of the gods." Amusement dripped from Vistomus Fulmen's tone.

Clouds of fog rolled over stacks of rocks. The hundreds of stone towers just inside the cave's mouth resembled a tiny city that Carnus Solaire half expected little spirits to poke their heads out of. The Heavenly Rock Cave was the kind of place where the air itself felt supernatural, and the reverence the locals held for the shrine could be smelled in the moisture.

An unamused hum was Carnus' response.

The voice of the tiny Japanese girl from town rang in his head. *The goddess of the sun, Amaterasu, sealed herself away in that cave. Be sure to make a wish when you stack your stones.*

PROLOGUE

As he began stepping with calculation through the maze of balanced rocks at his feet, he wondered if it was bad luck to kick them over. The reason for his visit wasn't some pilgrimage or sightseeing; there was a treasure to be found.

When no sound came from behind him except the running stream, Carnus paused. "You won't be joining me, Vistomus?"

"No," the powerful yet quiet voice returned. "There are circumstances that prevent me from entering."

Carnus nodded slowly, his shoulder-length brown hair brushing against his Mitad robes. The sun shone brightly behind him, but the cavern darkened past the wooden gate monument ahead. He ran his hand over his short, meticulously kept beard and then lit a Soul Sphere in his right hand. The burning indigo ball churned before him, illuminating the depths as he entered the sacred space.

Precise steps carried him past the countless mini stone shrines like stalagmites until he found the back of the main cavern. Flickering shadows cast in the blue light of his Soul Sphere revealed a large crack in the wall. He stepped forward to pass through it, finding the space more than adequate for his body.

On the other side of the aperture, he immediately felt the presence of Soul Energy different than his own. In the light of his sphere, a stream ran through this new room, and a small bamboo bridge lay before him.

He crossed it carefully, observing the chamber, as a nagging electric hum grew louder around him. He slid his hands along the ancient, polished railing.

What he sought would be found.

It had to be found.

After crossing the bridge, he came upon a stone door about half his height, lifted off the floor, and engraved with kanji and runes—clear markers from different time periods. Overgrown with moss, ten rays splayed out from a deep impression of the sun. Carvings of crows encircled it.

Carnus put his fingers to the cold, damp stone of the cave and cleared off the archaic art. He found the rays were no simple markings—they were inlaid with manus stones.

VISIONS AND POSSESSION

Immediately he focused his Soul Energy, sensing deeper, observing.

He felt the complex network of manus stones vibrating in response to his touch, sensing the door's internal latches. The ancient cogs within the door began turning in response to his manipulations of the engraved sun's rays.

He focused harder.

Sparks of sapphire and flashes of red flared from the door.

Innerworkings tumbled methodically.

The tension behind the engravings heightened, followed by a faint click into place as he nearly seized up the internal lock. The security mechanism preceded the Order of Soul Wielders by more eras than could be imagined, and Carnus knew even the best inlumes would struggle with such a lock.

All ten of his fingers continued to adjust pressure on the mechanism. They reached out to touch each manus stone spoke of the sun. He lit them up with varying amounts of his soul energy, causing blue and red light to dance on the room's walls, reflecting off the stream behind him and turning the modest cavern into a living-stained glass.

Clunk-clunk.

Ice ran down his neck.

The lock seized.

Carnus breathed slowly, trying to keep his head, and reversed the pressure of energy he had just applied. The delicate system yielded with a final turning, just a breath shy from locking its contents away permanently.

The door split down the middle and opened.

Inside, a pedestal displayed a single item: a blood-colored spherical gem—alive with a smokey black substance within. An unusual substitute for the twinkle that Carnus expected from such a magnificent artifact. Behind it was a carving on the back wall of a leaf-like eye shape that formed a circle from its edges.

"The Left Eye of Izanagi," he whispered.

That's what the local legends called it. The sun goddess had supposedly been birthed from the tears of her father's eye. Now, this piece of Izanagi lay in his daughter's cave of legend.

PROLOGUE

Carnus found the Japanese fable mildly entertaining. Perhaps it was true. It didn't matter. He knew the relic by the name of its collection: *The Tools of Karnak*. The eye was one of a set…but this chamber held only a single artifact.

His battle-weathered hands crossed the boundary and plucked the Eye from its pedestal, but upon his skin coming into contact with the gem, a shock jolted his body.

Consciousness became fuzzy. Body felt light. Perceptions dulled. A sense of being sucked in at a roaring speed. Sucked into…something.

Carnus forced himself to focus, or else he was sure he would die. As he did, he became acutely aware of his lack of embodiment. He was a disincarnate spirit as a foreign world solidified around him like a hyperreal painting. Then, he knew. This was another time, years ago, during the Fifth Primane-Viator War. He was in a memory, and it was not his own.

A voice bellowed in a deep baritone, but the words were unintelligible at first. It took intense concentration for him to make out the words, "Victory against the Viator is assured. The last of their forces are surrounded; however, our conduct in victory will determine how long the peace will live."

As if someone else's knowledge became his own, shoved uncomfortably into his head, he knew it had been the Hariban, Anzolo Primane, who spoke.

"Agreed, Anzolo," said another voice that Carnus instantly recognized. "However, your kindness is weakness. If you want true peace, then you must crush the Viator rebellion with finality. If you leave survivors, they will remember their enemy."

Carnus was shocked to hear Vistomus in the midst of a Primane war council. The implications had his mind reeling.

Anzolo refused the idea, "Hatred and brutality are the opposite of what I was advocating. We must allow those who surrender to return to their families and countrymen—"

"This is no time for weakness, Hariban Anzolo," Vistomus interrupted. A fur coat added bulk and presence to his otherwise lean body as his bald head and cold eyes gleamed in the nebulous gray room.

VISIONS AND POSSESSION

"While I respect your sentiment, there must be no question of which nation is superior in this struggle. The Primane must crush them."

The war council erupted with cries of dissent on both sides. Slowly, the murmurs for a lenient resolution gained ground.

The argument escalated until Anzolo Primane bellowed decisively, "Enough! This is a Primane matter. While the reinforcements and weapons Vistomus Fulmen provides are appreciated in our defense against the Viator attack, this is a decision for the Primane. The choice is for the king and his council. Visotmus, your profiteering from our struggle will be unaffected by the method of its end. I call for this council to be closed to outsiders."

The air crackled as Vistomus Fulmen's eyes narrowed. He bowed his head and said calmly, "Of course. I respect the decision of the Primane. This is a matter of your national sovereignty. I merely advise where welcome. My forces will support whichever way you proceed." The Mitad leader smirked at one corner of his mouth as he turned to leave.

Rapid panic spread within Carnus. *If this vision was true…there was no record of the Mitad involvement in the Fifth Primane-Viator War. The idea directly contradicted their backing of the Viator in the sixth war that followed three years later.*

His head spun at the implications.

The dream-like vision shifted.

The room disintegrated into wisps of the past before the vapors reformed.

Vistomus Fulmen was there again, now outside the council room. Carnus had no sense of how much time had passed since the war meeting, but the moments playing out before him felt connected like strands of a web.

Carnus watched as the younger version of his master inhaled deeply, preparing. The ashen-toned man waited, a quiet, calculating predator in his youth. The mulberry-pigmented stone of the southern nations made up the castle walls of the alley.

Anzolo crossed the dead winter grass and made his way toward the stone path where Vistomus lingered.

PROLOGUE

When he recognized who was standing in the shadows of the castle walls, Anzolo stopped, taken aback. "Vistomus…what are you still doing here? The troops have moved out for their final attack. There's no reason to remain."

"You're winning hearts, that much I must admit."

"*Won*." Anzolo's eyes narrowed. "My plan has been accepted, and the other haribans are carrying out the orders. The surrendered will be returned to their homeland tomorrow after our victory. But I must say, your constant contradiction in this matter has done you no favors in my mind."

Vistomus stepped forward; one hazel eye flecked with amethyst caught the light. He sighed, "I'm building something so much bigger than your minuscule mind can comprehend. Your well-intentioned attempt at charity is in my way."

Anzolo gritted his teeth. "Who do you think you are? I'll see to it that you and your bandits are never hired in—"

"You misunderstand, Hariban," Vistomus cut in. "Believe me when I say that your intentions are noble. I truly respect what you're seeking…admire it, in fact. However, I cannot allow you to go any further."

"What do you mean, *allow*?" Anzolo growled.

"You're a good man, but there is no place for such a person at this time," Vistomus insinuated with a tilt of his head and a pitiful purse of his lips.

Vistomus snapped his fingers.

Hot white light pierced down from the clouds.

Static charge lifted the hairs on Anzolo's forearms, and a pale glow bounced from sweaty cheekbones like glass under moonlight.

The sound came after.

Anzolo never heard it.

A worming root of lightning pierced the sky above and descended, meeting the Primane hariban at his temple.

With the buckling of Anzolo's knees, the memory that played out before Carnus wavered into a surreal mirage and vanished.

VISIONS AND POSSESSION

Alone again, Carnus held the Left Eye of Izanagi in the secret chamber of the Heavenly Rock Cave.

Vessels pulsed and ached fiercely with the pressure in his head as he held up the hunk of gemstone. The artifact beckoned to him, and Soul Energy simmered wildly in his core. The mere aura of one of the Tools of Karnak should have bewildered him, but instead his mind lingered on the vision it had given him.

Carnus was more than familiar with the historical events that followed after the memory-illusion. It was widely known that the Battle of Tacita was a slaughter. The entire Hamirate legion, the bravest warrior clan of his people, had been wiped out. None of the men who surrendered went home. It was a massacre that the Viator nation held in its eternal memory, fueling their disdain for the Primane people. The tale was told to every Viator child, and it fueled Carnus' own angry teenage years as he rose to the rank of hariban in the Viator military.

Vistomus achieved what he desired, Carnus seethed, clutching the legendary sphere of scarlet with trembling fingers.

His fury grew as he left the sacred door, traversed back over the bamboo bridge, through the crevasse, stepped into the cavern of stone towers, and made for the mouth of the cave.

The chirping of bugs and splashing of waters greeted him in the falling dusk as he crossed the threshold of the wooden monument. The delicate sounds of nature held an ominous calm that clashed with the burning inside him.

The waning sunlight revealed Vistomus on the other side of the shallow stream where they had parted ways, meditating under an overhanging rock formation.

Soul Energy platforms of the deepest indigo formed beneath Carnus' slow steps. He crossed the trickling body of water cautiously, contemplating how to approach his master after such disturbing revelations.

The bald man's eyes were closed, his garments hanging loose about his still frame.

One eye lazily cracked open.

"You succeeded?"

PROLOGUE

Carnus only nodded and held up the stone treasure.

Vistomus did not react to the appearance of the long-sought item from the collection of the Tools of Karnak. Instead, his single eye looked it over. "Well, what is it? I sensed your perturbed energy the moment you left the cave." His voice was mild yet held the undercurrent of a threat.

Carnus hesitated. "When I first touched Izanagi's Eye…I saw something…"

"What did you see that could shake you so, Carnus?"

"A memory."

"From the wars?"

"Not my war. Not my memory," Carnus admitted warily.

Both of Vistomus' eyes snapped open at that.

His pupils dilated.

"It was a vision from the Great Soul then?"

"From the Eye," Carnus said. He didn't believe in such things. He wasn't sure Vistomus did either. And yet… "It showed me something from the Fifth Primane-Viator War."

Vistomus waited for him to continue.

The ground beneath them began to tremble. Pebbles vibrated. The sensation meant violence from Carnus.

The apprentice continued, "Do you know how the Primane voted on the matter of the Battle of Tacita?"

"I've read that they were unanimous in their choice to exterminate the Hamirate clan," Vistomus said steadily.

"That's what is written…because someone wanted the history to say that. I know differently now. I saw Anzolo Primane won the appeal for a peaceful resolution."

The rumbling within the earth intensified.

Vistomus rose to his feet. "An intimidating display of your wielding, but I taught you to do that. I don't know why the Eye chose to show you things it should not, but the matter is too personal to you. You must understand the larger picture—"

VISIONS AND POSSESSION

"My original master's teacher, the last leader of the Hamirate, died that day." Carnus cut in with disdain that rained spittle as he leaned forward. "All the Hamirate died that day!"

"Not all. Your master and a few strays lived on."

"You caused that massacre! Of *my people!*"

"Yes." There was no pleasure nor remorse in Vistomus' simple reply.

Hate spread like kindling in Carnus' chest, building heat in his skull.

Indigo energy exploded from the overhanging rock, causing a slab to shear off above Vistomus. The disciplined master never looked up at the noise. His facial muscles didn't acknowledge the attack with even the slightest expression. He only lunged away from the falling rock with a shimmer of white Soul Energy at his feet, letting it smash to the ground where he had stood.

Vistomus' perception of Soul Energy was unrivaled, and Carnus cursed his master's innate gift at this moment. He thrust forward through the air with a rigid hand clenched like a claw, commanding his power through the solid rock. The energy burst forth from the ground, a mixture of deep blue light and stone.

Vistomus' white Soul Energy formed a protective barrier, shielding him from the collision.

Carnus stepped forward again and thrust out his other hand.

Another mass of glowing rocks attacked at Vistomus' feet, but he blocked it with a shimmering, colorless veil.

Huffing, Carnus calculated his next move as he caught his breath.

"My pupil, your ability to pass your Soul Energy through solid matter is a deadly force to face; however, you will need more conviction to put a single scratch on me."

"Then I'll show you my conviction," Carnus growled.

"You must see that slaying the Hamirate served two purposes." Vistomus continued, "Zeri the Great had come upon knowledge that could have stopped the Mitad from being born. I also required the Primane to win in that way for political reasons beyond your understanding—"

PROLOGUE

"I understand all I need to. You've lied to me. Laughed at me for the fool I was. All the while using me…for what? This?" Carnus held up the Eye of Izanagi.

"For the greater good of both worlds," Vistomus hummed, self-satisfied. "When the Viator were losing territory with you as high hariban, when the Order of Soul Wielders declined to intervene for your cause like a bureaucratic husk of their oath, *who came to your aid?*"

"You did, Vistomus," Carnus admitted, begrudging the reminder. "The Mitad offered us salvation. But now I'm left to wonder your true motivations."

"Carnus, the—"

"*No.* I will resign myself to wondering rather than entertain your lies!" Carnus' dark brown hair dripped with sweat as his nose crinkled. The ground tremored once more in response to his declaration.

A bolt of white lightning struck between the two, crackling with miniature forks and tongues of blinding electricity.

Vistomus warned, "This is your final chance to back down, Carnus."

"The way of the Hamirate doesn't allow for that."

"You left the true ways of your clan behind long ago."

The screech of a bird somewhere far overhead marked the beat of tension before the breaking.

"Never have. Never will," Carnus ground out.

Static filled the air and prickled skin.

The earth trembled deeply in response.

The forces of nature were caught under the spell of two great wielders.

Carnus struck first, sweeping his right foot forward; a javelin of indigo Soul Energy struck at Vistomus from behind, echoing the wielder's quick motion.

Vistomus quickly danced away, but the attack forced him into a roll to keep enough distance.

Crackle.

Before Carnus could manifest his next attack, Vistomus summoned more Soul Energy all around him. It wasn't the typical power of any wielder Carnus had ever met, but rather something external mixed with

VISIONS AND POSSESSION

Vistomus' aura—different from the way others wielded. Carnus had never understood that feeling.

Lightning cracked, descending from the sky, a rippling force that split the heavens and the earth.

Carnus dashed away, nearly losing his footing.

The strike had been a warning; the next one would surely bring his end.

The static sensation became palatable again, as if it lingered in Carnus' breath. Fear mixed with his venomous anger as he tensed for the onslaught.

A barrage of blinding bolts rained down, but with each branch of electric energy that struck the earth, the white light did not dissipate. Instead, a ring of Vistomus' Soul Energy formed rippling vines of lightning all around Carnus.

The apprentice was surrounded.

"Your talent is too great to waste on a premature death. That's why I chose you," Vistomus chided.

"You chose to assist the Viator for my wielding?" Carnus panted.

Zmmmm. Zmmmm.

The cage of lightning threatened to whip out at him with its wild, uncontrolled movements.

"Not just your wielding, but it certainly did catch my attention."

The lies. The manipulation. Years! The charade had gone on for years! Carnus grappled with the depth of the betrayal...the foundationally false pretense on which he had accepted his second wielding master...the thought of his ancestral clan being murdered by the actions of this man...every single member needlessly wiped away.

Newfound hatred scorched through his very core.

Carnus screamed through the popping symphony encircling him, "You forget you gave me Saida's mark!" Black ink crawled up his skin, spreading immediately to his neck. "That was your undoing, Vistomus! No one I've ever met could match your skill, but with the Mitad's Mark of the Chosen, I will best you!"

There was no reason to hold back.

PROLOGUE

A wave of indigo pulsed from Carnus in every direction, evaporating the cage of crackling light into wisps of soul, floating freely.

Hatred fully consumed Carnus as the inky mark began to spread across every inch of clear skin. Spikes of his indigo power, marred with black, projected from the ground.

The new barrage targeted Vistomus.

But the arrogant master remained still.

The Mark of the Chosen clawed up Carnus' face as he gave himself up to the waves of dark, manifested rage. The raw, wild power was untamed. Unearned. It fueled his shaking limbs.

A crushing wave of light crashed against Vistomus.

Pulverized earth rained from the air in the aftermath of the assault.

Carnus' body went rigid as his joints locked. The Mark darkened the veins around his eye sockets like a poison.

"I gave you the Mark of the Chosen," Vistomus said lightly, shrugging off everything Carnus had summoned against him. "It has been *your* undoing. It is no petty tool for revenge. Your emotions have opened you to its possession—*it has become your master rather than your tool.*"

The shadowy essence that stained Carnus' skin began to recede.

But it was not fully gone.

Instead, the cursed mark filled his eyes, turning them shades of darkest night. Dead, hollow eyes of pure black stared vacantly into the world.

"You have been consumed, and now you are mine," Vistomus said with a knowing smirk.

Then, the darkness drained back, like a diluted ink washing away.

When Carnus' irises returned, there was no light behind their tawny color. His dull stare was that of one imprisoned in his own body.

CHAPTER ONE

BLACK ELSU PATH

A mosaic of colors broke into the private study through stained glass, but Eos sat outside the reach of the early evening light.

In the month without his sister, the world had become a dull fog. The porcelain elsu statues appeared less grand, the shelves of precious books were uninteresting, what food he could swallow tasted like ash, and the pace of his day was a tedious struggle.

Even his induction as a member of the Order of Soul Wielders held less thrill than he had once hoped. He had lit the Record of the Order, placed his Soul Energy into the artifact, and become an anatus—an apprentice under the Inlume Aizo. It had been everything he had ever dreamed of. However, since that moment, he had not felt the urge to wield again. The spark of the momentous occasion could not overcome the grief and guilt he carried: his sister was gone, his father lost his arm, Jezca was missing—and he hadn't been strong enough to stop any of it.

CHAPTER ONE

Talus walked the castle halls with a different gate now, adjusting not only to the missing weight of his arm, but also to the missing weight of his daughter. The man was forever changed, and Eos wished he could go back in time and undo even just a moment of that fateful day…even if he was only able to give his father one more day with a whole body. One more hug with both arms. It was a dream that would never come true again.

And the dreams.

It was bad enough that his waking life was haunted by heartbreak and regret, but alone in the night, Eos' dreams were unbearable.

Sometimes they weren't even his own—

"I find you here yet again," Durath said from behind Eos. "Almost ready for dinner?"

Eos stirred, broken from his dark reverie.

The King's Son of Corleo had become something of a friend over the past weeks. While his parents and the inlumes gave Eos time and space to mourn Maxima, Durath met with him daily.

"I dreamed it again last night, Durath. It's becoming more frequent."

"About the priestess girl my father visited? Jezca?"

Eos nodded, his eyes lost in deep thought. He murmured more to himself than Durath, "Sometimes memories. Ones I saw in the Manus Temple when it first happened. Mostly repeats, but the new ones…they feel *present*. Like they're happening now, and she's in trouble. Worst of all, I can't decipher if the memories are mine until after I wake. Like I've lost my identity while the sequences play out."

Durath placed his massive hand on the table, distorting the stained-glass light. The myriad of colors cast over his fur cape.

"And you want to help this girl?"

"More than anything, but I have no clue as to where she is. If I must suffer these dreams, I wish they'd at least be useful and show me where to look."

"You know," Durath sighed, "I came to tell you that I asked Talus to include me on your coming expedition to this place called Earth. However, this conversation makes me think that you don't really want to go."

BLACK ELSU PATH

"I would gladly have you on the journey. But what I wish for and what must be done are different things. If I could, I'd hunt down my half-brother, avenge my sister by taking his head," Eos grit his teeth and squeezed the arms of his chair with crushing force, "then track down Jezca and rescue her from whatever it is that haunts these dreams…but I have a duty to follow the man who raised me back to Earth. Once Glenn fully recovers, we must investigate what Vistomus has done there. It's like I'm being pulled back to where I was raised by some unseen string."

"Pulled there?"

"Yes. Ever since Jezca and I connected, I've been…sensing possible paths." The woven paths he could take would lay themselves out in his mind. Cloudy. Imperfect. Still, he found every future led to one place. "It is inevitable I go to Earth. That much I know. Every other path would be a mistake."

"Eos, you should tell an inlume about these things. Maybe they could—"

"No. You know better, Durath. Propose that again, and I'll stop sharing these things with you." Eos paused for a breath, holding up his curse-marked hand against the glass tiles. "And that would be a shame. We haven't known each other long, but I'm sure I can trust you. Having no one to share these torments with would make it much worse."

Durath collapsed into the chair across from Eos. His scarred body filled the leather, and his dark hair swept back into a mane appropriate for his house sigil, the corcinth. The young warrior reminded Eos a great deal of the lion-like creatures.

The orphaned son of Ramath Leorix stroked his chin as he said, "When you pulled me out of that metus stone cage, *that hell*, I sensed you were different…and that I owed you my life. I would have died if I was in there much longer."

"It was Maxima's technique that saved you."

"Yet it was you who performed the Blood Ascension for the first time in many eras. Then, I watched those dark elsu you summoned assault Saida, and I knew I must follow you."

CHAPTER ONE

"I understand, but that darkness was not mine. It was this curse," Eos said, holding his arm out for examination.

"So, you've said…" Durath watched Eos carefully, choosing his next words thoughtfully. "There is a myth the Corleo people have…during the foundation of our kingdom, a darkness came over the Corleo plains. King Breuni Corleo, our founder, could not find a remedy."

"A darkness?" Eos echoed.

"The true meaning is lost to history. Could be disease or a scourge of some creature. I believe it was some kind of enemy tribe. We don't know. What is written is that a black elsu led Breuni deep into the mountains, to the king of the corcinth pride…a noble beast more ethereal than physical. They say this corcinth, named Maah, can walk both our world and the realm of the soul. Together, Maah and Breuni rid the darkness from the land and established the Corleo empire."

Eos contemplated the story for a while.

The comforting smell of parchment and cedar was always present in Talus' study, which is why Eos spent so much time there. Durath's story felt all the more grand in this setting, like it belonged bound in one of the rich leather volumes on the shelf.

"You believe I'm like this elsu that led Breuni?"

"Not exactly, but I believe the meaning in true myths can often be applied in our lives. I'm the heir of Corleo, and I've found my black elsu. It's not the bird's color, but the fact that it's set apart."

Eos hesitated to reveal the next details but decided Durath should know. "There is something else I haven't told you. I worried you'd read too much into it."

"Go on."

"When I was beside you in the metus stone cage, I entered my Soul Void. I faced a test there. One I was certain to lose, but I was visited by a…a spirit walker…a corcinth."

The heir of Corleo leaned forward and nearly fell from his chair. "Maah visited you? The king of the corcinths came to your aid?"

"Yes, but not of his own will. He had information for me. Your father asked him to visit and teach me something."

"My father *sent* Maah? Impossible," Durath sputtered, but as the words left his mouth, he knew the impossible must be true. "He never spoke to me of this ability or relationship to Maah."

Eos smirked, understanding what Ramath did not. "I've thought about it a lot these last few weeks. Now it connects. It was his inheritance. Now it is yours. I don't know how you learn to speak with this corcinth in the Soul Realm, but I believe your lineage may be able to. Perhaps, he'll come to you in time."

Holding his head in his hands, Durath stroked his dark brown hair back and stood.

"Eos, I have something in mind. I wasn't going to suggest it at first, as I know you must go to Earth once your friend recovers...but this conversation has convinced me. We must go back."

"Back?"

"To the site where the factories were destroyed. I've been thinking about it, and I want to recover some metus stone for studying if we can find any. You might be able to look for clues about Jezca. Maybe it will trigger some new kind of dream or show you some path in these visions you have."

Eos' golden eyes were afire at the idea.

Durath knew he had won Eos over, but there were formalities of protest they had to move through first.

"Talus would never allow it."

Durath chuckled deeply. "No. I suppose not."

"I saw you fight. There's nothing we shouldn't be able to handle together," Eos said, easing into the idea.

"Right. And the Mitad likely have no interest in a ruined manufacturing site that has been publicly exposed. It should be abandoned."

A cantium tablet lay at the edge of the table between them, the smoldering light of Soul Energy faded from the stone.

The configured text for the current news cycle read all about the scandals that had plagued house Bellator over the last month:

CHAPTER ONE

Mitad Conflict in Mircite Mountain Range. Invasion of Anite Failed. Returned King's Son, Eos, Defeated Alongside Talus Bellator. King's Daughter Missing; Rumored Dead?

The reports lent weight to Durath's claims. Eos' brooding contemplations grew darker. He had been a lifeless husk the last month. Maybe it was time to finally act.

Eos decided. "Then we go, and ask for forgiveness upon our return."

∞   ∞   ∞

The worry of repercussions had been at the forefront of his mind during the two-day journey from West Avem, but now that they were staring down the massive cliff face at the rubble of Mitad factories, nausea and anger replaced Eos' emotions.

He tasted bile as they approached the edge of the mountain top. Their travel had been nearly restless, leaving Eos' legs aching, but now he forgot that weariness.

Down there. That's where Maxima had drawn her last breath.

Plunged into a river.

Never to resurface.

"I know coming here isn't easy, Eos—" Durath began.

"No. I need to face it."

The reality set in on him in a new way. There was finality.

They let the mountain air whip at their faces for half an hour, observing with a cathartic numbness. They had agreed that scouting the area was the best plan. On first look, the site was abandoned to whatever ghosts remained.

Eos stared at the piles of rubble far below that were used to make weapons against him. Bullets for Anite. Metus stone to negate wielders. Their culmination was a wasteland of toxic water and debris.

They circled the edge of the area from the mountain top to root out any lingering Mitad members, but they found only the sound of the churning river and the croak of stone-frogs.

Durath's commanding stride befitted that of the mountain-man with a corinth sigil. There was little stealth to his movements, but the undefeated tournament warrior who had slain Mitad mirza and knocked down Saida had no need for it.

But trauma barraged Eos.

His time in the metus cage, his battle against Zala Alsar, Ares piercing Maxima, Talus losing his arm, Caldus falling to Yann Kilsig, and Jezca disappearing.

Too much had happened here. So many failures that he now had to face—haunting encounters with mental spirits.

Eventually, they agreed the site was clear enough to descend to the factory remains for scavenging. Eos didn't remember getting down, but the next time he broke from his trance of processing events, he was atop the mounds of stone and metal that had collapsed into the river.

"I figure the cages were on top of the building. Your father's final attack probably destroyed almost everything. The collapsing weight probably left nothing but fragments…but if the Mitad wanted to clear out of here…which I figure they did with all the attention we caused, then there have to be some fragments," Durath grumbled aloud as he turned over stones and chucked them down the slope.

Bricks clattered, momentum carrying them to a final splash in the river.

Eos had stopped turning over the pile. Every nerve in his body was on edge. Something was out there on the ridge. He was sure.

Scanning the horizon.

A monotony of gray stone, dew covered and unchanging.

A croaking symphony.

The oddly sweet blue lilac scent.

There!

A distant shuffling between rocks, high in the peaks.

Eos' eyesight became better than he had ever recalled it being. Even at this distance, he could see the face in the brief instant it looked down on him. The expression was cold and calculating.

"Ares!" Eos howled lowly.

A single crimson elsu manifested at his shoulder.

"Woah, woah," Durath slowed Eos with an open palm like he was calming a wild horse. "What do you think you're doing?"

CHAPTER ONE

"Look up there," Eos said and pointed.

Durath searched while holding Eos back.

"Now, let go of me," Eos' aggressively threatened.

"I don't see anything. Don't feel anything either."

"Ares is getting away! He was there! Between the sharp point and the collapsed wall," Eos pleaded, searching the same area he called out. The wings of his crimson elsu beat with the intent of attacking. However, there was nothing there now.

Durath turned and broke into Eos' space, coming close enough to feel his hot breath alternate against the icy bursts of wind.

"You're not in the right headspace. I don't see or sense anyone up there. It's just as likely that you're seeing what you want to see. I understand your pain—"

"No! He's there, and he needs to pay! You're giving him—"

Durath seized Eos by both shoulders. "I get it, Eos. I do. I want to see Saida out there for what he did to my father. I want to crush him in an idealized battle fantasy that I've dreamed up new variations of every night. But no one is up there. Certainly not Ares. And if he was, then the best thing we could do is flee before Mitad officers surround us."

Eos breathed heavy, heart-pounding exhales.

The heir of Corleo finished, "Now please, I can feel metus stone near us. Focus on that feeling from inside the cage."

The marbled energy above Eos' shoulder shot out at the location he'd sworn he saw Ares. Wings cut the air like molten razors, but Eos reigned in his temper and recalled the action. The elsu arced upside down and rounded back before fading away.

Durath was relieved. "Thank you. We don't need to make it known that we're here. Now let's finish this."

An hour later, they put on thick leather gloves and pulled out two short stubs of rod, the so-called *soul-negate* material. The sensation of their abilities weakening overwhelmed them, as their Observation Wielding dulled, their vigor faded.

They placed the horrible bars from the cage into a multi-layered silk bag within a thick, tan leather wrapping. The crushing feeling dampened the moment he drew the strings to tie it closed.

"Good job, boys. Ya come back to visit like g-g-good experiments. Drawn to my metus creation, I'd say."

They turned to see circular black glasses approaching on pale skin. Borne Ozen had been waiting. He continued, "I knew someone would c-c-come back. Been waiting for weeks. It was getting really boring 'round here."

Durath placed the bag of metus stones into Eos' hands. "Take these and keep them away from me. Make sure they get back to Anite no matter what."

Eos protested, "You think I'm going to let you take him on alone?"

Ozen let out a rattling chuckle and said, "Ready for a f-f-fight, it seems."

"Eos, the only wielding you've done in the past month was to travel here. You're out of fighting condition and in no mental state for this. Now, *keep that bag away from me.*"

Immediately, Eos knew he had been mistaken in neglecting his wielding over the last month of grief. A costly mistake.

"I'm not much of a f-f-fighter," Ozen stammered. His long black hair blew across his bleached face, "So tell me, before we battle…what was it like in the metus cage for that long? Were there any s-s-side effects? Long term. Permanent, I mean."

Green energy sparked to life around Durath and churned, taking a threatening shape. "You will pay dearly for putting me in that cage."

In response, a purple-black Soul Energy began bubbling out of the ground around Ozen. "Come now; you m-m-must have something to share. I need good data points."

"Data won't do you any good in a few minutes."

Eos backed away from the brewing fight.

The horns of a corcinth solidified mid-air before Durath, the color of emerald. The curled horns charged immediately for the Mitad scientist with a ferocity that had previously thrown Saida off his feet.

Borne Ozen was prepared. His energy frothed from the ground, limb-like and clambering. A mass of tentacle-looking arms whipped at the horns, seizing them mid-attack. Violet and emerald grappled between

CHAPTER ONE

the two fighters, humming with conflicting radiations. Fluorescent emissions of crackling air shot off the Soul Energies.

"Not a bad showing, Leorix b-b-boy. However, I want to know about your experience more than fight you," the Mirza said.

"Well, it's too late for that. Inside the cage was *hell*." Durath grunted as he fought to overwhelm Ozen's tentacles. "That's all you need to know before I send you there."

He punched forward both arms, and the horns snapped through the violet energy like brittle dry wheat in a field kicked over.

Ozen summoned all his manifested Soul Energy into one blockade. Into a glowing mass of twisting arms, oozing around Durath's attack, attempting to push it back.

"Well, hell is a start. But do you still f-f-feel its painful sensation linger? Even i-i-in its absence?"

"No, but you're about to!" Durath howled and sprinted forward at the mass of struggling Soul Energy. When he reached his own horns, he leaped.

With emerald glimmers at his feet, he bounded over the Soul Energies and hurled himself at Ozen.

He landed a mighty boot at the man's chest, crumpling his body.

His black hair splayed across the valley floor.

His circle glasses landed beside him, cracked.

Ozen coughed and gasped for air.

Durath stood atop him.

"Yes," the broken scientist wheezed, "I heard you were a brute in c-c-combat."

The boot heel dug deeper into Ozen.

But not for long.

The purple and black limbs constraining the horns multiplied.

New dark vines formed underneath Ozen and shot up.

They collided with Durath, who back peddled.

The Soul Energy lifted Ozen, attached to his back like a living cape, until he floated above them like some kind of underworld creature.

Limbs like toxic venom bubbled from him and emanated from the ground.

BLACK ELSU PATH

"F-f-fine. You won't give me information. But I'll t-t-take the last of the metus stone you found. Thought I c-c-collected it all." Ozen motioned with an open hand stretched out. Multiple projections of Soul Energy mimicked him as if to mock the two below his gaze.

Durath produced a new set of horns. Beneath them, the outline of a corcinth appeared, a visage in the trailing stream of emerald soul energy.

Eos thought he saw the corcinth snarl and bare its teeth, but the attack formed like an image seen in an hourglass as sand grains fell.

The particles of energy whirled and then charged.

His writhing arms of soul energy formed around Ozen in a cocoon of defense.

The scientist flew back as the corcinth strike landed.

Zmmmm.

The energies vibrated off each other and crackled through the ruins.

The corcinth form exploded and then faded, revealing Ozen as he emerged from the black shell of amorphous limbs.

Blood trickled from the corner of his lips. "Impressive b-b-brute. I think I'll take the metus stone and force the information out of you," Ozen slurred, beady eyes enraged.

Hundreds of arms bubbled out of the ground.

Ozen intended to end the conflict quickly.

The army of limbs rose up all around them as he hovered from on high.

Durath, unable to consider backing down from the middle of a fight, could only gather more emerald light, but the violet Soul Energy had emerged too fast at his feet.

He shifted, danced back clumsily, and dove into an evading roll.

Boom!

A crimson elsu broke into Ozen's periphery.

The burst of red launched him from his dark perch, but dozens of Soul Energy limbs reorganized and caught him.

The pale man rattled out a cough from his broken ribs. He stood again as his army of zombified energy refocused and jabbed for the two young men.

"I think that's enough," said a new fourth voice.

CHAPTER ONE

Eos and Durath turned their heads as they evaded to see a silver ponytail and sheathed short sword.

Scavok Alter stood with arms crossed and a bearded scowl. His yellow eyes cast his grumpy displeasure at all three on the battlefield.

The mass of purple energy receded into the ground.

Ozen shook his head and grunted, knowing he was outnumbered and vastly outmatched with Anite's master assassin joining the equation.

He fled, a trail of black-marbled violet surrounding him as he disappeared in a blur, back into the mountain cover.

"*Do not pursue. That's an order,*" Scavok said with steel in his command.

"But he—"

"I didn't ask. You two have the all the Soul Observational skills of a newborn pup. Your battle attracted crawlers. I sense more in the mountains to the south," Scavok pointed out sharply.

Eos muttered in confusion, "We checked the area when—"

"Apparently not very well. Now let's move."

Always calm, yet always irritable. Eos thought of Scavok like an old, scarred wolf, battle worn and weathered.

They followed him north, barely keeping pace with the masterful wielder's Soul Steps as he soared through cracks and over cliffs.

They had barely made it into the veil of the Sepeleo Mountains when Scavok came to an abrupt halt. He unsheathed his short sword. The winged hilt and anima blade beamed sunlight into the shadows. "We're not alone," his old voice murmured.

"No, you're not. I've been waiting for you to come out of that battle against the mirza," spoke a noble voice with no threat in it.

A balding man with dark eyes stepped into the mountain pass.

Scavok sheathed his blade and grumbled, "What in the name of the Great Soul is the Monte King's Whisper doing out here?"

"The Monte King's Whisper?" Eos breathed to Durath.

"Tavro Monte." Durath replied.

"Waiting. Observing. Hoping." Tavro nearly hummed his response to Scavok.

"For?"

"The same thing that I believe young master Eos was."

Scavok raised an eyebrow to Eos.

He replied to Scavok's expression honestly, "I was looking for evidence of what happened to Jezca."

"The priestess girl?" Scavok returned.

Tavro hummed again, "The future high priestess, Jezca Monte."

"And how did you know that's what he came for?"

Tavro laughed and replied, "How did you know where Eos and Durath had gone? We serve our kings with our talents. Mine is my network of information and intuition."

Jezca had written Tavro concerning the cracking of the Manus Temple's central chamber during her reading of Eos. It particularly struck Tavros, the way the future *tawas kajina* spoke of the Anite King's Son…and her mention of the memory exchange with the boy…

Scavok grunted, unsatisfied with the way this conversation was going.

Tavro continued, "Well, Eos, this is not the proper way I had hoped to greet you for the first time. However, time is short. The Mitad is moving everywhere."

"Technically they're right behind us," Scavok added, nearly rolling his eyes.

Tavro ignored the comment. "Did you find anything about the whereabouts of our priestess? My sources have only informed me that she went south with an arch-priest allied to the Mitad, but from there, the trail is cold. They could be in Corleo. They could be multiple kingdoms away, but regardless, I believe she went willingly."

Eos hesitated.

His mind stretched, reaching for the feeling of the dreams and the webs of possible paths and futures that sometimes came to him in nauseating visions.

Threads of white sand blew through the darkness of his thoughts.

Forming one string, then disintegrating into another.

There! He observed one life-line that held Jezca's aura.

It came with a wave of danger and panic, like in the shared memories he dreamed of, but the signal was always too short-lived.

And, like always, he could make nothing of it.

CHAPTER ONE

In his heart, he knew; his personal mission here had been fruitless. He discovered nothing new in his searching the valley rubble nor in his visions. His desire to find Jezca would have to wait as his destiny needed him back on Earth, and soon.

The vision he had lasted but a second, and Eos found himself quickly replying to Tavro's prompt, "No, we found nothing. But I have been having visions though...shared dreams," he offered.

"Oh?" Tavro insisted.

Scavok eyed Eos, as if reminding the King's Son that he should be more careful with such sensitive information.

Eos paid him no heed. If he couldn't stay here to help Jezca, at least someone else would, he hoped. "Since the time in the Eye of the Manus Gods...I've shared memories with her. We're connected. I can't see where she is, but she's in trouble. If she went willingly, then I don't think that's the case anymore."

Tavro bowed. "Thank you, King's Son. I'll continue the search, but if you learn more from these visions, please send a messenger elsu to me immediately. Lady Jezca has been a dear friend, and must be found at once. She's carrying half of the most important map on the Corland."

Scavok broke in, growing more irate by the second. "We shall send a message if we learn anything, but what is this half-map you speak of?"

"Knowledge is power, my friend. That is only for those who *preserve the knowledge*."

Scavok's brow wrinkled with concern when he realized that was all the Monte King's Whisper would say of the matter.

CHAPTER TWO

HASVELA'S CHOOSING

rey dresses and silk face-coverings glided around the Sanofem medical quarters as the healers moved from patient bed to patient bed like a hive organism. Soft lights from healing techniques would flare from behind curtains, tools and supplies would be carried in and out, and occasionally the quiet voices of the Sanofem would talk with their patients.

The senior healer on duty, Sirona, bowed to Eos and said from behind her half-veil, "King's Son, your companion Glenn has nearly made a full recovery and is almost ready to be awoken. As you already know, wounds inflicted by Soul Energy take a greater time to heal, but we believe he is nearly ready to be released; however, he will still need to prioritize his rest for a while longer."

Eos nodded and thanked the healer. He watched Glenn sleep peacefully. His strawberry-blonde beard had grown so long since Eos had seen him on Earth last, and his face was more haggard.

CHAPTER TWO

Whatever had happened, Eos was sure Vistomus Fulmen and the Mitad were at the root of it. He would know soon enough when Glenn finally awoke. The Sanofem had kept him in a state of induced unconsciousness ever since he had showed up, half-dead, on their doorstep a few weeks ago. They said it was best for the kind of healing the man would need. For the wounds he had endured.

While it pained Eos to come to terms with letting Jezca remain missing, he had warmed up to the idea of undermining whatever the Mitad had planned on Earth. That world had struggled enough to recover before the Mitad were added to the mixture. And it didn't matter which realm he did it on, defeating the Mitad in any capacity would bring Eos great pleasure. At least that was something he could throw himself into.

"Oh, Glenn," Eos whispered alone to himself. "If only Maxima could see you here. She probably would have had some healing technique she developed from an old book to try on you…I miss her. I bet you do, too."

A while later, he exited the medical building and passed through the archway carved with the emblem of a helix of Soul Energy around a chalice.

When he turned back to castle Alasedis' keep, Eos ran into his father's massive frame. Talus had been waiting outside for him.

"Are you so quick to relive the horrors of that day that you would return to Mircite without any plan or protection?" Talus bellowed, confronting his son for the first time since his return. "If I hadn't ordered Scavok to keep an eye on you, you'd likely be dead."

Eos' stomach sank.

"Father, I was careful, and Durath was with me."

"Your mother could have lost *two* of her children!" Talus stopped Eos' justification. "You could have asked for a regiment of reinforcements to go with you."

"You wouldn't have let me."

"No, I suppose not, but I may have sent an envoy to search in your place," Talus said as he adjusted his robust crimson cape, pulling it further over the broad shoulder with a pinned up tunic sleeve, now missing its right arm.

Eos' chest tightened at the sight. "Father, I *needed* to go back. I had to confront what happened there for myself, and to look for clues about Jezca. We brought back metus stone, didn't we?" He snapped back, more volatile than he had meant to be.

Talus sighed wearily. "I concede that your recklessness wasn't entirely fruitless in the Mircite valley. But do not overlook the risks and consequences. There is nothing worth the dangers you're throwing yourself into…especially when precautions could have been taken. I worry. *Your mother worries.* This isn't the way to handle your grief, Son."

Eos glowered.

The King's Son spoke through gritted teeth, and the dagger shaped scar crinkled in the corner of his eye as he lashed out. "You have *no idea what I'm handling.* You don't have the dreams I have every night!" Eos sounded more confrontational than he intended. Yet, inside, his heart was breaking with grief.

Talus considered chastising the young man, even screaming to shake some sense into him, but instead, he did the only thing a father could.

The two shared the grief and loss.

He reached out with his left arm and hugged Eos.

"I know, Eos. I lost her, too. But please, promise me you'll never return there and that you'll think of how to approach things more carefully. You're not alone."

With hesitation, Eos embraced Talus and whispered with teary eyes, "I promise."

He couldn't tell his father that the dreams he had were also of Jezca.

The Visrex of Wings wouldn't understand. It would only increase his worry and add to the level of watchfulness over Eos.

For now, Eos determined it was his burden to carry.

Talus smiled down at his son mildly. There was hurt and worry behind his eyes. "If you ever hope to become an inlume someday, you must act and think like one before The Order recognizes you with the rank."

Eos nodded with reluctant understanding.

CHAPTER TWO

His father continued, "You must learn to put aside your selfish desires and grandiose dreams of satisfying victories. Instead, consider long-term outcomes and the cascade of effects they could have. An inlume wouldn't chase the immediate desires in front of them. They'd pursue the most meaningful action for the good of the Order."

The weight of making a bad decision sat heavy in Eos' chest. Then, after a moment of quiet, he said, "I'll do better. The trip to the valley made me realize that there's no path I can take to find Jezca. She's gone, and we won't be brought together until another time."

"The Great Soul willing," Talus replied. "Now, in the spirit of responsibility, I have a final family ritual to perform with you before your friend awakes, and we make final preparations for our journey to Earth."

Eos' eyes widened with excitement. "What's the ritual?"

"You'll see this evening, but we'll have to get moving if we're going to be ready in time."

Eos followed in the massive steps of his father as they made their way across the castle grounds back to Alasedis' keep. They passed white marble stone spires and grass that looked made of gold in the burning fog of sunrise.

As they walked, Eos ventured, "You just asked me not to take unnecessary risks, but don't you think going back to Earth is risky, too?"

"It's incredibly risky. However, it must be done. And you won't be going alone. You'll have me, Aizo, and Scavok at your side. I shall also send Durath. You two have developed quite the bond, and he needs a task to distract him from the loss of Ramath as well, lest he run off recklessly again."

"I know. Durath told me he asked you to join before we left for Mircite. I'd be glad to have him with us."

"Then it's settled," Talus replied. "He's one of the most talented wielders of your age. He'll be asset to this group. You both will be."

Nodding with gratitude for an assignment he was sure he did not deserve, Eos managed to whisper, "Thank you, Father."

"But make no mistake, this will be a reconnaissance mission *only*. We will observe the situation, determine if the plans the Mitad have for Earth might affect Hperborea, and then we shall return to Anite. There will be no fighting if we can avoid it, no starting conflict with the Mitad, and no risk-taking. Do I make myself clear?"

"Yes. We're only going to Earth to gather information about what happened there," Eos replied quietly, trying to quell his thirst for vengeance in favor of the responsibility his father charged him with.

∞   ∞   ∞

They proceeded into Hasvela's Forrest through trunks of amber bark. It was a maze of trees blooming with silver veined foliage. The new leaves of spring created a thin but growing canopy.

A veiled priest of the Masruh Orthodox led the ceremonial procession. He wore garments of a royal purple, trimmed in elaborate silver foil patterned into intricate feather shapes.

Eos, Talus, Terrava, Aizo, and Inlume Spintha followed the priest with their hands folded and heads held reverently.

Upon clearing the trees and reaching the lake at the forest's heart, the priest lit an incense burner hanging from a chain.

He swung it as they walked, pouring incense from the three broken-sword-shaped holes in the burner. The golden orb spewed smoky fumes that smelled of frankincense and pine.

It made Eos' eyes water.

The trail of the aroma created a sacred sensation amongst the sublime imagery of the forest at sunset.

Shivers went down the back of Eos' neck as they made their way down the path toward the Ashva Pavilion on the border of the lake.

But then they passed it by.

The priest led them on, robes draping across the ground, arms ceaselessly moving the burner, all the way to the edge of the water.

Talus spoke with low reverence, "Eos, a companion elsu will now select you from the Ashva Tree. You will walk slowly over the surface of the water, place your hand on the trunk of Ashva at the center, then bend your knee and bow your head. There you will wait for the spirit of Hasvela to send you an elsu."

Adrenaline rushed through Eos.

CHAPTER TWO

This was the ritual of the Bellators.

To be chosen by the elsu.

To touch the sacred tree in the middle of the lake with roots in anima stone.

"First," the crackling old voice of the veiled priest said, "you must drink this so that the Great Soul may grant you the vision you need. Then you may approach the holy tree."

He held his purple sleeves up to the sky with an ornate vial in both hands and muttered some sort of prayer.

Eos could only make out the final line of the ancient language.

"Ama ruyat bialhima. May the Great Soul send you a watchful guardian, Eos," the priest said in a soft hum.

"What is it?" Eos asked.

"Hama. The wisdom of our ancestors. It will allow you to see what you must when entering this holiest of domains. Pray that the Great Soul grants you assurance of things you cannot see long after tonight."

Understanding little, Eos accepted the small potion flask and opened the gold cap hesitantly. He looked to his father for reassurance. Talus stuck out his chin, silently telling him to take the drink.

It was horribly bitter and earthy, but its effect was immediate within Eos.

His head became light, and a confusing sensation overcame him—a mixture of both sharp and cloudy, as if his senses were heightened, yet this new state of mind rejected everything he was sensing.

"May the Great Soul be with you and guide a wise companion to your side," the priest said in words that sounded like they were behind a layer of glass.

Eos responded with a phrase he heard the inlumes repeat over and over but had not understood until this moment, "The Great Soul is with us all."

The priest nodded, pleased with the response.

Walking over the surface of the lake, with crimson Soul Energy at his feet, each step felt like an eternity. He became lost in the complexity of the water and the nuance of his movement and wielding.

When he realized he was hyper-focusing, it felt like an hour had passed. Then it was time for the next step.

HASVELA'S CHOOSING

Everything around him looked…out of place…unnatural. It was as if the material world was an illusion, and the drink had uncovered this fact.

The potion was potent.

Unsure if it had been minutes or years, Eos finally stepped onto the shore of the island of the Ashva Tree.

What was I supposed to do now?

Touch the tree. Bend the knee. Bow.

Eos crossed the clearing.

A gust of wind slapped his face every few steps.

He recognized the movements as elsu going about at their incredible speed. *No. The hama drink had made him aware it was the elsu.*

Eos placed a palm on amber bark, on the trunk that was at least over a dozen of his arm-spans in circumference. The tree's canopy above was a small world unto itself. He saw pulses of electric light going through the bark like veins pumping life.

The tree was alive.

More than alive.

He saw the network of water distribution and roots like a ghost-projection implanted behind his eyelids.

Deep. Deep. Deep the roots reached.

Into the lake bottom, and beyond, throughout the entire forest.

Then the King's Son knelt with his head down at the foot of the tree and waited.

Wings beat all around him, but he did not look up.

Do you like my home, Son of Talus?

A gentle, feminine voice cooed, but the words were transmitted into his mind, not spoken out loud.

"It's more beautiful than anything I've ever seen."

It has served my children since before man walked this land. We have protected this forest long before Bellators learned to wield from the elsu. Before Morax formed the Order. Before the history you people have forgotten.

Now, you Bellators protect my forest in partnership with us. Will you do the same, young one?

CHAPTER TWO

"I…I will. If I'm given the chance to do so. May I ask, who are you?" Eos wondered, head still bowed, but knew the answer as soon as the words finished leaving his mouth.

You may rise, Eos.

He stood in his red dress-cloak, decorated with the Bellator family emblem of wings. When he turned, he saw a magnificent elsu whose wingspan was nearly as wide as the trunk of the Ashva Tree. However, this elsu seemed to be made of pure light.

Eos was sure he would have never been able to perceive the creature that seemed to be living, breathing Soul Energy itself, if it were not for the state of perception the hama potion had given him.

Never breaking eye contact for fear the splendid vision would vanish, he said, "Hasvela, I am honored by your presence." He spoke with absolute sincerity, each breath tense.

Yet another Bellator comes into my domain. I haven't had one that could see or speak to me since Pertinax. It seems you are gifted with perception and vision.

"If I am, I do not try to be. I'm not sure I want the gift, Great Mother of Elsu."

Which is exactly why you should have it. It is in your bloodline, after all.

Few of the bloodlines ever have a candidate that can manifest their inheritance.

Still, I sense a darkness in you that could lead you to misusing your gift.

Eos was silent.

You are well acquainted with this darkness? Hasvela seemed to sense. *Perhaps you shall tame it. I am assigning my greatest living son to be your companion. Faster than the wind and more intelligent than all my other children. His name is…well, I'll leave that to you. Maybe you can reclaim what your ancestors have forgotten.*

"Wait. Please, Hasvela," Eos urged, but the light-body shimmered into a sunset beam.

He nearly cried as her image disappeared.

Like a revelation in his genetic coding was once again lost.

A small elsu soared down in front of him, beat its wings, and hovered face-to-face. A lone blemish marked the pure white bird; a single patch of gold imprinted upon the snowy-white feathers, like a thumb had been placed over the graceful bird's head.

HASVELA'S CHOOSING

Eos instinctually reached out an arm for the elsu to perch on, and the mighty creature grasped his forearm with deadly talons, though they did not pierce his skin.

Then, he put his index finger before the bird's face.

Unsure why he had done it, Eos felt as if Hasvela's presence had guided him to make the strange gesture.

The bird bowed its head and touched the golden mark to Eos' finger.

My name is Ahktar. Swiftest and strongest among the elsu.

"I am Eos Bellator. Son of Talus Bellator."

I will be your eyes, Son of Talus, until you learn to use your own...and long after.

After the words came into his mind, he felt the potion's effects begin to fade. Ahktar did not speak again but rode on his shoulder as Eos Soul Stepped from the island and back to the main shore. As he did so, the heightened sense that everything material was made of so much more than words or thoughts could explain...dulled.

The holographic visuals tempered into ordinary sight.

When he stepped back onto shore, Eos' mind was sober.

The golden feather-crowned elsu still hovered at his shoulder.

Already waiting anxiously for his return, everyone's eyes widened in shock at the sight.

The priest fell to his knees and prostrated himself before the King's Son, now returned with Hasvela's chosen offspring.

Talus and Terrava bent a knee before Ahktar.

Spintha and Aizo immediately followed the King and Queen.

"*Tawasit Alsar. Aladima,*" the priest uttered in reverence, his face to the ground. "The ancient and high has selected your son. The Great Soul has made his will known this night. Eos is destined for great trials and even greater feats. This gift is a grace of the most special order."

Eos did not know what to say except to reveal what had happened. "Hasvela spoke to me. She gave me my companion and tasked me with—"

There were gasps at the revelation, and the priest interrupted, "Do not speak the words of Hasvela in public. This task is yours and yours alone. It may be discussed someday in private among Bellators."

CHAPTER TWO

They returned to castle Alasedis without another significant word, guided by the wrought iron lanterns, but Eos caught Talus beaming with excited pride—a contrast to the astonished, wary glances of the others.

Before parting, the Masruh priest said a final blessing over Eos and thanked the Great Soul for the blessings of the ritual.

Night had finally claimed the land when they at last came to rest at the banquet hall for dinner. As the double doors swung in, the aromas of a small feast greeted them.

So, too, did someone already at the table.

"Thought I would have to eat this whole banquet myself," Glenn jested weakly from his wooden chair, a mug of ale in hand.

"Glenn!" Eos exclaimed in shock, racing to his old friend's side, "You're awake?! You-you should be resting in the medical wing! What are you doing up?" Despite his words of concern, he was glad to see Glenn capable of moving around once again.

"We don't have time for any of that nonsense," Glenn rolled his eyes from over his mug. "I already had to make it past all those Sanofem women telling me to stay put." Eos gave the man's shoulders a jostling hug. Try as he might to hide it, Glenn seemed content with the warm contact from the boy he had helped to raise.

Aizo replied, "Those Sanofem women are the greatest healers in the land. You should heed their advice, but it is good to see you recovered."

Glenn sighed. "And I'm saying there's no time for that. I've already been asleep too long. Who knows what's happened in that time? Besides, they didn't let me have a single drink in that bed. This ale is holding me over, but I'll need something harder."

"So, this is the man who raised my children?" Terrava asked. "We owe you more than a drink, I'd say." The Queen clapped and ordered attendants to bring Glenn whatever he requested.

There was an anxious feeling in Eos' stomach. "Glenn, what do you mean, *'what's happened in that time?'*"

Glenn set his mug down and leaned over the table weakly.

"Emir Raggan and the Mitad have seized control of all of the North American Sector. And Vistomus Fulmen has disappeared overseas. Colonel Kane and I were imprisoned…" He paused, seeing the audience

HASVELA'S CHOOSING

in the hall hang on his every word, hypnotized by the introduction of his tale. "I believe we need to catch up over this meal. A lot has happened on Earth since you left. And none of it good. I'm gonna need whiskey."

The haggard man stroked his beard and prepared to recall the events of the Mitad's takeover of Earth.

CHAPTER THREE

TURN BACK THE CLOCK

The sharp edges of Glenn's cuffs cut into his wrists, but at least they had detained him with his hands in front of his body. He fidgeted in the spotlight of the morning sun through a stone-framed window. The brightness made him squint as he stared up at a panel of military generals and officers who surrounded him and Colonel Kane from on high. The soldiers that apprehended him as they returned to the base at Point Edward Castle had taken pity at first, giving him a flask to steady himself. But those few fiery gulps had already run dry, and if Glenn didn't have a drink soon, then he was going to lose his nerve.

"Colonel Kane," General Guren addressed the man standing in the center of the room next to Glenn. "This tribunal has gathered to investigate the potential conspiracy that has led to the murder of General Braxton. The evidence shows that your units were requested to assist General Braxton in a private meeting north of this base. It is then documented that you joined this mission without request and against orders. You returned with the civilian Glenn Parker the following day. As a result, General Braxton and eight other men were killed in action. Is this correct?"

"Yes, sir." Colonel Kane bit his lip hard to maintain his temper. Guren knew full well what kind of mission they had been on—delivering the Mellizo Glyph and ammunition to the Mitad. It was a traitorous and cowardly task, betraying his nation and caving to a foreign power.

"Please describe to us why you disobeyed the mission orders and participated yourself?"

"Sir, nearly every man and woman deployed to the field under my command was being sent on a mission that I found…*suspect*. I made sure the lives I'm responsible for were not being thrown away, and that they were not being forced to work against our sector's interests," he explained solemnly, a note of defeat lacing through his voice.

Glenn knew what that tone meant.

Colonel Kane had made it clear: General Guren would make a show at disposing Colonel Kane and simultaneously gain favor for his appointment as General of the North American Sector.

The room erupted in disbelief; some of it was feigned, and others were truly angered. Even the military police lining the doors shifted uncomfortably at the notion that General Braxton was betraying his sector.

Guren laughed under his breath while maintaining a straight face. His heavy brows against dark skin looked down with disdain. He knew he could bury Kane along this line. "A bold suggestion, Colonel. Without disclosing the nature of this top-secret mission, did you find that it compromised North American security?"

Colonel Kane hesitated as he parlayed his words, "I found that the end result of the mission severely compromised North America to foreign interests." *Foreign to this entire world, you fool*, Colonel Kane thought. "However, General Braxton's intent may be better described as well-intentioned but desperate."

General Guren's muddy gaze dug the knife in further. "Is this why you killed him?"

CHAPTER THREE

No one objected to the accusatorial and leading question. Guren could get away with nearly anything right now and he knew it.

"Sir, General Braxton was killed by a group calling themselves the Mitad. Specifically, a man named Kurt Fleischer committed the murder."

"So, you say. And yet we have evidence saying you conspired with this group yourself. I found you in the records room...digging into classified files without authorization."

The generals all stirred, upset at the impropriety.

"You did, sir. This was the first confirmation that the nature of the mission was suspect and convinced me that I must join to see for myself."

"The nature of the mission will be a separate inquiry," Guren said. There was a note of genuine interest in his voice, and Colonel Kane suspected that he didn't know the full extent of it himself. "What was the nature of Glenn Parker's role in this mission?"

It was Glenn's turn to bite his tongue. The urge to defend himself from this show of a trial was overwhelming, but Kane had prepped him to stay silent unless addressed directly. His fingers fiddled with the edges of Maxima's desert shawl that still hung around his neck—he had worn it ever since Eos gave it to him before their desert trek into Sires...after Braxton tried to put Maxima in the generator tank...*How long ago was that now? Just a few weeks back? Felt like another lifetime away already.*

"Glenn was part of a separate, independent attachment that arrived with Eos Bellator—whom I believe *you are already familiar with,*" Colonel Kane said with a tone that teased Guren in a way only he could understand. Guren had once vied to have Eos under his control but lost the bid to Kane. "Glenn played no active role in the mission except delivering Eos to the location and protecting General Braxton against Kurt Fleischer when they both were attacked."

He did his best to get Glenn out of any possible sentencing.

Their legs grew tired from standing for endless hours of tireless inquiry, but Glenn assumed that was intended. He squinted less and less as the bright sun waned. Eventually, only the dim refractions of the sunset came into the tribunal room.

TURN BACK THE CLOCK

Witnesses had testified about the events that occurred near Baker Lake without compromising the secret of wielders on Earth.

Friends and allies spoke to Kane's character while his enemies gave protest against him.

As the day dragged to an end, and Glenn's head began to pound, he finally perceived the display of it all; it mattered little what was testified or presented as evidence if the classified subject matter couldn't be spoken aloud. They were sacrifices in Guren's game, and the general likely already had the sway to accomplish his desires.

"We will reconvene tomorrow," General Guren said with exhaustion. "Take them back to their cells."

Colonel Kane and Glenn were walked out of the courtroom with heavy boots, low spirits, pure exhaustion, and the dismal reality of another day of similar questioning ahead of them.

$$\infty \qquad \infty \qquad \infty$$

The castle dungeon that was Glenn's jail cell shrunk in on him. The rations they had been given were abysmal, barely able to sustain his body. He supposed that this punishment came from General Guren's vindictive nature against Colonel Kane; Glenn had been associated with the Colonel, therefore, the cruel withholding treatment would be equally applied to the companion the Colonel returned with.

Glenn pressed his shaking body against the cell bars to cling to the tiny bit of dismal lighting that made it to his isolated box…and to avoid the smell of his own human waste and vomit in the opposite corner.

The guards never came to bring them to the next day of tribunal, and a fever had set in for Glenn. After weeks of being on the run and surviving battles he was never meant for, his immune system could take no more; the hurling up of his insides, the unbearable shivers and sweats through small fits of slumber, the headaches that pierced like a lobotomy performed with a dull glass shard from one of his long-gone shattered bottles…

Colonel Kane tried to talk to him from the neighboring cell, but the disembodied words were hardly a comfort. He seemed to hum a sad

CHAPTER THREE

tune. Rambled on about his lost friend Major Clark. Lamented his fiancée who passed away. The sounds were merely poor distractions from an execution sentence that surely loomed. *How many days had passed? Did the guards stop coming with rations?*

Glenn's fever dreams were a mixture of ghosts and waking hallucinations, but he saw *them* often. He didn't think he'd miss the two Soul Wielders he'd raised so much, but their absence in his life was a whole new experience, a hollow ache in his heart.

Their desert-tanned skin. A pair of curious golden eyes. A sweet sapphire gaze. That dark curse mark that stained the boy's right arm. Every detail of them he missed, but the possible notion of one day gathering the courage to see Eos and Maxima again sustained him through his haze of suffering. He had lost lovers, but this was like being separated from his own children. Glenn clenched the sacred Mellizo Glyph that Aizo had given him, glad he had been able to hide it from his captors. He clutched it as if it would bring them back from the other world they had departed to and take away his sickness all at the same time.

Vision fuzzy.

Fading.

Gray.

Gone.

Glenn's eyes flashed open. He felt… better. But his hunger and thirst came in with sharper clarity than before.

He let the chains of the Mellizo Glyph slip through his hands. Its cap was open, and dried blood crusted his palm where he must have nearly crushed the ebony-stone artifact in his unconscious struggle.

With saliva, he wiped the rune-covered vial clean as best he could and tucked it away carefully, like it was the greatest treasure he'd ever known.

That is insurance that you'll see them again.

Aizo had told him that…and more. Things he hardly believed, but he memorized every word of, often repeating them to himself.

A pair of guards eventually came down again, silent and wordless, giving scarce rations of bread and water and then leaving swiftly.

TURN BACK THE CLOCK

"Are we going to be stuck down here forever?" Colonel Kane called as they shut the way to the corridor.

There was no answer.

Something was wrong.

Glenn dashed for the food and drink at the edge of his bars, his parched throat needing the replenishment. "How long we been down here?" He croaked.

"Oh, good you're awake. Feeling better?"

Glenn swallowed. "Better is a stretch."

Colonel Kane reached for the tray they brought him. "You were out for a long time. Hoped you weren't dead. But to answer your question, I figure we've been down here several days now, though they haven't been feeding us regularly so there's no way to be exactly sure."

"We still on the chopping block?" Glenn ventured, wrapping Maxima's scarf tighter about him.

"Likely. But I honestly have no clue," Kane admitted warily. "We appear to have fallen off their priority list."

Shortly after those rations, they heard the sounds of gunfire and explosions outside for many hours. It was dull, muted and distant, but Colonel Kane knew the sounds of battle.

"Maybe Guren wasn't so popular as he thought. Didn't have the backing he'd hoped for. Sounds like insurrection," Colonel Kane muttered. "Maybe we'll be free before our execution date."

Food and water stopped coming altogether after that.

The two men soon found themselves arguing over how much time had passed without sustenance.

It was their only pastime between uneasy slumber.

"Whichever general took control, he doesn't seem to like us much...or even know we exist," Glenn mused, his lips cracked to the point of bleeding.

The cold stone floor of the dungeon faded for him again.

He was gone.

When he awoke, there was a canteen at the edge of his bars and a bowl of food that was hours cold. The overly warm water and stale rations were beyond compare to anything he could remember

CHAPTER THREE

consuming. He guzzled the water until it dripped from his chin and his stomach hurt.

"You awake, Glenn?" Colonel Kane asked.

"Something like that."

"Soldiers brought us the rations. I was half-asleep when they came. Couldn't make out who they were with in this lighting. Swear I saw tan britches…but that doesn't make any sense. That would be European Sector…I was half-delusional at the time anyway."

A few hours later, a voice murmured from outside Glenn's cell, "My God…"

Glenn looked up and couldn't believe what he was seeing.

"Shaun? Shaun Dunn?" He forced out weakly, as if seeing a dead man. His desert drinking buddy was standing outside the cell in shades of camouflage guerilla garb. An AR-15 rifle was slung over his shoulder, and a beard had overgrown his face.

Still, Glenn would recognize his friend anywhere.

So long ago, the days of the generator facility felt. How many lifetimes ago had he raised two orphan siblings while escaping to poker and drinking with his dune-dwelling friend?

"In the flesh. How did you get yourself in there, man? You look like hell," Shaun laughed sadistically. "Like the bottle finally drank you. Spit you back out, too, I'd say."

"Shaun, you beautiful desert rat—*I thought you died*…what do I know? Maybe I'm dead, too."

Colonel Kane confirmed from a cell over, "Not dead. We're living this nightmare together."

"The way we drink, I'm surprised we're both not dead either," Shaun chuckled. "I sure was close for a while, though. Haven't seen such a friendly face since…well, since I passed out face down during our last hoorah!"

Glenn realized the hand propping him up was planted firmly in his days-old dried vomit. He wiped it against his shirt and strained to wave his arm into a dramatized bow.

"Friendly face at your service, though we've established that I look as delightful as this place smells. What're you doing down here, Shaun?

TURN BACK THE CLOCK

And bring some more water! Oh, and whiskey. A whole handle if you can find it!"

"Probably best to keep sober for now, Glenn. You're lucky I found the water and rations my men left you there, but I'll look for more. With everything going on, getting extra of anything is near impossible. We're still securing the perimeter of Point Edward Castle. I have to say, I'm just as surprised to see you here, too. Weren't you babysitting when I last saw you? What happened to those kids?"

Glenn slumped back against the wall and said, "That's a long story I'd need more time to tell. You wouldn't mind breaking us out would ya?"

"I considered breaking you out when I first saw you, but I don't have the keys. We noticed your name logged into the prisoner book, and I came to have a look for myself—"

Colonel Kane broke in sharply, "Who is this *we?* Who is securing the perimeter?"

Shaun turned to the other cell, blinking in disbelief.

"Well, maybe you didn't hear the news down here, but the rest of the world knows already. Rebels overthrew the North American Sector's military regime. With Braxton dead, we seized on the chaos. Of course, our leader, Vistomus, is calling us *the Mitad* now. Funny name, but I won't complain."

Glenn's head pounded. "No. No. That can't be."

"Isn't it great?" Shaun let out joyfully, misunderstanding Glenn's reaction. "How many nights did we toast to that old mustached dog's death? Finally, Braxton and his lackeys are gone! The North American sector is liberated."

Yes, General Braxton was dead. Glenn personally witnessed Kurt Fleischer plunge a Soul Sphere into the man. Venomous-green light against maniacal beady eyes, the vile insanity of Kurt Fleischer lingered in Glenn's mind.

Now, Shaun was a member of the so-called rebellion—the Mitad!

"I came looking for you. Heard you'd been taken to Sires," Glenn said faintly, but internally, his anger grew.

CHAPTER THREE

Sires was the lie it was called, but it was really Laboratory 4, where Braxton had experimented on Aizo and developed the device of Maxima's imprisonment.

Glenn added, "But I was too late. They said you'd been taken into the lab already."

"Well, I'll be...you did all that for me?" Shaun was in disbelief.

Glenn repeated, "Like I said, it's all a long story."

Shaun laughed lightly, "My will to live was too strong. I led a breakout the night before I was scheduled for experimentation. Not that escape did us any good. Just about died in that desert, but rebels found us! Vistomus took us in and recruited us."

Glenn threw his head back against the stone once more. *Shaun thought he was being a hero with the Mitad...*

Visually apparent that Glenn's focus was drained by exhaustion, Shaun offered, "I tell you what. I'll search for more food and water for you both and then see about keys to get you out. Might take a while, though. It's chaos out there. I have no problem breaking an old buddy out...but as for your friend in uniform..."

Glenn quickly saved Colonel Kane, "We're both in here for directly working against Braxton. You could even say this man is responsible for his fall."

"Well shoot, why didn't you say that from the beginning? Only a few people know you're in here. If we get you both out soon, no one will think twice about why these cells are empty. Just give me some time."

Days passed without sign of the keys, but at least they had a steady stream of sustenance to regain their strength with Shaun's regular visits.

On the third day, Glenn was turning over the Mellizo Glyph, examining the runes patterned into each face of it...the larger rune in the center was a leaf-like shape, almost like an eye, with a spine that formed a circle around it...the mysteries of the artifact had him seriously contemplating their stagnant situation.

"You know, Axel," Glenn spoke for the first time that morning. "Aizo left me with something—one of the Hyperborean artifacts. *A Mellizo Glyph.*"

"Oh?" came Kane's response.

TURN BACK THE CLOCK

"Mhmm. He said it could teleport the user to Hyperborea—if they can make it past the Arctic Circle to activate it."

"That would be great if we were above the Arctic Circle," Kane chuckled darkly at the irony of it.

"Yeah, well, that's not all it does. It also grants a person the ability to *Soul Wield*, as Aizo called it. Use powers like Eos and Maxima did…if you perform the ritual."

"What kind of ritual is that?" Colonel Kane asked warily.

"Said you have to cut your finger and give it some of your blood. Then you can do what the Hyperboreans do."

There was silence for a while.

"Sounds like dabbling in things that shouldn't be in our world."

Glenn chuckled in agreement, "Yeah, but I think it's too late for that. The Mitad have taken over the North American Sector. Things that shouldn't be in our world have dabbled with us. So, I was thinking…if someone does the ritual, they would still need to learn how to use the ability…I'm not a fighter but…but maybe someone used to combat could figure it out."

Colonel Kane huffed in disbelief. "You want *me* to use this artifact?"

"Someone has to get us out of here, Colonel."

The prison went quiet again.

"Axel?" Glenn asked.

Kane practically growled, "Why didn't you mention this before? When we were nearly at death's door?"

"Didn't think it up as an option until just now."

There was silence again.

"Fine, I'll consider it. Let me see the thing."

Glenn shoved his body through the bars, dangling his arm as far as it would reach to the bars of the cell next to him. Kane did the same as the glyph swung on its chain to close the distance between hands.

Swing. Miss.

Swing. Miss.

Swing. *Catch.*

Colonel Kane pulled the Mellizo Glyph back into his cell.

CHAPTER THREE

Glenn waited anxiously for Kane to agree and report on the experience, but when he finally spoke again, he only said, "I'll stick to my guns and bullets. That wielding stuff is for Hyperboreans. Bullets are for soldiers. Besides, I have a feeling that whatever this is, it was only meant for you. Here."

Kane held his fist out of the cell again, the Mellizo Glyph dangling by its chain. Glenn reached hard, caught it on the second swing, and tucked it back into his pocket.

Trying to imagine what might happen, Glenn pondered if he would ever perform the ritual himself then. He recalled the struggles emotionally and physically that Eos underwent.

Would having that same power drag him into their world…their battles? Could he handle the mental requirements that it would demand? No. He was an engineer, not a super-powered warrior. But escape…he needed to escape.

Colonel Kane and Glenn sat back-to-back against the cell wall that separated them, contemplating the same question and all the weight that came with it: *how could they escape if the keys were never found?*

The next day, Shaun solved their problem for them.

"No food today?" Colonel Kane asked when Shaun appeared empty-handed the next morning.

"Better." Shaun swung a ring of keys around his finger.

∞   ∞   ∞

Bulbs flickered with instability—a string of hope draped down a tunnel of darkness that Glenn brought to life on a generator system he had devised.

The rapid cut between darkness and the artificial lights triggered a momentary recall to months before in the Point Edwards Castle jail cell. The hunger pangs, sickness, and dehydration amidst lights so similar to these still haunted him.

When Colonel Kane and his units managed to raid some of the Mitad's resources or negotiate with allies, there would be fuel for generators. It wasn't a ton of light, but it was better than trying to see by oil lamp or flashlight; when the bulbs were on, it would lift everyone's spirits.

The air was better now, too. Glenn had added ventilation and air conditioning to this third base of Kane's underground operational headquarters.

What remained of the Colonel's squads, and many North American loyalists, enlisted under Kane's command in the aftermath of the Mitad's coup. They did so either out of admiration for his leadership or disdain for what ruled in Braxton's place.

Colonel Kane had moved incredibly fast since Shaun Dunn had broken them out of General Guren's dungeon. Kane had numerous bugout contingencies in place: hidden vehicles and supplies, methods and locations of meeting his soldiers, contacts for acquiring supplies. His network and planning for such an event were astounding—but then again, his ambitions always threatened excommunication from North American military leadership.

Weeks had flown by in a flurry of activity as protocol and standard operations were established, until one day, Glenn found himself working on the lighting system for a third base. Days passed in the form of sweat and grime and wires since he had last spoken with Colonel Kane. The estimate was that his network of soldiers was already swelling to over five hundred in number.

The rumbling of the generator and the glow of yellow lights let Glenn know that this wing of the third base had electricity. For now.

Glenn fell back against the wall, feeling a weariness of heart that hadn't consumed him since Braxton had him construct Maxima's vessel of imprisonment. He stroked his growing strawberry-blonde beard and rubbed his forehead, adjusting the bandana he now wore—Maxima's repurposed desert scarf. He didn't consider himself a sentimental person, but he was grateful for the few things that had survived his misadventures thus far. If it wasn't for that and the Mellizo Glyph, it would be like Eos and Maxima never existed with him here on Earth at all.

From babysitting super-powered children to rebellion engineer.
The absurdity of his life made him laugh.

CHAPTER THREE

Supplies surrounded him in the newly stocked rations room.

To his disbelief, they even had a crate of liquor. Nine bottles of clear glass between wooden slats gleamed across the room at him, tempting his dry palate. There was a not-so-old twinge of desire that clashed painfully against his memories of being so deathly sick in that castle prison. He had not touched the wretched stuff since.

Probably vodka anyway. He hated vodka.

Boots clunked along the concrete corridor, and a navy pleated officer uniform came into the light.

"Well done, Glenn. This place is coming along faster than planned," Colonel Kane smiled with exhaustion behind a façade of vigor.

"For the *great leader himself* to grace me with his presence—I must have outdone myself."

"Come on now, Glenn. No need for that. I'm stretched thin between expanding our operations and infiltrating the Mitad's front with the rebels while keeping it all covert."

Glenn chuckled dryly. "I just figure you're overrun with new recruits and have a few more locations picked out for me to bring online."

There was a gleam from the man's bright-green eyes. "Can't I just check in on a friend who's helped me out more than I can thank him for?"

"That's most welcome," Glenn said, knowing Kane had surely chosen new bunker locations already.

"Operations aside, have you considered what you want to do next, Glenn?"

Glenn waited before responding. Hesitantly, he asked, "Next?"

"When you're done here. Eos and Maxima are gone. As far as I can tell, caring for them was the last decade of your life. And now you're dragged into this new resistance we have, but as a free man with no ties…I'm wondering what would be best for my friend in the long run, and if I can assist in any way."

Running his hand along a dust-layered table, Glenn hummed to himself and reflected. "You know…I don't think I've chosen a single thing in my life except which bottle to open next. My parents chose my career trajectory when I was younger. Then the war changed it all, and the path laid itself out with my natural abilities. Then Braxton came calling and thrust me into his little Hyperborean research project. Next thing I know, I was stuck with two super-powered kids. It sounds pathetic, but I wouldn't know what to do with a clean slate if I had one." He exhaled a half-laugh, half-sigh, at the insanity of his own life.

He had always embellished his own story to others. *The greatest engineer. The most in-demand researcher. The brightest mind.* But there was no need for that veneer next to the man he had starved alongside in prison. There was no need for masks with the harrowing bond they'd formed.

"The way I've heard it, you chose to watch over and protect those two kids. Probably one of the most selfless and impactful things anyone could ever do. Not to mention you risked a lot to get them back to Hyperborea."

"Yeah, well, cowardice prevented me from changing course to follow them. Easier to let the stream carry me here now, I suppose."

"I don't buy it, Glenn. You've said you have no one of significant relation to you here on Earth. Why stay adrift when you could go find them? You once told me that Glyph you carry is the key. I'd say it's a perfect time to write the next chapter of your story."

Glenn hesitated. "They've gone off to another world, Colonel—one which I don't have the birthright or powers to partake in."

Colonel Kane seemed to sense that had he said too much and patted Glenn on the back with a hardy thump. "No matter what you choose, I'm sure you'll find the next right path; we all do eventually. But, if you're truly set on staying here, then I have two more bases I want you to work on in the meantime. Among our newest recruits are some promising electricians and engineers. If you want to move on to other things, I'm happy to provide you with anything you ask for—within my ability. *But* if you decide to stay, I'd like you to lead our resources in expanding this operation to its largest and most important location."

Glenn nodded. "I've got a few more of these projects in me."

The remainder of the evening was a blur of memories that Glenn retained in some incoherent blend. Even as he experienced them, time seemed to cut from adrenaline rush to adrenaline rush.

It began with a commotion down the hall.

CHAPTER THREE

Then shots firing.

Explosions.

Flashes of Soul Energy.

Cries of pain.

A sense of the space filling with bodies.

Colonel Kane and a few others pulled his shocked-stiff body down the hall for better cover.

Glimpses of black cloaks in all directions.

Soul Energy flickers off the concrete walls.

A spraying of debris from ricocheting bullets.

In the middle of the chaos, Glenn saw gray female skin. Sunken flesh exaggerated high cheekbones in the low lighting. Her body was full and feminine under her open Mitad cloak, but her face was fierce, and her hair was shaved in the male military style. She cast out magenta whips of energy from each hand, cutting down soldiers as she strode down the hall, a shimmering power over her body—a shielding technique that Glenn knew could deflect bullets.

After the battle, Glenn would later learn she was called Mirza Morgana.

The last thing he saw of her was the sadistic curl of her black lipstick as she killed all in her path.

Glenn sprinted down halls with the Colonel and a handful of others, turning to avoid the sounds of battle. Colonel Kane had taken specific concern to get Glenn out alive. Protocol was in place for being discovered: exit paths, backup routes, and rendezvous points.

Colonel Kane turned a corner ahead of him with pistol raised.

Crack! Crack! Crack!

Bullets flew in both directions.

"Go back, Glenn!" he yelled as he reloaded his firearm.

Glenn didn't remember how many minutes it took them to get out of the building. Less than thirty, certainly, but the fear felt so long—a revolving montage of short, panicked moments and extended sprints of anxiety.

All of it paled in comparison by what happened at the exit.

TURN BACK THE CLOCK

As they neared the final door with three allies by their side, a group of Mitad members cut them off, emerged from the adjacent room, and nearly crashed into them.

Guns fired as Glenn was thrown to the ground.

Colonel Kane shot expertly, downing two Mitad.

The North American soldiers that accompanied them took fatal wounds.

Glenn and Colonel Kane were alone.

Kane dove against the wall.

His gun never dropped from its target.

Two more Mitad grunts went down.

As Glenn clambered against the concrete to stand, venomous-green light filled the hall. A voice he knew all too well sneered with surprise, "What are the chances? It seems I've been given another opportunity to kill you."

Beady eyes looked over silver glasses with side-parted blonde hair and a white vest under an open Mitad cloak—the terror inside Glenn ratcheted as he instantly recognized the man.

Kurt Fleischer was actively working with the Mitad now? Being trained?

The mad scientists' wielding was much faster than Glenn ever remembered it being.

A sickly-green Soul Sphere manifested in seconds.

The venom-light plunged at Glenn before he was on his feet.

Unbelievable heat and the smell of burnt flesh seized his senses. His ribs burned and cracked. The attack slid off his torso and brought a piece of the wall down behind him in a slab.

Fleischer summoned another sphere of Soul Energy and said as it grew, "You know if I think about it...I've wanted to do this since I was forced to work with you fifteen years ago. And when you intervened with Braxton and Maxima at the lab..."

The last standing Mitad soldier pointed his gun.

Glenn held out a weak hand, blood running down his entire torso, painting him red.

CHAPTER THREE

Colonel Kane took down the Mitad soldier before he could strike, but it cost him his last loaded bullet to do it. Then, without hesitating, he lunged forward and drove his shoulder violently into Kurt Fleischer.

The sickly soul energy guttered out. Glasses flew from his face and shattered.

North American and Mitad soldiers filled the hallway simultaneously.

Colonel Kane had no time for a close-quarter shoot-out. He hooked his arms under Glenn from behind and dragged him out the door.

The world was a vision funnel...muted sound...only the smell and sensation of his charred flesh...Glenn could hear words, but he couldn't make out anything meaningful...then the vaguely distant feeling of being lifted onto a stretcher...

He briefly came into consciousness long enough to comprehend he was receiving medical attention.

Mustering his will in an action that was mostly involuntary, he muttered, "Have to find...Eos and Maxima...Hyperborea."

Then he slept for many days.

CHAPTER FOUR

SAMURAI AND KAMI

Glenn shoveled down food and drink, barely seeming to stop for breath, as he recounted his tale. The massive dining hall seated only seven guests that night; Durath had been invited to join the celebration of Eos' elsu choosing.

"So, as I lay half-dead, the only thing I could think to do was find Eos and Maxima," he explained through a cheek-full of potatoes. He swallowed, "If wielding business had taken over Earth, I thought, then someone on Hyperborea must know what to do." He took another gulp of ale.

"How was it possible?" Eos asked. "How could you get here without a wielder opening the gate?"

Pausing his feasting, Glenn set down his mug and utensils and wiggled his fingers in the air like playing an imaginary harp. His brow wrinkled with intense concentration.

CHAPTER FOUR

"Is something wrong with him?" Durath jested. "What's he doing?"

"Not sure, but I think he's broken," Eos replied, perplexed.

Glenn held up his other hand with the index finger pointed in a gesture to wait. "Hold your insults. I've become a *powerful and mighty Soul Wielder* since you last abandoned me."

Continuing his bizarre behavior, Glenn began circling his hands around an imaginary sphere.

"Glenn!" Eos exclaimed. *The drink they brought out for him couldn't have taken hold that fast already!*

The strawberry-blond man dropped his hands and shrugged. "*Joking. Only joking.* Aizo left me the instructions for the Mellizo Glyph, but I couldn't bring myself to do it."

Aizo hummed with contemplation. "So, you didn't perform the ritual?"

Glenn shrugged. "No. At least, I don't think I did. One time when I woke in my prison cell, I found the Mellizo Glyph had my blood on it and the lid was open. Close call, but never noticed any changes, so I don't think any of *me* actually got inside it."

Eos' confusion had him leaning over the table now as he prodded, "Then *how* did you do it, Glenn?"

"Once I could walk again without bleeding out, Colonel Kane and I found a straggling Mitad wielder who couldn't perform the shield magic some of you can do. We Shanghaied him at gunpoint and made our way north—"

Durath raised a dark brow, "*Shanghaied?*"

Glenn sighed, annoyed with the interruption to his story. "A local colloquialism—*kidnapped,* for you Hyperboreans. We made the wielder open a portal past the Arctic Circle instead. And then I grabbed the Glyph and left the Mitad grunt Earth-side. I voted unharmed, but Colonel Kane voted for lead-filled. I wasn't about to argue as I stepped through the rift and held onto that Glyph for dear life."

"You killed him?" Durath snorted.

"Well, *I didn't.* That was Colonel Kane's handiwork. Unless you find it impressive that I killed him—then in which case, why yes. Yes, I did." Glenn was enjoying playing his crowd far too much.

SAMURAI AND KAMI

Finishing the tale, Glenn stifled his haughty smirk. "Aizo left a map with directions and some provisions where I dumped out on the Hyperborean-side, true to his word…and eventually, I stumbled half-dead into this place—*Anite*." He waved a hand about the room.

Talus spoke, "A brave journey, master Glenn. Tell me, do you truly wish to learn to wield Soul Energy?"

"Absolutely not," Glenn objected. "*Why do you think I made someone else make the portal?* I want no more of this trouble than what I've already told you. What I want is for you Hyperboreans to remove your Mitad mess from my world."

Aizo sighed, "If only it were so simple."

Talus explained over his third pint of ale, "As soon as you arrived with Emir Raggan's name on your lips, we began planning an expedition to Earth to investigate on your behalf. Everyone at this table, save my wife, will return to Earth—to gather information only. We cannot promise any action beyond that, but once we observe the situation, we can formulate a plan here on Hyperborea to hopefully rid both worlds of the Mitad for good."

Glenn nodded and stroked his rusted-gold beard. "I could ask no more than that."

Terrava eyed everyone in the room anxiously. She had just lost one child…and yet again, the other would go on another dangerous journey. The mother inside her screamed, but the Queen and Inlume looked on with the burden of responsibility.

It was that same look that observed her family and their companions departing two days later in the Alasedis courtyard before the portcullis gate. Talus, Eos, Durath, Glenn, Aizo, and Scavok all made final preparations, strapping themselves with heavy packs of travel supplies over their padded robes and light armor.

Eos embraced Terrava before putting on his pack.

"I'll be back soon, Mother."

"I know you will, Eos," Terrava said with strain.

"Before we head out," Talus announced to their party, "I have a gift for our noble guardian who protected my children."

CHAPTER FOUR

Talus lifted a long item, wrapped in a rich-green blanket, and held it out to Glenn, who received it and unfolded the cloth.

Inside, he found a wooden staff.

It was a curious but beautiful gift. The grain of the wood was white marbled with amber that turned into a decorative spiral like folded wings at the top.

"Amber wood from the trees of the Hasvela forest, imbued with a special essence inside," Talus beamed. "I believe our non-warrior friend should have something that could protect him in a time of need. It is one of a kind."

Everyone but Terrava, who already knew about the staff, looked on with confusion.

How could such a thing protect Glenn? Eos wondered.

Glenn examined the staff. "Thank you, Talus. It's a special gift. I can't say I understand it, though. Either you're preparing me to be a wizard or telling me I have a long hike ahead."

Talus laughed. "I do not know this word, *wizard*, but a long journey is certain. I'll explain in time."

Glenn nodded. He had learned to trust wielders when they had a plan, and he certainly wouldn't refuse such a fine present.

Talus turned to embrace his wife and gently held her face in his remaining hand.

"I won't be gone long, my love. We shall be back before you know it. If we are delayed for any reason, I'll personally return to Anite to update you."

Goodbyes faded into the dawn as they departed for the Sepeleo Mountains, the first stop before their return mission to Earth.

∞   ∞   ∞

It was not yet winter in the Akaishi Mountains, but at their altitude, the nights were well below freezing—this preserved flesh. Carnus looked over a gruesome scene against the tranquil backdrop of the snow-capped peaks and the soft-pink haze of early morning.

He shut his eyes and sighed at the tragedy.

SAMURAI AND KAMI

A lean woman quietly approached, settling beside him. She was hard in demeanor and physique, yet eloquent and beautiful beyond compare. Her white-blonde hair, streaked with strands the color of toffee, was pulled back into a tight bun and pinned with an ornate bar of gold and jade. She wore robes of red and white with thin threads of golden intricacies that formed chrysanthemum petals.

She nodded without turning her head from the gory sight, and greeted him with mild indifference, "Carnus."

The tone was a mask for the decades of relationship become strained.

Carnus stroked his dark beard, now heavily marked with gray, and returned the greeting likewise, never breaking his gaze away from what brought them together.

"Himiko."

"How dare you," the woman snapped, keeping her voice low so as not to startle the three samurai watching from a distance behind her. She spoke in English, so they could not understand.

"That's what they call you," Carnus gestured to the samurai. "I only addressed you by the part you play."

She turned her fierce maple-colored eyes at him.

A pang of nostalgic guilt swelled in him from the look.

"Fine," Carnus exhaled heavily. "Good to see you too, Grace."

They observed the remains of a human body. It was an older man— separated into two pieces and preserved by frost. All five individuals at the scene were accustomed to death and battles, yet a sense of dread hung in the dawn air.

"This far in the mountains," Grace fretted aloud. "Do you recognize him?"

They had both been called to investigate an unusual murder. It was too far into the domain of Saigo Takayoshi, which meant that the Mitad were suddenly moving against him after years of tolerance.

However, location was not the only reason Grace and Carnus had been summoned.

The man was severed in two, with most of the wound a burn mark.

CHAPTER FOUR

"I knew him. A manus weapon did this. It was wielder work," Carnus replied bitterly.

"Yes. This has Mitad fingerprints, no doubt. Who was he?"

"Father to a sick girl in one of the outer villages."

Thin, feminine eyebrows drew together in deep regret. "You healed her with Soul Energy?"

Carnus gave a solemn nod. "I tried my best."

"Did this father know where you hide?"

"Where I live? No."

"The Mitad know you're in these mountains, Carnus. They're coming for you one way or another."

The grizzled man was handsome, but visibly burdened which aged him far beyond his years. Still, something about the way he gritted his teeth in anger attracted Grace.

She hid the softness immediately.

Carnus snarled, "They'll never find me."

"No, but they'll kill innocents trying."

An animalistic growl responded.

One samurai stepped forward in concern saying, "Himiko-ojou."

She dismissed him in his native language and then said, "Carnus is a friend. There's no need to worry."

The samurai bowed his head, seeming to understand.

Carnus mustered up words in frustration, "Vistomus can't just leave me be. It's my destiny to be drawn back into this life."

Grace watched her old friend with a note of pain in her chest. He was broken—beaten down physically and spiritually. The look in his eyes was that of a soul that had been shattered. The pupils were a portal that reflected a man who had formerly been whole.

"You have the Left Eye of Izanagi. He will hunt you down to the ends of the world to get it. Our home world or this one. You must confront him eventually."

"This is our home world now, and I've sworn off the old ways. I'll do no more fighting and killing. My wielding is only for healing."

Grace scoffed, "That's only half of your clan's ways. The Hamirate training in you knows that. You can't abandon the warrior way."

SAMURAI AND KAMI

"I have," he growled, more in a reminder to himself than in response to Grace.

"Saigo is fighting a losing battle for Nippon-Wa. Vistomus holds full sway over Emperor Antoku now. You could save more lives and do more good using the Left Eye."

"I have no more appetite for death."

"Then let me use it!"

"*I said no!*"

There was a long silence.

Breaking sunlight cut the mountain ridges to pull back a receding shadow from the gruesome scene.

Carnus sighed. "Go back to Saigo and tell him what happened here. I'll decide what to do with my situation."

Grace glided across the rocks to face him.

"Saigo will ask you to fight."

"And I must refuse as I always have."

"He doesn't know the true power of the Left Eye, but he knows what you can do. We need wielders to hold back the Mitad. Vistomus has assigned a Mirza to every region. Some people worship and fear them like they do me. They're calling them Hanyos. If we don't turn this tide now, the Mitad—"

"If I fight, the curse will take hold again!" Carnus shouted, rousing the three samurai to grasp the hilt of their swords.

Grace shook her head, the motion telling the warriors to stand down; the movement mesmerized Carnus. It was a beauty and intellect he could have had in another life…another path.

He nearly started, wanting to reach out to hold her, but his arms fell in weakness.

Rose lips turned back to face him, moving with conviction. "You're stronger now. In here," she said, touching a finger to his temple, her fiery gaze holding his a moment longer than he could bare. "Farewell, Carnus."

Then, she turned to her men and said a few words, rousing them to their nearby steeds.

CHAPTER FOUR

"No. I'm not," Carnus whispered into the wind as Grace rode off on horseback to report their findings at Saigo's hidden mountain village.

∞   ∞   ∞

Cedar pillars and overhead cloisters opened to a mountain view filled with evergreen branches. Saigo sat in solemn contemplation beneath the roof of a restored Shinto shrine that served as his residence and the base of the Antoku Rebellion. His features were sharply handsome: eyebrows dark and brooding, jawline defined and masculine, hair pulled back in the samurai way, but his topknot was still a rich black color despite his age.

Grace stood at the doorway's threshold and waited for an acknowledgement to enter.

"Ah, Himiko-ojou. Please join me. I have awaited your return to help interpret this senseless death my men found. However, now I fear you must decipher more than that this morning." His English was excellent, though heavily accented.

"I will do my best to assist you, Saigo-dono."

"Tell me, Himiko, why is it that I trust you more than any samurai that serves me?"

Grace's lips curled slightly. Her beautiful features charmed every man in the village, but Saigo was the master of his desires and emotions. Such a shallow reason held no sway over his trust.

She moved across the wooden floor, sat beside him, and replied, "You must tell me that, Saigo-dono."

"You," he raised a finger to emphasize his point, "are not like Japanese men who serve me. They follow bushido because it is all they know. They follow me because they know only duty and honor. But you have joined us from a foreign land. Many ways other than bushido that you have known…"

Grace finished for him, "Yet, the way of the samurai has captured my heart."

A deep breath accompanied a slight head bow that acknowledged the correct answer. "You are both one of us and kami. Divine spirit."

SAMURAI AND KAMI

"Yes, so you've said before, Saigo. I remind you of your legend, and you call me Himiko."

"More than that. The people believe you to be her embodied again in our time."

"Saigo, I—"

"Forgive me, Himiko. Perhaps I ramble. However, it is only to say that your human nature may help me understand what I've seen in the mountains, but I hope your kami nature will tell me the meaning of a vision I've had."

Saigo's dark indigo robes were still, but Grace's red and white silks rustled with unease as she shifted.

"You've had a vision...and want me to interpret it? Forgive me, but I do not believe I am the best for this task. Perhaps your—"

"No!" Saigo's voice grew deep and full of concern. "My master, the Emperor, is dead. His child-heir sits on the Chrysanthemum Throne. The demon kami, Raijin, has swayed the Emperor and is unifying Nippon-Wa against the revived samurai way. Raijin's hanyo are crushing every region under their tyranny. Strange demon powers are used in these battles we now fight. *Nothing is in balance anymore.* You are the only one for the task."

Grace thought to herself in pause. *Yes, Vistomus Fulmen has swayed your child emperor, and his mirzas are slaying your samurai with Soul Wielding. This must all seem like some strange and terrible dream, dear Saigo.* Many more things she thought, but she only said, "It was Raijin's hanyo that killed the man in the mountains. Go ahead. Tell me your vision, my lord."

Another deep grunt came from Saigo as he went silent, pondering the body in the mountain and how to explain his daydream.

"I sat here and listened to the sounds of morning, but my thoughts were filled with darkness. I saw a man with only a left eye being chased by lightning. I knew...if he were struck, all of Nippon-Wa would fall, and many other lands would follow. For this, I shed a tear, but a great falcon came from across the ocean and caught the lightning in his talons. The lightning was captured, but it also struck the great bird."

"What did this falcon look like?"

"It was white like snow."

∞ 63 ∞

CHAPTER FOUR

Grace covered her mouth before it hung open.

She replied with a distant gaze, "We call this *the elsu*."

"Mmmm," Saigo rolled the name over in his mind with the hum.

"Did the elsu live?" Grace prompted carefully.

"I cannot say for another came with a magic staff and put out the lightning. This falcon fell from the sky, and I saw no more of any of them."

Soft eyes filled with dread of things to come before Grace shut them for a moment. When she reopened them, she explained, "These are signs from my world, but how they could come to be...I do not know. It should be impossible."

A subtle jut of the chin was Saigo's reluctant acceptance. However, one question remained in his mind. "This kami who possesses lightning...you and Raijin knew each other, did you not?"

"We did."

"Then why do *the Mitad* not come after you?"

"They...do, but I am not as important to them as Carnus," Grace answered. She hesitated to reveal anymore, but Saigo's fierce silence and piercing eyes called an explanation out of her. "I know their secrets, but I am stuck in this world now. Carnus stole something from them."

"Mmmm. And Carnus is also a kami like you, is he not?"

"Something like that."

"He heals our people. Why will he not fight alongside us? Has he no duty? No honor?"

Grace felt a resonance with the words. She agreed but couldn't say as much. Saigo's strong presence mesmerized her more than she wished, and she found herself saying, "Carnus is afraid."

"A coward?"

"He has killed many people. More than you could ever count. But when he uses his powers, it is possible for Raijin to control him. So, he has forsaken his warrior way."

"A *shizoku*...a warrior who has given up. Then he should commit seppuku and find his honor."

SAMURAI AND KAMI

"That is not our way, Saigo-dono. He wishes to help as many as he can without fighting. Sometimes there are meaningful paths—even for *shizoku*."

Saigo gave a slow shake of his head. "I do not understand your people's ways."

Grace smiled and laughed slightly. "I don't always understand them either."

Saigo mulled on his next words carefully. With particular caution, he said, "You...are a kami who embodies our ancient princess legend. I am a warrior leader. At times over the past years, I have felt a strong connection with you, Himiko-ojou. But I sense you love this mountain man who has lost his honor?"

Grace ran her fingers over the folds of her kimono. The wrinkles of soft fabric brought out a suppressed sigh. "There're paths that we cannot go down when we encounter them, and when we look back...they have diverged too much to return to."

A firm nod filled the contemplative silence.

"And this dead man we found in the mountain?"

"The Mitad are bringing weapons from our world here. You may call them *magical swords*, but we call them *manus swords*. They are made from special stone that can amplify our abilities."

Focused eyes grew wide, filled with the imagined horrors. "Our samurai cannot combat such a thing?"

"Not easily."

"You will teach them?"

"I'll...do what I can."

∞   ∞   ∞

Emperor Antoku sat in the recessed shadows of the Chrysanthemum Throne. Behind purple curtains and surrounded by ornate gold and red decorations sat a fifteen-year-old boy in vermillion ceremonial robes befitting of an emperor.

CHAPTER FOUR

His platform was edged by red rails and black painted wood, filled with Meiji-era dragons and cherry blossoms. Servants, attendants, and advisors lined the walls of his throne room.

Before him, seven men in black robes with the crimson Mitad crest lay prostrate at the foot of the boy's stage. An eighth man was in the same position at the head of the formation.

In highly proficient Japanese, the bald leader of the bowed men said, "Great Emperor, you honor us by giving us this audience and bestowing noble gifts upon your hanyo."

"Powerful Raijin," the boy answered in Japanese with an adolescent voice, "when the kami descended to this realm and revealed themselves fully, my father passed not long after. His attempt to unify Nippon-Wa, after the internal struggles of our sector, was in chaos. You and your servants have brought stability to my reign." His words were sincere but stumbling, like a nervous boy trying to remember a rehearsed speech written by his parents while under threat. "I present you with these weapons so that you may continue to defend Nippon-Wa from all invaders. You may rise."

"Hanyo," Vistomus addressed the seven mirzas behind him in English. "Each of you rules over a region of this land, serving me as I serve the Emperor. Our wills are united. To carry out this divine task, the Emperor has crafted a weapon for each of you—anima stone katana, blades of the finest quality."

The boy waved a small hand to his servants, and they bustled forward in their kimonos, carrying sheathed blades. One was placed before each mirza.

Together they leaned forward reverently on their knees and picked up the blades with arms extended. Each examined the metal with ashen-toned hands. Their peculiar skin color and amethyst eyes mystified the native people of Nippon-Wa, further cementing the mirza's status as divine beings in the nation.

Bysis pulled the hilt from its sheath and grinned from ear to ear at the magnificent red sheen that it held. His hulking frame made a show of putting the katana on display for the room.

SAMURAI AND KAMI

Diya was slight in build, and mild in her acceptance of the gift. She only removed the blade enough to honor customs, smiled with a crinkle of her yellow-flecked violet eyes against her caramel skin, and bowed her head.

Kallag nodded his head in satisfaction but showed no emotion, while Cyra, Zeres, and Artera accepted their swords graciously.

Rius was last to take hold of his katana. His pointed features received the gift as if it tasted bitter in his hands. His slender, boney fingers only removed the hilt enough to show a portion of the red anima before re-sheathing it, as if peeking into a box with disinterest. He glared with wild, slicked back hair that partially fell over his face as he gave the slightest, acceptable bow.

"These katana are a symbol to the people of each region that you are one of them, and rightfully rule with the Emperor's consent," Vistomus announced.

They had not yet made it back to their sliding-door rooms when Rius spoke in a low exhale, "Master, why do you let that boy gift us our own weapons forged in a new shape? It's demeaning to allow Antoku to lord over us like that."

Following closely behind Rius, Bysis grinned youthfully. His head was bald, his short-trimmed beard was bleached, and his body was so wide that the others walked in front or behind him in the narrow hall. With a bear-like hand clutched gleefully to the katana tied around his waist, he spoke in a slow, deep voice as if his words were searching for the thoughts they connected to. "Come on, Rius. I like these samurai weapons."

Rius scowled. "Stop having so much fun and have some pride, you big fool. These—"

"The Emperor and his advisors who control him have the full devotion of the nation," Vistomus did not raise his tone, but his voice commanded silence from his subordinates. "Nippon-Wa is named as such to unify the old and new ways. Antoku's father chose it to lead his people out of the wars that plagued Earth. With his blessing, we move unhindered and with unlimited resources."

Rius growled but held his tongue.

CHAPTER FOUR

"I am their lightning kami, Raijin. My mirza will play the hanyo warriors. And the Emperor's childlike mind will consider gods his beloved playthings. While under his watch, you must play the game, but after, you may run free in your given regions."

A suppressed, wicked smile crept across Rius' lips at the mention of running wild in *his* territory.

"You're such a pain, Rius," Diya complained, boredom in her voice. "You can't just be humble for a few seconds so you can live like a king? Typical."

A scowl grew deep crinkles on Rius' forehead, and he snarled his nose at the small girl with diamond-manus stone patterns on her cheekbones, stark against her night-kissed skin.

Vistomus had nothing more to say on the matter.

"Enough prattle. *My Hanyo of Kansai* has cut down an important man. Tell your fellow mirza what you've learned, Bysis."

The lumbering warrior laughed with innocent amusement at the notion of the old man he had killed in the Akaisha mountains.

Zeres' white mustache moved as he said, "Cut down in my region *without my order.*" His voice creaked with his age.

Bysis' mouth closed and tightened, and his eyes shot down to the floor.

"No need to chastise him, Zeres. He did well. Tell them, Bysis." Vistomus chided.

Bysis stuttered oafishly, "Well...the man had seen Carnus. The traitor has been playing doctor in the mountain villages."

"Did he know where Carnus was hiding?" Rius asked.

Bysis' head turned back and forth on his fat neck. "No. He lives alone in the mountains. The people think he's some mountain spirit."

Vistomus commanded, "Zeres, you'll surround the mountains in that region and monitor everyone who moves throughout that perimeter."

"Why don't we just tear down everything and everyone in the villages until we find Carnus?" Rius asked.

Shaking his head with disappointment, Vistomus explained, "And scare him deeper into the Akaishi? We can't kill him until we know where he has hidden the Left Eye. I must find leverage over him first. Until then, let *our Pursuer* work. Naith will be the only one to hunt within the area."

At that, they each retired behind the fusuma sliding doors of their rooms for the night, becoming the silhouettes of demons on the paper-paned walls of the Emperor's guest quarters.

CHAPTER FIVE

SOULBORN

The creaky moss-covered planks of an oceanside dock brought a nostalgic comfort to Ares. For a few minutes, he let himself be recalled into a daydream of childhood.

Salted wind.

Brittle boards.

Splashing waves against the rock.

His mother.

He had been an outcast, shunned and hidden away for the entirety of his childhood, but Terrava would allow him a respite when there was the opportunity. The two would go to the family vacation house, north, on the East Avem coast. It was here that he was allowed to feel truly free...temporarily.

SOUL BORN

But an immense presence was nearing, and she made no effort to conceal her approach; it was the angry aura of an inlume.

Wooden beams creaked below his feet as Ares left the dock and returned back to the stone path of the seashore cottage. Ocean spray dampened the hood around his neck as he reached the threshold of the sanctuary. The wetness clung to his skin as he awaited the inevitable.

Terrava always had an elegance to her movements, but she could be nearly undetectable when she wanted to. The pressure of her approaching Soul Energy suddenly went mute.

Ares stared at the extravagant painting of the Mother Elsu, Hasvela, with her pristine wings encompassing the Ashva Tree in the entry way. His mother had added the masterful art piece after his third visit. For that reason, he hadn't torn it down, though it brought strange, repressed feelings as he gazed.

The door creaked behind him.

"Why shouldn't I kill you before you have time to turn around, Ares?" Terrava asked, revealing the full weight of her Soul Energy aura to accompany the threat.

"Mother, if I had done something to deserve that, I wouldn't have met you here."

"You chose here for a reason. I expect you want the days gone by in this place to soften my heart."

Ares turned to his mother with his head down. There was a tiredness to his voice. "I only wanted neutral ground."

The slender woman strode up powerfully to her son, stared into his amethyst eyes, and struck him across the face with an open hand. "My daughter had just returned to me," her voice broke. It wasn't the inlume master speaking, but a heartbroken mother. "What right did you have to take her from me? *What right?*"

He forgot how frightening his mother was. The flickering peaks in her emotions gave her Soul Energy a deadly edge. She would likely defeat him if they fought right now. He could barely meet her sapphire gaze.

Within arm's reach on the table in the entry hall sat a brass sphere with layered, overlapping rings surrounding it, and smaller spheres on those rings. Ares picked it up, producing a short spark of gray energy

CHAPTER FIVE

upon contact. It was a child's plaything that he had practiced on endlessly during the rainy days of his youth. The combination of manus stone cores and magnets allowed the smaller sphere to orbit the center when one introduced the catalyst of a Soul Spark.

The spheres whirred to life on their tracks.

"There is something I want," Ares murmured, his focus on the contraption. "Saida promised it to me. Maxima was the price."

There was a loss for words until Terrava finally sputtered, "What is this? A plea for forgiveness? Is that what you—"

"No. Not that."

"Then you must have something up your sleeve to stop me from tearing you apart right now, or else you wouldn't have answered my letter after killing your own sister."

A thin smile crept on Ares' face as the orbital toy spun faster.

"Fear not. Death is only temporary."

The sound of Terrava's breath hitching was audible.

Brass spinning filled the void.

"Like this toy, someone unseen keeps everything moving. For the Mitad…it's…"

Terrava finished what Ares wouldn't say, "Your father."

A nod.

"I never saw his face, you know. When you were conceived."

Ares raised an eyebrow. "How is that possible?"

"If I weren't contemplating killing one of my children right now, perhaps there would be time for me to explain the circumstances of your birth."

The toy ceased moving.

"Well, there is plenty of time then."

Ares' hints finally clicked within Terrava as her searing gaze held his, sapphire searching amethyst. "Maxima…she…*is she alive?*"

Ares replayed in his head the conversation between Bellia and himself as they had trained her to teleport apples.

Bellia sighed, exasperated. "Why does it have to be so brief?"

"For my plan to work, we need to pull this off without a room full of people seeing, and it will have to be in the middle of a sequence of events."

SOUL BORN

"You make it sound like we're pulling off a heist."

Ares grunted. "Something like that."

"Can we at least find a way to slow the apple down?"

"No. It'll be coming much faster."

Ares remembered Zolo shoving a piece of metus stone into his palm at the edge of the river. Its deadening effect afflicted him before he had cast it into the water. Zolo had threatened to leave his apprenticeship if Ares went forward with his plan to kill Maxima.

"There is someone that I need to meet with. This path is the only way to get to him. You are my apprentice, Zolo...loyal as your finger has proven...so I will explain some of my plans to you. If you have the ears to listen."

Then he recalled the final act of his plan. It had required Bellia to be on the roof during the final battle at the river factories. Images of the action flooded his mind. Gray Soul Energy, in its dragon-like shape, had loomed before his sister.

"I want you to know," Ares said with a struggle, *"that I cared about you, Maxima. I was never planning to hurt you, but then...I was given this offer. There's one thing that I've always wanted."*

"And killing me will achieve it?" Maxima asked.

"There is someone that I need to kill. You're only a step in my path to fulfilling that. Unfortunately, my path...is in the darkness."

His Soul Energy had struck Maxima, but not before Bellia opened a small portal in front of her chest. The dragon had passed through her without ever touching her body. The poor girl had been too confused to comprehend. She had clutched her chest, trying to figure out what had happened. It had been too late; Ares pushed her over the ledge and into the river—where Bellia's portal had opened once more just under the water.

Returning to the present from his sequence of recollections, Ares' voice danced, "Yes, Mother. We really must thank Bellia. Her unique mastery of Soul Wielding is unparalleled. None of this would have been possible without her abilities."

Terrava was bewildered. "But Eos...Talus...they saw her *die*. Don't play me for a fool!"

CHAPTER FIVE

"They saw what I intended for them to see. *What they had to see.* The same thing Saida saw." Ares gestured to the open doorway beside him. "Maxima, please join us now."

Wearing a simple tunic dress of blue linen, the raven-haired girl emerged into the front hall of the manor. She had done as instructed and kept a damper on her Soul Energy so as not to be sensed until the right time. "Hello, Mother." She looked sheepishly at the two before her.

Terrava's heart leaped to gaze upon the whole and hale body of her own blood, come back from death now twice; once on Earth, now once on Hyperborea.

The Queen gave a cry as she lunged to embrace her child. She had no words amongst her flood of tears and stuttering breaths.

Ares' laced his ashen-gray fingers together. "Saida needed to believe that Maxima truly died. She must *remain dead.* Otherwise, I won't meet…my father. He wanted her dead, and someone from the Mitad was going to do it."

Maxima spoke, "Ares said no one could know that I was alive until we met. Not even family. So, I've remained hidden here. He's been kind to me, Mother. I'm alright."

Terrava's pupils quivered as she found her voice, "Ares…you've done a *good* thing; *you have protected your sister.* But why specifically her? Surely, Saida is not threatened by a mere anatus Soul Wielder?"

Ares ignored the compliments and the notion that he was noble. "I have reason to believe someone in the Mitad can evaluate a wielder's full potential before it has been reached. I've never met this person, but with how the Mitad have wanted to move against Maxima, I believe she somehow threatens…my father. Now, it's time you told me what really happened on that day: who is my father, Terrava?"

Terrava fell back into a dusty tufted couch, pulling Maxima to her side, never letting go of her daughter's hand. Her features pinched together and with searching, far-off eyes, she chose her words carefully.

"I was taken hostage during battle. It was the first major push by the Mitad against Anite. We underestimated them. *I underestimated them.* We know better now. They are a kingdom without borders. The Mitad emir and the Voro rival any inlume. So, I fell into their trap…one of their top members captured me in some kind of confinement made of Soul Energy. Like a black box. I was...in there for two weeks..."

"The Negotiator," Ares mumbled.

"Who?" Terrava asked.

"One of the Voro," Ares explained. "She goes by Lady Sugra and is called The Negotiator by others. They're a class of wielders, akin to inlumes in strength, who became drunk for more power. The Voro allowed themselves to be consumed in order to attain their ambitions. As a result, their consciousness is now one with *his*."

"Then she's the one. She's the one I'll find and..." Terrava didn't finish speaking her desire for revenge. She continued with her story instead. "I fought every single hour to escape. Nearly managed it many times. I cracked this *Negotiator's* prison walls on five occasions when she let her guard down or grew tired. Eventually, the constant use of her abilities to contain me drove her nearly mad. I heard her begging for something to be done but a distorted voice only told her to continue until the task was complete. I never saw who the voice belonged to during my captivity, but he was always the one giving orders. I assumed him to be in charge. I then heard him say that he was still preparing for the ritual.

"Then days after that, the Soul Energy wall Sugra kept over my body suddenly split down the middle and opened at my abdomen. A single finger of Soul Energy manifested and cut into me."

Terrava let go of her daughter's hand and stood. She lifted her blue silk top and shifted the band of leather at her waist to reveal a small, discolored scar below her belly button. "That finger cut shallow, just enough to draw blood. Then, it produced a Soul Energy more powerful than anything I've ever felt. It was..." she shuddered as she sat back down, her legs suddenly too weak as she recalled the feeling. "It was ancient and ferocious and masterful all at once."

Wind off the ocean whistled through the windows.

The memory clearly pained her.

"I...I...don't know what he did to me. It was like a seal. An invasion into my soul. The Soul Energy crept into my blood. Icy. Creatures in my veins." She winced, eyes squeezed shut. "His distorted voice in my head

CHAPTER FIVE

like someone possessed. To this day, I can't remember what he said. And then it all stopped. By the time Talus found their base and reached me, they had released me and disappeared already. Then nine months later, you were born."

Ares looked around the room, bewildered. His face was that of someone lost—an expression he had successfully hidden for years at a time. Maxima's eyes held deep sadness for what her mother endured.

"Then my father was...was what...?"

Terrava shrugged. "I don't know. I'd say you are a child of Soul Energy itself. Born from the Great Soul. The one you're seeking now is more your architect or catalyst than a true blood father."

It was Ares' turn to sit. He dropped into position next to his mother on the couch.

"That's impossible," he muttered.

"Yes," Terrava's voice was a whisper. "It is."

"I don't believe in a *Great Soul*. But a wielding technique that can create life...that I can hardly believe any more than your supreme God. It only makes it more important than ever that I meet the leader of the Mitad."

Maxima nodded in silent agreement.

"Thank you," Ares paused, "for telling me the truth."

Terrava rose and put an arm on her son's back.

He recoiled, inclined to escape the touch, but decided to allow it for a moment.

Ares stood and looked out the window at the darkening clouds. The signs of a storm painted the sky over the ocean. He closed his eyes and sighed.

This complicated things.

"There is another matter we must discuss before I go," Ares said. Amethyst eyes reflected off murky glass panes. "It's about the Priori."

It was nearly more than she could take in one sitting. Facing her daughter's death, seeing her revived, discussing Ares' supernatural conception, and now Ares speaking of the Priori of Karnak. The shock was slowing her ability to filter thoughts properly.

"How do you know about that?" Terrava asked warily.

SOUL BORN

Maxima remembered the back tattoo of a tree with a flame on her mother's back. It had been revealed in her private bath chamber when she had tasked Maxima with finding Caldus Lapithos.

The same grin crept onto Ares' face for a second time that day.

Arrogant. Pleased.

Confident in his conducting of the game, "I want to know what the Priori was after. Originally. And what Grace was looking for on Earth."

"That was the group you were in with Rebus?" Maxima asked her mother.

"Yes. That was long ago, but I still keep in contact. Just to stay informed of the Corland's secret world. The Priori seeks to uncover the Eras. Morax sought the same."

"Which is?" Ares prodded. Suddenly, the oceanside house was no longer nostalgic but confining—he had been here too long.

Softness.

Sentimentality.

It was weakening his mind.

Terrava bit her lip as she decided on how much to divulge. "For saving Maxima, here is what I can tell you. Try to understand that the Priori keeps knowledge distributed across the members. Only the top members know everything. Those like Grace and myself are only agents for the cause. What I can tell you is that there is a gateway between Earth and Hyperborea. Not one like Bellia creates."

"The Mellizo Glyphs," Ares said.

"That's how we returned to Hyperborea," Maxima confirmed.

Terrava nodded, "According to the knowledge I had access to, the Great Soul resided there, before the eras. Before time itself—"

"Nonsense."

"Just listen. You've always been too arrogant. If you don't fix it, then what you're seeking will be beyond your grasp."

Ares clenched his teeth but remained quiet.

Terrava continued, "A powerful wielding priest from the Lost Eras, named Karnak, found this…in between world…and within it, the Codex Stones."

"Which are?" Ares asked impatiently.

CHAPTER FIVE

"Monuments of manus stone that make the purest anima and animus look dull and useless in comparison. From the Codex Stones, he formed incredible artifacts."

"*Now that, I can believe.*"

Terrava frowned. "How do you know about those?" It was forbidden knowledge, even within the Priori.

Ares hesitated. Floorboards creaked beneath him, and the wind howled, urging him to leave before he revealed too much.

No.

This was his only chance outside of the cryptic puzzles that Salvaluc gave him.

"I have a few pages from Grace's journal. Copies of the original."

A gasp. Terrava's eyes widened. "Is she alive?"

"I couldn't say. She was looking for one of the artifacts from the Codex Stones. An eye. She called it an eye. Looking on Earth, it seemed."

"*The Left Eye of Izanagi,*" Terrava whispered, unable to contain her awe. "It was on Earth after all."

"Maybe. Appears that Grace played from every side. Mitad, Priori, and Necogen."

Agreeing, Terrava's tone became both saddened and awed, "She was a woman who lived on the edge. The knowledge of the Lost Era possessed her until she became entangled with every group trying to find it. The elders made use of her obsession. Grace was good at what she did. The best."

"She met multiple times with a member of the Mitad who almost became one of the Voro. A man named Carnus."

A slow nodding was the only response as Terrava processed. Her tongue hesitated to say the name. "Carnus Solaire…an infamous man. As dark as they come and as bad as they go."

"Voro. Comes with the title," Ares reminded bluntly. "But he didn't go all the way. Betrayed Vistomus from what I've heard. Anyway, I'm not after this eye. It's another artifact I want. There are only a few references to it, but someone in the Priori must know."

Terrava's sculpted dark eyebrow raised in curiosity.

"A weapon," Ares elaborated.

SOUL BORN

"They're all weapons of a sort, but I know which you mean. I also know who could have information on it. However, it depends on what you intend to do with it."

Ares looked at his younger sister and then to his mother, a devious gleam to his eyes. "I brought Maxima back to you. That should be payment enough."

The arrogant smile painted his face a third time that day.

∞   ∞   ∞

Maxima rested on the bed of her temporary accommodations. Terrava had arranged for her to be moved from the seaside cottage to south of East Avem, in a town on the outskirts called Old Cintish. It was an extravagant bedroom, spacious with fine oak furniture. Mirrors and paintings decorated the walls.

Still, it was her prison all the same.

She was to remain *dead* until notified otherwise.

Someone was supposed to come for her. Eventually. Her mother was attempting to recruit her old master back into active duty within the Order of Soul Wielders. But, if and when inlume Saier Fey could be found and convinced, was still undetermined. Until then, Terrava had ordered her daughter to remain out of sight.

The red ceramic corcinth mask of Caldus Lapithos sat on her bedside table. Ares had recovered it from the Mircite factory rubble. Its wicked grin and fierce horns didn't make her uneasy, though.

Instead, the mask made her think of Caldus.

A tear formed, nearly dropping from her eye. She wished she could have gotten to know the bold and reckless brother of Jezca. Terrava had previously tasked her with getting information from the son of Grace Lapithos, but she had grown to admire the heroic leader of the Red Corcinths as well. Before she knew it, Eos and Caldus had swept her into their attack on the Mitad.

It had been three days since Terrava had departed. Three days of lamentation and longing to be with her family again, with no end date to her isolation in sight—*it was all that Maxima could take.* Her chest

CHAPTER FIVE

constricted when she thought about her separation from the world for too long. The room felt too small to contain the dread she felt while those in Anite still believed she was dead.

The door to her quarters was being watched by royal guards disguised as private swords for hire. They delivered her meals, brought her anything she might need, and above all, made sure she remained in the room.

Maxima laced her fingers together and turned her hands out to pop her knuckles as she looked out the window. Then, she put on her leather boots, fastening them all the way up her shin. She turned to the navy curtains with a plan and began tearing away a piece.

It's just a quick trip outside.

Just a quick trip.

No harm. No one will know.

The curtain strip covered her face and nose better than expected. She tied the covering behind her raven hair, threw on her cloak, tucked the red corcinth mask away in her layers, and swung her legs out the open window.

A pang of regret hit her as she exited the second story of the inn. Maxima didn't want to contradict her mother, but the room was too claustrophobic for days on end with nothing but her thoughts and flashbacks of the events from the Mircite Valley incident to keep her company.

"Sorry, Mom," she murmured to herself as sapphire light formed at her feet, leading her to the ground of the village outside East Avem.

She found the town of Old Cintish quaint and peaceful as she passed the bakery, wishing she had coin to buy some sweets and the freedom to show her face. Suspicious looks came from the town's people, but she never stayed in one place long enough to be confronted.

The town square had a statue erected in honor of Vola Cintish. Maxima read the placard beneath the statue and remembered Talus' lore of the Order of Soul Wielders. This was the hometown of the Corlander who cofounded the Order under Morax. It seemed small and forgotten for such a historical place. Cintish's heavy brow looked out at the horizon with a bronze scroll in one hand and a long sword in the other.

SOUL BORN

"What am I doing here in your town, Cintish?" Maxima whispered to herself as she touched the raised words that told his story. "How did it end up like this?"

She felt under her cloak and touched the cold ceramic of Caldus' corcinth mask. Sadness drifted over her, and she longed run straight to castle Alasedis to reveal herself to Eos and Talus. She turned from the statue and continued with her exploration of the town.

Soon after she came upon a craftsman's workshop. The doors were thrown open because of the mild weather. The master of the shop was talking to his apprentice about an order for the region's legate, but Maxima didn't pay attention—she was mesmerized by the rich colors of clothes hanging to dry and the barrels of dye nearby them.

The dark pigment pools shimmered in the day's light, and she watched from a distance as the master and apprentice stirred an open barrel's tub. The deep blue color churned, and indigo cloaks hung behind it.

When the workers left for a break, Maxima found herself drifting into the open shop, wandering the expensive clothes, drying in rows, and staring into the tub of dye.

A dark reflection was cast back at her. She lowered her face covering. It was murky, but she felt a tiny bit of pride in her features, especially her hair, just like her mother's. She traced the faint scar over her lips—something she used to hide behind her desert scarf. Then, she pulled out Caldus' mask.

He was gone, and the red color didn't suit her.

She held it by the tie strings and let it soak in the indigo pigment while nervously watching the flimsy wooden door the two men had left through.

It had only been a few minutes before she heard, "What are you doing in my workshop, girl?"

Blood rushed into Maxima's head as she panicked and pulled the mask out. Then, she broke towards the exit.

"Get back here! You think you can freeload off my dyes? Nicola, go after her!"

CHAPTER FIVE

Maxima never saw the owner's face or Nicola's. She sprinted from the place with sweat dripping down her spine like melted ice.

Why had she done that? Too close. Too risky. Stupid.

When she stopped to catch her breath, she was multiple streets away from the craftsman's building and in the shadows of a side alley.

Her breathing settled, and the fire in her lungs dulled. She held up the corcinth mask to see parts of it had taken on the strong blue dye while other parts of the glaze had become a grayish-glacial color. Turning it over, she decided she liked the new look much more.

Maxima pulled her makeshift curtain-handkerchief back over her face before peeking out from the alley. She found a sign that read: *Cintish's Brew and Tavern.*

A disturbance of noise in front of the tavern worried her that Nicola had chased her this far, but she found something else entirely.

"You're not going to pay for dinner?" an old man with a prickling head of white hair and a hunched back asked at the tavern door.

Two men in black cloaks laughed with spite. "You're pushing your luck, old man. You know we eat free."

"This is the home village of Vola Cintish. We are proud wielders, and you should pay for what you ate," the old man said testily.

"Well, perhaps that shows you how far the Order has fallen. They can't even care for their founder's village. You do know who you're talking to, don't you?" One of the two men said in disbelief at the tavern owner's boldness.

There was a moment of hesitation before the old man responded, "Looks to me like two low-ranking thugs that the Mitad forgot to collect after their defeat at the Tenebrim Canyons."

The taller of the two Mitad members turned to his friend and said, "Perhaps we have to teach this senile man his place?"

"And remind him that he's late on protection money for the month," the other said as he pinned the tavern owner to the doorframe with his body and squeezed the owner's trembling pinky. "Perhaps losing this finger will remind you to pay on time." He threatened, then pried open the ring finger on the same wrinkled hand. "And we'll take this one next time if you don't have our money."

SOUL BORN

The two thugs burst into drunken laughter.

Maxima felt the anger rush over her. Everything the Mitad had done to her…taken from her…came bursting into her mind, making her more enraged than she remembered ever being. An urge to wipe out every member of the wretched group seized her. From Saida all the way down to these unranked hoodlums.

A hushed comment came from across the street, "When are the King's men going to come clean up this mess they left of the Mitad? It's been a month now."

A small crowd had formed to observe the scene as the Mitad man pulled out a dagger and pressed it to the pinned hand of the tavern owner.

The crowd murmured in distress, but no one did anything.

They're all just standing by and watching. They're going to let them hurt this old man. Cowards!

"That's enough," Maxima emerged from the alley. "I think he understands your point."

"Oh look, a little girly wants to learn a lesson too." The black cloak that wasn't roughing up the old man approached her. "What are you hiding under that face cloth girl—"

"I believe everyone here has had enough of you two. Why don't you leave before someone has to put you in your place?" Maxima hissed.

The Mitad soldier was quick. His arm grabbed Maxima's hair and yanked it painfully back, cranking her head down and throwing her to the ground.

"Go home before you die here."

Maxima lay face down in the dirt, shocked that the initial response had been so violent. Then, she touched her stinging cheeks. They were scraped and bare.

Bare!

The curtain cloth—it had fallen off.

Thinking quickly, she got to her knees with her head tucked and pulled the blue horned mask out from under her cloak. She feigned being wounded to give herself enough time to pull it over her face and tie it securely as she stood.

CHAPTER FIVE

"What the…?" The Mitad soldier asked. "Look at this freak."

The other ruffian turned, let the tavern owner slide to the ground with his digits still intact, and joined his partner. "What are you supposed to be?"

"You fools should have left when I asked," Maxima warned.

"She's gonna need a *special* kind of lesson," the tall one said, and both ruffians laughed drunkenly together.

Their amusement was cut short as a sapphire light reflected off the wicked smile of the blue corcinth mask. The air crackled, a dense aura of Soul Energy filled in the air, and Maxima pulled apart her glowing hands.

Fear suddenly flickered across their faces. They had meant to intimidate a few coins and a free meal out of an old man, not fight a Soul Wielder.

"L-l-look, girl. I don't know who you think you are, but Vizier Alsi runs this hole of a town now. If you start something, you'll have to answer to him."

Maxima smiled from under her mask, but the same devilish lion expression was all the Mitad members could see.

"Then whichever of you lives can tell your vizier that I look forward to testing his wielding abilities."

Sapphire orbs flew at each man, one after the other.

Bwoom. Bwoom.

They were small, quick attacks. That was still enough to tear a hole in the first man's chest. He flew into the street, bloodied and mangled.

The other slammed into the tavern wall, coughing and sputtering as his robe soaked through with blood. He stumbled to get away down the alley as best he could.

Maxima watched the pathetic retreat with cold eyes from behind her mask. Then she went to the old man and helped him to his feet.

There was fear in his eyes. Fear of both the Mitad and the fearsome warrior before him, but he managed to give a few words of gratitude. "Thank you…you…whoever you are." He touched his finger, bleeding from the dagger, and thanked the Great Soul for still having it attached to him.

Voices rose in the crowd that had witnessed the altercation.

"What was that?"

"Is she a member of the *Order?*"

"Do the Soul Wielders hide their identity?"

"Or wear masks?"

Maxima whipped around to see that the mass of witnesses was growing.

Panic.

She exploded from the street with Soul Energy at her feet. Without looking back, she fled the attention on her defeat of the unranked Mitad soldiers.

"Did you see that?"

"See what?"

"That girl with the mask! The Blue Corcinth."

CHAPTER SIX

BEACON STONE CALLING

An island within an island, that was castle Setudo. It was centered in a lake in the capital city, Loteal, on the island nation of Lenape. The roofs were entirely made of patinated copper, forming many domes and twisted spires made in turquoise panels that resembled a turtle shell. The entire structure created an effect like a myriad of strikingly colored turtle shells drifting towards the heavens.

Bellia could have teleported herself inside the castle but always chose to arrive across the moat gate first.

The arches of supporting chalky stone stretched a bridge one hundred meters across the lake to the sandy-pink walls of the castle.

The view gave her a nostalgia for her childhood. She felt at ease, thinking of a simpler time before her power had manifested.

A time where she could just *exist*.

No worries. No danger.

She clutched the carved, wooden sea turtle in her pocket, opened a portal, and stepped through the ring of writhing tendrils. When she emerged out the other side, tribal sea turtle banners surrounded her in the throne room.

The light honey skin of her father, a trait she had received little of, contrasted against the ornately carved throne. He sat between armrests with whittled faces of fearsome warriors amidst a chairback of spirals and tessellating patterns behind him. His hair was pulled up and tied high in the way of the warrior tribes, but the crown of his head, where his hairline would have started, was shaved to reveal the ink patterns of royalty.

"King Hika Tamat," Bellia said, putting her hand over her heart and bowing.

"Bell! You scare me every time you appear before me like that!" Her father let out a hearty laugh. "It's been too long since you last visited! My daughter has the greatest gift known to any living wielder and yet she hasn't visited in nearly a year." He teased.

"Please don't call me that, King Tamat. I'm not a child anymore. I've been abnormally busy with my work."

"You're still my firstborn. Can't my own blood at least call me father?" The King's smile faltered as he sensed something deeper to his daughter's sudden appearance. "Bell, you seem uneasy."

"Yes, I have news…I wish to stay for a few months, Father," Bellia said quietly.

The apprehension in King Tamat's deep voice echoed off the chamber ceiling when he asked, "The Mitad will allow this?"

"I will continue my work but return here when I am done each day…"

Tamat shifted forward. "Are you alright, Bell?" He asked, not as a king but as a concerned parent.

"You…you are to be a grandfather."

The King's hardened, warrior face eased into a warm smile. "My eldest daughter is with child?"

Bellia shifted her Mitad cloak aside, showing her far protruding abdomen. "Yes. I am."

CHAPTER SIX

That warm smile, as he beamed upon his daughter so near to giving birth, began to falter as he realized, "And who is my new son-in-law?" A tense mixture of fear and distaste colored his question.

"Ares Bellator. Though he would prefer not to be associated with his family name."

The man on the throne suddenly looked as old as his years. The remnants of his smile had melted into crinkling lines of concern. "The Son of the Mitad? Bellia...this is...unexpected." He searched for words by pondering aloud, "It will further ally the Mitad to our side, I suppose. Tell me, is Ares a good man?"

Bellia met her father's hazel eyes and said, "Ares is a *complicated* man. But I believe he is as good as his circumstances allow him to be. He cares for me, and I for him."

King Tamat bobbed his head repeatedly. "Then it is a good match for my daughter and our kingdom. Given our forced hand, it can't hurt to have additional favor with Saida and Vistomus. It will strengthen our trading position with Astor Bruinsma as well."

Bellia nodded weakly. She couldn't bring herself to reveal that the Mitad had met her relationship and child with extreme disapproval.

"Now, you haven't returned in so long, can I assume that there is a meeting of the cloaks on my island?" The King perceived wisely.

"Saida and Vistomus are both on their way as we speak. I came to give you as much warning as I could. Some emirs and Voro will arrive as well."

Kneading his brow he sighed, "A meeting of the highest cloaks. Well, there must be big things happening soon. Tell me...I have read the news of the Mircite Valley Incident on my cantium tablet. Ares' sister, the returned Bellator princess, is missing, presumed dead? Were you part of this plot?"

Bellia stood with pride. "I was there when it happened, but I took no part in murder. I saved a life. The Great Soul shall judge all other conflicts that happened."

The noble mask of a strong warrior-king became translucent. Bellia saw the worry and regret in her father's eyes. It was apparent that he wished he had different paths to choose from rather than having to send her to train under the Mitad. He longed for alternatives to fuel his economy other than the leteb plant that tied him to the Ignoble Lord Astor Bruinsma. And now King Tamat worried that his daughter was about to bear the child of such a conflicted lineage.

It was all abundantly clear in the old, warrior-king's face.

"Well, I'm thankful you were able to spare a life. I trust you'll make me aware of any significant outcome of this meeting?"

"If possible, I'll share anything that could affect Lenape."

Bellia bowed and left the room under the banner of her people, mentally preparing for the remaining Mitad members to gather in castle Setudo's private wing—where the organization had free reign.

Now, priestess Jezca Monte would be in the castle as well.

So many threads being woven.

Yet my child will take priority over them all.

She clutched the wooden turtle in her pocket once more.

∞   ∞   ∞

Salt hung in the air like seasoning for the lungs on the dock in the Lenape port of Tangar. Sun beat with near tropical heat. Waves struck rhythmically. Golden-blonde hair whipped across prominent cheekbones, and Jezca brushed it aside to keep it out of her eyes.

A staggeringly large cargo sea-strider was docked before her. The vessel had sails the size of other boats in the harbor, set like wings on a massive dragonfly.

The ship had the painted symbol Jezca learned to call *the Bruin*. It was a set of smoking pipes crossed to form an *X*, but the pipes' bowls were skulls. It was the emblem of the Ignoble Lord, Astor Bruinsma.

Astor stood at the edge of his ship deck, but the sun was at his back, making him an indiscernible blot of a shadow, looking down over his lined-up crew on the dock.

Blot was an accurate description.

The man was enormous—as wide as any four of the men below him and an extra foot taller. He was dressed no differently than his workers,

CHAPTER SIX

save for the fistful of gold rings that caught the sun on his deep-almond skin.

"Well, priestess, I must say I'm looking forward to seeing you in action," Astor's baritone voice boomed. "I have a taste for novelty. Drugs, food, companions…but especially wielding."

Saida leaned in and whispered into Jezca's ear, "Slowly approach the line of workers. Do not stop until you have tested them all."

She was supposed to use her powers to root out a traitor in Astor Bruinsma's crew. Someone had been stealing large amounts of leteb shipments and leaking money carrier routes to siphon gold from the revenue. Astor Bruinsma and the Mitad were allied in some way she had yet to understand.

"Am I to become a member of this criminal crew?" Jezca hissed with disgust. "I'm the future High Priestess—"

"May I remind you that you chose to be here?" Saida whispered harshly. "While you are with us, you are not some royal praying princess, *Tawas Kajina*. You're a girl earning information about her mother."

Her one exposed eye glared into Saida's red-amethyst irises; they communicated a disinterested impatience with her.

He was right, though. She had no choice if she wanted to find her mother.

Jezca scowled but strutted across the dock to the first man in line.

She reached up for his temple and held her breath at his sweaty stench. He recoiled at the sensation as she let a mist of pink Soul Energy escape her fingertip and invade his mind.

Astor snapped, "Hold still you mangy curs, or I'll throw you overboard halfway back to the Corland. Then we'll see if you like squirming enough to make it to shore alive." He cackled at the idea before breaking into a rattling smoker's cough.

Even with the threat, every man recoiled at Jezca's first contact.

Riselda Beltram, Astor's third in command, observed her carefully as if vetting the Priestess with doubt. She shaved the sides of her hair and looked as tough as any of the men before her.

No sign of betrayal in the woman.

Calm. No panic in the next person.

BEACON STONE CALLING

It wasn't this man either.

Her brief skims into each of their minds had not found anything of note. She moved on to a man in a blue knit cap. He rumbled a throaty groan of dissatisfaction as she probed his mind.

He's the one.

She casually moved to the next. Down the row with methodical cadence, willing herself to betray nothing of her discovery until she surveyed every last one like Saida—who watched on with indifference—had instructed. The man in the knit cap let a confident curl twist the corner of his mouth.

The last man gave her pause. *Not stealing from Astor...but this one had another agenda.* She heard the name *Fey* resounding in his thoughts. Probing to find more was going to make too much of a scene. She decided that a wild card in Astor's crew was not her problem.

"Name?" she asked coldly.

"Artu, my lady."

She lingered for a second longer to let the man know she was on to him.

"Well, it's not him." Jezca turned to Riselda and said, "But the one in the blue cap is your thief."

"Wha...what?" The thief protested, but it was short-lived. Riselda flipped a switchblade out. It flashed a yellow burst of Soul Energy as she drove it into the man.

The bellowing laugh from Astor above masked the cries of pain. "Very good, priestess girl! Very good. You passed the test. We had already found evidence of him being on the take from our rival."

Jezca was annoyed to be playing a part in the game at all, let alone for the Mitad and the Ignoble Lord of the drug trade.

"So, you feared I was working for them too?"

Again, Astor laughed as if enjoying a good performance. "No, dear girl, Saida would never dare allow such a thing. I questioned the authenticity of your ability." He popped each knuckle individually, flashing his gold-covered fingers and wrists. "Now I know. Saida, you have a special one on your hands."

CHAPTER SIX

Saida grunted as if he wasn't as sure or didn't care. He slicked back his hair, tucked his thumbs into his waistband, and said, "We've worked out a deal. Jezca will be with us for a time, and while she is, she'll do routine checks of your crew."

Jezca almost protested. Her lips moved, but then she thought of her mother.

She would endure it.

When they returned to the castle called Setudo, Saida escorted Jezca back to her room. Though they passed through corridors of elegant luxury, her mind was distant, and her demeanor withdrawn.

Saida mused, "Come now, Priestess, no need to be so dejected. You'll find life in castle Setudo quite comfortable."

"Indeed it's lovely…" Jezca mumbled. "Sorry, I've just been having strange dreams ever since—er, never mind," she caught herself. *Why was she speaking to the enemy about such things?* Her shared dreams with Eos Bellator were none of Saida's business.

They passed under a turtle-shell-trimmed arch that led to the guest wing of the castle. "Oh? What kind of dreams? My knowledge is vast. Perhaps—"

"I misspoke about a private manner," Jezca snapped, though after a few moments of silent walking, her curiosity got the better of her. "Besides, it's just nonsense anyway," she muttered. *But was it nonsense? The dreams of Eos felt so extremely real…like she was experiencing them herself.*

Saida pried, "I'm knowledgeable in what others consider nonsense as well."

"Well, unless you have been to another *world* that doesn't exist…a place called *Urte*…or something like that—"

"Earth?" Saida's eyebrow raised.

"How…did you…?" Jezca stammered.

"Girl, there are numerous distant lands, and I've been to many." They paused at the doors to her suite.

"Then, it's real?" Jezca's eyes narrowed on him suspiciously.

"Who was going there in your dream?" Saida pressured carefully.

Jezca knew that Saida would be *particularly* interested in the dreams of a priestess with *the sight* and tightened her lips. She had already revealed too much which was highly unusual for her. "Nobody. It was *just a strange dream.* I want to sleep."

Grabbing the handle, Jezca stormed into her room, but before she could slam the door shut, she froze.

She was not free, though Saida was right, it was a comfortable space; the room was clearly made for a noble, or at least a noble's favorite guest, but someone was already waiting for her within.

"Jezca," Saida said from behind her, "this is Bellia. She will be staying in the castle for the same duration I expect you will be. I thought you two might enjoy each other's company. She is King's Daughter of Lenape and a uniquely talented member of the Mitad."

Bellia was struck with awe at Jezca's anima stone right eye. The vibrant pink stole her attention. She had seen a few manus priests, but their dull-red stone eyes were no comparison.

"Stunning," Bellia said softly. "Pleased to meet you, Priestess. I look forward to having another wielding woman around while I visit my childhood home."

"Likewise," Jezca replied, but she scrutinized Bellia warily. Any member of the Mitad held equal weight in her eyes, heavily pregnant or no.

A mirza killed my brother...Yann Kilsig. They're all the same. Many heads of one body. Demons.

Jezca stretched out a hand to shake Bellia's.

*I'll have to be careful about this noble-born woman. As soon as I find mom...I'll kill them all...*Revenge permeated Jezca's thoughts. As she let go of Bellia's hand, she suppressed the urge to manifest Soul Energy and shove it into Saida's throat right there.

Instead, Jezca carefully rested her hand upon the pouch that hung from her belt, embroidered with the reverent hands of the priesthood below a manus stone emblem. It was a reminder of the path of peace.

Then, she noticed the desk in the room had something on it—another pouch. But this one was not like hers; it had the two-headed serpent of the Mitad on it.

The way of prayer and the way of the serpent.

CHAPTER SIX

She was appalled to realize that both appealed to her urges in different ways. She remembered Archpriest Mellitus leading her to Saida after the battle at Mircite.

Everything she had known was crumbling into lies.

More than anything, she felt alone.

Caldus was gone. The priesthood failed her. Only her assassin instincts remained consistent. She wanted more than anything to fall onto the softness of the bed nearby and not open her eyes for days…

But Saida and Bellia were in the room and a particular bag was on her desk. There was something else the Mitad wanted from her before the day was over.

A sensation crawled under Jezca's skin—a foreboding that raised the blonde hairs on her arm and stirred a fluttering in her stomach…it reminded her that she was among the Mitad in a foreign land. Their temporary truce should not allow her to lower her observational talents in sensing Soul Energy. It must always be on guard, and now it had her focusing on the Mitad bag.

Perhaps, the bag was focusing on her too…

Saida narrowed his eyes on Jezca and asked, "You can feel it, too? Such a keen talent for Observation."

"The Manus Order called it *the sight*," Jezca nearly growled.

"Yes, well…the rest of us call it Observation Wielding. Tell me, what do you sense?"

Jezca closed her eye. The world went dark, but she sensed the strobes of Soul Energy pulsing from the bag with the two-headed snake. Black and red rings of aura whispered into her mind.

"It's…it's ancient. Connected to others…like a network."

Saida prompted her, "Go ahead. Open it."

Jezca reached for the pouch and poured its contents onto the table, finding an onyx hunk of manus stone. The pyramid-shaped object was about the length of her pinky finger, and it fell with a dense clunk.

"A dull manus stone?" Jezca asked, slightly surprised.

"Much more than that. I want you to light it and tell us what your Observation Wielding reveals."

BEACON STONE CALLING

Jezca hesitated. Her curiosity and Manus Order upbringing nearly allowed her to proceed immediately, but she caught herself and said, "Why would I do this for you? I'm only here to reunite with my mother because the Mitad have her. I'm already doing you the favor of parsing through *the drug lord's crew*, but I am not here to solve all your mysteries. *You did murder my brother, after all.*" She tilted her head threateningly.

Saida sighed, "Ah yes, your hotheaded brother who led a masked rebellion group. I believe he led an attack on us, not the other way around. You also joined in on this attack, if my memory recalls correctly. Regrettable that your brother was a casualty before we could establish a relationship. Still, I'm willing to call all things even and forget that you contributed to the destruction *of my critical manufacturing facilities*," Saida growled lowly.

Bellia gave Jezca a slight raise of the eyebrows that said *this isn't the time or place for this confrontation.*

Relenting, Jezca gave a hum of agreement, but inside, her heart ached in the absence of her brother.

"Now, this is not merely a favor you're doing to see your mother," Saida worked to bring a soothing tone back into his voice. "This puzzle is more complex than can be explained just yet. But rest assured, what you sense here will be key to reuniting with Grace."

"I recommend you explain it *now,*" Jezca demanded petulantly, lacking any desire to respond with tact.

"In due time, Priestess. For now, you can either perform the act and report your findings or refuse and slow down your progress towards reuniting with Grace." Saida turned slightly as if considering leaving.

The young priestess acquiesced reluctantly, her curiosity winning over.

"It looks like a worthless stone. Barely capable of being considered manus grade at all," Jezca lied. On mere appearance, it was certainly true. However, with closed eyes and an open perception, there was much more under its surface.

"Oh, I doubt you believe that," Saida replied knowingly.

Pink mist drifted down from her extended fingers to onyx stone.

CHAPTER SIX

A veil was lifted when the Soul Energy mingled into the chunk of manus stone. The darkness peeled back from the edges like the fog of breath dissipating from a cold window, revealing a striking ruby color. Jezca marveled in wonder.

"Not much is known about them," Saida explained. "They're called Beacon Stones in the few ancient scrolls we've uncovered."

Liar.

Jezca focused her Observation on Saida as he spoke. He knew far more than he just claimed.

Energy continued streaming from Jezca until she completely purified the shard of the onyx shroud. Then the core began to burn a flaming scarlet.

A surge of Soul Energy overwhelmed her, a contrary, disorienting sensation, as if the energy flooded both into and out of her mind. She had experienced something similar to this before. This wasn't the same…but it reminded her of the memory exchange with Eos. There was something of her essence and someone else's in the phenomenon with the Beacon Stone.

A memory triggered. Her childhood days. An instance surfaced of her mother teaching her how to wield in private. Grace had been so proud of Jezca for being the top of her class in evaluations back in the Necogen village. As a reward, Grace had shown how her how to manifest a Soul Sphere at age five.

But the Soul Energy she felt right now…

Jezca honed her Observation to be sure.

Something…no, *someone* had called from the other side.

"Mom," she whispered as she matched the Soul Energy in the stone to the memory of the Soul Sphere lesson.

Saida's eyes lit up in satisfaction.

Then the darkness crept back over the stone.

"The artifact can only be used every couple of days," Saida explained.

No matter what Jezca tried, she couldn't halt the procession of onyx reclaiming the ruby color. The Beacon Stone had done its work and now she was locked out.

BEACON STONE CALLING

Sandy-pink stone, extravagant drapes, regal tapestries of battles for Lenape, and marble tables full of refreshment filled the private meeting room in castle Setudo. The hall burned with rose oil, and a fire crackled in a giant hearth. The luxury was greater than the King himself regularly enjoyed.

Saida sat in a velvet chair, thumbing through his half of Grace Lapithos' journal.

Vistomus Fulmen stared in quiet contemplation at the fire.

The Overseer, Jaco Hetfel, remained in hushed discussion with Lady Sugra, the Negotiator, near one of the multi-paned glass windows. His albino skin juxtaposed her raven hair and dark eye shadow.

The patter of rain filled the spaces between the popping of fire.

Emir Grimshaw gazed out another window, flicking spheres of his neon-red Soul Energy from his fingertip like a lighter to pass the time.

Ares had kicked his feet up on the blue sofa near the hearth, his eyes closed.

The time ticked away, only marked by the drops of water against glass, until finally, the doors opened. The last three members of the meeting joined the room.

A bleached, horned skull-helm entered.

Ares opened his eyes to glare at Naith Lelantos, the Pursuer, with his bone-elsu necklace, flaunting about like some gaudily costumed reaper.

"I see we're still letting certain *mirẓa* into a meeting of emirs and the Voro," Naith hissed.

Ares only answered with a rumbling growl.

A short, stocky man who reminded Ares of a crazed bulldog followed with Bellia in tow.

The doors closed, and Emir Raggan began, "Right. Apologies for the delay. Things on Earth are a bit frantic right now, but we'll have that sorted soon, eh?"

CHAPTER SIX

Saida looked up from the journal and welcomed Raggan. "I suspect you will. Your restructuring of their kingdom, *Japan*, has been extraordinary from what I hear."

"They were desperate for the structure...*after I killed their beloved emperor*. I gave them a taste of the old ways, and they ate it up," Emir Raggan explained pragmatically. "Told them we were their returned gods. Kami they call 'em. They even had a tale about a god who could tame lightnin'. So, I told their new child emperor that their *Raijin* was returning soon. And lo and behold, he did," he nodded to Vistomus who had yet to acknowledge the emir's arrival. Raggan went on, "The *Americans*, however, have been a different story." The man grunted to himself in annoyance, "Hmm. No, no, they are a more *complex* problem to solve. But solve it, I will."

Vistomus finally spoke without looking up from the fireplace, "I have no doubt in my mind."

"Lord Fulmen," Saida changed course, "perhaps you can start us off with an update of our search for Grace Lapithos and the Voro traitor." He spit the last words with disgust.

"My past months on the island with Naith have been fruitful," Vistomus reported casually. "And using the notes you've shared from Grace's journal, we've located Carnus' general area. However, I don't believe he has the Left Eye of Izanagi in his immediate possession. Perhaps it is hidden as a bargaining tool for his life. We haven't found him yet, but we're close. As for Grace, she remains as elusive as always."

Saida tapped his fingers on the meeting table, forming his thoughts carefully, "Finally...then we must force Carnus into revealing the Eye's location. He has no regard for his own life anymore. Do we have the leverage?"

Vistomus bowed his bald head in assurance, "I believe we do."

"Then you will act soon?"

"As soon as I believe we have nothing more to gain from waiting. His past relationship with Grace means he may still communicate with her from time to time. After he slips up in that way, *everything will be ours*."

The rain picked up, and gusts of wind seeped through cracks in the windowsills. The storm moved closer over the castle.

BEACON STONE CALLING

The windows flashed white, and the roll of muted thunder followed.

Naith added, his creaking voice like the grave, "I won't allow Carnus to escape. He's delaying the inevitable. It's only a matter of finding Grace's trail and where he hid the Left Eye."

"Good," Saida said, and stood to pace to the table at the center of the room. "The day when the Master ascends the throne is approaching. Grace's knowledge is essential, and the boy, Khasun, is nearly ready."

"I only ask that you decipher that journal and share its knowledge before that time. That…" Vistomus hesitated, "and there is, of course, her daughter to discuss."

The Overseer joined the conversation, "The Manus Priesthood handed her over to me after the Mircite Valley Incident. She came willingly and is resting in a chamber of this castle now." A small glowing crawler moved across his open palm. Its six legs rattled with a static-filled mechanical sound. "I am keeping eyes on her at all times." He held up the crawler on display.

Saida was pleased as he explained, "I'll oversee her work while here in Lenape. Vistomus, she said something interesting to me today— something you may need to prepare for."

Vistomus hummed and nodded for Saida to continue.

Rubbing the scars on his face, Saida revealed, "She mentioned that she had dreams…visions…of travelers going to a foreign world *called Earth*. Of course, she had no idea what she was saying, but I believe it's safe to assume you'll have visitors soon, Fulman. Make sure they don't interfere with our plans."

Sneering in disdain, Vistomus shook his head, "It's the Bellators, I would bet. They have a Mellizo Glyph. This Jezca girl will prove useful if so."

With a cold laugh, Saida agreed. "More than that, she'll help us put an end to Astor Bruinsma's losses. In return, he has nearly secured the Viator kingdom for us. With them, we'll gain a strategic foothold next to the northern kingdoms of Corland that are still out of our control. The Viator also have the facilities and resources in place for us to move to the next stage of our metus stone production."

CHAPTER SIX

Emir Raggan hummed, "Mmmm...so, the Mircite project was successful?"

"Extraordinarily so," Saida confirmed. "Our assault on Anite was premature and failed in objective, but I had calculated the chances of success to be slim. Nevertheless, it was an opportunity we had to take in order to test the waters. I had not planned to lose the metus stone factory, but at least that wretch, Talus Bellator, is now with one less arm and without a daughter. His reputation is in question, and he's on the back foot. Victory amongst the losses. Still, our plans are delayed, which makes taking Viator all the more necessary."

Emir Grimshaw kept his Soul Energy burning at his fingertips. "It doesn't really work, does it? Canceling out wielding with this *metus stone*?"

Saida reached under the long meeting table and produced a rod from the Mircite ruins with a handkerchief over his hand to avoid skin contact. He set it on the table, stroked back his hair, and rubbed his mustache. "I brought what remained of Borne Ozen's first trial on Durath Leorix. All of you, come and see for yourselves."

Grimshaw approached with arrogant curiosity, his right hand still brimming with neon-red Soul Energy. He placed his left hand on the bar of metus stone and pointed his right index finger at the window. The gesture threatened to let the storm in if he released his attack.

Pitter-patter-pitter-patter.

Rain came down.

No Soul Energy left from the Emir.

"Nothing," Grimshaw whispered to himself in astonishment. "That window should be shattered!"

Lady Sugra sauntered closer in her tight black dress. When she took her turn with the metus stone, nothing happened either. She only murmured, "Emptiness..."

Saida motioned for Raggan to approach next.

"No. Mmmm. No, thank you. That's unnatural, that is. I won' have anythin' to do with it."

A mustached smile and raised eyebrow met his comment.

"Suit yourself," Saida said and leaned on the top of the table. "Jaco, I am reassigning Borne Ozen to Emir Mina to begin work on new factories. I need you to maintain control over Corleo. It is our northernmost territory. With Ramath gone and Durath fled, it must become a stronghold. Keep the Leorix Queen a happy hostage, so the little lion-pup doesn't try anything."

The Overseer began to protest but was cut off.

"No, I understand you've lost your mirzas, but I have replacements in mind already. I'll have no mouth out of you."

The seven-foot albino man gave a deep bow. "Yes, Lord Saida. I look forward to leading Corleo with my new mirzas."

Saida nodded, pleased, and began his pacing once more. "Vistomus, there is another matter. What of the *domain?* Is it prepared? With the vessel found and the Left Eye of Izanagi within reach, we must be ready for the ritual."

Manus stone light mixed with the hearth's glow. It reflected softly off Vistomus' bald head, casting his face in deep shadows. "I've allied the kami with the Emperor-child of Nippon-Wa for many years now. My work has been tireless, especially the past months, and I believe we are ready. The Nature Energy around the Imperial Palace is finally suitable. I'll maintain the domain for the ritual until we have the Eye. Master M will not be disappointed."

There was a hushed uneasiness from the rest of the room at the mention of the ritual and Master M. It was as if a great taboo had been broken by even speaking of it.

The meeting carried on for another hour until Bellia requested leave. Ares was tempted to go to her but held fast to his indifference as he had been previously warned. Then, one by one, all the Mitad members departed to their quarters for the night. Soon, only Ares and Saida remained.

"I don't recall asking for you to keep me company, Ares," Saida growled.

Ares ignored the remark and stood over the table where Saida was working.

The well-dressed Mitad leader poured over Grace Lapithos' journal, refusing to look up. "If you want a closer look at these pages, you're better off sending your errand boy, Zolo, to sneak in here."

CHAPTER SIX

The comment caught Ares off guard.

Saida knew...Of course, he did. It shouldn't have been a surprise. Did he know that it had been copied? No. Zolo wouldn't have been allowed to live.

"I have no interest in reading women's diaries like you," Ares played it off. "I fulfilled my side of our deal."

A quill moved on paper, deciphering the journal text. It did not cease moving, nor did Saida break away as he said, "The Master is always busy. You will get your meeting."

Ares put his hands down near the parchment that Saida was writing on. "Don't jerk me around. I killed Maxima—*my own sister!* When will I meet my father?" He ground his teeth.

Finally, the quill stopped, and Saida raised his head to glare his former pupil down. "Don't make me shred your wielding techniques apart in this room. It's far too expensive to do here, but if you insist, I'll remind you how our bout on the Meteora balcony went."

Ares simmered a throaty growl.

"You'll get your meeting, but the Master is only able at particular times. When I know the time and place, I'll share it with you."

Ares relaxed his jaw.

"Fine."

The quill began moving again.

"Now, since we're discussing people that you've killed for me. I have another person I want dead."

"Salvaluc," Ares said knowingly.

Saida laughed deviously, "Yes, but I want to do this one *myself.*"

CHAPTER SEVEN

TUNED PERCEPTIONS

The subterranean sky tunnels projected warm light into the depths of Tenebrim. Salvaluc sat in meditation under the sun's channeled rays, his silver mustache and scraggly eyebrows glittering with silent wisdom. His mahogany robes contrasted against the man in a black cloak under the neighboring sky tunnel.

Ares attempted stillness of mind and body.

It didn't suit him.

"I've been given a time and location, Master Salvaluc," Ares said, barely above a whisper. When the provocation received no response, he continued, "I'm going to meet my father."

Salvaluc turned his head with mild irritation at Ares' disturbance. He was getting used to the regular occurrence after multiple visits from the Mitad mirza.

CHAPTER SEVEN

"I liked it better when you were meditating," Salvaluc grumbled, but there was a light, playful tone from the old inlume.

"Yes, and I liked it better when you were telling me about the Tools of Karnak."

The banter earned a smirk from the mustached master.

"Ares, you use this word *father* as if you are going to meet the man who shaped you. You've had many fathers of varying quality. The one's who've taught you, bonded with you, and shared meals with you. Sometimes it was me, other times Saida, and of course Talus—"

Ares cut the attempt to stir his emotions short, "Then what will you have me call him? Surely, you're interested in knowing what comes of our meeting?"

"It matters not what you call him but how you say it. I hear all the whimsy of the young boy I first met when you use the word, but this man is no friend or guide to you. I only wish to remind you that you are meeting someone more hostile than family. And yes, I do eagerly wait to learn about the leader of the Mitad. He has worked in shadows his entire life. Even the Priori know nothing of his true identity."

There was a moment of anticipation as Ares expected more. "Do you not have any advice? No warning or questions?"

Salvaluc closed his eyes once more and reminded Ares, "Why do we practice soul meditation?"

There was a sigh of exasperation. Ares mumbled, "We commune with the Great Soul through the light. We sit in silence under the sun to gain wisdom and discipline." He rattled the words off as if performing a repetitive task.

"That is my advice. Spend time in the stillness. You will know what must be said when you know yourself. The leader of the Mitad will speak with you, but he will not reveal his true name or face. If he does, then you would be wise to fear his reasoning."

Ares nodded. He settled his mind and searched for a place in the silence where he could feel comfortable.

Eyelids fell over amethyst irises.

Thunk.

A light slap struck his head.

TUNED PERCEPTIONS

He turned in surprise to see Salvaluc walking past him towards the cave-room's exit.

"Always wrong on your timing. Speaking when you should be quiet. Quiet and still when the time for meditation is over. You disrupted my practice already. Come on," Salvaluc beckoned for him to follow.

For anyone else, Ares would have threatened instant retaliation, but when it came to Salvaluc, he held a special, annoying reverence for the man. Salvaluc's aura humbled Ares—there was a mysterious charm to everything he said or did. It was as if allowing emotions like anger to come forward would prevent him from solving the next puzzle—and every sentence from the Inlume was a riddle with multiple depths.

Ares followed the flowing brown-red robe ahead of him. He knew better than to ask where they were going. So, he found himself leaving Tenebrim and climbing up the worn channels of stairs hidden in the canyon walls. They navigated the dark together, touching impressions in the walls to confirm their path and using Soul Energy rarely to light their way.

"Do you feel ready for your greatest task?" Salvaluc spoke in the shadows of the canyon.

The light pattering of their footsteps against endless sandstone filled the silence.

Dragging his hand against the rough, textured wall, Ares asked, "Do you mean confronting my father or finding one of the Tools of Karnak?"

Patter. Patter.

"I believe you will soon be a father, correct?"

Ares was glad the lack of sunlight hid his blushed face.

"Oh, that…" The young Mitad prodigy stopped walking. He debated revealing this vulnerability to an inlume. "Salvaluc…I…for the first time I can remember…I'm scared."

"That's a good first step."

Before Ares could say more, Salvaluc turned a corner and moved with a nimbleness that exceeded his age. Ares had to jog to keep up.

"Where are we going?" he finally gave in to asking.

CHAPTER SEVEN

Slightly out of breath, Ares paused as he rejoined Salvaluc, who stood motionless on a pink stone plateau. Sunlight peeked into the chambers of this canyon.

They were near the surface.

"Asking questions when we've arrived at the answer," Salvaluc mused without looking at Ares.

Ares crossed the canyon chasm on platforms of gray Soul Energy and met Salvaluc on the plateau.

Upon setting foot on the rock structure, he saw what they came for—blatant and obvious as if the thing had been invisible until he reached it.

The sunlight cut in a clean line that hid an archway of alabaster on the other side of the light. The form was natural, as if it sprung from the canyon organically, but its pure color gave it away as man-made. An opaque milky glass filled the arched gate.

"What is it?" Ares wondered aloud.

"A question wondered by the Priori since we were founded. We call them Makanla Gates. Please, touch it, but adjust your Observation; try to perceive the trail of Soul Energy that has long since dissipated."

Ares reached out a hesitant hand, confused.

At first there was nothing.

He pinched his eyebrows together and began digging beneath the surface level Observation, as if removing layers.

Tingling shock.

A vibratory wave pulsed through him.

The aura he sensed...it felt the most powerful inlume he'd ever encountered, but the frequency it existed at was different from most Soul Energy.

"Unless I had known to look for this sensation, I would have missed it...but it is beyond powerful...whatever it is. A layer of Soul Energy operating below our naturally tuned perceptions."

Salvaluc grunted with a nod.

"Why show this to me? Do you trust me with the Priori's secrets—even ones I did not seek?"

TUNED PERCEPTIONS

"I have communed with the Great Soul for a lifetime. I do not act of my own discretion here—against it, actually. However, this is the path that has been revealed to me. In time, you will find answers the Priori has long sought."

Ares grinned. "It sounds like you almost trust me, old man."

Salvaluc squinted. "I trust the way of the Great Soul, not the instrument he chooses to use. Don't forget, my knowledge is not free. I'm showing you a Makanla Gate as a gesture of goodwill. I will show you how to find the tool you seek, but first, you must find someone *for me*."

Ares hummed., "And why do you think I know where this person is?"

"Because Grace Lapithos was working with the Mitad. Find Grace, and I'll teach you where to find one of the Tools of Karnak."

Ares paused and contemplated the implications.

"I don't know where she is, but I know who does. I have a certain wolf for an ally who might be able to help." Ares laughed, "The people call him a half-demon in their tongue."

Salvaluc stroked his mustache, pleased at Ares' agreement to cooperate. "*A half-demon wolf?* You keep interesting company indeed, Ares. Then do what you must."

∞   ∞   ∞

"Right. You may be wonderin' what you're doin' in the capital building of the North American Sector. I agree. Too much white. Hard to clean up blood. Americans and their stark-white buildings," Emir Raggan grumbled.

Sergeant Malin looked up without being able to lift his head all the way. Blood dripped down his lips. His hulking body was limp in the chair he was tied to.

"Ain't much of a...a mystery," Malin snarled sarcastically.

"Well, since you're aware of your situation, shall we get on with it? I'd prefer we beat you in someplace a little less classy, but the information will come out of you just the same," Raggan said.

CHAPTER SEVEN

Malin took in his surroundings.

White walls, brass light fixtures, and maple furniture filled a stuffy office inside the U.S. Capitol Building. The room smelled musty and neglected, but Malin could hardly breathe through his broken nose.

The soldier grinned tightly though a swollen black eye, "Get on with it. I'm ready to have some fun."

"This will be different, mmm?" Raggan mumbled. "My mirza beat you physically, but I will teach you pain with Soul Wielding. You will learn. Then, you will speak. After that, we'll decide what to do with you. Let's start with location. Where is Colonel Axel Kane hidin'?"

"Oh, wielding. Gonna do the magic on me, huh?"

Emir Raggan stroked his beard and cocked an eyebrow.

"What do you know 'bout wielding?"

Malin didn't try to raise his head again, but managed to say, "I worked alongside Eos Bellator. Seen all the magic I need to see."

"Then you know that I can and will make you talk."

"You can try," Malin said and jerked at the ropes tying him.

Raggan leaned in close, neck jutted out, so that Malin could see the pale blue of his eyes flecked by amethyst. His wrinkled brow was like a raging bulldog's. "Right. I am, by nature, a very peaceful man, but I can be brought to...*great violence*," he said with heavy breath.

"Get on with it then," Malin shot back. "I'm feeling a lot more *talked* to than I am *tortured* right now." He grinned tightly again, splitting his lip further.

Conjuring up a pale emerald mist from undulating fingers, Raggan let the Soul Energy touch Malin's forehead.

"Not the face! Don't start with my face! I need to look good after this. Ladies won't want me ugly," Malin jerked as far away as he could.

He screamed.

The energy's heat was so intense he lost the ability to differentiate between the extremes of hot and cold. The sensation was a wavering reality of pain that was simultaneous fire and frostbite setting into his skin.

TUNED PERCEPTIONS

"This pain is just for my entertainment, yeah? I'll soften you up, but then I'll go inside there to get what I want," the Emir said and pressed his index finger into the burn mark on his captive's brow.

Between screaming, Malin muttered, "Devers gave me…grief. Told me ten grenades was…too much, but—agghh!—I was right! Always—agghh!—am right. More grenades…always the answer."

"Think of yourself as a real funny, tough man? Won' be thinkin' anythin' is funny ever again before long." Emir Raggan relented briefly in his ministrations.

"Lighten up…didn't get your name, Scruffy," Malin jested between his shallow, labored breaths. "You prefer Scruffy or Mad Dog? Got that look in your eyes like you're real…real wild. I respect that."

The emerald light came again.

Malin's shadow danced shakily against the white walls behind him. "Wait! Wait," he huffed, out of breath from screaming. "It doesn't matter if I tell you where Colonel Kane is."

Raggan drawled, "Isn't that convenient?"

"We have many locations…It's a network. You'll get one of them and spook everyone off. They'll abandon them all within the hour. No way for me to know which they're using right now," Malin lied, still grappling with the after effects of pain.

"Mmmm," the emir grunted.

"I don't know what you want me to say. They set it up like that in case one of us was interrogated."

Raggan paced, tapping his fingers on crossed arms. "Lucky for you, I believe that but no…no…that won't do. We've learned that intel on Kane already. Mmmmm. You have a few more seconds to give me somethin' more useful. Else we go into your mind."

Panic set in. Malin couldn't take much more physical pain and didn't want to find out what else the Mitad leader could do.

The stocky figure loomed over him.

The room suddenly felt so small that the walls were pressing in. There wasn't enough space between Malin and the glowing embers of emerald Soul Energy that fluttered about.

Malin thought carefully about his options.

CHAPTER SEVEN

As the threat of Soul Energy reached closer to his face, he decided on his next words—

But he didn't get to use them.

"Ah, Emir Raggan, they told me I'd find you here. Having too much fun, I see," a young voice, dripping with arrogance, said.

"Ares, aren't you on the wrong world?" Raggan asked, recognizing the voice without turning around.

"I'm on business from Saida."

"Saida sent you?" the emir's voice rasped and rolled playfully, almost mocking the young mirza.

Ares pursed his lips in annoyance. "Saida gave me a mission. The mission led me here."

"Well, it'll have to wait, won' it? Unless you think you can get *this one* to talk faster than me."

"By all means. I won't interrupt your torture session," Ares smirked and tossed up his open hands to gesture that he wouldn't disturb Raggan's work.

Malin intervened before Raggan could continue, "Look, if you want to get me on your side, pain ain't the way."

Raggan raised an eyebrow with an expression that said he would only wait a few seconds to hear Malin out.

"See, I'll do a lot of things for free, or a pretty woman, or if I get to do killin', or—" Malin realized his rambling was about to earn him excessive pain, so he skipped ahead, "but I don't betray my friends."

An aggravated grunt accompanied the searing pain of Soul Energy that once again threatened to cook his skin.

"Except!" Malin tried to finish, "Except if for the right amount of money!"

"Tryin' to extort me when I can just kill you? Not wise, yeah, soldier?"

"Look, I can hand Colonel Kane over on a platter, but you have to buy off my conscience. You want his rebellion ended. I want a pile of money. Win-win."

Raggan stepped back, taking his flow of Soul Energy with him, as he set about pacing again.

TUNED PERCEPTIONS

Finally, the Bulldog looked to Ares and said, "Negotiate with this idiot and then find me to discuss your mission. Try not to kill him, right?"

Ares smirked and glared at the tied-up soldier. "Notice how he said *try?*"

∞   ∞   ∞

The two weeks in Colonel Kane's network of underground bunkers had been far from the excitement Eos had imagined a return to Earth would be. Instead, it had consisted of either Aizo or Scavok alternating between lectures:

"You're not to join this mission, Eos."

"Do not leave the bunker, Eos."

"Do not attract attention today, Eos."

Glenn kept busy improving the ventilation and air-conditioning in their hideouts, while Scavok and Aizo were away most of the time with Talus. Eos was left with Durath and Corporal Devers. They appeared to be assigned to watch him.

"Let's summarize what we've learned," Eos said to Durath as he gestured to a world map spread out on a part of the wall. Over the last two weeks, Eos had meticulously covered it with pins connected to strings and names marking important facts and keys to their current situation.

Devers sighed, "You've done that a few more times than necessary already."

Eos ignored him, extending his pointer stick. He tapped the tip at a name with many connecting strings over North America "Vistomus Fulmen has been missing since the Mitad took over the North American Sector. Emir Raggan led the takeover under the guise of their partnership with the European Sector. Raggan's three mirzas on the continent here are the siblings Morgana, Virgio, and Wyan." *Tap. Tap. Tap.* "None of their abilities are known, but they've divided territories." Eos pointed at the East Coast of the North American landmass. "Virgio oversees the northeast from the U.S. capitol building, Morgana is securing the southern states, and Wyan is working on capturing the middle, where the

∞ 111 ∞

CHAPTER SEVEN

remaining holdouts from the previous military regime are making their last stand under General Guren." Eos then tapped on the shattered West Coast. "Meanwhile, we believe the Mitad is operating from a position of power off the West Coast in the Asian Sector." His stick swiped across the Pacific Ocean to the island of Japan.

Ahktar perched on Eos' shoulder.

The white feathers were the only thing in the entire bunker that appeared clean. The smell of oil and dust permeated the place, and there was a constant hum of a makeshift electrical system powered by generators.

Durath leaned back in his chair calmly, not saying a word.

"Give it a rest, Eos. Please," Devers sighed. "You can go over all the facts until you're blue in the face, but in the end you're going to have to be patient until your dad and crew return. I know you want to be out there helping investigate the Mitad and finding Malin and Grant, but this is a different situation than before. Why don't you tell me more about this Hyperborea place? It was your goal for your entire life to get there, and I've barely heard you utter a word about it since you've returned."

"I can't give it a rest, Corporal. The Mitad killed my sister, and now they're taking over the world I grew up on while spreading chaos on the one where I was born. *I need to be out there helping.*"

Durath finally spoke with a friendly groan as he pulled his fur cape around his muscled frame and ran his fingers through its texture, "Eos, enough. You're King's Son of Anite and only heir to your father. You have connected the people of Earth and Hyperborea, helped smooth the path for us. You're allowed to be here as an emissary, but anything more than that is reckless. I'll remined you that *the Mitad killed my father and stole my kingdom, too.* You think I want to be sitting here anymore than you? We have been instructed to wait, so for now, we wait."

Eos grumbled but respected Durath too much to argue.

"So, everyone on your home world can do this wielding like you?" Devers asked, trying to change the subject.

"Most of them." Eos shrugged.

TUNED PERCEPTIONS

"Any fancy wielding weapons on Hyperborea that we could use to retake North America back from the Mitad?" Devers' question was more of a passing curiosity to fill the time than a serious notion.

"Sure."

Devers' paused. "Really?"

"If you have an army of wielders to use them," Eos said, blunting the spark of hope the idea provided.

"Well, you got any spare wielders you can loan us, considering the worst ones from your home world are running around like rats here?"

Durath answered, "You're looking at them. The five of us are considerably strong on our world. But there's no efficient way to get an army over here, and most Hyperboreans can't wield Soul Energy as warriors."

Devers clicked his tongue, teasing, "Well, maybe we *should* send you both out into battle if this is all the reinforcements we get."

Eos had enough of the meaningless banter.

"I'm going up to let Ahktar fly and get some air."

Corporal Devers stood with Eos, "All right, let's go." Before Eos could protest, he finished, "You know Colonel Kane's orders. Neither of you goes outside alone."

The dimly lit gray brick pillars, and the web-like system of condensation-covered pipes that ran along the underground hideout, fell away as the trio climbed the stairs to the outside world.

Sunlight hit Eos' skin, and the sight of greenery eased his mind.

Ahktar screeched with relief to be able to spread his wings, and Durath cast back his cape in the rays of light.

Devers followed behind Eos and watched in amazement as the elsu beat its wings and swiftly became a small blot against the sun, accompanied by an audible *crack*, breaking the sound barrier.

"Unbelievable that such a creature exists," Devers marveled.

"You'd see many things that would drop your jaw like Ahktar on Hyperborea. And just as many would have you wishing never to see them again."

It was only a few minutes before they were joined by Glenn, who stepped outside with his winged staff in hand. He spoke, slightly out of

CHAPTER SEVEN

breath, "You'll want to see this for yourself. Captain Draven has returned."

Devers jumped to attention at the news.

Sorry, Ahktar, we need to return inside.

There was a screech, a *woosh*, and then the elsu was back on Eos' shoulder mere moments later.

"Did they find him?" Eos asked in excitement as they headed back underground.

"Yeah. They got Malin out of there alive."

"Thank God. I thought we might have finally lost the brute," Devers said with a relieved exhale. They ducked under hastily hung electrical wires. "What's with the new walking stick, Glenn? You didn't have that when you left."

Glenn smirked, "When you're surrounded by wielders, you get strange gifts. Talus told me to keep it on me. Not to mention my knees aren't getting any younger." He strode forward with his wing-topped staff.

There was a strange look of not understanding, but Devers continued, "Right. Well, I'm sure it'll come in great use if the guys with magic start a fight with you."

Glenn chuckled but said no more.

After weaving through shadowed hallways, they found Colonel Kane standing at anxious attention. His hands were behind his back with military poise, but his boot was impatiently tapping the concrete floor.

"You made it back just in time," Kane said without taking his eyes off the door ahead.

Devers replied, "Yes, Colonel. Glenn told us the news—"

The metal hinges creaked, and a puff of smoke preceded a tall blonde man with a cigarette hanging from his lips. Captain Draven held the door with one hand and helped Malin into the room, supporting him with his other arm.

When Draven saw Eos, his eyes lit up. Once through the door, he removed the cigarette with his free hand and said, "Well, I'll be...Kid! I heard you were back over the comms but didn't think you'd be the first face I saw next to the Colonel."

TUNED PERCEPTIONS

"Hello, Captain. It's good to see you again," Eos said, a deep smile breaking across his lips. Memories of his service under Draven came over him. It had been a defining period in his life, marked by his sacrifices during the rescue attempts of Major Seth Skye.

"Eos," slurred Malin, his face badly swollen and purple. There were burn marks over his forehead and temple, and he could only open one eye. "Wish you could see me...better time. An...ugly sigh' righ' now." The long sideburns and stocky stature were immediately identifiable. His speech was less so, with his mouth unable to finish the syllables of all his words.

"You're looking prettier than ever, Malin. Glad you're alive." Eos returned.

That nearly got a chuckle out of the half-conscious soldier, but fractured ribs prevented anything more than an amused exhale.

"Colonel," Draven said with a salute.

Kane smiled with gratitude at his returned comrade. "First things first. Put that cigarette out. You know better. No smoking down here. I'll waive your punishment on account of the merit of this rescue."

"Right. Sorry, sir." Draven put out the stub on the doorframe and let it fall to the ground.

"Sergeant, it's good to have you back alive," Colonel Kane said to Malin. "Let's get you a medic and some rest. I'll need a full debrief as soon as you're able."

"Yes, sir. Bes' do it now. I think I'm gonna sleep for a week straigh' af'er."

The steely yellow-green eyes and side-swept bangs of Lieutenant Olivia Skye entered the room with a small group of soldiers that Eos didn't recognize.

"Sir," she saluted sharply. "Perimeter secured. No evidence that we were followed after the rescue."

"Excellent, Lieutenant. And where is Corporal Grant?"

There was a solemn pause from everyone.

"Corporal Grant was fatally wounded during the extraction, sir. He...he didn't make it out of Mitad hands," Skye said with strain.

CHAPTER SEVEN

Colonel Kane bowed his head and spoke what Eos had been thinking, "The Mitad have taken Major Clark, Corporal Grant, and so many other good soldiers. We will be sure to repay them many times over. We'll hold a memorial for him."

Eos remembered Corporal Grant alongside Major Clark during his first confrontation against Ares. He'd also been right by his side at the battle of Orford.

Eos ground his teeth together, enraged.

The debrief continued, but Eos was lost in contemplation.

The Mitad must pay. Death after death at their hands.

Revenge tainted his every thought for the rest of the night.

Eos found himself back in his bunk where all the Hyperboreans shared a sleeping quarter. Durath had been asking questions about his time in the North American Sector's military, about how Earth guns worked, and about the ways the remaining nations were ruled after the Fracture War. He had been doing all he could the last few weeks to learn about this foreign world.

But tonight, Eos only gave absent-minded, automatic responses.

It wasn't until Talus embraced his son that he snapped back into the room, back into his body. His father, Aizo, and Scavok returned from multiple days of reconnaissance.

The five Hyperboreans reunited, sitting at the edge of their metal-frame beds and discussed.

"We've learned all we can from our visit to Earth," Talus said, leaning back on the support of his one arm. "With the situation as it is back on the Corland…I doubt we could spare any resources to assist Colonel Kane. His rebellion is a fraction of a force against the joint Mitad and European Sector alliance."

Durath grunted. "The whole place is a mess. If I'm permitted to speak, King Bellator? Recovering the situation would require taking down an Emir and maybe even Vistomus Fulmen himself."

Aizo agreed, "The boy's right. There's little we can do for the situation. We assisted secretly in the rescue of one of their kidnapped officers. Perhaps we can offer some parting assistance, but nothing more."

TUNED PERCEPTIONS

"No," Eos protested. "These are my people as much as Anite is my home. We can't leave them to be ruled by Emir Raggan."

A brooding, silver mane of hair rose from his bed. Scavok growled with irritation, "Emotions have nothing to do with it, King's Son. Think like the Order of Soul Wielders requires of you. We didn't come here to strike a blow against the Mitad. We came to learn what they've accomplished and what they want. Information was the objective."

Eos scowled at the master assassin. His face was scarred by battle-earned wisdom, and his attitude was molded by having to choose between those battles. Yet, Eos could only think of what Ares had done to Maxima. What Tessio had done to Major Clark. The staff of Rohl Ford killing Benedir. The blade of Yann Kilsig piercing Caldus. Saida's strings of light slicing off Talus' arm. The face of Malin in the hallway earlier, and the fact that he would never see Corporal Grant again...

"The Mitad *are* weak, Father," Eos pleaded. "They have a small group spread thin here. Our presence is unknown. Perhaps we could strike them before—"

"Perhaps!" Talus bellowed. "Perhaps we could deal a damaging blow to the Mitad before we return home. It would feel satisfying no doubt. Satisfying to set them back after all they've done, right?" He leaned forward and stroked the multiple strands of his braided beard, a look of disappointment in his golden-brown eyes. "But perhaps you did not understand the oath you took."

Eos glared resentfully and said, "*I believe in the right for all to make for themselves a free life.*"

Talus sighed. "Son, this is not how you achieve that mission. Now, you promised me after your return to Mircite..."

Before he could protest more, Eos caught an advising glance from Durath. He only responded by saying, "Whatever you decide is best, Father."

Durath asked, "With that decided, did you find the information you were seeking? We know what the Mitad have accomplished, but do we know *why* Vistomus has long since abandoned the North American Sector? It seems he left everything to Raggan, even his moment of victory?"

CHAPTER SEVEN

Scavok grumbled with dissatisfaction. "We have only clues and hints. We're unable to decipher them ourselves, but perhaps Terrava or Salvaluc can provide answers back home."

"Why them? What do they know that the King and his master assassin wouldn't?" Eos asked suspiciously. "They're all the way back in Hyperborea."

Talus returned, "Sometimes, you must rely on other inlumes to be knowledgeable where you are not. One man cannot be a master of every domain. There are things the Mitad are after that I know little of. With that said, I think it's best we establish a regular check-in schedule with Colonel Kane to monitor the situation here on Earth."

"Agreed," said Scavok decidedly.

The feeling of heart-drop was apparent on Eos' face.

"Don't worry, Eos," Aizo said, "We're not abandoning your friends. When the proper time comes to help, or if this information leads to something more, we'll return. The Mitad will never take Hyperborea and we won't allow their hold on Earth for long."

Eos accepted the notion was the best he would get for the time being.

There was quiet in the room after that, except for the occasional murmurings between Scavok and Talus. Durath grew contemplative between polishing Caldus' manus daggers and staring intensely into the golden corcinth pendant usually clasped to his cape. Aizo had begun to write in the bound book that he always carried with him, while Scavok and Talus had moved further into their quarters to plot in private. Eos was left snapping spheres of crimson Soul Energy to life in his palm, then letting it fall into vapor on his bed sheets.

The hum of electrical equipment combined with the humid stuffy air left Eos restless. His mind wandered to dark places, and temptations flirted with his will to hold fast to his vows.

It was tempting to try and attack the Mitad.

Revenge would be satisfying, even if he just picked off a few low-ranking members.

Breaking his cycle of dark thoughts, he found himself shocked at how far his own fantasy went with visions of reckless violence.

TUNED PERCEPTIONS

The night passed as he stared into the marbled orb of light in his hand. Eventually, only Eos and Aizo remained in the sleeping quarters.

Aizo put down his quill and turned to his pupil.

"You know, Eos, I believe I find myself in a situation similar to you. It's not like a mentor to talk about such things with his student, but I don't think anyone else could answer the questions that are tugging at me."

The mischievous eyes of his master were suddenly painted with the grief that he had been holding inside. Eos couldn't place what Aizo meant.

"What do you mean? Similar to me?"

Aizo rubbed at the temples between his wild tufts of hair and sighed, "Mourning someone lost to you."

Eos let the words hang until Aizo was ready to say more.

"I...I only fell in love with one woman in all my life. Here...on Earth. But our destinies were on different worlds. You see, we fell in love in the days of our youth when your father and I explored this world with abandon...before the war. He would allow me to take the Mellizo Glyph to visit, but I still had duties in Anondorn."

"Who...who was she?"

"You've already met her. A long, long time ago."

A shocked wave of connection came over Eos. *"Miss Lori?"* he asked, realizing what had always been evident but never noticed.

"Yes, Lori Lee. However, when the time approached for me to make a decision, I stalled. She couldn't wait on me forever—a man disappearing for months...sometimes years. I understood. When I came back the final time, it was to hide you and Maxima." There was a long pause before he could bring himself to finish with a broken-heart, "She had a son by then, and I planned to turn myself in to Braxton to evade the Voro members after me. The only way to keep you both safe and vanish from their relentless search..." his voice drifted to a whisper.

"Aizo, I'm so sorry," Eos said, feeling the pain of his master's sacrifice and unfulfilled romance.

"Being back on Earth again...do you think there is any chance—any at all—that I could find her?"

CHAPTER SEVEN

"Aizo…I'm sorry, but that's not possible."

"How can you be sure?"

"Her son, Jace, was like a brother to us. Max and I lost touch when Braxton took us, but recently we found him again. He revealed that Lori had passed away in one of General Braxton's work camps years ago."

Tears were at the corners of Aizo's creased eyes. Eos had never seen anything but sagely inlume wisdom or goofy jest from his teacher.

It stunned him to see his master so devastated.

Aizo replied, "Then, her son…Could I find him? Perhaps I can meet him, do something for him, that I couldn't for her."

Eos hesitated, watching the last vapors of red light sift through his fingertips. "You could, but not here. Jace was the one who stole the Mellizo Glyph back from Vistomus and gave it to me in the desert. But now he's on Hyperborea working for the Mitad."

Aizo nearly fell from his chair. "How is that possible?"

"He escaped the same work camp as his mom and was taken in by Vistomus' rebel-front group here on Earth. He became an apprentice of sorts under," Eos paused, struggling to admit it, "under my brother."

"Ares?" Aizo asked in disbelief.

Eos nodded. "The times Max and I ran into him, he meant us no harm though. Helped us, even. I believe Jace is still good, despite his allegiances."

"The will of the Great Soul appears stranger and stranger to me as my years go on. I cannot understand the ways." Aizo turned away, lost in the past and threads of possibilities that couldn't be. He murmured to himself, so low that Eos could barely hear him say, "If Jace is on Hyperborea and with the Mitad, then I must find him."

Eos didn't have any words for the moment. There seemed nothing that he could say to comfort Aizo. Fortunately, Durath returned, followed by Scavok and Talus.

Talus announced, "Colonel Kane has asked us to assist him in one matter tomorrow. After that, we will leave Earth the following morning."

Two days. That is all I have left on Earth, thought Eos.

It felt wrong to leave so soon and with the state of things in chaos. *Bwooom!*

TUNED PERCEPTIONS

A muffled explosion rocked the walls of the room.

Concrete debris fell from the ceiling; the powder dusted Eos' head.

Everyone lurched into high alert, with Durath and Eos scanning the room for a cause.

The three elders in the room remained still, however.

Ahktar screeched and beat his wings.

Aizo snapped, "Focus your Observation! You don't have time to be looking around when you should be *sensing* what happened. Your perception must improve if you really want to chase the Mitad."

Eos and Durath closed their eyes.

They were novices, unskilled in the ways of the inlumes.

Pressure.

Intense pressure of foreign Soul Energy.

It was nothing like Saida or Vistomus'. Perhaps on par with what Eos felt from Rohl Ford in the mountain pass, but there were multiple sources. He felt Ahktar guiding his inner vision.

Like the new presence was a heavy thumb of electricity pressing in on his forehead, Eos sensed them. However, the signal faded in and out of his awareness.

"Wielders?" Eos wondered aloud.

Bwoom. Bwoom.

"Mitad," Durath growled.

CHAPTER EIGHT

RELUCTANT TEACHER

Old Cintish was quiet and peaceful coming out of winter. The bright pink blossoms of spring renewed life on the forest trail in a canopy of vibrant unfolding petals like berries exploding open.

Terrava walked along a lesser-known trail that she and her inlume master frequented in past hexades.

"The situation is delicate. Eos and Maxima have returned to Hyperborea—"

"For that, I'm overjoyed, Terrava," a little woman interrupted as she walked alongside the Queen of Anite. To a new eye, her exact age couldn't be guessed. Her chestnut hair was layered with a deceptive platinum that looked almost like highlights rather than the marks of age, and the wrinkles at the corners of her warm cinnamon eyes were the only hints that the woman was well into her sixties.

RELUCTANT TEACHER

"Master Fey! Would you stop walking like that? It makes you look older than you are, and I know you don't hunch like an old woman."

"Who me? Perhaps you don't call on your old master enough to know these things?" Saier Fey said with sly, teasing eyes.

"Even if you were easier to find, I have a feeling you'd have run out on me today if I didn't beg for this meeting. You really must get past this recluse phase and rejoin the active members of the Order. Your talents are wasted here."

"I'm retired," Fey said bluntly.

"Even an advisory role on the Inlume Council would—"

"Not a chance," Fey cut her off again.

Terrava felt a vein pulse in annoyance on her forehead.

Fey's fingers found the silver dragon-hoop earrings that bit at her earlobes and adjusted them. Her tunic sleeve fell enough to reveal a sickly-purple and scarlet blood bruise on her slender forearm. It was unlike any wound that Terrava had ever seen.

"What is *that?*" Terrava asked, concerned.

Fey was quick to pull her sleeve down to her wrist.

"Minor injury. You fall when you're my age. Don't heal as fast as I used to. It's rude to point out such things, Terrava. I taught you better."

Calming herself, the Anite Queen changed the topic, "As I was saying, Master, Maxima was presumed killed on Saida's orders. She must remain that way, or else the Mitad member who faked her death will be compromised."

"That is a problem. Might I suggest you train her in private then? A few years of training in secret wouldn't be bad for the girl," Fey said with a hum, pleased at her suggestion.

The sweet scent that floated along the perfect weather couldn't overcome Terrava's irritation. She was beginning to remember why she hadn't minded her master disappearing to become a career hermit. Even the slowness of their walking pace was aggravating.

Master Fey is hobbling slowly on purpose.

"Maxima must hide outside of Anondorn to avoid any attention. But a life of hiding behind Castle Alasedis' walls is not the life I want for my newly returned daughter. Meanwhile, I must attend to my duties in

CHAPTER EIGHT

Anondorn," Terrava explained with a sigh. "Please...teach Maxima for a while, at least until she can return to public life."

"*I'm retired.* I don't deal with matters of the Order, and I don't do babysitting," Fey snapped.

"I'm not asking the great inlume Saier Fey to take on a new apprentice for the Order of Soul Wielders," Terrava said with a pleading tone. "I'm asking the woman was like a mother to me to look after my daughter."

Old brows crinkled with weariness.

Fey relented, "Fine. I'll do you this favor and watch over Maxima—*temporarily.* That's all, mind you. I'm not her inlume teacher. I won't make an errant of her."

Terrava's expression softened. "Thank you, Master. This—"

Snap. Zmmmm.

Terrava's expression of gratitude was refused as Saier Fey snapped her fingers. Topaz-gold energy zipped from her hand.

She stood up straight, and the elderly arm shot out with a speed that mocked the hobbling manner she had been moving in. Her eyes never broke from Terrava's.

A palm-sized piece of fruit dropped into her hand, severed from the branch by her Soul Energy.

"A Cintish spring-apkle. The first of the season. A delicious gift of the forest."

Fey bit into the peach-colored flesh, and juice ran down her lip.

"You're going to drag me into your messes again, aren't you, Terrava? Can't a little old woman find some peace?"

"Perhaps you could, Master. If that's what you *actually* wanted."

"When did I teach my protegee to talk back with such disrespect?"

∞   ∞   ∞

Maxima hugged her mother goodbye as she stepped back toward the door of the inn bedroom.

"I'll send word when you can expect Master Fey to arrive. She hasn't committed to an exact day yet, but she's nearby and has agreed to watch over you," Terrava explained. "Please be patient a few more days until then, my dear. I know this has been difficult for you, alone here, but it's the safest place for you to hide out."

"I understand, Mother."

Terrava glanced out the window, but something else caught her eye. "What happened to your curtain?"

Maxima tried not to blush in surprise as her face heated up. "Oh, that? I...I...was bored and trying to exercise. I fell and grabbed it, but the curtain...may have ripped."

She wasn't sure if the words were believable or if she had spoken so fast that it betrayed her. Lying to her mother was a step too far, but she couldn't admit she had disobeyed either.

"Not to worry, I'll have the innkeeper replace it. He's an old friend." She turned to go but stopped, "One more thing, Maxima. The innkeeper told me that some Mitad ruffians have been driven away from this town the other day by a mysterious Soul Wielder locals are calling the Blue Corcinth. If I had known any Mitad would still be lingering this far into Anite months after the battle, I wouldn't have brought you here. But I feel it is too risky to move you just yet. I would advise it best to minimize your walks outside until Master Fey arrives. Keep to this inn as much as you can."

Maxima nearly choked as she replied, "As you wish, mother."

"You're acting strange, dear. Are you sure that you're okay here?"

She had taken out another Mitad gangster in the streets since her first encounter. The Blue Corcinth persona was perhaps getting out of control, but Maxima was having too much fun roaming the town as a vigilante.

And tonight, she had an appointment.

Hours after Terrava left, Maxima pulled the grinning ceramic mask from her drawer, threw her legs out the window, and glided on planes of sapphire light into town.

Dusk hung over blossoming trees and shingled rooftops. The smell of dinner preparations filled the small town, and the chirp of bugs in the distance cried out an announcement of summer's approach as Maxima navigated the back alleys of Old Cintish.

CHAPTER EIGHT

She struck her knuckles against the backdoor of the Cintish Brew and Tavern.

"Hello, Fion," she greeted the old man whose life she had saved days before. "Is he here?"

"Yes, that cursed vizier, Alsi, is playing cards with his underlings. He hasn't stirred up any trouble yet. Thrown a few glasses against the wall, but that's it so far. A few more hours, a couple more drinks, and a losing hand—and I'm sure he'll be tearing the place up again and threatening to kill my patrons."

Fion led her through the kitchen. The women cooking paused to gape at the walking myth before them, but the tavern owner urged them back to work. He led the *Blue Corcinth* to a sliding panel in the pantry that opened to a hidden compartment in the wall.

Tonight, Maxima would rid the town of the Mitad menace for good.

Thin slits behind the bar taps gave her covert visibility of the tavern and its gambling table. As she observed the situation, someone approached the game.

A small woman with streaks of platinum-brown amidst waves of bushy dark hair approached the crew of sinister figures.

Vizier Alsi looked up from his hand with a long, silent gaze.

"What are we playing gentlemen, Wielder's Draw? Got room at the table for a fifth?" the woman asked.

Alsi did not respond but pointed at the empty chair, apparently accepting the new player. The Mitad leader raked in a stack of coins from the hand just played and began to deal again.

"Well, wait a minute. High card deals, doesn't it?" Her voice was mild and innocent.

His beady eyes stared from between black sideburns and nodded toward the deck. Each member at the table drew, and Alsi tilted his head with pleasure as he revealed his high card: an errant wielder with a wreath of two broken swords and horned lion emblems in the corners.

Then, Alsi gave an extravagant show of reshuffling the cards, smirking slightly. Cards fluttered from hand to hand as he cut the deck, repeating the smooth motion over and over. Flutter, cut, flutter, cut; his showy flair evoked whistles of awe from his men. He then presented the deck to the newcomer, as was custom.

"No cut," the old woman said. Her small silver-hoop earrings shimmered from the angle Maxima watched. The tiny head of a dragon bit each earlobe.

Cards flew to each player, and then Alsi rolled a dice across the table.

The six-sided stone landed with a horse emblem facing up.

"Keeper bonus is the elsu," Alsi announced.

Without looking at the hand before her, the woman said, "I fold."

A few at the table grumbled. The woman had gone out of her way to cause a reshuffle without even playing the hand.

Minutes later, Alsi was pulling in another stack of coins.

The dealing moved to the woman.

She flicked the cards from hand to hand even faster than Alsi had, sending a stream fluttering into the middle of the deck. The cards rotated as she contorted her fingers and went to shuffling with only one hand while eyeing Alsi audaciously.

Tension built with the flapping of cards.

Each tap of the deck on the table caused uncomfortable glances from each of Alsi's underlings.

One of the men let out a surprised laugh as the deck appeared to flutter upward and float itself into her opposite hand above it.

A sharp grunt from the Vizier cut the amusement short.

Maxima rubbed her eyes as she swore the cards shimmered a glowing topaz color momentarily.

The bar's patrons were mesmerized by the show being put on.

"Bartender!" the old woman called rudely. "Another round for me."

Fion's son answered, "If you wish, Ma'am, but this will be your tenth round. Are you sure you don't want to slow down?"

"I'll judge that for myself, thanks," she said with a slight slur and began to deal. Her wrist flicked, the dice landed, and she announced, "Sunkaw keeper bonus."

All five at the table pondered their hands seriously.

A giddy look came over the underlings.

Each tried to suppress their pleasure at their cards.

CHAPTER EIGHT

Alsi remained stone-faced.

The clinking of glasses and pouring of drinks ceased in anticipation.

"Opening for ten jital," the first underling said.

"Make that fifty," the next Mitad member countered.

"One hundred," Alsi said when it came to him.

The old woman never looked up as she said, "Two hundred."

The rest of the table matched.

She dealt the next set of cards to those who slapped the table.

Again, each member tried to suppress their giddiness.

The betting began high, but Alsi raised another hundred.

The pot of money on the table was now a massive stack that had cost most of the men half of their pile of bronze and silver coins.

Alsi flipped his cards and revealed something that clearly pleased him. The hand drowned out the smiles on each of his men's faces.

Three anatus cards with elsu crests in the corners lay on the table.

"Three of a kind. No bonus." It seemed that even though everyone had an unusually great hand, the Vizier was victorious again.

He gulped down his drink and reached for the heap of coins with sweaty hands.

The woman interrupted him by flipping over a ten with the corcinth crest.

Everyone's mouths hung open, waiting.

Maxima could feel their anticipation as she teased the final card.

The men all threw themselves back in their chairs as she revealed the winning hand. "Three tens and the sunkaw bonus."

The crowd at the table laughed in disbelief at the luck of the round, but Alsi quieted everyone with a violent look that panned from one end of the tavern to the other.

"I say you're cheatin', little lady," he accused lowly.

She looked him in the face with an innocent expression.

"You think so?" she asked as if she was genuinely curious as well.

"I think so," he said threateningly.

"Hmm," she hummed and proceeded to gather the cards.

Vizier Alsi stood.

"Why don't we get that next drink at the bar? *On me.*"

RELUCTANT TEACHER

He strutted to the bar in his long black pants, boots clunking slowly as men threw themselves out of their chairs to clear space for him.

The small woman stood to accept the threat.

Maxima noticed something tied to her waist under her baggy mauve cloak. It was well hidden, but large enough that it was noticeable with the movement of her right leg. She stumbled forward to the bar with a less than sober wobble and looked up, a foot shorter than the looming dark-haired man.

Fion's son began to pour.

Alsi threw a dagger onto the bar. "The drink helps with pain. Though it looks like you've already had more than enough for the night. I'll only take one finger if you admit you cheated and hand over the money you stole."

She played up her femininity as she made an expression that wordlessly said, *Who me? Cheating? Never.*

But she merely replied, "Better pour him a double then."

The entire tavern gasped and braced themselves with many shuffling to get away.

Alsi's gray-toned hand picked up the knife and turned it over carefully so that the blade gleamed before his prey.

Maxima noted the cheap animus stone that only gilded the weapon's edge.

Falling forward, the woman's small frame appeared to reach for her drink but instead missed and struck Alsi's wrist.

The blade slipped from his grasp and clattered on the table.

This woman's not what she seems, Maxima thought.

There was a look of genuine surprise on the woman's face. Her kohl-penciled eyes widened in delay as if the alcohol was slowing her perception.

She picked up the knife, turned the point toward herself, and roughly shoved the handle back into Alsi's hand, wrapping his fingers around it for him. Her unbound chestnut-gray hair bobbed wildly as she nodded, pleased to complete a lesson on holding knives.

Alsi growled, "You have a death wish, little lady. Now I'll let you choose which limb I cut off after I get my money back."

CHAPTER EIGHT

Fion broke in, "Please, Ma'am, no need to pay your tab. Just give Alsi his money, and let's have peace."

"No," Alsi rumbled, looming over her. "She's past that point, but she'll give me the money…alive or dead."

The woman's bright-cinnamon eyes smiled up at the tall thug as she raised her glass wordlessly and drank.

Alsi, for his part, allowed the action to continue until the mug was empty out of his own sheer disbelief.

Then, she drank her second glass.

Finally, she reached across and drank Alsi's glass without pausing.

A foam-covered upper lip greeted the Mitad Vizier.

Alsi's animus knife poked her chest.

She burped in answer.

The knife dug in more and drew a spot of blood.

Maxima dashed from her hidden spot, through the kitchen, and to the bar before violence could break out. All the way there, she thought, *This woman has natural poise but presents herself as an old, slovenly, gambling drunk. She is more than meets the eye. I will not stand idly by.*

The kitchen door swung open.

The silent patrons, frozen on the edges of the room, looked away from the unfolding scene at the bar to witness a blue corcinth mask standing in the doorway.

Audible gasps came.

The tavern was split between those who wanted to witness the most exciting thing to happen in Old Cintish in their lifetime, and those who ran out the door in fear for their life.

"That's enough, Vizier Alsi," Maxima's voice waivered with fluctuating confidence. She widened her stance. "I've heard of how you torment this town and this tavern. Now it's old women, too? You won't harm her."

Vizier Alsi chewed on his lip and rolled his wrist so that his blade danced towards Maxima's direction. He looked as if he had been half-hoping to run into the blue-masked vigilante.

If Maxima wasn't mistaken, the woman next to him had a similar expression.

RELUCTANT TEACHER

"You sure about that?" Alsi challenged.

Maxima said from behind the mask, "Fight me and find out. So, let's take this outside."

His narrow nose twitched with anticipation, and Alsi licked his lips with over-confidence. "I've heard of you, Blue Corcinth. Few of my men have gone missing. Townspeople say it was you that did it." He let the words drift through the room for a while and then twirled his dagger towards the door. "After you."

Maxima exited the tavern, never letting Alsi leave her peripheral vision the entire time.

The Vizier followed but tapped the point of his blade at the woman who had downed his drink and taken his money. "You too, drunken hag. I'm still collecting my money." He nodded his head to the door.

The woman hunched over and stumbled on his command with a mischievous smirk that never left her lips.

Outside, Maxima and Alsi stared each other down.

Through the eyeholes of the ceramic mask, she observed the long dark character before her. She could sense it, the arrogance and bloodlust permeating from him, almost strong enough to be a scent. It curled her nose.

He looked down at the small female frame hidden behind the devilish blue-gray grin of a corcinth. She gave away no emotion from her sapphire eyes and still body, but her hands were ready to wield—that much, he was sure.

The four underlings from the card table walked down the steps with the old woman stumbling behind them.

"No, boys, stay right there. I want this *Blue Corcinth* for myself."

Maxima said nothing.

Her black hair fluttered behind her in the evening breeze.

Alsi twirled his dagger nonchalantly.

The Blue Corcinth waited with fingers touching, almost as if in prayer. The moisture of her breath condensed on the inside of the mask. Each damp exhale made her more aware of the situation.

Alsi held out his other hand in a clawed shape turned up.

Dark red sparks lit in his palm.

CHAPTER EIGHT

Immediately, Soul Energy filled it.

Simultaneously, a red glow emitted weakly from his blade in his other hand.

Maxima's fingers separated in quick response; five streams of blue light morphed into a single sphere.

Then, the sapphire orb split into two.

Alsi launched his sphere at Maxima as if probing for her response.

She slipped past the blast, evading to the side.

The Vizier had closed the distance in the seconds she had spent watching the red sphere fly by.

Maxima released her first Soul Sphere, but Alsi had expected it.

He rolled around her with experienced footing and brought the knife in with a thrust.

There was space between the dagger and Maxima as she slid back, but something happened that she wasn't expecting.

A beam of Soul Energy projected off the animus stone.

The blade's energy now filled the gap of inches that had narrowly saved Maxima from being sliced—the dagger's edge extended with red light.

The warm drip of blood met the sting of broken skin.

Maxima did not let the pain of it go to waste.

She flung her second sphere, and Alsi was too close to dodge.

His chest took the brunt of it as sapphire exploded him back.

"Looky there," he rose up, panting from the severe wound she had just delt him, "the Blue Corcinth packs a punch. Guess I can't play around with you for too long."

His clothes were seared in a mix of blood and cloth to his chest, but he manifested another Soul Sphere quickly and adjusted his dagger position.

There was a disturbance of screams and thuds from the tavern porch.

Maxima glanced briefly at the source of the noise.

The four men from the card table were collapsed on the floor. By the time her brain comprehended that, a blur whipped past her.

RELUCTANT TEACHER

She turned back to the Vizier, but the small old woman was between them. As she landed on the ground, a long-handled weapon emerged from under her cloak. Its onyx blade was straight on one side and curved on the outer edge like a leaf attached to a spear's pole.

It swung with incredible speed as it was held by a single hand.

The curved edge pressed against Alsi's chest.

"Woah! Woah! What is it with the women in this town? One at a time, ladies. Boys, why don't you show…" Alsi noticed his subordinates piled on the stairs in a heap. "Well, I don't know how you did that or who you are—"

Alsi thrust his dagger forward mid-sentence to catch his new opponent off guard.

With the edge of her palm and two fingers pointed up, the woman thrust out her hand and connected with Alsi's wrist for a second time that night.

A subtle topaz vapor lit where the two touched.

The glow of Alsi's dagger died.

"The name is Inlume Saier Fey."

Alsi's ugly mouth gaped at the name.

He shook his dagger as if it were a broken device that needed to be reminded to turn on.

It remained unlit.

"*Wha-what did you do to it?*"

He made to fling a Soul Sphere forward in panic, but Saier Fay struck his arm just above the Soul Energy before he could release it.

The weak red light died down to sifting faded tendrils.

"To it?" Inlume Fey asked with a chiding tone. "No. To *you*," she said with no hint of drunkenness in her voice or movements.

Alsi clutched at the air as he tried to bring forth his Soul Energy.

"Blocking Soul Energy pathways only works on the narrow channels of weaker wielders. Are you so feeble, Vizier?"

"No. No. No," Alsi said, stumbling back as the tip of her long glaive pointed at him. He fell to the ground, tripping back, and her weapon followed, never leaving his chest.

CHAPTER EIGHT

"This blade has the highest-grade anima stone at its core, but let your final thoughts contemplate the fact that I need not activate it to defeat you. I didn't even need to manifest my Soul Energy."

Lips moved, but no words came to him as Alsi tried to comprehend his position.

The glaive plunged into his chest.

A dull spurt of breath was all that Alsi could manage. His last sight before he went still was the silver dragons that decorated Fey's ears.

"Now, Blue Corcinth, if that is what I'm to call you," Fey turned to Maxima. "I'd like a private word. And as for you pathetic Mitad lumps that served this weak man, go back to your remaining members and warn them that I'll kill any Mitad members that are still within the borders of Anite by morning." She did not glance their way as she threatened.

The underlings struggled to their feet in a daze.

"Best get moving. It's a long way to the border before tomorrow." She grinned to herself, "Oh, and be careful that Salvaluc doesn't catch you in his territory. I hear he isn't taking hostages after you forced your way through his kingdom."

The cheers and gossip of the townspeople still rang in Maxima's head long after they had slipped back into room at the inn where she was staying.

Stunned by the Inlume's appearance, Maxima marveled that the legendary Soul Wielder, Saier Fey, was in *her quarters*.

"Mother told me you'd be coming…but…"

"But you didn't expect me to be hunting down Mitad members? Or that I'd heard of a rumored wielder of blue Soul Energy that went around town this last week in a mask?"

Maxima nodded.

"First, let's get this straight. Your mother asked me to do a favor. I'm retired. I don't do new students. This is strictly a temporary arrangement."

"Oh. Okay," Maxima was both mesmerized and caught off guard by the demeanor of her mother's teacher.

RELUCTANT TEACHER

"Good. Next matter, you went behind your mother's back, threw yourself into danger confronting the Mitad, and risked ruining your cover." Fey glared as if coaxing a confession out of Maxima.

"I know," Maxima said softly, her head down. Saier Fey intimidated her far more than even her mother.

"Don't look so gloomy. I had fun, didn't you?"

Maxima's brows curled in confusion.

Saier Fey laughed, "Terrava has become quite the proper queen since her young, wild days. If you ask me, I think she's gotten a little *boring*. But I think the two of us can find some fun to pass the time," she hinted with a smirk.

Maxima blinked in disbelief. The inlume was giving her psychological whiplash.

"But I warn you, Maxima, don't think about getting in the way of my drinking or gambling. If you sound like Terrava even once—"

"I promise. I won't," Maxima assured her immediately, but then eased into asking, "So, that wasn't an act?"

"Girl, I've cleaned out the pockets of nearly every tavern with a card table in East Anite and every kingdom north of Terspar." Fey winked mischievously. "Not one of them ever knew I was an inlume, either."

Maxima's eyes narrowed. She thought back to how the cards swam through the air in Fey's hands and the faint shimmer of topaz she had seen.

"They probably didn't know you were cheating."

"Sharp eyes girl. If you're lucky, maybe I'll teach you a few card tricks, too."

CHAPTER NINE

WISDOM AND PRICE

"The Mitad, *here?*" Eos asked, alarmed. He knew it was true no sooner than the words left his mouth. He felt it with his improving Observation of Soul Energy.

Aizo responded with annoyance, "Don't ask questions you've already sensed an answer to. Now everyone, prepare yourselves."

"On me," Scavok said, leading his king and the party to the door with his blade drawn.

Rumbles of Soul Energy explosions shook the underground bunker. Gunfire pinged through the base. Echoes of conflict chirped maddeningly. It prevented Eos' focus from lasting more than a second before a cold rush of adrenaline would wash over again and again.

Pressed against the wall, with vapors of Soul Energy trailing from each person's hand, they followed Scavok. The sounds of ricocheting bullets grew louder and the presence of foreign Soul Energy became nearer.

Scavok peaked around the door frame to see Colonel Kane ordering soldiers from behind the cover of unloaded supply crates. With suppressing fire, they held the advancing black cloaks back as best as they could, but the Mitad soldiers were breaking through on the other side. Soul Spheres and yellow whips of energy created too much chaos for guns alone to hold at bay.

A vine of light split the crate that covered Colonel Kane.

It exploded, and packages of military meals were scattered across the room.

Kane dove away from the shrapnel, sprinting in a crouch to meet Scavok at the door.

Through the splinters of crates, Eos saw the source of the attack. A gray-skinned woman with high cheekbones and a vicious frown wielded a saffron energy.

Mirza Morgana made eye contact through the field of airborne fragments.

Colonel Kane breathed heavily as he leaned against the wall, rifle in hand. Despite bleeding from a gash on his neck, his eyes were intensely focused. "Mitad everywhere. We're compromised."

Scavok's silver ponytail danced as he shook his head with regret. He faced Talus and shouted over the sounds of battle, "Get everyone out. There are too many unknowns in these close quarters."

Talus nodded, accepting his master tactician's guidance.

"Colonel," Scavok said without turning, "Order your men to fall back and escape."

"How do you propose—" the Colonel's response was cut short.

"I'm going to hold them all back and then collapse the place in on itself," Scavok's voice was steady. "The Mitad will escape the way they came in, but they'll have to dig their way out. It'll buy us time so we can get away. We need to move now!"

Colonel Kane relented and dashed back into the room to command his men.

CHAPTER NINE

Two fingers waved the Hyperboreans to fall back from the action as Scavok's sword glowed an icy color. He marched into the battle as the others moved for the back exit.

Everything that followed happened in slow motion for Eos.

A swarm of retreating North American uniforms filled his vision.

An ice-blue net of Scavok's barrier technique filled the room's opposite end behind them.

Eos looked back and saw through the shrapnel a flurry of glowing violence amidst the mass of fleeing bodies.

Tell-tale amethyst eyes and a head of wavy, jet-black hair glinted from a man on the other side of the ice-blue net. Pale-gray chains flowed across the room from him and struck Scavok's barricade.

Zmmm!

Energies clashed and screeched.

The ghostly light of links rattled across Scavok's glacial blue.

Ares was here.

Eos was filled with a euphoria that desired revenge.

He turned from the group and moved against the crowd, back to the battle instead.

His father's only arm caught Eos by the wrist.

"Where do you think you're going?!" Talus yelled as he pulled his son back.

"Ares is in there! I saw him!"

Dragging Eos forcefully, Talus replied, "Even if he is, we *must* get out *now*." The look in his father's eyes pleaded with Eos to remember his promise. "Be wise! Think like an inlume and not like a child!"

The words caused a burning sensation in Eos' chest as he looked back to the ice-net.

He was certain in the next moment that Ares' eyes caught his. There was a squint of recognition before Eos was swept away by his father's pull and the push of fleeing bodies. He tried to wrench around, to look back once more, but Ares was gone from his sliver of vision.

This time was different. Not like the return to Mircite Valley.

Ares really was here.

WISDOM AND PRICE

Moments later and they were finally outside, running over grassy hills under the slim moonlight of a place Colone Kane had called *Maryland*. Many North American troops had just encountered Soul Energy for the first time—and Eos could hear the fear of it in their panicked breathing. Colonel Kane gave instructions about where to rally and what direction to keep heading.

The pounding of boots, the howl of the wind, and the chipping of the nocturnal wildlife filled the frantic night. Eos looked up to Talus alongside him, then to Durath. He assumed Aizo, Scavok, and Glenn were among their numbers somewhere. No one dared to speak if it was not necessary. They could no longer hear the explosions of battle in the bunker now miles behind them when a transport of vehicles Colonel Kane had gotten word to finally intercepted them.

The Colonel had a plan. Always another plan. But he prayed in whispers that the Mitad had compromised only one location and not all the other hideouts.

Hours passed as they rode into farmland on the outskirts of Washington D.C. Then, the last miles to their next hiding place were done on foot. Eos didn't even register how tired he was as they shuffled wearily into an underground bunker nestled in the countryside.

The surviving troops huddled together, awaiting orders. Meanwhile, Colonel Kane had radioed his other bases to prepare them for the possibility of compromised locations.

Malin tried to catch his breath against the far wall, opposite of Eos.

"I haven't done so much runnin' in years. Just after getting rescued, too. Can't catch a ruttin' break," the burly man said to himself though labored breaths.

The words caught Colonel Kane's attention and stoked a wave of anger lying under the calm surface. He rushed to the newly rescued man with an accusing look etched into every line of his face and wrenched him by the collar.

"Ay! Ouch! Colonel, what are you doing—ow! Easy."

Colonel Kane dragged the bruised and burn-bandaged face through the doorway to a supply room and threw Malin against the wall so the rest of the troops could not see. His personal guards followed after him.

CHAPTER NINE

Eos got as close as he could without being turned away by Kane's men at the door.

Inside the room, Malin's nose flared. "What do you think you're doing to me, Colonel?"

"You tell me, Malin. We rescue you. Save you from torture. You tell us you didn't crack, but our location is compromised only hours after your return. Tell me how that works."

Malin's eyes went wide, and he raised his hands in an easing motion. "Woah, Colonel. That's crazy talk—"

"I hope it is, but I need to be sure."

"They beat me, tortured me with Soul Energy, and offered me all kinds of things, but I wouldn't give in. I was loyal, sir!" Malin said, trembling. He recalled his final conversation with the Mitad.

Ares smirked and glared at Malin as Emir Raggan made to leave the room.

"Notice how he said try?" Ares continued the interrogation.

"Try offering me something worth spilling information for. How about that?" Malin spat.

Ares nearly broke his jaw for the comment.

"Fine. How much does one offer in this situation, Raggan?" Ares caught the Emir before he disappeared beyond the threshold. "I know nothing of Earth money."

Speaking loud enough for Malin to hear, the Emir answered, "I'll pay him a million dollars if the information turns out. That seems to be a number these American dogs like."

Malin coughed with laughter that hurt his broken ribs. "Aww hell, is that all? I was thinking more like an equal share of your empire," he teased with a wheeze, knowing it would earn him more pain.

Ares became furious when he realized Malin had no intention of accepting a bribe but quickly calmed himself. "I have a better idea of what to do with this broken jester."

Malin looked up at Colonel Kane like a wounded puppy. "Sir, I told Ares they'd have to make me equal partners over the Mitad if they wanted me to give up your location. Beat me real good for it, too."

"If that's true, Malin, then there must be another explanation for why they came down on us moments after your return." Colonel Kane looked to the two soldiers in the room with them and ordered, "Strip search him."

"Sir! Now that just ain't fair."

Eos pushed into the doorway guards and yelled into the room, "Malin, did you say Ares? Did you speak with my brother?"

Colonel Kane motioned for the guards to let Eos in.

The embarrassed man was half-undressed when he said, "Eos! Tell the Colonel, I wouldn't betray us all to the Mitad!"

"Did you say my brother is here on Earth? I thought I saw him during the raid...but I'm not sure I can trust what I'm seeing these days."

Malin looked him over with confusion as soldiers tore through his clothes and bag. "Yeah, kid. Ares is here—"

"Where?"

"They held me at the Capital Building. They've made the place into their house now," Malin answered in his underwear.

Colonel Kane quieted him, "That's enough. Eos, whatever you're thinking—*don't*."

"He killed my sister, Colonel. I have to go after him. Wouldn't you do the same for Major Clark's killer?" Eos asked, unblinking.

Hesitating, Colonel Kane tried to find the right reply, but was interrupted by the search.

"Sir, the only thing unusual in his possession...is this," the soldier said, holding out a shard of gemstone. "It was in his pants pocket."

Malin looked confused and tried to defend himself, "Colonel, I swear I don't know what that is. I'm not much of a rock collector."

Eos moved to the stone and said in a solemn tone. "I know what it is." He touched it, letting a tiny stream of Soul Energy drip to the manus shard. Rays of light refracted inside it, and the soldier dropped the stone, recoiling.

"What could the Mitad do with this type of gem?" Colonel Kane asked.

"Nothing..." Eos whispered to himself, "Except...Maxima once said Ares had a special ability that allowed him to track her down in the middle of the desert." His eyes lit up. "I don't know how he could do it, but Ares may have planted that as a way to track us."

CHAPTER NINE

Grabbing the stone from the floor, Eos bolted for Scavok who had silently entered the room at some point. He shoved it into his hand. "Scavok, take this manus stone as far away from here as possible and light it. I think Ares is using it to track us!"

The moment recognition crossed his face, Scavok's silver mane of hair was flowing behind him as he sprinted from the room in a blur of Soul Step speed.

"Will they find us? I can send out the order to evacuate now if needed," Kane said urgently.

"No," Eos calmed him. "If they had already found us, we'd know. Scavok will throw them off. We're safe...but Colonel, there's something I need to understand. Do you have a map of the area that I could use?" Vengeful plotting flashed in his golden eyes.

"Of course," Kane accommodated Eos for whatever he had in mind, thinking it was related to being tracked.

Minutes later, Eos was analyzing a local map that Colonel Kane had unpinned from his office wall. Base coordinates were circled, major supply routes were highlighted, and most importantly, it showed their location relative to the Capital Building that Malin had mentioned.

Eos did not wait long.

The moment everyone was distracted in conversation and planning, he slipped away, Soul Stepping into the night.

When Scavok returned, he reported, "I lit the stone miles from here. It should throw them off if they're pursuing us."

Talus placed a hand on his friend's shoulder. "Thank you, Scavok. Your quick action may have saved everyone here."

Scavok replied, "And Eos' recognition of how they found us. He did well..."

"Where is Eos?" Durath asked, looking around.

Talus searched the room and muttered, "He was just over at that table ten minutes ago."

"Where did you say the Mitad have taken over, Colonel Kane?" Scavok asked in an anticipating growl.

The Colonel answered, "The Capitol Building. Not far from here."

"Show us exactly," Scavok urged.

WISDOM AND PRICE

The weary Colonel pointed on the map.

Durath and Scavok looked down in horror as they recognized how short such a journey would be with Soul Step.

"He wouldn't be so foolish, would he?" Scavok asked.

"What are you saying?" Talus worried.

"He's going after his brother," Scavok said grimly.

CHAPTER TEN

FEIGNED DUEL

The gray clouds of dawn hung like a somber veil overhead as Eos Soul Stepped according to the mental map he had constructed in his head. He knew his target's relative distance and that it was a distinctly white-domed building. Colonel Kane had revealed that much.

His blood ran hot through his veins as he remembered Maxima falling into the river.

Never coming up again.

There had been no goodbye to his best friend.

No look of remorse from his twisted half-brother.

In fact, it had been a face of devious pride.

The curse mark on Eos' arm burned up into his shoulder. This time, he welcomed the pain.

After half an hour of bursting through the sunrise sky, propelled by Soul Energy, he had entered the heart of the city, high above the streets and buildings. Eos saw more lights through windows than he had ever seen in his life. The city was enormous and moving, even as it woke up to start the day.

The white dome drew nearer, as did his second guessing. Approaching the Mitad directly was not the action of a future inlume. Yet, fierce loyalty to his sister and anger overrode his common sense.

The building came into full view as he soared past the giant obelisk monument and landed in front of the Capitol Building.

They had expected him. Felt his Soul Energy approaching.

A brooding figure in a hat and cloak waited with an aura of power that made Eos' skin tingle. But behind this man was the reason he had come so recklessly; seeing Ares made Eos ignore all the panicked warning signs firing in his head.

Emir Raggan looked at Eos from under the prominent brim of a hat he wore, as if weighing his worth on a scale and finding the boy wanting. He stood on the lawn of the Capital Building with the porcelain white dome filling the view behind him. The man's throat rattled as if about to speak, but let a rasping growl do all his communication instead.

Ares faced his half-brother with a look of wicked curiosity, lips curling as if debating how to disassemble a toy.

"Ziah," Ares referred to Emir Raggan by his first name, "let me handle my brother."

Eos glowered. His heart and thoughts were heavy, his jaw clenched like a vice, and his throat burned from tension.

Raggan grumbled in the affirmative, and Ares raised his eyebrows in shock. "I didn't think you'd be so accommodating."

"Mmm. The Master said I can't kill the pup yet, I have no interest in 'em, and he's 'bout to bring two of the most powerful inlumes and their friends down upon us when they come lookin' to reign 'em in.," Raggan said, his eyes going wide with lips thrust out as he nodded at his dislike of the idea.

"Looks like it's just the two of us for some personal time, brother," Ares said, his smile flashing fiendishly.

"I couldn't ask for anything more," Eos seethed.

CHAPTER TEN

Emir Raggan rumbled, "Right, but I fancy this buildin', yeah? So, keep it out there in the grass. I won't be cleanin' up any messes or havin' you destroy my new headquarters."

"You heard the man, Eos. Raggan, I know Bellia is watching. Keep her at a safe distance, please."

Eos didn't trust that Raggan was only observing, and he didn't understand what he meant by *'the Master said I can't kill him'*. However, his desire for revenge burned through any hesitancy to fight or concern with consequences.

"Ares, I'll give you one chance to apologize and show you regret what you did—*if you're even capable of that*—before I send you to face Maxima." The curse mark on his arm flared with his declaration, threatening to climb higher into his chest.

"Oh, I don't think you could possibly do that," Ares teased.

Looking over Ares' shoulder, Eos noticed that Raggan was joined by other cloaked figures. But for Eos in his cloud of all-consuming rage, he and Ares were brothers alone under a bleak sky.

"Then, we don't have anything to say. You've taken away…my best friend in the entire world." Eos felt tears welling up as he said it.

Ares twisted his chin to crack his neck and rotated his shoulders, making a display as he warmed up for battle. "Oh, I have more to say, but you may entertain me with a little duel first. When you're breathing on your knees, Eos, wondering which gasp will be your last…then I'll have repaid you my pain. I'll have no interest in rivalry anymore. Maxima—"

"Don't say her name!" Eos ordered, the promise of murder in his voice.

Strangely, Ares didn't smirk or return with any arrogant comment. Instead, he only nodded with something in his eyes that resembled understanding.

Ahktar's cry pierced the sunrise as he hovered far above Eos, observing as he circled.

Shall I assist you? Ahktar's voice echoed in Eos's mind.

No. This is a battle I must face alone. Thank you, Ahktar.

So be it, but calm the darkness rising in you.

FEIGNED DUEL

The snow-white bird glided higher, and Ares glanced at it warily.

"Tell me one last thing, Ares," Eos said, crimson Soul Energy beginning to leech from his hands. "*Why?* You have a grudge against me, sure. But her? You saved her from Braxton once..." Eos pleaded with searching eyes, hoping to understand. Praying there was something untrue about what had happened. "*Why?*" he whispered again.

"I have someone I want to meet. She was the price. It's really as simple as that."

"Does family mean so little to you that your sister's life is a bargaining piece?"

A glow of pale-gray light came from Ares' sleeves as he murmured solemnly, "How else can I seize what I want in this world?"

The point of Ares' chain whip shot across the space between them, whistling through the air.

Eos rolled to the right. As the chain passed by him, he forced his breath to slow into a controlled rhythm.

The links of glowing Soul Energy bent around and arced back at Eos again. He dodged to the grass, nearly clipping the attack with his back.

As he stood back up, unscathed, he continued to control his exhales as he had with Talus in the ice-cold river during training at Fanum Ortus. Rage still coursed through him, and his cursed arm burned hotter, but he harnessed it all with a technique of calm and focus.

A crimson elsu manifested, and a glaze of red shimmered over his cursed hand as it flung out. He grasped the chain whip as it reeled by.

The gray Soul Energy melted into beads where his soul-gloved hand closed on it. The chain reformed as it retracted back to Ares. The separated links evaporated into steam.

"Stop messing around, Ares! Bring out your cursed beast, and let's settle this. Show me your Severance!" Eos' golden glare was unbroken as his dark hair waved across his face.

Ares let out a short, conceited laugh. "No. I don't think that's necessary when I can fight you..." he said while stepping onto platforms of Soul Energy, "from up here." He pushed off and circled Eos from above.

Eos cast out his Soul Elsu in pursuit.

CHAPTER TEN

Chains sliced the air.

A crimson-covered hand deflected.

Zmmm. The high-frequency clash rang out.

Again. Again!

The dance continued as Ares fought from the high ground while dodging the winged attack.

Blinding flares of distant red and gray illuminated the white façade of the Captical Building, as Raggan stood atop the steps with Morgana and two other mirzas at his side. They waited patiently, anticipating what was to come while they spectated the duel out on the grass beyond.

A stray bolt of tangled Soul Energies split from an eruption between the brothers and landed squarely on a column of the building sending chucks of marble flying.

"Ay!" Raggan boomed out, gazing at the destruction. "I said keep it on the lawn! You two take out another one of my pillars and I'll kill the both of you! Mmmm," the Emir grumbled impatiently, suddenly Observing a shift in pressure. His prediction was correct. "Yeah, well, here they come. Yeah. Right on time. Mhmm."

A minute later, Talus, Aizo, Scavok, and Durath skidded to a halt in their Soul Step and looked up the white marble stairs at the Mitad coalition that awaited them.

Talus' face was pained by his Observational wielding as he felt Eos' rage echo through the clashes of his Soul Energy, though the King could not take his eyes off the emir-level threat.

"What is this, Emir?" Talus demanded.

"Ah!" Raggan said with play in his gruff voice. "So, you recognize me? What an honor. Well, this," he gestured with his chin to the lawn, "this is your son being reckless, yeah?"

Talus listened with suspicion. "That I can agree with."

"All fueled by revenge and anger. A poor excuse for a member of the Order. He'll get you all killed."

"Then why do you just stand there?" Aizo asked out of turn.

"That…" Raggan pointed at the distant battle as Soul Energies clashed, "is a brotherly dispute that I'm allowin' to play out, just like you will."

FEIGNED DUEL

Talus raised an eyebrow of disbelief.

Raggan continued, "And this…" he pointed at the group around Talus, then himself, waving his finger in a circle, "is what I call mutually assured destruction, yeah? I know I could kill you, Talus. Morgana here could handle Scavok. But Aizo could choose to kill either of us while we're distracted. Before Wyan or Virgio here could stop him. Ramath's boy…well…he's just a wild card."

"You're awfully confident that you could take me down. That's a mistake, Emir," Talus challenged.

"Believe what you will, one-armed King, but I propose we stand here, watch the show bein' put on, accept the result, and all live to see another day. Meanwhile, you can just be thankful that Lord Vistomus is away." Raggan nodded to himself and moved his jaw as if chewing on the words.

Aizo urged, "Talus, we can put a stop to this!"

"No," Talus conceded. "He's right. There will be casualties on both sides. Eos must deal with the consequences of his actions. However, Emir Raggan, *I will intervene to save my son if required.*"

Raggan continued to nod disrespectfully with a look of superiority and stroked his beard. "We'll see about that, one-armed King."

Zmmm.

Eos' crimson Soul-Elsu cornered, swooped down, and pinned Ares against his own airborne momentum.

Fearing the blow, Ares redirected his Soul Chain to the bird.

The blade tip wrapped around the elsu, but the bird was so fast that it got within range to do damage.

Booom!

It erupted in a bubbling explosion that spread until the edge of the blast reached Ares. He was sent tumbling from his Soul Step and sliding across the grass until a tree stopped his body.

Eos seethed. He was losing his breath control as the curse mark burned through him. The dense layer of energy required to deflect Ares' chain with his hand was wearing on him. It was a technique he had not yet mastered, and it required an intense focus. He spent far more of his capacity on it than he should have due to inefficiency.

CHAPTER TEN

Ares stood, groaning, and slumped against the tree opposite their audience on the steps—out of view of the Mitad.

The opportunity to strike was apparent.

"Wait!" Ares cautioned Eos.

"Did you wait before you killed Maxima?"

Ares ignored the question. "I have what you're here for."

"What do you know about why I'm here?"

"I know why you're *all* here, on *Earth*," Ares said with labored words. He chuckled through his pain and pulled a folded stack of parchment from his robe. "These are copies of Raggan's recent letters and notes regarding…some of the Mitad's current pursuits."

Eos prodded impatiently, "Why would you give me your boss's letters? You better have more lies than that if you want to save your life."

"If you win this fight, the letters are yours. "

Eos hesitated. "Why?"

"Because you came here to find out what the Mitad is after. This is your best shot at real answers. If you get those answers," Ares grunted and held his ribs, "then you're doing some of my work for me. There's a man who was possessed entirely by this curse you and I seem to share, and yet he came back from it. He also has an important weapon that Vistomus wants."

As if in response to the mere mention of it, Eos' Curse Mark flared again, the searing pain from his arm shooting well into his chest. He knew he couldn't keep it at bay for much longer. He wasn't even sure he wanted to. He eyed his brother suspiciously and asked, "And you want that weapon too?" He knew Ares never acted on charity. Always for selfishness and gain.

Ares rolled his eyes in annoyance and taunted Eos, "Look, if you can't win this fight, then I'll send you to join your sister."

Eos howled then at the callous words, and in response the Curse Mark suddenly stretched across his abdomen and up his neck. The rage of his grief had pushed back the seal that kept it in check, and he welcomed the rush of dark power taking hold.

"I'll make you bring out that dragon form, Ares! No holding back. That way you die knowing I'm the better wielder!"

FEIGNED DUEL

"You're so lucky I haven't killed you already, Eos. It is beyond tempting," Ares snarled.

Crackle! Five crimson-black elsu flashed to life around Eos.

The Curse Mark crawled in flame-like tongues through Ares' chain until it became black and morphed. The shape expanded and wriggled into the body of Ares' Severence. The wolfish snout and floating whiskers emerged at the end of the chain as the dragon took form. The dark energy marbled it, just as it did in Eos' elsu.

"This is what you wanted?!" Ares bellowed, the dark flames licking around his neck. "Now you'll regret it."

The jaws of his weapon snapped at the air, zipping forward in a serpentine path.

Eos cast one of his elsu at the rushing dragon.

Feathered wings beat, and then the crimson and ink-marbled bird soared at Ares in a blur of speed.

Jaws opened.

Beak pointed. Wings tucked.

Soul Energies hummed their strange crashing sound, like metallic ringing and static popping buried in a symphony of explosion as Ares' creature bit down on the elsu.

Red light emitted from its mouth as Eos' Soul Energy erupted.

The gray-black beast broke form momentarily.

The air smelled burnt after.

Ares' energy reformed, and the creature weaved in place, eager to attack. It faced down the four hovering elsu remaining.

The feathered creatures suddenly burst away with a speed that cracked the air. Within seconds they became blots against the clouds.

"Abandoned by your own soul?" Ares jeered.

Eos ignored him and covered both hands in marbled inky-crimson Soul Energy.

The dragon bared its teeth and came at Eos.

The fangs widened over him.

They bit down.

Zmmmm.

CHAPTER TEN

Soul Energies repelled each other as Eos grasped the upper and lower jaw with each of his soul-covered hands. The layer of protection he formed over his arms cast sparks as he held back the attack with a pained grunt.

His muscles tensed as blood pumped through the veins his arms, resisting the closing fangs. Eos knew he only had seconds to act. His Solido was pulsing light but fading as too much of his Soul Energy had flown out of sight in the clouds.

Eos was at his limit and running low on energy.

A peculiar look crossed Ares' face as he glanced distractedly towards the sky. He let out a single exhale of silent amusement. He sensed Eos' energy out in the distance, preparing for something. *The four elsu were not gone at all.*

The curse mark crawled over the skin of both brothers, writhing alive, as they exerted themselves, pushing beyond their physical limitations to match each other while struggling not to be consumed by the darkness wholly. The ink-like scrawl lapped at their faces, manifesting their deepest drives.

Eos by his hate.

Ares by his ambition.

However, where the inky-flames halted at Ares' jawline, they edged dangerously near to Eos' eyes.

Whispering to himself, Ares said, "Make it look good. Otherwise, I'll have to kill you."

A peculiar look crossed Eos as his final attack unfolded.

Crack.

Crack. Crack. Crack!

The four black Soul Elsu beat their wings a single time each, rupturing the sound barrier and cutting the air with such a swiftness that it would be missed with a blink.

Ares let his dragon fade and raised a total Solido defense. The veil of pale Soul Energy wrapped around him as he released his use of the curse mark.

Because once the elsu had moved, there was no time to react.

FEIGNED DUEL

They were missiles locked onto their target and moving faster than any living creature on the planet. From all directions they came for Ares and struck.

The eruption of tainted crimson was magnificent.

It curled in a cloud that bubbled to the height of the capital dome, casting its dreadful illumination upon the white building.

Formless, tainted crimson illuminated the white building.

When the blast faded seconds later, Ares' Solido was thin, like it was stretched to protect more surface area than he had intended.

Finally, it collapsed, extinguishing into a haze on the scorched grass around him.

Ares nodded slowly in recognition of the power. He tried to speak, but the strain of surviving such an attack left him with a voice that was cracked and weak.

"We made it...look convincing. Yes," he said, nodding slightly to himself. "Next time we meet...*brother*...I'll show you my true strength." His long, raven hair fell over his face as he stumbled forward.

The curse covered Eos' cheeks and forehead with its inky tendrils as he panted from exertion and said, "There's not going to be another fight for you."

"Yes...there will."

Violet energy sparkled to life in a ring between them.

A portal opened.

"No!" Eos screamed. "Don't you dare. *Coward!*"

It was too late. When the violet ring of light shrunk away, no one was standing behind it.

"Bellia!" Eos called angrily into the emptiness, knowing she was behind Ares' escape once more.

The emotional haze clouding his vision began to falter, enough for Eos' reasoning to return. He noticed his friends and family alongside him in the smoking remains of the ruined lawn. The curse mark was already retreating as exhaustion tempered him, but the wriggling tendrils on Eos' neck were still on display for all.

Talus looked ready to finish Eos off himself.

Scavok was visibly uneasy at being in enemy territory.

CHAPTER TEN

Durath and Aizo projected a profound disappointment as they met his gaze.

"Perhaps I was mistaken when I associated you with the black elsu that led King Breuni," Durath said with his maroon fur cape dancing behind him in the breeze.

"Let's go. Now, Eos," Talus barked.

Eos didn't move. The stack of letters tied with string at the tree's base held his attention—*one of the only trees that survived the battle.*

Aizo added, "If I am to be your inlume, Eos, I need a member of the Order—not an undisciplined child. You've put us all at risk."

"We need to go," Scavok snapped as he scanned the horizon. "Mitad members are gathering out there."

Talus grabbed Eos' arm to lead him out of his trance.

Eos ripped away from his father's grip and ran for the tree.

"No!" Talus ordered him.

"We need to take this with us," Eos explained hurriedly and retrieved what Ares had left behind.

The next thing he knew, they were Soul Stepping away from the battle site at a pace Eos could barely keep up with. He saw Scavok peel off from the pack to deal with the Mitad members trailing them.

Scavok secured the secrecy of their return, confident that the Mitad had not decerned their location as they made it back to Colonel Kane's contingency bunker.

Deep under layers of concrete, Eos stood before the group—on trial with his trustworthiness under scrutiny.

"No anatus of the Order has ever been so...so...so reckless, foolish, and willing to endanger his own family," Talus' chastisement was laced with pleading. He searched for rationality to explain Eos' actions.

Scavok merely looked furious, but even his expression was less painful than the hurt on his father's face. Worse still was Durath's disdain. His pinched eyebrows questioned whether Eos was worthy of his commitment to following the Bellator King's son. He weighed the balance of owing his life to a talented, wielder prodigy, one who matched his people's legend, over owing it to an impulsive irresponsible boy.

FEIGNED DUEL

Aizo broke in, "Talus, I think Eos has had enough excitement for one day. Why don't you talk to him as a father tomorrow when we've all calmed down? Then, as his inlume, I will remind him of his responsibilities as a member of the Order."

Talus resisted the urge to contradict Eos' inlume teacher for a few moments before finally relenting with a nod.

Eos silently thanked Aizo for his generous rescue.

"You made a terrible decision today, but for now, let's read the fruits of your risk-taking," Aizo continued. "We all came here on the same mission. Shall we find out what Emir Raggan has written in communications with Vistomus and Saida?"

Scavok made a disgruntled noise and said, "Yes, let's. First, however, we should hear why Ares gave these documents so willingly and determine if we should give any credence to their legitimacy." He swung his silver ponytail and retrieved the bundle of paper from the center table.

"Yes," Talus hummed. "Why *would* Ares help us after everything he's done? More than likely its misinformation to lead us into a trap."

The room searched for an answer in anxious contemplation.

The flicker of unstable lighting and the dreary drip of leaking pipes filled the uneasy silence while they pondered.

"I know why," Eos finally said, a loathing in his tone. All attention waited for his explanation. "Ares pursues his own gain at all times. He didn't fight me like I wanted. Instead, he ensured I received these letters and explained he wants two things from us…from me."

Eos sulked as he despised his half-brother, lost in thoughts of bitter exhaustion, but Scavok prodded him along. "What were these things he told you?"

Trying to explain as best he understood the cryptic motivations, Eos responded, "First, that we both share this curse they call *the Mark of the Chosen*. The Mitad is after a man that has been fully consumed by it and lived. Apparently, the man came back from that and understands this curse. Ares knows I need that information." Eos flexed his blackened hand, now burning with the pricking sensation of thousands of hot needles from its recent use, and placed it on the table for his companions

CHAPTER TEN

to appreciate. Remnants of the curse still freckled his face. "So, he expects I'll do the research he can't."

Talus spoke with a wounded edge, "Always scheming, that boy. Being so lost in his attempt to understand himself makes him more dangerous than even his raw power does."

"Aye, and for that reason, I believe there may be truth in Eos' explanation. Let's hear the second thing that Ares revealed," Scavok continued.

"Well, it wasn't much, but Ares said the Mitad is after a weapon...and I believe he wants it as well. Something in these letters must tell us how to find it."

Scavok stroked the short beard he had grown during his time on Earth and tapped the hilt of his sword with his other hand, the wheels in his head clearly churning. "For that to be true, the Mitad must be withholding that knowledge of this weapon from him. In both cases, Ares is acting like a rogue element, playing as a mirza, as long as it gets him closer to his real pursuits."

They deliberated through the day into the evening, taking turns for rest, as they read the letters and notes aloud numerous times, picking over lines of interest, arguing over the meaning of certain words, and brainstorming the best action to take in response.

Talus thought aloud, "So, these letters reveal Vistomus is in a land called previously called *Japan* but referred to now as *Nippon-Wa*."

"Yes," Aizo agreed. "It explains why Vistomus was not there to tip the scales to our slaughter at the base last night, or even during our fight for the Mellizo Glyphs at Lake Baker so many months back. To think the legendary Viator hariban, Carnus Solaire, is the man they search for on this island nation."

"My father met with Carnus Solaire in his younger days, during the Primane-Viator wars," Durath added. "He asked for Corleo support in his war. My father respected him greatly...to imagine he was corrupted to such a level that the Mitad possessed him entirely with this curse..."

Scavok snarled, "It seems no one is beyond their reach. Their filthy roots grow everywhere...across the Corland...across all of Earth...even within Anite."

FEIGNED DUEL

Eos' eyes fluttered open groggily. He'd bounced around between states of sleep, shame, and excitement at uncovering the Mitad's intentions. Even his lucid dreams were captured by the fantastical elements the letters contained. "What about this weapon? Tools of Karnak? Eye of Izanagi?" He yawned. "The ability to see the flow...the flow of...what was it again?"

Talus and Aizo shared a knowing look that silently communicated more than what they were willing to speak on, but Talus revealed some of his knowledge, "The Tools of Karnak were thought to be a legend from long ago, even before the Era of Lost History. This ancient power they refer to as *The Flow of All Things* is terribly concerning. I must go back to Hyperborea immediately to discuss this matter with Terrava. I believe she has contacts who may know more about these things."

Suspicion rose up in Eos. "Why would Mother know more about this than you?"

Talus hesitated, adding to Eos' suspicion. "Terrava has knowledge of disciplines that I...eh...never pursued myself and that you need not concern yourself with."

Eos tried to break in, "But—"

Talus cut him off, continuing, "Now, it is clear that some action must be taken regarding all these revelations in the land of Nippon-Wa."

Aizo sighed, "Yes. We must further understand this Mark of the Chosen and how to overcome it." Eos lifted his eyelids at the idea while fighting off another wave of exhaustion. His inlume master continued, "Unfortunately, I believe Eos needs to be present if his case is to be examined—*if* we can find Carnus. Jezca's sight in the Manus Temple gave us hints about its nature, but we can't miss the opportunity to know what it accomplishes when it takes over completely. How Carnus conquered it is likely the key we need."

There was a knock at the door.

Durath let in a tired Colonel Kane and Glenn, who wore his melancholy about the Hyperboreans leaving publicly.

"Just checking in for the night. Tomorrow is your last day with us, so let me know if you need anything," Kane said. His body attempted to maintain an upright and optimistic posture, but the weight of the Mitad

CHAPTER TEN

attack and his responsibilities pulled on him visibly. He wanted to say more, but Talus spoke over him.

"Colonel, just the right time. We may have a change of plans."

"Oh?" Colonel Kane was taken aback by the news.

"We have learned of Mitad activities that require us to go to a place called...*Nippon-Wa*. Do you know of this nation?"

Glenn's expression turned to interest.

Colonel Kane nodded sternly. "I do; I have traveled to Japan in my younger days and have contacts there. It's a country in turmoil with strange rumors coming across the sea. If you're looking for my recommendation, I can't advise you to seek it out."

"I've always wanted to see Nippon-Wa," Glenn said aloud to himself while running his thumb over the metal wings of his staff.

Talus stroked his beard. "I don't imagine anyone would be advised to go to a land controlled by the Mitad...but say we must go there, could you help us?"

Colonel Kane pinched the bridge of his nose, pulling his eyebrows together and sighed. "I suppose I could. If my contacts remain as I last spoke to them, you could be there in two weeks or so."

"We would be grateful," Talus said. "It may help untangle this web the Mitad has created across your world."

"Very well. I'll prepare a debrief of what I know about Nippon-Wa and schedule your transportation," Colonel Kane acquiesced.

After that, the Colonel left, but Glenn remained with the Hyperboreans. Feeling the taut pull of fate separating him again so soon, Colonel Kane's pep-talk from not so long ago echoed in his mind once more. *Choosing his own path, for once.* Before Glenn could second guess it, his voice asked softly, "Would you consider taking me along? I've wanted to visit Nippon-Wa since I was a boy. I promise...I'll stay out of your way."

The King of Anite looked at the man who had raised Eos and Maxima. "Master Glenn, you sell yourself short. Perhaps you'll be of more assistance than you expect. You're welcome to join us on this trip, if you so choose."

FEIGNED DUEL

An eager grin crept over Glenn's bearded face. "Thank you. I'll do whatever I can and won't be in your way."

Talus continued with his planning and preparation. "I must go back to Hyperborea briefly. I promised Terrava I would check-in," he informed them. "I will arrange a separate trip to meet you on this island nation. Wait for me and I will join you with the information we need about this weapon not long after."

"Are you certain?" Aizo questioned.

"Yes. I want Scavok to have as much time as possible to get to know this new land. Understand its geography, internalize its power structures, discover the extent of the Mitad's involvement, and perhaps learn of possible locations of Carnus or this woman, *Grace*. There is nowhere safer for Eos and Durath than under your protection, Aizo, with Scavok nearby."

Eos' teacher bowed, "Then, we will go to Nippon-Wa ahead of you and await your arrival, my king."

CHAPTER ELEVEN

THE NECOGEN SCHOLAR

Panic swelled in Jezca's mind. She looked across at a young girl with sapphire eyes. *Sister*. She felt the word inside her. Blood rolled down the girl's chin from a split lip. *Jace*. The boy over Maxima was not much older. Needle in hand, he held down the squirming girl to stitch her lip. *Panic*. Flashes of an accident and screaming. Jezca tried to focus…to remember how the injury had happened, but a soft knocking sound caused the vision to waver.

Jezca shook off sleep as a golden beam from the open curtain hit her face. The dream was not from her own imagination or memory. This had been happening at least once a week. She wondered if Eos was experiencing the same. She figured he must be if they went through the same memory swap in the Manus Temple.

The knocking that came through her dream had been from the waking world. It came again at her door.

The priestess sat up from her bed and went to the door, still in her rich blue dress with her Manus Temple broach and belt. She had fallen asleep in the middle of the day, and her veil was still on, adorned by the golden circlet and fine wreathes of gold chain.

"Sorry, Jezca. I didn't realize you were sleeping," Bellia said as she took in the priestess' sleepy yawn. She brushed her silvery-blonde fringe back behind her ear as she balanced a stack of books under her other arm, nestled against her pronounced stomach. Jezca let her in.

"Only drifted off. A nap," Jezca murmured, straightening up. "Might I ask why you're here?"

"Saida wants me to observe each time you light the Beacon Stone," Bellia reminded mildly. Jezca's animus eye always appeared to be staring into her true intentions, but whether the eye being able to actually see into her thoughts was real or just her imagination, Bellia had not decided. "I took the opportunity to bring you some books. These are a few of my favorites. This one is from a place called Earth."

Jezca nodded with melancholy in her slow movement.

Earth! That's the place from my dream of Eos.

'…there are numerous distant lands, and I've been to many,' Saida had said about the foreign place. Bellia is part of the Mitad…Best to play ignorant.

"Thanks. Never heard of Earth," she murmured and sat at her desk to light the onyx gemstone that lay on it.

"No, I don't suppose you have. How are you settling into my home of Setudo?"

"I'm watched like a prisoner. My brother was killed. I want to find my mother. Perhaps settling isn't the best description," Jezca responded sarcastically.

"Fair enough," Bellia said and placed the stack of books on the table. "Well, I brought you *A History of Lenape*, so you can learn about the island; *The Wielder and the Wanderer,* which is a popular children's tale here; the book from Earth is rather romantic; and here's some Manus Priesthood prayer books and scriptures that I was able to find in our library."

The only response was a quiet nod. Then, Jezca let pink mist drift from her hands to the stone. Her eye glowed to match and cast a pink overlay on her golden-blonde hair. The Beacon Stone revealed its ruby color briefly as sparks whirled inside her right eye.

CHAPTER ELEVEN

Jezca sighed as the onyx color spread back over the surface after just a few seconds.

"What did your *sight* tell you?"

"Nothing. I can identify my mom's energy but that's it. The stone lit up once from the other side, but something was in the way. Normally, I could get an idea of where the person is or what they're doing from their Soul Energy…but it's like she's too far away."

Bellia hummed knowingly. She waited a moment to decide whether she was revealing too much. "That's because she is. Grace is on another world."

"Another world? Like…*Earth?*" Jezca connected the dots skeptically.

"Yes."

"How do you know that?"

"This is between us, but I worked with Grace a few times. I didn't know her well, but I did know her."

Jezca's eyes narrowed. "Why are you telling me this?"

"Because I'm about as stuck as you are," Bellia rubbed her swollen belly tenderly. "I'm due to have a child that the Mitad is not thrilled about. My staying here in my father's castle is for Saida to keep an eye on me as much as it is for my safety."

"Why?"

"My child's father is one of the Mitad's greatest tools…as a result he's not allowed to have attachments. And yet he's…" Bellia trailed. "Just my situation is a difficult place to be in."

Jezca nodded her head, beginning to understand.

"Us women have to help each other out in this world," Bellia said with a friendly smile. "And Saida promised to help you find Grace. I'm making sure he makes good on that promise."

"I…appreciate that," Jezca gave an exhale. The suspicion didn't wholly leave her body, but she did recognize Bellia's effort with this peace offering. The priestess couldn't resist asking, "What was Grace like? And why did she go missing?"

"Grace was brilliant," Bellia mused. "Perhaps the most intelligent woman in all of the Corland. She could read and write in a dozen languages, including ancient ones that no one else understands. She was as talented of a wielder as she was a scholar."

"A *Scholar?* We were assassins. Necogen doesn't have *scholars*," Jezca scoffed, doubting Bellia's description.

"True, but as she began taking missions that sent her further away from Necogen, she became obsessed with learning, particularly about the Lost Era. Eventually, her obsession with that lost knowledge got her tangled up with a group called the Priori of Karnak. At the same time, she was taking on assassinations for high pay, along with missions to smuggle information for the Mitad. That's how I met her."

Jezca leaned forward. "What is the Priori of Karnak, and why would my mom work for you?"

"Necogen assassins take the highest paying jobs; you know that. As for the Priori, they are a secretive group. No one knows who the members are or what exactly they want. However, we do know they possess lost knowledge…including information on ancient weapons that the Mitad also want."

"So, my mom knew about these weapons?"

"Some of them. She had found clues to a few of their locations. We call them the Tools of Karnak, and the Beacon Stones are minor tools of Karnak's creation, according to legend. The one we were seeking back then was on Earth."

"What is *Earth?* Is it another continent like the Burning Lands?"

"No, it's like another planet out in the stars."

"Impossible," Jezca muttered and began twisting the metal rings on her fingers as she reevaluated everything she thought she knew.

Bellia brushed her fair hair behind her ears. "It's not. I've been to Earth many times. If you analyze the truth of what your Observation Wielding has revealed, you would know it to be true as well."

Jezca reflected on what her sight had observed. Grace's energy was not contactable because she was further away than any distance Jezca had ever felt. That much was certain.

Her umber eye narrowed and her lips pursed. "Saida's been lying this whole time. What am I doing here if he's looking for my mom just like me?"

CHAPTER ELEVEN

Bellia calmed her down, "The Mitad know where she went missing and are searching Earth for her. Saida didn't lie. We're your only hope of finding Grace. Each time you light those stones, our people on Earth have a better chance of locating her."

"Why wouldn't she come back herself?" Jezca asked suspiciously and raised her mental wall once again.

Bellia sighed, "I don't know. Her last mission went badly. I wasn't there, but I've heard the rumors. She lived and fled but went missing after that. That's all I know."

Jezca bit her lip and closed her eyes. She muttered in disbelief, "A Necogen scholar. Who's ever heard of such a thing? Thank you, Bellia." She picked up the onyx Beacon Stone and turned it over, examining it for some kind of clue that she had missed. It vibrated with a living energy in her hand but remained locked.

∞   ∞   ∞

Grace ran with urgency, flying across the tatami floor mats. She sensed the Soul Energy from across Saigo's castle. There was never so much as a spark to be perceived in the Akaishi Mountains and yet she knew what she felt in this moment.

She threw herself at her bedroom table and pulled open the second drawer frantically, dumping out the contents of a silk bag. Her prized possession rolled onto the surface like a pyramid-shaped die. It had been the first confirmation of her research on the Tools of Karnak, though a minor one with many identical pieces. Still, it represented tangible proof of what the Priori sought.

There was still a sparkling ruby glimmer in the Beacon Stone when she picked it up.

A tear fell, wetting the relic.

The energy was familiar, a match for her own, and yet far more. She recognized that it belonged to her daughter.

How? How does Jezca call out to me across worlds after all these years?

A beautiful moment of hope burned in her stomach like the warmth of a first sip of saki. Her daughter was alive and seeking her.

THE NECOGEN SCHOLAR

The sensation fell to vacant despair.

Separate worlds. No way to bridge them.

She put the stone and bag back in the drawer.

For the first time in years, she remembered who she truly was. A desire to actively seek a way home was rekindled—something she had long given up hope on.

Later that day, she bowed at Saigo's entranceway.

"Himiko-ojou, a pleasant surprise."

"Saigo-dono, I've come to discuss Saitani's letter. You do not have much longer to decide."

"Mmm. Walk with me," Saigo said and rose from his table.

They walked under the irimoya temple roofs and along the bamboo engawa walkway surrounding the edges outside Saigo's private quarters. It bordered a rock garden with sakura trees and paper lanterns. They paced along it in a slow, meditative path as Grace awaited Saigo to initiate the conversation.

"I value your advice greatly, Himiko. Saitani Umetaro has no love for the bushido-restoration movement. Even when my dear friend, Emperor Toba, was still alive, Saitani was open about his dislike for the return of the samurai way. We were always in conflict. Now we share a common enemy, but his ways are not mine," Saigo said, almost in contemplation to himself more than to Grace.

"The Mitad is too powerful now for you to face alone, Saigo-dono. These *hanyo* that Emperor Antoku has given free rein to...they make the Emperor's army and guns the least of your worries."

"True. My warriors do not have many battles left if the hanyo target us. We will be wiped out. Our battles must be picked wisely."

Grace nodded in agreement, the charms on her gold and jade hairpins bobbing with her. "Is stopping a large shipment of guns and ammunition from reaching Antoku's forces not important enough?"

"Are they any better in the hands of Saitani? He leads a modern rebellion from the cities, but would he not advise the Emperor to destroy the samurai if he gains control? Antoku is so young...merely a figurehead for whomever can impress their will on him." The lines around Saigo's dark earth-colored eyes deepened as he fretted.

CHAPTER ELEVEN

Grace smiled gently. "Perhaps he would, but perhaps not…if Saigo's samurai help in repelling Raijin and his hanyo from Nippon-Wa, then you would be welcomed on a new council for the Emperor, just as you were with his father."

Saigo grunted his acknowledgment, still deliberating.

Grace continued, "Not to mention weapons pointed *at* the hanyo are better than *in* the hands of the hanyo."

"You are correct, Himiko. But I must have strict plans and contingencies to avoid many of my men dying. I will tell Saitani that the samurai will come to his aid, but only with tactical precision, and in certain areas we agree upon."

"Very wise, Saigo-dono," Grace agreed. Then she broached the next topic carefully, "You wanted me to prepare your forces to battle the hanyo, and I am doing my best, but there is only so much they can do with steel against kami powers. I believe you should ask for the *Ise shinshoku* to join you. I could make the request. Kikujiro and I train together sometimes. It would not be—"

"You ask priests to become warriors?" Saigo scoffed.

"They have their guards."

"Pacifist priests trained in theory."

"They are your people's natural connection to the kami! You trained Kikujiro yourself in the way of the sword. He is strong," Grace reasoned.

"Kikujiro chose to follow his mother's path. He knows nothing of bushido. You may request their aid, but I expect little. Whatever Carnus' artifact is capable of, I only know the priests guard it for him. Then again…" Saigo reflected, as if remembering, "You are kami, and qualified to be their supreme priestess…you may be the only one that can sway them to war."

Grace bowed, "I will do my best, Saigo-dono. I may be able to convince them in time for Saitani's raid, but regardless the war must be decided someday soon, and you will need the Ise shinshoku on your side."

"I fear even the shinshoku combined with your ability and Carnus would not be enough," Saigo admitted.

THE NECOGEN SCHOLAR

"Perhaps, but we will make our stand nonetheless. *Maybe an elsu will catch lightning*," she mused in reference to his vision.

Three days later, Grace had left the Akaishi Mountains and made her way south to the Mie Prefecture. She traveled slowly, resting often between her stints of Soul Step. It gave her time to take in the rice patties reflecting like glass staircases up the green-covered peaks and mountains that poked through the mists of the countryside.

At the end of her journey, she found herself bowing under the white-washed timber of the torii gate of Ise Grand Shrine.

She then crossed a bridge of the same wood, swallowing down her heart-racing awe at the massive scale of the walkway, and passed under another torii gate where she was greeted with the deepest bow from two on-negi, the junior Shinto priests, and the shrine maidens waiting on the other side. The women folded their bodies in reverence, their white miko tops meeting their red pleated pants, revealing their hair ribbons.

Most would not make eye contact with her, for her reputation preceded her—only the senior priests would would meet her gaze.

Despite this, Grace always felt calmed by the atmosphere at the Ise Grand Shrine. World wars were fought, regimes changed in Nippon-Wa's rich history, revolutions washed over the island in waves, and yet the Shinto way remained through it all—an unmovable boulder revealed each time those waves pulled back. The religious movement was now in more favor than it had been in the last hundred years due to the previous emperor, Toba, unifying the modernity of Nippon with the ancient culture stemming from the land known as Wa. He laid a path for the nation to live harmoniously in the post-Fracture War world.

Revealing herself to Nippon-Wa as the first *kami* to come forward earned Grace a lot of complications. She matched the resurfacing myths at the time to an incredible degree: the Queen of Wa, Himiko, a direct descendent of their great goddess Amaterasu. Their ancient sorceress queen was lost to history, but Grace was the reincarnation of their imagination and need.

Walking elegantly through the beauty of the shrine, Grace both dearly loved this land and resented the role they had cast upon her. She washed her hands with a ladle in the purifying basin, then made her bows

CHAPTER ELEVEN

and passes through the outer and inner shrines. It was an act of respect, playing the character her life had morphed into.

Soon, Kikujiro met her in his traditional robes. He greeted her with the same reverence he would have shown to the Emperor.

His masculine face resembled Saigo's, though his features were narrower and younger. He wore the garments of his position, the supreme priest.

They spoke in Japanese.

"Himiko-ojou, you honor us with your visit. Please walk with me." They left the heart of the sanctuary and sauntered to the edge of the ocean against a cloudy, purple-dusk sky. The sound of splashing filled the silence until he continued, "I am always pleased to be graced by your beauty—in fact, I wish you would visit more. It brings a renewed vigor to our priests and maidens to have a direct descendent so connected to Amaterasu walk amongst us. You are both royalty and kami. Yet, I find myself with dread at the reason for your visit."

Grace raised an eyebrow. "You assume to know why I've come, Kikujiro?"

"The Emperor has sent envoys repeatedly, asking me to convince my father to end his rebellion. The conflict must end soon, regardless of the victor. You are here to urge me to give you what I cannot."

They walked past frog statues bordering the salt water and peered out at two rock formations joined by sacred rope. They leaned into each other, almost as if they were reaching across the rope for thousands of years, and a torii gate sat atop the larger left monolith.

"You assume too much," Grace replied. "As I have always made clear, I believe you should turn over the Left Eye of Izanagi. It could be used to end this war—"

Kikujiro interrupted, "End it with death and violence on a scale that could erase all of Tokyo. That is not our way. Amaterasu was created from Izanagi's Left Eye. It belongs in the custody of the priests of Amaterasu."

Grace groaned slightly in aggravation. "Instead, you let death and violence occur daily as Raijin takes hold of your land." *If only she could convince them to despise Vistomus Fulmen under his guise of "lightning god" as much as she did.* "Yet, I am not here to ask you to give up what Carnus has tasked you to hide. It is futile, and I lost that dream years ago. No...I'm here asking you and your warriors to assist your father. Saigo will lose this war within the year now that Emperor Antoku has appointed authority to the hanyo."

The mention of the mirza, those that his people perceived as half-demons, made Kikujiro clench his jaw. His distaste for their power usurpation was as palatable as the salt in the evening air.

"My father chose the sword and I the priesthood. Why would I go against my ways for his?" Kikujiro asked.

"I have asked for the Left Eye to defeat Raijin and accepted your refusal. But when Raijin learns you know where it is—he will burn this shrine down and murder everyone in it. He is not one of your people, not your kami, nor a friend of the Emperor. *He only whispers poisons in his ear.* Now, your mother trained you to wield Soul Energy, as is your clan's secret birth rite. Over the last five years, I've taught you to be a formidable warrior. Do not pretend you are a man of only peace. Raijin will take away everything you hold dear if you do not act now," Grace said forcefully.

Kikujiro's bloodline had retained some ancient wielding lineage from a time that far preceded any history Grace could track down.

They had maintained the purity enough that he and a few other shinshoku of his clan could wield. They had always been warriors in secret, taught to defend the shrine in difficult times, though the art was nearly lost until Grace had rejuvenated it in recent years.

She did not know how a wielding lineage ended up in Japan, but she suspected it was an effect dating back to Karnak's time or earlier.

The sun blazed past the cloud bank in a neon orange haze between the two rock formations as it fell toward the horizon.

Thinking, Kikujiro sighed and eventually conceded. "I will not fight for my father...but when the direct descendent of my temple's kami makes a request...and the fate of Izanagi's Left Eye is at stake, I will serve my bloodline—*my mother's bloodline.* However, only me! The other four clan guardians will protect the Eye. Tell me, will this win your war?"

CHAPTER ELEVEN

Grace shook her head. "Even if you gave us the four wielders from your clan...they still need training. It would not win our war...no. However, you may sway a critical raid—and that could distract Raijin from Izanagi's Eye for a little longer."

Kikujiro gave a throaty grunt of acknowledgment that sounded like his father. "I have conditions for this work, Himiko-ojou."

"Ask, and I will do what I can."

"As you respect my role in protecting the Eye, I accept that you will not take me back with you to Takamagahara, though it is my deepest desire to see the realm of the kami. So, you leave me with smaller requests...I want to understand the power of the Eye. More than anything, I crave to understand the way of my ancestors. I also want a duel here and now. To test my abilities against yours before my fellow shinshoku see me in battle."

Grace smiled, "Very well. I will give you this duel, but you and the others should train with Saigo's men under my tutelage. With wielders in their ranks, they will be much more effective."

Kikujiro bowed deeply. "As you wish Himiko-ojou. And the power of the Eye?"

"I'll tell you what I know. Soon, but not tonight."

The two disappeared down the coastline, away from the shrine, so that the two rope-joined rocks became a small shadow against the sunset.

Kikujiro swirled his stiffened hands around his core in a Tai Chi-like gesture.

Grace struck first to set her student on the backfoot as vibrant pink Soul Energy manifested in a slash at his shoulder.

The supreme priest perceived the energy a second before it cut into him and shielded his shoulder with a veil of blue, so similiar to the shade of the ocean splashing beside them.

Zmmm.

Their energies clashed in the first strike of the duel.

Kikujiro's protective layer then swirled into a shape like levitating water as his limbs moved in a dance. His arms whirled, and his knee came up, preceding a lunge that sent the Soul Energy towards Grace like a liquid whip.

THE NECOGEN SCHOLAR

They sparred, again and again, pink and blue against the setting sun on the coast of Nippon-Wa.

The flow of energies was an extension of their bodies, an expression of combat and art and dance.

Grace weaved and shuffled as the whip of energy disconnected from Kikujiro and snapped around her. After a few evasions, she would turn the momentum back by forcing him to defend.

"You fight like you are trying to demonstrate the eloquence and mastery of your skills. But you'll have to redirect that martial arts nature into deadly intent on the battlefield," Grace chided him.

Blood dripped from torn fabric in Kikujiro's robe sleeves as Grace punished him for his missteps with superficial wounds.

This continued until they were shadows against the coast.

The bout ended with Kikujiro stumbling to a knee to dodge but looking up to find a barrier of searing hot pink light at his throat.

He put his head down, conceded, and thanked Grace for the lesson.

"Meet me with your men in one week at Saigo's castle," Grace said as she helped him up. "We have much to do."

CHAPTER TWELVE

VIOLET ASH VOW

Catavelum, the capital of Caracta, was a mesmerizing place filled with the bustling sounds of a thriving populace, the crash of hundreds of waterfalls, and the white-gold of pillars and domes layered on top of each other amongst the spires.

It was the city Terrava hailed from, the home of the Caerule family—half of Maxima's bloodline.

Holding onto the rail of a sea strider, Maxima watched the crashing falls of Caracta Bay through the clay holes of the blue corcinth mask. Some were not much bigger than a person in width, but others were larger than the castle at the kingdom's heart. The vessel had taken her and Fey down the east coast of Anite into Caracta.

The ship workers and captain had warily eyed her when she boarded, wearing the grinning corcinth disguise. However, Saier Fey was so revered and well-known that none dared to comment on the inlume's travel companion. Maxima heard their uneasy murmurs when they thought she was out of earshot, though.

"They say the rivers that made the Tenebrim canyons now flow east through Caracta to join the Sharfamilh ocean. To do so, they must fall a great distance," Fey explained while leaning on the sea strider's rail. "Welcome to Catavelum, your mother's home city…and mine."

They passed the clamoring of dock workers and ships being anchored and found themselves heading toward the royal castle's private port. White stone trimmed in gold made up the tiered tower surrounded by waterfalls except for a small portion facing the bay. Columns stacked on successively narrower circles of pillars, reaching higher than the waters, until the white dome nearly touched the clouds.

"When will you tell me why we are here?" Maxima asked as they walked down the private boardwalk and across a one-hundred-meter walkway of smooth ivory rock to an entourage of welcoming guards.

The little woman hobbled slightly along, hinting at the age her looks didn't fully show. However, Maxima knew it was only a disguise to keep everyone off guard. The inlume smiled slyly and asked, "You've seen your mother's tattoo, yes?"

Maxima nodded. "A tree with a flame in the center?"

"Yes. That is the tree of knowledge and a reminder that the flame of hidden knowledge must be preserved by us wielders."

"Inlumes?" Maxima questioned.

"There are inlumes among us, but no—we are a secret order of scholars, preserving ancient knowledge and uncovering lost truths. I have been called for an urgent meeting, and I'm not allowed to let you out of my sight. So, you will be attending."

"This secret group will allow it?"

Fey laughed, "I am one of the most revered members of the Priori of Karnak alongside Salvaluc, Roana, and Gibrali. If I choose to initiate you, they will accept. If I ask for you to attend, they will vote, and Salvaluc and Gibrali have always gone out of their way for me. I was quite the beauty in my younger days." She winked at Maxima.

CHAPTER TWELVE

Saier Fey had a timeless attractiveness, but Maxima knew better. Her behavior and disposition betrayed any eloquence her natural beauty presented.

The guards wore silver armor, pointed and scrawled with detailed lines and the rearing horse crest of the royal family, as they waited in stillness for the two guests who stood before them.

Golden-topaz light appeared around Fey's head in a circlet of Soul Energy that formed three broken swords at the forehead. The crown of an inlume prompted the guards to place their hands over their hearts and bow to the master Soul Wielder.

"Welcome, Master Fey," the captain of the regiment said as if greeting a hero returned from battle.

They turned in unison and marched towards a pointed arch that was the private entrance to the castle. Blinding sunlight reflected off the roof and redirected Maxima's gaze; however, a shadow caught her attention. Atop the ring of waterfalls, a muscular creature moved on four legs. Maxima couldn't be sure if it was a glow coming from where it ran or the surface water deflecting sunlight. She shook her head and blinked to make sure what she saw was real. When she focused again, there was only the foaming crest of water before gravity bent it.

"Master Fey, did you see…?"

Fey continued walking and said without turning her head, "You saw something above the Tristurium Falls? It was no illusion—wild horses roam the land above us. The sunkaw are watchers and friends of the Caerule family's realm. They are a royal breed, chief among the plain's horses. The stallions of that line are legend to wield with their hoofs." Fey smiled as she looked to see Maxima's mouth hang open.

"On top of the water? Like Soul Step?" The girl sputtered from behind her mask.

"Well…they roam in the royal pools according to legend, so only nobles could tell you for sure," Fey said with a grin that teased she knew much more. "Perhaps you can ask King Gibrali. Then again, they're so fast that you may have just caught the best view of them."

Maxima frowned. Fey must be having fun teasing her. It was in her nature to drink, gamble, and tease after all. *An unlikely teacher*, she thought.

VIOLET ASH VOW

They were led down tunnels of white stone lined with a brilliant turquoise accent that looked almost crystalline. Every twenty feet, a miniature fountain was built into the wall in an alcove, filling the halls with echoes of soft trickling.

It was peaceful...and strangely welcoming.

Maxima found some piece inside her, deep in her marrow, resonate with the world she had stepped into, and she desired to touch the falls and meet the sunkaw horses.

Then, they entered a banquet hall. Equestrian banners of blue lined the walls between portraits of nobility. At the head of the room stood a man with tanned skin and hair as black as Maxima's, swept back and parted in the middle.

King Gibrali wore a simple crown, a band around his head with sharp points at the front and the back made of black metal. It was inlaid with a rippled gold pattern of darker rings like Damascus steel. It brought to mind a pool of liquid gold.

A twinkle of joy sparked in the King's eyes as he greeted Saier Fey with a bow. She returned by kneeling before Gibrali Caerule and asking, "My king bows to an old inlume?"

"Come now, Master Fey, an inlume and senior of the Priori has more titles than this king. You've always had my admiration since our youth," he said with a flirtatious tease in his voice. "And who might our masked guest be? I must say, no one has been so bold as to meet with me while disguising their identity."

Fey rose and said seriously, "She is my apprentice and will be joining the summit if you all consent."

King Gibrali's eyebrows raised. "Master Fey...I...I thought you were retired as an inlume teacher? I do not doubt your judgement but newcomers may not join a Priori summit. It isn't done."

"*I am retired*," Fey said wearily. "But this is done as a special request of the Order. Tell no one of it. Her usefulness to the Priori must be trusted on my recommendation. Besides, you don't often deny me, Gibrali."

The King nodded. "Of course, then it will be done after a vote. Who are we welcoming into our ranks?"

CHAPTER TWELVE

Maxima resisted her instinct to reply to her uncle honestly.

Fey winced at this.

Layering a second breach of custom would be difficult. "You may call her the Blue Corcinth. Due to the nature of her mission, her identity must be kept secret. It is a matter of life and death." Seeing the disbelief on his face, Fey added, "This is not a request of the Order, rather *a demand of your sister.*"

At that, Gibrali swallowed his forming sentence and pursed his lips instead. "Of course," he yielded. "Nothing could be more in Terrava's nature than that. I must consent, especially after the tragedy she has recently been dealt."

"Thank you for honoring me with your accommodations, King Gibrali," Maxima said reverently.

"Anyone Master Fey entrusts with a mission on behalf of both the Order and my sister is welcome in Catavelum. Still, it may be—"

"Gibrali, let the girl join us," a fourth voice, aged and heavily accented but strong and calm, interrupted from behind the hanging tapestry of the ancestral Caerule family tree. "I have already deciphered her identity. If you have not, you disappoint me." A man with a silver head of hair and mustache entered the room. He wore simple mahogany robes with an air of mischief about his sage demeanor.

"Master Salvaluc…who?" The King's confusion was evident.

"Never mind *who* she is. The Blue Corcinth has already made a name for herself in Old Cintish driving out the Mitad." Salvaluc's voice creaked in amusement, "Though I believe that may be the least of your feats against them in the past months." His smile grew.

Maxima smiled sheepishly behind her mask, grateful that they could not see the blush that surely colored her cheeks.

"Come. The others are waiting," Salvaluc disappeared behind the tapestry again. Fey, Maxima, and King Gibrali Caerule followed behind the hanging cloth.

The woven fabric contained a myriad of running and rearing steeds, each following numerous more as the branches of descendants grew. They flowed from the first crowned horse, which had the name Tiglath Caerule curled in white threads on a black body. Maxima passed by, wondering if her name was at the far end of the decorative herd of Caerule relatives.

Fey stopped her as the men continued on ahead, out of hearing distance.

"Before we enter, Maxima, I must ask you: what do you want most? I am about to drag you into a new world of secret knowledge. While you're under my watch, you will be tied to my affairs. Anything beyond attending them is your choice, but I'd like to know where your desires lay so that I can guide you for the time we are together."

Surprised by the sudden confrontation, Maxima asked, "What do I...want?"

"Yes. What does your heart call you to do?"

The question was a lot for Maxima to consider so unexpectedly. "I suppose I want most to see my brother and family. For them to know I'm alive."

Fey waved her hand. "You're a king's daughter and an anatus of the Order. You are called to duty beyond these simple impulsive things. You must rise above base desires and bear the responsibility of your calling. Now, are you drawn to serve the Order of Soul Wielders primarily as a wielder? Or do you want to become part of a pursuit of knowledge beyond the veil of even the Order?"

Maxima was nervous to answer. She wished for a moment that she had her old scarf to put to her mouth, but at least she had her mask to hide behind as she choose her next words carefully. "Master Fey, that's too much to consider so unexpectedly. I don't know that I can make a decision like that without knowing more."

"And yet, you will often be called to make decisions on instinct. I'm trying to understand your instinct right now. You don't have to decide immediately, but the time is fast coming when you will have to choose what you want to pursue."

Maxima was unsure but whispered, "Yes, Master Fey."

Do I want to become an inlume?

Do I want to pursue this secret world offered before me?

CHAPTER TWELVE

They turned through hidden chambers until a false wall slid back and revealed the base of the Tristurium Falls. This edge of the castle was near the churning foam, only one hundred meters of turquoise water away.

The seasoned wielders confidently walked over the surface following an invisible path known only to them, and Maxima mirrored their Soul Step. When they approached the falls, Salvaluc created a shield of white Soul Energy to deflect the spray of mist.

As they drew closer toward the shroud of water, Maxima resisted the urge to ask questions. Her curiosity tugged at her psyche, but the desire to not embarrass herself with childish inquisitiveness won out.

Salvaluc held his shield of energy to create a tunnel through the crashing cascade, revealing a staircase built into the cliff wall behind the waters. He gestured for Maxima to hurry through, following Fey and Gibrali.

The group then ascended the stairs beneath a *hurr*-ing sound that muted everything else—a soothing song of white noise to hide their steps.

Finally, they passed through an entrance in the face of the rock and found a door with ancient writing that Maxima didn't recognize. An inlay of anima stone twinkled like sapphires as Salvaluc placed his hand on the design of a tree of knowledge with its branches and roots forming a circular emblem. The silver-haired inlume closed his eyes as he focused on directing his energy into the internal locking mechanisms of the door.

With a blue flash, a heavy array of locks clunked open, and the doors parted to a cavern with a floor made entirely of sparkling azure rock. The blue mineral deposit glittered under the lighting stones affixed around the room, marbling the walls and ceiling in veins of deep blue, sprouting from all surfaces like shelves of fungi in leaf-like plumes.

The center of the room contained a circle of ten seats built into the floor, fashioned from the blue rock, surrounding a miniature tree with twisting gnarled branches and violet leaves. The pale tan trunk had grown around a chunk of anima stone, not quite engulfing it, and its roots spread through the cave floor.

VIOLET ASH VOW

Maxima stood in front of a chair adjacent to Fey, copying the actions of the other members of the Priori of Karnak. Two other members were already waiting for them to arrive.

"Half answered the summoning on short notice, and it appears we have a newcomer," Roana said coldly, clearly annoyed by both facts. Her eyes gave the demeanor of one who is constantly displeased, a stark contrast to the distracting light pink of her dyed hair. She was far younger than the others, but her disposition was full of confidence in her right to be there amongst elders and masters.

Fey explained, "She's under my protection and welcomed here by the vote of Salvaluc and King Gibrali."

Gibrali stammered, "I didn't—well I...I suppose the combined trust of Fey, Terrava, and Salvaluc earns my vote."

Salvaluc nodded with a wise smile, giving his approval.

"Pushover," Roana chided the King. "And the mask?"

"An unfortunate requirement that is more burden to her than us. She is performing operations that require her identity to be kept secret, even here," Fey said softly.

A displeased huff was Roana's response. "Well, even with Tavro's vote, that's not enough to disagree with you three."

Tavro spoke his first words of the gathering, "However, I would vote in the affirmative. I believe I've solved the identity of our guest and wish to keep it secret as well."

The pink-haired woman bristled as she changed the subject, "Well, is this everyone? Looks like Caracta, Tenebrim, Terspar, and Monte have made it here. Where are the others?"

"Peladan was detained on errands for the King," Tavro said.

Salvaluc responded, "I don't like the others' absence; however, we must get started." The elder Priori leader walked to the miniature tree and lit it with a spiral of white Soul Energy that danced around the anima stone in the trunk like an excited sprite before lighting the gem. He spoke deep and commandingly, "Knowledge is power."

Fey stepped up to the tree as Salvaluc returned and took his seat. "Power must be preserved, and knowledge retained," she answered the mantra and manifested her topaz light.

CHAPTER TWELVE

Each member lit the stone with their personal Soul Energies and repeated the response—Gibrali, Roana, and then Tavro. Finally, Maxima glanced at Fey, asking with tensed body language and the slight gesture of upturned hands.

"All members of the meeting must answer the call," Fey commanded.

Maxima approached the center, lit the stone, and spoke the words, "Power must be preserved, and knowledge retained."

"I called this gathering of the Priori in urgency," Salvaluc announced. "Last week, I visited the Makanla Gate in Tenebrim. I sensed it was active...vibrating with an intensity that I hadn't felt before. So, I posted a guard there to watch it. When I returned, I found him..." the old man paused. His serene disposition was upset by the thought of what happened. "He was dead. Killed in the way they do...*Drained!*"

"Impossible!" Tavro interjected immediately. "That's just a myth. Someone else must have been in your territory. Perhaps a vengeance for your assistance in Anite?"

Salvaluc answered with a firm tone of chastisement, "No. We must not allow the knowledge we preserve to become only myth. They may not have been seen in our lifetime, but we must not discount the knowledge we have gathered from Karnak's time. The texts warn of what comes from the Makanla Gates."

Maxima's head whirled at the new words she had no reference for.

Roana agreed, "I have felt the new energy at the Makanla Gate in Terspar. It is alive like I've never seen before. Something new is happening to them."

"Or something very old," Fey agreed.

"If...if *they* are moving on Hyperborea again, then what do you suggest, Master Salvaluc?" Tavro wondered.

"We post a guard at every known gate with a signaling system to warn if one activates."

Gibrali was shocked, "Master, that would be a death sentence for them if what you say is true."

"Yes. Let's hope what I say is not true, then. We must monitor this threat," Savaluc said. He raised his hand in front of his chest and held it there. "I vote yes. We put watchmen at every gate."

The room fell silent.

Roana repeated Salvaluc's gesture. Fey followed.

Tavro looked grim as he also voted yes.

Finally, Gibrali said, "You'll need my vote with only five here. I request that we bring all texts and scrolls concerning the Makanla Gates to this room for analysis. That is my condition."

"Agreed. We shall put out an order for the watch and a call for knowledge to be copied and brought to Catavelum. Let it be done," Salvaluc finalized the matter and then plucked a violet leaf from the tree and turned it to ash in his hand with a flash of Soul Energy. He smeared it with his thumb and left a vibrant stain down the inside of his forearm. Then, he passed the ashes to Fey. After every member recognized the vote with the gesture, the remaining ashes were sprinkled over the tree.

Roana moved to the next issue. "I possess one beacon stone from the set left behind by Grace Lapithos. Master Salvaluc has tasked me with watching over it. For the first time, it has been lit."

Fey and Gibrali let out an audible gasp.

"More than that," Roana continued, "It's been lit multiple times by two different sources."

Salvaluc hummed in contemplation as he parsed the meaning of the multiple lightings. "You believe Grace lit her stone? Can you be certain?"

"Yes. I recognized her Soul Energy…but it was so distant. Almost infinitely so. Like a person without a location."

There was a crinkle in Salvaluc's brow as his expression softened to appreciation for the long-hoped-for news. "Then she is alive. Thank the Great Soul."

Roana returned with a sneer, "You may thank the Great Soul, but I will not until she's returned safely—and we have no idea where she is."

There was a knowing smile on the old man's face. "My source within the Mitad has procured that information for me."

"Spill it," Fey said with a snap.

CHAPTER TWELVE

There was hesitation. With lips that hung searching for the right words, Salvaluc decided only one was necessary.

"Earth."

It was Tavro who reacted first. "Salvaluc, you're determined to bring every myth to reality today. This cannot be!"

Roana was astonished as she let out, "The land of legend? So, that's why she's gone missing?"

"No," Salvaluc answered. "That's where she went missing. Why she went missing is the Mitad. However, this information is of no use to us by itself. The ancient texts say we must possess a Mellizo Glyph to travel between worlds. Unfortunately, we have neither knowledge of their location nor the ability to obtain them."

"*If* Earth actually exists...the Mellizo Glyphs were last thought to be in possession of the Order," Tavro said. "If we set our resources to it—"

Maxima broke in, saying, "I know where both Mellizo Glyphs are located, and I can assure you that Earth is very real."

Roana cast her cold gaze on Maxima with a new interest. "So, our newest member is here for a reason, after all. Do tell, masked one."

"One is in the hands of the Mitad," Maxima admitted sadly as she recalled the mountain pass in the Pacem Derex Fingers collapsing with Benedir and Eos trapped on the opposite side from her. "The other is on Earth."

King Gibrali was amazed and couldn't help but whisper, "Who are you, girl?"

Maxima announced to the room, "I am the Blue Corcinth...until I am allowed to be free again."

Gibrali nodded, knowing he should not have asked the question.

"And how can you be sure of the Mellizo Glyph locations?" Roana asked with suspicion.

"I saw Mirza Rohl Ford steal one. The other was used recently by members of the Order of Soul Wielders to travel to Earth. That is all I can say," Maxima said.

"Who are you?" Roana repeated Gibrali's words, perplexed.

Fey stepped forward. "With that said, there is no way of obtaining a glyph or traveling to Earth. I only know of two ways to get to Earth: Mellizo Glyph ritual or the Mitad's wielder named Bellia who can replicate their ability. We have access to neither. However, I have infiltrators in a certain Ignoble Lord's crew. This informant has reported to me the whereabouts of Grace's daughter."

Tavro jumped at the words. "Jezca? Where have the Mitad taken her?"

Fey nodded. "Yes, I have located Jezca. She left with the Mitad for reasons I could not determine. She's now off the west coast of the Corland on Lenape."

Tavro frowned and protested, "There's no way that she'd voluntarily leave with the Mitad. It may appear that way to you, but they have just killed her brother!"

Maxima had spent little time with the priestess that had entered Eos' mind in the Manus Temple, but she was shocked to hear she had left with the Mitad after the Mircite Valley incident. She knew all too well that Caldus died in battle against Yann Kilsig. She wondered if Eos knew what had happened to Jezca.

No. If Eos knew, he would have rushed after her recklessly. That is his way. Instead, he went to Earth.

"Regardless of why she is on Lenape," Fey said, "she is in a Mitad den now. King Tamat has let his island nation become more publicly overrun by Mitad than even Corleo. Not to mention *the Bruin* hangs over all his ports."

"We must go after her," Maxima burst out. She was surprised that the thought had left her lips before her mind could restrain it.

A thin eyebrow raised on Fey's head. "A bold statement. Who do you propose infiltrates an island that Saida and his emir use as their vacation home?"

"And why should we risk so much for a girl who went willingly with the Mitad?" Roana asked with a scoff.

Maxima felt all the eyes in the room focused on her. She chewed her lip until a frustration built up enough to push back.

CHAPTER TWELVE

She didn't know why she did it. It was a desire that was nearly as reckless as what Eos would have wanted. Perhaps it was her Bellator blood. Finally, the Bellator King's Daughter asked, "Grace was your friend, wasn't she? What have you done for her daughter? Would you be able to look her in the eyes after she returns from Earth and tell her you left Jezca to the Mitad?"

Tavro sighed, "You don't understand. She fled Necogen. We didn't even know she was Grace's daughter until many years after she had joined the priesthood. I did all I could for her from afar."

"That was your mistake," Maxima said bluntly. "I've witnessed her powers firsthand. There is no knowledge she could not extract, no target whose mind she could not penetrate. Her gift is everything the Priori needs for their mission. Power preserved? Knowledge retained? Is that what you tell yourselves?"

"Listen, *New Girl*," Roana growled, "I don't know who you think you are, but these are complex matters that your simple mind can't comprehend. You better have a stronger reason if you want any of us to enter Lenape."

Tavro drug his hands down his face, pulling his skin as he prepared to release a confession. "Enough, Roana. I have all the reason we need. The Blue Corcinth is right. Jezca is Grace's daughter and has all the skills to lead Priori meetings one day. Plus…she…has half of Grace's journal." His facial muscles contorted as he cringed at the final words.

"What?" Gibrali snapped. "You gave it to her? Tremlay is dead. The Mitad must have both halves now!"

"She had the best chance of any of us at deciphering it," Tavro explained wearily. "I felt it was her birthright. At the time, hiding it amongst the Manus Priesthood was an extremely conservative plan."

Fey said calmly, "They won't have it yet. The girl won't give it to them freely I'd wager, but it is right under their nose. She must be extracted immediately."

Maxima wanted to scream out. She wanted to demand to know what was in the journal and what Grace had knowledge of, but she knew it would expose her unworthiness to be at the Priori gathering.

VIOLET ASH VOW

Salvaluc spoke, "None of us here can go. Convincing a member not attending this meeting would be difficult. Do you volunteer, Master Fey?"

Fey's eyes squinted. "You know I'm retired from that kind of work."

Salvaluc shot back with a friendly overtone, "I heard you were retired from taking on students as well. Yet here you are with a student and a contact inside Astor Bruinsma's crew."

"Don't do this to me, Salvaluc. Don't test me," Fey responded with a heavy breath of dissatisfaction.

"Maybe it's better to ask a younger member," Salvaluc goaded her. "Perhaps, gambling and drinking are a better way to live out your last days. The Great Soul could have no higher calling for you."

"Curse you, Salvaluc. Your tongue is as silver as your hair."

Maxima interjected, "We'll go."

Fey whipped her head to her pupil, her eyes flashing in warning, and her lips pulled tight.

"We'll do no such thing—" Fey didn't finish before Maxima stepped forward.

The Blue Corcinth looked over the violet leaves and plucked one. Then, she lit it in a sapphire blaze in her palm and repeated the ceremonial gesture to seal commitment with the ashes.

Maxima held the ashes out to Saier Fey.

The aging woman shook her head and looked up at Maxima. "You have no idea what you've done. You've just made a vow before the Priori. You will be hunted if you stray from your task."

Maxima extended the ashes toward her master again.

"Then we will not stray from this task."

∞   ∞   ∞

Terrava ran her fingers through the fountains in the interior gardens of castle Alasedis. The warmth of the pools and the trickling of water from the white marble rings comforted her. She sat among the flowers and greenery, waiting and fretting.

CHAPTER TWELVE

Talus had sent his messenger elsu, Hermios, ahead of him to tell her he had returned alone to discuss plans on Earth.

As she waited for her husband's arrival, the Queen was left to wonder what had happened to her family on the distant world of Earth. Even more worryingly, Talus had called for the Ignoble Lord Xaro Monte to join them. The manus stone industry magnate had been vacationing abroad in Anite, though he was seldom seen. She notified his staff of the requested meeting and was surprised to find that he had just returned from the beaches of West Avem.

Xaro could hardly decline his hosts. He had shown a new interest in Anite noble affairs ever since repelling the Mitad from their failed invasion at the foot of the Sepeleo mountains.

The Ignoble Lord of the manus mines had been an asset, crushing the invading Mitad with a righteous anger, but Terrava didn't fully trust him.

It was Talus who arrived first. When the garden doors opened, Terrava embraced her husband, clenching him with all her might.

"Why have you returned alone? Where is our son...and the others?" she pleaded for answers.

"They are safe. Do not fear. Our investigation on Earth has been fruitful, but it has led to a new twist in our plans."

Terrava's eyes fell, already knowing that she wouldn't approve of this unwelcome *twist in plans*. "This will mean more than scouting for information, won't it?"

Talus placed his arm against the wall of a pool and stared at his reflection. He was aging and missing a limb. The threat of the Mitad and the weight of the crown...it all wore his body down. Yet, what path was there that didn't lead to conflict against the Mitad?

"We discovered that Vistomus Fulmen has moved to an island nation on Earth called Nippon-Wa. There he is after Carnus Solaire and—"

"The Viator Hariban who turned to the Mitad...is alive?" Terrava asked with a hushed surprise.

"Not only does he live, but he has evaded Vistomus and his hunter, Naith, on Earth for all these years. We learned he was once entirely possessed by the same curse that Eos has. Yet somehow, he has resisted it all these years."

"So, you're going on another dangerous mission in pursuit of a cure to Saida's curse?" Terrava asked angrily. "Need I remind you what happened on the last attempt?" Terrava's hard eyes softened with aching affection for her husband. "You came back to me so injured...If you lose even a strand of your beard this time, I'll hunt down Vistomus myself!"

"My Dear, I am less one arm and one daughter as a reminder—but Carnus overcame his curse! We learned from Jezca Monte that the curse is a fragment of some dark, foreign power that seeks to control Eos' mind. The stronger our son becomes, the greater the danger. Aizo's seal can only hold the curse at bay for so long. Every day is a battle for Eos...but if Carnus knows how to fight it, then we must learn from him, or else you may lose two children to the Mitad."

Terrava winced, but then a smile crept over her. "My King, something has happened while you were away...I met with Ares."

Talus' mouth opened in a search for words, but it took seconds to overcome his shock. Finally, standing tall and stroking his thick braided beard, he muttered, "That wretched boy is busy. He was seen on Earth as well."

"He brought Maxima to me! She is alive, Talus!" Terrava cried out, overwhelmed by joy.

Again, Talus found no words. "But...I saw...he...that can't be."

"Maxima is alive! I have had to leave her under the protection of Master Fey. Ares was assigned to kill her, but instead he faked her death. He had kept her safe all this time."

Talus was weeping before she finished. Huge tears streamed down his rough cheeks. "Thank the Great Soul." He fell to his knees in gratitude with arms out. "I don't know what Ares is up to, but for this, I will forgive him for everything he has done in the past."

After explaining that Maxima must remain dead to the world until the time comes, Terrava went into a quiet catharsis in her husband's arm, nestled against his chest. As he held her in the tranquility of the gardens,

CHAPTER TWELVE

the exhaustion from the spectrum of emotional revelations settled upon them.

Eventually, Talus spoke again, "I have not finished telling you everything from Earth. Vistomus is not only after Carnus in Nippon-Wa. He also seeks your old friend, Grace Lapithos. The two of them stole away something called the Left Eye of Izanagi."

Terrava covered her mouth as if speaking the name was equivalent to seeing Grace's ghost. "She's been found? I had given up hope."

Talus winked at the Queen. "We must never give up hope. But with this news, it's time you told me about the Tools of Karnak and all the Priori's secrets. I cannot go back to Earth empty handed."

Terrava stammered as she processed, "The Flow of All Things…that's what she called it. Grace was the expert on the Tools of Karnak. I knew little of them besides what she revealed to me in passing but I can tell you what I do know. They precede our written history. Artifacts from the Lost Era. They are the most powerful weapons ever created. The Left Eye of Izanagi is the name it came to have, but its power she called *the Flow of All Things*. The treasured eyes of the Manus Priesthood, even the rarest *blessed manus eye* that Jezca Monte uses, is only an imitation of the long-lost Eyes of Izanagi."

Talus nodded, "Do you know what that means, this *Flow of All Things?*"

"Only partially. You have heard of the way that the Krog people wield on their homeland?"

"The art is lost here on the Corland, but I know the legends of Nature Wielding: A living Soul Energy of the Great Soul that passes through all, man and nature. Though, I've hardly believed in it."

Terrava continued, "It's real. The Krogs call it *Nature's Pulse*, and the Priori has confirmed it. The Flow of All Things is some sort of vision…insight into both Soul Energy and Nature's Pulse. I was pulled from the Priori too early to learn the deeper secrets. But one time we found a scroll with a warning. Then that warning began appearing in the most unlikely of places."

"A warning?" Talus mused. "What kind?"

"Beware the *Sahar Alakil*."

VIOLET ASH VOW

Golden eyes searched for understanding. "The...Sahar...Al...?"

"Sahar Alakil. Grace told me it translated to *stone eater* in the ancient tongue of the Lost Era."

A relieved laugh answered. "Terrava, my love, you were beginning to make me nervous. I will most certainly fear a man with teeth that strong." The King slapped his leg with amusement.

The feminine lines of Terrava's face remained stoic. "It was a grave omen that haunted us, Talus. Other texts used another word. *Ruyah Alakil. Sight Eater.* The omen said more: Beware the Sahar Alakil who becomes *Ro-hatam...one of the shattered.* Grace would never tell me everything. Her understanding...and the things she had seen on her missions...the name terrified her. It was no joke to her. Or me."

Talus pulled the padded leather of his empty sleeve and adjusted the light chainmail under his tunic as he considered the matter more seriously. "Forgive my light heartedness. Are you telling me that something fearsome out there consumes manus stones?"

Terrava replied warily, "Or *someone.* And they seek certain stones above all. Stones that give *sight*—we have a guest."

Talus sensed the immense presence outside the door before the knock came.

Xaro Monte entered the inner garden, his brilliant white hair flowing in a mane behind him along with the fur-trimmed black coat he used as a cape. His white beard blended into the ever present cloud of smoke as he puffed his anima stone pipe. It created a glow of navy blue around him as he approached.

"Forgive me, King Talus. I had hardly unpacked from my trip to West Avem when I received your summons. Beautiful city West Avem. Best beaches on the north side of the Corland," Xaro bellowed across the room.

"Thank you for meeting my request on short notice, Xaro. I'm glad your time in Anite has been restful. I called you here on crucial business. Seeing that you know about my son's curse, and you helped to fight off the Mitad horde at the Sepeleo mountains, and that the Mitad have now encroached deeply into your mines, I believe we may have enough common interests to form an alliance."

CHAPTER TWELVE

Xaro sat across from the rulers of Anite on a bench of twisting carvings. His arm was thrown casually over the backrest as he smoked, and his thickly belted tunic was open so that his muscular chest showed its scars. "Aye, King Talus. I'd say we have a common cause."

On closer inspection, between fading rounds of smoke, Talus noticed something off about Xaro's face. "I must confess, I'm surprised the Mitad's actions haven't spurred you to reclaim your mines." There was a tilt of analysis in the King's head before he asked, "Xaro, are you well? Your face…"

"Oh, this?" Xaro touched his cheek. Flecks of what appeared to be dull manus stone protruded from under his skin in scale-like patches. His cheekbone and forehead were dotted with the marks. "I must confess, Talus; I could face down any inlume without the slightest fear. No wielder alive could threaten me…and yet…all the wielding power in the world does not stop age and illness. I'm near the end. That's why I'm here taking this break. What you see is the result of decades in the mines. A rare condition that I can no longer hide."

Talus was disturbed. "We have the best medical wielders on Corland here in Anite. Let the Sanofem take a look—"

"No. It's too late for that," Xaro cut him short.

"With all the inlume knowledge, there is surely someone—"

Xaro snapped, "I said no! I am one of the richest men on the Corland. You think I haven't already consulted the greatest healers? Let this old man die his way."

Stunned, Talus nodded.

"I apologize, Xaro. I didn't mean to intrude in personal affairs."

"Not to worry, King Bellator. I apologize for losing my temper. Now, as for this alliance, I am open to hear what you propose. And as a show of good faith, I have information for you. It pertains to your long-time rival family, the Cassions."

Sadness and shame seized Talus. "Whatever grievance they have against me, it is justified. I was not able to protect Benedir."

Calculating steel-blue eyes peered through smoke. "They'll leverage that exact softness against you, Talus. Whispers and rumors swirl while you're away."

VIOLET ASH VOW

"We can handle the rumors," Terrava objected. "Scipio ensures that any unsettled whispers are turned for the positive. The people love their King."

"They love their King, no doubt. However, Jullian Cassion has used his son's death to sway enough legates against you in your absence, Talus. He plans to recall you from your throne. With the ninth legate seat empty, a breaking voter will be selected, and it will be the man who lost his son to the Mitad under the current king's watch. Julian's vote against you will break a tie."

Talus ran his hand under the trickling fountain they sat upon and let out a heavy sigh. "Then, I must assign a replacement for the ninth seat before I leave again. Then I will find a way to make amends to Julian."

A hearty laugh turned into a smoker's cough. "That soft heart has no end, Talus. The man wants to use his son's death to drive a knife in your back, and you're concerned with making amends?"

Terrava knew where the conversation about alliances was heading, and she was wary of it. "Talus, you must select someone close to the family. A Bellator, or at least an ally you can be certain of."

"Xaro has brought me this news in time to prevent the recall," Talus began.

"It should be a citizen of *Anite*," Terrava tensely replied.

"We don't know who Julian has swayed. Xaro is heralded across the kingdom for his fight alongside you."

The Monte mining mogul let out a stream of smoke from his lips. "I'll do it, Talus. But only temporarily. I will have been away too long. I'll retain your throne for you...then I must settle my affairs." He tapped the patches of stoney scales on his cheek. "I'll give you a few weeks, but then I will find rest in the mines that created my empire."

The King of Anite nodded to his wife to reassure her. "It'll require a few extra days here, but it must be done."

Xaro stroked his beard. "We still have other matters of this alliance to discuss. I hear the Mitad are forming an army in the southern kingdoms."

CHAPTER TWELVE

The anima stone pipe illuminated again, as the dying Ignoble Lord laid out plans that he intended to see outlive him. Indigo Soul Energy refracted in the haze of leteb powder and glimmered off the pools.

CHAPTER THIRTEEN

JOURNEY TO NIPPON-WA

The voyage to Nippon-Wa lasted two weeks. Colonel Kane had explained that there were few foreigners these days on the island. Air travel was out of the question if they wanted to keep their arrival covert. Kane had put them on a small cargo vessel that would sneak them into the port of Yokohama.

On the night of the third day, when Eos had gotten used to the rubber feeling in his legs from the constant churn of waves, he found himself alone with his inlume master. Aizo had given him some minor drills to practice, but Eos remained quiet and reserved through them. Since the incident with his brother, he felt that the others were annoyed with him at the best of times.

That wasn't the only reason he kept to himself, though.

It was his shame.

CHAPTER THIRTEEN

The emotion pulled on his heart with each glance from Aizo, Scavok, and Durath. Only Glenn appeared to hold no grudge as they sailed across the Pacific.

Durath's coldness hurt the most. When he saw Eos first wield against Saida after breaking out of the metus stone cage, he had decided to follow Eos. Now there was uncertainty in that decision, and Eos was determined to restore Durath's faith in him—determined restore all their faiths in him.

After Eos' half-hearted drills, Aizo instructed Eos to practice a special meditation. He cleared his mind and focused only on the Soul Energy in his core, exciting his Soul Reservoir to a bubbling, frothy sensation and then calming the way Aizo had taught him.

Aizo read and wrote, paying little attention to Eos during his practice.

Then, after what felt like hours of silence, Aizo finally said, "We must talk about your duel with Ares."

Eos opened his eyes and let his Soul Energy fall to rest. It was the first time since the incident that Aizo confronted him directly.

Aizo continued. "What you did was reckless, and it endangered the entire party. We could have had all-out war with Emir Raggan in that city. Not all of us would have left alive had Raggan not called for a truce."

Eos replied, trying not to raise his voice in anger, "I understand, and I'm sorry. But that was my only chance to face Ares and make him pay for what he did. I shouldn't have done it, but I couldn't let him go unpunished after what he did to Maxima…" his voice trailed in disgrace. "You shouldn't have come after me. I didn't want to put any of you in danger."

"Do you think Talus felt any differently? Does a father not feel the same desire for revenge when his daughter is murdered? Yet, he stilled his rage. Do you know why?" Aizo asked.

Eos remained silent.

Aizo spoke calmly, but the words were harsh. "Because Talus knows his duty as a Soul Wielder of the Order. Do you, Eos? '*I will use wisdom granted by the Divine Soul to guide my wielding.*' That is the vow you took. Now, I'm going to give you two choices. Do not take them lightly."

"Yes, Aizo," Eos mumbled.

"You can either leave the Order and find a new teacher—"

"No! Anything else. I'm sorry, Azio," Eos begged.

"Or, you will show your commitment to the virtue of wisdom and temper your impulses."

Eos only nodded vigorously to signal his agreement with the latter choice.

Aizo looked upon him grimly.

The ship's metal walls were already suffocating, and Eos craved open land. The dread in the pit of his stomach felt like it filled the entire room and left no space for him.

Then, Aizo sighed a weary breath, saying, "You probably think that an old inlume like me couldn't possibly understand how you feel." He closed the book he was reading. "But I'll let you in on a little secret. When I was younger than you, I also made my share of foolish decisions." A faint smile crinkled his eyes.

Eos raised an eyebrow. "The Right Hand of the King made foolish decisions?"

"There was a time, before I knew your father, when I was what's called a golan—of a petty street gang. Eventually, I became their leader. Picking pockets, stealing food, starting brawls in the streets…" Aizo let out a short stomach laugh. "I caused trouble for myself and everyone around me."

"Then how…?"

"How did I end up the King's Right Hand?"

Eos nodded.

"King Bekrin prepared his sons to lead by sending them into the trenches. He set Rebus to conquering barbarians and tasked Talus with cleaning up street the gangs in Anondorn. Though, Rebus was always sticking his fingers in Talus' assignments. It just so happened that your father started by taking on my rival. Got himself into a battle against a dangerous wielder before he was ready. I bailed him out." There was a twinkle in Aizo's eyes, as if he remembered the time more fondly than he was trying to articulate for his lesson. "After that, he smooth-talked me into cleaning up the streets with him. It was that, or I could have the royal guard after me." He shrugged with a childish grin.

"So, you were a criminal, Aizo?" Eos asked in disbelief.

"You didn't think I could be as much trouble as I am today without a past, did you?" Aizo slapped Eos on the back. "Your father and I quickly became best friends, trying to outdo Rebus in Bekrin's eyes. Soon, I was welcomed into the family. But yes...I made poor decisions before all of that. Street brawls, revenge, impulsive choices, endangering others..."

"And then you just stopped all that?"

"The Bellators recognized my wielding talent. After proving myself on adventures with your father, I was invited into the Order. When you come from rummaging on the streets for your next meal as an orphan, you appreciate when the Great Soul presents you with an opportunity at a better life. I never looked back after taking that oath."

"How old were you?"

"About your age. Now, if you intend to stay in the Order, I need you to follow in your master's footsteps. I know you and Maxima were all alone on Earth growing up, but you're part of something larger than yourself now. I don't want you to waste this opportunity. You're a talented anatus, Eos. Maybe the most talented in your generation that I've seen."

A serious shift crept into Eos's reply, "I won't let you down, Aizo. I want to be an inlume like you and Father. I swear, I won't mess up again."

"Good. I believe you. Now, this trip to Nippon-Wa may be more dangerous than your time in Mircite. You'll have the addition of Durath, Scavok, and me, but we're in a foreign land under the control of the Mitad. I need one more promise from you...do not call upon your curse mark. The seal I placed is weakening, and I fear how much longer it will protect you."

"Yes. I'll keep my right arm hidden and my wielding suppressed, as you've taught me. But how will we search for Carnus and Grace if we have nowhere to start? Raggan's letters don't reveal anything more than Nippon-Wa. An entire nation is a large place."

JOURNEY TO NIPPON-WA

"We'll meet with Colonel Kane's contact Saitani Umetaro. He is an underground leader against the current regime in Nippon-Wa. If anyone knows about wielders on the island, it's him. We need only start there. Scavok will do the rest. Great Soul willing, that will lead us to one of them at least. We just need to remain hidden and undetected while we wait for your father to return."

Eos longed to see the shoreline and imagined what Nippon-Wa would look like. Colonel Kane had called it Japan, and that old name was what Eos had read in books, but he hardly knew what to expect.

Aizo's expression was one of internal debate. His lips pursed, and his eyes wandered. "I think…it must be done," he said to himself more than Eos.

"What must be done?"

"It's dangerous with your curse mark strengthening and this manifestation of soul you've encountered in your Void—"

"Zala," Eos said.

"Yes, but I believe you need to confront your next gates. You'll need even greater combat abilities if we run into trouble in Nippon-Wa."

"You mean it?" Eos asked boyishly. He had assumed learning new skills would have been out of the question considering his recent failings.

A long exhale preceded Aizo gathering his composure and saying, "It seems your path requires we rush the process." Aizo grinned teasingly. "Unless you'd prefer to continue basic exercises as punishment for the remainder of our voyage."

Eos laughed and shook his head, grateful to be working on his Soul Wielder abilities again.

"Good. The third gate deals with confidence and willpower. It is hindered by the emotion of shame. We'll only begin the preparations for now, but before we leave Nippon-Wa, I hope you'll have gained control over this next inner gate," Aizo began.

The weeks wore on with mediation on the third gate of the soul, but Aizo insisted that Eos avoid confronting anything directly in the Soul Void. Eos was reluctant but obeyed. He kept his appetite for wielding satiated with long bouts of Solido practice.

CHAPTER THIRTEEN

He couldn't remember how many sparking orange punches he had received deep within the ship's hull, but it was in the hundreds as Aizo tested Eos' ability to generate a veil of defensive Soul Energy.

"Denser. Don't hold back. Solido is a technique about converting one hundred percent of your resources to defense. Imagine a layer of armor over your skin. Now make it appear from that excited state you've been practicing."

They also practiced what Aizo termed *Quick Manifest*, improving Eos' speed at summoning his crimson elsu.

The days bled together, differentiated when Durath requested to join the lessons.

Zmmm. Crackle.

Durath's fist, coated in emerald light, slammed into Eos.

A shimmering crimson cloak of Solido defended the strike.

Eos dug his feet into the ground and was pleased he didn't slide back. He grinned in response to the punch. Two more came at his body.

Thud. Zmmm.

Shards of red Soul Energy splintered off with each blow.

"Durath, I can tell you're trying now. I swear that one tickled," Eos said through gritted teeth. The taunt was spoken from a clenched diaphragm struggling to hold air as Eos defended with every bit of strength he had.

Then, it was Eos' turn. He launched a fierce series of punches against a deep green veil. His body didn't have the mass to throw behind his physical attack, but he spun up his Soul Energy to pack more into the strike.

The concussion rattled the walls of the small cabin room.

Durath choked out, "I'm not your girlfriend, Eos. Stop trying to tease me with your gentle touch."

Eos grinned. He had missed his friend.

The two slugged it out in their Solido practice. With each back and forth the walls rattled more, and the intensity of the clashing energies increased.

"I think I may have felt something," Eos laughed in pain.

JOURNEY TO NIPPON-WA

Durath received the next few punches with his eyes closed. "Did you do it yet? I didn't feel anything. Don't give me any hints."

The two wielders trained until Aizo stopped them, saying, "That's enough, boys. The ship crew is going to investigate at this rate. Raise your Solido one more time, and we'll call it a day."

They did as instructed.

Crimson and emerald shone on the walls while Aizo threw a quick jab at both Durath and Eos. Though nonchalant and physically unintimidating, they felt the extreme weight of Aizo's Soul Energy pressing down on them as orange sparks scattered off his knuckles.

The crimson shield shattered entirely, leaving Eos clutching his chest as if his life force had just been sucked out of him when his Solido had broken. He stumbled to lean on the nearby bed.

Durath's Solido didn't fail entirely, but Aizo put a hole in it where his fist landed, and cracks ran up and down the layer of green energy. The Corleo King's Son recalled his Soul Energy to salvage what he could, but he felt the air and zeal sucked out of him.

"All those taunts, and you boys couldn't stand up to a little jab from an old man," Aizo mocked.

The two students accepted the chastisement, knowing better. Their teacher had gone all out on them while acting like his attack had been weak and playful. Aizo always kept them on their toes.

There was little to do between training and watching Ahktar fly off the deck. So, Eos rested for much of the journey.

He dreamed often—most nights of Maxima. Occasionally memories included Jace. Others were nightmares from his childhood, of experimentation with Braxton and Fleischer. Twice he dreamed things that were not his own. Those belonged to the beautiful priestess with the manus stone eye. He wondered daily where Jezca could have gone after the Mircite Valley battle.

Waves often tested Eos' balance and stomach. Salt permeated everything as the mist of the sea found its way into every room of the ship. Then, one day atop the deck, Ahktar returned from a flight. Gliding in a blur of speed, the snow-white elsu returned to Eos' outstretched forearm.

CHAPTER THIRTEEN

Land.

Ahktar rarely communicated with Eos in words; usually the creature would send sensations or ideas. He would get intuitions of messages appearing in his thoughts, planted there by his elsu companion.

Only a few hours later, the island nation's coastline came into view. Soon, they were sailing by a distant red torii gate that stood above the water. As they approached the new country, the painted red beams and curved roof against the sunset were a mystical greeting. Eos had only ever seen pictures of this land, but upon witnessing this strange architecture in person, it dawned on him that Nippon-Wa would be entirely different from any kingdom he had yet seen. The image was imprinted on his mind until they reached the shore.

Glenn stood in awe by his side as well. He had wanted to see such a sight for his entire life.

Their breath condensed over the ship's rails as the chill bit them with a humid-winter sting. Eos' face became numb at the cold, but he hardly noticed it because of his excitement.

They idled into the edge of Yokohama harbor later that evening with engines on low under the cover of darkness. The crew met with dock workers and began unloading cargo.

Eos and the others watched from their cabin window as cranes operated and workers lifted. Finally, after minutes of nothing but the sounds of labor, the door cracked open.

"Hoods up. Don't let your faces be seen," the crew worker whispered into the cabin. "Follow these two, and they'll take you the rest of the way."

Two Japanese men greeted them with heads bowed.

"Welcome to Nippon-Wa. We are pleased to receive Colonel Kane's friends. I am Minoru," said a tall, lanky man in his late forties with hair pulled back into a short ponytail. His beard was scraggly and salted with gray, and his facial features were flat and weathered. The foreign accent was mild, and his words were easy to understand.

"And I am Kamatari. Please follow us," said the shorter companion of similar age. He had thinning hair and a heavy, round body. Both men spoke smoothly; only faint hints revealed their Japanese native tongue.

JOURNEY TO NIPPON-WA

"Thank you," Aizo said as they followed out the door with hoods pulled over their faces. "I heard this nation was closed off, but your English is very good."

"Yes," responded Minoru, "Kamatari and I speak English primarily. Years at sea on international vessels."

Kamatari waddled along to keep up with the fast pace as they descended the ship and moved across the dock. "Enough conversation. Wait until we get into the van."

"Don't be rude to our guests," Minoru said in a harsh whisper. "Sorry, but Raijin's soldiers are all over the harbor and borders. The Hanyo, Rius, has increased patrol this month—"

"Hush, fool," Kamatari whispered.

"Sometimes, I don't know why I put up with you," Minoru complained.

Kamatari and Minoru led them through the port and to a back alley where a black van waited for them. The entire way, Kamatari scanned the shadows and dock workers for anyone paying too much attention to their group of seven men.

Once the van door closed, Scavok asked, "Who is this Raijin you mentioned? And what is *hanyo*?"

"Oh no. No one told you before you came? Raijin is the kami who—"

Minoru was cut off again.

"Kami?" Scavok asked.

"They're foreigners, you fool," Kamatari chided. "They don't know our ways or words yet."

"You don't have to always refer to me as a fool!" Minoru complained.

"I'd be lying if I didn't," Kamatari chuckled.

Minoru continued as he kept his thin hands on the wheel, "Apologies. Kami are what you would call...hmmm...gods in the North American Sector. Fifteen years ago, the kami descended onto Nippon-Wa publicly. The Herald of Raijin announced himself. They were seldom seen at first, but eventually they worked their way into the Imperial Court's graces. When Emperor Antoku's father died, Raijin arrived, just

CHAPTER THIRTEEN

as the kami in the top hat had prophesized. Raijin rose to power alongside the boy emperor. He is said to be the lighting kami, though I've never seen his abilities for myself."

Scavok grunted and said, "Vistomus."

"Oh, you know of him? Does he have another name in the North American Sector?"

"Something like that," Scavok replied. "And the hanyo?"

"They are the demi-gods who serve Raijin and the Emperor. They have each taken watch over a region of Nippon-Wa. Here in the Kanto region, Rius is the hanyo in charge. A dangerous and terrifying man."

"Coward," Kamatari said under his breath, drumming his fingers on his big belly.

"Rius would kill you with just a look, Kamatari. Don't pretend to be brave."

Kamatari grunted and huffed in disagreement.

Scavok turned to Aizo and said, "The Mitad's mirza, I'd guess."

"Most certainly," Aizo agreed.

The drive was short, and within fifteen minutes, they arrived at a small house with a sweeping gable roof. It was a small white plaster building with latticed windows.

"This is your house, Minoru?" Eos asked.

"Not exactly," the thin man replied. "This is one of Saitani-dono's buildings near the docks. As dock workers, we spend much of our time here, but we have homes and families further inland."

"Take these," Kamatari handed each of them domed bamboo hats. "Traditional kasa hats. Common these days. Just wear it until you get inside. We'll go two at a time, staggered by a few minutes. If we're being watched for any reason, we don't want the large group to attract attention."

"Would a group like ours attract Raijin's men?" Glenn asked.

Kamatari frowned. "You'd have chinpira investigating a bunch of gaijin straight off the docks," he said incredulously. "Raijin's thugs are looking for something like that to report."

"I hate to say it, but Kamatari is right," Minoru agreed.

JOURNEY TO NIPPON-WA

"I'm always right, Minoru. Now, why don't you lead in our first guest."

Just as planned, sets of two by two in staggered timings, they walked up the driveway and into the Japanese house with their pointed bamboo headwear covering most of their faces.

Once all were settled within, they sat on cushioned floor mats at a short-legged dinner table called a chabudai. Minoru served them a meal of pork udon, and they warmed themselves on the soup during further introductions.

"It has been many years since I've spoken with Colonel Kane in person," Minoru said, "but I hear that the North American Sector is in considerable trouble. European Sector invasion has become irreversible, they say."

Aizo sighed, "Your Raijin is at work in that invasion effort, it seems. We're here to meet with Saitani Umetaro and learn about Raijin's activities here in Nippon-Wa. It may help us understand what he's after and lead us to some friends we're looking for."

"Friends in Nippon-Wa?" Kamatari asked, raising his bowl to his mouth.

Aizo nodded. "Yes, a woman named Grace Lapithos. You may refer to her as a...*kami*. We don't believe she would be allied with Raijin."

Minoru and Kamatari shared a glance over their noodles and paused their slurping momentarily.

"Do you know of her?" Aizo asked excitedly.

"No. Not personally," Minoru explained. "But there is a woman kami known as Himiko. She works for Saigo-dono. We wouldn't know where to find her, but Saitani-dono may. However, he doesn't get along with Saigo-dono."

Kamatari nearly spat out his noodles and laughed. "I'll say! Saigo and Saitani would kill each other if they weren't both trying to kill Raijin."

Scavok squinted. "Why is that?"

Minoru replied, "A difference of lifestyles and political views—"

"Both were advisors for most of their lives to Emperor Antoku's father," Kamatari interrupted. "Saitani is a modern man. We fight with guns and politics. Saigo is a stiff-necked samurai who can't let go of his

CHAPTER THIRTEEN

old ways. He fights with his sword and honor. Had quite an influence on Antoku's father, though. Led to a resurgence in samurai and Shinto culture. Saitani thought he stole political power by swaying the previous emperor with his fantasies of times gone by." He laughed again loudly, "And yet both ended up having all their political power stolen by Raijin."

Scavok asked, "When will we meet the great Saitani?"

There was a second of pause. Kamatari and Minoru looked at each other as if trying to decide together.

Minoru spoke. "Saitani-dono is a very busy and secretive man. It may be a while before he has time to receive you. There is a strategic attack coming up for our movement. I do not think he will see you until after that."

"When is that? Colonel Kane said we could meet Saitani," Scavok pressed, irritated. He sensed a misunderstanding in timing and importance.

"Well...I'd estimate two weeks at least. If Saitani finishes his plan and has time in his schedule...I'd say within a month is likely," Minoru calculated as he spoke, stroking his patchy beard.

Scavok's scarred and hardened face was emotionless, save for the disdain in his pupils. "We must speak with Saitani sooner. We know the Raijin's motives here in Nippon-Wa and must begin our search for Grace Lapithos immediately."

Kamatari shrugged, "Saitani is a busy and important man. You'll have to accept that he'll see you when he wishes it. He has been notified of your arrival and will contact us when he is ready to meet."

Nearly hourly, over the next two days, Scavok demanded to begin his investigation. However, Minoru assured them that Saitani would assume their cover was compromised if Scavok did so, resulting in no meeting at all. A low growl came from Scavok every so often as he eyed the door. His silver ponytail swished back and forth as he paced, gripping the hilt of his short sword. Eos feared his patience wouldn't last another day.

They feasted on noodles and rice and freshly caught seafood for breakfast, lunch, and dinner. Their garments were replaced with ones that blended in with the people of Nippon-Wa. An indigo kimono was given to each of them, worn open over a black cotton shirt in the modern style. It hung like a cardigan above loose-fitting but narrow pants that matched.

By the third day, Eos was nearly as eager to leave the close quarters as Scavok; the lack of anything to do but sleep or eat frayed on the boy's last nerve. His visit to Earth had consisted of more waiting in bunkers and hiding places than he had ever imagined when he left Hyperborea.

And anytime he did sleep, his dreams haunted him again.

Maxima falling underwater. Never resurfacing.

Then, visions of Jezca. They were more recent as far as he could tell, maybe even current—and always the same. She translated notes from half of a journal and studied some kind of manus stone. She'd light it in every dream. He could feel her desperate hope, though he knew not what she hoped for or why so desperately. Her emotions seeped into his senses like a toxin, overwhelming his unconscious world until he lost all sense of self. She was anxious and scared. As a result, so was he.

Every dream made his curse burn, and the black ink-like mark would wriggle up his arm each time he awoke in a frantic state. He kept the curse mark completely covered using gloves, but inwardly he struggled. Opening his third and fourth gates was proving impossible with the dreams he was having. His meditations and training exercises were constantly distracted from the lack of real rest.

Knock. Knock.

Knuckles on the door woke Eos from another dream. Minoru gestured to the ground frantically. All at once the group dashed into action, just as they had rehearsed, lifted the dinner table, opened a false floor, and climbed down into a hidden chamber beneath the bamboo mats.

"Coming! One moment," Kamatari called as he stood by the door.

Minoru helped cover their hiding place and reassembled the room.

Eos, Durath, Aizo, and Glenn were left in darkness.

"Humiliating," Durath whispered. "Nothing but Vistomus himself could threaten a group of wielders like us, yet we hide like cowards."

"Don't be so sure," Aizo murmured.

CHAPTER THIRTEEN

Glenn complained quietly, "I think this is quite representative of our time in Nippon-Wa so far."

"Where's Scavok? He's not here," Eos realized.

Above, Kamatari hissed, "*Chinpira!* I knew we shouldn't have taken in the gaijin."

"Oh no," Minoru fretted. "Don't say such things. You were happy when they arrived."

"Was not."

"Liar."

"Fool."

The two bickered in aggressive whispers until the moment Kamatari opened the front door.

A formal black kimono with the crest of a red two-headed snake stood before them. A bamboo hat obscured the chinpira's face. Only a scarred gray chin and thin lips showed beneath the shadow of the woven covering.

At his waist was the sheathed steel of a katana.

Minoru bowed deeply with fear. His voice quivered as he said, "Great warrior, what brings you to our lowly house?"

The Mitad Vizier turned his head back and forth, slowly scanning. He took his time before responding. "There are reports of foreigners seen in the area."

Minoru responded, "Sir, we have not seen any gaijin. They are not welcome in Nippon-Wa and would be reported immediately."

Click.

The Mitad warrior flicked the hilt of his sword with his thumb. It was an obvious threat, though he would use Soul Energy if he intended to act on it. The blade was only a showpiece for the people they lorded over.

He stepped into the house without being welcomed in.

"Reports of foreigners...in this house."

How could they have known? Eos wondered from under the floor. The windows of the house were small, and they minded to stay away from them. They had arrived by night, covered their faces, and had not left the house.

JOURNEY TO NIPPON-WA

The Mitad's watch must be everywhere.

Light sparked from the Vizier's fingertips as he snapped his fingers. The small show of supernatural abilities had Minoru cowering in fear and Kamatari staring at the floor.

Minoru pleaded, "Sir, if we had any information, we would share it with you, but as you can see, there is no one here."

"I've been watching the docks all week. We were warned of their arrival. You cannot hide them. Five foreigners entered this place."

Kamatari clicked his tongue in disbelief.

They had been tracked the entire time.

The man in the black kimono continued, "Tell me where you've hidden them now, or neither of you will ever walk out of that door again. This is an order on behalf of Emperor Antoku and Lord Raijin. Hiding these—"

His words were cut short by a flash of icy blue.

Safisay, Scavok's short sword, pierced through the Vizier's abdomen. He gave a grunt of shocked pain and then a gurgle before his head turned back. With wide eyes he glimpsed the silver mane of his assassin.

Scavok withdrew the sword, and the Mitad warrior collapsed, clutching his stomach in his final moments. The master assassin quickly cleaned and re-sheathed his blade so that the winged hilt hung at his waist once more.

Minoru and Kamatari fell to the floor, pressing their foreheads against the mats in worship.

"Why did you not tell us that you were kami?" Minoru cried out in awe.

Scavok grunted and began moving the table to uncover his companions.

Kamatari scrambled to assist, tripping over himself in his rush to be of service to the kami that had saved his life.

"And you said they would be trouble," Minoru taunted his friend.

"I never said anything of the sort," Kamatari denied.

The two nearly hissed at each other as they bickered while working to open the secret compartment.

CHAPTER THIRTEEN

"This is incredible!" Minoru exclaimed as he provided an arm to lift the four men from their hiding place. "Are you all kami?"

"Four of us are wielde—er—kami, as you say," Scavok answered.

"No one told us that kami would be coming to meet with Saitani. Even he must not know this! For he would wish to meet with you immediately," Kamatari said excitedly.

"Good," Scavok said. "Then let us meet him as soon as possible."

"Of course!" Minoru said with his head bobbing. "We would be honored to escort the four kami and their servant to Saitani's location."

Glenn frowned, "I'm no servant."

"My apologies. We would be honored to escort the four kami and their pet," Minoru said in complete earnest.

Glenn rolled his eyes and grumbled, "I'm beginning to regret coming on this journey."

Aizo laughed. "He's our companion."

"Ah, an honored companion it is," Minoru corrected himself.

All eyes fell on the bloody body on the floor of the small living room. It dragged down the moment of levity.

Scavok said, "This location is compromised. He was alone, but Mitad will be crawling through here in a few hours when their friend does not return."

Kamatari nodded, "I will call ahead to let Saitani know the great news. Then, I will head to the docks to make this body disappear. It will buy us some time."

"Gather your things. Let's be off in ten minutes," Minoru said. "We must meet with Saitani immediately. This will change everything. Raijin's terror will not go unchecked."

The sunset tinted the paper windows of the house pink-orange, and a puddle of blood stained the bamboo floor with scarlet as the Hyperboreans prepared to accelerate their journey into Nippon-Wa.

CHAPTER FOURTEEN

FLESH AND SOUL

After the success of the metus stone experiment in Mircite, Saida gave Zolo a private research space in Harcath Castle in the Corleo capital city, Aritrea.

His esteem and status had increased substantially in Saida's eyes—to the point that Saida ordered the chief engineer of Aritrea Mining Company, Palino, to be at Zolo's service. This left him with nearly unlimited access to tools, knowledge, and manus stone resources.

"Are you going to share what you're working on now?" Ares asked Zolo as he paced around the worktable.

The space was a mixture of a mechanical workshop, a chemist's laboratory, a manus smith's forge, and a library. Research notebooks and dozens of leather-bound tomes lay open across the room. Ares couldn't imagine reading them all in his lifetime, let alone keeping track of the knowledge in each one in the way Zolo did.

CHAPTER FOURTEEN

Ares' young wielder devotee consumed information more than food, to the point that Ares wondered if Zolo really did sustain himself on written words.

Tools lay across his multiple workbenches, strewn about for numerous ongoing projects. Disassembled firearms from Earth, animus stone swords, and anima shards surrounded him while vials and tubes lined the back wall, full of active experiments. As Zolo developed his wielding abilities, the variety of projects and ideas he worked on multiplied.

When no immediate response came from the hyper-focused researcher hunched over his latest wild idea, Ares muttered, "We need to get this place organized. Maybe an assistant or two would help."

"No," Zolo said without looking up. "Assistants would slow me down right now, Master Ares. Besides, I don't want to share all my ideas. At least not yet. And no, I'm not going to tell you about this if there's a crawler within a mile of here. The Overseer's wretched spies are everywhere. He sees everything through them. *Hears everything too.* He's got the best vision of any blind man in history."

Ares closed his eyes and used his Observation of Soul Energy. His mind's eye perceived the spider-like creatures of static-white energy roaming the castle.

Inside the walls like spies.

Outside the walls like watchful sentries.

"I've searched the castle twice, Zolo. There are none close enough to hear us. So, we're safe for now."

"Good. I don't want the Overseer or Saida to know about this yet. It's my best invention…if it works, that is. I'm not sure if I'll be the only one who can use it anyways. I may be able to make a more general application of it, but for now, it's only my manifestation of Soul Energy that will make it work—"

There was a flash of brilliant orange as Zolo dripped his Soul Energy over something.

Pftt!

Sizzle—

Bang!

FLESH AND SOUL

A small explosion startled Ares and left Zolo's ears ringing.

"Not quite right. Too volatile. Need to adjust the ratio down," Zolo said while running his hand through his golden-brown hair and scribbling down his future adjustments.

"Is that...gunpowder...and...?" Ares wondered aloud.

"Gunpowder and crushed animus stone powder. Yes. That's exactly what it is. Way too much anima stone in that mixture. Not stable. Or maybe missing a stabilizing component."

"And Saida thinks *I'm* risky. He should see this place," Ares said to himself.

"Oh, he has. He said the same thing but gave me free reign." Zolo silently sketched a few more lines in his journal before asking, "So, Master Ares, how is Bellia doing?"

"I just came from Lenape actually. She's healthy and coming along well. The birth should be soon, though she's still quite moody about having to downplay our relationship in public," Ares answered cooly, but his head was swimming with thoughts of the future. None of Salvaluc's wisdom or riddles soothed the reality of becoming a father.

"Understandably so. That's a relief that there's no health complication at least," Zolo said. "And what of your meeting with *him*?" It was a question that hung with anticipation and mystery.

Ares examined the spring of a disassembled rifle. Then, he moved to a dagger with repeating layers of anima and animus stone. The blade shimmered with alternating blues and reds.

"That's why I'm here today. Saida called me to Aritrea because he has news."

Zolo finally stopped working. He looked up and stammered, "Well...that's great! That's great, I think. Isn't it?"

"Yes. I've wanted to meet my father for the longest time. But now that it's finally about to happen, I'm at a loss for words." Ares leaned over the table and massaged his forehead.

"Well, I have a few ideas for you. What is the Mitad trying to achieve as our end goal? Outside of the standard issue propaganda that we feed the underlings, I mean. And why did he want Maxima dead but Eos alive?

CHAPTER FOURTEEN

And what's the secret behind Vistomus Fulmen's wielding? It doesn't feel right. Not like Saida's or anyone else's—"

"Zolo," Ares cut him off. "I was thinking of starting simpler. More along the lines of why he hasn't been a part of my life. *Hi, Dad. Thanks for making me into your outcast creation and abandoning me. Mind explaining that?* Something easier before prying up the Mitad's deepest secrets," Ares gave a sorry half-smile. "Besides, I don't think I'll be doing much of the talking. Guessing it'll be more a listening event," he said with annoyance.

"Right. That's probably a better place to start than my suggestion. Go with that," Zolo chuckled and then ducked his head down to resume mixing his powders.

Ares leaned over Zolo's shoulder and watched him work.

"How is your wielding practice coming along? You're not neglecting it for this, are you?" Ares gestured to the worktable.

Zolo put down his tools and pointed his index finger at Ares.

A small slit of orange Soul Energy protruded from the fingertip like a scalpel. It waivered as he tried to maintain the form. "I never miss a day of my exercises, Master Ares. I promised."

"Not bad," Ares said, shaking his head. "Do you have time to sleep?"

"Occasionally."

The room was quiet except for the clinking of Zolo's tools.

The acrid smell of chemical solvents, lead, and grease all mixed in the room. None were strong enough to overwhelm the others, but each took turns revealing itself to make Ares' nose twitch. He sat back and kicked his feet onto the table as the evening wore on under the flicker of stone lights.

Zolo wiped his brow and finally stopped work for the day.

There hadn't been another explosion, which Ares assumed was a positive indication.

"Master Ares, have you decided on a name?"

"For?"

"Your child. What else."

"Mmm."

"That's not a name."

"You pry too much, Zolo." Ares stood.

FLESH AND SOUL

"Well, you'll find out soon enough anyway." Zolo wiped his hands on the cloth he kept on his belt. He began to close up shop for the night.

"If it's a boy…Gideon," Ares finally responded. "If it's a girl…ahh, Bellia can choose."

A knock interrupted.

Saida strutted in, slicking back his dark parted hair that curled around his neck. He looked at Ares with an emotionless expression, his gray skin dull under the stone lights, his ruby-flecked eyes piercing across the room.

"You got what you wanted, boy. The Master will meet with you," Saida said. Then his eyes flicked back above his eyelids briefly as if possessed. When his pupils met Ares again a moment later, his voice was changed. It was deeper and rasping as his facial muscles tightened. "I will meet you in Pacem Derex. The day after tomorrow. Ask for my servant, Ardern, at the old Talinadu House that Saida took you to when you were younger."

Then, Saida's expression relaxed, and his voice returned to normal. "You heard the Master. Don't take for granted your opportunity. If it weren't for your birth circumstances, you wouldn't get the chance."

Ares exhaled sharply but didn't squander the moment with hot-headed remarks. "What shall I call the Master when I speak to him?"

"He goes only by *Master M*."

∞   ∞   ∞

Ares wandered the streets of Pacem Derex. The town had never recovered from the revolution he had helped incite there.

The Mitad had led an uprising in the town that still showed to this day on the city's south side. Some buildings had been burned and never rebuilt in the poorer districts. Passing over the white marbled gates at the city entrance, he noticed a few spires were still damaged.

The building that used to hold the Council of Races sessions was now used as a den for black market sales. It's exterior was dirty and untarnished. The massive pillars and double doors still towered with magnificence, looming with the height of eight men, an arm clutching a

CHAPTER FOURTEEN

sword on one side and a reverse image holding a dangling olive branch on the other.

He scoffed internally at it. What a joke the council had been—rife with bribes, political favors, and feigned goodwill.

There was no remorse in his heart for tearing apart the fools and their superficial excuse to further their power games, but looking at the city, he felt the slightest twinge of disappointment that the place had not recovered properly. He saw more of the mixed-race Mezclado in the streets than ever before, homeless and hungry.

The Krog race may have seized power, but it was mainly in the form of roving street gangs. He had to run his chain through the leader of one group on his way to find Ardern. The rest of the thugs scattered after that.

The streets smelled of trash and ashes, but the wealthy districts had reclaimed their former glory. Their red stone facades and gold-painted trims had been restored, and their gates built higher than before.

The wave of feelings pulled on Ares from multiple directions as he recalled his memories here. He had escaped the castle and hid in the city at Saida's residence on various occasions. They called it the Talinadu House—some shamanic term from the Dacian continent.

Now he stood outside it again. Years had passed since he had seen its walls, decorated with the sharp symbolic Mezclado patterns in white paint against the gray slate stone.

There was an immense pressure of Soul Energy coming from the place, though the passing citizens seemed unaware. To them, it was nothing more than a strange sense of dread—a standing of the hairs on the back of their neck they couldn't explain. The people of Pacem Derex were non-wielding ostaka, weak craftsman wielders, or untrained gangsters who used Soul Energy to threaten more than for combat.

But to Ares, there was a presence inside so powerful that its pressure threatened to bring down the house's walls. What made it worse was that the wielder was at rest. Almost like he was sleeping, and still the tremendous power was evident.

He asked for Ardern when he met the guard at the gate.

FLESH AND SOUL

The guard nodded as if knowing the name was evidence enough and opened the iron gate. Ares crossed the courtyard to the rounded wooden door adorned with the eight-pointed bronze star of one of the ancient Krog religions. Studying it intensely, Ares traced his finger around the white painted serpent body that surrounded the star.

He realized he had been delaying opening the door to the Talinadu House with his long trip around the city; not to reminisce but to procrastinate the encounter ahead.

His whole life, Ares had fantasized about this moment. Whether killing the man he was about to meet in revenge-blinded anger or being filled with a warming sensation at speaking to his father—the daydream depended on the year of his life during which he had imagined it.

Now, Salvaluc's cryptic whispers and sagely hints filled him with doubt.

Behind this door, he wanted to be reassured of the Mitad's purpose. Of his purpose. To know he had not met with Master M for all these years of life because of a fundamentally principled reason.

His soul knew.

The understanding that the reason would not be sufficient had been growing like a prescient vision.

Yet, he could do nothing but proceed.

Come. A voice spoke into his mind from down the weathered red-painted entrance hallway. The voice chilled his stomach and raised his defensive instincts. At the end of the dimly lit hall, he found a wooden door with paint worn by time to the point that only flakes of color remained in grooves.

Enter.

He grasped a tarnished handle and turned it.

Walking into the room was like being smacked by a first punch to the nose. The aura of Master M was palpable. It made Ares take his first step away from the entrance rather than through it.

Iron lanterns hung from stakes in each corner of the room, spreading a weak stone-light through orange-tinted panes of glass. The light was not enough to reveal the room entirely, but the area was aglow with radiance from the center.

CHAPTER FOURTEEN

Three figures were before Ares.

A small boy huddled on the floor at the foot of a reclined chair. He wore white robes and sat with his feet tucked and arms wrapped around them. His dull black hair fell over his forehead in an unkept pile.

Above him was a man in square spectacles, old and wrinkled. He stood with his arms stretched out and golden Soul Energy trickling from his spotted palms in some Sanofem-derived technique. The tan cloak that fell to his knees was pressed with some subtle star pattern that Ares didn't recognize.

His golden Soul Energy veiled the man in the reclined chair, who sat like a medical patient. His body glowed in a dense shell of yellow. Not one feature or detail of clothing was visible of the cocooned man. Yet, Ares knew—this was the leader of the Mitad.

His voice was deep but strangely inviting, save for the rasp of a lifelong smoker of the betel pipes. Ares had expected a more god-like voice. Something like the one that entered his mind and commanded him into the room, but this was the voice of a man.

"Welcome, Ares, Son of the Mitad."

His aura of Soul Energy spoke for him.

The imposing force that had nearly pushed him out of the room now hit him like waves at the edge of a beach made of acid.

Each pulse of the man's life force announced his danger and command.

Ares fell to a knee instinctively at such an aura.

"I…was told to seek Ardern, and he would lead me to…Master M."

"You have found both. Ardern, please lower the treatment intensity for a moment," the reclined man said.

Ardern nodded and reduced the stream of golden energy coming from his extended hands.

"You may stand, Ares."

"Thank you, Master M. I've been looking forward to finally meeting you," Ares said. It was sincere, but there was a bitter taste in his mouth. Underlying resentment was bubbling up, and he had to actively suppress it.

FLESH AND SOUL

"I'm sure you have. You did well in eliminating your half-sister, so I have granted you this chance."

Ares kept from making eye contact with the pulsing rings of gold that morphed over a human body and said, "I must ask..."

"Go ahead."

"Why her and not Eos?"

There was a genuine laugh from the chair.

"A good question. I wanted both for their Bloodline Inheritance, but I realized it was impossible. Maxima became a liability. Watch!" Master M's voice twisted into a diabolical pitch as he finished. He turned a golden Soul Energy-covered hand up and clenched his fingers inward.

Ardern frowned with exhaustion, but he did not fear saying, "My Lord, I need you *not* to wield while I'm working on you."

Master M laughed deeply again, entertained by the man's annoyance. It was a rumbling laugh, like a rockslide down a mountain.

"It'll only be a moment, Ardern."

Ares' limbs seized and locked up. He tried to move, but he couldn't command his own body.

Then, he felt the negative emotions that allowed his curse mark to take control. The Mark of the Chosen spread a burning of hatred, anger, and suffering that tainted the mind and body.

This time, those feelings did not overwhelm him.

Worse, they concentrated into a single point in his core, impossible to ignore—but still, he felt the curse mark clawing up his back. Then his chest and arms.

Ink-like flames scrawled up his neck.

When the tendrils of black touched his face, he felt despair.

Movement was impossible, and there was a sense of being possessed—another presence was violating his soul.

On the floor, the curled-up boy's eyes went wide with interest.

"The strongest wielders on Hyperborea could fight this to some degree, resist it perhaps. But *my Mark of the Chosen* has claim on any who are host to it. That is...except for Eos. You see, Maxima saw to that. Somehow...as an infant..."

CHAPTER FOURTEEN

"*Tchh*," Ares struggled through a rigidly locked jaw. "How...is that...possible?" The curse moved for his eyeballs.

"I asked myself that for years. Then, I found my answer while combing through Saida's memories. When he conjured the mark on Eos, there was a mistake. His concentration was broken!" Master M growled. He recalled the memory, both not his own and yet fully available as if he had experienced it himself.

Ares' curse filled eyes shared the vision with Master M.

Saida slashed his finger across the young Eos' face.

A flash of white Soul Energy on the tip of his sharp nail.

Maxima, tiny and uncoordinated, reacted to her brother's scream.

A tiny arm lashed out!

It struck Saida in the face.

For an instant, a spark of blue came into existence.

"Maxima, as an infant, manifested her Soul Energy in response to her brother's scream...forever creating a weakness in my hold on the boy." Master M eased his fingers and released the curse's control over Ares. "Continue, Ardern."

The black flames receded from Ares' face, and his arms could move again. He realized he could breathe fully as well. In the panic of being possessed, he hadn't noticed his breathing had nearly ceased.

Ares gasped and spoke, "Then, a great vulnerability has been eliminated."

The glowing head nodded slightly, its movement restricted by whatever Ardern was doing. "Yes, yes. But get on with it. Why did you want to see me? The real reason. No games."

There was a childlike feeling that came over Ares. He felt vulnerable and young again. All the hardened emotions that he had learned over the years fell away.

He tried to rebuild his interior wall in that moment.

To catch the falling pieces of his emotional shield.

To cover up his inner boy.

But it came out in a torrent.

FLESH AND SOUL

"You're my father! How could you never meet your own son? Why is it now that we're meeting? Twenty-four years and you never wanted to meet me?" Ares cried out.

There was loathing in Master M's voice as if he despised the emotions on display. "I saw you through Saida and Vistomus. I did not need anything more. You're not *my offspring*. I merely facilitated your creation."

"How…how can you say that?" Ares asked, feeling like his body was caving in and his bones cracking at the delivery of such a crushingly cold statement.

Master M hummed while both pondering and demeaning Ares. "Do you know the truth of the creation of our world?"

The tortured look on Ares' face did not change. Only a shake of his head showed his confusion.

"I thought not. You must not have listened to Talus when he told it. Well, his understanding of a portion of it. The Order loves to tell the creation of Hyperborea by the Great Soul. They only know a piece of the full truth. Though a few inlumes and knowledge-preserving groups know more of the whole story."

"And what is the truth?" Ares spat, unhappy with the distraction from his topic of focus.

"Oh, I think you should take more interest if you want to understand what you are, arrogant boy. In the beginning," Master M boomed with a storytelling rhythm in his words, "the Great Soul created Earth, its inhabitants, and seven beings of pure Soul Energy called the Danaqi. They were revered and turned to myths in all the cultures of ancient times. Mostly before the Lost Era…but some of the myth lives on in part today. The Great Soul then created Hyperborea and its inhabitants and gave the Danaqi directions to watch over and guide the worlds, but only on Hyperborea could they play like the Great Soul himself and *create*. So, they began weaving great creations and teaching the beings of Hyperborea to Soul Wield."

Ares feigned interest in the story just enough to keep the man who ran the Mitad talking. Meanwhile, Ardern resumed his strange work.

CHAPTER FOURTEEN

"For one of the Danaqi…guiding wielding was not enough. He wanted to create like the Great Soul. So, Noximor created a race that could dominate humans. In what remains of the writings, they are called Kenat. The other six went to the Great Soul and asked permission to balance the world. It was granted, and together they created a single being named Karnak. This divine being created tools and imbued special wielding traits in the men of Corland."

Ares became acutely focused and asked in a blurt, "Then the Priori of Karnak…?"

"Yes. The Priori is a thorn in my side. They preserve much of this history and attempt to piece together the Lost Era."

"And you know what happened in the Lost Era, Master M?"

"My knowledge alone."

"How could you know such things?"

"*I simply know*," Master M said plainly.

Ares shook his head with a huff of displeasure at the brief responses. "What does this have to do with me?"

Master M laughed, but this time it was slow and immensely pleased at his position of insight. "You see, I have spent my extremely long life hunting knowledge. The descendants of the Kenat became a priesthood before the Lost Era. They infiltrated nations, twisted empires, and bent wills. Most of all, they documented their abilities and everything Noximor gifted them with to submit humans to their will."

Ares was emotional and impulsive, but he was also sharp. He saw where the narrative was leading, and it made him even angrier. "You copied their techniques, didn't you? To create me. You tried to imitate Noximor."

Master M interjected with a viciousness to his voice. "Try? Imitate? I do not *try* at anything. You were my first use of the technique of Noximor. I channeled his will to create you!"

Ares' pupils vibrated, his hands shook, and he looked at his skin with a disturbed recognition of what he was for the first time. There was no father waiting to meet his talented wielding son with pride. There was only a man playing with forbidden knowledge who had set aside his first attempt.

FLESH AND SOUL

"W-w-why?"

"I have been called to a mission and need many resources to complete it. I have a unique ability to see the potential in everything," Master M said with a matter-of-fact confidence. "Terrava was the only one capable of enduring such a trial. Once-in-a-generation combination of genetic potential and realized abilities. So, I chose her and created you from flesh and soul."

The messy-haired boy smirked and repeated words like an infant imitating his parents. "Once...in...a generation!" he exclaimed. His tiny pupils were glazed over, and his expression was blank.

Ares scowled, and his voice went low.

Something caught his curiosity—it didn't sit right.

The room was filled with the Son of the Mitad, the leader of the Mitad, the healer, and... "Who's this child?"

Master M tilted his head down at the boy, a glowing golden shape wreathed in rings of pulsing energy. He spoke kindly to the child, "You are so much more than that." Then, Master M turned back to Ares and replied, "I call him Khasun. From an ancient language on my mother's side. He was traumatized when I found him. Looking at him, you would never know, but he is far beyond your mother, Terrava's, potential. I can confidently say he is once in an era. Two hundred and fifty-six years," he stated the numbers with a dull numbness, "that's how often a talent like you comes along, Khasun. And I found you while the opportunity was ripe."

"Two hundred...fifty...six," the boy echoed.

Ares spoke with sarcasm lining his words.

"What kind of *talent* is that?"

Master M appeared not to hear Ares' question, or at least not answer it directly. "You needn't worry yourself with Khasun. You see, he is headed to Earth soon."

"Earth?" Ares mumbled.

"If your potential is limited to repeating me with a questioning tone, I'd say you have outlived your usefulness, Son of the Mitad."

CHAPTER FOURTEEN

Ares was tempted to retort. He wanted to release all his anger and disgust, but his scarred neck and shoulder tingled to remind him what Vistomus had done to teach him not to talk back.

"Repeat!" Khasun exclaimed as if learning new words.

Master M let Ares bite his tongue until it bled before finishing, "But we both know that's not true. I originally envisioned a role for you…but this boy of fortune has filled that. However, you possess a special Bloodline Inheritance."

"You're setting me up to repeat you again," Ares said with a smirk.

Behind the shroud of healing energy, Master M let out an amused exhaled and then continued, "You see, my time to ascend the throne is near. I nearly have the pieces in place, but I am old, Ares. Older than you know. This body is failing me. I'm kept healthy enough to wield only by the work of Corland's greatest healer, Ardern."

So that's what this is. Master M hides his name with secrets and his face with a healing treatment.

The orange glow of the room's corners was suddenly too weak for Ares' liking. The golden stream from Ardern made Master M the source of light. There was nowhere to hide from the radiating veil.

His thoughts wandered to places he didn't expect.

A disgust for his own birth.

Then, images of Salvaluc meditating.

He realized he desired now the peace of mind and unmovable resolve that the Tenebrim's inlume leader had. Without it, he felt naked in the crushing aura of Master M.

Thoughts of his son.

The round bump that Bellia's belly had become.

Emotions he was not allowed to feel.

Love for the only woman that understood him.

Suddenly, Ares was too far from Bellia and his unborn child.

Finally, Ares broke from his trance, fixated on the hum of Ardern's treatment.

"If you allowed me to speak to you…it wasn't because I killed Maxima. What do you want from me? What is your end game?"

FLESH AND SOUL

Master M clapped his hands together, disrupting the veil over them momentarily. Ares saw skin that was falling apart in patches.

"Now, that's what I expected from your intellect, Ares. Very good. The Mitad's end game...*my knowledge.* Why did I call you here? To plant seeds. They have now been planted. Also, to urge you. My time is coming near. You must complete your training, but you are becoming weak of mind. Your resolve is failing. I'm going to instill it back in you. Your attachments are undoing my creation. That sickening fondness for Bellia, and now I sense you developing far too much admiration for Salvaluc."

"Bellia will be mother to my child!" Ares protested, "And my time with Salvaluc is only at the order of Saida. I am strengthening the Mitad."

"You say, but I sense weakness in you."

The words were perfect provocations to Ares' ego.

"*No. Never,*" he denied passionately.

"Learn what you can from Salvaluc. Pursue whatever it is you're seeking. Then, kill your bonds. Just like you did with Maxima."

Ares gritted his teeth until he thought they might crack. He nodded in agreement.

"Remember you carry the Mark of the Chosen...my *tide of power.* Know what it did to you today when I summoned."

Ares shivered at the thought of being possessed by it again. He said in a low tone, "I will not fail you—"

"And!" Master M boomed with a final command that echoed off the ceiling. "Your son will take my mark upon his birth. He will be mine."

Frozen, Ares searched for words.

Master M left no question. No room for response.

His immense aura of Soul Energy was released.

It caused his golden healing veil to waiver.

The walls creaked.

When the weight of it reached Ares, it was like being slammed in the chest. Only wielding against the leader of the Mitad could have stopped him from being flung back by such a force.

He had no intention of fighting such an imposing menace, even if Master M was being kept alive by Ardern's treatment. The surprise of it gave him no time to question that instinct.

CHAPTER FOURTEEN

The door was thrown open before he reached it, and Ares fell to the floor in the hallway as it shut again after him.

Sitting in the dark, facing the worn door, he contemplated the options left to him and the knowledge that had just been implanted in his mind.

CHAPTER FIFTEEN

THE NEW KAMI

Silver mist pulsed with the neon agitations of city nightlife as they drove. None of them had seen anything like it. Even Glenn, who had seen more of Earth over his life, was not prepared for the vibrant display that consumed more electricity in a night than most portions of the North American sector would see in a year.

The Hyperboreans marveled at the pink and green mirages that shimmered around them as they drove through the Yokohama streets. Japanese kanji symbols flickered, lanterns danced in the wind under the turquoise storefront awnings, and every alleyway was a cluttered ecosystem of signs and shimmering reflections. Eos had never seen a big city in its fully functioning capacity during all his time in the North American Sector.

Signs blinked in vibrant Japanese characters that only Minoru and Kamatari could read. Lines of cars rushed by in streaks of light, and every

CHAPTER FIFTEEN

building was glowing with life. It was a prosperity Eos hadn't imagined during his childhood on Earth.

"I don't like moving so fast in these metal Earth boxes," Scavok muttered, looking sick and avoiding staring out the vehicle's window.

Eos realized the Hyperborea natives had never been in a car before, much less seen electricity on this scale, though Aizo was more familiar from his travels between worlds.

Durath pressed against the window and said, "Like millions of manus light stones…"

"Yes", Aizo agreed. "It's a beautiful and strange sight. Though, I agree with Scavok on our method of travel. So much stop and go at high speed."

Minoru bowed his head as he looked back from the passenger seat. "Forgive us, great kami. We cannot walk on the sky like you, so we must travel like this to Master Saitani."

The busiest area fell behind them, and the constant stirring of the inner city quieted. After an hour of driving, they exited the vehicle into the soft luminescence of red paper lanterns over damp concrete, the scent of street vendors frying, and the buzz of streetlights.

They were led by their two guides up a gray staircase under the shadow of green ceramic roofs with their bamboo hats pulled low over their faces.

They entered a business building, flat, , sharp, and concrete. Quickly, they were led past security guards, through badge-locked doors, under oak crossbeams, and through sliding glass until they were lost from the turns as they navigated deeper. Finally, the group entered through parted doors into a conference room.

The floors were tatami mats, and the back wall contained the crest of three cranes forming a circle—white feathers on blue background. A series of low individual tables lined the room's walls with seat cushions on the floor at each one.

Some seats were taken by stern-faced men dressed in formal robes, but they were waiting for someone. The intrusion of six new members was unwelcome. Scowls and shrewd glances greeted them as Minoru

THE NEW KAMI

bowed and announced in Japanese, "Forgive our intrusion. We have brought guests for Master Saitani."

Behind them, a deep, slow voice spoke in accented English, "And who told you that I wanted guests?"

The six turned to see a large man, heavy and tall, in a gray-striped suit smoking a cigar as he addressed them. His thin eyes creased to glare from behind the vapor of his exhale.

Kamatari jumped but then settled into a bow and said without lifting his head, "Master Saitani, we don't mean to intrude—"

"Yet, you intrude," Saitani bellowed over him. "This location is now compromised, even if these are friends of Colonel Kane."

"Please, sir," Kamatari stuttered. "We have brought them t-t-to meet you as an emergency."

"Oh?" Saitani ran his empty hand over his short black hair, streaked with gray on the sides.

"They are kami, sir." Kamatari turned his bow to the Hyperboreans.

Silence gripped the meeting space.

The fidgeting of the room's occupants ceased.

Saitani took a long draw from his cigar.

"Is that true...kami?"

Aizo stepped forward and bowed less deeply than Kamatari, who had still not raised his head. "We are what you call kami, and we have come to speak with Saitani. My name is Aizo Mudar."

The rebel leader looked the group up and down as if unimpressed by their pronouncement of being kami. "The gods have returned, yet they bow to a mere mortal like me and speak the tongue of another continent. How did I get the great fortune of having such kami in my presence?" There was a monotone way of speaking where reverence should have been.

Wisely, Aizo decided to cut to the point that would interest the unmoved leader. He assumed a straight posture, reversing his bow, and flicked his fingers apart.

Orange sparks scattered from his hand like his skin was made of flint. The inlume resisted the curl of his lips into a sly smile as the meeting room's members shuddered at the show of Soul Energy.

CHAPTER FIFTEEN

"We have come from our world to yours. I only show the sign of respect used in Nippon-Wa. In our world, the one you know as Raijin also troubles us. In that, our interests are aligned," Aizo enticed Saitani.

Smoke parted from a thin mustache, and Saitani walked to his seat at the head of the room. He put his cigar out on an ashtray and gestured to empty tables.

"Then, by all means, have a seat. I'm pleased to see that *not all kami plot against Nippon-Wa.*"

No sooner had they all found cushions to sit on, another figure entered the room. This time, it was a man two decades younger than Saitani with long black hair and the draping white sleeves of formal vestment robes. He bowed to Saitani upon his entrance, and the seated leader made the grand gesture of dipping his head in return.

"Ah, Kikujiro, now we have a proper representative to speak with our new guests," Saitani bellowed.

Kikujiro spoke softly and said in English, "I don't understand, Sir. Who are our new guests?"

"We are graced by kami, and they prefer English. Imagine that," Saitani responded with a hearty laugh.

Kikujiro's face was overwhelmed with surprise. He stammered, "T-t-this is unexpected. It changes everything." Falling to the floor, he prostrated himself before the four guests. "I have kept the purifications and adorations at Ise Grand Shrine. We have continually made the offerings and prayers and hoped for the day of your arrival since the first kami revealed herself."

Scavok and Aizo exchanged raised eyebrows.

Saitani intervened between the facedown man and the Hyperboreans. "You see," he explained, "Kikujiro here is a high Shinto priest...shinshoku as we call them. He keeps a sacred space for you, kami."

Aizo adapted as best he could to the foreign culture and rapidly changing circumstances. "Kikujiro, we appreciate your...devotion to our people."

THE NEW KAMI

The last vapors of smoke wafted in front of Saitani from his ashtray as he interjected, "Kikujiro, you just missed a display of their godly powers."

Remaining prostrate, the Shinto priest returned, "I wouldn't dare to ask them to demonstrate their power for spectacle."

"A devout man. Rightly so," Saitani nodded with a grin. "Though I suspect you will see a demonstration soon enough. While you prefer to bow to these great warriors—I prefer to negotiate. So tell us, Aizo, why have the kami returned to Nippon-Wa? I would prefer if they all returned to Takamagahara where they came from."

"You mustn't speak to them like that," Kikujiro urged, rising to his feet and approaching his empty seat and table.

This time, Scavok responded, using his rhetoric skills, "That's quite alright, noble priest. We have come to Saitani, and he prefers the language of business. If that is how he would speak to us after our journey from Ta-kama-ga-hara," he tried to replicate the choppy sharp pronunciation that he assumed referred to Hyperborea, "then he will receive only the fruits of business. You, Priest, shall receive based on your reverence."

A dissatisfied grunt preceded Saitani repeating, "Again, I ask what purpose the kami have in our world."

"We have many purposes. I suspect the one you call Raijin is here for an artifact of our world that was left in Nippon-Wa long ago," Aizo answered.

Kikujiro's tan eyes widened at the words.

Aizo continued, "We've come to learn what Raijin has accomplished here and to meet with Lord Saigo, who may know about a female kami that has been stranded here."

Kikujiro mouthed breathlessly, "Himiko-ojou."

"You know her?" Aizo asked.

Saitani interjected, "Lord Saigo is an old associate of mine and father of Kikujiro, who is aiding me in an important raid tomorrow. We could introduce you, but..." Kikujiro shot a warning glance as if Saitani was being too bold while the stern man went back to his cigar, "we must ask

CHAPTER FIFTEEN

for your assistance. Kami would ensure our success, and the thought of rivals will slow down Raijin's plans."

Scavok nodded, "It could be done. If you can introduce us to your father, Kikujiro, we will gladly assist you. Saitani, what is the nature of this raid?"

"Simple," the large man grunted. "Emperor Antoku's military strategists have a large warehouse of firearms that will be transferred tomorrow. We intend to intercept them. I have exhausted my fortune procuring our weapons from China. We must have these weapons to fight off Raijin and his hanyo. Without them, we are hopelessly underpowered and Raijin's regime grows stronger."

Stroking a face of silver stubble, Scavok nodded. "Do they anticipate your attack?"

"Unlikely. My source is a long-time friend. The guards will be standard for the cargo."

Aizo frowned. He sighed internally as he felt the pull of the Nippon-Wa conflict drawing them all into a deeper web of complexities. "Scavok and I will assist you. The other three stay here."

"Aizo—" Eos began but was silenced with a glance. He could see the Durath's disappointment matched his own.

"They are not here to be warriors. They must be kept safe. Far away from the danger," Aizo demanded.

"Of course, we respect the wishes of the kami. They can remain with me for the raid. Two will be more than enough. Don't you agree, Kikujiro?"

The son of Saigo nodded and smiled with his eyes. "Hai, Saitani-dono. The might of two great kami will be formidable indeed. I must alert my father that there will be two assisting us. His men will be nearing soon."

Saitani agreed. "Go. We must be in position by morning."

The slender priest with long dark hair bowed and left with the parting words, "It is an honor to meet the new kami. I look forward to fighting alongside you tomorrow."

Leaning into Eos' ear, Aizo whispered, "Tomorrow, I need you to be a disciplined anatus of the Order of Soul Wielders. Your instincts may want to join us, but we are vulnerable with only Durath by your side. If anything happens tomorrow, promise me. *Do not fight. Flee to safety. Above all—do not use your curse mark.*"

The Hyperboreans sat through the entire meeting, but by night, Aizo and Scavok were preparing with Saitani's tacticians for the raid the next morning.

Eos, Durath, and Glenn left with Saitani to his safehouse.

Constantly, Eos reminded himself that he was a member of the Order. He couldn't afford another mistake like the one he'd made against Ares, and so he repeated Aizo's words in his head.

Do not fight. Don not use your curse mark.

∞   ∞   ∞

The murky dusk left the ensemble of Soul Wielders, Saitani's armed soldiers, and Saigo's small samurai unit sitting at the tree line's shadow outside the warehouse holding Emperor Antoku's new shipment of firearms.

The group of twelve rebels were defected soldiers dressed in all black with modern body armor and helmets that melded with the darkness. They were a small group of elite infiltration specialists.

Walking tactfully, their fingers were on the edge of their rifle receivers above the trigger guard. They moved like well-trained ghosts, but it was the samurai that had Scavok on edge. He was familiar with assassins and military men—comfortable even.

Saigo's eight warriors barely resembled humans.

The samurai moved silently despite their full body armor that was crafted in the spirit of the old ways. But unlike the old ways, the plates were bulletproof ceramic, and the connecting pieces were joints of composite material.

Their facemasks were black and contorted like demon faces with crested antlers or dragons adorning their helmets. Tassels dangled over their breastplates, and a skirt of shielding draped over their greaves. Some had katanas at their side. Others gripped ornate spears with half-moon blades beneath the spearhead.

CHAPTER FIFTEEN

At the front of them all, stood a set of rich jade-colored armor. Kikujiro stood with a serpent-like dragon adorning the top of his helmet above the rich green yoroi uniform.

It was a small, specialized infiltration team. However, Saigo and a unit of horse riders waited further back in the forest to provide greater numbers if needed during the getaway of the heist.

The muffled pops of suppressed rounds pelted the air.

Four exterior guards fell to the ground outside the warehouse. The muzzle flashes glowed like short-lived embers in the pre-morning haze. Then, a speaker crackled at low volume.

"In position. The route is clear," the words warbled in Japanese before the radio cut to silence.

Kikujiro nodded in a slow, clean motion and walked out of the forest's edge with Saitani's men by his side.

Aizo and Scavok closed the distance in a few seconds with flashes of Soul Energy that caused the soldiers to shudder and the samurai to pause in awe.

When the twenty men joined the two who had cleared the perimeter guards, the group pressed against the wall for cover. The lead soldiers signaled in points and gestures to each other as they broke open the door.

Murmurs and a scuffling of boots came from inside.

Shots echoed through the lofty building as the soldiers found cover inside and engaged the guards.

Brief cries of pain bleated in the morning air, but it wasn't until Saigo's men charged into the warehouse that screams of horror filled the air.

The reputation of the samurai proceeded them.

Bullets glanced off their armor.

Twisted fanged smiles and monstrous ceramic scowls charged forth. It was imagery that the people of Nippon-Wa had only read about.

Scavok observed the artful stances and movement as the samurai gripped their katana and spears with both hands and cut down everyone in their path.

Their advance was methodical and relentless.

THE NEW KAMI

There were a dozen of Emperor Antoku's guards inside, lined around rows of crates.

Aizo and Saigo watched with a glaze of thin Soul Energy shimmering over them to deflect stray bullets. It had been agreed that they would only intervene in case of emergency. So far, the raid appeared to be a swift victory bolstered by the mere presence of the so-called kami.

However, the precision of the surprise attack caught Antoku's soldiers unready, and they were quickly slain.

"Pull the trucks into position. Room cleared," the Japanese leader spoke sharply into his microphone. The Hyperboreans did not know the words but understood their meaning.

The cargo trucks would be nearing the loading docks according to plan.

The rebels began checking crates. They spoke in whispers amongst themselves, confirming their loot was there as the samurai scanned the room through the slits of their masks.

The docks rolled open, and four trucks backed in without pause.

Crates were lifted, and the loading began.

Too easy. But then again, Saitani's informant had given them information the Emperor would have assumed was known only to him and his closest advisors.

Scavok knew better than to expect a victory before his sword was drawn, and his intuition proved correct.

The pressure of wielding aura crept into the warehouse.

The air became thick and heavy to Aizo and Scavok's senses, and their Observation sensed two presences enter the room with no intention of hiding themselves.

Aizo nodded to Scavok, and the two split off from each other as planned. Orange sparks jumped from Aizo's fingers, and Scavok drew his short sword, Safisay.

"Can I kill them now, Diya?" bellowed a voice so deep it sounded like it had been muffled.

There was a shrill sigh, and a female voice complained, "You really don't understand the element of surprise, do you, Bysis? Why do I have to get partnered with the idiot?"

CHAPTER FIFTEEN

All eyes in the room shot up to see two figures in black kimonos with red crests of the Mitad walking on air overhead. They crossed above the crates, moving with Soul Energy glimmering beneath their feet and katanas at their sides.

The male voice belonged to a man with a giant's proportions. His frame was nearly seven feet tall and as wide as three men. His head was shaved bald, his skin a dark ash-toned caramel, and his eyebrows and sharp beard were bleached to give his face the look of an unnatural, menacing giant with sunken eyes.

"Diya, you always have to insult me," he said with slow words as he gripped his katana giddily. "This will be like crushing ants."

The woman by his side was tiny in comparison, and her skin was as dark as dusk. Her black hair was chopped short above the shoulders, and the amethyst of her pure-blood Krog eyes was not a solid color. Instead, it was marbled with yellow, making her irises glow as they reflected the light of her bubbling purple Soul Energy.

"You insult yourself every time you open your mouth. Now, hurry up. You're bleeding aura so fast it's suffocating them," Diya snarled. There was a trail of white crystals in the shape of diamonds at the corner of each of her eyes.

Scavok's sword glowed an icy blue in preparation.

Aizo implanted orange Soul Energy into the crates before him.

There was little time before the lumbering giant demonstrated incredible speed at drawing his blade. It burned a brilliant silver light as the manus blade cut the air. The Soul Energy projected out from the swing, bloated and sloppy—but immensely powerful.

The three soldiers near the blade's attack were sliced in half, and the wall behind them exploded, opening to the sky.

There were screams in the native language.

Aizo only understood the word: hanyo.

The leader yelled into his microphone as he slid for cover, ordering the trucks to flee with the little cargo they had loaded. The engines rattled and turned over, but the trucks did not move.

Shadowy-purple Soul Energy crackled and crawled in thorny vines around the tires and frames. The twisting energy sang in a high-pitched hum as it manifested around the metal, scorching the paint with its heat and locking the vehicles in place.

Diya grinned as she commanded the purple light with tensed fingers. "The great kami, Raijin, ordered no weapons to leave this facility. I don't know if you people understand my language, but you'll understand this one!" she cackled quietly. Her thorned vines sprouted from the ground and gripped at feet. Soldiers screamed and tore at their ankles as the creeping energy burned their skin.

"They may not, but I do," Scavok said. He raised his sword, and its metal became a blinding white. "I recognize you, *witch*," he hissed.

Diya's thin lips curled, and she snarled, "Oh? You know me, do you?"

Scavok rotated his blade overhead and swung it in a full circle.

Icy blue light streamed from it as he pointed it at the mirza, Diya. He spoke with rage in his heart and pain in his voice, "I know your kind, and I saw you in battle. You were there—in Pacem Derex!"

Soul Energy shot across the room at Diya and cast out in a net of ethereal threads that wrapped around her like a large cage.

The vines retracted from the soldiers as Scavok's net surrounded her. They reappeared, rising from the ground to strangle out the threads of blue light and hold the cage at bay before it could constrict around her.

"Silver hair, a scarred face, and that sword with a winged hilt," Diya said in a teasing tone. "You must be King Bellator's dog."

"Aye, witch. Don't think I take that as an insult. I serve my king proudly."

Zmmm. The energies clashed in a dissonance against each other, tangled and flashing in conflict.

"A dog who knows his place. I was warned you might be here, Scavok Alter. Yes, I helped overthrow your faux-peace regime at the battle of Pacem Derex." Light glinted off the yellow of her eyes as they widened with wild a thirst for blood.

"Then, I'll enjoy putting you down," Scavok grunted, increasing the intensity of his Soul Energy's pressure as it began to wilt the violet vines.

"You call me a witch, so you must know that an acolyte of the Sisters of Noxim has many skills in her arsenal," Diya said and touched the

CHAPTER FIFTEEN

diamond tattoos under her eyes. The shards of high purity anima stone activated, implanted in her sharp cheekbones underneath the ink. With her face glowing from under the skin, she teased with a snarl, "You have no idea the darkness I possess, assassin dog."

"I have something of an idea," Scavok returned, his voice gruff and unyielding.

The tendrils of violet suddenly swelled and enveloped Scavok's stream of energy.

On the other side of the building, Bysis swung his sword again. This time the projected blast of Soul Energy was far wider, enough to take out half of the soldiers and samurai in the room.

As the wave came at them, Aizo raised a wall of neon orange.

He had expected it to hold against his opponent's wild swinging attack, but in nullifying it, his shroud of protection was shattered into fragments of brilliant dust. Aizo's quick reaction spared lives, but the katana's swings was brutal and overwhelming.

Aizo tried to diffuse the battle, "Mirza of the Mitad, hold your blade. I am Aizo—"

Bysis cried out, "Aizo Mudar! I've heard of you. It's been ages since Vistomus let me have some fun! Killing ants gets boring," Bysis said in a slow voice that emphasized his simple-mindedness.

The brute has no fear and a love for violence.

Aizo ran his fingers along more crates as he walked confidently towards Bysis. Orange sparks sprayed from the contact. This duel could be won, that much he was certain, but it would be long and labored— and there was no margin for error. In the meantime, their cargo trucks were destroyed, and their casualties were growing.

Bysis lumbered forward. His foot found Aizo's Soul Energy, planted stealthily between them. The Mirza was like a beast with an iron hide— he tilted and moaned, but his skin gleamed silver as he protected himself. He fell into the nearest stack of crates and found more of Aizo's implanted energy.

Swinging his blade chaotically without any sign of refined swordsmanship, Bysis lashed out in response to the pain. Another silver projection rippled forth.

THE NEW KAMI

Aizo turned to his Observation Wielding, knowing a single direct blow would be lethal. He did not raise a defense, but instead shifted his stance and slipped to the side of the attack.

"Slow and loud. Your rage telegraphs your attacks," Aizo mused.

Bysis roared in outrage. "I want you to see this one coming, Inlume!"

Diving into the attack, Aizo closed the distance between himself and the bleach-bearded giant. He had no intention of winning. Their mission was to retrieve the weapons, and their means of doing so was gone.

Tangerine light bathed Aizo's sturdy body.

The Inlume's hand produced a dense coating of Soul Energy.

The katana sent out a final wave, but its metal found Aizo's Solido-coated hands. He gripped the manus-forged blade!

The clash of energies rang out, and the blade glowed white as Aizo overwhelmed its mediocre quality with a flood from his Soul Reservoir.

"You're going to need to find another sword." Aizo smirked.

A perplexed look crossed Bysis' face for a single second.

The metal shattered.

So too did the coat of protection around Aizo's arms.

He was left defenseless.

"Kikujiro!" Aizo urged.

Jade armor appeared around the aisle of crates.

Ocean-blue energy slithered through the air in a vine as Kikujiro wove his technique toward Bysis' now empty hands.

It slashed like a whip at the Mirzas shoulder.

Bysis' arm fell at his feet amongst the broken shards of his katana. He let out a pained howl and crashed into the stack of crates. They came down around him and created an echoing cacophony of noise.

"Our objective is lost," Aizo called to Scavok. "Best to retreat for now! Let's go straight back to Saitani's. If they knew we were here, then their location could be compromised too!" He stomped his foot, raising a splashing wall of neon orange that littered the air between the Soul Wielders and the Mitad members with a field of mines.

The surviving soldiers and samurai abandoned the warehouse, following Nippon-Wa's newest kami back into the forest.

CHAPTER SIXTEEN

MANIFEST VISION

The end of Saitani's cigar glowed a hot red-orange as he looked over Glenn, Durath, and Eos. They waited inside a nearby safe house location, safely away from the raid that Scavok and Aizo were participating in.

Eos creased his brow, muttering, "Visiting Nippon-Wa has been a lot more sitting around, waiting, and hiding than I expected."

Durath reclined against the wall, his maroon cape draped over his Japanese robes. He gave a dry laugh, "I'm forced to admit...I agree."

"Was hoping for a bit more sightseeing myself," Glenn grumbled while rubbing the wings on his staff in his boredom.

"Maybe I'm being forced to practice discipline through boredom for punishment," Eos said.

MANIFEST VISION

Brushing his dark mahogany hair from over his closed eyes, Durath stroked his chiseled jawline and mused, "Then I'm being punished right alongside you."

Saitani tossed out an arm with smoke streaming from his hand. "Now, gentleman," he said with a noticeable accent, "You could pretend to enjoy my company a little more."

Eos' face went warm as he realized he had slighted Saitani's hospitality. "Please, Saitani, we did not mean to be unappreciative of you welcoming us. It's just that, recently, we've been told to stand to the side."

"Ah, I understand. You two want some excitement. It is of little consolation, but perhaps I can show you some artifacts of my family that would be of interest? Waiting for news of the raid is no more fun for me than it is for you."

Eos nodded. "I would like that, Saitani. Thank you."

Durath tilted his head as if weighing something in his mind. He had been keeping his distance from Glenn for days, and he eyed the winged staff wearily. "I'll pass. I have some things on my mind, but I appreciate your hospitality."

"I came to see the culture of Nippon-Wa," Glenn said and stood to join Eos. Durath appeared unusually pleased as their non-wielding companion turned and left.

The three strolled down a wooden hall with white walls and maple cross beams. Screens of green and gold Meiji-era-styled landscapes decorated the elaborate sliding doors of rooms they passed. Then, they came upon an entrance with a white cap of Mount Fuji and the gnarled trunk and twisting branches of a cherry blossom.

"This is a private room that holds treasured relics of my family," Saitani said as he pulled back the screen. Inside, the walls were lined with spears, katanas, scrolls, and paintings. The air smelled of pine and cherry, and the space was dramatically lit to showcase its contents.

It was a miniature museum with a suit of black studded samurai armor in a display case at the center. The face grinned at Eos with an open mouth and a haunting expression under the adornment of a crescent moon.

CHAPTER SIXTEEN

Saitani explained, "This is a recovered piece from my ancestor who led at the battle of Sekigahara. Behind it is one of our nation's oldest paintings—a pride of my collection from the Heian Period." The hanging scroll depicted a man bathing in a river with a loose-flowing caricature form. From his eyes and nose streamed red smoke that turned into various shapes. The left eye morphed into the sun, the right eye into the moon, and the curls of ink formed waves from his nose. "This, as I'm sure a kami like you is familiar, is the great kami, Izanagni, from whom the three precious kami were fathered in the river Tachibana." The ink was faded, but it only added to the mystic character of the ancient art.

Eos didn't blink as he scanned the room. "It's beautiful, Saitani. I'm grateful you shared this with us."

A particular spear caught his eye on the wall.

Saitani hummed, "Yes, of course. You see, I am much like Kikujiro, who has ties to Shinto's peaceful ways and the samurai's warrior ways. Kikujiro chose the priest's path. I merely observe each path and navigate as best I can."

"A wise choice, master Saitani," Glenn agreed.

"You see, I was dear friends with Kikujiro's priestess mother, and I worked alongside Lord Saigo. We were advisors to Emperor Toba, father to our current child emperor, Antoku. I respect bushido, the warrior's way. However, *unlike Saigo*, I can keep my nostalgia for the past and my vision for the future from mixing to the point where I can't tell them apart."

"You don't like the way Saigo sees things?" Eos asked, trying to piece together relationships like looking at a torn map with missing fragments.

"It is not the way forward for Nippon-Wa. Too much of Saigo's influence wore off on Emperor Toba..." Saitani shook his head sadly. "He clung to the old ways religiously. But, I babble on. It matters not. My dear Lord Toba died soon after that cursed Raijin entered our land."

"Vistomus..." Eos hissed lowly.

"What's that?" Saitani tilted his head.

"A name we use for the lightning kami."

MANIFEST VISION

Saitani massaged his brow as if exhausted. "Yes, you have your own names. I don't suppose you recognize the painting of Izanagi either. The people of Nippon-Wa may project our myths and beliefs upon you people, but I have not been tricked. I know Raijin is no Japanese god." The heavy man glanced at his companions to judge their reaction. His was giddy with entertainment.

Eos was shocked at the revelation. He caught a terrified expression on Glenn's bearded face.

"So…you don't believe we are kami?" Eos asked.

"I believe you people are from another place. I believe you have incredible god-like powers. I do not believe you are our ancestors' gods, nor are you even familiar with Japanese ways. Raijin, or Vis-too-moos," Saitani struggled to pronounce the Hyperborean's name in his thick accent, "came here for his own reasons and seized power from the people mistaking him for a kami. He poisoned the mind of Toba's advisors with fantasies of greater power. Then, he killed my dear friend and sat himself at the same table as that poor child, Antoku."

Eos didn't know how to respond at first but eventually found the words to say, "I'm deeply sorry for what has happened to your nation. Vistomus has caused similar tragedies on our world. His group killed my sister."

"Then we share in tragedy, young Eos. You will stay to rid the land of him and his hanyo, then?"

With hesitation, Eos admitted, "We've only come to understand his purpose in Nippon-Wa. Five of us cannot overthrow Vistomus and all his men alone. We came for the woman you call Himiko, though we know her as Grace. Perhaps she can show us a weakness in Vistomus' plans."

Eos stepped closer to a spear with a crystal blade. Its handle was ancient worn silver tarnished by fifty generations.

Saitani looked through the glass pane at the samurai armor, longing for a possibility where such traditions and simple ways were possible. "I had hoped you would take all the kami away with you when you left. It all started with that woman, Himiko. With the revival of the ancient kingdom name of Wa, she was fresh in our people's imaginations. A sorceress queen. When she displayed the powers of a kami to Lord Saigo, rumors ran wild. Many believed that she had returned from the heavenly realm of Takamagahara to reclaim her kingdom. Fools," he spat.

"If she was the first to arrive, she must know why Vistomus is here. Have you met her?" Eos asked.

"Only a few times, and only in passing. You will meet her soon, so long as Lord Saigo agrees."

Eos nodded. "Saitani, this spear…"

"Ah, good eye, young Eos. That is a crystal blade from the oldest of days we have recorded. The only of its kind."

"It's manus stone."

"You are familiar with this kind of weapon?" Saitani asked without understanding.

Eos lit the spear blade.

The flash of red made their host jump. His shock quickly turned to a joyous fascination.

"Beautiful. The powers of the kami are truly not of this world."

A pang of warning split Eos' skull like a momentary migraine. It was a sensation that came from outside his body.

Ahktar!

The pain of caution came from his companion elsu, alerting him to a threat—something the white bird could see as it flew watchful circles above the building.

Attacker.

He understood that much.

"Saitani, I think we need to go!" Eos urged.

"What do you mean?"

"It's not safe. Someone—"

"There's nothing to worry about. No one but your companions know you are here, and my guards…" Saitani's voice dropped as the sound of gunshots and struggle came from down the hall. He squatted low and pressed himself against the wall.

A voice sharp with playful aggression called down the corridor, "I felt a manus stone flash with Soul Energy down there. Hard to miss when I haven't sensed that in months."

MANIFEST VISION

Eos braced himself and prepared his energy so that it was beading up at his fingertips and stirring in his core.

The intruder entered the room with a sword in his belt and a hand casually in the pockets of his black cloak. Instead of a hood, his Mitad uniform had a collar, which he chose to leave flipped up. His crooked grin spread across his face like a wolf baring its fangs, and his were eyes animalistic with unpredictability. He ran his hand through his wild shoulder-length brown hair and said with a melody, "I found you, Eos."

"Glenn. Saitani. Get away from here now," Eos ordered.

"Who...?" Saitani wondered.

"I'm what you people call a hanyo," the Mitad Mirza said. "Rius Yama is my name. If you two run fast enough, I'll let you live. I only have business with Eos."

Saitani and Glenn hesitated, looking to Eos for confirmation.

Eos nodded. "It's fine, Glenn. I'll handle this."

Glenn sighed with worried lines creased on his face. He hesitated, gripping his winged staff as if contemplating trying to help Eos somehow, but he relented and obeyed.

"Now that they're out of the way, Lord Vistomus would like to speak with you. He wants me to bring you to him, peacefully...or by force. Personally, I'm hoping for the second option. I'd like to see what the Bellator name is made out of." His voice was calm but menacing.

"I have no interest in meeting with Vistomus. He can come to me if he wants to talk," the Bellator King's Son spat.

"That's what I wanted to hear!"

Eos' mind raced. He remembered his promise to Aizo that he would not battle and use his curse mark again. That he would flee from danger...*but would that be possible here?* "Rius, let's take this outside; there's no need to cause excess destruction." Despite his guilty urge to obey Aizo's orders...he felt a wild impulse to test himself against this Mitad soldier. Something about Rius' overconfidence tempted Eos to knock that ego down.

Rius shrugged nonchalantly and flipped out his hand. Blue-white Soul Energy, like a stream of flame, came from his palm. He made no

CHAPTER SIXTEEN

attempt to give form to the energy. Instead, it flowed and erupted against the side wall of the room.

Spear poles snapped, the wall crumbled, and everything touched by the Soul Energy charred and cracked. The blast left a hole in the wall that exposed the early morning sky beginning to brighten.

"After you," Rius said arrogantly.

Eos frowned and walked out of the building on layers of crimson that levitated him in the air. He descended while glancing over his back nervously.

"Don't worry, Bellator boy. I'll put a hole in you while looking you in the eyes."

Eos snarled, "You might hurt yourself trying."

"Watch it. Vistomus only needs you to be able to talk. I don't think he cares if you ever walk again."

They were both outside, a reasonable distance from Saitani's Japanese castle, and descending on a clearing near the forest.

Rius touched the ground with his hands casually in his pocket. "You're sloppy. No control over your aura. I can feel your Soul Energy announcing exactly how strong you are, and I'm not impressed. I hope the son of Talus Bellator has more to offer."

Eos couldn't gauge his opponent's power precisely, but he feared he was outmatched. He let his energy flicker around him like a swarm of fireflies and focused on purifying his soul's inner gates. Fear, guilt, and shame drifted away from him as a rush of efficient Soul Energy flow energized within.

Can I intimidate him to back down? Definitely not. Rius is looking for a fight. I could run…no.

Three red elsu crackled into being before Eos. His black hair whipped in the wind over his forehead, and his golden eyes reflected the wings of his creation.

"Right to it! That's what I like to see," Rius cackled but never removed his hands from his pocket.

The first elsu snapped its wings against the air and shot at the Mitad mirza.

Rius only smiled.

MANIFEST VISION

An icy shimmer protected his body as the elsu collided.

When the blast faded, Rius remained unphased.

"Best hurry and use the Mark of the Chosen that Saida gave you. My viziers are in the building. If you don't stop them, they might kill your friends."

The words broke through Eos' calm demeanor. They broke his flow state as fear and panic tugged at his thoughts.

There's no avoiding the fight here.

Sorry, Aizo. I don't know what else to do.

Then, he felt darkness seize his mind. Unwillingly, the curse mark began to throb and crawl up his arm. It pulsed like flames charring his skin and clawed for control.

At the sudden change in demeanor, Rius was shocked. "That's not good, Bellator. You barely have any free will left. Makes it easier for Vistomus, I suppose."

The curse's ink color overwhelmed the elsu.

"And what does he want with me?" Eos growled.

With hands still hidden, Rius shrugged. "Beats me. Ask him yourself. Now, if you don't show me something impressive…" He lifted one hand out and snapped his fingers. "…my pet is going to eat you alive." A neon sky-blue glow shimmered in the air like a specter and then solidified into a four-legged shape. A massive wolf-like beast formed, half the height of Rius and with paws the size of a human head. Its fangs bared, but instead of a growl, the electric hum of Soul Energy rippled out.

Aizo's words echoed in his head. He had promised to run… not to use his curse again, but it was acting on its own at the slightest loss of emotional control.

The ache was moving into his bones.

The two elsu turned completely dark and flew at Rius with a speed Eos would not have been able to command ordinarily.

They were on the Mirza before he could blink. The speed allowed for no evasion or counterattack. A bubbling black explosion engulfed him as he raised his Solido and let his Soul Energy wolf fade.

CHAPTER SIXTEEN

Rius stepped through the blast, gasping through clenched teeth. His black kimono was torn, and a long gash striped his chest where the elsu attack had penetrated his still-forming defensive technique.

Eos expected anger or pained rage, but as the blood dripped down from chest wound to stomach, Rius only grinned maniacally.

A mixture of relief that the attack had landed and bloodlust filled Eos. The curse mark moved toward the whites of his eyes.

"That's more like it," Rius yelled. Then, his expression turned into a frown. "I see the look of victory in your eyes. You think you're on my level? I'll teach you."

The ice-blue wolf reemerged in a sprint. Its paws thrust off the ground as it leaped at Eos. He raised a layer of crimson over his arms to try and block the beast, planning to grab hold of it if he was able.

As it neared him, it opened its jaws wide.

A Soul Sphere formed in its mouth.

It let out an electric howl.

A beam of azure light pulsed from the wolf's mouth seconds before it would have reached him.

Eos was no master of Solido and was slow with the skill.

The crimson did not manifest in time to save his life—it was the dark veil of his curse that acted for him.

He was protected enough to survive the attack but flew back from the clash and bounced off the ground like a thrown ragdoll.

"You're a wild one, Bellator. But no match for me. Without the Mark of the Chosen, you're nothing special."

Eos heaved himself up. His body was burning between throbs of numbness. "Well, let me catch your interest," he roared, followed by a rapid succession of sounds like bullwhips cracking.

Black elsu surrounded him as his vision faded and willpower weakened.

Still, Aizo's command lingered as a last echo in his free mind.

...*Promise me. Do not fight. Flee to safety. Above all—do not use your curse mark.*

MANIFEST VISION

Eos felt Ahktar's chastisement in his head as well. His elsu companion was far overhead, but he sensed the bird would soon intervene on his behalf as he lost control of himself.

Momentarily, his mind regained clarity, and he longed to bottle up the curse and return it beneath the surface of his wielding.

He wished he could obey Aizo's directions.

Veins of black crept into his eyelids.

Rius shook his head and said, "It looks like you can't keep this up much longer. I was told to bring you back—"

Emerald light shaped like a pair of corcinth horns slammed into the Mirza.

Durath ran to Eos as his Soul Energy blindsided Rius.

The sight of his friend gave Eos relief. It was enough to release the dark elsu back into ether and untense his rigid body for a moment.

"Eos, I won't tell Aizo that you used the curse—but you have to leave now," Durath said, holding Eos by the shoulders to support him as he wobbled.

"But..." Eos stammered through foggy thoughts.

"Go now! I can handle this one myself."

Rius stood and stretched out his limbs after receiving the mighty blow. "I've heard about you, former king's son gone rogue. No one told me you were on Earth, though. What happened to my men?"

Durath glared with palpable murderous hatred.

"One dead. One may still be alive. I chose to get here rather than finish him. But, you should know, my greatest joy now is hunting you people."

There was an arrogant huff from Rius as he said, "And you should know Vistomus has no requirement for you to remain alive."

The world was a pulsing migraine.

Half-blind.

Burning.

Impulse mixing with duty.

Fight blurring flight.

Eos' promise broke through it all thanks to Durath's intrusion. It had been enough to restore his thinking capacity. He heard no more of

CHAPTER SIXTEEN

the conversation between the Corleo King's Son and Rius. His instincts led him at reckless speed in Aizo's direction. He knew roughly where the raid was to occur from the planning maps. It was only fifteen minutes at the blistering pace of his adrenaline-fueled Soul Step.

Crimson twisted with black smeared across the morning palette as Eos ran. When he stopped, he was at the warehouse of the raid. He didn't remember getting there, only his intent to do so, and fell back against a tree at the forest's edge.

He used his Observation of Soul Energy as best he could. The sensation was like noisy pounding distortions interrupting a clear signal as the curse mark flared up.

No one had pursued. Durath must have detained Rius successfully.

But numerous pressures were coming from the warehouse. Something was wrong...battle was ensuing inside.

Ahktar called out to him with a screech overhead. He was grateful for the noble creature. He felt clarity returning faster with the consolation of his companion.

What to do? Aizo would scold him for jumping from one battle into another. But what if theirs was going poorly?

It didn't matter what he chose because there was no time for a decision. Ahktar sent him a ping of warning. The elsu had seen something in the tree line.

No sooner had the warning gone out, two pairs of hands grabbed him from behind and pulled him down.

He heard deep voices speaking in a foreign language, repeating the word *hanyo*. Cranking his head back, he saw his captors as he struggled against being dragged deeper into the foliage.

The two men wore suits of samurai armor like the one Saitani had shown him that morning. Helms covered their faces and looked down at Eos struggling with twisted intimidating ceramic scowls.

Eos wriggled and fought, but his captors had immobilized his arms as they pulled him.

They threw him roughly to the ground.

He jolted up, ready for a fight.

All around him were samurai.

MANIFEST VISION

Gauntlets, helmets, and blades circled him. Quickly, he estimated eight men surrounded him—two with spears pointed down at his chest. He slid back as they pushed the steel tips closer, shouting intensely in Japanese.

A boot stepped on his shoulder, halting him. The spears came close enough to raise panic. Eos' face burned, and he realized that his curse mark must have been apparent for all to see on his neck.

The word *hanyo* kept floating through the forest in the mix of masculine voices behind masks.

These people knew their enemy. The Mitad had invaded their land, and the curse mark must be known to them. Eos' mind raced for options as he realized an entire unit of warriors thought he was a member of the Mitad.

There was a second of stillness as foreign murmuring died down, panting excited breathing filled the morning, and the circle parted.

A warrior on horseback approached.

"We will slay you, demon kami. You may know that your death was at the hands of Saigo Takayoshi's *bushi dan* as punishment for your invasion of my homeland and the murder of my emperor."

Saigo looked down from his horse with his mask hanging over his chest, revealing his brooding dark eyebrows and sharp jawline. His facial hair had grown in, giving his glare an even fiercer look as if judging every blade of grass for its proper place. The antler-like crest caught a sunbeam through the canopy, making Eos cover his eyes.

There was a sharp bark of orders that Eos couldn't understand, and the spears withdrew while Saigo dismounted.

A metallic ring pierced the silence as his blade glided out of its sheath.

All the samurai did the same. Spears and katana danced around him like fangs ready to bite.

Eos' heart pounded, and his skin burned. He managed to say, "I'm not one of the hanyo."

"You have their mark. You use the powers of a kami to travel. You may defend yourself if you choose, or accept death honorably…if Raijin and his warriors know anything of that word."

Eos pleaded, "They have no honor, but I am not one of them."

CHAPTER SIXTEEN

"We shall see, kami."

Saigo's heavy boots slid back.

The first steel swung.

A blur of deadly intent came from Saigo.

Barely dodging the blow, Eos rolled to his feet.

He formed a small Soul Sphere that cast a red and black light on the contorted ceramic faces around him and illuminated Saigo.

"There it is. You are kami."

Another swing came, and Eos flung the energy at his attacker this time. It connected. The resulting explosion shattered armor, sent the warrior flying, and knocked over the next closest samurai. He had not intended to kill with the blast, but he was badly outnumbered and losing control of his discernment due to the curse mark. If it didn't end shortly, he would have to increase his force.

Saigo stood from the blow and charged.

Steel sliced.

Dodge. Roll. Pant. Soul Sphere.

The actions came instinctually as they tried to cut him down, but he fought like a wild animal. Some orbs of light connected, but many were slip-dodged by expert movement that had trained to evade such attacks.

Eos worried that the curse would possess him entirely if he used his crimson elsu. He fought two enemies fronts simultaneously—Saigo's samurai and his inner demon that claimed his skin.

Both were poised to finish him.

The flurry of attacks continued as the suits of armor dodged his hastily formed attacks.

The blades and spears pinned him down against a tree.

Saigo's unyielding eyes faced him as two spears dug into his chest, pricking his skin.

Finally, there was a Japanese command that halted the blades from plunging.

"*Matte!*" Saigo barked.

Eos prepared to give in to his curse. He had no other option.

Aizo couldn't chastise him if he was dead at the hands of the samurai.

Brown eyes stared into his.

MANIFEST VISION

The point of the spears awaited the kill command.

A sudden relief swept over Eos. Something told him help was on the way and eased his mind.

Ahktar. He knew before the elsu acted.

A fearless cry rang out like a warbling siren, and a streak of white light cut through the forest. The samurai all paused and turned their eyes to the canopy as if anticipating a predator above them.

Saigo shuddered. His blood went cold as his premonition warned him that a spirit was in the woods. His vision of the man with only a left eye came to mind, and he couldn't shake the image away.

Then the elsu came through again. This time, it slowed when it reached the group of armored men, enough for them to glimpse the bird's shape briefly.

Its claws reached down and tore at Saigo's face.

Flesh came away. Blood ran over his eye.

In his shock and pain, his sight left him as his face bled.

In place of his sight was the vision of the bird that caught lightning in its claws and saved Nippon-Wa. He remembered what Grace had told him while interpreting the dream.

"White...elsu..." he murmured in his blindness.

Eos thanked Ahktar silently, grateful his life had been spared even for a moment longer. Still, spears pricked his chest, but the samurai leader's words gave him pause.

Saigo knows what Ahktar was.

The phrase allowed Eos to lower his guard enough for the curse to recede some down to his collarbone.

Saigo wiped the warm stream of blood from his face and saw his men surrounding him to aid his wound. In his native tongue, Saigo gave the order to detain Eos and take him back to their castle in the Akaishi Mountains.

The spears withdrew some, and Eos fell to the ground, exhausted. He provided no struggle—he was already unconscious when the samurai began to tie him.

CHAPTER SIXTEEN

Saigo dabbed his wound with two fingers in disbelief as he scanned the shadows for the mysterious creature that had manifested out of his dream.

CHAPTER SEVENTEEN

UNSEEN CHASE

S aier Fey let her glaive blade show as they traveled. It warded off any bandits or unsavory characters from approaching.

Maxima had followed for three days of Soul Step and two of a mostly silent caravan ride west. Now, Fey's silver dragon earrings glinted as strands of her platinum hair twisted in the wind. Maxima struggled to keep pace with the speed at which she generated platforms under her feet. Fuchsia color flashed in and out of existence beneath the short inlume.

Her pace has been faster today; more uneasy, Maxima thought.

Before she dyed it blue, the ceramic corcinth mask tied to her waist had belonged to Caldus Lapithos. Fey decided that Maxima did not need to wear it in the uninhabited plains north of Terrspar.

The rhythm of the mask bouncing against her hip kept time.

CHAPTER SEVENTEEN

They rested opposite of the Monte capital of Petramon, on the south side of the Sepeleo Mountain range. The massive wall of jagged blue-gray teeth bit at the overcast sky as far as they could see to the west. Maxima remembered visiting Petramurus Castle and the Manus Temple in the Monte capital city on the other side of the mountains last spring.

It felt like years ago.

She had died to the world on the northern edge of the Winter Aisle. There was a bittersweetness to it. She wished more than anything to see Eos again—to be publicly alive and embrace her family. However, it was a price she would endure for Ares and the liberation of Mircite that was achieved.

During their rest period, Saier Fey was more talkative than she had been the previous day.

"Your mother tells me she was working on overcoming timidness when she trained you last," Fey said, bringing up the idea of wielding training for the first time since they had left Caracta.

"Are we going to be training?"

"I didn't say that."

Maxima grinned, "But you did say training."

The old wielder sighed wearily. "I suppose I did. Might as well make use of the time we have together while I'm roped into this."

With a playful shrug, Maxima added, "You did promise my mother."

Rolling up her sleeve, Fey revealed the faded stain of the violet ashes she had smeared on her forearm. "There's a bit more than that binding us together now, thanks to your impulsive choice."

Maxima's gentle eyes beamed. "Well, to answer your question, yes. Mother was teaching me to overcome what she called my *timid instincts* if I wanted to be a warrior of the Order."

"Caerule nonsense if you ask me. While under my care, you take my advice, and apparently, not all of my lessons penetrated Terrava's thick skull," Fey said while sipping from her leather canteen. While Maxima's contained water, she smelled a more potent liquid inside Fey's flask.

Maxima nodded unintentionally, eager to hear an alternative.

Fey continued, "Sure, hone your weakness enough that it won't hinder you, but play to your strengths, I say. There are plenty of bold and daring Soul Wielders in the Order who will jump headfirst into a conflict. Most of them are dimwitted men, mind you. There is wisdom in a subtle and covert approach to wielding."

"There is?" Maxima asked, holding on to new hope in each word.

"Of course! Look at my style in Old Cintish. I let that fool believe I was a feeble drunk gambler—"

"You were drunk, though, weren't you?"

"Besides the point, Maxima. I only revealed my skills when required. There are plenty of errants and inlumes you could pass by in the streets without noticing. There are scholars who research new techniques, warriors who utilize their perceived restraint as a weapon, and assassins who reveal themselves when it is too late for their opponent."

"I could be like that," Maxima agreed eagerly.

"After observing you, I believe so. However, you bleed your aura like carrying a bucket of water with holes in it. So, the first thing I need to teach you is to suppress your energy's presence."

They spent thirty minutes practicing the stilling of Soul Energy so that Maxima's aura was suppressed. She visualized the reservoir of energy at her core churning and then practiced slowing its movement. Doing the exercise while singularly focused and stationary was difficult enough that she couldn't imagine mastering the technique while moving about and interacting as Fey had in Old Cintish.

They slept under the stars in the open golden fields. The nights were mild, the plains were empty, and they encountered no one that day or the next. Only nature's creatures crossed their path.

With little to break up the steady monotony of the foothills, Maxima spent much of the time observing Fey.

The Inlume's frantic pace increased, and she constantly scanned the area and checked over her shoulders for threats.

On their first break during the sixth day, Fey said, "I may have retired from most duties as an inlume, but I didn't stop my work. As I've initiated you…and you've volunteered for the responsibility of finding Jezca Lapithos…there is some baseline knowledge you should understand."

CHAPTER SEVENTEEN

Maxima looked up from her meditative position. "So, you chose the work of the Priori over the Order of Soul Wielders? Why—"

Fey cut her off, "No. Listen and talk while keeping your energy suppressed. Practice. You'll need to be much better by the time we get to Lenape."

Maxima nodded and visualized the frothing Soul Energy calming inside her.

Fey began, "The Priori of Karnak is committed to tracing down a lost knowledge and a forgotten history that I believe is becoming increasingly urgent to understand."

"Because of the Makanla Gate and the Mitad?" Maxima repeated the word that was a focus of the Priori meeting without a clue as to what it meant in reality.

The corners of Fey's eyes crinkled. "Perceptive as usual, Maxima. A Makanla Gate activating has me worried. I'm also certain the Saida and Vistomus are pursuing the Tools of Karnak while hunting members of the Priori to keep us from making progress."

"What are the Tools of Karnak?"

Fey tugged at a silver chain around her neck as she responded, "That requires some explanation. The Priori has concluded that most religions on Hyperborea, ancient and modern, believe in a supreme creator force that is the source of both Earth and Hyperborea…and the first high beings he formed were called Danaqi in the old religion. Even your father's faith of the Masruh Orthodox has references in their texts to seven beings of pure light. One of these high beings fell from grace."

Maxima closed her eyes to focus on her aura suppression while speaking. "I read about this in one of the books in Father's library. They call him Noximor, correct?"

"That is one of his names. He tried to replicate the work of the Great Soul and created a race called the Kenat. To balance out this evil, the other six Danaqi asked the Great Soul for permission to create something that could undo Noximor's domination of Hyperborea. So, it is said, that Karnak was born."

"So, you…trace down information about Karnak?" Maxima asked slowly, trying to understand properly.

UNSEEN CHASE

"Yes. A large portion of history is missing due to the work of the Kenat. The Lost Era, some have labeled it. Karnak crafted immensely powerful items from the purest manus stone vein. Grace Lapithos and I were tracking down and understanding these tools. I'm sure you have read some amount on Absolute Severence?"

Maxima nodded, speaking with careful word choice to not disturb her quieted Soul Energy. "I have. It's the end technique of a Soul Wielder's Severence practice: fully accessing all of one's energy in a state with all seven inner gates purified. But it's more hypothetical than a real technique. No one purifies beyond the sixth gate. The updated versions of Magnan's writings state that it is unknown if any inlume has actually achieved such a state."

Fey took a bite from a loaf of bread and nibbled on cheese they had been sustaining themselves on for the past three days. "You're well-read. I'm impressed. What isn't written publicly is that it has been achieved as far back as Morax and even further. Only a rare few can realize that potential. It provides access to what I've learned to call a Bloodline Inheritance. Karnak's tools simulate these abilities without needing to purify one's gates. Powerful and risky weapons that were necessary to defeat the Kenat."

"And the Kenat…they were defeated?"

Fey was quiet for a sustained period before she murmured, "I believe both the Priori and the Mitad are trying to figure that out." She packed up the food and flask, resecured her boots, and motioned for Maxima to do the same in preparation for the next leg of their journey. She tugged nervously on the chain around her neck.

Maxima stretched her legs. Her endurance was excellent, but somehow, she couldn't match the agility of the much older inlume. Lactic acid was building in her legs after days of Soul Step. She adjusted her dark outer tunic, tightened the leather straps of the armor over her doublet, and fastened her laces as she asked, "Then…the Makanla Gates…are related to all this?" she asked.

"Even I don't have definitive answers to that mystery. I have suspicions that they are remnants of the Kenat. There are myths found in ancient scrolls, but they're inconsistent and sparse on details. Grace

CHAPTER SEVENTEEN

had solved much more than I have, but her knowledge is now in Jezca's hands and under the Mitad's nose."

"Which is why you agreed to this task, isn't it?"

Fey's small pointed chin only moved up once in affirmation.

"I promised your mother I'd look after you. I've spent my life working towards the knowledge Grace acquired. It must be protected at all costs. She had a unique placement working for all sides and extracting what she wanted from each. Her mind was on another level from any other member of the Priori. She decoded more of ancient languages on her own than the rest of us combined."

They ran again.

Sapphire and cherry blossom light streaked the foothills as the two women crossed through the edge of Terrspar.

Her frequency of glancing over her shoulder and scanning for threats began to resemble paranoia to Maxima.

The Inlume's hand began drifting towards the hilt of her glaive blade. They hadn't traveled far before she said, "I had hoped we could make it to the Viator border. I have infiltrators in Astor Bruinsma's crews that could smuggle us into Lenape from rivers in the Viator strip. Unfortunately, we're being followed. I expect our pursuer to catch us before we reach the Viator Strip."

Maxima swiveled her head about but saw nothing. She tuned her Observation but sensed no living being as far as her sensing could reach.

What does Fey sense that I cannot?

Another fifteen minutes passed, and Maxima began to worry. Her intuition told her danger was all around her, but her Observation of Soul Energy sensed nothing.

A speck of landscape appeared in her periphery; a shade too dark to be part of the mountain. As she focused on the distortion, it moved alongside them in the distance.

"Great Soul forsaken us. *Alam hazan*," Fey swore in the ancient language. "You see it now? It's only tracking, but it revealed itself. I expect an attack soon."

"Attack?" Maxima asked with distress in her voice. "What is *it*? What's out there, and why can't I sense it?"

UNSEEN CHASE

"We call them the Unseen. The old texts allude to such things as the Bishiwal. This one has been following me for months. I fought it off once. Thought I lost it for good after Old Cintish. Then, I noticed it tracking us on our way out of Caracta. Wasn't sure, but yesterday I became certain."

Maxima struggled to swallow her saliva as fear bunched in her throat. *Something only referred to as the Unseen—that even the highest-level wielder could only fight off and evade.* As Fey increased their speed to a sprint, Maxima managed to ask, "Why can't my Observation sense this Unseen?"

Old eyes squinted solemnly, evaluating their situation. "Re-tune your perception. Focus on the faint Soul Energy all around us."

Maxima obeyed. No longer did she consciously search for another person on the horizon. Instead, she allowed the energy all around to reveal its subtle presence. There was a natural flow at work in the world...in all life. She could not wield it, but it was there all the same.

There!

At the crags, she noticed a disturbance in nature's energy. It was as if a hole had been punched in the network of Soul Energy. It was more of a void than a being.

The sensation made her shiver.

"There's something...missing..." she mumbled.

Fey agreed and slowed to a halt.

"We can't outrun it. When it comes, I want you to stay far back. Wear your mask so that it cannot recognize your face. No matter what, I want you to run, even if I'm defeated—"

"Don't talk like that, Master Fey! I can help you—"

"No! Survive at all costs. If you fight it, you become its enemy. You must get to Jezca and recover Gracc's journal."

The Bishiwal came.

Like a missing piece of paper on a map.

The energy of Hyperborea warped around it as if evading.

Closer.

Fey moved to it at a walk, distancing herself from Maxima.

When it was upon her, Fey drew her onyx blade.

CHAPTER SEVENTEEN

Navy robes with golden trim lined with stars fluttered around the Bishiwal. A mask like pearl moonlight covered its face—an unsettling tangle of veins and roots that changed from milky white to pink-marbled silver as the light reflected off it. The twisting organic pattern to the mask was repulsive, and Maxima could hardly look at it.

Combined with the sensation of blotting out the flow of life around it, the Bishiwal's appearance made Maxima's stomach lurch.

There was a radiant flicker of Soul Energy, but instead of a light color like the mask, their pursuer's energy was a muddy brown-red like dried blood.

Each finger extended into a foot-long blade of Soul Energy like a set of claws.

Talons of light shone against Fey's manus stone core glaive.

The two shimmered in a standoff that Maxima counted with her heartbeat.

The Bishiwal sprang first.

Its right arm struck out with gold stars fluttering behind the five talons.

Fey's right knee bent as it took her weight, and her left foot swept in a half circle to brace herself as her half-leaf-shaped blade met the Bishiwal.

The glaive glittered with topaz Soul Energy in the clash.

The creature was incredibly agile—as if weightless.

The familiar twang of energies humming against each other echoed through the empty plains.

The Bishiwal's left arm swung in a follow-up attack.

Fey parried the blow by striking its forearm with her own before the razors of light could find her flesh.

Swing. Clash.

Parry. Dodge.

The dance of battle continued as Maxima watched, biting her lip and percolating sapphire light at her fingertips.

The Bishiwal advanced with its dreadful mask of roots like metallic milk looming above Fey's tiny figure. It attacked with relentless speed as if it could not grow exhausted from repeated vicious swinging strikes.

UNSEEN CHASE

The glaive cut in and out as it deflected blows.

Fey was only on the defensive.

Her aggressor was ravenous with its onslaught.

But then, she managed to position herself for a controlled block. The Bishiwal came in too close to maneuver its long claws.

With her middle and index fingers pointed and the other three curled, she struck her open palm against its shoulder with a flash of her Soul Energy on contact.

The arm went limp.

Claws faded.

Maxima recognized the immobilizing technique. Fey had blocked Vizier Alsi's wielding in Old Cintish. Now, it not only prevented wielding in the afflicted arm but also paralyzed it.

Maxima pumped her arms in silent excitement that Fey had finally turned the momentum.

The onyx blade made its first offensive slash.

The Bishiwal backpedaled as its single arm of muddied energy claws sparked against the glaive's edge.

Fey drove it back until she drew the remaining arm too low.

She swung the long pole up.

The blade found its target!

A topaz-colored glow shattered the Bishiwal's mask.

The creature recoiled in inhuman stutters backward.

Its limbs rattled and body squirmed under the cloak.

The mask fell away.

The strike had been deep enough to sever its head down the center, but when the Bishiwal's face was revealed...there was only a featureless blot resembling Soul Energy beneath.

The contours of a face were there—but no features completed it. Only the same Soul Energy like coagulated blood swirled in the form of a head.

Maxima's jaw hung loosely at the horrid site.

Inhuman and revolting, the creature vibrated and shimmered momentarily as if recomposing itself.

Then, its claws returned on both hands.

CHAPTER SEVENTEEN

It had overcome Fey's energy paralysis technique.

The terrible mass had absorbed the full-frontal strike.

Now, it lurched forward relentlessly.

Zmmm. Zmm.

Fey protected herself in panic.

Each time she lost ground and slowed.

The faceless one lurched its head with a muted light smoldering where eyes should have been as its bladed fingers glanced Fey's arm.

There was a warmth of blood and a sizzle of burning skin.

She was losing, and her techniques targeting the internal flow of Soul Energy through the human body were ineffective against the being that appeared to have no true body.

As Fey's strength and speed faded, the Blue Corcinth stepped in.

A wall of blue droplets, each the size of a fist, swirled between the two combatants.

The Bishiwal clashed against a floating sapphire orb and was met with a violent explosion. It did no harm but paused the furious assailant.

In the seconds it bought them, the array of Soul Spheres enveloped the inhuman creature.

Maxima looked through the holes in her ceramic mask and realized they had only this moment before the Bishiwal broke through the trick.

"Now!" she urged her master.

Fey was already raising her blade.

She brought it down in a mighty slash that projected out a massive flare of Soul Energy.

The wave of rose light smashed into Maxima's makeshift cage.

The eruption tore through the Bishiwal's entire body.

The cloak and shattered mask lay on the ground, charred.

A mist of brown-red rolled away from the scene. It whipped in the wind and slithered back towards the mountains.

"You did it," Maxima breathed with stress easing from her.

"No. I've broken it once before, and it returned. Now it will come after both of us. We must run!"

They fled, sprinting in spite of their muscles aching.

UNSEEN CHASE

The nightmarish image of the Bishiwal turned off Maxima's rational mind and compelled her onward in a rush of adrenaline.

When they finally stopped to gasp for air, it took a full minute before either could speak.

The Master Inlume managed to say, "We're near the border. We must lose it and get on our boat before it can track us down again."

"What was that?" Maxima blurted in a whisper with a dry throat and empty lungs. Her pupils quivered, and hands shook.

Fey pinched her eyebrows with her fingers.

"We don't know for sure. Something left behind by the Kenat...or sent by them."

Maxima threw up her hands, "Why is it after you then?"

There was a moment of hesitation as Fey thought. Her breathing slowed, and she removed the chain from around her neck.

The Inlume held out a leather pouch to Maxima.

Raven hair blew wildly behind the blue corcinth mask. She had not removed it in their urgency but now lifted it from her face.

Opening the pouch, Maxima dumped its contents into her hand.

"Careful!" Fey urged. "Do not look into it. Tilt it away from your face."

A shard like glass, the size of her palm, fell out.

Maxima squinted cautiously at her turned-out hand.

She was cupping a fragment of mirror.

Fey explained quietly, "It's a shard from Amaterasu's Mirror—one of Karnak's Tools. That's how some legends refer to it, at least. We call it the Holy Penitus Ostium."

Maxima's eyes widened with recognition of the word. She slipped the fragment back into its bag.

"You're familiar with the word?" Fey asked. She laughed to herself knowingly. "Of course you are. You'll make a fine addition to the Priori, Maxima."

"During our night at Fanum Ortus...during our initiation into the Order...Eos found a mirror that pulled him into a Soul Void," Maxima explained

CHAPTER SEVENTEEN

Fey's head tilted. "Oh? Now that is interesting. You can tell me more once we're in the Viator strip." She closed her eyes and cast her Observation out to distances Maxima couldn't hope of perceiving. "I sense that rotten thing already reforming. We must go. When we reach our boat, I will teach you about this piece of Amaterasu's Mirror. On its own, it can draw you into your Soul Void in an instant. I can't fathom what the whole mirror would do. But Grace was investigating exactly that. Now, let's be off."

Maxima followed her master's Soul Step, shuddering at the thought of the Bishiwal on their trail.

CHAPTER EIGHTEEN

HAUNTED AND HUNTED

Vistomus Fulmen rose from a reverent bow and stared past the red railing and stylized dragons painted on ancient wood. Behind the façade was the young boy who sat on the chrysanthemum throne.

"Do it again, powerful Raijin," Emperor Antoku commanded in his adolescent voice.

The advisors on either side of the throne platform shifted uncomfortably at the request. They fidgeted with their black caps, a fusion of the kanmuri formal court-wear and modern headwear, like peacocks.

"As you wish, my emperor," Vistomus responded with a small bow. Then, he held out his hand and flexed his pointed nails.

There was a crackling and popping around the bald man as the air grew heavy.

Flash.

The room erupted with thunder.

CHAPTER EIGHTEEN

A bolt of pure white lightning ran from the ceiling to the palm of Vistomus' hand. He clutched it in curled fingers, a sphere of plasma wielded in his palm. The bright energy cast highlights on his pointed chin and the contour of his sharp brow.

The boy laughed giddily and clapped his hands as if pleased by a new toy.

"My Lord," one advisor whispered loudly, warning in shame, "The kami have not returned to be commanded like servants."

The Emperor frowned and huffed.

"Quite alright. It reminds the Emperor of the strength he has at his command with the kami on his side," Vistomus said, carefully reminding the Emperor's court that the kami's alliance was not guaranteed.

"Raijin, what do you wish to request of me?" Antoku asked. Every word from the boy's mouth was like a trained student attempting to pass a test. His speech was constantly searching for authority.

"The time has come, Emperor Antoku. You must put down this rebellion once and for all," Vistomus answered calmly.

At that, there was a nodding of advisors and court members. They signaled their agreement silently under the cherry blossoms painted in the throne room.

Emperor Antoku saw the excitement of his two highest advisors but asked suspiciously, "How do you propose I end the rebellion?"

Vistomus paused for three seconds before answering, "You have a problem with samurai. I happen to know that lightning cures samurai." He displayed vaporous light in his hand. "Announce to all of Nippon-Wa that Raijin and his hanyo have full war powers to put down the bushi and Saigo."

Antoku gripped his chair and tightened his lips. "Saigo was a loyal court member to my father, he taught me bushido, and he still has a position on this council."

Vistomus interrupted the Emperor to remind him, "Which he has not attended for over a year."

Antoku was silent at this for a while. He pondered as his eyes wandered, searching for support, but found none in the throne room. This time, he spoke with a confidence Vistomus had not heard before.

HAUNTED AND HUNTED

"He has told me that the rebellion is his lesson for me. I value his dissenting opinion."

The nostalgic loyalty to Saigo made Vistomus furious, but he masked it with a smile. "Perhaps it is time to let go of the old ways. Nippon-Wa cannot unify in your father's vision if Saigo continues to tear it down. Grant me this, and I will bring you Saitani's head as well. All of Nippon-Wa will glorify their emperor once again."

Whispers fell into Antoku's ears from both sides.

"You cannot deny the kami, my Lord."

"His offer is wise. Saigo must be stopped."

The advisors exchanged sly glances and nodded to Vistomus in secret communication that their words would work like poison on the boy's mind.

Antoku rubbed his forehead daintily as he fretted.

"I will consult my council and decide before the next moon."

"Very wise, Emperor Antoku," Vistomus answered a bow but fumed silently as he parted from the throne room.

Back in his private wing of the Imperial Palace, he strutted back and forth across his room, plotting.

He sat at his low tea table with eyes closed. His meditation came with difficulty today. Thoughts wandered like floating debris. Before he could settle in fully, he noticed the entrance of two of his hanyo.

Allowing them to wait, kneeling on one knee, he observed their aura for a few minutes. Rius' Soul Energy was erratic and aggravated as if still seeking an opponent to duel with. Diya was broodily calm—as he expected from a Sister of Noxim.

Finally, after letting them tremble before him, Vistomus addressed the two, "I've read the report, but I'd like to hear in your own words. How did the mission go? Diya first."

Diya looked up from above her diamond-patterned cheekbone tattoos. She spoke cautiously, "My Lord, we fulfilled our objective. No weapons were stolen, and we distracted Aizo Mudar and Scavok Alter. However, a third wielder appeared and caught us off guard. It would seem a man named Kikujiro can also wield. He is well trained, but his Soul Energy is not particularly strong. I had my viziers investigate...and

CHAPTER EIGHTEEN

they determined he is the son of Saigo. Also…Bysis was injured in the attack. The idiot was reckless and lost his focus."

"So, I've heard. Our healers are working on him now," Vistomus hummed. "You succeeded in keeping the weapons from the rebels. Well done, Diya. If Bysis does not make a full recovery, he will be replaced. This matter of Saigo's son interests me greatly. Find out more about him. I want a full report, including his whereabouts."

"Yes, My Lord," Diya bowed her head.

"And you, Rius?"

Scowling as if seeking to defend his honor from every direction, Rius reported, "I located and confronted Eos Bellator. He refused to come peacefully to meet with you. We battled, but the fight was interrupted. Durath Leorix is here in Nippon-Wa as well."

The doors slid open again, and a Mezclado woman in Mitad kimono entered. Her blond hair starkly contrasted with her dark skin, and she had a muscular frame that drew attention when she walked into any room.

Rius growled at the interruption.

Before he could speak, Vistomus calmed him, "It's quite alright, Rius. I asked for Mila to join us."

Mila assumed the line of bent knees and bowed before her master. She received a callous glare from the hot-headed mirza next to her.

"*As I was saying*," Rius continued, "Durath Leorix interrupted my battle and allowed Eos to escape—"

Vistomus peered over his mirza with increased interest. "I was not aware the Loerix King's Son was part of the party that came to Earth. This changes the math some. How strong was he? Did he live up to his rumors?"

Rius put his head down as he responded, "He was a wielder who lives up to his praises. However, I was unable to crush him properly as I was trying to pursue Eos Bellator. By the time I knocked Durath down for the first time, Eos' trail was cold."

"Then you failed in both convincing Eos to meet with me and subduing him after his refusal?"

HAUNTED AND HUNTED

Tensing his whole body, Rius defended himself with a rigid expression, "Master, there were complications that I could not have foreseen."

"Did you take Artera with you as I suggested?"

Rius' cold eyes glanced to the side of the room as he admitted, "I didn't need her to defeat Eos."

"Yet you did not defeat Eos."

"I was not told Durath would be there!"

"You went in unprepared against my advice," Vistomus said calmly. "Mila, on the other hand, has exceeded expectations. She has obeyed and led Naith to information that has narrowed our search for Carnus in the Akaishi Mountains."

"May that traitor perish," Rius spat.

Vistomus' voice was blunt and laced with finality. "He will face judgment soon. However, the matter at hand is leadership and success. Mila will be promoted to mirza. You may report to her starting today." He then turned and sipped on steaming tea nonchalantly.

Shaking, Rius stood. "Master…" he said while his fists trembled. "How can you—"

Vistomus moved his eyes to stare at Rius without turning his head. With the glare came a rumbling as if static was building charge in the room before striking.

Rius turned his head. He knew better. Every mirza had heard the story of what happened to Ares when he had spoken disrespectfully and out of turn. Lord Vistomus had struck Ares with lightning and left a scar on his neck to remind everyone.

"Thank you," Mila said proudly, "I will not let you down, Lord Vistomus. Rius, we will discuss your place in my command after this meeting." The last words were sharp and pointed, twisting in Rius' gut as he digested them.

"*Your command?*" he asked incredulously. "My task was to bring Eos Bellator here. I will carry out that mission."

"Yes, *my command*. You're a wild animal that can't control himself." Mila stood and faced Rius. They were the same height, and she had more muscle than his lean frame. "I will put you to use where you can accomplish your missions."

With his lip twitching, Rius shoved his hands into his pockets to restrain himself. He sauntered towards the door with haughty arrogance in every strut.

Mila called out to him, "Do not leave until Lord Fulmen has dismissed you!"

Rius turned, whipping his long brown hair in the process.

In an instant, there was a crackle of icy blue.

Soul Energy glazed his hand, which was pointed rigidly like a spear.

Before Mila could blink, Rius plunged the Soul Energy-layered arm into her abdomen.

Her eyes widened in shock before she lurched in pain.

Violence was not allowed between mirza, least of all before Lord Vistomus. Mila had not expected the attack, nor had her Observation sensed the snap in Soul Energy that preceded Rius' ferocity.

The shimmering blue hand pierced through Mila's back, dripping with blood. He withdrew his hand and shook off the vibrant red liquid before letting his Soul Energy fade.

Mila coughed weakly and fell to the ground.

Rius stood over her and scoffed, "You're making a mess of Lord Vistomus' room, Mila. It's quite rude."

Diya sprang to her feet. "How dare you! It is forbidden to do such a thing. And in front of Lord Vistomus. You will not leave this room alive for disrespecting our master."

Rius only put his hands back in his pockets and shrugged.

"Bring it on, Diya. Your anima stone implants will make a nice trophy." Rius smirked, knowing he had triggered Diya. "But before that...Lord Vistomus, it seems you're in need of another mirza to fill Mila's place."

Vistomus allowed his full aura to push both Diya and Rius unexpectedly to their knees once more. "Enough," he said with detached nuetrality, though the pressure of his Soul Energy spoke his anger for him. "Explain to me why I should let you walk out of this room alive, Rius."

HAUNTED AND HUNTED

A wolfish smirk replied, "If she couldn't raise a defense to such a simple attack, she had no place as a mirza. She would have been a danger to the rest of us and you in a battle. I did us all a favor."

Vistomus looked on, neither refuting nor accepting what Rius said. He only flared his nostrils while contemplating.

Thin lips and handsome features smiled back Vistomus as if a murder had not just occurred. "I promised you Eos Bellator. So, I will go and find him."

"See that you do not return without him, or it will be your last day breathing, Rius." Vistomus resumed drinking his tea. Without looking at his mirzas, he said, "Diya, I want you to alert the others that Master M is sending Khasun to Nippon-Wa shortly."

Diya nearly choked at the news. "So soon? But-but-we haven't..."

The Mitad leader inhaled the steam of tea, savoring it. The conversation appeared only to have a minor part of his attention. Finally, he hummed and said, "Yes, it's imperative that we locate the Left Eye immediately. We will not delay the Master's plans. Time is short."

∞   ∞   ∞

The Sixth Primane-Viator war had been raging for five years now. The Viator side was weaker and losing ground, but the brilliant tactician Carnus Solaire had led his people to unprecedented victories against impossible odds.

Carnus strutted from the Viator royal chamber with pride in every step. He had been promoted to the highest rank of hariban. Combined with his universal favor among the common people of the kingdom and his upbringing as one of the Hamirate Clan—descended directly from Zeri the Great, no less—meant that the King of Viator had given him nearly equal power.

If only the Hamirate had survived the Battle of Tacita, he thought.

Rage mixed with pride.

The Hamirate teachings said this was the deadliest combination for the soul. Yet, how could he feel anything less? He had been bestowed

CHAPTER EIGHTEEN

the sway of a king to combat the Primane aggressors who had slain his people, heritage, and culture.

With the original warrior force of the Hamirate, he would have secured victory, but only a few straggling fragments of the clan lived today.

The history and memory were a toxin in his heart.

Carnus remembered well his master leaving with Zeri the Great to Tacita to make a final stand in the Fifth Primane-Viator war. Still only ten at the time, he had been left behind while his brotherhood was eviscerated and hunted.

As these thoughts settled and his mind cleared, he repeated the teachings of Zeri, who would say: *Pray as if everything depends on the Great Soul. Work as though it depends on you alone.* He did as he was taught. He petitioned in his heart for a means of victory and plotted maneuvers that he would lead himself.

The rank of hariban would give him the freedom to take the risks necessary for success.

As he plotted over a map with wooden figures representing troops and supplies, he saw something was missing. He needed a key strength at the forefront of the upcoming battle. The victory path was clear in his mind, yet the required spearhead was obscured.

A particular, rapid rhythm knocked at his office door.

He had been expecting it for days, and it couldn't come soon enough. As his security detail opened the door, Prax the inlume entered. In those days, Prax wore his caramel hair shaven on the sides and long on the top. His clenched jaw and cold blue eyes spoke of urgency before words could.

Carnus poured him a glass of the finest whiskey. It usually softened the gruff demeanor of the inlume.

Reclining in a mahogany chair, Prax spoke with a detached and formal tone, "I hear a congratulation is in order, Hariban Carnus Solaire."

"Indeed. I'm honored with the promotion. It'll allow me to lead the Viator to victory and end this senseless bloodshed. I hope you come with news that will aid me," Carnus said. He stroked his black stubble as he evaluated the Inlume's guarded expression.

Prax swirled his glass in the air and savored his sip. As thoughts turned over in his mind, the whiskey warmed his throat. "I come with the Order's offer. It is a steep price, I know."

"Tell me."

"If you publicly join the Order of Soul Wielders, we will provide you with undercover errant ranked warriors to aid your efforts," Prax explained.

Carnus scoffed. "Is that all? *Chaos to order. Path of light,*" he mocked the creed of the Order. "What's that all about? Hollow words and empty promises?"

Prax closed his eyes and tightened his lips, pained by his own offer. "I know—"

"*You don't know!* The Primane slaughtered my people! The Hamirate were exterminated! Now thousands are dying in another senseless war, and the Order could end it with the commitment of a few inlumes. The threat alone would cause the Primane to surrender."

"There is something in the creed about setting aside the influence of nations and kingdoms too. The Order should have aided the Hamirate back then, that I freely admit. But there are innocents and justifications on both sides now. The Order cannot make enemies and alliances in messy vengeance wars. The offer stands. I'll leave my messenger elsu with you. Send word by the next month, or we will assume you have rejected the offer."

Prax set down his half-drunken glass and strutted out.

"Worthless, cowardly, spineless, fake honor..." Carnus' words chased out the stoic Prax. The glass shattered against the closed-door seconds after the inlume was gone.

For three days, the disbelief and feeling of abandonment by the supposed highest order for good on the Hyperborean Corland swirled around Carnus as he went about his duties and settled into his position as hariban.

CHAPTER EIGHTEEN

The King's pressure was immediately upon him to lay out a new winning strategy, and the other hariban were not shy with their hostility towards him.

When the next guest passed through his office doors, it was one of the few surviving Hamirate that entered. His spiritual brother waited under the charcoal-colored stone walls.

Carnus sat at work behind his desk under dual banners on equal levels. To the left was the Hamirate crest of a sword wrapped in an olive branch surrounded by seven stars. To the right was the Viator flag, royal purple with two fighting fish curled around the sails of a sea-strider sprouting from a golden crown.

"Brother Naith," Carnus welcomed Naith Lelantos.

The ashen-toned pale face approached, gaunt and weary. Naith's messy auburn hair was strewn over his forehead as if he had just sprinted into the room. Most likely, he had. Naith was a specialist of the Hamirate Clan—a master of Soul Step with profound Observation Wielding abilities. He was one of the few wielders that Carnus feared a duel with. He wasn't nearly as strong, but his speed and perception made him a difficult opponent.

"Brother Carnus, or should I say Hariban Carnus now? You climb the ranks so quickly it's hard to keep up with your titles," Naith laughed as he eased into a seat at Carnus' gesture. His black tunic was in stark contrast to the paleness of his skin. Corcinth horns were woven onto his shoulder, a symbol of his time spent in the Sepeleo mountains amongst Corleo barbarian tribes.

"Before one of the Hamirate's most elite guardians, the title means little," Carnus bowed his head slightly.

"Being the most of anything amongst an extinct clan is hardly worthy of praise," Naith humbled himself, though he was recognized and feared even in the Hamirate clan's prime. At the Battle of Tacita, he had slain thirty men before having to flee.

"Please, Naith, tell me you bring word of an alliance that could replace those feeble half-hearts that call themselves wielders."

HAUNTED AND HUNTED

Naith grinned a devilish smile. There was danger in his face but also promise. "I brought a guest who is waiting outside your doors at this very moment."

Carnus gestured for his guards to allow in Naith's companion.

He had a clean-shaven head and cold eyes. His demeanor was a juxtaposition of perfectly calm and incredibly threatening all at once.

"Hello Carnus Solaire. I've been an admirer from afar. My name is Vistomus Fulmen, and I'd like to offer you what assistance the Mitad can provide to your noble campaign against the Primane's advances." Vistomus' voice was smooth and convincing.

"The Mitad?" Carnus asked in his deep voice. His eyes narrowed into a squint, and his chin tilted. "Haven't heard of it before."

"We're not well known yet. However, I can commit fifty skilled wielders from the southern Krog nations…should that be acceptable to your national perceptions," Vistomus offered.

Carnus gave a single-syllable laugh. "You should know that the Viator have no racial prejudices. I am grateful for your offer, Mr. Fulmen, and your admiration. I don't know you or your organization, so what price do you ask for such a force?"

Vistomus spread out his hands to reveal himself unarmed, "I ask only your friendship, Carnus. And that's not all I offer," he said with a twist in his tone to tempt Carnus.

Not buying the authenticity of the Mitad alliance, Carnus replied cautiously, "Please. Do tell."

"It's something you can't pass up, Carnus," Naith interjected. I know warriors who would sacrifice their family for such a gift!"

"Well, I wouldn't sacrifice my family for anything, Naith. You know that."

"Only a figure of speech, Carnus. Listen to the man."

Vistomus sat down before receiving an invitation.

"Carnus, I offer you a unique wielding gift. An offer of *power and might beyond imagination.*"

"Oh…my imagination is quite good," Carnus said suspiciously.

"Then picture, if you will, a new source of Soul Energy in addition to your own. One that will fill your veins with the fire of vigor and multiply your wielding many times over." There was a hum of excitement in Vistomus' voice.

"And this is free too, I assume?"

"You assume correctly, Carnus. You see, I want the Mitad unit to lead your next campaign. The spreading reputation of our strength will be payment enough. I have many wielders who have accepted the Mitad's enhancement now."

"So, you're seeking glory and risking your organization's best as payment? And you sweeten the deal with some kind of…what? Ancient forbidden wielding technique?" Carnus said in a monotone, careful not to give away how desperately he needed the addition of fifty skilled wielders.

"Precisely. The Mitad's Master has knowledge that would tantalize even the best inlumes. Yet, we are opposed to their falsely noble public face. Instead, we offer our alliance to the mixed races, the Krogs, and the moral underdogs who have a real need but no voice," Vistomus said, his words dripping with a sweetness he knew Carnus craved to hear.

A realization dawned on Carnus. He turned to Naith, "You've taken this offer, haven't you? The *enhancement*, I mean."

Naith bobbed his head in confirmation.

Then, he held up his hand as if displaying his palm.

Like living ink, a black flame crawled over his skin. It spread until it was entirely black, like the midnight sky from sleeve to fingertip.

"My Soul Step in twice is fast. My Observation extends to new distances and perceives subtleties I couldn't have trained for in a lifetime…" Naith turned his hand over as if examining some foreign artifact that wasn't attached to his own body. "I never wield without the Mitad's gift," he cooed.

"And if I don't want this enhancement? Just the unit of wielders during battle?" Carnus asked.

Vistomus put the tips of his fingers together. The Viator Hariban sensed unstated terms hidden in the agreement.

"It's a package deal, but the Mark of the Chosen will give a prodigy like yourself the additional wielding might equal to all fifty of my men. It will take you to unparalleled heights. My offer is, therefore, the power of one hundred men. It's generous, you must admit."

"Extremely. I'll take that into consideration," Carnus rasped and nodded ever so slightly.

Naith added, "I will personally be leading this unit from the Mitad. The Primane can't overrun us in the next battle. If they do, the Viator kingdom is lost."

Again, Carnus nodded in slow, steady motions. He found no words for his options. He could either concede to the Order of Soul Wielder or this new group calling themselves the Mitad.

Submit to humiliation and covert, half-hearted assistance, or accept the risk of a new organization and the consequences of their dark enhancement. The fact that one of the remaining Hamirate brothers had already tested the gift made Carnus consider the deal. However, his intuition sent pings of warning under his skin.

"I can see you need time to consider," Vistomus said. I'll be here in Viator for two days. Take this," he placed a piece of paper containing a blood-red serpent with heads at both ends. "It is special ink. Light it with your Soul Energy; I'll be near enough to perceive when you have. I'll receive your answer at that time."

Carnus stroked his beard wearily and tapped his thumb against the strange symbol that evening as he debated his options. His stomach ached at the unideal choices.

Hexades had passed since Naith introduced Vistomus.

Twenty-eight Earth years, Carnus mused. *Forty Hyperborean years.*

Now, in Nippon-Wa, Carnus remembered the encounter from his youthful days as a hariban. How he wished he could go back and undo his choice. He and Vistomus had been partners and something approximating friends. They had ventured to foreign lands and worlds, hunted relics, and turned the tides of wars together...but all that changed when he learned the truth of the Fifth Primane-Viator war.

When he had touched the Left Eye of Izanagi, and the vision of the past was given to him, Vistomus had resorted to possession and manipulation to maintain their working relationship.

CHAPTER EIGHTEEN

Tears welled up in Carnus' eyes as he thought about the unforgivable sins he had committed while under the control of his curse mark. He had spent years fading between one of the Voro and a sovereign wielder fighting not to be consumed.

For those sins, he could never make amends.

Not with himself. Not with the world.

He sat in a tiny forest shack—the residence of a hermit. His posessions were simple, and the space was minimal. It was tucked deep in the woods of the Akaishi Mountains.

A teapot boiled over a makeshift fireplace. The heat warmed Carnus' extremities, and the crackle comforted him as he faced the demons of his past in solitude.

A knock struck the flimsy cabin door.

It startled him so much that he spilled boiling water on the dirt floor. He shuffled frantically.

On a few occasions, Grace would visit. The number of times could be counted on his hands, and she always warned with her aura before she arrived. No villagers knew where to find him. He would disappear in a flash of Soul Step after treating their ill and wounded.

Who?

There was a wave of aura that threatened danger. Its heavy weight was like the smell of decay, communicating that death approached.

From behind the door, a teasing voice sang, "What did the Zeri the Great often say? In hiding from others, you hide from yourself, but the Great Soul sees all?"

Carnus' head fell against the other side of the door in defeat.

He had been found, and the time of peace had come to an end.

Refortifying his mind, he let his face go emotionless and braced for what came next. Carnus opened the door to see the bleached skull helm and bone necklace that proclaimed Naith Lelantos' arrival.

"It's been a long time, Naith."

"Not for lack of trying on my side. Years, I've been tracking you. I just never believed you could reduce yourself to living in this squalor to evade me." The fabric strips covering his face waivered in the breeze, and he spit from behind the mask to show his disgust.

HAUNTED AND HUNTED

"I will not fight you, Naith."

There was a gritty cackle. "I'm well aware of that fact. Your cowardice is renowned these days amongst the Mitad. You know why I've come. What's your answer?"

"I can't offer you tea, then?" Carnus asked in a low, gruff voice.

"Understand this, *Traitor*. Now that we have you, we will not kill you first. I know this is hard for you, and because of our Hamirate brotherhood—"

"Don't pretend like you have anything left of the Hamirate creed in you. I know what you've become. It's all Saida's curse in there...tainting your mind," Carnus growled.

Naith hissed but continued, "For our history, I will give you one week to think things over...if I can manage to convince Vistomus to be patient that long."

"I gave the Left Eye of Izanagi away so I could not know its location. You're wasting your time with me."

The bird bones rattled on Naith's chest.

"Then you will give me the name of who you left it with. After your week of grace, Zeres will begin wiping a village off the map each day until you give us what we want."

Carnus closed his eyes and pinched his face in pain.

Naith continued, "Yes, we know how much you love the little villagers. I've had to hunt them down and interrogate the ones you've healed at great pain. Eventually, it led me to you."

"You, scum..."

"Call me what you want, but you can't make up for the things you've done. This," Naith gestured to the hut, "All this is pathetic. You were a great hariban feared across the Corland."

There was a glare of contention between the two. Dark, wounded eyes met shadows behind the skull mask.

Carnus only nodded repeatedly and pressed his hands together at his lips.

Naith spoke bluntly, "One week. Then villagers die. Whether you give the information willingly or not, Vistomus will determine your

CHAPTER EIGHTEEN

punishment. Perhaps he will allow you back…but I expect…he will call upon Lady Sugra to sentence you."

No. Vistomus would not use Lady Sugra to perform my execution. He would do it himself. Carnus knew the vendetta was too personal.

The image of Naith waivered. As if an illusion had faded in the mist, he was gone. His Soul Step, under the possession of the Mark of the Chosen, made him a ghost.

The forest life chirped, mocking Carnus with its continuous tempo that was unchanged as the last fragments of his soul chipped and shattered. He fell to his knees, broken in spirit.

CHAPTER NINETEEN

ESSENCE OF LIFE

The next time Eos was conscious, he was not awake among the living. Instead, he found himself deep in his inner world. The Soul Void had claimed him from his extremely stressed physical state, and he had slipped away inside himself.

Looking around, Eos found himself in a forested mountain valley that he understood to be in Nippon-Wa. The place would have been beautiful, worthy of resting to marvel at nature for an entire day—but the scenery was marred by ink-colored liquid dripping from everything down to each blade of grass. The world of his Soul Void was weeping an oil-like sludge with the consistency of molasses.

As he expected, Zala Alsar appeared, walking toward Eos with a slow, methodical Soul Step. His white mask, streaked with a pattern of red, covered his face as Eos was accustomed to, and his silver-streaked hair flowed behind him against the contrast of his black cloak.

"You've really done it this time, Eos," Zala muttered.

CHAPTER NINETEEN

Eos reflected on the decaying state around him. His small patch of untainted grass was being encroached upon as the oozing black bubbled to a simmer all around him.

"I did this?"

"Oh yes. You did this and so much more."

Summoning crimson energy at his feet, Eos stepped above the ground to avoid the sludge. He thought quickly about how to react to his inner realm being overwhelmed by darkness.

"Last time I was here, I did not have the Order of Soul Wielders' anatus crown." Eos activated his mark of membership.

Light twisted around his head in a circlet that held a broken sword like a cross at its center above his forehead. "Now, I am a member of the Order under inlume Aizo Mudar."

A hearty laugh like one would at a child who misunderstood an important lesson was the response. "Having a crown and being worthy of it are entirely different things. You don't act like a member of the Order. You lack discipline, which is why I will take control and rule you soon."

Eos cast his gaze down at the pit like tar below.

Zala continued, "You throw your life away for a chance at revenge, are consumed by your anger, and risk your friends and family for a chance to satiate your base emotions." He threw his hands up in a grand gesture to the entire area. "And this is your reward. Wear your crown and imitate all you like."

"You're wrong!" Eos yelled in reaction.

"Am I? The Mark of the Chosen has invaded everything in here. How can it be anything but true?"

Eos breathed heavily as he began to panic. He balled his hands into fists and asked, "So what now; do we fight again? Is that why I'm here?"

"That won't be necessary. I'll be the king, and you'll only be the vessel soon enough. Look around you."

The anxiety grew in Eos' chest. He remembered his previous journeys in the Soul Void.

Falling into nothingness only to summon the crimson elsu to catch him.

ESSENCE OF LIFE

Accepting the curse as relief from Zala when Jezca had probed his mind. Only to be interrupted by the memory swap they shared.

Then battling Zala after meeting the corcinth spirit.

Somehow, he knew this time was different.

Each time before, Zala was testing him as if looking for a weakness in Eos' mental armor. Now, the masked man appeared fully confident he had won their constant struggle.

Eos looked down to see the curse mark climbing over itself to reach his foot. The mass of ink was morphing into strands that stretched toward him. He jumped, avoiding contact.

Penitus Ostium, he thought. *It's like when I was pulled into the mirror at Fanum Ortus.* He recalled the same substance had attacked, held at bay by the wielding of the young boy he had met there.

Eos summoned a sphere and threw it into the longest-reaching arm of the mass below.

Gurgle.

The curse swallowed the energy and dulled the red light to a weakly lit vapor.

"No, that won't work at all. The Mark of the Chosen will only feed off attempts like that," Zala said, amused.

The dark ooze shot up and latched onto Eos' foot. It burned his skin as it seeped through his boot.

He broke free and sprinted away from the growing trunk of the curse. Closing his eyes to think of a solution, Eos shook from exhaustion. The weakness in his body from the physical world carried over here. He pleaded for guidance in his thoughts.

An emblem came to Eos' mind. It glowed in his closed eyelids as he thought, a recollection from his first time in the Soul Void: a glowing triangle made of two nested halves with a flame in the center—the symbol of the Human Essence.

He summoned it to him in the same way he did to manifest Soul Energy.

The world shuddered ever so slightly.

Eos wielded with all the intention he could.

CHAPTER NINETEEN

Strands of black whipped towards him as the base of the curse welled up and rolled across the ground like a wave.

There was a burst of red behind his eyelids.

I am here, a voice said in his mind.

Opening his eyes, a crimson elsu hovered above the valley. Its massive form dwarfed him.

But the strands of black did not slow.

They hurled towards him.

Eos raised Solido over his entire body.

The tendrils of curse smashed against him.

They clashed, trying to break down his barrier.

"Please! Help me," Eos let out.

The wings, like lava, beat steadily, unmoved by the plea.

Zala mocked him, "Why should it help you? Who are you calling out to? Do you know yourself? Do you know your Essence? No, you do not because you lack the humility and discipline. It's all about you and your external desires."

Arms of the curse seized his limbs and morphed over his skin.

It burned. A torment both physical and mental.

Searing heat like an injection of fire and hate into the veins.

Pain.

Eos' eyes watered in fear as he fought.

As the curse engulfed his torso, he cried out in the most desperation he had felt since Maxima's death, "Please. I'm sorry. I've never even asked the name of the power I draw upon."

The noble bird of pure Soul Energy bowed its head.

Narruh Risha, it spoke into his mind as Ahktar did.

The molten ink immersed him up to the face.

He felt the toxin in his skin, veins, and thoughts.

Resisting the constant resounding urge that toyed with his thoughts to give in to his hate and selfish pursuits, he thought for a moment: *It would be easier this way.*

But then he imagined Aizo and Talus looking over him as he gave in to the easy path—one he had promised to avoid.

ESSENCE OF LIFE

"Narruh Risha," he called into the Soul Void as he lost vision to the Mark of the Chosen, "I will become a better man. Worthy of my name, Bellator. I will know my Essence, and together we'll overcome this darkness."

Golden beams radiated from Narruh's eyes. The massive creature fluttered its wings in rapid succession. Crimson spread from every feather and blanketed the land. Like staring at the sun, Eos saw the pulse through his closed eyes.

The curse mark retreated from his skin and fled from him.

Red mist hung over the entire area, repelling the curse into the shadows. As the last traces of it disappeared, Eos saw the Soul Void in its current manifestation.

In a courtyard of green, sakura blossoms were beginning to bloom like pink snowflakes against pale blue skies. Each tree was a unique twisting homage to the unique beauty of Nippon-Wa, and they were staggered among the *toro*, stone pedestal lanterns. He stood at the foot of a magnificent castle before jade folds of the mountains like earth had grown over the ridges of a fallen kimono. Decorative beams arched under the curved irimoya gable roof above bamboo porches.

A single teardrop of sapphire Soul Energy was rotating at the center of one of the stone lanterns. Eos nearly cried as he felt the freedom from the receded curse and saw the perfect drop of Soul Energy that he knew belonged to his sister.

"Maxima..." he whispered.

Some of her remains in you, but only a little now. I was able to use of it...this time. You will not be so lucky again.

Narruh's words came to him telepathically.

"I don't understand, but thank you," Eos said humbly.

For the first time in recent memory, Eos had found a place worthy of resting at and the peace of mind to allow it.

The serenity was short-lived.

The castle and mountains faded, as did Narruh and Zala.

The masked man smiled with his eyes and said, "You may be able to access your Bloodline Inheritance after all."

The words drifted into a white abyss and nothingness.

CHAPTER NINETEEN

From this visionary trip to the Soul Void, Eos woke to mahogany walls and slatted screen doors on futon bedding.

His last waking moments returned to him, and he jolted up, ready for battle. The samurai hands dragging him, immobilized. The spears and katanas pointed. The suits of armor ready to kill. Ahktar attacking their leader to give Eos a few extra seconds of life.

"Rest easy, little hanyo," Saigo hummed in accented assurance. "You are only a guest. Not a prisoner."

Eos moved his body to make sure he was not restrained in any way. True to the fierce-eyed samurai's words, he was free.

Saigo's clean-cut, brooding face and masculine jawline were marred by a bandage over his forehead and traces of dried blood at the edges of the cloth.

Ahktar! Eos turned his head about the room in concern. His instincts calmed, and he remembered how to call his companion elsu. He sensed Ahktar's presence circling overhead outside the building. As soon as he connected with the bird, he understood that Ahktar had been watching over him for a long time.

Eos' gaze drifted back to the bandages over Saigo's right eye.

Saigo touched the cloth gently as Eos noticed it.

"Ah, this. Your friend has left me with a deep scar. Down to the bone with those talons. I'm fortunate I did not lose an eye."

"If you can still see, it's because Ahktar chose to spare your sight. It was only a warning," Eos said coldly.

"Hmmm," Saigo returned with no interest in rushing the conversation. Instead, he cast his sight out the window and observed the clouds against the mountaintop for a while. Then, he continued, "What is this white falcon to you?"

"They're called elsu, and they are the symbol of my family—the bird of my people."

Again, Saigo took a long pause before musing to himself as he recited, "*Catching lightning in a troubled land, the white wings fly free like mine. Yet, fate constrains both our hands.*"

Eos only questioned the heavily accented poem with a squint.

ESSENCE OF LIFE

"It is a poem I wrote based on a dream I had of this...*elsu* of your people," Saigo explained. "So, my vision may come to be true, but you have the mark of the hanyo." The samurai master's look was a distrusting and curious expression.

"This?" Eos held up his blackened hand. "I didn't ask for it. The man you call Raijin is an enemy of my family."

"Oh?"

"It is a curse that I must carry," Eos said, rubbing his hand with pained memories of the suffering it caused and the darkness it spread over his Soul Void.

A soft voice came from the doorway behind Eos.

"If the Mitad gave you the Mark of the Chosen against your will, then it is even more reason that you must not wield Soul Energy. I took care of you the best I could, but I am no healer, and their curse has almost taken hold."

Eloquent and dainty, a woman stood at the room's entrance in red and white robes. She had striking blonde hair that reminded Eos of the priestess from the Manus Temple in the Monte kingdom. Behind her soft and beautiful exterior, a lurking danger in her demeanor kept Eos on edge.

"Who are you people, and where am I?" Eos asked.

"The people here call me Himiko, and you have been asleep for a week. We cared for you here in the Akaishi Mountain citadel."

"Forgive my rudeness. I am Saigo Takayoshi, leader of the samurai and free people of Nippon-Wa, servant of the late emperor, Tuba," the stern samurai smiled slightly and bowed his head in greeting.

"My name..." Eos responded, feeling obliged to introduce himself, "is Eos Bellator, son of Talus Bellator. I have come to your country searching for Grace Lapithos and a man who can tell me about this curse. We want to understand what evil Raijin is spreading through Nippon-Wa."

Saigo grunted in approval, "Welcome, friend. I must apologize for mistaking you as one of the hanyo. I am grateful to meet another kami not aligned with Raijin."

CHAPTER NINETEEN

The woman who had introduced herself as Himiko smiled. "You have found her, Bellator King's Son. I am Grace...or was once...in a previous life on Hyperborea, but that was so many years ago. As for the man you seek, his name is Carnus Solaire. He may be able to help you, but it may take some time before I can convince him to come here."

"You're Grace?" Eos asked in disbelief. "We came here because we learned the Mitad are after you and something they call the Left Eye of Izanagi. We want to know more about it and my curse!"

Grace pursed her lips in pain. "If Anite has sent a king's party to Earth, then things on Hyperborea must be worse than I left them. I never thought I would meet another Hyperborean besides the Mitad for the rest of my life." She put a thin hand over her mouth as the reality set in on her. "I've been separated for so long...I gave up hope that I would ever return."

Eos explained, "The Mitad have grown their reach on Hyperborea just as much as here on Earth. We are trying to understand their true goals, which is why we must learn about this Eye of Izanagi. My father will return soon with a Mellizo Glyph. I know there are many in Hyperborea who have awaited your return...if that is what you want."

Grace struggled for words and her eyes watered. "I...I...you should rest, King's Son. You're weak and distressed. I will ask Carnus to join us and examine your curse mark. Then, we can discuss the Mitad and the Eye." The tone and darting of Grace's eyes told Eos she held closely guarded knowledge. He was sure that this woman had secrets about the Mitad and much more.

Processing the words, Eos felt the weariness in his body. Sleep became so enticing that he let the heaviness of his eyes drag them closed momentarily.

"You have caused quite a stir of Soul Energy in your sleep. Let's hope you have a calmer rest now, or else there will be Mitad mirza searching these mountains soon," Grace said. "We will have to teach you to better suppress your aura."

Saigo saw Eos drifting away and said, "Rest, Eos Bellator. When you wake, I will show you our people and our way."

ESSENCE OF LIFE

As he slept, Eos dreamed of training as an assassin in a village he had never been to, called Necogen. Yet, he knew its cliff boundaries, its teachers with the title Domin, and its bitter winter winds. He became lucid enough in this dream to realize that it was not his memory, and this caused him to feel guilty for not telling Grace Lapithos of her children's fate.

The thoughts lasted only moments, and he slipped back into Jezca's ephemeral tapestry of memories, loosely stitched together in the world of sleep.

When he woke, a castle servant brought him food and tea. He nourished himself on steamed rice and freshly caught fish with strange eating utensils. He grasped the two sticks in each hand, and fumbled with his meal until he resorted to eating with his hands like a savage, which matched his ravenous hunger after a week of being kept alive by Saigo's servants. He scraped the last grains of sticky rice with his fingers as Saigo entered.

The stern samurai raised a scabbed eyebrow and shook his head.

"There is much to teach you about our ways. The white elsu feeds with his fingers...unexpected. Come," Saigo said, clapping his hands together, "Get dressed."

Eos walked through the castle grounds in a simple gray-blue kimono, his stride struggling to keep up with Saigo's.

They passed stone lantern pedestals like the one he had dreamed about, sakura trees that had yet to blossom, and the rounded ends of the dark green clay roof. Past it all, lush mountainside rolled through a web of mist.

They spoke little at first, but Saigo led him with an escort of retainers outside the castle walls and into the surrounding village. Eos was in awe of how much nature surrounded the Akaishi Mountain citadel.

As they passed children running and yelling in play, women at work carrying food and clothes, and men chopping wood and practicing with swords, Eos asked, "What is this place, and why is it so...different from where we entered Nippon-Wa?"

Saigo smiled proudly. "This is the village hidden in Chichibu. Out there in Tokyo and Yokohama is the modern world. Here we find peace

CHAPTER NINETEEN

in the simple ways of tradition. From up in these mountains, you can see everything as it should be. Honor and harmony in all we do—in work, family, and battle."

Eos observed a culture profoundly different from anything he had ever experienced. For months since Maxima's death, restlessness haunted him. Stress, nervousness, and sorrow weighed down his every move.

Yet, amongst tall grass and simple people...he felt a serene peace that stilled his weary spirit.

They approached a field of training swordsmen who were repeating their swings again and again under the scrutiny of their instructor.

"Where is Grace?" Eos asked.

"Doing her work and finding the cowardly kami you call Carnus," Saigo said plainly as he brought Eos to the sword instructor. "Nakazawa will teach you kenjutsu."

Eos gave a questioning look.

"The way of the sword."

Remembering his lessons with shooting firearms under Major Clark, Eos embarrassedly turned down the offer, "No. I couldn't. Soul Energy is what I fight with...my powers. You know..." Eos lifted the wrapping over his arm that concealed his curse mark. "I couldn't—"

"Nakazawa will teach you. You know how to fight like a kami, but that mark Raijin gave you troubles your spirit. You are not at peace. The katana will teach you discipline and the way of life."

Eos looked at the line of men swinging wooden swords with elegance and power. Though he protested, something about the crisp movements of the katana that called him.

Seeing Eos' gaze linger, Saigo nodded. "Good. Practice. I will return this evening for you."

Square-faced with a short black beard, Nakazawa taught him to bow and handed him a wooden katana. His every move was met with suspicious looks. He came to understand the village whispered of him as something akin to a hanyo living with them.

ESSENCE OF LIFE

Still, Nakazawa instructed him, though harsher than he did the others. The swings of the blade and dance of footwork had him forgetting himself entirely, lost in the flow of the art form.

What began as becoming present in the art of kenjutsu evolved into losing himself to the way of bushido. Carefully prepared matcha tea started his mornings. His daily scenery was walking past farmers working in the rice paddies on his way to and from sword lessons. The sessions were exhausting to the point he collapsed asleep after dinner each night, still recovering from his coma. But the days brought inner tranquility to his psyche that he had forgotten existed.

Though it had been bothering him, he found the opportune moment and confidence to address his quiet yet intense samurai host after his third day of lessons.

Over a bowl of steamed rice, pickled vegetables, and skewered chicken, Eos asked, "Saigo, do my companions know I'm here? I must tell them what happened, and return soon."

Saigo ate another bite while Eos fumbled with his chopsticks. He then sipped his sake contemplatively, taking his time before responding.

"Saitani is furious that we brought you back here, but he is preoccupied after his failed raid and the attack on his home. Aizo knows you are here, but there is no need to rush. Are you not enjoying our village and our ways?"

"I am. More than I thought was possible, but I must return to my master and let him know everything that happened. Why hasn't he come here?"

"Accept everything just the way it is," Saigo mused over his sake cup. "Your father has returned. He and Aizo have business with Saitani to finish. He knows you are safe and healthy. They are doing what they must. There are multiple paths to the top of a mountain, and your path is here. You sought Himiko, *your Grace Lapithos*, and you have found her. She will return with Carnus to examine your hanyo curse."

Eos nibbled at his food clumsily with chopsticks. He remembered his orders to pursue duty and not desire. "Can I write to them at least?"

"Writing to them is no problem; however, it seems the hanyo are making extraordinary moves and have new authority. One of the strongest among them, Zeres, now blocks the mountain pass. Villagers have also seen their assassin demon with a skull helm. Delivering the message will take time."

"Then, Ahktar can deliver it. My elsu will find my father and deliver it in a day."

Saigo nodded once, communicating only what was necessary. "Then, it shall be done. You will write your letter after our meal. However, the matter of traveling in or out of the mountain is more difficult. Any movement out of the mountains will be monitored. Himiko said your kami presence would be felt, and you are in no condition for that battle against the hanyo."

Closing his eyes, Eos accepted the answer. "Just a letter, then."

That evening, he picked up a bamboo-handled writing brush and dipped it into the *yatate*, a pipe-shaped inkwell. He composed his thoughts and touched the brush tip to paper. Ink splotches spread, but he found a flow that put legible words on the page. He felt a vulnerability in communicating with writing.

The paper could not judge nor chastise him.

Ink spread, and his experiences bled from the brush.

Aizo,

I awoke from a nightmare. The Mitad's curse mark has been draining my spirit and body, but Saigo has taken good care of me. Something strange has happened here. I don't know how to describe these unusual people and their way of life other than peaceful. The samurai have shown me much that I do not understand, but I have found it stills my mind. I'm learning their techniques with the sword. They devote themselves to a set of principles here, and though I don't understand it yet, I enjoy it much more than expected. It's as if they have distilled the essence of life into a state of mind that is reflected in all they do.

I can say that I've had both my most difficult and most restful sleep in the Akasihi Mountains under Saigo's roof.

Grace Lapithos is here. She will return soon with Carnus, and they will examine my curse. I fear what they will tell me. Its influence is growing beyond my control, and I haven't wielded since I arrived.

ESSENCE OF LIFE

Saigo has told me that Visotmus' mirza are guarding the way in and out of the mountain. So, I only send this letter, though I wish to rejoin you as soon as possible. For now, I wait for Carnus and Grace to deliver my verdict...

Eos continued writing until he had filled the parchment. Then, he tied the rolled letter to Ahktar's leg and fed him seeds from a pouch he always kept at his waist.

There was a streak across the stars as Ahktar's wings disappeared.

The following day, Eos practiced katana drills facing his samurai partner among a line of robes.

They dueled.

Wooden practice weapons clunked as swings were blocked in a rapid sequence that he struggled to keep up with. His sword barely made it into position for the first three movements of the series. The fourth swing came around the side, but his coordination was too slow. He accepted his bruise on the arm with a grunt but did not let the pain show to the others.

Nakazawa laughed to one of the other instructors as he watched and said something in Japanese.

Eos did not turn his head but watched the mockery from the corner of his eye.

His partner, Kanbai, said in rough English, "Nakazawa say your technique is ugly."

Eos clenched his teeth and resumed his stance. "Hai," he returned.

He accepted the criticism and found himself forgetting the stray dog treatment from the mountain natives. They hid their concern behind courtesy and discipline, but he knew they viewed him warily as some kind of unwelcomed kami guest.

It didn't matter.

The sword and fresh air allowed him to slip out of his head and into a state of efficiency where he was only movement and purpose. It reminded him of wielding Soul Energy and was the closest thing to it he could practice.

"The katana is extension of you," Nakazawa repeated as he did every day in choppy English and adjusted Eos' arm and grip angle.

CHAPTER NINETEEN

That evening, Eos enjoyed tea with Saigo in the garden.

"Do you know what our name means?" Saigo asked.

Eos shook his head from side to side as he lifted his teacup.

"Bushido—way of the warrior. Honor, discipline, and duty. You have observed the bushi and their way, but we are not just *bushi*. We are samurai, and that means *to serve*."

"And what do you serve?" Eos asked.

Saigo paused for a while, sipping tea and reflecting.

He ran his hands through his sleek black hair and said finally, "I served my master, Emperor Toba, with my sword and my advice on his council. Now, I serve his heir, Antoku."

Eos nearly spit out his tea in surprise but tried to stifle his expression. "Saigo...you tell me Antoku is your master, and you serve him by being in open rebellion against him?"

Sighing, Saigo looked out the window with pain in his eyes as he explained, "I provide my advice to the Emperor. If he did not value it, he would have had me killed before now. I advised against letting Raijin into his inner circle, but other advisors insisted. He is only a child. Their pressure was too great for the poor boy, but out of respect for his father's love for me, he allows my rebellion. It is a piece of advice for him to contemplate always."

The complex workings of Japanese respect and duty confused Eos. He couldn't understand how a nation's leader could allow rebellion and keep the rebellion's leader on his council. "I don't understand your people's ways. And Saitani...?"

"Saitani was removed from the council, even before his rebellion. If he is caught, he will be executed. Antoku has a love for me that spares my life for a while longer. I tutored him in the way of the sword and horse riding. He practiced his English speaking with me during our lessons. I saw him more than his own father. An emperor is a busy man...but Emperor Toba was killed. Poisoned by the twisted workings of Raijin, though I don't know exactly how it was done. My oldest friend...lost in an evil kami's plot."

The profound sadness in Saigo's voice stirred Eos. It was as if a hole was cut in Saigo's core, and he was only a fragment of the man he had been. That incomplete man served out his duty with the last of his remaining lifespan out of honor in the narrow path that was left to him.

Saigo finished bitterly, "I want you to take Raijin and his hanyo back to Takamagahara and free this land."

Eos' stomach boiled. It was a sensation he had not felt since he walked with Caldus through the hospital shacks in the Mircite Valley. A mixture of fury and compassion called him to action, but reality weighed on his emotions.

"I...I would love nothing more than to defeat him and restore Nippon-Wa, but..." Eos raised his blackened hand and rubbed it as if it were an old aching scar. "I don't know if I can wield Soul Energy again."

They finished their tea in silence.

Finding solace in the way of the samurai, Eos picked up his practice sword and repeated the movements he learned on the castle grounds against the pastel sunset that melted orange and pink between mountaintops.

He continued on this way, slashing and blocking while reciting the oath of the Order of Soul Wielders. His mind would wander to dark places. Maxima. Dreams of Jezca. Fear of the curse mark. Thoughts of Talus' lost arm. Wondering if his mother worried while he was gone.

But the sword movement would only allow such thoughts for seconds before they were washed away. Half an hour passed in the meditative state until the orange sky gave way to night, and he heard a call from Saigo on the castle porch.

"Eos, Grace has returned with Carnus. It is time to examine that arm of yours."

CHAPTER TWENTY

THE WITNESS OF POLYCA

Guiding her platinum hair behind her ear so it wouldn't be in her way, Jezca Lapithos sat in her isolated Setudo castle room. She scanned the pages of her mother's journal, lost in contemplation about the contents, and only remembered to glance around with paranoia occasionally to assure herself she wasn't being watched.

Grace's intellect was on a level beyond the greatest minds on Corland if the codex that was her journal was any indication. She had constructed her own hieroglyphic alphabet to protect the information contained in the broken binding.

That was only the first layer of defense. Once Jezca had broken down the character system, she found that the words were in the ancient tongue. Most living scholars were not fluent enough to read and write in it. However, she could recognize the language thanks to her training at the Manus Temple with the priests. Still, she only had the vocabulary of her prayers and memorized passages. It was incomplete knowledge at the root of a cryptic system.

She could not take full credit for deciphering—at least, she didn't believe she could. It had taken three months to understand the alphabetic system, but the real breakthrough had come when communing through the beacon stones.

It was as if Grace understood what she was working on and planted the knowledge in her daughter's head. After that, the translation of Jezca's half of the journal became increasingly easier. Each day she lit the onyx gems and revealed their true ruby color, she treasured the art of interpretation. It was the closest thing to a conversation with her mother that she had.

In her official reports to Saida and Bellia, she only reported vague sensations of her mother, too distant to make anything out.

Some names were repeated often in the text.

Danaqi—an ancient word she knew as the angelic servants in the Masruh Orthodox and other religions.

Kenat—this she did not know.

Morax—the text focused large chunks of prose on the founder of the Order of Soul Wielders. However, the way Grace wrote about the historical figure was strange. It was as if she believed his actions were still playing out to this day, perhaps through some kind of secret organization. Unfortunately, she could not interpret much more.

Karnak—she understood he had been some mythological hero of renown in many eras past. It seemed he worked against the Kenat and left behind items that Grace was hunting.

Noximor—the evil one. Enemy of the manus gods and the Great Soul. It mattered not which religion; all the most ancient texts would name him in some variation as the antithesis of good in the world.

The words in between were mostly still untranslated, leaving sentence fragments and hints among illustrations and diagrams. The process strained Jezca's mind, but her rose-pink manus stone eye flickered with light as she worked.

A knock on the door.

CHAPTER TWENTY

Jezca had lost track of time. The sun was setting through her window, and it was the hour when Bellia called on her. She hurriedly closed the half-book and shoved it under her dress, where she kept it at all times.

Bellia entered after Jezca's invite. She was far along in the pregnancy now, and the bulge in her belly caused her to alter her walk.

With her hand on her unborn child, Bellia closed her eyes and said, "Good evening, Jezca." Her voice went quiet. "I came to observe the lighting of the beacon stones as usual...but I also have important news."

Jezca nodded, still distrustful. "Go ahead."

"Saida knows you have half of your mother's journal. When he returns next, he plans to take it and force you to reveal its secrets."

With her heart beating in her throat, Jezca stammered, "H-h-how could he know? Why would you tell me this?" The ornate golden circlet chains rattled as she shook her head.

"I'm unsure, but Saida knows. He has spies. Some emir and Voro have ways of seeing what you're doing if they choose." Then, Bellia's voice dropped to a whisper as she held her thin, dainty fingers over her child-to-be. "I will be a mother soon. My allegiance to the Mitad is waning with each day closer. There was another girl once who I did not help when I wished I could have. I won't make that mistake again." Bellia thought back to Maxima in the arctic hideout where the Mitad had been smuggling weapons shipments and how she had played a part in deceiving the young girl.

It left her a pinging regret as she recalled Tessio sedating Maxima. She had repaid the mistake at Mircite, but she would not betray her morals for Vistomus or Saida ever again if she could help it.

"What should I do," Jezca asked herself. "I'll fight him—kill him if I—"

"No. You mustn't attempt it," Bellia hissed. "You are an incredible wielder, no doubt, but Saida is in another league. I'll think of something. Give me time. I just need a little time."

In a trance of despondency, Jezca lit the beacon stones as she did every night. Then, she felt weary and dismissed Bellia without any conversation. She fell onto her bed, huddled against the beacon stones and the journal that pressed against her skin.

Sleep quality was poor most nights in Setudo. Jezca longed to speak with her brother one more time—to say things left unsaid. Yet, it was often her connection with the bold and talented Bellator King's Son that would jolt her awake. Tonight was no exception.

That night she saw through his eyes again, though past or present, she was unsure. Perhaps, it was only a figment of imagination, but she couldn't be sure these days. Her grasp on reality was slipping, and her perceptions were dissociating.

At sea, sailing past a torii gate. She had never seen such a structure, red wooden beams with a bowed roof, but the name appeared in her head as if Eos' knowledge was spilling over to her in the dream world.

Castles unlike anything she had ever seen. Little stone statues that reminded her faintly of the manus shrines used in Necogen and parts of the Winter Aisle. Foreign swords clashing in a society of warrior peoples. It was a strange discontinuous montage that jarred her senses.

Then, darkness.

The curse inside Eos that she had peered into.

The energy that had caused a crack in the Eye of the Manus Temple…its influence was growing.

It loomed in her dreams like a specter, and she knew it was taking greater possession of Eos. Like black smoke, it formed a screen that blurred the visions.

In a final glimpse into Eos' mind, she woke from a coma on a floor bed and spoke words that she did not control to a man who she identified with the word *samurai*. Her memory failed on what they spoke of, but all that mattered was the woman in the doorway when she turned around.

"You have found her…I am Grace…or was once…in a previous life on Hyperborea."

Tears poured uncontrollably down her face as she lay awake in bed for the rest of the night.

∞   ∞   ∞

CHAPTER TWENTY

"Do you know every king in Corland?" Maxima asked from behind her blue corcinth mask. She had worn the disguise as ordered, but worried it drew attention—which it did, but it also turned away more glances than it attracted.

After her first few days of practicing Fey's techniques of disappearing aura, Maxima found that she was nearly invisible to the common passerby and inadept wielding minds of the populace. They would look past her more often than not. Still, she was constantly scanning crowds and alleyways for the faceless horror of the Bishiwal.

Its form haunted her waking moments.

Around corners and between moving bodies, she'd imagine it.

But it would turn its head and reveal a commoner or an illusion of the light. Each instant of her mind's trickery gave her shivers.

Saier Fey's eyes crinkled with a nostalgic delight. "No, only half of them. At least five kings tried to court me in my youth."

Maxima had learned not to entertain Fey's jokingly egotistical comments more than was required. "Well, hopefully, you didn't reject Lenape's king in the past. We'll need him to like us."

Suppressing her soul's aura had become second nature to Maxima during her weeks in Lenape. Stealth practice was a constant assignment, and her talents were prodigy level.

The two of them could now pass through the Ignoble King Astor Bruinsma's warehouses unnoticed and slip behind guards without drawing the slightest suspicion.

"Oh, he has a soft spot for me," Fey said with a wink.

Observing shipments coming and going had led to their spying on a meeting with King Hika Tamat's go-between for personal royal supply lines.

That, in turn, led to contact with the head servant at castle Setudo. She had confirmed that a new girl was being protected within the castle walls.

From there, Fey was quick to contact King Tamat.

He was kind enough to grant a secret audience.

Now, they walked towards the patinated copper domes and twisted spires that resembled floating turtle shells dancing under the clouds.

THE WITNESS OF POLYCA

They crossed the bridge leading to the lake's center where castle Setudo sat. The guards had anticipated them and led them into the castle to meet a tiny woman, shorter than Saier Fey. Her face was hard, and her hands weathered. She bowed to the guests.

Her voice was soft but had an uneducated rhythm. "My name is Anahera. I will lead you through private corridors to King Tamat. He wishes you to be seen by as few as possible in the castle. He said you are...special guests."

Fey nodded. "Thank you, Anahera."

They immediately entered a side door and were led through a narrow passageway tiled with teal-blue ceramic like ocean water. After wandering through twists and turns, doors and secret corridors, behind statues, and through swinging bookshelves, they found themselves in the hall of the king.

Sea turtle banners draped around them. Patinated copper shields lined the walls between marbled pillars. A navy-colored carpet ran to the throne chair where King Tamat sat on his carved seat.

His brown brow furled with amusement, and his lips curled, suppressing a laugh as his belly moved.

"Master Fey, I haven't seen you in what, six or seven years?"

Fey and Maxima bowed to the Lenape King.

"True. It's been too long, Hika. Not that I hold all the blame. You've turned this island paradise into a den for two-headed snakes and pipe-crossed flags. Not so welcoming for an old inlume."

The king threw back his head and bellowed a burst of deep laughter as he tossed his tattooed arms up in admission. "Fey, you're as sharp as ever and just as beautiful as I remembered you. You're a welcome sight from these weary eyes. I think we both know it would take an army of inlumes to say no when the Mitad's emirs are at your door and Astor Bruinsma wants to do business. Perhaps that's why you and your masked Soul Wielder student are here? To liberate my kingdom with the great righteousness of the Order?"

"No, this old bag of bones is retired from the Order. Haven't you heard?"

CHAPTER TWENTY

King Tamat's eyebrows raised with his tattooed head. He scoffed and said, "Heard but did not believe. A waste."

Sinking into her performance and hunching a bit more, Fey sighed, "I don't wield much these days, and this is not my student. I only came for research purposes. She is my assistant and keeps my notes as a skilled scribe. We request access to your libraries."

"You know I could never say no to you, Fey," King Tamat said in a playful tone. The teasing was short-lived as his voice fell, "But I must warn, you must leave the island immediately after. I can have a boat ready for you tomorrow morning. You were right that my throne has become a web for spiders. Saida and others will demand that you are held for questioning. Best if you take what you need and save vacation for another time. Things have gotten...difficult. I find myself like a prisoner whose cell walls are closing in these days. So few moves left. Little room to maneuver."

"A king should never be a prisoner to his own throne, Hika. You know the game and its rules, yet you dabbled with the Mitad anyway," Fey said somberly. "We thank you for your hospitality and will use the time in your library well. Perhaps I can visit again when times are better."

"Perhaps, but I see storm clouds rolling in, not clearing up. You and the Mitad both know what's at the heart of Lenape."

After congratulating King Tamat on becoming a grandfather soon and making other minor talk, Anahera led them through a passage behind the king's throne.

They descended a spiral of stairs until Maxima lost count of the steps, and she sensed they were deep below the king's chamber. The castle's servant lit their way.

The soft artificial glow of lighting stones began as Anahera released effortless streams of Soul Energy. A liquid wavering followed each light from the water-filled alcoves they were mounted in.

"I am not allowed any further. This is the entrance to the Grand Library of Lenape," Anahera announced. She left them at a giant tortoise carving with its mouth open as the doorway.

Maxima and Fey entered a circular chamber. It was not particularly large, but the walls overflowed with tomes and scrolls. The shelves were crafted to look like golden-pink coral that branched towards the domed ceiling, which shimmered with the blue light of anima stone embedded in a painted sea. It created an underwater effect that relaxed those who entered the Grand Setudo Library.

Fey led Maxima to the center of the room and explained the indexing system and how to find certain kinds of texts.

Then she said, "There is vast and secret knowledge here. In ancient times, this library was so remote that the most valuable and elusive writings were accumulated here. Now, I believe Saida has been removing certain works from circulation and keeping them for his private study. The combination means we could spend a year here but we only get one day."

Maxima bobbed her head in acknowledgment, and they set to work. She found it difficult to resist opening every book she laid eyes on. Each title stamped into a spine or inked into the edge of a scroll case enticed her imagination.

Her mission was to learn about the Bishiwal and the Makanla Gates.

Information was scarce. She mostly stumbled upon references that were more legend and myth in translated editions from ancient languages.

"It says here that the Bishiwal come from *between worlds and between gates*...whatever that could mean," Maxima read aloud. "All these references are more like fairy tales and poetic myths."

"Write it down. Keep good notes and continue digging."

"Have you found anything yet?"

Fey looked up, confused as if she had only been half listening.

"Find anything? About the Bishiwal? No. I'm in search of other knowledge. That is your task, and I have my own."

Perplexed, Maxima probed further. "I thought we were here to understand what is coming out of the Makanla Gates?"

"I never said those words. *You* are researching that."

"And you are looking for...?"

"Priori business. Personal suspicions," Fey said absent-mindedly without looking up. Seeing Maxima's visible displeasure, she continued, "You are aware of the founders of the Order of Soul Wielders, yes?"

CHAPTER TWENTY

"Morax chose three. Cintish the Corlander, Jaruus the Krog, and Straquil the Mezclado. Which one betrayed Morax, in the end, is left to debate," Maxima recited.

Spreading open a new scroll with wide eyes, Fey nodded. "Good. I expected that from your level of intellect." She smoothed a curling edge of the paper. "I suspect that Morax found a new interest in his last year. The sixth era is of particular interest to the Priori."

"The Lost History," Maxima murmured.

"Yes. Writings from Morax are nearly impossible to find. Someone has been collecting and destroying them...or so I thought. Many such pieces of history were being gathered here. Saida and Vistomus do not lead the Mitad, they are more akin to a rank you could call high emir, but whoever does is directing them to erase Morax into only a myth of oral tradition. I suspect the Mitad master was doing this before Saida and Vistomus were involved. Instead of destroying the knowledge, some of it has been hidden here. A private library at the heart of a castle on a lake in the middle of an island that the Mitad control."

"And King Tamat...just let us in?"

Fey said with a wink and a smirk, "I told you I have charm. Besides, he has no idea that Saida has been collecting Morax's writings down here. He allows the Mitad to operate freely so long as they protect his island and don't interfere with his reign."

"And you want to know who really killed Morax and why they did it?" Maxima asked.

"I want to know what Morax found in the Lost History that led to his death. He may have been just as responsible for his own death as his disciples."

"How...could he...?"

"Never mind that. Time is short. Learn what you can. We may not see inside these walls again for a long time."

Maxima obeyed.

Even Maxima's voracious appetite for knowledge could not keep her head from falling over her books as the night wore on. The passing of time was marked only by the flickering of lighting stones, too numerous to count.

THE WITNESS OF POLYCA

A particular marking in a book roused her into an adrenaline-fueled fury. A character appeared on the page, not from the alphabet of any language she knew or had seen. Yet she recognized it!

Excitedly, she pulled her personal bound notes from one of her pouches and opened them to the writings from her night in Fanum Ortus. She recalled shattering the mirror that Eos had warned her about, reading for the first time about the technique of Blood Ascension in the *Philosophi and Disciplines of Magnan.*

But, more than those memories, she couldn't shake the image of paintings surrounding the map of Corland that had been hidden behing glass and under tapestry.

She set her notes down side-by-side with *Journeys of Maco Vasga Vol. II.* Sure enough, the rune in Vasga's second volume matched one in her notes that correlated to a remote place in the Vale of Aleric.

Vasga had written about his encounter with a crystal gate at a location he had only marked with this rune.

Progress! Still, something about the runes was familiar enough to bother her. Foreign shapes teased her with knowledge that was just out of reach.

There were so many symbols that she doubted they could all be Makanla Gates. Then, there were the paintings. The familiar landscapes and architecture that hung around the encased map in Fanum Ortus had reminded her of something that made no sense.

Pictures she had seen about foreign lands on Earth came to mind. Now, she only had brief notes about the painting descriptions and the rune she found in each frame's corner. *Huge stones in a circle on a green plane. Red wooden shrine with a small roof in the ocean. Pyramids of sand; three small; three large.*

Later, against the resistance of prolonged tiredness, she found an encased scroll. The symbol of the Order was upon the weathered bronze cylinder, and white skull shapes adorned the top and bottom. When she tried to open the endcap, it would not budge.

"Ah," Fey cooed as she leaned over to look at it. "A rare find. Allow me." The short Inlume moved around her stack of books and held the scroll case.

CHAPTER TWENTY

A circlet of topaz pink scrawled around Fey's head, made of soft light. It matched the case's emblem as three broken swords floated above her forehead.

With the touch of her thumb at the center of the case's symbol and a spark of Soul Energy that bounced off the metal, the protection mechanism clicked to life.

Fey twisted the cap and removed the scroll. "An inlume's lock. Well designed and effective. Trying to force your way in would likely damage the aged paper inside."

She spread the rolled parchment with thin hands and held it open as she read old words that Maxima didn't know.

"Someone has added a title to the work in a different handwriting. They called it *The Witness of Polyca*. The original author wrote in code, but it's simple, and the handwriting is rushed."

Fey's eyes darted from line to line as her mind churned to calculate the meaning hidden in ink. "It seems Polyca was one of Straquil's first and most favored students at the founding of the Order of Soul Wielders. This...is..." her voice cracked in disbelief, "the written account of the murder of Morax. It says here that Polyca went to call on his master late one night to discuss a new technique. However, Straquil was arguing with Morax in Straquil's private reliquary room that night. He hid out of fear of embarrassing his masters by witnessing their feud. He turned away, but there was a flash of Soul Energy. When he looked again, Morax lay dead on the ground."

"That's terrible," Maxima said bitterly.

"I know too well what happened to Polyca the following morning. In my research, multiple texts report that he was found dead. He is known as Polyca the Eclipsed, for his legacy and story is overlooked by Morax's funeral."

"Poor Polyca," Maxima whispered. "It seems Straquil killed more than one that night to cover his tracks."

"But why? It makes no sense. Morax himself was of mixed blood and known to favor Straquil." Fey fell back into her chair, exhausted. In the weakening stone light, the creases of her forehead appeared deeper and her hair duller, as if her weariness was releasing some spell on her age.

After a minute of silence, Maxima asked, "Master Fey, I apologize if this is asking too much…"

"Go on."

"Why do you pursue knowledge of the Priori—knowledge about the origin of the Order—so fervently? Yet, you have set aside your role in the Order itself. Why?"

A single heavy exhale was the only answer at first. Then, slowly, Saier Fey muttered, "I had a daughter. An errant on her way to becoming a fine inlume. She trained with your mother. Eventually, she became tangled in a mission that quickly escalated in scale and danger…" The lighting dimmed as Fey neglected to replenish the stones around the walls. Her voice creaked with age and sorrow that she never showed publicly. "I…lost her."

Wanting to console, Maxima raised a comforting hand.

"I want no pity, child. Back then, I wanted revenge. I wanted retribution. The other inlumes only bickered and cautioned. My passion for the Order died with each passing week they took no action and assigned no resources to aid us. The mission had led us three, Terrava, Jakka, and I, into the world of the Priori. We met Salvaluc and Rebus Bellator."

"But Rebus—"

Fey cut off Maxima, "Died? Yes, there were many casualties in this hidden world we discovered. Uncovering Sacrum Crypts attracts more than one kind of danger. Terrava and Rebus' love was kindled and extinguished far too quickly. That led to Terrava being forced to abandon anything to do with the Priori of Karnak, not that the Caerule family knew us by that name. I trained your mother to inlume after that, but our relationship was strained."

"Then you retired from the Order?" Maxima asked with compassionate hurt written on her face.

"One can never retire. It is a lifetime membership revoked only by excommunication. I contemplated earning that for a while. But no, I slowly became an inactive member. Took on no new students or

CHAPTER TWENTY

missions. My purpose was found with the Priori. It stilled my rage enough to carry on. I need no kind or consoling words from you. That's in the past. We're here wasting time in a library that we won't access again. What have you found on the Makanla Gates?" Fey lifted her sleeve and reminded Maxima of their purpose by exposing her violet-stained forearm.

Maxima resisted her natural urge to try comforting or empathizing with her master. She was too proud, stubborn, and brash to accept it. Instead, Maxima laced her fingers together, turned them out, and cracked her knuckles.

"I've found an explorer named Marco Vasga was marking the locations of what he called crystal monuments," Maxima explained.

"Good. We're out of time. Find everything you can that Vasga wrote and carry it up to our room," Fey ordered irritably.

"Can we do that?"

"Ask for forgiveness on your own time. I just gave you permission. King Tamat will understand...*if he ever finds out.*"

When they were above ground again, the melting orange waver of sunrise beams disrupted the shadows through castle windows. They arrived at their designated room, which Anahera had prepared with two made beds.

Exhaustion set in with a twinge of regret as Maxima looked at the bed she wouldn't get to sleep in.

"Now what?" she asked, knowing the time for sleep was passed, and the plan did not involve getting on the boat King Tamat had prepared for them.

Fey sat on the bed and closed her eyes.

"I wait. You hide," Fey said, moving the haul of scrolls under the bed, out of sight. "We need to find Jezca. I will be the bait, and you will search. They will reveal who the Mitad has left here, and that person will likely guard me. It will hopefully just be a locked door if I put on a good act. You will wait in the storage room until I give you the signal, which will mean it is time for you to find Jezca."

Less than an hour later, Anahera was left with her jaw hanging open when she saw Saier Fey still in her quarters.

THE WITNESS OF POLYCA

"You were supposed to be returning to the mainland by now!" the servant exclaimed.

Fey smiled warmly. "Turns out I left some important research material in town. I sent my assistant to get them; she'll return this afternoon."

Anahera shook her head furiously. "You mustn't remain here. King Tamat is reporting to the Mitad about your visit right now! They'll come to investigate your room within the hour to be sure. So leave now, or you will have to face *the Negotiator*!"

Playing up her retired, innocent persona, Fey only nodded again. "I have nothing to hide, child. Let them investigate. All they will find is that my research venture here is complete. By tomorrow I'll be off the island."

Anahera whispered something to herself in the ancient tongue. It was a passed down peasant butchery of the language, but Fey understood it to be a plead for the Great Soul to watch over someone facing certain danger.

"Even King Tamat can't save you now. Be careful," Anahera said in a low voice and rushed from the room.

As predicted, a drift of haunting aura came down the hall within the hour. The presence brought a chill as it neared Fey's door.

The room was thrown open.

A dress the color of nearly dark wine rushed in.

Fey saw a deep burgundy dahlia pinned to Lady Sugra's hair when she entered. By reputation and rumor, Fey immediately knew who was watching over castle Setudo.

Her mind crawled in rejection of the presence.

"Inlume Saier Fey, your presence in Lenape is unexpected. To what do we owe the honor?" Lady Sugra asked in a cool, raspy voice.

Voro! Her inner voice shrieked at her, but her logic prevailed as she greeted the Mitad officer like a feeble old woman.

"You didn't have the manners to introduce yourself, but by reputation, I can assume you are the one they call the Negotiator." Fey rose from the bed shakily, putting a hand on the bedpost to assist her. She stood with a slight hunch in her back, making her height diminished and her demeanor feeble. "I can assure you, it is little honor to have this

CHAPTER TWENTY

old wielder in your library. I am retired from the Order. Here only to do research."

"No one retires from the Order," Lady Sugra hissed.

"I did," Fey shrugged.

"Tell me why you're here and where your partner is, Fey."

"I came to research some curiosities that would bore you. Old age leaves me entertained by the most mundane topics. Did you know that Terrspar was explored by—"

"Enough. Where is your companion? King Hamat said there were two."

"I was set to leave this morning but realized I left an important piece of my research in town. My assistant is fetching it now. I don't move quickly anymore," Fey shuffled to the desk to sit.

Lady Sugra's eyes narrowed in suspicion. A shadowy violet spread from her feet as she stood in the doorway. "I don't know what trick you're playing at, but no inlume is foolish enough to walk onto this island unaware of who runs it."

The notion was correct, but Fey controlled her aura to such a masterful degree that it must have been perceived as dull and unthreatening. Fey put her hands up, "Only research. I mean no threat to you."

The maroon-black Soul Energy sprang from Lady Sugra's feet.

"No games! I will know if you're lying."

The walls turned black.

Soul Energy layered the boundaries of the room.

Streams of energy sprouted from the floor and pinned her to the wall by her wrists. The aura pulsed a violent funeral hymn into Fey's mind as the murderous intent was palpable. Despite this, she kept her wielding abilities suppressed, giving no indication she was anything other than retired and out of practice.

Suddenly, Fey was in Lady Sugra's shadowy coffin.

Her wrists burned, and Fey could smell the scent of her skin charring. She grunted frailly.

So, this is the horror that poor Terrava faced for days on end. It is a wonder she kept her sanity.

THE WITNESS OF POLYCA

Lady Sugra shrieked with pleasure. "What? Can an inlume not defend herself?"

"Haven't wielded in years. I-I'm," Fey let out a pained moan, "I'm retired."

Instantly the coffin shrunk around her until the Master Inlume was contained in a cramped box of Soul Energy. It suffocated and squeezed her.

In that moment—Fey knew that her wielding skillset did not allow her to defend against such an attack once it was around her.

Her life now depended on the believability of her acting.

For seconds, death neared with each breath that used up her available oxygen. The container shrunk so that it threatened to break her arms.

Still, she knew her best move was to continue with the plan.

Anything else would endanger Maxima and end their chance of finding Jezca.

In that last moment, Saier Fey was surrounded by darkness, unable to breathe, the world collapsing around her...and she only saw her daughter's face.

Soon Jakka. Soon.

"For your sake, you better not be lying."

The Negotiator released her Soul Energy, freeing Fey.

She fell to her hands and knees, coughing and gasping.

Lady Sugra sneered, "How far you've fallen from your reputation. They say you were quite something in your younger days, but I could crush you like an insect now. Your room will remain locked. Saida will be here in two days to decide your fate. Do not try anything, or you will relive my Shadow Coffin for as long as your body can cling to life."

Soon, my daughter. But not yet, it seems.

A flare of aura pulsed so that Maxima could sense it from the storage room at the end of the hall. She stretched briefly, stiff from her rest on the floor where she had waited patiently.

Then, she brought the blue corcinth mask down over her face. The sinister aura coming from down the hall had worried her. It was powerful

CHAPTER TWENTY

enough to threaten any inlume, but Fey's signal to her was calm and unbothered.

Knocking gently, Maxima whispered at the door, "Master Fey, are you alright?" She tried to turn the door handle, but it was locked. "I'll look for the keys to get…"

Her words fell as pink Soul Energy slithered through the door crack, up to the doorknob, and into the keyhole. The internal mechanism clicked as the energy wavered.

Fey opened the door.

Maxima was speechless.

"You'll have to teach me how to do that," she said in awe.

"Not all my secrets are for you," the Inlume teased, but her breath was heavy as if she had gone through an ordeal. "Now, there's no time. You must search for Jezca. To keep up my harmless appearance to the Mitad, I will remain here. Don't let your face be seen. Suppress your aura at all times." She placed her hands on Maxima's shoulders. "You can do this. I'll be observing the castle for any wielding that could reveal her location."

The ceramic horns bobbed up and down. "Yes, Master Fey."

Maxima set to sneaking through the castle, keeping her aura lowered to nothing more than a minor irregularity for anyone scanning with Observation Wielding.

First, she planned to watch the servant's quarters. Anahera had revealed that Jezca was indeed under Setudo's patinated copper roofs. Maxima recalled roughly where the servants worked from when they entered Setudo. Surely, one must attend to her room, even if it was only to deliver a meal to a prisoner.

Creeping near the wall, Maxima moved silently. She darted behind statues and down hallways, watching for castle dwellers and Mitad cloaks.

She found very few of either. The west wing of Lenape's fortress was mostly empty. Twice, however, she had to duck behind pillars to avoid being seen as someone ventured into the same hall as her.

The second time, she was confident that the waddling royal had seen her. Reacting in panic, she squeezed her aura down so that it was a pinprick against the backdrop of an entire fortress. Then, she collapsed it down even more as she hid. It was as if she had done more than hide her wielding presence—the man did not see her at all though his eyes surely crossed her as she fell behind a chalky stone column.

After half an hour of watching the disappointingly uneventful servant's quarters, Maxima decided to wander. Down a hall of Tamat family portraits, through a room of decorative spears and war displays, and past the delicious kitchen that smelled of simmering citrus.

Lamenting her lack of success, she became distinctly aware of another wielder approaching. Her face went cold at the surprise, and she gripped the mask to her face as she dashed down another hall.

The Mitad member moved slowly but made the same turn Maxima had.

Again, her path was followed.

A third time.

Maxima accepted that this was a pursuer, and a rush of fear flooded her. Her suppressed aura swelled into a signal at that moment, and she moved faster.

It was too late. By the time she sensed the use of Soul Energy, the Mitad member had closed the distance down the hall with Soul Step.

A delicate hand touched her back from behind.

"Wait," the voice said softly.

Maxima recoiled to see that Bellia stood behind her.

Slight relief came to her tense muscles, and she relaxed some.

"I know that aura," Bellia murmured, squinting her amethyst eyes at the masked figure before her. "Maxima! What are you doing here?"

"Bellia, thank the Great Soul, it's only you. I can explain—"

"You're going to blow our entire illusion. You're supposed to be hiding somewhere, anywhere as far away from the Mitad as possible."

"Yes," Maxima said slowly and put up her index fingers. "I was, but then something came up. We need to find Jezca Monte...and...you know, I owe you a huge debt. I never had a chance to thank you. Ares told me you were responsible for faking my death at the Mircite factory."

"Well, this is not how you should be thanking me!" Bellia raised her voice but remembered to drop it back to a whisper. "You are going to get us all killed!" she said, gesturing to her pregnant form.

CHAPTER TWENTY

"Oh wow! You're pregnant," Maxima said in shock. "I'm-I'm going to be an aunt?"

"That is beside the point," Bellia sighed.

Maxima refocused, realizing she was exposed if anyone saw them. "Look, Bellia. I wanted to kill you for what happened on Earth. Now, I owe you my life. And something has happened that I can't explain, but we need to find Jezca, and we know she's here."

Bellia brushed back her blonde hair over high cheekbones and said sadly, "Yes, I hope I've made amends for what happened on Earth. I couldn't act freely back then."

"And you can now?" Maxima asked, confused.

Waving her hand over her belly, Bellia let out an exhaling laugh. "I have other concerns to weigh in my calculations these days. Now, I'm guessing you're here because of Jezca's half of the journal. Saida knows, and I believe he's on his way here to confiscate it."

"That can't happen. Where is Jezca being kept?"

"Well, unless you think of a way to prevent it without betrayal being obvious, we'll all be hunted and executed by Lady Sugra. I'm transporting Saida here tomorrow evening. Then, he will take it from Jezca to complete the journal."

Sapphire eyes wavered as Maxima said with fierce certainty, "We can't allow that to happen. Please, Bellia, just take me to Jezca, and we will figure out a way."

Bellia muttered to herself, "If only it were that simple." As she said it, her lips pursed in thought. "Actually, it may be possible, but you'll need to do exactly as I say. For now, go back to your inlume's room. I will take you to Jezca when Lady Sugra leaves the castle this evening."

Pupils locked on each other as the two wielders analyzed the risk they were taking.

Maxima nodded. "You betrayed me once on Earth but gave me a second chance at life here on Hyperborea. I'll trust your more recent action, but if you think about crossing us—"

"I swear on my unborn child that I will take you to Jezca tonight and show you how you can all leave here without exposing yourself. For now,

THE WITNESS OF POLYCA

I must get to an appointment," Bellia said in a rush. "I'll see you at sundown."

The pregnant wielder held up two fingers as if performing an incantation and drew a small circle in the air.

With no delay, a violet beam of Soul Energy cut through the hall. It melted space itself as it zipped into a circle with smokey tendrils drifting from the trail.

The area enclosed in the violet light became a portal.

Through it, Maxima could no longer see Bellia where she stood. Like a mirror that showed another world, she observed a small boy huddled on the floor with his arms around his knees.

Zmmmm.

The portal ripped apart and snapped into itself as it closed.

Maxima stood alone.

When she returned, she found Fey meditating at the foot of her bed. The Inlume Master looked tranquil and more youthful than usual as new day's light cast a golden hue over her.

After explaining the situation, Fey only responded by saying, "All we can do is wait, then. Sit. Join me."

Obeying, Maxima crossed her legs and sat across from Fey.

Tired hands removed the pouch from around Fey's neck.

She removed the mirror shard tenderly and placed it on the floor between them.

"Ready your mind and steady your Soul Reservoir. It is time for you to use this piece of the Holy Penitus Ostium. You will need to prepare for anything that could happen tonight. This will not be easy. What is holy should be revered but also feared. For it brings about great tests and attracts powerful darkness."

Swallowing suddenly became difficult. Maxima frowned. "It's dangerous to use?"

"Extremely. But I don't know if I'll have another opportunity to guide you soon. Those who call it Amaterasu's Mirror also say that you will confront your shadows in it. That you may become trapped in its reflection."

"Is it true?" Maxima asked hesitantly.

CHAPTER TWENTY

"I have found it to be exactly true in my experience. Don't fear. I'll be here to direct you through the experience."

Maxima reached slowly and picked up the mirror piece.

It was smaller than her palm, so unthreatening and unnoteworthy. Yet, the moment her gaze cast into it, she felt a buzz of Soul Energy.

The sensation was like a choir of angelic voices and siren calls simultaneously ringing out under her skin. When she looked into the mirror—it was no longer a reflection but a window. She saw out into the room where she had sat with Fey.

The melodic hum of Soul Energy was no longer in her head but all around her. She released the glass in shock.

And it hovered in the air exactly where she released it.

She remembered the word Fey had used once for this place.

Soul Void.

CHAPTER TWENTY-ONE

HANYO PATHS

White foam and blue brushstrokes fell from a mountain scene in the painting across from Vistomus. He stared at it patiently.

Two mirzas waited in front of his table. They attempted to admire the painting as Vistomus did, but their interest in the art was brief.

A lanky, boyish face turned in his Mitad robe, twisting his neck back to look at his superior. "Lord Vistomus, forgive me for not understanding, but why are we all observing this waterfall?"

Vistomus was unwavering in his focus.

"Kallag, I think we're waiting for something else. The painting just happens to be there," the second Mirza said. He had a black ponytail and long nose.

"Cyra is correct, Kallag. Sometimes you worry me," Vistomus murmured as he sipped tea.

Kallag blushed and turned his yellow-green eyes back to the area of focus.

CHAPTER TWENTY-ONE

After another minute, there was a crackling jolt.

A violet portal opened up and appeared to rip apart the canvas of the waterfall before engulfing half the wall.

Two figures stepped through Bellia's portal.

The first was tall with straw-like hair and a face sharply gaunt like whittled wood. His expression was curled and soured as he stepped into the Tokyo castle and looked down at his leg.

A small, messy-haired boy clung to his pants like a toddler—though he was around fifteen years old by his looks.

"Welcome, Tessio," Vistomus said with a hint of awe in his voice. The cause was clear. He could not break his gaze from the young boy. "And welcome, Khasun. We've been anticipating your arrival."

Khasun hid behind Tessio, keeping his ash-toned face concealed. As he peaked out at the strangers, his pupils stole the room. They were a vibrant magenta that was speckled hypnotically with ruby. Where most Mezclado and Krog ethnicities had eyes described as amethyst, this child's were more pure and piercing from behind strands of black hair.

"Whoa, Tessio. I didn't know you were babysitting. Who's the kid?" Kallag said with innocent curiosity.

Cyra leaned in with interest, studying the child. He stroked his chin and exclaimed, "Those eyes…he's not just any kid. That's a Dacian. He looks like he's from a noble bloodline too."

"Now, now, Cyra. Let's not talk about our guest in front of him. You are correct. This is Khasun, the special elect of Master M." At the name, Kallag, Cyra, and Tessio's faces went pale and stiff. Visotmus continued, "He is the purest of Krog bloodlines, though not noble. He descends from their shamans."

"Wakahin," Khasun mumbled slowly.

Cyra was taken aback at the name. "I've heard legends about that Dacian tribe. They wield completely differently from us on the Corland. I believe they call it Nature's Pulse. Is that right, Kahsun?"

The boy only glared and gripped Tessio's pants tighter.

"Not a friendly one. That's for sure," Cyra huffed.

HANYO PATHS

Tessio broke free of the child's grasp, strode forward, and placed his bat-winged spear on the floor as he knelt before Lord Vistomus. The action forced Khasun's grip to break free.

"Rise, Tessio," Vistomus commanded. Then he addressed his other mirza, "Kallag, you've witnessed Tessio's abilities before, have you not?"

"Yes, Lord Vistomus."

"How would you describe them?"

Kallag put his index finger to his lip as he thought. "Well, I'd say he projects his spear...but it's not exactly like most manus stone weapons. It looks more like the spear itself extends."

Vistomus' teeth showed in a rare smile. "Good. Tessio, please demonstrate. Pierce the painting behind you."

Tessio bowed. Then, he whirled his spear as if warming up. Sitting in a low stance, he gripped the winged blade at the middle of the pole.

His palms glowed a light blue.

It spread to the metal of the spear handle.

The entire spear became illuminated as if the metal was molten.

Blue, then white.

Then, it tripled in length in a blink.

The canvas tore, and the waterfall painting was left with a hole as the spear returned to its normal state.

Khasun stumbled back in fright.

"I barely saw it," Cyra mumbled.

"Incredible," Kallag added.

"What did you see happen?" Vistomus asked.

Shaking his ponytail, Cyra speculated, "Well, it was like a manus stone attack, but closer to an afterimage of his spear than a projection. It's as if the weapon actually grew for a moment...but that's impossible."

"Is it? Tessio, come here," Vistomus called. "You've completed your training with the Sisters of Noxim, have you not?"

Bowing his head low, Tessio answered, "I have, Master. I've learned to push my technique further than ever."

"Take this anima stone and hand it to me without removing it from under the table." The Mitad Lord showed a sapphire-colored stone but held it out beneath the bamboo slab.

CHAPTER TWENTY-ONE

Once Tessio took the sapphire gem, Vistomus' hands waited above the table to receive it.

Tessio's hazel eyes focused intensely and then closed.

The black tendrils of the Mark of the Chosen filled his veins.

The curse mark darkened the veins in his face.

The stone flashed.

Blue spun on the walls in tessellations of the anima stone's surface cuts. It grew so bright that it appeared to lose form.

The gem became like a ghostly afterimage as it shook in Tessio's palm.

He raised it to the underside of the table and then pressed.

The violently vibrating stone passed through.

It disappeared into the wood.

As he continued to push, it emerged through the other side.

When the bright display of wielding ended, Vistomus plucked the stone from beside his teacup, pleased.

"The ability to vibrate at the molecular level with Soul Energy. So potent that the amplification of manus stones allows you to manipulate the physical form itself. Tessio, you have done well and proven your worth as a mirza."

Kallag beamed in amazement. "I get it! That spear is entirely manus stone at the core. When you force open your fourth gate with the Mark of the Chosen, you can even vibrate the thin metal layer around it." The teen Mirza had a boyish charm and curiosity, genuinely amazed by Tessio's skills. He whistled and added, "Must be one seriously *expensive* spear."

"Perceptive," Tessio muttered. He was not pleased to publicly reveal so much about his Severence but could not disobey Vistomus.

Flicking his ponytail while thinking, Cyra spoke, "Lord Vistomus, forgive me for not understanding, but why are we here? And why have you brought Tessio and this Dacian child to Nippon-Wa?"

Vistomus laughed a single weak exhale. "Tessio and Khasun have important work to do—Master M's work." A note of sadness dripped in Vistomus' voice after that. His words held a nostalgia that was lost on the others. "Khasun will be the heir to my legacy. Master M chose me

HANYO PATHS

for a unique purpose. It is a purpose that has played out, and now Khasun will build upon my efforts." He knelt at eye level with the boy. "You have great things ahead of you, Khasun. I will teach you."

A look of confusion was painted on Kallag's brow. He spoke with uncertainty. "Lord Vistomus, I...I'm still not sure why Cyra and I are here."

"Can't say I understand either," Cyra muttered.

Vistomus turned to them, "You two will be security for Tessio and Khasun when they perform Master M's work. They will be vulnerable, and you two are particularly suited to defending them."

Cyra stroked his cheekbones, "Are you expecting someone to try and stop them?"

"Their task requires the Left Eye of Izanagi. When we obtain it, you can be certain that Saigo and Saitani will make a final push against us. Talus and his band of intrusive Soul Wielders will likely provide their support." Vistomus turned and looked gravely over them. "So, yes. I expect...*conflict*. You will defend Khasun as if he is Master M himself. If his body is harmed, you will be punished as if Master M was harmed."

With head bowed, Cyra accepted the task. "I understand."

"Before that, I have another mission for you. Bysis and Diya successfully defended a weapons warehouse. We must keep those guns out of that Saitani pest's hands. With enough guns, Saitani could provide a military problem for Emperor Antoku. Combined with Saigo's honor and reputation, there is the making of a full rebellion. The weapons are at a choke point, and I expect them to need protection."

An hour after being dismissed from Vistomus' gathering, Cyra made his way to the far west wing of the Emperor's castle. In the basement, there was a medical facility. He found Bysis there, lying on a floor mat.

Bysis glared at the wall with pent-up anger and his shoulder bandaged where the arm should have been. His robe and a new katana lay at his bedside.

"That Kikujiro guy got you good, Bysis."

"Mmm," the brute grunted.

"How long they have you in here for?"

CHAPTER TWENTY-ONE

"Too long. Getting restless. They don't want me to reopen my wounds, but I'll be back to full strength in another few days. Nurse doesn't know what she's talking about."

"Back to full strength? My friend, you're missing an entire arm. I've advocated for you to Vistomus, but he's going to give your title to someone else," Cyra clicked his tongue sadly. "I left you a new manus katana while you were sleeping though."

Bysis finally looked at his visitor. "Nah," he grunted slowly and sat up. "I've had nothing to do but work on this technique for the past few days."

Silver light sprouted from his bandages in veins of writhing Soul Energy. They joined together into solid form, only for more strings to sprout.

An arm of Soul Energy took shape.

Bysis flexed the fingers of his newly formed hand.

They shone like headlights behind mist, and he grinned.

"It takes a lot of energy and focus, so it weakens my other blasts," he paused, grabbed his katana, and unsheathed it as he stood. Then, continuing, he bellowed, "But I find my blade swings are even more powerful!"

The lumbering giant wound back the blade in a ferocious motion worthy of the half-demon name, hanyo, and swordsmanship that was more eloquent than could be expected from his bulky body.

The blade shone as he prepared a demonstration.

Cyra leaped in front of the swing.

The blade came down with a pulse of light emitting from it.

Dull gray-blue Soul Energy formed a wall between the two.

Zmmmm! The Soul Energy wave rushed from the metal and collided with Cyra's shield of slate blue.

The attack sizzled against the barrier but instantly shrunk. It receded into the defensive technique like a sheet of paper being crumpled. It snapped into a condensed form and then sucked into Cyra's energy.

The slate-colored wall splintered like a shattered Solido that had been overcome, but as the fragments broke away, the silver light re-emerged in the spaces in between.

HANYO PATHS

Bysis' attack became a tamed layer that held all the pieces suspended before bleeding into and then becoming Cyra's misty gray-blue color.

Cyra summoned the energy back into his hands and scolded Bysis, "Idiot, we can't damage the Emperor's castle like that! We'd never be allowed back." Though he had recalled Soul Energy, he clenched something physical in his grip.

Bysis let out an energetic belly chuckle. "I knew you'd use that ability. You never let me destroy things." He curled one bleached eyebrow as his slow mind worked. "Well, wasn't worried either way. Don't care if I'm invited back here anyway."

Exhaling with exasperation, Cyra complained, "That was a strong attack. I almost couldn't contain it, Bysis."

Laughing even more, Bysis explained, "That was nothing. Just a sample."

Cyra's face went pale.

"You know?" Bysis strode for the door. "I'm feeling healed up already. I'm done sitting around here."

The massive frame starkly contrasted Cyra's average height and long limbs as they walked out the door together.

The silver arm faded away into luminous vapors.

∞   ∞   ∞

A raspy breath slowly escaped dark lips and condemned life without forming any words. Zeres Teritus looked down the patchwork of greenery and brown cliff at a small village seated in the valley below. He stood like a specter against the mountain backdrop. His looming figure cast an impending death sentence—his left eye was scarred closed from battles decades ago, but his right was fixed on the huts.

"The end comes quickly," he finally murmured in a gurgling slur of words. His silver mane of shoulder length hair waved in the wind as a rotting smell blew through the valley. "You may thank your hermit wielder's cowardice."

CHAPTER TWENTY-ONE

The open sky above him was overcast like gray paint bleeding through paper. Something in the mood of the sky tore his memories back to thirty years ago.

Back then, Visotmus had slaughtered his personal guard and intruded on his throne room, which consisted of a stone chair seated on a mountain plateau.

Vistomus Fulmen had stood calmly, staring Zeres in his one good eye. Three bodies lay at his feet, on display to slow any inclination towards violence.

"Great Barbarian King of Cavnan, Zeres the Harbinger," Vistomus said with a tease. "That is what they call you. I did not wish to kill your men, but they left me no choice."

"Mmmm. Yes, you come alone," Zeres rasped, "into my castle. Most impressive."

The bald head tilted as Visotmus asked, "Castle? You call this plateau a castle? There isn't even a roof."

"Everything under the sky...as far as I can see, belongs to me. *My castle*. I am a king."

Vistomus stepped over the fallen bodies of Zeres' guards, making sure to raise his eyebrows just enough to question the claim without outright denying the large man. "I've heard your unified tribes force King Oriq to bend the knee to you. Yet, you allow him to keep his castle while you remain here?"

The scarred, arrogant face sneered. "Diplomacy and formalities are his domain...for now. He will pay his tithes to the true king, and I will allow him to wear a decorative crown and gather my tithes for me."

"A wise choice..." Vistomus raised his tone with anticipation. "Still, my observers have noted that you have sent multiple military detachments back toward the capital."

Zeres laughed silently. His chest heaved as a malicious grin spread. "Boredom has its price. They are a gift so that he may have better luck in our next battle."

Deranged.

HANYO PATHS

Vistomus held his tongue from his true thoughts. The madness of this barbarian lord impressed him. He couldn't help but let his thin lips smirk.

"Now, Mitad leader, is it? You have one chance to walk out of here alive. State your purpose and then bend the knee to Zeres Teritus, King Under the Open Sky."

Spreading his hands open innocently, Vistomus began, "Perhaps the thirst created by your insatiable boredom can be quenched, Zeres. You seek a grander purpose and new challenges in battle. Serving in the Mitad could provide that—"

There was a bellowing, slurred grunt. Two thick fingers waved, barely raised from his armrest. Two giants strode from behind the throne. The curved blade edges of their scimitars were immediately brandished, glowing red with Soul Energy.

The massive frames moved slowly, allowing time for their size to dwarf their enemy's ego as it did in every conflict. However, this lone man only looked at them with a mild expression and eyes gleaming with an expectation of some kind of deal.

The two guards exchanged perturbed looks, their brutish brows furling. Then, they shuffled forward aggressively.

A black-cloaked arm responded with a sweeping martial arts motion, coming across Vistomus' core and extending out with fingers pointed and palms up.

The cloak snapped with the sharpness of the gesture.

Air crackled.

Plasma flittered in the atmosphere.

Lightning emerged from the ionizing air.

Purplish-white arcs shrieked, ripping apart the sky.

Bolts pierced the space between the men and found their skulls. Both went limp. Collapsed. Lifeless.

It only took seconds, but Zeres was left alone on his throne. His expression contained no concern for his fallen men. Instead, his nose curled in a defiant look.

Crackle-Boom!

CHAPTER TWENTY-ONE

Again, Vistomus summoned forth energy in the form of plasma-lightning. This time, it was marbled with black veins.

It struck the solitary throne!

Zeres' hand glowed like a manus stone where the lightning connected. It had been a warning—only a hand. *This time.* He did not grunt in pain nor acknowledge the wound other than to clutch the blackened hand with his unwounded one.

"I offer you purpose, Zeres. Power beyond your imagination comes with that purpose. You will make an excellent officer in the Mitad."

All these years later, Zeres' hand was still marred. He had never regained the use of it beyond twitching his fingers. A strong desire to kill bubbled up in his chest. His scars ached across his body, and his thoughts switched in a moment of distraction to Vistomus. *I'll kill that man one day. I am the King Under the Open Sky!*

The task at hand regained his focus. The stench of decay honed his thoughts back to the Japanese village below. How strange to have become a warlord feared to be half-demon in a foreign world. This was not *his* open sky. It was some bizarre *ostaka* world where neither the peasants nor the lords could wield Soul Energy.

Insects before me. I am a warrior king!

Soul Energy drifted from his crippled hand, dark as shadows on a moonless night. It spread down the cliff like billowing smoke.

I am a benevolent king. Those who run quickly may be spared.

Over the next ten minutes, a wall of Soul Energy crept to the edge of the village, scorching and razing everything in its path. Peasants and workers had begun to take notice of the evil manifestation descending on them. They gawked and pointed and yelled amongst themselves.

The first buildings it reached began to crumble.

It proceeded, a miasma that rolled into the village at a speed that could be escaped with a jog, but many were caught unaware.

Screams of horror, pain, and death echoed up to Zeres.

He neither took pleasure nor felt any remorse in the devastation. The grass roofs and tilled lands were beneath his status. Its inhabitants were nobodies in a foreign land that held no value to him.

Orders. This was merely business.

HANYO PATHS

Thirty minutes later, he exhaled with annoyance as he looked over the ashen field of rubble and bones. *Not a single wielder to challenge me in this whole nation. Once we have the Left Eye...then I can leave this ostaka land.*

Zeres' barrel chest blurred through the sky as he followed Naith's directions. The Voro member known as the Pursuer had pleaded to handle the situation himself, but Vistomus had already decided. They would push Carnus to divulge information about the location of the Left Eye sooner. Zeres would be the instrument to apply pressure.

Naith was too familiar, too intertwined with his Hamirate brother.

Zeres slowed his hulking body outside the hermit's hut and marveled at the squalor of the once-great Hariban of the Viator Kingdom.

He offered no knock. No greeting was given.

Only the slow roll of his Soul Energy under the flimsy wooden door announced his presence.

Inside, Carnus felt the ominous aura before he saw it. When the smokey-black energy crawled under his door, dread sank through his entire body as if being pulled to the bottom of the ocean with weights around his ankles. He knew well who the aura belonged to. Zeres' arrival meant only one thing for him.

Outside the door, the voice drawled in a deep gurgle of words, "Naith was too generous with his offer, dear Carnus. Vistomus says your time is up now. The nearest village has been erased. It is time to end this game."

The energy reached his fire as he pressed himself against the wall to distance himself from the crawling death. The fire whipped with life below his tea kettle, but when Zeres' Soul Energy reached it, the intense heat died, and the light was snuffed.

The kettle's stand crumbled, and the metal vessel fell into the darkness and turned to singed dust with the last embers of firelight.

Carnus bowed his head.

He cursed the Great Soul and the Hamirate teachings, which told him to trust the divine plan. Stroking his silvering beard with absolute exhaustion, he tried to see the work of the Great Soul in this wickedness.

He cursed life itself. Most of all, he swore aloud his hatred for Vistomus Fulmen—the perpetrator of his ruin.

CHAPTER TWENTY-ONE

Carnus searched his soul for the last remaining pieces that hadn't been crushed and pulverized by his possession under the Mark of the Chosen. He gathered that remaining reflection of his essence to face the end of his journey.

So many lives lost in that one village—people Carnus had shared meals with, healed, and loved. More villages would follow, he knew. He had to stop the death now before becoming responsible for an entirely new massacre.

"Yeah. Alright," he growled with a renewed desire for vengeance kindling.

∞   ∞   ∞

The anti-hanyo movement had grown to an unhealthy rage across Nippon-Wa. Protests and rallies had become commonplace. Though, they usually scattered upon the first hint of authority cracking down. That was until one week ago when Vistomus replaced all politicians who had friendly pasts with Saigo Takayoshi.

To the citizens, this was an act beyond disrespect for the old ways. It signaled Emperor Antoku giving the kami political power to undo the democratic process. Riots spread across the country.

The Tokyo cityscape was now marred with fires. The Metropolitan government building was facing a mob of angry citizens and flames lapping at the building's edge from the concrete. Fire reflected in the glass panes of the looming forty-five-story building.

Rius Yama and Artera Kyte sat on a nearby rooftop, watching the scene. Rius' long brown hair flowed in the wind at this height.

Artera smirked. "So, Vistomus won't let you back in at all?"

Thin lips pursed as Rius grunted in affirmation. "Not until I bring back Eos Bellator."

Artera's skin was not just the ashen tone of the Mezclado but also had a caramel base. Her hair was so dark that it had a violet hue and was pulled back into a tight bun. She was tiny in frame, less than five feet. However, confidence exuded in her voice and body language as she kicked her legs over the edge of the Tokyo roof.

HANYO PATHS

"Should've brought me," Artera chided.

"I wanted to take Eos alone."

"How'd that go?"

Rius clicked his tongue to disregard the question. He cracked his neck. "I have a plan. I learned where he's hiding."

Artera looked at Rius with insulted eyes. "Will you allow me to help you this time?"

Rius stood so his toes hung off the ledge, ten stories above the ground. The rioters clashed with police across the street. The respectful and peace-loving people of Nippon-Wa had overcome their honorable nature in rage against Vitomus' takeover. Their roars and cries were getting on his nerves.

"If you don't get in the way, Ara, you can join me."

Hurt was etched on Artera's face—not from the insult but from the distance of her companion.

"In fact," he continued, "I'm planning to take all my serving viziers with me. And yours. The duel is mine, but everyone else will be in my way."

"So, you want me and the viziers to allow you to capture Eos?" Artera curled one side of her mouth in begrudging acceptance. "You know that I'm a mirza too, right?"

White-blue Soul Energy flickered around Rius as he stepped off the roof. Planes of energy supported his feet. He continued without looking back at Artera, "Don't compare our skills, Ara. I have kept you around as a friend, but I could challenge Vistomus and Raggan." He thrust his chin up haughtily. "In single combat, no one can threaten me."

Rolling her eyes, Artera sighed. "Any of the other *hanyo*," she used their Nippon-Wa title sarcastically, "would be willing to fight to the death over that statement. I know Zeres wouldn't take kindly to the claim."

"Let them. Not one of them impresses me. A lumbering idiot, an old barbarian with a crippled hand, a demonic witch who buries manus stones in her skin, a kid who throws a decent punch, and defensive specialist with no bite…"

"Reckless and ruthless, Rius. Besides," Artera continued, "I only said that I also rank as a mirza meaning that you should rely on me more."

CHAPTER TWENTY-ONE

She looked at his fiercely handsome figure as he loomed over the protest. Her gaze lingered longer than intended, and she caught herself. "If you say back off—I will not get in your way. If you say lay down my life, it is yours. It has been that way since we were teens. Tell me, though. After you defeat Eos, will that get you closer to your goal?"

Rius huffed and threw his head back. "So dramatic, Ara. I get it. You want to fight beside me, and you will this time. This time…yes…I'll be closer to finding who ran the slave house. I need to get closer to Vistomus and Saida." He paused for a while as the frenzy below grew. "Your decision to pursue the general Inner Path instead of Severance perplexed me for as long as we have known each other, but I must admit it comes in handy at times like this."

"Remind me, how many of the Inner Path arts you've mastered, Rius?" Artera jabbed. "Not everyone is suited to Severence. I have mastered seven of the Inner Path arts. That is enough to contend with anyone who has opened even the fourth gate of their soul."

Rius grinned back wolfishly and ordered, "Well, let's see one of them now, raise your walls."

"This is not going to gain any favor with the people."

"I don't need their love—just fear," Rius snarled.

Artera pressed her palms together, folded her fingers in a complex mudra and focused. Her hands glowed white.

"Inner Path Twenty-Eight—Soul Barrier," she mumbled with the slightest movement of her pecan-colored lips.

In the distance, sheets of snow-like Soul Energy raised around the rioting populace. They were immediately caged. It took only moments for them to realize and begin pounding against the walls of Soul Energy.

Contact with Artera's Soul Barrier burned their skin, and their panic grew as shrieks of pain sounded inside.

Artera's technique was so perfected that even most errant-level Soul Wielders couldn't crack the barrier. The mob of ostaka could do nothing but injure themselves against it.

Three icy blue forms manifested around Rius. They flickered like ghostly creatures, solidifying into the shape of wolves and then wavering unstably. They ran ahead of him as he casually descended on planes of Soul Step towards the confined crowd.

His wolves bound ahead of him, paws stamping at the air.

Their tails painted the skyline with afterimages of blue light.

They leaped into the den of imprisoned rioters with a static crackling as their growl. The claws and fangs set to work immediately, tearing through the flesh of all in their path.

Blood sprayed in a scarlet mist.

The Soul Barrier became a boundary for death.

Rius stood above the white walls and watched with a sadistic grin. He called down, "Lord Raijin tolerates no disobedience. For rebellion, there will only be death."

Over the cries, moans, and iron smell of the blood-filled air, Artera joined Rius with a cold expression. She looked at the scene of brutality with indifference. "So, where will we find Eos?"

Soul Energy zipped around in feral blurs.

Bodies were torn, and final breaths were exhaled.

When the cobalt creatures ceased moving, they stood upon a pile of corpses. Then, Rius released them into vapor.

"He's with the samurai. Cowering in the mountains with Saigo and his sword carrying ostaka."

Artera's technique was released, and crimson ran in the street.

"How did you find him?"

"I had a couple vizier of mine in the woods outside the weapons storehouse that got raided. I wanted to know how it turned out. One of them caught Eos' trail…until a bunch of samurai got involved. I let Naith pick up the scent from there."

Frowning, Artera questioned Rius' ethics, "You left scouts outside a raid that resulted in Bysis losing an arm, but you didn't have them assist in defending the weapons?"

At this, Rius howled with laughter. "I take particular pleasure in knowing that great oaf lost an arm while my men stood by!"

"You're sadistic, you know that?" Artera smirked.

"Oh, Ara. I know you despise the other *hanyo* as much as I do. Don't play loyal with me."

CHAPTER TWENTY-ONE

They left the scene behind them as they stepped on planes of Soul Energy into the sky. Blood and corpses reflected off the multitude of repeating government building windows beneath them.

Thinking pensively, Artera thought back to all her years with Rius. She would help him achieve his goals, no matter what. Despite her dislike for Rius' arrogance, she couldn't deny his formidable combat ability and wicked charisma. It magnetized her to his presence.

Ruthless. He always leaves a trail of death wherever he goes. This Eos Bellator better be something special, or he will be a bloodstain in Rius' path.

CHAPTER TWENTY-TWO

FRACTURE ORIGIN

Thin paper screens and sliding doors faced Eos and Saigo as they waited, seated on zabuton floor cushions under the wooden roof beams.

Saigo ran a hand over his freshly shaved face. Whatever weighed on his mind was apparent, but instead of voicing it, he said to Eos, "Aizo will join us shortly. I received word that he intends to arrive this evening, maybe even before Grace."

Eos' golden eyes lit up. He smiled and replied, "I've missed him."

An hour later, the screened door slid back.

Grace's white-blonde hair was pulled back into a bun, pinned with gold and jade. Her red and white robes fell around her like a work of art. Beside her was a man worn around the edges and battered inside. He wore his exhaustion like a piece of crumpled up paper that had been smoothed out again. His every movement was stiff and calculated.

CHAPTER TWENTY-TWO

Black hair streaked with gray parted in the middle down to the shoulder. Steel eyes quivered over a simple, earthy-tan kimono. At his waist was a sheathed katana. He would have never been allowed into Saigo's castle with such a weapon, but they had entered through the sky using Soul Step.

Saigo bowed his head slightly, "Welcome Himiko-ojou and Carnus-san. We have eagerly awaited you."

Both fell to their knees and bowed prostrate to show the deepest respect, then joined Saigo and Eos on the zabuton cushions.

Carnus spoke in a deep rasp, "Thank you, Saigo-sama. Forgive my long absence. I have been...unwell." His speech had a growl to it that was not aggressive, rather it matched his rough demeanor. He was a man of few words and blunt speech.

"You are most welcome back in my castle, powerful kami," Saigo indulged him. "I see you've found a weapon after all these years."

Nodding his head, Carnus explained, "An old manus blade I had buried. The hanyo have come to visit me...a precaution. I don't wield anymore."

"We need more than precautions these days," Saigo gestured to the raven-haired young man beside him. "This is Eos Bellator, son of Talus Bellator. I believe that name means something among the kami."

"It does. It's an honor to meet you here in Nippon-Wa, King's Son." Carnus bowed his head, fully engrained in the ways of the island nation now.

Eos activated his anatus crown with a single crimson broken sword at his forehead. It was a gesture that Aizo had taught him to use as greeting to respectable wielders. "Likewise, Carnus Solaire." Despite the widening of Carnus' eyes and humble nature, Eos was deeply afraid of what was to come.

"I haven't seen the crown of the Order in a lifetime..." Carnus' rumbling voice trailed off. He saw the tension in Eos forehead and around his lips. "I know why I'm here. Because you have a curse. The same one I have. What I tell you will not be pleasant...but the Hamirate Clan have a saying from Zeri the Great. It was spoken to me during my time of need. He told me, 'Be at peace. The Great Soul will shield you from suffering or give you the strength to bear it.'" The humble warrior paused again and grimaced. "We're the same. The Great Soul has chosen for us to be bearers."

A clap came from the doorway.

"Zeri the Great's wisdom is for the ages. I return to his collection of philosophy often," a wily voice chimed.

"Aizo!" Eos exclaimed and nearly jumped from his seat to greet his inlume master.

A guard escorted Aizo into the room. He bowed deeply to Saigo and said, "Hello, my boy. I'm glad to see you recovered after your run in with the mirza. And Master Saigo, I thank you for taking care of my young disciple."

"It is an honor, though I nearly killed him first," Saigo mused.

"I've been tempted many times and nearly done the same. A common urge," Aizo assure him with a sly grin.

"Aizo Mudar?" Grace and Carnus echoed in shock.

The inlume flashed his circlet of Soul Energy with three broken swords and grinned. "At your service. Quite the meeting of famous wielders in one strange foreign land, but let's not dwell on it. We've been on a long journey to find Grace Lapithos and Carnus Solaire."

Nodding stoically, Carnus agreed. "Let's begin then. Eos, I'm going to ask you to open as many gates of your soul as you possibly can. Perform the most advanced form of Severence you're capable of." He put his callused hand up and touched two fingers to Eos' forehead.

Eos hesitated. He looked down at his blackened hand wearily. "What if I can't..."

"Can't control it?" Carnus finished. "I don't expect you to. Stop wielding the moment you lose control."

Aizo's wild bronze hair bobbed as he nodded in reassurance to Eos.

Clearing his mind, Eos obeyed. He manifested crimson light, but it was immediately marbled with a black fire. *Emotions calm. I'm in control.* The image of his soul essence came alive as the blazing avian Soul Energy filled his mind. For a moment, unnoticed by Eos, his natural energy's color overcame the darkness.

CHAPTER TWENTY-TWO

Then, he pushed further. A Soul Elsu crackled into being under the timber ceilings. It circled its master overhead as the curse spread over it.

Carnus did not remove his touch on Eos' head. His Observation Wielding worked through the silence, deciphering internally what Eos' skin was already revealing as the Mark of the Chosen spread.

Before it reached his face and the elsu turned to a majority of foreign energy, Carnus commanded him, "Enough."

Soul Energy abated.

The room hung on Carnus breathing. He clenched his chiseled jaw and frowned with psychological pain.

"Do you know of the Voro?" he asked.

"I've heard of them. They're members of the Mitad?"

A bitter grunt answered first. "When you lose yourself to the Mark of the Chosen entirely, you lose your consciousness, your willpower, and…your individuality. If you give in all the way, the Master's power is granted to you in greater portion, but you lose yourself. Your mind becomes linked to the Master's. Your wielding becomes subject to his whims. You become a mere puppet. A tool for his purposes."

Aizo mumbled, "That is the meaning of Voro?"

"Yes, they are the ones who are lost to this curse...some by choice. Others by lust for power. As formidable as any emir or more so. They are special agents who operate outside of the Mitad's standard hierarchy," Carnus returned. "I was once like you, Eos. Then, I almost became one of them. Once you get to that point, there is no turning back!" he whispered fiercely.

"Then how," Eos' voice waivered with grim anticipation, "…how do I remove it?"

A straight forward answer was not given immediately. Instead, Carnus grasped Eos' wrist, opened his hand so his palm towards the roof, and tapped it with his fingers.

Eos sensed the faint frothing of Observation Wielding. It was not so noticeable as manifesting Soul Energy exteriorly, but it produced distant vague pulse, like a lighthouse through a thick fog.

"Your work?" Carnus asked, turning to Aizo.

"Yes. Long ago. When he was only a child."

FRACTURE ORIGIN

"Good. It's good. This seal has kept him from becoming one of the Voro." The gray-blue eyes turned to Eos once more. "You best thank your master. He has saved your life many times over. The curse is accumulating in your arm because Aizo's seal prevents it from having free reign through your Soul Reservoir. Now, that seal is weakened. Whatever you do, don't break it entirely."

"Or what?" Eos' voice filled with dread.

"Or you must contend with Master M's energy…and lose yourself most likely."

Eos was getting frustrated. "Who is this Master M? And why haven't you told me how to get rid of the Mark of the Chosen? You're healed from it now, right?" The words flooded out more aggressively than intended. Years of searching for answers had him impatient in the final seconds.

Carnus turned away, looking sadly at Grace's beauty.

Grace picked up where Carnus struggled to speak. Her words were soft and careful, but wise. "Master M is the leader of the Mitad. He commands Saida and Vistomus, who are the only two members to push into the domain of the Voro and yet maintain control—mastered the Mark of the Chosen, you could say. They are still tied to Master M as far as I can tell, but retain their individual soul and will. No one knows who Master M is. I'm not even sure Saida and Vistomus do. They just carry out his plans. Neither of us have met him, though I have my suspicions."

Aizo hummed worriedly. "We shall discuss those suspicions at another time, Grace. There is much about the Mitad, the Tools of Karnak, and the Priori that we need to know. But first, Eos' curse." He tilted his chin at Carnus.

"I never removed or overcame the Mark of the Chosen in any sense. Merely suppressed it." Carnus looked up sheepishly, "I told you we're bearers, Eos. It's a part of us. We're flawed and must remain that way. Always fighting. Always on the edge," his words trailed off as he remembered painful memories. The corners of his eyes crinkled as he said through clenched teeth. "I have not wielded in twenty-three years. I will not let myself fall over that cliff and hurt anyone else. We can control our emotions and call upon our soul's essence, but that is only a way to delay and slow the creeping possession. If you wield purely…avoid even the slightest use of the curse…but the temptation is nearly impossible to avoid when battle instincts take over."

Eos fell back off his cushion. "What do you mean? Are you telling me we came all this way…*for nothing?*" He looked at his cursed hand in horror, desperately wanting to tear it off and face whatever agony was required to be done with his burden.

"Not for nothing," Carnus reached out to Eos. "I can teach you how to suppress it. But you will have to be careful wielding from now on."

"If your techniques worked," Eos' voice raised, "then why don't you use them? Why don't you wield anymore? Saigo says you gave up the warrior ways and live the life of a hermit avoiding all danger and conflict! That doesn't sound like suppressing the curse. That's running from it."

Carnus' hands shook. The words pierced his heart.

With a parched voice, he conceded. "You're right, King's Son. I am running. Hiding. *A coward.*" He turned slightly to hide his face from Grace. "But you must understand…I've done things no human can imagine. I've committed atrocities that can't be atoned for. So, I choose to live out my last days in some semblance of peace, asking for forgiveness that I don't deserve, and trying to bring some tiny bit of good to the people of Nippon-Wa."

Aizo squinted and said slowly, but commandingly with Soul Energy dripping from his voice, "Carnus Solaire, I ask that you explain what you've done to deserve such a fate. Your story may give us insight that we need."

Carnus stared despondently at the floor.

"Please," Aizo urged. The Inlume's request tempting the silent, defeated man.

Grace cut in. "It's time, Carnus. Explain it to them."

The two exchanged a look like long lost lovers seeing each other after years of hardship apart. There was a pleading in Grace's face that melted the hardened man's walls.

Carnus heaved, holding his head in his hands, and began to recount his tale.

FRACTURE ORIGIN

∞   ∞   ∞

Storm clouds blotted out the light over the Pacific Ocean as Carnus stood at the foot of an aircraft carrier galley deck.

Jets swarmed overhead, roaring against the gray heavens above. The machines were foreign to him. Unnatural. Mechanical. *Wrong.*

Carnus clutched a gemstone above the tumultuous sea. He held the purest blood-red gem he'd ever seen, but it did not glimmer. Instead of a manus stone sparkle, the Left Eye of Izanagi refracted a smokey black substance inside.

Weathered hands shook. His heavy brow crinkled in mourning and submission to fate. He had chosen his path all those years ago in Viator when Naith had introduced him to Vistomus. The offer had been inescapable—he faced certain salvation for his battered army if he accepted the Mitad's aid.

However, it came with a personal consequence sold as a gift.

The Mark of the Chosen. That's what Vistomus called it. The Master had taken an ancient primal wielding technique belonging to the Kenat and attempted to replicate it.

Carnus had read the that Grace Lapithos' gathered texts.

They had studied the curse mark together for the past year in secret. It had been a work that bound them. She would hunt for information, translate ancient texts, analyze Carnus in extremely rare private moments where they could touch skin to skin without any Mitad gaze.

One day they had uncovered a text from a kingdom they had never heard of. One that didn't exist on the maps, no matter how old or who the cartographer was. No wielder's map revealed it, but Amytis had existed according to one of Grace's most reliable historians from the Thirteenth Era.

Grace explained that her missions with Vistomus had revealed coveted knowledge, and she feared they would kill her for coming to understand too much. The pair had been plotting their escape for months. It would be together. To the plains of Terrspar. But Vistomus was careful to have one of them bound to him at all times…keeping one of them always on Earth…by tying them with obligations to Mitad

CHAPTER TWENTY-TWO

missions where their lives were on the line...by enticing Grace with a new piece of knowledge that she couldn't resist pursuing. His webs were never ending.

The last piece of forbidden knowledge came from a surviving scroll of Amytis. The Kenat had developed a technique called *Noximor's Tide*. Grace had broken her vow, as she often did, and read the text before handing it over to Vistomus—a choice that had been critical to her efforts.

Vistomus had destroyed the scroll immediately.

Now, on the edge of the battleship, teetering on the roll of agitated waves, Carnus felt a rising burn in his veins. His throat tightened at the sensation.

It was Master M's mimicry of a technique, but for all he knew...he could have some remnant *Noximor's Tide* polluting his Soul Resevoir. The notion caused him to shiver despite the fire under his skin; consumed by flame yet without warmth or light.

He wanted to tear off his flesh, extract every ounce of blood and Soul Energy from himself and purify. Start again.

Oh, what he'd give to begin anew.

That time is past, Carnus, he managed to tell himself through the agony of his existence.

The dark smoke churned in the Left Eye of Izanagi.

A perfectly calm and composed voice came from behind.

"It's time, Carnus. With this, we will cripple the North American Sector. Their regime has stood in my way for decades now. With this, they will bend the knee to our proxy empire. While they concede to the Asian Sector, they bow to the Mitad."

Soul Energy spiraled in Carnus' palm against his will.

The ruby stone flashed as if waking from a long slumber, pulsing and fading.

"No, Vistomus. We can find another way. The North Americans are weak. Their empire is crumbling, and soon enough, we will have military victory. There are other paths—"

Lightning shot down into the ocean before them.

Crackle-boom!

FRACTURE ORIGIN

Pure white and teeming with aura. It silenced Carnus' protest.

"There is no other way! Unless you want to get on the front lines and slaughter every soldier on the continent yourself, this must be done. It is quicker. Easier."

Carnus' begged internally. He cried out in horror at his fate.

"I won't, Vistomu—AGHH!" his words became a choking wretch as his veins turned black and the Mark of the Chosen rose to the surface of his skin. The living poison moved like ink up his body.

"No! STOP! Thi-th…" Carnus' voice became that of a man on his deathbed as he wheezed, "I won't… let you…"

"Let me? Dear, Carnus. We've been through too much together for you to be so foolish. You'll perform this task for me, or I'll use your body like a puppet."

The steel eyes and black beard quivered as Carnus raised the Left Eye of Izanagi against the strain of his muscles fighting.

Ruby light flashed.

Black smoke churned and whizzed in the stone.

Soul Energy filled the Tool of Karnak.

For an instant, the energy shone in the symbol of a leaf-like eye. Carnus knew it well; it had been drawn on the secret room where he had discovered the artifact.

Then the light snapped, funneling into Carnus' chest.

His consciousness spun, and he became nauseous.

Whether feeding its energy into him or sucking his out like a black hole, he couldn't tell.

The sensation was too intense, and his senses were too disoriented.

The power contained in the Left Eye was too much to contend with. It battled with the curse mark inside him, threatening to break his body into a million vibrating pieces.

He knew then that he had to accept the light of the manus stone, or else something far worse would happen. So, he relented and allowed himself to bend to the curse and wield with the Left Eye of Izanagi.

It was an instant of weakness.

Pain and the face of his mortality had overwhelmed his will. The hauntings of his previous sins under the manipulation of the Mark of the

CHAPTER TWENTY-TWO

Chosen caused him to doubt himself. He forgot the teachings of his master, Zeri the Great. He did not trust the workings of the Great Soul as Zeri had instructed.

There could be no forgiveness for a man like him.

His soul was tainted.

His soul was…his soul…

In that moment, he forgot the name of his soul's essence.

Broken, he relented.

Carnus' vision went white.

Then, everything he could see was made of effervescent particles. It was too much to comprehend. A force similar to Soul Energy was alive in everything, everywhere. It interacted with every atom of matter. It flowed through all space and time. Not conscious like the Soul Energy in human souls, but potent all the same.

Like sand made of pure light, the world sifted through his perceptions, shaping and reshaping, bouncing, repelling, and attracting. It was an infinitely complex show put on in black and white.

And it was all-encompassing.

For hundreds of miles, he could see the flow.

All that raw information compressed into his mind like molten metal poured into a cast. He was sure he was screaming uncontrollably as the data flooded him…out there in the conscious world. However, through the perception of the Left Eye of Izanagi, there was nothing else.

Carnus knew the name.

They had uncovered it together, what was whispered about by only select inlumes and explorers. The Dacian Shamans—the continent of origin for the Krog race—were said to wield using an external flow of energy that existed outside of human beings. It was far weaker than wielding Soul Energy but magnitudes more abundant.

The Dacians had explained it to the first Corlanders.

They called it *Nature's Path*.

The west coast of the United States undulated before his awareness. Carnus perceived the shelves of continental mass below the surface. The thermal energy frothing beneath. Light particles moved underneath the continent with their own currents, a procession of miniature spirits—

billions of grains like sand being carried by the wind beneath the window of human perception.

The task at hand possessed him.

Though he now willed against it with all his heart, he had allowed the process to start. The Mark of the Chosen commanded him. His indigo Soul Energy crashed out of his body and into the realm only known to the Dacian shamans.

Indigo poured into the colorless world, staining it.

The Soul Energy traveled hundreds of miles.

The Left Eye's terrifying power augmented his normal abilities. It was more than he had ever used in any battle, more than he thought he possessed in his entire Soul Reservoir.

When he knew his limit to be drained—the force extracted more from him.

His skin felt brittle. Blood thin. Lifeforce dull.

I'm dying.

It's too much.

Vistomus is taking it all.

When he felt like no more than a husk, he sensed his body fall to its knees...out there...in the distant material world.

But here! In the realm of Nature's Path, a shroud of his Soul Energy the size of entire states was snaking through the continental flows.

No. Please no! Don't make me do this.

By the Great Soul, don't let this happen. I can't bear it.

My soul will shatter. It will turn to ash!

His pleads were heard by an infinite void.

Carnus felt his arms lift in a gesture like a puppet. Strings of possession compelled him.

The blue light ignited.

It fractured the flow of Nature's Path that had been for hundreds of thousands of years.

The continent creaked. The land moaned. The coast sheered.

The United States fractured.

An entire coast fell into the ocean that day.

CHAPTER TWENTY-TWO

It was the psychological scar as much as the physical act that later gave name to the conflict: The Fracture War.

Then, after an eternity in this state, Carnus was released.

Thin and vapid, he opened his eyes to the ocean. Severely weakened, he could still sense the tsunamis and catastrophes far away across the Pacific Ocean.

Tears flowed relentlessly.

"It is done, Carnus. Your tears can't undo their demise," Vistomus said callously.

"How many," Carnus' voice broke while asking. "How many did I just *murder*? How many tens of thousands did you force me to kill?"

"Enough to win a war. That is the correct amount."

Vistomus left after that. He allowed Carnus to keep the Left Eye, never wanting to touch it himself.

The curse mark began again, claiming his skin and veins. His head fell back while his body remained rigid. Vistomus was no longer commanding the curse. He knew that. It had gained victory over him, just as Vistomus had taken conquest over North America.

The Mark of the Chosen was advancing; a scavenger over a corpse.

A pitter-patter of soft running feet came.

Grace dove for him and held his seizing body.

"Carnus? What is this?" she begged while holding him. "Tell me what you've done. I can feel it out there. *Something terrible.*"

The solemn man tilted his head to Grace.

"Please...Grace...I'm sorry..."

She held his face in her gentle embrace and mourned for him. "You have to live, Carnus. We have to escape together," she cried.

Black crept up his neck with no resistance.

"Fight. Fight it! Remember who you are. Remember the wielder that I love," she admitted for the first time. It had remained an unspoken truth. Understood, but never verbalized.

The curse paused for an instant. As it quivered, she knew what must be done before it advanced to his brain.

FRACTURE ORIGIN

Grace Lapithos caressed the handsome, broken bearded man. She plucked the instrument of his undoing from his cold hands and placed it in her pocket.

Then, she leaned in and touched her lips to his.

"I love you, Carnus Solaire. Remember yourself. Remember your soul. You are one of the greatest wielders of our Era. This will not defeat you."

Carnus' eyes came alive, and he kissed her back.

Her soft lips kindled a will to live, and her words called the name of his soul to mind.

The Mark of the Chosen receded.

The two wielders knelt on the ship deck together as the gray skies cast down droplets. The sound of doom echoed like a screaming demon as the ocean was sucked into the hole where the West Coast had broken off and sunk. The air smelled burnt as if the event had putrefied the sky.

Though he was barely clinging to life, Carnus' Observation could sense the crystallization of his Soul Energy underneath the United States.

It was a fusion of his imprint with Nature's Path where the genocide had occurred, and it echoed throughout the land. It was a permanent signature of his hellish work.

The Viator Hariban turned emir of the Mitad, Carnus Solaire, was now on the brink of becoming one of the Voro. He lay limp—a broken man with a soul scattered beneath the land he had massacred.

∞   ∞   ∞

Mouths hung aghast. The only face not in shock was the one that had been there with Carnus through the ordeal. Grace knew the truth. She had lived it and kept it secret between them for twenty-three years. She had stranded herself in Nippon-Wa for it. Her face was etched with a morose blend of regretful compassion and pained loss.

In coping with the reality of what he had done in the Fracture War, Carnus was only a shell of the man she loved. He hid from the world and himself, denying happiness and pleasure as a penance.

CHAPTER TWENTY-TWO

Saigo's scabbed face tilted uncomfortably as he processed aloud, "You were...the source of the fracture? You sunk the West Coast of the United States?"

Dead eyes looked back as Carnus nodded, only enough for the motion to be noticeable.

In an act of love, Grace intervened. "He was merely the vessel for Master M's work. Noximor's evil pours through all of time. Here...now...in our time, through the Kenat's ancient wielding spells imitated by the Mitad's crude curse."

Aizo stared with resolve. "May the Great Soul act through us to end that flow of darkness."

"It doesn't matter how you frame it!" Carnus growled. "*Yes. It was me.* I was too weak to stop it, and that's enough for the guilt to rest on my head." He seized his robe and tore it off his shoulders so that it fell at his waist. His bare torso was exposed. Thin, striated muscle was revealed, but it was marred. The left pectoral muscle, rib cage, and upper abdomen were all covered by withered, gray skin. It was like of rash of stone and decay had spread from his heart. "I did it...and this is my token to never forget my skins."

Silence.

"What is that?" Eos asked, disturbed by the disfiguration.

Carnus pulled his robe back on. "The consequences of a rebound—a conflict between two natural enemies: the Tide and the Eye. Something I gladly wear to remind me that I must dedicate my life to making amends."

Saigo finally countered. "Then why don't you fight back? Draw that kami sword at your waist! Recover the Left Eye of Izanagi. Use it to defeat Raijin! That would make amends for the role you played."

Carnus shook his head with eyelids shut tight. "No, it would not bring back any of the tens of thousands who died."

"It would stop those who will die here. In this time! In Nippon-Wa!" Saigo raised his voice. "The hanyo just slaughtered every member of a protest in Tokyo. Antoku has bent his knee to Raijin. Only his favor for me, has kept them from leading a direct attack in these mountains. These kami have replaced our political leaders. Our emperor's favor will not last. Many more will die before Raijin is done. *War is coming!*"

"Don't you understand? I can't. If I wield again, I will become possessed. If I retrieve the Eye, it will end up in Vistomus' hands. One way or another..." Carnus' voice trailed off. Then, he admitted the second weight on his soul. "Besides, they know now. I met with Kikujiro and told him that the Mitad will come for him. Vistomus knows now that the shinshoku of Ise Grand Shrine hid the Eye. The Mitad will hunt the Shinto priests now."

Saigo put his head down. "My son..."

Carnus shook his head. "I'm...I'm sorry, Saigo. Truly, I am. I didn't want to put your son in danger. I had a child, lost a world apart from me. I would never—"

"Enough! Kikujiro knows honor and duty. I taught him. He would never turn down such a task when it is the responsibility of his bloodline. Unlike you, he is bushi in his heart. Even if he is shinshoku on the outside." The noble lord of the mountain stronghold stared off. "Do what you must, my samurai-priest son."

Aizo changed the subject, "As we speak, Scavok and Talus are leading Saitani's men in a final mission. Saitani speaks every day of the coming battle. He doesn't have the favor or protection of Antoku and knows the hanyo will kill him soon. So, he wanted me to carry a message to you, Saigo: his last stand will be in a few months."

Saigo bowed. "Hai!" he bellowed with his Japanese affirmation. "My bushi and I will lay down our life to teach the emperor one last lesson and resist Raijin's influence in our land. The only question is: which kami will join me?" He turned his stern and heavy gaze around the room.

"I cannot wield anymore," Carnus uttered solemnly.

"Can't or won't?" Saigo pressed.

Once more, Aizo cut in. "I may have a solution to that. Carnus, what if I offered you a seal like the one Eos has? That would allow you at least one more fight."

Disbelief filled Carnus. He searched for the proper response. He had given up, receded into himself, forgone wielding. Grasping for words, he nodded and said, "Then, Vistomus would face me one more time. I accept, but I have a private request about this seal. Perhaps…I can stop Vistomus from ever getting his hands on the Left Eye."

Saigo smiled. "Then it shall be done," he said with a clap. "Perhaps we can find a bushi heart in you, Carnus."

Aizo continued, "Then it is agreed, but I must ask…what would happen if Vistomus obtained this artifact of Karnak?"

Grace hummed. "Disaster. It contains a power called the Flow of All Things. With it, one can see the flow of Nature's Pulse, the living energy that exists all around us. Carnus was able to fracture a continent due to the quality and essence of his Severance. It was a potent and synergistic combination. How he knew that Carnus was capable of such a feat is beyond my imagination…needless to say, Vistomus will have plans for it that will be nearly as catastrophic."

Eos finally spoke. "We came here to learn about my curse mark and the Left Eye of Izanagi so that we could understand the Mitad's plans," he addressed his inlume master hesitantly, knowing that he had stretched his limits too far already. He would keep his promise to act according to his inlume's orders, but he had to try. "Aizo, we can't allow them to gain such a powerful item and advance their plan. We have an opportunity to prevent something terrible and possibly free a nation from their grasp at the same time…but I know we also did not come here prepared for battle."

"We did not," Aizo affirmed. "Our mission was for research only. You've already rushed headlong into danger and risked the party's safety once."

"And I swore that I wouldn't do that again. I'm asking you, can we allow the Mitad to advance their plans and have the Left Eye of Izanagi? To me, it sounds worse than if we handed over the Mellizo Glyphs."

Grace added, "I came here for *only research*. It cost me everything. A lifetime away from my homeland and my children as the Mitad advanced their agenda. There are times when one must make a stand."

Conflicted, Aizo shook away the emotional impulses. "Saigo, I cannot commit to anything tonight. We'll consult with our king, Talus. He will decide."

Saigo grunted with a nod of understanding.

FRACTURE ORIGIN

Eos' mind was heavy with the knowledge he held. It pulled with a dread to match the Mark of the Chosen having no cure. He thought of his dreams and his shared memories with Jezca Monte.

No, that was her adoptive name. She is Jezca Lapithos.

Twin daggers of manus stone and a corinth mask plagued him now. He grimaced as he faced the long-stranded mother.

"Grace..." Eos began hesitantly.

"What is it, Bellator King's Son?" she asked softly, anticipating the weight of his tone.

"On Hyperborea, I traveled to the Monte Kingdom to search for answers to this curse. There I met a woman who is the future high priestess of the Manus Priesthood. She is the most talented wielder of my age, they say. And her beauty is beyond compare," Eos blushed as the words slipped out. "We became bound together through wielding. Later, I met her brother. He was a brave and noble-hearted rebel who resisted the Mitad's presence." Here, he paused.

Grace's lips quivered as if she could read the meaning of the words. "I was raised in a hidden village in the mountains south of the Monte Kingdom; I know the area well."

"Necogen," Eos said slowly, "I've...been there in my dreams. I've seen the Domins training assassins and the old ways of offering Soul Energy to the manus stone fragments."

At this, Aizo questioned, "In your dreams, you've been there? You haven't told me about this, Eos."

Eos shook his head. "Ever since the incident in the temple, I've been dreaming *her dreams*. I've been seeing *her memories* in my sleep."

"By the Great Soul...You should have told me earlier." Aizo whispered, knowing Eos had so many burdens laid on him at once. He felt a ping of guilt for being so hard on the boy. He was struggling with losing his sister, succumbing to an ancient wielding spell tied to the Kenat, and even in his dreams, he was being haunted.

Grace spoke again, her words shaking. "These dreams...the siblings you met...tell me their names. Please," she urged.

"Jezca and Caldus."

CHAPTER TWENTY-TWO

"The Great Soul is good! My children." Grace cried out. Her chest heaved, and tears streamed down her cheeks.

Eos' face tightened. He struggled to deliver the tragic news, "I'm sorry, Grace. Caldus…was a bold leader, and it was an honor to fight alongside him, but…a mirza…killed him. Take some solace knowing that he was avenged."

The tears flowed furiously now.

Joy mixed with disbelief and grief all at once. "Then, I only have one living child, and she is the future high priestess?"

"Yes. Jezca lives."

Nodding repeatedly, Grace breathed in gasps and braced herself against the doorway, saying, "It is enough—a blessing. I never thought I'd see my children again. I was so sure. Then the constellation stones spoke to me." She revealed an onyx rock from her pocket. "Jezca's been reaching out to me from across worlds. I knew it was her Soul Energy that spoke to me." She closed her eyes. "I have a path back to Hyperborea and a living child waiting for me. That is reason enough to fight the Mitad!"

Eos didn't understand the rock she called a constellation stone but smiled at the woman's fire in the face of tragic news.

"But tonight, you must tell me about my children."

"Of course, Grace," Eos answered.

The warbling call of a Japanese wren sang through the castle walls. Its chirp was warm and melodic, but the echo in the rafters had a distorted quality. It rang like a premonition of coming trials.

There is no cure for the Mark of the Chosen.

Vistomus is going to take the Left Eye of Izanagi.

There is no cure. This is forever.

Eos' thoughts were jumbled like the bird's echoed singing. He longed for the comfort and confidence of his sister.

Major Clark. Caldus. Maxima. How many others? How many more?

The Mitad must be stopped.

Eos calmed his mind in the presence of so many wielding masters and reminded himself of his oath. It had been an anchor for him. Repeating it reassured him when fear took hold.

FRACTURE ORIGIN

Sometimes the entire vow.

Often, just a few lines.

I believe in the right for all to make for themselves a free life.

I will use wisdom granted by the Divine Soul to guide my wielding towards this belief.

I will transform chaos into order.

I will pursue the path of light.

He repeated the lines in his mind.

The chirp of the wren went quiet.

CHAPTER TWENTY-THREE

ETERNAL STRUGGLE

Teal light broke through gaps in the Tenebrim canyon channels, tinting Ares' ashen-toned skin. He sat before the alabaster arch of the Makanla Gate. Thoughts whirred by faster than he could grab onto them. New impulses, worries, and fascinations had his mind racing while his body remained still.

Allow them to pass by. Observe the thoughts. He repeated the instructions but grumbled in his throat at the tedious task.

"I found her, Master Salvaluc," Ares murmured excitedly.

"We are meditating," the Inlume replied.

There were only a few seconds of silence before the intrigue tainted Salvaluc's practice. "You're like an infectious child," he sighed. Curiosity about his lost friend won him over. "You found Grace?"

Ares kept his eyes closed, feigning meditation practice. "Please, don't let me break your focus," he provoked the Tenebrim leader.

ETERNAL STRUGGLE

"You've already ruined that."

"An inlume could never be so easily distracted by—"

"Did you find Grace?"

Ares smirked and turned to Salvaluc. "I found her. At least I found out where Raggan and Vistomus believe she is. They're focused on Carnus Solaire, but there are mentions of her as well."

Salvaluc gave up the session and threw a brown-robed arm over his propped-up knee. He clenched his jaw as if trying to contain his emotions with pure willpower.

"But you did not confirm she is alive for yourself?"

"No. I left the pieces in place for my little brother to do that for me. I left him with the evidence. He doesn't have the discipline not to pursue it. It's beyond him."

Salvaluc chuckled. "Ahhh, Ares lecturing on discipline. A day of paradoxes."

Ares grew annoyed at the teasing, but as usual, he found just enough intrigue in the puzzle of a man and his riddles to suppress his instinctual aggression. "Do you want to know or not?"

Salvaluc turned out an open hand, signaling Ares to continue.

"Grace ran away with the Hamirate Hariban from Viator. They stole an item called the Left Eye of Izanagi." Salvaluc's eyes widened at this, but he said nothing to interrupt. "But they're trapped on an island nation on Earth. I assume they have no choice but to spend their years hiding among the people there."

Salvaluc stroked his bushy white brows and relented, "It is in the hands of the Great Soul then. I have no way to cross worlds." His head sank, and he mumbled prayer in the old language.

While he did this, Ares stood up and inspected the otherworldly gate. His wavy locks and handsome face were muddled in the opaque milky glass that filled the archway. He tapped the stone structure mindlessly as he thought.

"How long are we taking the guard duty? We've been out here for hours," Ares complained. "There's something else I wanted to tell you…in exchange for solid information from you this time."

Salvaluc nodded, still lost in concerned thought for Grace.

CHAPTER TWENTY-THREE

"I've learned that Saida is amassing an army for Master M in the south. They are allying with the Sisters of Noxim. I'm planning to see it for myself, but it's difficult without good reason, and I don't want to be seen prying there without cause. Emir Valrea is leading this army Gualpine."

"That can't be!" Salvaluc recoiled into a crouch and stood. "I've heard nothing from Inlume Cyprin or any of our covert Priori members there. If that were true, it would require an immediate assembly of the Council of Soul Wielders to prepare!"

"Then you best do less meditation and more assembling," Ares hummed with amusement.

"That can't be true..."

"That's all you're getting from me, Old Man. Your turn."

Salvaluc frowned. Now he was plotting and connecting unrelated and undisclosed events in his mind as if frantically piecing together the validity of Ares' warning. Finally, he ceased stroking his silver mustache and gave Ares the hint he sought.

"There is a Scarum Crypt in Lenape. I've confirmed it's there. However, I'm still gathering the exact details from my Priori sources. I believe I'll have what you need to start your search by the next month."

Ares grinned devilishly. "You're going to send me into mythical places guarded by Crypt Keepers? You really want to get rid of me for good, don't you? And in Lenape, of all places. What a rat's nest. Under Saida's nose this whole time. No, he probably has an inclination. Must be why he chose the spot. But Astor Bruinsma will be a thorn to work around."

Salvaluc raised an eyebrow and crinkled his forehead. "Don't go dying that easily. I'd feel almost guilty if you did because of my information."

Ares cast a doubting look.

"The Ignoble Lord of the drug trade routes," the Inlume chewed on the words. "He will be a dangerous presence to navigate. No doubt, he also has some mind about the Sacrum Crypt, though it's likely little more than a treasure hunt to him."

ETERNAL STRUGGLE

"Don't tell me the Priori are searching for it too?" Ares said with exasperation.

"No. Too many enemies in Lenape. We seek knowledge not death."

Tuning his perceptions to the resonant energy of the Makanla Gate, Ares sensed the vibrations that lived in the moon-colored stone.

Subtle. Ancient. Otherworldly. And yet...

Something about the energy was familiar and matched his.

Salvaluc interrupted his interaction with the arch, "Have you thought about your most important task ahead?"

A low sigh responded, knowing where his mentor was headed. He decided not to make it so easy on the inlume. "Discovering Master M's identity? It has crossed my mind."

"Ah, yes. Pursuit of base urges and grudges is the first lesson I impart to my students."

"I know, Master Salvaluc. I've taken it to heart and will not let you down," Ares bantered.

"At least you finally called me Master."

Catching himself, Ares quickly retorted, "You must have misheard. Hearing does fade with age. And *old man* could be mistaken for *master* with all the years you've lived."

"How joyous to know my student has nearly mastered my second tenant of disrespect and a loose tongue."

"But you did call me student."

The silver head tilted, perplexed, as Salvaluc said, "Perhaps your thoughts were running wild, and it is you who misheard. Your ego inflates beyond your head. Then, it's easy to hear *student* when I said *burdensome brat.*"

Ares' lips twitched at the returned slander. "I'll have you know this *brat* has weighed carefully and made a responsible decision to set aside the pursuit of Master M."

"Really?"

"Yes, I realized that I've neglected paying back the Bellators for too long. Father and son."

"Perfect, you've internalized my third tenant of a death wish."

"Neither could threaten me, Salvaluc. Hardly a death wish."

CHAPTER TWENTY-THREE

Shaking his head in amazement at the arrogance, Salvaluc clicked his tongue. "The man who wiped out the Mitad's factories and held off Saida with only one arm? Surely, he will cower before you, Ares. And do you believe Eos is sitting around idly? It's time for you to progress in your wielding training without the crutch of the Mark of the Chosen if you hope to try that."

Ares grunted. "Gideon," was all he responded.

"Gideon?"

"That's what I'll name my son. I've decided to protect him from a life in the Mitad. There will be no mark placed upon him." Ares ground his teeth together and placed his hand on the Makanla Gate once more. He bowed his head and closed his eyes, pained.

"How will you ensure that? Ares, the time is coming for you to look inward and answer the difficult questions. Ares, Son of the Mitad? Ares Bellator? Or someone else entirely? What do you want?"

"There are things I have to do!" Ares growled, his temper flaring. Soul Energy bubbled at his core as the precarious future was laid out before him. "My fate—"

"Your fate? Or the fate others have tried branding on your spirit? You have a path of happiness and love open to you." Salvaluc shook his head. "But do you have the strength to choose it?"

"You make it sound so simple. Strength is all I have!" Ares pounded his fist against the gate. "It's all I've ever had. That's why I must get even stronger!"

"True strength is in your character and grace, not your violence. There is only one way to save your child from the kind of life you've lived."

"Aghhh!" Ares screamed and pounded the gateway again as Salvaluc turned away. The milky stone that filled the arch flashed a blinding white as his hand struck it. The space beneath the arch radiated like the pink of an oil slick. The nearly unperceivable vibrations increased until they beat in Ares' skull like a taut drum.

Thrum! It resonated behind his forehead.

Thrum. Thrum! He stumbled back.

Through Makanla Gate, a form emerged.

ETERNAL STRUGGLE

Muddy red.

Claws the color of dried blood penetrated the threshold.

They glowed like muted Soul Energy, but when Ares viewed them through his tuned Observation, the long phalanges scraped through space like some kind of inverted energy.

Where the inhuman shape reached through, it was as if Soul Energy was repelled.

Salvaluc was pale with horror. His mouth hung open, and his instincts were slowed. "Unseen...Bishiwal," he whispered.

Then, suddenly, the gate's light died. The portal closed and returned to stone, and the creature's claws that had reached through turned to dust and vanished.

"What...?" Ares couldn't form a thought that communicated what he had just seen.

"Ares," Salvaluc turned with a stone expression, "this is why we are watching the Makanla Gates. Entities lost to myth and crumbling scroll-lore have been rumored to be returning. It appears *you* just caused a reaction somehow."

"Me? How could I?" Ares examined his hands in erratic disbelief. Salvaluc took him by the shoulders and locked eyes.

"An eternal divine struggle has been playing out since the beginning of time. Inside you, a child born of Soul Energy, I believe there is a microcosm that mirrors it. I need you to make me a promise *right now*."

Ares was disturbed by both the words and the shaken demeanor of the Inlume. "What, Master Salvaluc?" He found himself quivering with stuttered breath.

"You have been forcing open your inner gates long enough. Severance is dangerous business. Many wielders have died from reaching too far. Do not leave Tenebrim until you've finished training with me to open your fourth gate without the Mitad's curse."

"Now?" Ares stuttered. "Why now?"

"Events are unfolding too quickly. You think I don't know why Saida allows you to visit me?" Salvaluc's words made Ares go pale. He continued, "I've known Saida far longer than you've imagined. I know how his twisted mind works. You will have to decide soon. Perhaps you

CHAPTER TWENTY-THREE

will not be given a choice at all. I must impart what knowledge I can to assist you while I'm still here. If the Bishiwals are returning, then we are short on time. With an army building in Gaulpine...there is even less time than I thought."

Ares looked at the pale stone arch. It no longer had a mysterious intrigue—instead, he was shaking at the implications he didn't understand.

Fading light trickled down the canyon, and the crevasse was drawn back into the shadows of setting dusk.

"Promise me, Ares!"

∞   ∞   ∞

Bellia stroked her delicate fingers over Ares' hardened back muscles. She traced the lines of the elsu legend inked in his skin with a pondering hum.

Her room was decorated with the regality of a king's daughter, though it felt like an illusion to her. She was more an ambassador for the Mitad than a member of the Tamat royal family these days. The luxurious fabrics, expensive paintings, and golden statues were a preservation for her father more than anything—a nostalgic reminder of a time of innocence.

"Saida won't like that you're here. With me. Like this," Bellia murmured as she stood from her bed and sauntered to an intricately crafted silver, turtle-shell music box. She opened the hinged box, propping the shell open to reveal a rotating dancer inside. As the chiming notes rang out, her seventh birthday gift recalled her mind to childhood. *She had wanted to be a dancer...all those years ago.*

Then, the Tamat King's Daughter placed her hand on her belly as her child kicked in her stomach. *How far away those days were. How simple things were then.*

Violet rings. Disappearing objects. Rooms with missing furniture.

She had begun manifesting her wielding with absolutely no control not long after she had received the music box.

ETERNAL STRUGGLE

Ares muttered in a deep, contemplative voice, "He'll dislike what I'm planning to do next so much that this won't even cross his mind. Besides, he's on the coast, in Amufaga, doing business with Astor Bruinsma. Only *that witch* stayed behind. And she fears me more than I fear her."

You have a path of happiness and love open to you.

Do you have the strength to choose it?

Salvaluc's words echoed with a persistent nudge in his mind.

Ares joined Bellia near her bedside table as the music box slowed its notes and the wound energy of the spring began to die out.

Brushing her striking blond hair back, Bellia stared into Ares' amethyst eyes. "We both had such isolated childhoods. I kept tearing holes in the castle…hurting people…disappearing things unintentionally as I came of age. My father hid me away for my own good until a suitable wielding master was found." Bellia let out a single syllable of bitter laugh. "You were the illegitimate son that your father was ashamed of. *We were feared*…but we found each other."

The music stopped, and Bellia closed the silver shell case.

Ares took Bellia's hands in his.

Look inward and answer the difficult questions. What do you want? There is only one way to save your child from the kind of life you've lived. Ares cursed the old man silently for haunting his mind with his morality.

"I love you, Bellia. Please understand, what I'm doing is for us and our child. I won't be back before it's time."

Fingers squeezed against Ares as Bellia drew close to him.

Bellia sensed a grave undertone. "Why now? It's so close."

Ares' eyelids fell with somber responsibility weighing on him. His voice was low as he answered, "I must train with Salvaluc. Something is happening, and it's bigger than just the Mitad or the Order—but when you can, teleport to Tenebrim, to Salvaluc's keep. I prepared a midwife for you. Salvaluc will keep you and Gideon safe. I'd have you come now, but I don't want to raise suspicion until the last possible moment. I'll be there waiting."

A weak smile received the answer. Bellia knew the birth could come any day now. "You're sure it's a boy?"

CHAPTER TWENTY-THREE

A guilty shrug came with the reply, "An intuition. Maybe Salvaluc's training is doing me some good."

"Saida will never allow—"

"Leave that to me. I'll take care of everything."

"That's always your answer these days."

"Don't I always come through? It's safer for you this way. You know if I told you everything Saida might catch on. I promise soon this distance will end. We'll be together."

The world had been pressing in lately, and she needed to hear his reassurance as the ache in her shoulder scar flared and the child within kicked again.

"One more thing," Ares began as he gently tucked a strand of Bellia's hair behind her ear.

"Yes?" she asked expectantly.

"When can you see your father next?"

"Maybe tomorrow? Why?"

"There's something I need you to look into when Saida and the others are out of the castle. Salvaluc told me that there's a Sacrum Crypt here on Lenape. I want you to probe your father for knowledge of it. If anyone would know, it's King Hika. I know it's a lot to ask, but the time is nearing when I'll need that information to protect you." He looked at Bellia's belly and corrected himself, "Us. We're a family now."

Bellia is my only weakness, Ares thought. *Saida was right about that much. But this weakness is my one treasure. Even Master M won't take that away from me.*

CHAPTER TWENTY-FOUR

NEGATION WINGS

A convoy of ten Japanese military trucks waited behind the cover of rich green maple trees, just out of range of being noticed by watchtowers. Glenn sat between Durath and Kamatari in the passenger row behind their driver, Minoru. The four waited tensely in body armor for the signal of Talus, Scavok, and the elite unit leading the weapons depot infiltration beyond the tree line.

"I can't believe we were dragged into this. Sure, I have driving skills, but I am not a combat specialist. This is beyond our responsibilities. It's dangerous!" Minoru grumbled from the front seat, his thin body, short ponytail, and scraggly graying beard rotating as he scanned through the windows with paranoia.

"You think *I'm* a combat specialist?" Glenn muttered.

Minoru huffed, "Then why are we here?"

"We are bound to Glenn's protection. He is the kami's favorite pet—" Kamatari caught himself as Glenn scowled and prepared to reprimand him, "*honored servant*, and our duty is to stay by him as Saitani ordered."

"I'm not a servant for the last time," Glenn said, strumming his winged staff with annoyance.

Durath eyed Talus' gift warily.

Minoru sighed, "That's why *we're* here, but why is *Glenn* here?"

"Doesn't concern you." Kamatari peered out his passenger window, just as nervous as his companion.

Squinting, Minoru protested, "It certainly does concern me—and you! We're in the middle of a raid."

"More like at the outer edge of a raid, *watching*," Durath chided.

Glenn tried to end the bickering. He was on edge as it was, and the two extras in the vehicle only added to his apprehension. "Talus has a special task for me in case things go badly. I don't want to be here anymore than you. I came to Nippon-Wa to sightsee, not to get mixed up in Soul Wielder battles and raiding the Emperor's weapon depots."

"What could you possibly do to assist in a battle of kami?" Minoru whined. "Pets—servan—ah—regular humans would be crushed instantly."

"*Want to find out?*" Glenn threatened, tapping the decorative top of the staff in his palm. "I didn't ask for either of you to be here."

Kamatari rubbed his round nose and taunted his companion, "Saigo's samurai warriors fight against the kami."

Minoru groaned, "Well, suit me up with armor and hand me a katana. Then I'll feel *much better* about our situation."

The handheld radio mounted to the dashboard crackled to life. "King's Son of Leorix, we're ready for you," Scavok's voice came through in a distorted static tone.

Durath opened the door and leaned out. "Well, it's been a pleasure listening to you bicker like old women about who's the bigger coward, but I have business inside. *Being useful*." He was about to exit but leaned back in, eyed Glenn, and nodded acceptingly. "I understand why you're here. That staff's been making me uncomfortable for weeks now. You have to be the one to hold it."

NEGATION WINGS

Minoru peered back at the white amber grain of the staff. He couldn't see the details from the driver's seat, but Durath's comment had his curiosity. "What is it?" he asked inquisitively.

"A staff," Glenn grumbled.

"A special kami-staff?" Minoru asked childishly.

"*Just a staff.*" Glenn's irritation grew.

The weathered Japanese man craned around the headrest to take a closer look.

Kamatari kicked his seat from behind.

"Ow!"

"Mind your business, fool," Kamatari chastised.

"I just wanted to see it!"

"Now you've seen it. Leave Glenn alone."

"Well, you get a closer look from back there," Minoru groaned. He fidgeted with his body armor. "I'm the one driving you. I should at least get to see it. Does it have special kami powers?"

Glenn ran his thumb over the wings, scrunched his face in annoyance, and grasped the wooden handle made from the sacred trees of the Hasvela forest.

The metal wings came over the seat and tapped the driver on his head. "Ow!" Minoru exclaimed again.

"Did you feel it?" Glenn asked. "That's its power."

Minoru patted himself down as if checking for some kind of magic spell that had been cast over him. Feeling his arms, he whispered, "I think…I…"

"It makes idiots shut up," Glenn cut him off.

Boom!

An explosion shook the truck.

In a deep voice, Minoru commanded, "Enough, both of you. That's the first signal. Durath just took out the security gate."

∞   ∞   ∞

CHAPTER TWENTY-FOUR

Scavok's short sword, Safisay, glowed glacial blue and pierced metal as if it was made of sand. The brilliant blade slid around the door lock until it came loose.

Behind him were Talus and ten men in black infiltration garb and tactical body plate carriers. Their rifles were at the ready, pointed to the ground with fingers just above the trigger guard. Four security watchmen lay at their feet, taken out by Saitani's men to clear the way for the two kami.

The instant the door popped open, the ten moved with trained prowess. The leader scanned the entrance with his barrel from behind the wall, located cover, and signaled his men to enter.

Talus followed behind with a slow strut and the sheen of Soul Energy over his body to protect him from possible bullets. His braided auburn beard bounced on his chest, and his left arm swung in his lavender Japanese robe while the right sleeve was tied at his shoulder stump.

Scavok watched his king's back as they entered, his Solido raised.

Vast gray metal walls and hanging industrial lighting gave the warehouse a dull hollow ambiance. The concrete dampened their steps as they moved through the pungent smell of oil and gunpowder. A few hundred feet ahead was the prize they sought. Munitions cans, rifle crates, rockets, and all the strange weapon technologies of Earth lay before them.

No sooner than the two Anite wielders joined the ten behind a stack of pallets, gunfire broke out.

"I counted thirty," Scavok returned to cover as bullets flew around them. One zipped into his Solido, evaporating with a momentary electric hum against the defensive layer. "No—" his scarred face went rigid.

Saitani's infiltration unit engaged with the guards. Cries rang out as the first men were wounded on both sides.

"I feel them," Talus acknowledged. His body tensed in preparation for battle. "Two of Vistomus' mirza." They revealed their presence, though the King's eyes couldn't find them yet.

NEGATION WINGS

Lowering his Solido, Talus created a crimson wall ahead of the ten men. As they had practiced, they recognized the supernatural kami power and advanced behind its protection.

They moved methodically as bullets rained against the glowing wall. It stopped the projectiles from reaching any of them as they closed the distance to the nearest stack of crates and supplies.

The enemy soldiers yelled out in their native language in shock. They were witnessing an impossible feat of inhuman abilities that caused their weapons to be useless.

"Ready!" Talus announced.

The veil fell, and Saitani's soldiers used the moment of shock to take out half of the exposed guards.

Closer. The mirzas are coming closer!

Talus sensed the auras of the Mitad officers becoming clearer in his Observation and more hostile as they approached the conflict.

Scavok's silver mane disappeared like flowing wind, smooth and intangible, as he stepped behind enemy lines. The soldiers behind cover fell one by one as his short blade went to work. He performed the required task, slicing, stabbing, and moving like smoke through his targets.

When the last pained exclamation fell silent, the gunfire followed. "Cleared," Scavok called out before stepping into view.

Of the men that entered with them, six remained. With weapons ready, they cautiously stepped into the open and watched their periphery.

"There are even more weapons than reported. This'll be enough to lead an attack on the Emperor's forces," the lead soldier said in a deep voice, pleased that their effort had been fruitful. "But how are we going to get them all to the trucks before reinforcements arrive?"

The piercing haunt came like papercuts to the mind. It chilled Talus' skin as he recognized the powerful aura closing in.

They're closing in. Talus nodded in warning to his master assassin.

"Leave that to us. Some of the reinforcements are already here," Scavok growled.

Talus perceived the gleam of steel sliding out from a sheath behind a silver form of Soul Energy.

CHAPTER TWENTY-FOUR

Bwooom!

A projection of a manus-core katana roared forth.

It was more intense than any manus blade strike Talus had ever witnessed. He was sure it would have instantly overpowered even the champion black-armored knight of Anite, Gondul. Whoever was wielding it could have taken on an entire unit of Anite's vangar swordsman.

Talus' throat grew tight. He hadn't expected the brutal assault to be so quick. The speed of the sword draw, proficiency of the Soul Energy projection, and raw, heavy aura were a combination he was unprepared for.

Too fast for such strength!

The silver wave rushed past him in an instant, finding the six living soldiers where they stood in the open.

By the time he blinked, the blast of energy had engulfed the men in a raging silvery inferno.

There were no screams.

No attempts to evade.

No final thoughts.

The six were erased instantly by the overwhelming aura flash of an elite wielder.

"I like working with you much better, Kallag. That witch, Diya, was so controlling," Bysis bellowed in his slow, dim drawl.

Kallag smiled. "Kill them all, Bysis. I won't tell you to hold back." His blond hair swayed, and his boyish face was too innocent for the statement.

"I'll take the elsu with a clipped wing," Bysis chuckled as he lumbered toward Talus. His sword arm was made entirely of Soul Energy, and he twirled his katana with it.

Standing across from the Anite King, Bysis looked down at Talus from an additional six inches of height. Talus was taller than most men at six feet, but Bysis was a giant in stature. "We match, Anite King. Well...almost," he laughed and showed off his artificial limb.

Kallag was left with his opponent. He beamed excitedly for the fight and said, "I guess that leaves us."

NEGATION WINGS

Scavok's gray eyebrows twitched, and his nose snarled, giving him a wolf-like resemblance amidst his beard and mane. "Suppose it does," he replied dryly and readied his short sword.

Noting the young man did not carry a katana like Bysis, Scavok asked, "No weapon for you?"

"No, I like to get my hands dirty."

Scavok observed Kallag's hands. They were permanently swollen with calluses as if beaten thousands of times against stone. Then, the young Mirza removed the top of his black kimono robes so that he stood uncovered in his baggy hakama pants.

A striated body was revealed, every sinew taught as if ready to strike, and his arms were covered in the ink of tattoos. Arcs and squares ran up his arms, surrounding sets of forked runes that marked his skin like magic symbols of some fearsome ancient people.

"The Eastern Isles...you're a Vurangian," Scavok remarked from the ink patterns.

"An assassin who knows his cultures," Kallag belittled. "Good, then you know my people's reputation. You have no need to hold back." Though too far to connect any physical blow, Kallag assumed a sparring stance and threw out a jab.

The moment his shoulder wound up, Sacavok recoiled.

He felt the overwhelming aura potential build.

An orange-yellow glow covered Kallag's fist.

The marigold Soul Energy shot from the callused knuckles.

Scavok raised his icy blue Solido.

The electric clash hummed through his chest.

Kallag grinned, letting Scavok know that the vicious blow was only a playful probe to discover Scavok's reaction time and defensive ability.

The wicked flash of Kallag's teeth curdled Scavok's stomach. This was a boy raised in brutal hand-to-hand combat and weapon warfare of a raider people. His training was in wielding, and he only needed his hands.

Scavok knew he had to quickly apply pressure in the fight to slow Kallag's momentum and confidence.

CHAPTER TWENTY-FOUR

Soul Energy sprouted at his feet, crystallizing into fleeting afterimages where he once stood. Scavok closed five paces in a single second. It was a costly exertion to move that quickly, but it accomplished what he needed.

The expression on Kallag's face became tensed, displaying his surprise at the speed and fluidity of Scavok's footwork.

The sword, Safisay, came crashing down in Kallag's periphery.

Marigold energy coated his tattooed forearms as he defended himself with raised arms. He brought up both and positioned them to parry a series of three swings from the blade.

The energies ran against each other, sparking and sounding out in a shrill shriek.

As he fell out of range from the attacks, Kallag noticed the shallowest of cuts near his wrist. The combatant's eyes locked as the blond young man licked a small trickle of blood.

"Not bad. You got through my defenses," Kallag acknowledged as his tongue found the taste of salt and iron.

Scavok held his blade in its readied position, its edge slicing his vision of the shirtless Mirza.

A series of jabs responded.

Orange-yellow burst out in a merciless flurry.

The projection of his punches connected with Scavok's glowing swings faster than he could orient his sword. The first two bursts he cut through, deflating the Soul Energy with his own, channeled through the manus blade.

Defending left his wrists throbbing.

The pain slowed his maneuvering, and the following three strikes connected with his hastily raised defensive layer.

The concussions jolted Scavok in his bones and left him feeling like his body was a struck tuning fork reverberating unstably.

Knowing he could not let Kallag press the advantage, he summoned a net of energy from his hands. The manus sword's animus core aided him in weaving it into existence faster than he normally would have been able.

Kallag's boyish features got too close.

NEGATION WINGS

He was almost within physical striking distance—which Scavok was sure would crush his body regardless of any hastily formed defense.

The Mirza reeled back a fist.

As he released, he found his limbs hindered. His torso slammed into the curling net of Scavok's Severance. It tightened around him, searing his chest with heat, as Scavok thrust his sword through the pockets in his trap.

Behind him, he heard the massive explosions of Talus' conflict with Bysis.

Talus unfolded his crimson wings from around himself like parting a veil of lava. The feathered texture of his Severance flowed and bristled at his command. For a brief moment, he allowed himself to glance away from the enemy.

The western metal wall of the warehouse had a smoking hole in it. Bysis' katana projection had been more than Talus' abilities could neutralize. The wings had wrapped around his body and protected him, but the excessive aura couldn't be absorbed entirely. It had rolled around him and continued out of the building.

A section of the roof creaked and drooped down over the missing wall. Bysis' laugh echoed the groaning structure.

"So, one arm, but you still get two wings. As for me, I made myself a new arm." The giant rotated his sword around to put his forearm on display. It churned like a kaleidoscope of moonlight. "They call you the Visrex of Wings, but I think your reputation is greater than your wielding."

Talus did not entertain the taunting.

"Why are you trying to stop us?" Talus tried to navigate the situation in a way that might diffuse the fight, but he had little hope. The brute before him appeared of low intellect and had a lust for blood.

Above all, he needed to keep the fight from destroying their weapons cache.

"Vistomus helps Emperor Antoku," Bysis said with a shrug. "The pesky little runt said the Earth weapons must be protected."

"You don't like the Emperor?" Talus delayed his opponent, circling and backing away as he said it until Bysis followed.

CHAPTER TWENTY-FOUR

"Stop stalling, Talus. Not much of a warrior king. I don't know why we take orders from that child, but I leave politics to Vistomus. At least it means I get to kill you." Bysis' broad face curled in joy.

Now he's out of the way. My line of attack is clear.

With no crates behind the Mirza, Talus raised his arm. "For your boldness, I'll give you the fight you crave." He let it fall, initiating a wave of translucent ruby that separated from the wings that spread out from his back.

The ghostly outline of Soul Energy wings launched like a drifting phantom silhouette from his body.

Crack!

It rushed at Bysis with the speed of an elsu in flight.

Boom!

Crimson found its mark instantly.

Bysis' slow mind could not react in the milliseconds it took for the space between the men to close. He only fed his artificial arm out of instinct. It was the only thing between his flesh and the sizzling tsunami of feathered Soul Energy.

The pale light vaporized as Talus' attack struck it.

His enormous body took the blow, and he bounced across the edge of the warehouse like a stone skipping water.

The brute stood, cracked his neck, and manifested his limb once more before picking up his sword.

Talus saw Bysis' clothes were in tatters and his skin was burned beneath. His Observation sensed the luminous arm had blunted the attack, but only that. Much of the assault had reached Bysis' body, and his Solido had not raised above the skin.

Talus realized the monstrous Mirza had taken the blast head-on and shaken it off like an annoyance.

His resilience is inhuman.

Enraged, Bysis charged like a wild boar. His steel glinted red against Talus' wings and swung with his dash. His bleached hair trailed behind him.

Pearled light radiated from him as he ran.

Booooom!!

NEGATION WINGS

The south wall shattered.

Outside, Minoru drove the armored cargo truck behind a line of nine others. They passed through the violently destroyed gate and over the cracked and pitted road.

Glenn knew it was Durath's work.

Directly ahead of them, the warehouse's upper level exploded, covering the ramp up to it in rubble. It gave them an access point, but their orders were to proceed to the lower-level bays.

"We should turn around!" Minoru cried. "Look at that. A kami battlefield is no place for normal people like us. It's madness! *We're going to die.*"

Kamatari strung together sharp Japanese words that Glenn could interpret as swearing from the tone. The truck bounced and jolted over the gate debris.

"You're a coward, Minoru…but I can't disagree. Curse the Emperor and his akuma demons."

Glenn clenched his body in dread. He had every urge to agree and demand they avoid the troublesome wielders and their dangers.

The only two he cared about were Eos and Maxima—at least, that's what his self-preservation instinct convinced him of. Now, Maxima was gone, and Eos had nothing to do with this raid. Yet, Talus had entrusted him with a task. It was a responsibility that called him to more…and he wasn't certain he could rise to meet it.

His strawberry blond brows twitched in annoyance, at his companions complaining and his own internal pull toward danger despite his nature. He growled with irritation. *"Drive!"*

They neared the lower bay doors. There were enough loading docks for all their vehicles to approach at once.

Inside the loading zone, Ramath waited for Scavok's signal.

His maroon fur cape hung from his stocky shoulders as his Soul Energy bristled energetically at his fingertips. Rich emerald green light arced in jolts up his forearms and into the sleeves of his gray tunic.

A voice called to him from far across the warehouse. It was a calm, almost amused tone. "Whatever you're planning down here, I can't let you do it."

CHAPTER TWENTY-FOUR

Durath flexed his knuckles in anticipation as a long-nosed man with a black ponytail and pale-gray skin approached in a black kimono with the Mitad's crest on his chest.

"Afraid I have work to do," Durath said.

Cyra shrugged and tilted his head in understanding. "I was hoping we could both just stay here and talk while they fought upstairs, but if you insist, I'll have to stop you. I don't enjoy fighting men with your reputation" He slipped his fingers into his left sleeve, fidgeted momentarily, and then tossed his hand out as if flinging invisible objects before him.

A wall of slate blue energy spanned out around Cyra.

"Straight to defense?" Durath questioned. "This won't be any fun at all."

"No, it won't be for either of us," Cyra sighed.

Emerald shimmered before Durath and swirled into a pair of corcinth horns—the crest of the Leorix family. "Well, you people stole my kingdom," he growled. "So, saying I won't enjoy this would be a lie."

The horns charged forward like a battering ram!

Cyra's expression was unmoved.

Zmmm! The Soul Energies met in a head on clash.

Durath expected an explosion of sparks and heat from the density of his attack against the wall of the Mirza's Soul Energy...but none came.

Instead, there was an extinguishing sound as his horns crumpled into the veil, folded into a compressed mist, and then disappeared into the muted blue light.

"What...?" Durath was at a loss for words.

Veins of emerald pulsed through Cyra's creation momentarily and then merged with it. Durath's Observation could sense the wall becoming stronger as it swallowed his attack.

Cyra raised a proud eyebrow and said, "You're a skilled opponent— far too much for me to duel with, but I don't have to win this."

Above them, Talus weathered swing after swing from Bysis' katana. Silver light bled around his wings like a wave crashing over a boat in a storm. However, Talus was not overwhelmed; instead, he was calculating while in awe at the Mirza's bottomless reservoir of Soul Energy.

NEGATION WINGS

When the barrage let up, he commended his opponent, "In terms of raw strength, you're not far off from Saida." At this, Bysis lips spread in a goofy grin. It was quickly erased, however, as Talus added, "But in terms of style and cunning, you're like a child staring at the reflection of the moon thinking you can reach out and grab it."

"I won't fall for your taunts, old man. You'll wear down eventually, but tell me this while you await your execution: why do you help these people of Nippon-Wa? What do you care about this island's fate?"

Talus glared fiercely as he declared, "I believe in the right for all to make for themselves a free life. I pursue the path of light. I uphold the Order of Soul Wielders so that they may defend all others. *That is the oath I swore!* I've seen enough destruction and death from the Mitad to not allow you another victory, however small. Wherever that may be. You've taken much from me and from innocents, but no more. I will not allow you to advance your path any longer!"

Bysis rolled his eyes and ran his hand over his braid. "Ahhh, the noble king. Such a dull bunch you inlumes of the Order are."

"Allow me to demonstrate something to you, Mirza. It is something my wife's master showed me once. I had to adapt it to be my own."

The feathers of Talus' crimson wings rustled and stood up.

Then, the projectiles shot across the warehouse!

Nearly one hundred flew as the wings faded away. Of the assault, ninety-seven were hollow forms no more than mere illusions, but the dim-witted brute didn't have the time or ability to perceive that.

Bysis chopped wildly at the blur of red that met him.

The three feathers that Talus had concentrated his will on found their mark in Bysis' massive shoulder as the rest were swatted away or evaporated on contact with the man's durable body.

The silver arm began to waiver and shrivel.

Clatter. The katana fell to the ground.

Suddenly, Bysis was looking at a mirror image of himself in Talus. His Soul Energy arm had dissipated. "Wh-what did you do?"

Talus knew that copying the Severance of another inlume was ineffective and folly in most cases; however, this was a situation where it was called for. With his adaptation of Saier Fey's technique, he could

CHAPTER TWENTY-FOUR

cripple the flow of Soul Energy in an extremely specific way—and it cost him nearly all of his bandwidth for wielding. Whereas Fey could cripple an opponent and keep fighting with further wielding abilities, Talus could only replicate the effect when focusing the majority of his aura on maintaining it.

Knowing how limited the technique was and how little time it bought them, Talus yelled out, "Scavok, I've slowed him down. Do it now!"

Scavok cursed in the Anite way, "Great Soul forsake us, Talus. I wasn't ready yet!" He took two blows from Kallag. The second penetrated his defenses enough to crack a rib.

Wasting no time, the silver-maned assassin cleared his mind in preparation for the complicated task before him. He elevated his Observation momentarily, taking in every surface of the warehouse. Then, his short sword flashed blindingly as he augmented his Severance with the manus stone blade.

Thrusting it down, Scavok stabbed Safisay into the floor!

Immediately a web of ice-blue spread across the room, weaving a grid under every crate and supply box.

The blade pierced through the ground, shining its light above Durath.

The signal!

The young wielder caught the message from the corner of his eyes. Durath formed a shimmering corcinth head. It wavered violently—then the beastly apparition charged at Cyra.

Undisturbed, the Mirza watched with calculation, prepared to absorb yet another attack from Durath. However, the corcinth manifestation turned before it collided with his defenses!

It changed course and burst into the ceiling.

The explosion was like a roar.

Concrete rained down as the floor fell out from above.

Emerald Solido raised over Durath's body, and Cyra redirected his wall in a hasty attempt to protect himself from being crushed.

NEGATION WINGS

Above, Scavok wrapped Kallag in layer after layer of his Soul Energy nets. They crawled over the blond youth as he projected out his marigold energy to keep the restraint from fully entrapping him.

The old assassin grunted as he struggled to maintain and coordinate the superhuman amount of Soul Energy. All he could do was stand still and occupy Kallag as his web descended to the first floor, carrying their loot below.

Saitani's men opened the hatch doors to the loading docks and prepared to receive the goods.

The crates were carried to the far end of the lower room by Scavok's Soul Energy as Durath and Cyra emerged from their protections, surrounded by rubble.

The multitude of crates was nearly at the edge of the building but suddenly fell to the ground! The glacial light that held them up vanished.

Scavok grunted as a punch escaped through the net and connected with his chest, throwing him to the ground. He coughed, searching for breath as Kallag broke free.

Beside him, Talus dodged attacks from Bysis, who had given up trying to swat away the blood-red feathers stuck in his shoulder. Instead, he screamed, launching beams of Soul Energy from his open mouth with each growl like a primal animal.

Talus danced and dodged, only able to send out weak projections while he suppressed Bysis' sword arm from reappearing.

Below, Cyra was the first to move.

He sprinted across the room to the bay doors on planes of Soul Energy faster than Durath could react. His gray-blue glow spread out with the flick of his wrist in front of all the openings—trapping most of Saitani's soldiers inside as they loaded the trucks.

Kamatari waddled into the wall, carrying a crate with the assistance of other men in body armor.

Minoru turned in panic. "I knew we shouldn't have come in here! Kami magic and I do not mix."

Everything being carried was abruptly dropped as they panicked into drawing their firearms and pointing at the Mirza.

CHAPTER TWENTY-FOUR

Cyra, ever calm, surrounded himself with Soul Energy armor while maintaining a barricade on the exits.

Bullets flattened against him, falling to the floor at his feet.

"Last warning, Durath, son of Ramath," Cyra called across the room. "End this raid and leave, or I will slaughter every man here."

"Well, isn't that a generous offer," Durath spat. "A man of peace, I take it?"

"I have orders to protect the weapons, nothing more. My defenses are impenetrable, even against a wielder such as yourself. The weapons aren't leaving, and it's only a matter of time until my companions above overwhelm Talus and Scavok. I'll leave you with no one to load the trucks. You lose."

Glenn paced forward. His boots took uneasy steps as he clasped his pale staff, leading with the iron-colored wings. Whispers muttered from his lips as he pleaded with a higher power to see him through this trial of courage. "That bearded giant of a king better be sure," he grumbled, approached Cyra's side, and remembered Talus demonstrating the functionality.

"One more step and you will walk no more, *ostaka*," Cyra warned, using the slur against non-wielders.

Glenn continued without saying a word. It was everything he could do to keep moving his feet. He looked with uncertainty to Durath, who nodded to reassure him.

Steely-blue light burst out at Glenn in a spike.

Flinching, Glenn turned away and held out his staff as if trying to smash an insect he was deathly afraid of.

The Soul Energy faded as it neared Glenn, evaporating like the water of a forge when molten metal is plunged into it. The blue-gray glow vanished as it approached the point of the staff.

Fear gripped Cyra. He turned his head in horror. "What...?"

Glenn faced his target with renewed bravery and laughed in disbelief that it had worked. "That's right," he stammered in awe that he was alive. "Who's still walking? A lot of talk if that's all you could do. Now you are going to lower that wall and—"

"Glenn!" Durath yelled. "Just do it!"

NEGATION WINGS

"Fine," the strawberry-bearded man sighed with disappointment. He thrust the metal wings into Cyra, whose Solido vanished, negated.

The roar of rushing Soul Energy went by Glenn's face as an emerald manifestation of a horned lion slammed into the defenseless Mirza.

Cyra slid across the ground, unconscious, before he came to rest. His long black hair was splayed messily about the concrete.

Glenn twirled his staff proudly as he joined Durath.

The Leorix King's Son glared with trauma vibrating in his pupils and clenched his jaw. "*Keep that metus stone away from me,*" he warned. "The rest of you, load the trucks up!"

"That's a strange way to say thank you," Glenn complained.

Durath looked over the unconscious Mirza. "Cheap trick," he mumbled to himself. "But your master used metus stone on me. Only fair. You offered to spare lives, so I'll return the favor this once."

Above the blown-out ceiling, Talus weaved his mass between Bysis' attacks. His heavy footwork danced swiftly enough to keep him uninjured. Meanwhile, Scavok was losing ground against Kallag, who managed to get within range.

Now he was able to obstruct Scavok's blade.

Breathing with cracked ribs, Scavok absorbed another projected punch, this one much more powerful than the previous blows he had deflected. The force threw him down the pit to where he had lowered the weapon crates.

Scavok rose to his feet. The room was empty, and only the tail lights of disappearing trucks shone past the destroyed gates.

Alone on the pavement outside, he saw Durath taking out a fleet of reinforcement vehicles that had arrived. Explosions rang in the sky as the Emperor's military trucks and backup soldiers were left in flames. The phantom mirage of a corcinth trampled everything before it.

The Soul Energy beast leaped into the air.

Through the bay door, the next thing Scavok saw was two helicopters plummeting to the ground. Their eruption into the asphalt woke Scavok from his momentary stupor just in time as Kallag descended on him.

CHAPTER TWENTY-FOUR

"Talus!" the Master Assassin cried out. "It's time to go. Durath is holding the gate!"

Kallag landed before Scavok with an innocent smile. "Well, you must have pulled something cheap to do that to Cyra." The expression turned grim. His pupils vibrated, his lips went thin, and his head turned down as the young man's knuckles went white. "*I won't forgive you for that.*"

Talus' voice shook the room as he landed in a furious jump from the floor above. His beard bounced, and his knees flexed until he was nearly kneeling to brace his fall on crimson planes of energy. "I'm afraid you'll have to save that for another time."

Ruby red wings grew behind him.

The lumbering silver-armed giant fell to join them.

Gunfire splattered the soundscape outside, split by occasional explosions and the crackling of Durath's Soul Energy.

Marigold Soul Energy burned like heat waves around Kallag's fists. "What makes you say that, Anite King?" He thrust forward a flurry of punches that were immediately joined by the silver projection of Bysis' katana.

The majestic wings fluttered to a folded position that resembled a shield between the two parties. Talus' auburn eyes looked at his friend with the reflection of their enemies' Soul Energies in the gloss of his whites.

"Go, Scavok. Take Durath. I'll be right behind you. This is going to empty my Soul Reservoir. I'll save just enough to Soul Step to the truck convoy."

The feathers of his wings turned out like molten lava porcupine quills—all pointed at Bysis and Kallag.

Slowly, then suddenly.

An immense barrage of Soul Energy feathers drowned out the two mirzas. The pelting did not cease as Talus spent every last drop of his reserve.

Each feather point was an explosion from the Visrex of Wings—a brilliant attack that required the victim's complete focus on Solido to survive.

The King intended to leave nothing to spare.

NEGATION WINGS

Their enemy was immobilized, and their layer of protective light was cracking.

Talus doubted it would be enough to finish them. More tactic would be required for that, but Bysis and Kallag were paralyzed under the rain of elsu feathers as Talus turned to join the faraway convoy.

He skated on planes of light; his focus split between sprinting and maintaining the volley of crimson behind him. Yet, despite his intense attention to technique, the quiet voice in the back of his mind ran wild.

He missed his daughter and worried for his son.

Aizo's with Eos now. He's safe.

Maxima's with Fey. Safe.

They're safe.

Still, Eos' advancing curse mark and recent lashing out had weighed on him for weeks. He couldn't imagine the anguish his son felt. He had to let Eos know Maxima was alive.

As the vision of the trucks finally came into view minutes later, his thoughts shifted to the fate of Nippon-Wa and the Left Eye of Izanagi.

Such a powerful artifact. Vistomus can't get it, no matter what. The Flow of All Things must remain out of his grasp.

When he finally reached a truck and slipped inside the fast-moving vehicle, he mourned the violence.

Soon, Son. We will put this business of the Mitad and the evils they spread behind us. We will be a family in a thriving, peaceful kingdom. Then you and Maxima can focus on your noble journey to become inlumes. Soon.

CHAPTER TWENTY-FIVE

THE BLUE CORCINTH

Polished onyx, like burnt mirrors, surrounded Maxima in every direction. It was a maze of glossy black stone as far as she could see. Every path led to a new expanse that was never-ending. Her reflection was on every surface, distorted and dark enough to only see her shape but not make out any details.

The air had a charred flavor every time she opened her mouth, and there was a hum to the world as if a single note had been strummed on an instrument and left to ring for eternity.

As she wandered this inner world, loneliness began to suffocate her. She realized that the place wasn't the source. The Holy Penitus Ostium fragment, as the Order of Soul Wielders called it, had merely magnified the isolation that was building inside her.

She began to wander faster until she turned through onyx aisles at a panicked jog. Here, she was truly alone. Outside, in the physical world, she had Fey to provide some comfort while she masqueraded as dead. Here, there were only obscure reflections.

Maxima slowed as she turned all around, taking in how lost she was as hours melted together. Eventually, her back fell against the polished walls, and she slid to the floor. It was here, curled up, that she knew who she longed for more than anyone. Her mother and father would have brought tears flowing if they had been here. Zolo's green eyes lingered in her mind. Even Ares, who she barely understood, would have been a welcomed presence.

But above all, her heart cried out for her brother.

Eos. You're worlds away thinking that I died.

At this, salty tears splashed on black stone, bringing out a violet hue. Her raven-haired head fell into her arms as she wept.

Eos...I will get out of here and find you.

That inspiration kept her from absolute despair.

She dried her eyes with the silky fabric of her teal Lenape dress and turned to her wielding to Observation. She sensed Soul Energy loosely tied to every feature inside this shard of Amaterasu's Mirror.

It was faint but familiar. It was hers and pulsed like blood vessels through the rocks—all leading further inward. Some paths were weaker, and the trail would die off. Others were like arteries, coursing consistently.

Maxima stood and followed the flow.

The newly illuminated path gave her the motivation to trudge forward. She resolved to follow it to its end and find a way out.

Faster and faster, she traced the coursing Soul Energy through the lifeless terrain. Sapphire light glinted beneath her feet as she flew past murky, mirror-world versions of herself that disappeared around jagged edges and rematerialized in dozens of far-off surfaces.

Then, she reached it—the heart of the mirror realm. The faint rhythm of what she tracked became vivid, like finding words after days without speaking. The source of aura was a slab of stone, perfectly smooth and twenty feet tall. It was opaque, unlike every other surface around her. There was no reflection in the onyx-frosted glass.

CHAPTER TWENTY-FIVE

Daring to hope for a way out or anything that would end the solitary confinement, Maxima reached out for it. As she did, she sensed a presence within. When her lightly tanned skin met the cool surface, a spark of Soul Energy jumped from her fingertip.

Another flicker of blue sprang from the stone.

The two lights met at the interface of the cloudy glass and her fingertip. At the instant of union, the fogginess receded and peeled back like melting ice. It revealed a mirror of perfect night. No color disturbed the infinite blacks it held, save her image.

Her reflection looked back. Slim figure, elegant dress with subtly woven flowers in the sleeves that clung practical and tight in case combat was needed, hair that morphed into the mirror's color, and a face—*there was no face! There should have been sapphire eyes and a faint scar over pink lips!*

Clutching her face, she felt for the missing features in the image shown to her. She tried to scream but couldn't find a sound to make. The crawling in her skin calmed when her fingers felt the contours of eyes, nose, and lips that the horrifying reflection did not reveal.

As her fright receded, the reflection conjured a blue smoke.

It formed into a veil over her head, though nothing was before her physical face.

Then, it materialized into the blue corcinth mask that she had donned over the past weeks to hide herself.

Her mirror image began to move on its own.

Clasping. Pulling. Clawing. Anything to remove the mask.

To return to Maxima Bellator.

A whispering laugh filled the air.

"You can have your identity back. You can reclaim your life," the air hissed at her. Suddenly the mask was gone, but she was turned away, looking over a body. Upon closer inspection, she saw the deceased was Ares. He lay lifeless at her feet.

Maxima lost her breath momentarily. Then she choked out, "No. I can't. Not after what Ares did for me."

The mask returned with a fierce grin.

THE BLUE CORCINTH

"Even if it keeps you separated from everyone you love? Even if it costs Eos believing you're dead?" the voice tempted from the other side of the glass.

Maxima's emotions died in a cathartic realization.

"Yes," she murmured. "I'll do what is required until I can be Maxima Bellator again."

The mask floated away from her reflection's face and past the surface of polished stone.

It pushed beyond the glass, escaping from inside.

Manifesting before Maxima as a real object, it faced her.

Maxima back peddled in horror. Her instincts screamed to run from such an unnatural occurrence, but something about her steadfast nature and knowing where she stood kept her from looking away.

Sapphire mist formed a body-like shape so that the mask had an incorporeal form as it hovered before her.

"That's not what you really want, is it?" the thing said.

Seconds passed as she hesitated.

"I want to return to Master Fey."

"You're in here with me. Out there, you're just a dead girl who everyone has forgotten. Forget the weight of consequences. You deserve to be yourself again."

"No," she countered firmly.

The masked humanoid form did not try to speak again.

It lashed out!

Misty blue Soul Energy flashed before Maxima.

Instinctually, she summoned a wave of her light to block the attack. *Zmmm!* They clashed with a harmonic hum that resonated in all the rocks around them.

Confused and off guard, Maxima kept her distance as attacks multiplied. Embers of blue sparked on the ground as they clashed.

Maneuvering with skill and agility, she danced around the onslaught of lashes, blocking as needed.

Each time, she became more tempted to return an attack.

Yet, something stayed her violence.

The energy didn't feel foreign and aggressive.

CHAPTER TWENTY-FIVE

It felt like it was her own.

She grunted as she braced against an attack.

Parrying every lurch and stretch of the mask's advance, she found a moment of delay. In that second, she followed a guiding instinct below her conscious thoughts and reached for the corcinth face.

Her hand seized the ceramic grin.

The mass of Soul Energy paused at the action.

"I will be the Blue Corcinth *for as long as required.*"

Maxima lit a bit of Soul Energy in her palm.

It formed a glowing layer over the horned mask.

Then, the mask lost its physical form.

The blue-dyed clay turned to pure light, and it absorbed into her palm until she was left alone again inside Amaterasu's Mirror.

"Well done," the voice whistled one final time as it washed away.

Maxima accepted her state and caught her breath.

As her exhales slowed, the world of onyx stone faded.

Maxima was sitting before Fey.

There was a quality to her Soul Energy that was more still and vibrant after the experience in the void of the Holy Penitus Ostium fragment. She tenderly touched the mask at her side, remembering Caldus and accepting it as her temporary identity. There was peace with the acknowledgment, as if she knew it was a path she was meant to be on.

"Welcome back, Maxima," Fey greeted her. "It's done."

The raven hair bounced with certainty as Maxima nodded.

Fey explained, "Whatever you overcame in there…it will allow you to access deeper into your essence. It may manifest the next time you wield Soul Energy, months from now, or in a stressful battle, but your Severence will develop new forms."

The door opened before Maxima could respond.

Bellia entered, her dress falling over her pregnant belly in a purple and blue flutter of cloth with white sea turtle patterns waving as she moved.

"It's time. We must go now," Bellia urged.

THE BLUE CORCINTH

Fey retrieved her long-handled blade from its hiding place under the bed, gathered her bag of stolen scrolls, and placed the mirror fragment back in the pouch around her neck.

They followed the trail of blond hair and high cheekbones moving elegantly through grand halls despite the late stage of her pregnancy. Within five minutes, they were in Jezca's quarters.

Maxima met Jezca with a broken smile. They looked at each other with a bond formed by their experience in the Mircite Valley. Jezca's crystal pink eye glowed with recognition.

"I thought you were dead," Jezca whispered.

"Everyone thinks I'm dead," Maxima smirked slightly.

"What...?"

"The Priori of Karnak decided to find you and rescue you from the Mitad, Jezca Lapithos," Fey said. "Tavro and the Priori Council entrusted us with the task. We mustn't let you or your mother's journal fall to the enemy."

Jezca hesitated. Platinum hair fell over her manus stone eye as she glanced away. "I...I came here by choice. I'm trying to find my mom. They know where she is." She pulled a black stone from her pocket.

Fey's eyes went wide. "Is that a constellation stone?"

"It's my mother's. She's all I have left now. With Caldus gone..." Jezca clutched the stone to her chest sadly.

Maxima hugged the priestess and said, "I haven't seen my brother since the battle either."

Jezca did not resist the gesture, but made no attempt to return it.

"Grace's constellation stone?" Fey wondered aloud.

Jezca nodded, but her gaze fell on the painted corcinth face tied to Maxima's waist. "Is that...?"

"It's Caldus' mask," Maxima confirmed.

"But it's blue now?"

Maxima smiled, a little embarrassed. "I may have changed the color a bit."

For the first time in months, Jezca laughed genuinely. "It suits you that way."

"Did you find her?" Fey interrupted.

CHAPTER TWENTY-FIVE

"Not exactly. Mom communicated through it, but it's so far away, wherever she is. It's like hearing an echo and not being able to understand the words."

"That only makes sense. I received word from Master Salvaluc's messenger elsu on our way to Lenape. Grace is trapped on Earth—a kingdom called Nippon-Wa."

Maxima's expression tensed at the words. Her rough comprehension of Earth geography pieced together what that meant—*the island nation across the Pacific Ocean.*

"I know," Jezca said. "Bellia told me that's where they lost her and where they still search for her. They're using me to get closer to her. I figure if it works...I won't tell them, and I'll go after her myself. So far, nothing. I've had more luck through Eos."

"Eos?" Maxima asked with concern.

"Our dreams are tied together. Ever since the night at the Manus Temple where we cracked the roof, I see memories—his memories...when I sleep. Some of them are from childhood. A few feel current. I think he's with my mom in this land you called Nippon-Wa. They're just flashes. There was a red wooden archway in the ocean and then armored men with swords fighting him. Then...I saw my mom in the doorway talking with Eos. It was only a few seconds, but I've been seeing these sequences a lot lately—especially that strange gate. Red pillars with a curved roof," Jezca muttered and squinted as she tried to recall the details.

Again, Maxima's mind was churning. The description was familiar, but she didn't know why. *Where have I seen that before?*

Bellia interjected, "As much as I'd love to let you all keep talking, Saida is on his way back to the castle this evening. He could arrive earlier than I anticipated—*and then we would all be dead.* He's somewhere on the island's coast for business with Astor Bruinsma. Lady Sugra is away. This is our window to move. Now I don't expect you have a boat off Lenape? There's no time to try and coordinate one now."

Fey shook her head. "No, and the distance is too great to Soul Step. We'd drown without land to rest on."

"Then I only see one way of possibly escaping," Bellia said hesitantly.

THE BLUE CORCINTH

"You use your powers to get us off the island?" Maxima asked with a hopeful eyebrow raised.

"That would get us all killed. I'm under the same curse as your brother. All ranking Mitad members are. Saida would instantly know that I've used my power. Probably even know where I move you to. He'd kill me and my child but probably force me to help hunt you down first."

Fey rubbed her temples as she thought. "Then what do you propose besides a fight to the death against the man who took Talus Bellators arm?"

"The King will cover for us. He's always had a soft spot for you, Fey. As far as anyone will know, I've fallen ill, and he's been by my side all day. There was no possible way that I could have communicated with you. Especially not to tell you that he has hidden the Mellizo Glyph in his office vault behind the painting."

The notion perplexed Maxima. She chewed her lip as the reality of their desperate situation set in. "How would that help us? We could only use it to cross worlds if we were in the Sepeleo Mountains. The Mellizo Glyph only works in specific locations."

"Not exactly. I don't understand it, but Saida has said there are ways to use it from anywhere. I've only caught parts of his discussions, but he mentioned a coordinate system and being able to travel anywhere with it."

Coordinates. Red roofed pillars.

Pieces of a tapestry were weaving together in Maxima's head. She couldn't see the entire vision nor how the strands were connected, yet she held onto threads forming some grand image. She laced her fingers together in concentration and flexed them out, cracking her knuckles as she waded through the puzzle.

"Even if that's true," Fey reasoned, "we'd still have to solve how to use it before Saida arrives."

Bellia shrugged apologetically. "You should have left the island on the boat my father prepared for you. This is the best I can offer. I'm taking far too much risk as it is. Now, I must get to my sickbed so that my story has evidence. I'll tell you how to get to Saida's office. The rest is up to you."

CHAPTER TWENTY-FIVE

"It could be our only chance to get the Mellizo Glyph back," Maxima reasoned. "We may not get another, and the last thing we want to fight is Vistomus or Saida…or worse with the addition of the glyph's power."

Fey grunted in agreement and gestured for Maxima to put on her mask. Only jet-black hair showed as the anatus Soul Wielder donned her Blue Corcinth identity.

They traveled together most of the way, but Bellia left them to find Saida's private room on their own. When she parted, Bellia told them, "At the end of this hallway, you'll find a staircase. Take it up two floors. Then follow that to the northmost room. You'll know it by a banner hanging beside the door of a crescent moon around a sword."

"That's the crest of the Atilsha family," Fey murmured.

"You better get there quick. You don't have much time. Saida could be in the castle *now* for all we know," Bellia gave a final warning before parting.

The stretch of hall was immense. It took them five minutes to cross it, passing thousands of hexagon-like stones that created a turtle shell pattern on the walls around oval windows. The staircase spiraled, and the three women sprinted up the twisting steps.

An aura crept over them, causing the hair on their arms and neck to rise. It was malevolent and volatile.

They ran faster, planes of energy manifesting under their feet as they climbed the last step. Out the windows of the castle's sixth story, they could overlook Setudo's royal lake.

The aura closed in on them.

The walls were lined with maps and drapery, but Maxima had no time to observe the tribal patterns and rich oceanic colors.

"No matter what," Fey exclaimed to Maxima, "you must not wield. Let no one perceive your Soul Energy!"

Maxima became worried, "Why would I need to wield? That aura…" Maxima's panting breath was muffled as they made for the end of the hall.

Zmmm! Soul Energy ripped the air apart before them.

THE BLUE CORCINTH

Strings of mauve light striped the hallway like dozens of thin, vibrating prison bars. They stretched from floor to ceiling, strobing white at the core with muddied purple edges where the plasma-like energy bit at the air.

"In such a rush that you couldn't take time to see me, Saier Fey?" Saida called tauntingly from behind them. "I knew it smelled of inlume in here. Can't stand the self-righteous stench." He let strings of light slowly stream from his fingertips toward the three women, teasing his control.

They broke their sprint, stumbling uncontrollably to avoid colliding with the blockade. Jezca whirled and fell to the side, Maxima rolled her ankle with the deceleration, and Fey nimbly jumped against the wall of strings with Soul Energy at her feet to rebound off of and protect her.

Saier Fey straightened her posture and gripped the hilt of her polearm blade from under her cloak.

"Saida," she said with a bitter nod.

"That's all you have to say to me, you withered-up inlume? I can't imagine you're taking a casual run for exercise in the exact direction of my office? With *my favorite little priestess*, no less."

Fey growled, "We did our research before we came here."

"Apparently, someone's been talking too much in this castle. I'll have to make sure they never talk again. I don't suppose you'd save me the trouble of investigating?" Saida clicked his mouth chidingly.

"Afraid not," Fey said tersely.

Light broke through a rounded window, centered on where she stood like a spotlight, while Saida loomed in shadow with only his extended hands teasing lines of Soul Energy in the sunlight. His murderous mustached expression hid out of the sun's beam.

Saida shook his head of tawny hair in amusement. "So, you chose Castle Setudo as your place and my hand as your method to die. It'll be an honor to put an expired relic like you to pasture, Saier."

"You're a stain on your bloodline, Saida," she crowed.

"You act as if that's an insult."

CHAPTER TWENTY-FIVE

Fey glanced back momentarily as she said, "I'll hold Saida off as long as I can. Jezca, give everything you have to breaking through that barrier. Keep advancing no matter what!"

Saida didn't let the words finish echoing in the halls before he whipped a rope of five wound light-strings from his fingertip and sent them piercing toward Fey.

The short inlume ducked, spun on her toes while sweeping her right leg out for balance, and twirled her blade from her waist.

The black leaf-shaped blade cut up. Its edge glowed topaz.

It met Saida's Soul Energy in a cacophony of vibrating, aggravated humming. The air was scented with a singed odor as inlume and Mitad powers collided.

The strings snapped, and the separated pieces faded, but Saida only produced more. All the while, he maintained his barricade behind her.

Jezca let loose, sending jagged pulses of her energy against it as if an invisible creature was running its magical claws through the air. The pink and purple lights clashed violently.

Saida's bars waivered but did not fail. She continued a flurry of attacks, throwing her arms into the motion as it reinforced her mental command of the Soul Energy.

Maxima stood against the wall, feeling helpless.

Her nature swelled, tempted to wield and help in the fight, but she had sworn against it. Fey's wisdom must have known the best path.

Still, the urge was bubbling up within her. She channeled the willpower and anxiousness into her thoughts as she ran through her mental register of all the notes she had ever written; every book page, character of foreign language, symbol, and rune she had ever seen. They flowed through her visualization as she parsed for something useful to answer their need for an exit.

Jezca's relentless attacks paid off. Between the distraction of Saida's duel and the strength of her attacks, the bars of violet energy wavered and broke.

The long black blade swung, advancing on the distracted Mitad leader. He flashed a layer of Solido over his body as Fey closed the distance.

THE BLUE CORCINTH

The glaive rang out in a disharmonious screech against his defensive layer. It was short-lived.

Strings bent towards Fey the moment she recovered her blade, forcing her to dodge back on planes of light to avoid being skewered.

The three women advanced down the hall as the path cleared.

It was quickly blocked.

The mauve bars sprung from the floor.

Jezca resumed her barrage with desperate fury.

Fey swung her glaive masterfully.

The rhythm of the battle was set.

The barrier would break.

Fey would give up her advantage to proceed towards Saida's office.

Saida would recover his advantage and the wall of strings.

They flowed in a procession of Soul Energy cords against the glowing blade. All the while, Maxima was thumbing frantically through her volume of research notes like a mad scientist on the verge of a breakthrough that could save her life.

Zmmm!

Energies rang out through the north wing of the castle. The office door with the crescent-wrapped sword banner was within sight. Just one more break of the barrier would get them within reach.

Saida realized how close they were and launched a set of cords at the Blue Corcinth. With the unbelievable mastery of a savant wielder, he maintained the wall, clashed with Fey, and now sent violet death flickering toward the masked woman.

Fey cried out in warning.

Maxima's eyes dilated in instant realization.

The underhanded tactic was effective.

Maxima's focus was on her notes. A revelation had just come to her, but it distracted her fighting instincts. She didn't even think to override Fey's instructions by wielding.

She was perfectly vulnerable, unable to react in time.

The thin arm of the master inlume extended.

Her long-handled glaive slipped through a loose grip.

Yellow-gold flashed from its edge as she did so.

CHAPTER TWENTY-FIVE

A wave of Soul Energy burst forth as the blade flew!

It split Saida's strings and saved Maxima from certain death.

The black metal pierced the stone wall and lodged in it. In the seconds that followed, Fey was exposed and weaponless.

Saida went for her chest with an attack.

Jezca saw the moment of distraction as his attack failed to reach Maxima. She struck! Her claws of light scarred the air. They manifested at his neck but found his shoulder as he moved.

A deep grunt of pain came as Saida bled through his black canvas coat. With the pain, he chose to drop his attack on Fey to preserve the obstacle between them and his office.

Saier Fey seized the opportunity. She slid in, small and swift.

Her index and middle fingers were pointed, thrusting into Saida's shoulder and bicep repeatedly. Skillful motions blurred as her hands worked.

Six strikes in under two seconds.

She rolled away, grabbed the hilt of her blade, and yanked it from the wall.

The barrier fell.

Raising his arm, Saida became confused.

"You hag witch!" he cried. "My wielding!"

"Yes, I cut off the Soul Energy channels in your arm," Fey said, pleased. A proud smile stretched across her face.

"Gesture only brings clarity to wielding," Saida said grimly. "That's what they teach. You should know I'm far beyond the need for that!" he rumbled with hatred.

While his wall was down, Jezca and Maxima bolted for the heavy oak office door.

Jezca wasted no time testing if the door was locked. Her Soul Energy melted through the door handle and shattered the wall where the locking mechanism would have been. She kicked her way through as she got to the room.

Reaching the office only enraged Saida further.

He relented, giving up on preventing their entrance. Instead, his brow furled, his mustache quivered, and he turned his intent on killing

THE BLUE CORCINTH

Fey. The twisted scowl was magnified by the ugly scar that created a trench on his chin and cheek.

With each focused blow, Fey was thrown back.

Saida's arm hung limp, but he did not need it to form his weapons. His wielding skill required no physical motion, only harnessed hatred and years of honed mental technique as the strings manifested around him.

Hundreds of threads formed like a living loom.

"I'll hold him off. Get it quickly!" Fey screamed as she became overwhelmed by a multitude of light beams shrieking their electric drone. Waves of rose-pink light emanated from her blade and around her body in rapid succession to parry. With every flash of her energy, she slid back.

Inside the office, ivy-colored drapes hung from the walls and framed the magnificent view of Setudo Lake. Saida's walnut desk was stained black, and a huge battle scene painting with a castle on fire hung on the wall.

Jezca tore it from the wall as Bellia had instructed, revealing a safe. There was no locking mechanism to turn on the face nor handle with which to open it.

The priestess knew a wielder's safe would be lined with enough anima stone to absorb far more Soul Energy than she had time or endurance to expend.

Maxima spread her bound notes out on the table, piecing together the answer to the Mellizo Glyph mystery that had been in her head all along. She began rotating the book and twisting her head to view it from different angles.

Every second mattered. Each thought pattern was crucial.

No wasted moments. Absolute focus.

"The red wooden gate! The painting! It's a dial," Maxima exclaimed, overjoyed at her private revelation. "It's a rune dial!" She stared at the sketch of the tool she found during her initiation night in Fanum Ortus. It consisted of concentric rings subdivided into small sections with runes.

"That's great, but right now, I need silence," Jezca muttered. Her animus stone eye was bright like fire in her skull as she touched her fingers to the two-headed snake raised on the surface with ruby eyes.

CHAPTER TWENTY-FIVE

The psychic priestess went to work. With her gemstone eye lit, she saw through the metal surface with her perception.

The notched wheels gilded in manus stone were as apparent in her mind as if she was seeing them exposed on the table. Her Soul Energy drifted into the snake eyes and began carefully turning the notched wheels of the vault.

"Apparently I'm the only one who can't pick locks around here," Maxima mumbled aloud.

A scream of wounded agony came from outside the room.

Fey resisted the urge to clutch her bicep, which now had a thin hole through it. The action would have been the death of her.

Inlume instincts took over.

She ignored the gushing wound and used her good arm to swing her glaive in a motion that would have cut Saida in half had he not dodged.

The two stared each other down like wild animals.

"Jezca, I hope you're almost done," Fey cried out.

Saida stalked Fey as she backed into a wall. "What? You think you can break into *my* safe and somehow get away with *my* treasure alive? This is the end of the road for you, Fey. Weak. Old. Washed up. Just like your Order of Soul Wielders."

Inside the room, Jezca said to herself, "Got it!"

The blond priestess pressed in the door panel, and it sprung open, revealing papers, money, and a rectangular vial relic. She plucked it, examining the tiny pressed etchings of symbols that marked all sides of it.

The artifact was made of a dark-hued marble with each engraved rune highlighted in white and two larger, prominent markings of the Human Essence and the two spheres with encircling tails.

Jezca set it on the desk while Maxima was still working frantically. Her sapphire eyes flickered between pages, holding her fingers in multiple places to mark different parts of the notes she was coordinating.

Maxima pulled the Mellizo Glyph over her sketch of the dial from Fanum Ortus' library shelf.

The symbols were a match, just as she had suspected!

THE BLUE CORINTH

"It's a coordinate system," Maxima spoke aloud. "I don't know how it works entirely, but the red wooden gate painting had runes in the corner like a signature."

Soul Energy clashed outside the room's walls.

Jezca didn't understand anything being said but urged, "We have to hurry. I don't think your inlume will hold up much longer."

"I'm going as fast as I can," Maxima said with strain. She turned over the dark artifact and let the slightest drop of energy bleed from her fingertip. The sapphire Soul Energy lit up a central rune. "This one should allow for resetting the coordinates."

She lit three more symbols with the smallest amount of energy required. They glowed as if light was escaping from the core of the Mellizo Glyph, brightly shining through the stone. "There! Those should get us there."

The brilliant anatus wielder gathered her notes as the glyph shone from four runes. She tucked her belongings into her side bag and commanded, "Jezca, open the Mellizo Glyph and fill it with Soul Energy! I've set it for Nippon-Wa...I hope."

Jezca didn't understand, but she didn't hesitate.

Outside, Fey was cornered. Her chestnut hair was pressed against the window. Her eyes creased in the corners as she searched for a path out.

Violet Strings pierced the wall on either side of Fey as Saida gloated before his kill. "I'll give Salvaluc your regards, Fey. I'll tell him you fought well. Not nearly the feeble hag you project to the world these days," he sneered from the other side of the hallway.

"You never deserved Salvaluc," Fey retorted, shifting her feet and one-handed glaive grip as she distracted the Mitad leader. "He's many times over the wielder and the man you are. Remember that when you are looking up at me with my sword pointed down on you." Blood was soaking her sleeve, dyeing it a rich crimson-brown.

Saida laughed hard. "Strange words to part this world with, but that's your choice." He contorted the fingers on his functioning arm and commanded his strings for a final plunge into Fey.

The Inlume's glaive flashed with preemptive light.

CHAPTER TWENTY-FIVE

The onyx blade swung into the ground.

The floor exploded!

Rocks crumbled. Debris sank as pink light plunged the sixth floor into the room below.

Saida's bearded mouth let out a startled yell.

His strings of light scattered to stabilize his fall.

Looking up from a pile of rubble, the last thing he saw was the tip of Fey's glaive pointed down at him. She could have chosen to advance in the moment of advantage—to send a wave of Soul Energy through the hole. Instead, she seized the opportunity for escape and turned to join Jezca and Maxima with the Mellizo Glyph.

CHAPTER TWENTY-SIX

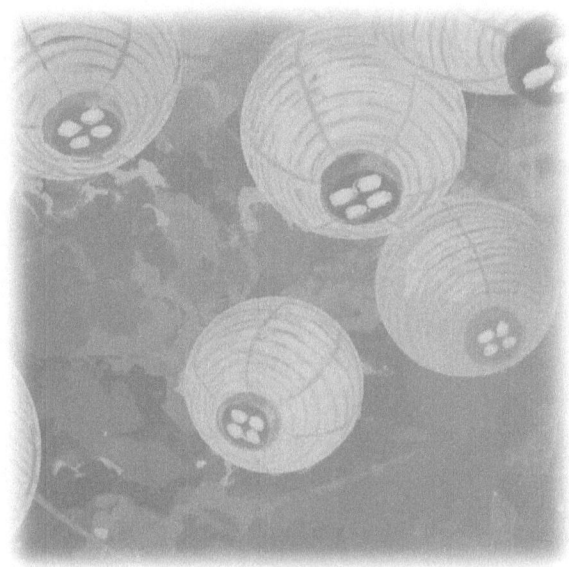

VOID TEMPTATIONS

Raked sand twisted in curling patterns at the edge of a pond. Paper lanterns were strung to create a soft glow above the brighter toro pedestal flickers as dusk made its first creep into the day.

Eos sat cross-legged before Aizo as the tranquil sound of a small waterfall pattered behind him, washing out the distant sounds of Saigo's castle.

"Aizo, these dreams are becoming more frequent. Last night...I saw things that weren't possible...but it was so real."

Stroking his graying copper facial hair, Aizo grunted and nodded. "These are the dreams of the priestess girl? Grace's daughter?"

Eos rubbed his cursed arm nervously. "Yes. It felt like all the others—real! But this time, I saw Caldus. His corcinth mask, at least...it

CHAPTER TWENTY-SIX

was a different color. Blue. Like…" he trailed off, daring not to speak what it reminded him of.

Like the color of Maxima's Soul Energy.

Aizo's eyes remained closed, and his eyebrows pulled together. He had spent the entirety of the previous day placing a seal on Carnus and half the afternoon doing maintenance on Eos' seal. It had weakened to the point of barely being recognizable, but Aizo wove his Soul Energy to repair the best he could.

This diversion was more than Aizo had the capacity to interpret. "I'll ponder the meaning of this dream. For now, you must clear your mind, my anatus. Release your thoughts and worries and find your Soul Void. You need to master your emotions and impulses further if we have any hope of you wielding again without losing yourself to the curse mark."

Exhale. Inhale.

Soon, Eos' heartbeat and breathing rhythm left no room for straying ideas and wandering thoughts. He welcomed it. Saigo's bushi lifestyle was encapsulated in this private garden. The inner peace was a blessing. Between his dreams, his curse, and the struggle with the Mitad, his conscious, logical thinking was a constant stressor.

Badum. Badum. Heartbeat filled his ears.

Without opening his eyes, he saw everything emerge around him in a ghostlike mirage. The garden, with its sand and lanterns, shimmered in a haze solidifying smoke.

His master was no longer before him.

A dark form emerged in Aizo's absence.

Cloaked and masked, Zala Alsar stared back at him.

Echoing from outside his inner realm, Aizo's voice instructed him, "Focus on the feeling in your core. There, your willpower rests, and your shame weighs on you. This is the third gate of your soul."

Zala laughed dismissively during a pause of silence.

Aizo continued, "What are your greatest disappointments? What shames do you carry?"

A battering of regret tied Eos' core in an anxious knot.

If only he could undo his past decisions.

VOID TEMPTATIONS

He had rushed headlong into Saida's factories at Mircite. Eos' leadership had brought Caldus to his death. *Gone.* His beloved sister. *Gone.* Then, he had returned to that marred site, only to be saved by Scavok. Even before that…Major Clark. *Gone.* How did he act in response to these mistakes? The thought of his recklessness made him nauseous. He wanted to hide, from his master, his father, Durath, and even himself.

He had followed this streak of irresponsibility by charging straight after Ares on Earth—no regard for his companion's safety or even his own life. Rage had consumed him.

Aizo's instruction soothed him. "You must accept those mistakes and embrace humility. Only in humbleness can you overcome your shame, accept yourself, and improve going forward."

Zala stalked around before him as if he could barely contain himself to listen to Aizo's words. "Are you really going to listen to the senile man and his ramblings about humility? What could come of it? Vistomus is going to find the Left Eye of Izanagi any day now, and Aizo wants to sit around here, hiding from the conflict that must occur."

Eos' forehead twitched in contemplation. "What would you suggest, Zala? Aizo is wise."

"No, Aizo is stuck in his dogma. You have the ability to stop Vistomus yourself. I can show you how to use that curse properly! Take Durath—he's bound to you by oath. Stop Vistomus before he gains the power to destroy all of Nippon-Wa. Then, he'll unleash it on Anite."

Minutes passed as he was locked in internal debate and conflict about Zala's temptations. Time warped as if he was stuck in a loop of torment.

"I would put myself and everyone else in so much danger. It would be like my battle with Ares, only worse!" Eos rationalized.

"You can walk through it successfully. Let me guide you. The alternative is to give Vistomus exactly what he wants. It would be letting him win."

Eos let his temptation and fears slip away.

CHAPTER TWENTY-SIX

Humility. Aizo's words guided his intuition. "No. The wisdom of the inlumes is greater than mine. My selfish choices have had consequences that I can't let happen again. No matter what."

A wave of relief warmed Eos.

Zala's suggestions ceased.

Soul Energy flowed within him more purely. It was as if he had been drinking from a tainted pool that suddenly became clear.

Aizo sensed it. "Hold onto the clarity that comes from humility, Eos. It will be a never-ending battle. Even I struggle daily with it, but in time, you will set aside pride. Its temptations will only be a fleeting desire. Now, move your focus to your heart. It's where you hold your grief. I'm sure there is much pain kept here."

The moment Eos' attention reached the heart, a pang of longing for Maxima nearly broke him.

"It hurts. *So badly,*" Eos whispered in a cracked voice.

"I know, Eos. It's good to be sad for a time, to miss her. But you have to release that sadness so you can function at your full potential. It's what Maxima would have wanted. Release your loss and let the pain flow away. Being free of pain does not mean forgetting. It means remembering in a way that honors her."

Eos held the memory of his sister dearly in his mind.

Aizo's voice became distant after that. It was a faraway guide.

He was *here.* In the Soul Void. *With Zala.* The realm became more real than the outside world in his current perception. The smokey forms in his surroundings condensed into more vivid matter.

Zala's white mask floated to Eos above a mass of black fabric.

Pale gray hands gestured out as if simultaneously casting and revealing. The dark sleeve undulated before him, and when it pulled away, a blue spark hovered between them like an embryo of light.

"Maxima," Eos whispered.

Zala nodded.

A sickening premonition followed. Darkness percolated within him—a venomous tide cresting after the nausea of the prior gate-opening experience.

Eos noticed a bubbling at his feet.

VOID TEMPTATIONS

The curse was bleeding through the blades of grass and indentions of sand. The ooze was a weeping wound on everything around them.

Beneath the wisp of fluttering blue, the curse gathered.

It clambered in beads towards Maxima's remnant light.

The boundary of sapphire glow repelled the dark substance.

An inky mass formed like an egg shell at the outer boundary as if a magnetic force was repelling the curse from tainting the wisp. However, the glow was weak and faltering.

Zala called from the other side of the spark, "The last traces of her are fading. Soon it won't be enough to hold back the curse."

Pangs of longing.

Piercing despair.

Maxima's last light was disappearing. How could he save it…hold on to it…preserve it?

Release your loss. Let the pain flow away.

Eos obeyed his inlume's direction. It was not easy, nor was he efficient at it, but he attempted.

The shell of oily substance beaded up further, nearly encompassing the blue. Eos panicked momentarily, and in that instant, Maxima's light was almost snuffed.

No. Honor her by functioning at your full potential.

Eos realized what was required.

"Narruh Risha," he summoned. "Save what's left of Maxima. Please." The words were low and firm in their request. No sooner than his lips closed, the crimson elsu descended over the closing black sphere.

Narruh's wings bristled like tongues of flames and wrapped around the struggle. The red became blinding white and drove the curse back.

Then, crimson flowed in feathered streams into the sapphire light. They marbled together like they had where it all began—at the generator complex in the desert.

The Soul Energy expanded, multiplying in volume. Maxima's share was not diluted; it grew with the churning orb and increased in intensity.

The field of rays drove back the curse into the ground.

Accumulated beads scattered.

Then, the curse receded entirely as if time had reversed.

CHAPTER TWENTY-SIX

When the last drop of curse returned under the Soul Void's ground, the fiery elsu of his soul hovered above, a kaleidoscope of Soul Energy.

"Thank you, Narruh."

Eos turned to Zala, who paced nearby, watching the development curiously. "What I have left of her is enough. Maxima will always be a part of me. No matter what."

Relinquishing his previous words, Zala spread out his arms.

"So it is. Most impressive, Eos. You maintain control another day, but I'll be waiting for you to slip up. If you do, I will protect us where you cannot."

Zala's image wavered. Then, there was only the glow of lanterns under dusk. When Eos looked up, he was in the real garden, and Aizo smiled at him warmly.

"How do you feel, Eos?"

"Better," Eos said softly as if waking up. He examined his arm. The burning sensation had left him. He recalled what Grace had called the curse—its true name. "Noximor's Tide is under control. For now. I think I can wield again." He produced a flame of pure crimson to demonstrate his hypothesis.

"You had me so worried. This is a relief," Aizo sighed, his expression relaxing. "This trip to Nippon-Wa has been far more than we signed up for. To be expected of such a search, I suppose. Come. Let's return to Saigo for the night. We can train your wielding tomorrow."

Lantern reflections glistened like fairy lights on the pond's surface as they left the garden. Eos felt a particular appreciation for the lifestyle he had emersed himself in for a brief time, but something loomed that he couldn't place.

The sense of foreboding hid in the darkness at the fray of the beige paper lanterns' diffused illuminations.

His time in the Akaishi mountains was ending.

When they reached the front courtyard, Saigo's men were drinking and dueling in a square lined with more bamboo-framed lamps. The shadows of blades and robed figures cast long across the pavestone walkway. The men were drinking and cheering, mingling their mirth with the clash of steel.

VOID TEMPTATIONS

Saigo looked stoically at his warriors but curled the corners of his lips slightly at the Hyperboreans approaching. "Ah, Aizo and Eos. So glad you joined us. Perhaps you would like to demonstrate your swordsmanship in a match?"

The invitation went unanswered as Eos and Aizo froze.

Their Observation aura picked up on the approach of a wielder.

The individual was nearing at a speed only possible with Soul Step and had no regard for hiding aura.

"Saigo, someone is coming!" Aizo called lowly.

The bald samurai master gave a curt nod and gestured to his men. The hands of all bushi present went to the hilt of their weapons as they anticipated the threat.

Swords clicked, releasing from their hilt; prepared to be drawn.

Anticipation filled the dusk.

Eyes darted in every direction into the day's dying light.

Eos prepared to manifest Soul Energy, but Aizo slowed him with a slightly raised hand.

"Let's see who it is first. I sense franticness but not hostility," the Inlume hummed.

The newcomer approached from the castle's courtyard entrance, running under wooden gates and past stone effigies without pause or reverence. He wore priestly robes with flowing white sleeves that rippled behind him like moonlight streams alongside his long black hair.

Sword grips eased. Tense bodies relaxed with a few chuckles.

Kikujiro fell before his father, gasping for breath.

"My son, what brings you in such a state?" The samurai father asked in his native tongue, shaken. His intuition wrinkled in the corners of his eyes.

"Carnus warned me..." the High Priest searched for enough air to finish his sentence in English for the kami to hear. "...he told me the kami would be coming for the Ise Shrine...I couldn't move the Eye in time. Raijin came with his hanyo. We were outnumbered...my...my men are dead."

Aizo's eyes widened as his bronze beard blew in the night breeze. "The Left Eye of Izanagi? What happened to it?"

CHAPTER TWENTY-SIX

Kikujiro found the strength to stand. His hair fell over his face, disheveled, as he said, "Raijin has taken the Eye. I had no choice. He was destroying the shrine and murdering the innocent. I stood no chance against him——"

Saigo growled, "That is no reason to hand over the greatest weapon to Raijin! You meet death as it comes to you. Honor consumes fear. Have I taught you nothing?"

Eyes like a hunted animal darted between the Soul Wielders and samurai. Kikujiro's voice cracked weakly, "I could not be as strong as you, Father. I'm not you! The most I can do is warn everyone. We should all flee the island! Whatever the kami are planning, I overheard Raijin saying, 'the boy will be prepared for the Eye in one week'. He could use it to kill us all!"

"Perhaps," Aizo broke in. "Carnus was able to use it to sink nations, but that is not Vistomus' ability. He could cause destruction, but not in the same way. We should consult with Carnus. Whatever Vistomus has planned, it must be stopped quickly. It could prevent countless deaths."

Saigo glowered with heavy shadows under his facial features. "And will you kami act now? Or will you still leave us to our doom against the forces of Raijin?"

Aizo hesitated. Instinct told him to burst out in response that he would go to battle, but experience held his tongue as he measured in his mind. After seconds of pause, he admitted, "It must be decided by King Talus."

The sharply masculine features were stoic against the answer. No facial muscle moved in the stillness of the tension. Finally, he muttered, "We will defend Nippon-Wa to our dying breath—with or without you, gaijin kami!"

Fwip!

The building tension released at the sound of an arrow flying through the evening. As it flew past their heads, ripples of aura emerged in the shadows around them.

Five. Ten. No, twenty?

Eos couldn't get a read on the exact number of wielders that had stealthily surrounded them.

VOID TEMPTATIONS

Booom!

The streaking glow of the manus stone arrowhead pierced the paper lantern nearest them and erupted into a ball of fire as the projectile exploded with precharged Soul Energy.

"Saigo!" Aizo called in warning. It was enough to awaken Saigo's instincts from the calm evening only moments ago.

The samurai turned his head, perceived the premonition of aura and mass coming, and slipped his body just out of the path of the following arrow.

Fwip! Fwip!

The samurai master had dodged, but a nearby swordsman was not so lucky. Another arrow followed and consumed him in a bloody explosion when it pierced his chest.

Katanas drew throughout the courtyard, and the samurai turned so they faced the threat outside the castle. The mountain's shadows held a greedy reaper's appetite.

Their assailants hid at the threshold of the castle's light.

Three more arrows released.

This time katanas swung with the swiftness and precision of a lifetime dedicated to the art of the sword. The arrows were all deflected into the night sky.

Eruptions overhead. Soul Energy glittered like fireworks.

In the darkness, Rius ran his hand through his shoulder-length hair to tame it behind his head as he watched the bushi cut manus stone arrows from their trajectory. He turned to Artera, annoyed.

"I don't know a swordsman on Hyperborea who could do something like that. Mere ostaka cutting down arrows." Rius clicked his tongue with disgust. "This will be messy, but Eos is within my reach."

Artera warned anxiously. "That's an inlume down there. Aizo Mudar. We're going to have to extract Eos quickly."

Rius waved two gangly fingers forward.

Black cloaks rushed into the night like shadows come to life.

The combined forces of Rius and Artera's vizier wielders advanced on the ring of samurai. Their mirza commanders sauntered behind them.

Manus blades descended.

CHAPTER TWENTY-SIX

A Soul Sphere fell on them as Mitad officers flooded the courtyard. Eos sensed the attack was weak, paling in comparison to what he could form in a second, but it was more than enough to end the unarmored samurai's life.

The bushi looked up in awe as the orb fell on them.

Eos froze, panicking as he tried to determine a counter.

An indigo wall rose over the area as Carnus sprinted to them.

The Soul Sphere erupted against it.

Both energies vaporized and dissipated in the sky.

Carnus cursed in the ancient tongue as he had learned from grace. "I'm beyond rusty, but the seal is working well, Aizo. I can wield again." There was a slight laugh as he marveled at being able to manifest Soul Energy without the curse mark flaring up to possess him. The experience was so profound…after all these years. It brought a layer of liquid welling up in his eyes.

"Just don't overdo it," Aizo warned. "There are stronger auras out there. Mirza."

Carnus nodded as he assumed a martial arts stance next to the inlume. "My Observation has not dulled. I sense them well."

Grace was not far behind Carnus, and her ornate kimono joined them with a silk flutter. "It seems the Mitad is forcing our hand."

"They have the Eye," Saigo announced.

"What?" Carnus burst out. He realized that Kikujiro was amongst them. The situation crystallized in his mind. "This is the worst scenario—"

Aizo barked out with command, "We'll settle it after. Mirzas are nearly upon us."

There was a single second in which Eos exhaled during the tension left by Aizo's warning. In the instant air escaped his lips—chaos erupted.

Mitad kimonos surrounded them. Black cloth rushed at the circle of samurai with glowing swords and Soul Spheres in hand.

Clang!

Boom! Screams and grunts accompanied the katanas and Soul Energy clashes. Grace and Carnus did their best to defend the Mitad's Soul

VOID TEMPTATIONS

Energy attacks, shielding against spheres of light and redirecting projections of manus blades.

Carnus stomped and directed two fists up in a tight punching motion. As he did, a pillar of glowing earth rose from the ground to form a barrier between a samurai and his attacker as a wave of dull green light slashed forward.

Grace parried a Soul Sphere with a thin veil of magenta. She was a scholar far more than a warrior these days, but she had been trained in the Necogen way of assassins. Handling viziers was well within her capability.

Swords clashed near her as one black robe overwhelmed a broad-faced samurai. He parried with his blade expertly, but the added strength of the imbued manus sword was more than he had prepared for.

The purple-pink energy manifested like daggers of pure flame from her hands as she spun in a crouch into the vizier's striking range, coming up below his arms and stabbing her Soul Energy just below his armpit.

The vizier's blade arm fell.

The samurai finished the job, cleaving down on the man.

Carnus and Grace could not assist every duel and ambush taking place—they were far outnumbered, and the samurai had been drawn all across the castle lawn.

But not all of the bushi warriors required protection or assistance. Many were going swing for swing with the low-ranking Mitad officers, compensating for their lack of wielding with a lifetime of skill with the katana and footwork that was unmatched.

Steel carved through the air between sakura trees and lanterns.

Saigo struck with crisp cuts that whistled as he backed an opponent into a trunk and slew him.

Their two strongest approach, Ahktar spoke into Eos' mind from high above the castle.

At the west end of the courtyard, Aizo intercepted the two Mirza while Eos hung closely behind him with a crimson elsu ready over his shoulder.

CHAPTER TWENTY-SIX

Artera's dark caramel-gray skin contrasted with Rius' pale ashen tone. They appeared complete opposites; Rius towered over Artera from behind, two full heads taller than her.

The small Mitad Mirza cursed as she perceived Aizo's first trap. Particles of Soul Energy were all around them on the grass and pavestones, hidden within the matter itself.

"Watch your step," Artera warned as they slowed their sprint.

"You think I don't sense that? C'mon, Ara. I'm not a complete barbarian—my Observation worked well enough to get us out of the factories and through the Battle of Sekira."

She rolled her eyes. "I'll hold off the inlume. I can't promise you for how long, so don't play with your prey."

A wolfish grin answered her.

The two leaped over the minefield of Aizo's Soul Energy.

Aizo cast two handfuls of glowing orange dirt between himself and the Mitad members. The dust gleamed like a fine spray of gemstone powder, then turned completely ordinary and hung in the air.

"Stay back, and don't strain yourself yet, Eos! You only just regained control of your wielding. Don't let that curse get ahold again. I just got you back. Can't face Talus and tell him I've lost you already," Aizo bellowed.

Eos nodded without taking his eyes off the approaching cloaks. They maneuvered over the ground with Soul Step, but Aizo's air attack scattered as they did.

The masterful Inlume did something Eos didn't know was possible—perhaps it wasn't possible for anyone else.

The Soul Energy imbued in the dust suddenly dampened. His Observation sensed Aizo's overwhelming power; he saw the ghostlike scattering on the courtyard's edge, but the piercing aura in the air suddenly became undetectable. It was as if Aizo could cloak only certain portions of his energy as he chose—and while it was away from his body.

Rius and Artera swerved in the air where they had last perceived Soul Energy. It was enough to buy them an extra step, but no more. They could advance no better than navigating a labyrinth in the dark.

VOID TEMPTATIONS

A sunrise orange erupted, throwing the two Mirzas back from the courtyard. The explosion enveloped the sounds of minor Soul Spheres and clashing blades.

The night suddenly tasted of electric char.

Rius screamed in frustration.

Cobalt wolves rose from the ground at the summon of his clenched hands. Before they were fully formed, the wavering beasts dashed into the night.

Boom. Boom.

They sacrificed themselves against Aizo's invisible obstacles.

"Take care of the old man. I want him dead," Rius barked. He charged forward through the cleared path his canine manifestations had made.

With a heavy sigh, Artera mumbled, "I'll do what I can."

Moving faster than even Rius' wolves, Artera closed the distance to Aizo as he cast a shining fissure of Soul Energy across the ground in a wave.

The small woman rolled around it nimbly. She stood from her dodging maneuver with a glow in her hand, and moved with intention and precision.

Inner Path Sixteen—Outer Containment!

Artera darted around Aizo's back with a stream of snow-white Soul Energy weaving around him in a ring. She sprung back as she wielded the bead of light into a complete circle.Then, there was a bright flash, and the Soul Energy clung to his skin.

Aizo could feel his Soul Energy bubble at the surface, ready to be summoned, yet it would not come. Sparks escaped in frantic and uncontrolled jitters. His limbs became heavy.

Wiry eyebrows pulled together as Aizo's eyes narrowed. He slid into a fighting stance, prepared to defend himself in hand-to-hand combat, and said, "That's an advanced technique of the Inner Path. I haven't seen its kind in decades."

"And you'll never see it again," Artera retorted.

CHAPTER TWENTY-SIX

"You won't be able to wield while maintaining this," Aizo said through gritted teeth as he exerted twice the effort he was accustomed to just to move.

"I don't need to." Artera drew a curved dagger from her cloaked waist. "Besides, killing you is only a bonus. We're not here for an old inlume."

Aizo's expression dropped to a heavy contemplation. He prepared to defend a knife fight with his body weighed down and his wielding incapacitated. Behind him, he caught the motions of Saigo parrying a glowing manus sword.

The light reflected in Artera's pupils as she lunged at Aizo.

Not far from Aizo, Eos met Rius before he stepped into the courtyard. A pack of specter-like wolves prowled around him, their paws bristling as if their fur was a neon electric hologram.

The last time he met Rius, Eos had been eager to test himself—and he had paid a terrible price. Now, he was in one of his favorite locations he'd ever spent time in. Somewhere he felt true peace. A place his soul was at ease.

Yet, the courtyard was burning, and samurai were crying out for their last time all around him. The Akaishi Mountains and their inhabitants had tempered his headstrong nature and desire to fight.

"You didn't impress me much last time, little Bellator," Rius taunted from within the circle of his soul Energy creations. "Do you want to end this chaos now and come with me? Durath Leorix won't be saving you this time, and your master is a bit tied up at the moment."

For a second, Eos almost felt a *yes* leave his lips.

"I would prefer that if it spared the men here," Eos said with a calm that held a brewing storm. "But you know I can't do that, and you've already destroyed and killed more than can be forgiven here."

Rius threw his head back, swept his fingers through his long maple hair, and laughed. "Well, bring out your curse then. It didn't do you any good last time, but maybe I'll let you have a few minutes of playtime."

Eos' golden eyes did not waiver. "I don't need it. I have a few more tricks to show you, and that scar I left on your chest says otherwise."

The cobalt wolves stilled as they bared their teeth at Eos.

VOID TEMPTATIONS

Rius' eyes narrowed.

Four crimson elsu hovered around Eos, their feathers marbled with gold. He could keep up the technique for a few seconds. *Better use it wisely.*

Cobalt and crimson stood against each other.

Their energy forms were unwavering.

The wielders' burning eyes were locked by adrenaline.

The Soul Energy elsu broke first!

Red elsu beat their wings in a single movement that propelled them faster than eyes could follow. Even Rius' Observation couldn't keep up with the speed of attack. Trying to track the jolting blurs of aura was so disorienting that the Mirza gave up entirely. Instead, he went on the attack. His wolves snarled as they leaped at Eos.

Zmmm! Crimson forms blurred through the air. The streams of golden afterimage sliced the pack of wolves.

Though outnumbered, the elsu's swiftness made up for the difference. The birds flew with such magnificent speed that it appeared to be an entire flock attacking.

The cobalt wolves wavered as they were struck repeatedly.

Again. Again. *Again!*

The elsu barrage swarmed, making the night sky erupt like firecrackers as they traveled faster than sound.

Eos commanded one of the four to change trajectory.

It cut towards Rius, appearing at his chest as if it had teleported.

Fiery energy cut him in his already wounded chest like a molten slash. Then, it struck again from the other side in an instant!

"You think you can challenge me?" Rius swore and growled, swinging his arm out to order his wolves.

On the third elsu assault against Rius, the wraithlike wolf sprung off its haunches and snapped its jaws, catching the elsu out of the air and extinguishing it into feathery vapor.

Behind Eos, Aizo struggled against the Inner Path restraints. He had been caught by Artera's dagger a few times, but the wounds were shallow glances.

Finding air was becoming a labor as her technique weighed his body down. Reacting required exerting every muscle fiber to its fullest extent.

CHAPTER TWENTY-SIX

The drain refocused his mind on finding a way to end the fight as his copper hair gleamed in the reflection of a nearly connected dagger swipe.

A mischievous grin spread across the Inlume's face.

During their battle, Aizo had combed his memories for clues to undo the technique's influence. Piecing together how it worked, he beamed and said, "That's enough of this game, I think."

Artera paused a moment in her surprise at the confident statement. She adjusted her grip on the dagger hilt and spat, "I don't think you have any say in that, Aizo Mudar."

"Ah, but I do!" he teased, holding out his index finger.

His finger glowed orange at the tip. Soul Energy couldn't leave his body, but he could concentrate it at the surface. He had knowledge of the Inner Path arts, studying them in his early training days under Talus' father, Bekrin. He never progressed in them—few Soul Wielders who could perform Severence did—but he understood how many worked. Now, he had brilliantly deciphered how to reverse it.

Spinning on the ball of his foot, Aizo traced the circle of white energy that Artera had formed in reverse. As he did, he performed a complex manipulation of his inner Soul Reservoir. The Sixteenth Inner Path technique was peeled back throughout his body.

The grin on his face went from playful to victorious.

Sparks shot out all around Aizo like from a campfire.

Artera hopped back to distance herself from the Inlume's minefield. Time was up.

The Mitad had lost their advantage in the ambush. Then, a gift came that bought her a few seconds. Artera's eyes betrayed her anticipation as she watched behind Aizo.

A vizier with a shaved head stepped over a samurai's motionless body and drove his sword toward Aizo's back.

Saigo had anticipated the cowardly action the moment his companion had fallen. Unfortunately, he was too far to act.

Aizo turned to see the blade coming at him, glowing a muddy gray light with heat that he could feel as it approached.

Solido began to form over his body, but not in time.

Saigo's katana cut through the night.

VOID TEMPTATIONS

It picked up a paper lantern with its steel tip and carried it with a masterful swing. The contained flame soared through the space between Saigo and the Mitad swordsman.

The backstabbing blade did not reach Aizo.

The lantern struck the black robe, and fire engulfed his ribcage.

Aizo stomped laterally with the edge of his foot, sending a rush of tangerine energy through the stones. The glowing veins caught the stumbling man and erupted in a blast that swallowed the black cloak entirely.

Artera cried out in the distraction, "Rius, we have to go!"

The hot-headed Mirza hesitated only a second before nodding and ordering, "Fine. Do it now, Ara."

Artera put her caramel-toned fingers together so that her hands formed an open triangle in the space between them. She put the gesture to her face and peered through the triangle, focusing on Eos.

The motion uneased Eos enough to steal his attention from Rius. In that time, the wolves evaporated into an ether of cobalt Soul Energy that recalled to the Mirza. The blue mist formed around him—the pressure of his aura surged with such a heavy presence that it froze Eos.

The shroud formed over Rius, much like Solido, but this was no defensive technique. His body morphed as if a hologram was merging with him, phasing in and out of his humanity and replacing it with a wolf-like form.

His ears streamed into canine points with the distortion of Soul Energy. Brown hair glowed a cool blue. His irises became white. Hands became claws, and his legs were like haunches—all while cobalt static jolted over him like bristling fur.

"You're not the only one with speed," Rius howled.

The wolfish Rius shot at him from a crouch.

Eos raised his layer of Solido, but he had never been gifted at the skill. It was weakly formed, even for his aptitude.

The Mirza was unbelievably fast in his new form.

Vision could not track where he had gone.

An instant later, Rius appeared at Eos' side, his Soul Energy revving in a growl as he plunged his right arm into Eos.

CHAPTER TWENTY-SIX

Zmmmm! The thick aura was as vicious as it was intimidating. Raven hair fell over his eyes as Eos crumpled from the blow. Crimson Solido shattered around him.

He was thrown in Artera's direction.

The woman was prepared to receive him.

Snow white Soul Energy cast out from her unmoving hands.

Inner Path Ten—Inner Containment!

A cube of energy grew around Eos' shocked body.

His vision went white as he became surrounded by the Inner Path technique. Spitting blood from his bitten lip, he struck out feebly with a glowing fist. There was no room to wind up his strike as the cube shrunk in on him. His powers crackled against the wall but did no damage.

In his wolf hybrid form, Rius sprinted to the cube and lifted it. In the distance, Kikujiro came running to his father's side.

"You're going to take *him*? You can't!" Kikujiro yelled furiously at the Mirza.

White eyes glared with insane feral madness.

"Enough, we're done here," Rius screamed into the blood-stained night. Then, he propelled himself with his prisoner in tow.

Immediately, Aizo and Kikujiro chased.

Kikujiro could almost keep up. The weight of carrying Eos slowed the Mirza down. But it wasn't enough. He felt the distance grow after the first few steps.

Aizo reached out to grab the wire hangar of one of the lanterns, thinking of how Saigo had assisted him. He sprinted ahead, but not after Rius—the clever Inlume set his sight on Artera as they moved up the mountainside.

The fire inside the paper cover became brighter than any other lantern, filled with Aizo's energy. The flame swelled and scorched his hand for an instant.

He gained on the retreating woman.

Greenery rushed by.

A single misstep and he would crash into a tree at deadly speed.

VOID TEMPTATIONS

There! Aizo felt his distance to Artera close enough to cast out the lantern. It flew, a speeding flame eating at the frame that contained it as it soared through the foliage and darkness.

The cube of white was dimming as Rius fled.

It connected with Artera's back and spread in an augmented inferno as Aizo's Soul Energy was delivered through the blaze.

The Tenth Inner Path crumbled.

Eos tumbled to the forest floor.

Swearing turned into a frustrated growl as Rius lost his hostage.

Kikujiro joined behind Eos with threads of weaving of Soul Energy floating before him. They faced off against Rius together.

"I didn't even get to show you what I could really do," Eos taunted, wiping blood from his lips as he stood.

Rius howled with laughter. "Next time we face, kid, let's settle it and fight to the death." He glowered furiously at Eos. Then, he spat with dark amusement. "This plan went to hell. Vistomus still wants to speak with you. Maybe you'll approach him of your own free will—if I don't kill you first. But for now, I'll just take this one!"

Diving in a blitz of feral speed, Rius grabbed Kikujiro and hurled him with unnatural strength at Artera.

The woman was stumbling away from Aizo as fast as she could. Her back and arm were burnt, and her Soul Energy was nearly depleted.

A single hand came up to make the same gesture she had before, but only half the triangle was made this time. Still, the white cube formed well enough, this time around Kikujiro.

The warrior priest's face was blank. It was so still that Eos couldn't tell if his expression was shock or acceptance. White enveloped him, and Rius scooped up his prisoner as he had done to Eos.

With Eos forming and elsu and Aizo approaching, Artera deployed her final technique of the ambush. Her hands overlapped, palms facing out at the two Soul Wielders. Through the searing pain of her charred skin, she closed her brilliant magenta eyes.

Her hands shone like a struck match. Then the flash increased until Eos' vision was like staring directly into the sun on a summer day. The white flare was blinding.

CHAPTER TWENTY-SIX

Eos' head pulsed as his sight was overwhelmed by the flare.

It took nearly ten seconds for him to recover. All the while, he searched the area with his aura Observation for intentions of a counterattack.

Ahktar spoke to him, *Fleeing!*

When the pulsing in his temples ceased, Eos found Aizo had also looked into the disorienting technique. It had bought the crucial seconds the two Mirzas needed.

Aizo scanned the area. Rius was moving with Soul Step speed at the outer edges of his perception radius. Artera was not far behind, but her aura was fading. Aizo had seen a wielder at the end of their Soul Reservoir many times before—and Artera was wielding on fumes. The surviving viziers from the failed ambush dotted the cliffs behind Rius.

Aizo's sturdy grip held Eos' shoulder as his apprentice started to pursue. "No, Eos. Rius is already too far away. The rest are meaningless to go after, and we don't know what else is hiding out there in wait for us."

"But, Aizo! They took Kikujiro. He-he…" Eos struggled to process what he saw. "He didn't even fight back. Just…gone."

"He was caught off guard by a superior wielder. I've seen it before. They took him alive for a reason. We'll get our chance to save him, no doubt. But we'll have to walk into a trap to do it. Come on. Back to Saigo's castle to check on the wounded."

Following his master in silence, Eos returned to the village in a stupor. His legs dragged with sparking streaks against the night.

The Mitad kept taking and taking.

The Left Eye of Izanagi with its power—the Flow of All Things.

Saigo's only son.

Something had to slow their progression of victories.

The bitterness welled up in him, but he cast it aside immediately, conscious of his thin control over the Tide of Noximor inside him. Such unchecked emotions would leave him unable to wield again. Even so, there was an instinct in him that craved to know who would walk away from a duel between him and Rius.

VOID TEMPTATIONS

"Aizo…we have to get Kikujiro back and stop Visotmus from using the Eye," Eos stated firmly as they neared the remaining lantern lights.

"Your father must decide that."

They returned to flame-scorched stone and bushi robes that would never rise again. The Mitad stain on Nippon-Wa had reached the Akaishi Mountains.

CHAPTER TWENTY-SEVEN

SAKI PSUEDOCIDE

"My son!" Talus bellowed emotionally as he rose from his personal chabudai table in one of Saitani's many meeting rooms. The mass of his burgundy kimono made the tiny tea table look like a toy.

Eos received his father's embrace. The braided auburn beard smacked him in the face, but he couldn't have been happier.

They were surrounded by murals of Saitani's family crest of cranes over a tatami floor. Tea tables were organized so that Saitani sat at the head of the room in front of green silk drapes with three tables running down both sides of him, facing each other for a meeting.

Talus held his son by the shoulders, saying, "I'm beyond grateful that Saigo took care of you and helped you recover. I was so worried! You had me ready to take everyone into the mountains to get you back safely. With Mirza Zeres, and his henchmen crawling through the woods, we thought it best to let Aizo take the long path around the Akaishi Mountains. Forgive me for leaving you so long."

Eos smiled with a contemplative quietness that his father wasn't used to seeing in him before revealing, "Actually, Father, I missed you, but the time with the samurai taught me much about being a Soul Wielder. Their philosophy…the bushido…has impacted me in ways I can't explain."

Nodding with recognition, Talus was satisfied. "I can see that. You have a different demeanor about you…more measured."

Glenn slapped Eos on the back warmly. "You gave us all a scare. I always said you were destructive, but I'm starting to think I can't see you anymore without everything going to chaos!"

Laughing, Eos shook his head. "I'm beginning to agree with you, Glenn."

Durath stood with his fur cap trailing as he joined them. "Rius was unlike anyone I've ever fought to have taken the blow you gave him, battled me, and still chased you down again. Welcome back, Eos."

The Corleo King's Son brought a wide smile to Eos' face. "Thank you, Durath. Without your aid, I would have been lost to my curse mark."

"I vowed to follow the black elsu," Durath shrugged nonchalantly. "My father would have wanted it this way. The Corleo have always served the Bellator."

The two clasped forearms in a brotherly embrace.

The image gave Talus a wave of nostalgia for his youthful days with Ramath.

Saitani smoothed the sleeves of his gray suit and removed a cigar from his lips to boom with a heavy accent, "Eos! Aizo! I am pleased to have you both back. It is an honor to have all of *Talus' kami*," he gave a playful wink, "back under my roof. I'm humbled."

Then, Saitani bowed his head to the table and said with deep regret in his voice, "However, I must beg your apology for allowing our previous meeting to become compromised by the hanyo, Rius."

Returning the solemn tone, Eos answered, "Rius was after me. He pursued me into the mountains and even attacked Saigo's castle while I was there. You have no blame, Saitani."

CHAPTER TWENTY-SEVEN

After a long inhale of his cigar, Saitani bobbed his head. "Then, I am glad his efforts failed twice. Come. We must discuss matters. Your journey should have been easy. My spies tell me that Zeres and all the hanyo have been recalled to the Imperial Palace."

"It was," Aizo confirmed. "I trust you received my letter about the events of the attack and Saigo's appeal?"

"I have," Saitani muttered gravely. "The loss of his son into Raijin's hands is a tragedy. The loss of this powerful kami artifact is even worse for all of Nippon-Wa. Please, sit." He gestured to the short tables to either side of him.

To his great pleasure, Talus had saved Eos a seat between himself and Scavok. Aizo sat across from Talus with Durath and Glenn trailing him.

"Gentlemen," Saitani declared to start the meeting. He stood, bowed slowly, and then picked up a bottle of saki. "This is my finest bottle of gingjo saki. We will drink the first cup to Eos' return." He poured for everyone and raised his white ceramic cup. The room followed the gesture, and they swallowed their drink together.

Again, Saitani bowed and refilled the cups.

He continued, "This second drink honors Kikujiro with Siago's tradition. The samurai always drink before a battle. Let us discuss and drink together if it is battle that we decide."

Glenn's cheeks went flush from the alcohol, and his voice sang with delight, "That was delicious. I'd be willing to commit to battle for another glass."

Durath hummed with pleasure as the warmth ran down his throat. "It may take a few more drinks to buy my alliance, but I second that, Glenn. I must take some back home with me."

Saitani responded kindly but with an apprehension underneath his words. "When this business is finished, I will send you home with as much saki as you'd like." He cleared his throat and put out his cigar.

The last wisps of smoke passed him before he continued with a heavy Japanese accent, "Saigo and I have always disagreed on the direction to take Nippon-Wa. I always advocated for a future of progress forward, while he is rooted to tradition and nostalgia. Still, we share many values and a love for our country. Raijin has taken our independence and our identity as a people. He grafted his lies onto our history and myths and imprisoned our beloved Emperor Antoku in illusions."

"Then you've decided to join Saigo's battle?" Talus asked.

"There was never a question. The course was set when the hanyo took Kikujiro and stole Izanagi's Left Eye. He will dominate us forever if we do not stop him here and now." Saitani's eyes closed with exhaustion. "A surprise assault now is the best chance we may have. When new kami appeared, and I learned you were not allied with Raijin, I knew this conflict was drawing near. Now…it has come. We will need your power."

Talus gave a strained hum.

In that moment, the lines on his face appeared deeper, and the sprouting array of gray hairs became more noticeable to Eos. His father had been considering the decision every waking moment and wore it plainly.

Scavok and Aizo awaited their king's words anxiously.

"We came to Earth to gather information only. That information led us to Nippon-Wa," Talus sighed heavily. "I promised my wife that we would avoid conflict and return safely…I have a kingdom of my own to protect…"

Saitani gripped his extinguished cigar as his lips pressed together.

Eos held his breath in anticipation. *Surely, Father will not sit back and allow the people here to go on oppressed—killed by the Mitad. He couldn't allow Vistomus to fulfill his plans with the Eye…could he?*

Talus' eyes expressed his mind's every measure of the risks.

Beware the Suhar Alakil. Stone Eater. Terrava's revelations sat in the pit of his stomach. He realized, he now felt some of the despair that Grace Lapithos had experienced at the name. *Ruyah Alakil. Sight Eater.* If it hadn't been for Terrava's warning, he wouldn't have know which path was correct. *I can't allow Vistomus the sight of the Left Eye of Izanagi.*

"With what said," Talus continued, "what I've seen here cannot go unanswered. The group we know as the Mitad, whom you call Raijin and his hanyo, have spread oppression in our homelands and now yours too.

CHAPTER TWENTY-SEVEN

With the Left Eye in their possession, they will only accelerate their cancerous spread. We must act," the Visrex of Wings finished decisively.

Saitani's tobacco-stained teeth showed as he grinned.

"I serve my king," Scavok answered.

"As do I," Aizo echoed.

Durath threw his cape back and nodded. "My life is the Bellator's. I will fight alongside you gladly against the enemy of the Leorix."

Before Eos could join the call to arms, Talus bellowed, "However, I swore to Terrava that Eos would be unharmed. I've weighed this matter in my heart and couldn't bear to lose you, Eos."

Lamp lights flickered behind them, setting Eos' tense expression in shadows as he lowered his head. Before this journey, he would have instantly contradicted the King. He would have argued with heartfelt pleading to join the fight and free the people of Nippon-Wa, just as he had attempted at Mircite...but he had seen the fruits of that rash decision.

Eos had learned from his inlume master and Saigo's bushido.

He knew his duty as a Soul Wielder of the Order and remembered his promise to Aizo of obedience and temperance of his impulses.

With gut-wrenching disagreement, Eos spoke calmly, "I understand, Father." His raven hair fell over his eyes, and his cursed hand clenched as he fought for self-control.

"Good," Talus smiled proudly. "Unfortunately, what I want and what must be done are different matters. This is our chance to strike Vistomus down while he is separated from his emirs and has only seven mirzas. We can't hold back anything in recovering one of the Tools of Karnak. You've become a formidable wielder, my son. We'll need your strength on the battlefield."

Eos' golden eyes lit up, and he couldn't hide his childish grin. He put away the whimsical expression as quickly as he could and said, "It will be an honor to fight alongside you, Father."

Auburn braids bobbed with Talus' affirmation, and he finished, "If your life falls into any serious danger, I want you to run. After all Terrava and I have been through, we can't lose you. Promise me you'll consider your own life above all in this battle."

"I promise," Eos assured him.

"Then together, it will be an honor to defeat Vistomus Fulmen, the cursed man who calls himself the kami Raijin–and purge this land of his stain!" Talus exclaimed as he raised his saki glass.

They all drank.

More was discussed, but Eos' head swam with his father's affirmation in front of everyone at the war meeting, and his body was warm with the tingle of liquor.

Soon after the meeting, he stood alone with Talus on a balcony atop Saigo's castle. It had traditional Japanese architecture, and they shared silence under a curved roof and interlocked beams as they looked out over the inner garden courtyard. The glow of blue paper lanterns bounced against the bonsai trees and fountains below.

The cold was seeping into the evening with the smell of pine and incense. There was a stillness that Eos had learned to savor during his time in the mountains with Saigo. It was an appreciation for peace in the full knowledge of the coming war.

"You know, Eos," Talus said without turning his head from the glowing garden, "I wasn't sure if I should allow you to join this battle, but you listened to my words and accepted my judgment. I knew then that I could trust you on the battlefield."

"I won't let you down," Eos assured. "I'm grateful you're allowing me to help repel the Mitad from this country. I've seen them ruin so many lands already…I can't imagine letting them take another…allowing more to suffer as we have."

Talus smiled sadly. "This is war, Eos. We will cast them out here, but they will take more lands, there will be further death and suffering, and we will have to sacrifice even more before it's over. For now, I want to share one piece of hope as we go into this battle."

"Yes, Father?"

"You must live. Not because I have lost one child to the Mitad already…but because Maxima lives, and you must return to your sister after this."

Eos' arms fell from the wooden railing weakly.

His pupils quivered, and his eyebrows drew together.

CHAPTER TWENTY-SEVEN

He found the strength to lift one arm and unconsciously touch the dagger-shaped scar under his cheek tenderly as he asked, "How is that possible?" He dared not hope in something he knew to be impossible. "I watched her fall in that river! I watched Ares kill her," he forced out with his jaw clenched.

Talus let the words hang in the evening air as he pondered for himself why his fallen-away son had defied the Mitad for his Bellator blood. His deep voice broke as he explained in disbelief, "Ares saved her. I don't know why, but he faked her death. Terrava met with Maxima while we were away. Her life must be kept secret for now...but..." The huge Visrex of Wings' eyes watered as he finished, "...Maxima lives."

Eos wept.

He had even more reason to fight now—to see his sister again. The taste of salty tears rolling on his lips captured his miraculous joy.

∞ ∞ ∞

Stacked like bricks laid by giants, shipping containers towered in multicolored arrays. Minoru and Kamatari felt lost in the seaport storage labyrinth as the salty ocean air clung to their skin.

"I have a feeling like we're being watched," Minoru whispered, though no one else was nearby.

"Quiet, coward, you're always nervous when we're receiving inventory," Kamatari said bluntly while stroking his dull, thinning black hair. He waddled through the row of orange and blue corrugated steel. "Here it is."

Minoru stopped behind Kamatari as they found the white spray paint markings of three cranes in a circle—Saitani Umetarō's family crest.

"Always insulting," Minoru complained as they opened the doors to the container. "Chinpira are crawling around these docks looking for trouble. I wouldn't be surprised if there's a hanyo watching tonight with what's coming. I've heard a lot of dock workers have gone missing and been interrogated in the past week."

Kamatari scoffed, "A hanyo wouldn't waste the time it would take to kill us, and we can handle any of their underlings if we have to." He smiled confidently and tapped the holster under his thick navy winter robes.

The pair entered the dark rectangular metal shell and examined the ammunition crates. Kamatari continued, "Now, the truck should be here in fifteen minutes to unload this cargo. See if you can't contain your fear until then."

Before Minoru could respond, a shadow cast across him, darkening his view with an elongated humanoid shape. However, as the form enveloped him, he realized the head had horns sprouting from it.

Minoru's hands shook as his thoughts about the horned intruder behind him ran wild. "*Hanyo*," his voice quivered to Kamatari, but he didn't let his fear prevent him from adding with a hiss, "I told you!"

Kamatari whipped around faster than would be expected of his heavy body, drew his pistol, and raised the muzzle toward the intruder.

A young woman stood at the mouth of the container. She was no taller than him and had raven hair. Her soft blue cloak was foreign with leather accessories and fur trim, but it was her face that struck him momentarily speechless—she wore a sapphire-colored mask resembling a horned lion.

The girl spoke, "Careful, Fey, that's a *gun*. It's a weap—"

A short woman with chestnut hair and wrinkles in the corners of her eyes stepped around the open door and joined the masked girl. "I've read plenty on the weapons they use here. *Barbaric*," the older woman, called Fey, scoffed.

"Not one more step," Kamatari ordered in a deep voice that tried to be authoritative but wavered enough to betray him when he observed the long-handled glaive at her waist.

"Did Emperor Antoku send you?"

Fey chuckled, "No emperor sent us. Now point that weapon down. I'm not here to fight you."

The gun did not move, but Kamatari's plump finger moved closer to the trigger. "Then...you're hanyo?"

"Hanyo?" The young woman asked, confused.

"You approach us here and expect us to believe you don't serve Raijin?" Kamatari huffed.

CHAPTER TWENTY-SEVEN

Minoru blurted, "Of course they're hanyo! Look at that mask."

Fey tried once more to calm the two men. "We don't know this Raijin, nor do we know this word *hanyo*. We're here looking for someone, and we think you might be able to help us find him."

"H-h-how did you find us?" Minoru wondered aloud.

The raven-haired girl answered, "We've been monitoring the docks for weeks. One of us is particularly talented at getting information from the workers here."

There was a flash of topaz at their feet.

Kamatari felt a sharp pain in the back of his shoulder.

His arm went limp.

The gun clattered on the container floor.

In horror, Kamatari turned to see Fey behind him. The woman had appeared to teleport in an instant.

Kami! This was proof.

Kamatari's neck went cold, realizing the worst situation had occurred.

Falling to the floor prostrate, Minoru's ponytail whipped about his back as he cried out, "Great Kami! Please spare us. Tell us what you want."

"There's a plague of kami in Nippon-Wa. Starting to think they aren't so special," Kamatari muttered. He turned slowly with his functioning arm out to show his surrender.

"What are these, *kami*?" Fey asked. "I've heard others here use that word."

Minoru stuttered, "So you speak like our k-k-kami allies. They call themselves b-b-by another name. Soul...Soul Wie...eh." His words drifted as he tried to recall the name.

"Soul Wielders?" The masked girl asked.

"Yes!" Minoru exclaimed. "That's it. I can't be expected to remember such strange names under pressure."

Fey caught Kamatari crouching slightly as if to grab his gun with his one functioning hand. "Don't move a muscle, or I'll do the same to your left arm."

SAKI PSUEDOCIDE

"Kamatari! Don't disrespect these kami! They're our allies," Minoru pleaded with his friend.

Kamatari shot a fierce look back at Minoru, still on the floor, and spoke through gritted teeth. "Allies? Great, then perhaps they can make my arm work again?"

Ignoring this, Fey tried once more. She spoke reassuringly, "We are searching for our friends. Their names are Talus and Eos Bellator. We believe, from the information we've gathered, that they may be allied with your boss, Saitani."

At this, the two men's eyes lit up.

"See!" Minoru exclaimed at Kamatari. "You're so quick to the draw, but they're friends."

"You're the one who thought we were being followed by hanyo, fool," Kamatari hissed back.

A third woman entered the container. She had blonde hair and high cheekbones, but what caught both men's attention was the rose-pink gemstone that she had in her right eye. It glimmered into the shadows with a light of its own.

The newcomer spoke urgently, "We have to hurry. I went into the guard's mind at the end of the alley. They're expecting a pickup of their wares any minute now."

Minoru's mouth moved without speaking a few times before his astonished lips could form words. "Incredible...you're the very image of Himiko-oujo." He bowed again with his forehead to the floor.

"We just need another minute. Almost done, Jezca," Maxima answered. She adjusted her mask and bent down to Minoru. "So, you call us friends. Then you know where we can find Talus and Eos? We only mean peace. They're our allies."

The lanky man nodded vigorously. "I do! Well...I did. I don't know where they are now, but I know where they will be."

"Riddles?" Maxima tilted her head. Her sapphire eyes pierced through Minoru, and he cowered beneath the intimidating mask hovering over him.

"No! No Riddles. We were with them yesterday, but we all went our separate ways. Talus, Eos, Scavok, and their servant, Glenn."

CHAPTER TWENTY-SEVEN

Maxima snickered uncontrollably at that.

Minoru continued, "There is a great battle coming in two days. They will all be at the Royal Palace as it goes under siege, and the noble kami will try to rid this land of Raijin and his evil hanyo."

Fey broke in, "And you can take us to this *royal palace* where the battle is to take place?"

Minoru nodded vigorously.

The masked girl sighed. "How is it that Eos gets involved in a battle everywhere he goes?"

Fey chided, "Terrava said they came to Earth on reconnaissance, but boys have an appetite for violence and war."

Kamatari raised his voice to a friendly begging tone. "This is wonderful. Since we're all friends here, can we fix my arm?"

"The effect will fade in a few hours," Fey disregarded the comment.

Kamatari's jaw went slack in exasperation.

Minoru squinted at his companion. "Don't expect me to load your share of the crates just because you were trigger-happy."

Fey addressed the two younger women, "It seems we located Eos. Your dreams of the red wooden gate were correct, Jezca. Now, we must meet them on a battlefield."

CHAPTER TWENTY-EIGHT

EYE AGAINST THE TIDE

Darus and Cyra stared once again at the Meiji period waterfall painting that hung in Vistomus Fulmen's quarters within the Emperor's castle. This time, they were joined by Bysis, and all three faced the judgment of their master, known to Nippon-Wa as Raijin.

The roar of a mass protest was a constant droning background noise that seeped through the castle walls. After four days, the sounds mingled with the smell of lantern fires and the nervous pacing of all the servants throughout the castle to create a constant sense of apprehension.

"Bysis, you come to me with failure," Vistomus began. Words dripped from his lips with calm intimidation matched by the dull pressure of his soul's heavy aura. He allowed it to flare enough for the three mirzas to feel its weight like a palpable specter. "I ordered Emperor Antoku's weapons be protected—"

Bysis broke in with a bumble, "Master, I did as I was told! I faced the Visrex of Wings," there was a pleading in his oafish voice. "I might have defeated him too, but the weapons were taken while I fought him. Then, they all fled."

Vistomus' lip curled in a snarl, "If you cut me off again, I'll burn your tongue out. *Might have defeated Talus?* The weapons *were taken*, and that is the point. You failed to defeat Talus and prevent the theft. Your failure is collective. Three of my mirzas! And still, you couldn't complete your task."

Bysis bowed his bleached head and put his only hand over his heart to show remorse without taking the risk of speaking.

Continuing, Vistomus showed a tinge of mercy in his tone, "You succeeded with Diya in your mission before this, and it cost you an arm. I have not forgotten that sacrifice. Consider your blood debt for failure wiped clean…"

The hulking, one-armed Mirza sighed aloud more than he meant to, relieved that he could keep his only remaining upper limb.

"However, fail me again in the upcoming battle, and death will be your punishment."

Vistomus Fulmen turned his chastisement to the boyish-faced blonde between Bysis and Cyra. "Kallag, what have you to say for yourself? Is Talus' master assassin more than a mighty Vurangian warrior trained by the Mitad can handle?"

The young man's eyes were glazed over, and his head was low. "Master, I have returned with shame. It's better for a Vurangian to die in the honor of battle—which I would have gladly accepted had my opponent not run away the moment his objective was complete. Scavok Alter was a formidable opponent." He rubbed his calloused hands with slow movements, fantasizing about landing the strikes he had been unable to.

Vistomus' pointed hand shot out and clutched Kallag's jaw. The bald wielder turned his apprentice's head as if examining bruised fruit. "It is that exact attitude that will allow you to keep your rank as mirza and lessen your blood debt."

There was a burst of white light between hand and face, accompanied by a static charge in the air. Intense heat overcame Kallag, and a shock came that was so immensely painful that it quickly became a numb throbbing.

He nearly went unconscious from the blow, but the scent of his scorched flesh triggered a fear response, and kept him awake.

Kallag fell to a knee, resisting with all his strength not to succumb to the burn wound on his face.

Returning to his low bamboo table, Vistomus lifted a Japanese oni mask. It was a disfigured open grin of fangs and harsh features that covered everything below the eyes. He held it out to the Mirza, who was hunched over in pain before him. "Kallag, I spared you with only a surface scar to remind you of the price of failure. The people of this nation call my mirzas: *hanyo*. Half-demons. Wear this over the wound and embody their myth. I still have great expectations for you. During the upcoming ceremony, I expect you to protect Khasun above your own life."

Outstretched hands accepted the oni mask.

Straining to speak without using his damaged facial muscles, Kallag sputtered through a locked jaw, "I will not fail."

Vistomus' attention turned to Cyra, finally.

"I acknowledge my defeat and accept my punishment, Lord Vistomus," Cyra bellowed in an attempt to get ahead of any consequences he owed.

"Your defeat..." Vistomus paced with his hands behind his back. His face was contorted with the pinched lines of weighing a decision, "...was not entirely your own. I weigh all my moves carefully, so defeat is the tiniest of probability. However, nowhere in my calculation did I plan for Saida's metus stone experiment to have fallen into Talus' hands, let alone end with it used against us here on Earth."

Cyra's palms began to sweat, and he became cold as he recalled the sensation of being touched by the ostaka's winged staff.

"It was...like being faced with something worse than death."

Vistomus hummed in response. "Yes, metus stone negates Soul Energy. It is a horror to experience, which is why he had an ostaka carry it. Cunning, Talus."

CHAPTER TWENTY-EIGHT

With his dark ponytail swaying as he shook his head in anguish, Cyra seethed, "If I find that man, I swear to kill him, Master."

"It's best you do. Even I have no ability to withstand the metus stone," Vistomus acknowledged. "Your loss was partially due to the failure of our brethren in the Mircite Valley. You will play the key role in two days, creating the barrier around Khasun and Tessio. If Khasun's ceremony is completed, then your debt is forgiven."

"Thank you, Master. My *Invincible Soul Barrier* has never been broken by another wielder. Khasun will be safe."

The dampened cries of the rioters outside the castle carried on like the chirping of bugs on a summer night. Their yelling and drumming irritated Vistomus to the point of a headache. Thousands of peasants were echoing day after day.

Endless noise.

The protest captured his focus so much that he couldn't concentrate again until the sound of golden dragon fountains between rows of perfectly pruned bonsai trees brought him back into the present moment an hour later.

The members of the imperial guard knew Vistomus by sight.

The black military uniforms stood aside, opening the grand red doors crested in gold for the kami walking among them. They avoided eye contact; it was said Raijin would strike you with lighting for staring.

Emperor Antoku sat beneath the phoenixes that adorned his throne canopy, dressed in a miniature military uniform with chords and medals like a child playing dress up. His advisors stood behind him. They whispered to themselves in secret conversation as Vistomus approached the throne.

The cursed formalities of politics and institutions.

Vistomus bowed deeply, but not as deeply as the Emperor, and his advisors returned the gesture. *I have the Left Eye of Izanagi. Their treasure is mine. A few more days and no one can take it. Then, these formalities will end.*

Emperor Antoku spoke after a minute of patient silence with the tone of an adolescent trying to command a deeper voice, "Great Raijin, you have your treasure that has been trapped for so long in our mortal realm. Tell me, what will you do with it?"

EYE AGAINST THE TIDE

"I will use it to see what even the other kami cannot see, your Imperial Majesty. However, the Left Eye of Izanagi is not for me to possess but a gift for someone better suited to its powers," Vistomus spoke calmly.

"This must be a special kami for Raijin to honor them with such a treasure," Antoku responded.

"Indeed. The most special. Now, your Imperial Majesty…" Vistomus cleared his throat and attempted to raise his tone to a child's level without being condescending, "…I have requested this audience to ask you once more to grant me full military powers to eliminate the surge of Saigo and his new kami friends."

Minutes passed as Antoku's advisors spoke behind their sleeves into his ear. The whispers echoed indiscernible in the openness of the throne room.

Finally, Antoku answered, "My advisors tell me this must be done to save our kingdom. *However, I believe* that is only your offer to make them like you…a kami…that is speaking through them."

The Emperor's advisors took a step back behind the throne nervously and glanced at each other with guilt painting their previously stoic faces.

Vitsomus' jaw clenched.

Perceptive little brat. It smelled of Saigo's influence.

Continuing after an appropriate pause to catch all parties off guard, Antoku said, "I gave your hanyo the governors' powers and title of Daishōfu. This has resulted in uprisings in every prefecture–to which," his voice raised angrily, "your hanyo slaughtered my people. Japanese blood has been spilled unnecessarily, and trust has been lost! As evidenced by the riots outside these walls."

Vistomus' eyebrow twitched.

Rius' insolent bloodshed was a poor match for the disposition of Nippon-Wa. He better bring Eos to me, or I will have his head!

"Your Imperial Majesty, I admit that one hanyo was particularly rash–"

"*Violent,*" Antoku corrected with a cracking voice.

CHAPTER TWENTY-EIGHT

"Mmmm. Yes. The excess bloodshed was a political mistake, but the lives of the peasants are forfeit if they go against the kami. *Do not forget that fact.*"

Antoku could not argue with the hierarchy of gods and men. He nodded, his juvenile mind turning, grasping for the words he needed against such a formidable man. "More measured terms are required."

Changing his approach, Vistomus cooed, "Perhaps an Emperor as great as you would like to be made a kami? The greatest kami in Nippon-Wa after Raijin? When I return to Takamagahara, you will be invincible for all your days."

Again, the young boy returned to silence, and it looked as if tears would come to his eyes any second. "My father was a great man, and he made Saigo my mentor. *Greatest. Invincible. Those are merely words. An emperor must be detached from desires.* That's what he told me. Saigo has acquired many kami of his own, according to reports. Your dispute is now between kami. My advisors tell me that an army is marching this way to fight for the abolishment of kami in Nippon-Wa's Royal Court. When they arrive, you may have full authority to wage your war. Then, your kind can settle their own matters. If you are victorious or defeated…it will be decided by kami—not men."

Vistomus nearly growled in irritation but, instead, rolled it into a smile and bowed. "Thank you, Emperor Antoku. You will soon see that my power is unmatched. Allied with me, you will have peace and unquestioned leadership."

Antoku interjected one last time, "Peace?" A hesitant grimace crossed his face. "My advisors believe that the gates of the castle will be torn down by tomorrow by the protesters if I cannot appease the people. I will not allow my military to use violence against them when I share their anger and distaste for the bloodshed caused by the hanyo, Rius. I will permit you to put down Saigo's kami, but first, you must send away the protestors at my gate."

It was a clever ploy. Antoku knew that violence would have to be used, but it was better aid to Saigo's cause if his leadership was seen as the hostage to the violent lightning kami.

EYE AGAINST THE TIDE

If Raijin used excessive violence, it would further justify the protests. Most importantly, it would send them away before Siago and Saitani's war began.

"I know *just the method*," Vistomus declared.

Vistomus left the meeting with the Emperor and retrieved his treasure. The Emperor's condition would be fulfilled.

The whipping wind and the blaring noise of riots in the open air replaced the royal fountain splashing.

Standing on dark green patinated tiles at the peak of the Imperial Palace roof, the man fearfully called the lightning god observed the moat-encased Tokyo Imperial Grounds. To the north, protesters had overwhelmed the barricades and taken over Kita-no-maru Park, filling up the Inui-mon Gate, where the citizens and soldiers faced each other from only feet away.

To the east, the Kokyo Gaien Garden and Edo Downhill Gate faced the same swell of angry bodies.

From the southern Sakurada-mon Gate all the way around to the western Hanzomon Gate, the road around the moat was filled, going back to the Kioicho skyscraper...perhaps further.

The clusters of bodies blurred in the horizon.

The peaceful and honorable people of Nippon-Wa had reached their limit. The seizure of the kingdom's governor positions by kami, whom they perceived as demons, was a step too far in their traditional minds.

Against the clear blue-gray sky of the chilly afternoon, a single lightning bolt came down on the castle.

From a distance, it appeared like a sign from the heavens, but the bolt never struck a roof tile. Vistomus Fulmen caught it in his hand and pulsed repeated streams of electricity overhead to gather the attention of tens of thousands.

The citizens looked at the Imperial Palace's strobing rooftop with awed outbursts that turned to concerned frenzy as they processed the rooftop figure.

CHAPTER TWENTY-EIGHT

Vistomus saw the physical masses of protestors, the royal gardens, and all the traditional Japanese castle architecture throughout the grounds, but he saw *so much more!*

In his fist, he clutched the Left Eye of Izanagi.

Its scarlet hue churned internally with a dull, smoky color.

The darkness was like an inverted refraction of light.

To Vistomus, the world was all the material that a person could perceive with eyes and sense, but it was layered with a substance that resembled Soul Energy!

There was a flow to nature that even the most sensitive wielder's perception could not grasp. In any one space, the amount of energy was tiny, like pollen in the spring air—but it moved in unison everywhere.

There were rivers of this flow that swam like ether tides through all of the physical world. It was always there, but the Left Eye of Izangi opened a window to its user's mind that allowed this revelation.

"So, this is the power Karnak called The Flow of All Things…" Vistomus whispered to himself, mesmerized by his access to this new dimension.

His lightning came down again, but his focus was no longer on the protesters and their panic. Rather, he was lost in the realization that his summoned lightning jumped from pollen-like spec to spec and traced this flow of nature's energy.

He understood the principle of the technique. After all, he had invented it under the guidance of Master M. He knew he was blending Soul Wielding with the method of the Krog shamanic tribes called Nature's Pulse–stretching his wielding as far as he could until it approximated their way.

Now, he could see the interaction!

His Soul Energy was mingling with this other dimension–and he could witness it! But there were limits to such transmutations of the Human Essence and Nature's Pulse, and he could see his abilities were merely an imitation of what was possible.

There is a burning in my arm. Where I'm holding this magnificent artifact, it's on fire…

The thought of his pain was detached from him.

EYE AGAINST THE TIDE

The pain was there, but *down there*—in his physical body. And his mind was up in the realm where Nature's Path could be read like the runes of a foreign book.

The horrified and superstitious cacophony broke into his conscious perception and pulled him back into observing the material world.

His task for the child Emperor was at hand.

Then, he could eliminate Talus and his allies while they had no wielder army, and it would be politically sanctioned. After that, Khasun would complete the ritual, and the need for any political masquerade would be over—he could replace Antoku's advisors instead of merely influencing them.

First, the Downhill Gate to the East.

Lightning struck the crowd in a nightmarish web of forked electricity. Its charge eviscerated the insulation between the tightly packed bodies.

Bolts jumped from air to skin and tore through the crowd with a vicious fluidity.

The attack proceeded clockwise; a prowling micro-storm that brought instant death.

Vistomus summoned all the power vested in him by the Tide of Noximor. He allowed the curse to marble his skin, for he required it's augmentation to manipulate so much Soul Energy through the newly revealed channels of etheric dust.

A wealth of aura frothed within him.

His lightning storm increased!

The Sakurada-mon Gate was next. Then, every turn of the street leading to the western Hanzomon Gate.

Brilliant crackling light spread in a blinding wave.

All Vistomus saw was the beautiful fractal dissipation and multiplication of his Soul Energy through the vantage of the Flow of All Things.

The showering wall of white death finished its circumnavigation of the Imperial Palace grounds and turned the Inui-mon Gate and the park behind it into a field of ash, burned flesh, and scarred earth.

He did not kill them all. Only the ring closest to the palace.

CHAPTER TWENTY-EIGHT

It was all that was required to scatter them permanently.

The Smiting of Raijin, as it would be remembered, was complete.

Vistomus Fulmen allowed his vision of the Flow of All Things to fade. As it relinquished, he became acutely aware of the pain in his hand that clung to the Left Eye.

His skin felt like it had been drained of moisture and then lit with a match. Glancing at it, he saw his hand was withered and frail. His normally ashen Mezclado complexion was now charred.

The fingers in his right hand would barely respond as he commanded, and scales of his skin were flaking like a relic that had aged one hundred years in an instant.

"The Tide of Noximor and the Tools of Karnak. Natural enemies," he uttered hollowly as he internalized the damage he had done to himself. "A small price."

CHAPTER TWENTY-NINE

FEATHER AND FANG

When the small samurai army marched through Shibuya City on the western outskirts of Tokyo, the Imperial Military had attempted to block their route into Tokyo. However, the throngs of uprising citizens joined the march so that the nearly thousand samurai became surrounded by tens of thousands of Japanese commoners.

The people rallied around their traditions, manifesting like a risen ghost that epitomized their roots. They clamored to the symbol of ancient resistance against the modern infiltration of Raijin and his hanyo.

The pious movement was further fed on the rumor of a small unit of kami amongst the bushi warriors. The story of their clash against the hanyo was told in mythicized wonder through the crowds.

Given their strict rules of engagement from Emperor Antoku, there was little the Imperial Military could do to slow the procession of

CHAPTER TWENTY-NINE

traditional yoroi armor fitted with modern bulletproof plates, katanas, and horses from coming to rest at Meiji Jingu shrine.

The Shinto priests welcomed them with reverence, for Saigo had ushered in the Shinto restoration alongside Antoku's father, Emperor Toba.

Only the torii gate of the shrine and an hour's march stood between the samurai and the western edge of the Imperial Palace. The legion of citizens, empowered by the historic march into a quasi-religious frenzy, surrounded the entire border of Meiji Jingu with hundreds of bodies of depth to their encampment.

To the south of the Imperial Palace, Saitani's rebel army had brought nearly ten thousand soldiers to the foot of Tokyo Tower in Minato City. They had decentralized their gathering points with months of preparation, distributed their weapons stores over the past years, and risen like smoke through a grate in the streets of Meguro and Shinagawa, south of Tokyo, into an army that solidified like the evenfall.

Saitani had not commanded the awe or devotion that Saigo did during his approach, but he didn't need to. The samurai had captured the attention of the vast majority of the Emperor's forces and rendered them useless against the mingled civilians and samurai—all the while, Saitani's network of rebel units gathered in coordination.

The rebellion had slipped through the military watch deployments like water through a net.

A blazing yellow sunset melted into purples as the crowds parted to allow a single car through to the Meiji Jingu's eastern entrance.

Saigo's black greaves approached the outer gate upon the news of a messenger from Emperor Antoku. He wore the full armor of the bushi: midnight-colored gauntlets, spaulders, and breastplate with the flared antlers of a kabuto helmet adorned with a golden komainu head. The mythical lion-dog bared its fangs from atop his head.

The samurai leader stopped before the torii gate.

He waited beneath its two thick wooden beams and gently upward curved arch with cold, anticipating eyes, scanning like a predator.

A small guard of five samurai waited in the distance behind him, as did an entourage of kami dressed in traditional battle kimonos.

FEATHER AND FANG

A man in a white robe skimmed across the shrine path. His black Shinto eboshi cap faded into the dusk as he approached under the canopy of trees.

Only four vizier Mitad members trailed behind the messenger priest. The red crest of the two-headed serpent was woven in red on their chests.

Saigo's fearsome gaze and stiff jaw softened at what he saw.

The priest motioned for his guards to fall behind as he continued on, stopping just at the threshold of the torii gate.

Father and son stared at each other from opposite sides.

"Kikujiro…" Saigo whispered weakly and searched his son's expression for an explanation but received none.

With a somber voice and no line of emotion on his face, Kikujiro stated, "Father, I come as a messenger for Raijin and Emperor Antoku." He held out a wax-sealed letter without making eye contact with his father.

Saigo's scarred hands crossed the boundary of the gate to his son to receive the Emperor's message. They paused momentarily on the other side. His dark eyes narrowed as his brow drew down. In deep throaty Japanese, he addressed his son.

"You have not come to return to us?"

Instead of answering the suspicion directly, Kikujiro pretended to be lost in focus on something on the horizon. "Courage. Honesty. Justice…your bushido code has its values it sees as truths. But you know, Father, I've observed one absolute truth. The kami are superior to the rest of us. If they want to, they have the right to rule however they desire."

Saigo grunted in disapproval and pulled his arms back across the torii gate. "Loyalty. Honor. Mercy. You forget my favorite of the tenants of bushido. My son…is lost to me?"

Kikujiro was motionless as he replied in Japanese, "When Raijin came to the Grand Ise for the Left Eye, I handed it over to him with no resistance. He could have erased the shrine and every innocent life in it but chose to spare us all if I gave up *their* artifact. It belongs to the kami, so I returned it. In exchange, Raijin will take me to Sekigahara and teach

CHAPTER TWENTY-NINE

me the art of *wielding Soul Energy*." He spoke the last word in English, imitating how the Emperor's kami pronounced it. "After he left, a hanyo named Rius came to me and made plans to take me back to the palace after I warned you to flee Nippon-Wa. What happened the night of the attack was his fulfillment of our agreement…though I had no idea Rius followed me to your castle."

Without breaking the look of disdain, Saigo raised two fingers over his head and waived them in a signal for Talus to join him. The tall Anite King approached and looked over the two men, his beard falling to the top of Kikujiro's head.

Changing to English, Saigo explained, "My son has brought a letter from the Emperor." He slid his thumb under the red wax pressed with a chrysanthemum emblem. The seal broke, and he read aloud, translating:

Saigo Sensei,

I have the deepest respect for the ways of the samurai and all you taught me growing up. I hold the same love for you that Emperor Toba did. Perhaps more, since you are all that remains in this world that still reminds me of my late father.

Emperor Toba was caught between two worlds: the ancient roots of Japan and the modern world that had washed it away. He united the two in balance. Now, I am caught between two entirely different worlds: the one my father created and the world of Takamagahara that has descended upon us. I fear it is impossible to find the balance as Emperor Toba did.

Raijin has worked himself into the minds of everyone around me. I have prevented him from attacking you directly until now, but I have granted Raijin and his hanyo war powers. If kami are to rule this world, then it will be decided here in this battle. I hear rumors that you have found new kami allied to your cause. If this is true, we will let the kami decide our fate.

I take this march against my castle as your ultimate advice on my council.

Make your advice heard.
Free Nippon-Wa if you are able.
Perhaps you will find the balance that I cannot.

FEATHER AND FANG

Your loyal student,

His Majesty the Emperor Antoku

Saigo let the letter fall to his side. "Talus, it seems you will have the full force of Raijin to contend against." His eyelids fell, and a sigh escaped his dignified posture. "We will retake the throne, kill the corrupt advisors who cornered my Emperor, free Antoku, and expel Raijin from Nippon-Wa."

Talus reaffirmed, "We will, Saigo."

The fully armored samurai spoke softly to himself, "My son has betrayed me and joined Raijin's side."

Kikujiro finally looked his father in the eyes and responded in English for Talus to hear as well. "I am part kami...if only a small part. I have chosen one side of my bloodline. Out of respect, I warned you that the Eye was stolen and that you should flee. I knew you would not, so I offer you one last mercy as a son." His voice lowered, out of range of the Mitad guards in the distance behind him, "Raijin has begun a ceremony with the Left Eye of Izanagi. It is taking place in the Fuijima Yagura at the Edo ruins."

"You offer me aid? Even after betrayal?" Saigo questioned.

Kikujiro nodded. "My fate is tied to the Eye. It always has been. Now, the relic may return to the kami which deserves it most...gods willing, with minimal civilian casualties." He turned with priestly poise and disappeared behind his security guards.

"And if you are wrong about the side you chose?" Saigo cried out.

"Then I will perform seppuku."

∞   ∞   ∞

The wielders of the rebellion against Raijin stood on planes of light far above the marching legion of samurai. Below, Saigo proceeded towards the wall of the Imperial Military with a methodical and

CHAPTER TWENTY-NINE

undeterrable pace from the west. Similarly, Saitani's forces amassed before the southern barricade of soldiers.

The morning air enlivened the lungs of all eight as they surveyed the battleground from the dawn clouds.

Glenn stood on the crimson floor beneath Talus and chattered, "I was n-n-not made for this! My *normal* body is made for walking on the *ground*, not this freaky floating in the air!" He shook as he clutched the light, manus-laced chainmail that hung under the Anite armor at Talus' chest. The white elsu emblem marked his steel plate, but underneath the protective Hyperborean layers, he wore the kimono of Saigo's people.

"We'll be heading down in a moment," Talus reassured. "You all know your groups and your missions. We'll approach the *Edo Ruins* from three directions. Our target is the white guard building on the stone wall that Kikujiro called *Fujima Tower*."

Their gaze went far to the eastern side of the Imperial Palace grounds. Over the Hanzomon Gate at the western edge, across the immense green lawns, around the Imperial Palace, and in the Edo Castle Ruins, their objective waited. Atop an ancient, sloped stone wall nearly as tall as the building itself, perched the white walls and three-tiered sloping green roofs of the Fujima Yagura.

From the southern Sakurada-mon Gate, the distance was no closer. Only the northern Inui-mon Gate created a shorter path.

Talus continued, "We'll enter low, just over the wall to minimize our aura. If we can sneak through on foot to Fujima Tower without alerting the seven mirzas to our presence, then we'll have succeeded."

"If we can do that," Scavok muttered, "I'll be sure that Kikujiro's information was a trap, and they'll all ambush us all at once. I scouted early this morning. I felt their presence throughout the grounds. Vistomus is ensuring there is no way to approach safely...and that Voro wraith...I sensed his presence everywhere."

"Naith," Carnus growled. His Hamirate brother waited over the castle walls.

Clapping to regain everyone's focus, Talus bellowed, "Retrieve the Left Eye of Izanagi. Defeat the Mitad, expel them from Nippon-Wa, preserve Saigo's bushido way, and free Emperor Antoku. Above all, *survive*. Send a flare of Soul Energy if you're in danger. If things go badly, flee back to the shrine." The Anite King turned to Eos, "Especially you, Eos. You're skilled. We need you in this mission, but I don't want you to take any excess risks. If that curse becomes a problem—"

"I know, Father. I'll be cautious," Eos assured him.

"He'll be fine, Talus," Aizo patted Eos on the back. "He's got *my* training, a bolstered seal, Carnus to monitor the curse, and *your* stubbornness to assure his victory."

For a moment, Talus was quiet, but he decided it was enough. With a firm nod, he ordered before he could second guess himself, "So he will. I'll see you all at Fujima Tower then."

Aizo punched Eos' shoulder with a pre-battle grin and set off with Savok south. To Eos, it was a sign of confidence from his inlume master.

Talus leaned into Eos and masked his unease with a playful wink. "Best not to tell your mother that you were involved today. Stick with Durath. Heed Carnus about your curse." He accepted Eos' nod.

Before the groups split, Durath spoke. "One last thing…Grace, I have something to give you. These belonged to Caldus. I picked them up at the battle in Mircite. I suppose they're best in your hands now."

Grace received a set of skull-handled daggers with sheathed manus stone blades. Her mouth widened as she realized what she held. "Amon's Daggers! By the stones…Caldus was a bold child." She clutched them over her heart, praying silently, and whispered with trembling lips, "Thank you, Leorix King's Son. I'll treasure them."

Then Talus took Glenn on his back and led Grace toward the north gate.

"I believe it's our turn," Carnus muttered with subtle reluctance as he rubbed his scarred chest. "Stay close. If we come across one of Visotmus' mirzas, I'll deal with them."

Durath grabbed his mane of oak-colored hair and cracked his neck. "Well, just don't keep them all to yourself, Carnus. I want to let a few of them taste righteous Leorix anger."

Eos grinned as Durath's infectious fire for battle spread. "You two can have them all…there's only one mirza I care to fight." A flood of manus arrows flooded his memory. He remembered that ice-blue wolf.

CHAPTER TWENTY-NINE

Durath laughed as they followed Carnus toward the Imperial Castle grounds. "Hoping for a third bout?"

"Not hoping…but ready," Eos answered.

In a hushed note of solemnity, Carnus confided, "If…if I don't make it back from this battle for any reason, I…have a son I left behind on Hyperborea. His name is Koda. I have in my kimono an inheritance and letter for him…"

Taken aback slightly, Durath and Eos were at a loss for words.

"Carnus…what—" Eos started.

"We're going into battle against Vistomus Fulmen! Do not treat this like play or some game," Carnus' voice trailed as his temper settled to a calmer tone. "Just promise me that you'll find Koda and do this for me if I don't make it back to Hyperborea."

They descended over the roofed gate from on high as Carnus sent a wave of Soul Energy out over the perimeter to distract from their exact entrance location. Eos sensed Scavok and Talus do the same so that the entire border was alight with a noise of aura.

The three touched ground not far past the wall. The remainder of the journey would be on foot, and the slowness of moving through a battle zone without Soul Step gave him anxiety. They crossed stone bridges and kept to tree cover most of the time. It was nearly two miles to their destination when avoiding buildings and open paths.

The greenery rushed by in Eos' peripheral   as they approached a large pond. They intended to divert north of it, but Carnus held up a halting palm. The two boys stopped just behind him, breathing heavily.

"Running without Soul Energy is a real drag—"

"Shhh," Carnus hushed them with closed eyes.

Something rushed through the trees near them.

Too fast for wind.

The rush came twice more. First behind them. Then north.

It was the warning of a cat playing with dinner.

Eos closed his eyes and let his Observation spread out.

Whoosh!

FEATHER AND FANG

He only caught flashes of energy that gave away a location, but from the intense speed moved, Eos knew he was only picking up on a long-gone trail by the time he recognized it.

Then, the aura slowed to a perceivable pace.

The owner *wanted* to be tracked this time.

A haunting figure drifted before them.

His cloak was like a reaper's garb beneath his bleached bone helm with curled horns and the bone necklace that rattled over his chest as he came to rest. Strips of cloth fluttered over his lower face, hiding whatever remained of his humanity beneath.

The voice rasped like sifting gravel from behind the helm, "Well, well, Carnus. It appears you found your courage again. Did you remember how to wield too?" Naith teased. "Or did you just come for your execution?"

"Naith," Carnus growled lowly as he nodded in cautious greeting.

"Sorry about our deal, *brother*. I tried to buy you more time, but Vistomus sent in his dog, Zeres, early. Nothing I could do, but seeing as you're here now, I don't think it much matters."

Carnus glowered, his dark beard and topknot catching the sunrise as his pupils quivered. "Those people were *my friends*. That village was my refuge for many years. You had no right—"

"I'd say take it up with the *King Under the Open Sky*," Naith mocked Zeres' self-bestowed title, "but I don't think you'll get the chance. It's a shame, Carnus. You were great once. We could have carried on a new Hamirate legacy."

If only I had turned down Naith that day. Turned down Vistomus and his offers. How far I've strayed from the path because of that one decision.

"*No.* I was self-centered and power hungry."

The bleached bone shook with laughter. "When did you become such a self-righteous, pious bore? You were ruthless once. I liked that Carnus better. So, let me remind you how it's done. Which of you three would like to be first to part from this life?"

The form of black and bone wavered before them.

Like a ghost fading back into the daylight, Naith vanished.

CHAPTER TWENTY-NINE

Then, he reappeared before Eos and cooed, "The Anite boy that I pursued for so long here on Earth? Shall I reclaim the prize that Aizo hid all those years ago?"

Again, Naith vanished, only to reappear before Durath. "Or..." his voice teased a higher note, "should I end the Leorix lineage?"

Before Durath could comprehend the speed of Naith's Soul Step, the phantom of a man patted the corcinth broach that strung from the shoulders of the fur cape.

Durath lunged with furious arms but caught only the hazy light of dawn.

"Or perhaps my Hamirate brother would like to go first to spare himself having to watch the young ones die," Naith baited Carnus as the strips of cloth fluttered where his mouth should have been.

"Boys," Carnus bellowed with urgency. "Do exactly as we planned."

Eos was still in shock from the Voro's speed as he questioned, "Are you sure you can—"

"*Now!*" Carnus screamed so hard his throat strained.

The Viator Hariban brought his palms together and curled his fingers near his chest in a flash of indigo Soul Energy. Carnus stomped forward, sending his pressed palms out in a striking gesture that rippled through the ground.

The earth trembled.

The ground fissured in an instant.

Indigo flared from the cracks.

Slabs of rock rose, carrying the momentum of Carnus' thrust as they spiraled around Naith.

The Voro was completely entombed in a cone of rock.

Crimson and emerald Soul energy blazed a trail into the distance as Eos and Durath rushed ahead while Naith was confined.

It had only bought them ten seconds, but it was enough.

Carnus was left alone with his encased Hamirate brother.

A burst of Soul Energy, black and thick like sludge, punctured the stone spiral around Naith Lelantos. A spiderweb of cracks filled with the cursed energy, and Carnus' dome shattered within seconds.

FEATHER AND FANG

Naith relies entirely on the curse. Of course. Voro. He welcomes the possession…probably lives for it after so long under its influence.

A silver gauntlet with ruby scrollwork adorned Naith's outstretched hand, but this metal covering was special. It had only one sharp phalange, ridged with the red gleam of animus stone like a giant stinger protruding from his index finger.

"So, you can wield after all, eh pacifist?" The gravelly voice emerged from the shadowed containment.

Carnus nodded. His jaw was stiff. His words were measured. Each forced through his rigid lips. "A man becomes master of himself by governing his passions. Command them or be enslaved by them."

"More ramblings from the old man?" Naith sighed with exaggerated exasperation.

"I recall Zeri the Great's *ramblings* in my thoughts daily. Fear and loathing became my passions—my jailors—but I have been given one last chance to remember who I am."

"Well, I remember who you *were*. Though I doubt there is much left," Naith chided. "They call me *the Pursuer*. And you were once formidable, so I've broken out my hunting gauntlet for you."

"I'm honored," Carnus spat with sarcasm.

The Voro vanished.

Traces of the haunting Soul Energy everywhere.

Too fast. Carnus whirled, trying to track it.

He sensed the aura flash in front of him a fraction of a second before Naith appeared.

The hunting gauntlet pierced toward his heart.

Not good. Defense. All there's time for.

Indigo light solidified over Carnus' body.

A vaporous stream of black bled from the stinger-like index finger's animus stone as it attacked.

The tip of the gauntlet finger sparked against Carnus' Solido.

The cursed energy magnified Naith's speed and striking power, and the animus stone-crested gauntlet further amplified it.

Just in time—Pain!

The Solido did not shatter. It did not break.

CHAPTER TWENTY-NINE

A clean hole the size of a finger broke through it.

In a panic, Carnus shifted away as his defense failed.

It was enough movement to change the gauntlet's trajectory to his shoulder.

He felt the excruciating sensation of searing hot Soul Energy piercing bone. Carnus wanted to puke from the pain.

"I was aiming for your heart. A pity. It would have been faster for you," Naith mocked.

Carnus knew he had to disrupt his enemy's concentration, or he was a dead man. The speed was too much to deal with. Naith had been known in the Hamirate Brotherhood for his Soul Step. With the Tide of Noximor flowing through him, it now resembled teleportation to the slowness of the human eye.

His shoulder wouldn't move. *Useless. This arm is done.*

It didn't matter. Carnus had a purpose on this battlefield that superseded all else.

"Cute necklace, Naith. Did you find a dead bird that you took a liking to?"

Naith's skull helm shook.

Good. It worked. He's a prideful man.

"I caught an elsu mid-flight. A testament to my great speed, which you just witnessed. How did it feel?"

Carnus turned his sharp exhale of pain into an ugly laugh. "Tickled a bit. So, you collect dead things you find on the road. With a skull that small for your helmet, that must have been a sickly corcinth cub, or is that just a prop you had made?"

The strips of fabric over Naith's mouth fluttered angrily as he exhaled. "Joke all you want! These are your last words. I'm sure Zeri the Great had a quote you can remember about the proper time for words and actions."

Naith was rattled. It was working.

The two fingers of Carnus' lame arm flicked inconspicuously at his side as Naith continued.

FEATHER AND FANG

"If you want to know, I hunted a corcinth and took its cub from it during the battle as my prize. Scarred the beast up badly. It may still be limping around—"

A strip of rocky earth, coated in indigo energy, shot out near the foot of Naith's black cloak. It struck him in his hip and knocked him back.

The Voro hobbled upright again as Carnus lunged forward with another strike.

Naith dodged as the next jutting ground attack struck a mirage.

"You're going to regret that cheap blow, Carnus."

"I regret a lot of things, Naith. Nothing I do this day will be one of them."

∞   ∞   ∞

Eos and Durath didn't backtrack. They had promised not to, but it didn't change the fact that their actions sat like a rock in Eos' stomach.

"I know we promised," Eos muttered as they skated over the grass with Soul Step, "but together, we could have beaten that Voro."

The gold chain of Durath's corcinth cape pendant bounced against his chest. "Carnus knew what he was getting into. Seemed like they had history anyway. Our mission is to get to the Eye as fast as possible. Vistomus is using it for his purposes as we speak."

Using it for what? Eos wondered.

Trees streaked by in their vision.

They neared the Imperial Palace. Through pruned hedges. Over mossy ponds. Through the scent of sweet garden air.

Yet there was a sense of anticipation in Eos.

The palace's tile roof was set against a graying sky.

The dampness of the morning dew clung to Eos' wrapped arm. The humidity clung to the outside of his skin, but beneath, it met the tingling of his Soul Energy bubbling forth in warning.

Another is coming. Ahktar circled overhead, a pure white blot against the clouds.

"Wait," Eos stalled their approach.

Whoosh!

CHAPTER TWENTY-NINE

An icy blue form ran by off to Eos' left. It was half-wolf and half-ghost; its legs materialized enough to prowl in warning before it vanished.

"He's here," Eos called out lowly.

Durath hummed in acknowledgment, "I feel the aura. You know who it is?"

"Rius," Eos said bluntly.

The lanky Mirza clapped his hands, appearing from behind the pillar lantern on the bridge ahead of them. "Excellent, Bellator. So perceptive. What gave it away? Could it be the Soul Energy wolf?" He teased with an arrogant dance in his tone.

"I swore an oath to protect you, Eos," Durath declared in a low voice. "You go ahead. I'll hold him off."

"No," Eos replied as Rius sauntered closer. "Even if he'd let one of us by...I'll stay to fight him."

Durath nearly choked on the thought. "Eos! You're supposed—"

"It's fine. I've faced him twice now. I know his techniques and his personality. I can take him, Durath."

Rius ran his hand through his long russet hair, pulled his collar against his neck, and settled his hands in his pockets. His piercing gray-green eyes, above pronounced, masculine cheekbones, were hyper-focused on Eos with unblinking concentration.

"The corcinth brute can go ahead. I won't stop him. I only have business with Eos...besides, it's your funeral. Vistomus awaits whichever fool reaches his *precious Left Eye*," Rius mocked the object of their conflict.

"I don't like it, Eos," Durath growled. "He wants this fight too much."

"Go. We have a mission. It's best served if I fight Rius," Eos commanded. His voice was unwavering, laced with Soul Energy that frothed within him. "Besides, he'll let you pass. Not me."

Sighing heavily, Durath muttered, "Bellators." Emerald flashed. His fur cape fluttered as the Leorix King's Son sprinted off. Before getting out of earshot, he turned back and called, "I better see you at the Fujima

Tower. Or our deals off. I won't follow the black elsu if he can't beat a wielding imitator like him."

Rius waved his middle finger over his shoulder at Durath but remained staring at Eos. "Better get going, little corinth boy, or my offer is withdrawn, and I'll kill *you* first."

Eos gave a firm nod to Durath, and his friend was gone.

Once Durath was safely out of distance for Rius to change his mind, Eos asked, "So you're just going to let him get to the Eye? I thought all the *hanyo* were supposed to be protecting it."

Rius curled one corner of his mouth in a snarl. "Not really my concern. I just want my fight with you." He kept his hands in his pockets. Three Soul Energy wolves shimmered into physical form around him. They stalked around him with a sharp electric sound. "Show me why Vistomus is so obsessed with you."

"I'd like to know that myself," Eos spat as he formed six crimson elsu that hovered above him. "You don't seem the loyal type, and you strike me as a loner. Why are you here in Nippon-Wa at all?"

"Less talk. More wielding. Or does the Order not teach that these days?" The Mirza smirked with dripping confidence. The three wolves turned to face Eos simultaneously. "Get serious. Use the Mark of the Chosen, or this won't last more than a few seconds."

"Guess you could say I gave that up."

"How boring."

But I still have some tricks you haven't seen. Eos held his tongue from revealing anything further. *We didn't have enough time in our last fight.*

Eos sent two of his elsu into the sky as four Soul Energy birds swarmed and distracted Rius in a flurry of cutting paths. Their wings streaked golden behind the red feathered wings. They slashed around the Mirza, but his wolves snapped and leaped, diverting any direct blows.

A few connected, giving Rius surface-level cuts, but he accepted them as if the pain was only a pre-fight ritual.

"Enough!" Rius flicked his chin and commanded one of his creatures. It lurched into the air, snapping up one of the crimson elsu in its glowing teeth. He made a show out of keeping his hands in his pockets.

CHAPTER TWENTY-NINE

The pair exploded in a flash of red and blue that became vaporous glowing smoke.

"You can have twice as many birds as my wolves, but it won't be nearly enough." Rius clicked his tongue.

The three remaining elsu hovered just out of distance of the icy-blue canine manifestations.

"*DO IT!*" Rius screamed with a twist of insanity. He tore down the neck of his black cloak to show his scarred chest. "Show me the power that can do this!"

"No," Eos whispered. His elsu swarmed again.

They cut in bursts. Slashes of intense heat swelled.

Cracks of speed pulsed through the air.

Rius was unphased. His Solido formed over his arms as he swatted the elsu that got past his wolves. His reactions were superhuman.

Wisps of Soul Energy drifted from his eyes as his pupils dilated and darted, tracking the paths of the three elsu as best he could.

As he clawed at one whose wings came within striking distance, he threw it off him and darted at Eos.

There was no time to dodge, so Eos threw up a veil of light.

Zmmm!

Rius' coated arm punched with enough momentum to send Eos on his back and coughing for air.

"Pathetic. You were disappointing without the curse mark—"

Crack!

One of the distant elsu descended from Rius' blind spot in the sky. Rius turned his head in realization of Eos' plan.

In the final moment before contact, the Mirza managed to summon one of his two wolves to leap between him and the attack, though only with enough time to throw its body against him as a shield.

Bwoom!

Thrown down in a violent eruption of fire, Rius let out a scream.

It was guttural and one of frustration, not pain—anger at being bested by tactic when Eos was clearly demonstrating weaker wielding. He wiped blood from the corner of his mouth and got to his hands and knees with his remaining wolf wavering like smoke in the wind beside him.

Eos stood, looking down on him.

"I'll ask again, Rius. What are you doing with the Mitad? Doesn't seem your style."

Rius spat a mouthful of blood. "You don't know a thing about *my style*. The Mitad offered me power." His wolf stabilized and became marbled with black. He caught his breath and finished, "You've tasted it. I need it for someone I'm hunting. If you'd seen things like I have, you wouldn't turn down the opportunity for information and strength."

Eos' jet-black hair twisted in the wind as his three elsu threatened over his shoulder. "I've seen a lot, and it's taught me that there are much more important things than power alone."

"*Pffft*," Rius snarled. "Spoken like a spoiled kingling. I'm no inlume holy paragon. Morality is for the weak to negotiate for power. *Strong steps on weak*. I was weak once, but now I'm strong. Let me show you."

The wolf evaporated into wafting energy that swirled around Rius, forming a shroud around him. It curdled black and morphed around him as his humanity became wolf-like.

His irises became white. Claws formed over his hands in ice-blue marbled with black ink. He crouched on all fours as Soul Energy bristled over him.

"I don't want to kill you, Rius," Eos warned. "You deserve it for attacking Saigo and his samurai. All that death, and for what?"

Rius growled with an animalistic pitch. "Nothing will stand between me and my quarry. I'm hunting Ignoble prey. You're just a step in proving myself." His long hair shook as he lost control to the curse. "The Mitad…a step to the information I need. I have nothing to justify to you."

But to justify to yourself? Eos mused.

Rius jolted at him.

His new hybrid-wolf form enhanced his speed and power to levels that Eos couldn't keep up with.

It was perceivable. But just barely.

CHAPTER TWENTY-NINE

Eos coated himself in crimson just in time to feel the air leave him. He doubled over, trying to shift out of the way of another attack, but his body was overcome with pain.

Animalistic eyes met him as the glowing form of a half-man rushed past him.

For a moment, the temptation flickered in Eos' heart.

It would be easier. *So much easier!*

Just for a moment.

The curse would win him this battle.

Path of light. I'm going to be an inlume. Eos reminded himself.

He shifted again, just enough to prevent Rius' rippling arm from piercing his chest. Instead, the claws found his Solido-coated arm, braced against his side.

It had to have been at least fractured.

The ache was intense. Every thought was interrupted halfway by the throb. In between, he managed to summon light around his feet and recoil away a few steps to distance himself.

Use it! In his pain, he was certain that he had made a mistake.

The curse was the best path.

No. Stick to the plan.

Eos searched his mind. He still had his four total elsu remaining.

Shame. Humility pushes out shame. Aizo knows best. The curse will consume me. Release guilt.

Thoughts ran in an unfettered stream of panic surrounded by pain in Eos.

Ice-blue light came at him again.

There was distance this time. He had a split second.

He rolled to the ground, nearly throwing up as he jarred his injured arm, but he managed to avoid another blow.

Rius' outstretched claws were held out in a delay of pulling back his attack after assuming he'd connect with flesh.

Now!

Eos' energy rushed within him, purified as Aizo had taught him.

There was a crackling like thousands of particles accumulating static charge.

FEATHER AND FANG

Eos' three elsu on the battlefield were torn apart.

The avian forms burst into hundreds of molten forms.

Rius whipped his head around in every direction.

Feathers.

He was surrounded by an uncountable number of Soul Energy feathers. They fluttered around him like sakura petals falling in the Japanese autumn.

There was enough time for his eyes to widen and his jaw to hang slightly. The fierce eyes wavered.

The waves of Eos' technique came at him like a tsunami.

A mass of feathers rushed over Rius.

Golden-red Soul Energy bit the Mirza's skin like blade cuts being made to every part of his body. Over. And over.

It was a relentless torrent of crimson feathers.

Blood filled his mouth. It dripped from every limb as his wolf-like form fell away to a crumbling attempt at Solido.

The only relief from Eos' Severence came after the assault reached a crescendo and the swarm of light exploded on all sides of him.

Eos did not smile at his victory. It was not nearly as sweet as he had hoped. His skills were proven, but there was something about Rius' forced personality that he *almost* sympathized with.

"You were wrong, Rius. The strong can also protect the weak."

The look in Rius' cold gray-green eyes was of genuine tragic wonder. He searched for an answer to how the impossible had happened. Lips moved, but no words came.

Rius Yama was on his knees, bleeding from nearly every part of his body and surrounded by shattered Soul Energy.

"I refuse," Rius whispered. "I won't lose to you."

Pitch black filled his eyes and crawled up his skin.

His features became wolfish again. Ears pointed. Skin like fur.

But now it was dripping with the sludgy viscosity of the curse.

It granted even greater speed and a second gasp of life for the defeated Mirza.

Before Eos could perceive the movement, the hand tainted by the Tide of Noximor was around his throat and lifting him off the ground.

CHAPTER TWENTY-NINE

"Can't...lose..." Rius mumbled as if possessed. "Must avenge...Ara needs me...can't end here."

Demonic black eyes looked lifelessly into Eos.

Despite the hand constricting his throat, Eos was at peace. His body relaxed.

Rius squeezed and pulled back his hand, ready to pierce Eos through the chest.

Crack!

Soul Energy wings broke the sound barrier as Eos' sixth and final elsu emerged through the clouds.

It struck Rius in the back and exploded!

Both Eos and Rius were caught in the explosion, but Rius' cursed body shielded Eos.

The heat was intense. Even through Rius, it scalded his skin.

Eos rolled the limp Mirza off him as he rose, finally victorious.

He wasn't sure if Rius was alive, but he didn't have time to care for his enemy now. The Left Eye of Izanagi awaited.

With a sad nod, Eos murmured, "It was a good battle, Rius."

He hoped the man did not die, but Rius had reaped the deserved consequences.

Rius was left bleeding on the ground. His body broken. His will crumpled. His life fading.

I'm sorry, Ganz. I won't be avenging you.

I'm going to die, aren't I?

Ara...I'm sorry...Ara...

CHAPTER THIRTY

HAMIRATE BROTHERS

The ashen fields north of the Imperial Palace filled Talus with dread. It was as if there had been a smiting around the Emperor's property, and the chastisement had turned to rage outside the Inui-mon Gate. Trees were turned to charred stumps, shattered and broken.

The outer ring of destruction all around the imperial walls was noticeable from the sky, and the blackened park filled the trio's vision as they descended upon it.

Talus released Glenn from his back and handed him his winged staff as Grace touched down beside them.

"Vistomus…" Grace observed with a solemn whisper.

"Explains why we didn't get a welcoming party. Whatever was here before was burned to nothing," Glenn murmured.

CHAPTER THIRTY

"I don't expect we get much further without Vistomus or his mirzas greeting us. I sense battles everywhere. Soul Energy to the west with Carnus…and the south with Aizo and Scavok. We're already close. Look there," Talus directed them to look across the moat. "That's the ancient castle, the Edo Ruins, behind those trees. We'll get there on foot. If our aura wasn't sensed as we crossed over, we might make it to Fujima Tower."

The Anite King stroked his braided auburn beard and nodded to affirm his decision. They followed the road, undisturbed, and crossed an ancient stone bridge, stained with one thousand years of dirt and overgrown with the greenery across the moat. Pine and leaves drooped and leaned to shield the Edo Castle remains.

An eerie silence surrounded them. It was a buffer to the distant gunfire of Saigo and Saitani's battles. Soul Energy clashed with samurai swords and rebel guns just three miles away. Wielding crackled from the Imperial Castle grounds, but it was distant rumbling as they proceeded through rows of bamboo gardens.

They exited into a clearing at the base of the Edo Castle ruins.

It was a cobbling of rectangular foundation stones that had darkened and discolored unevenly throughout the ages. Atop it, there was no structure—only the base tiers remained.

But where a castle had once been, ages ago, stood a mirza.

His black, serpent-crested cloak flowed in the wind from chest to knee in a rolling mass of cloth. His hair was like smoke, with a mustache to match. Gold hung from his neck, waist, and wrists with kingly status, and his fingers glittered with gemstones, though his left hand was withered and deformed.

"You wear the elsu," the Mirza called down from atop the ruins. "Could it be a great king sneaks around in Lord Vistomus' territory?" The face was cut with the lines of time and a life of battle, and his mustache moved slowly as the words came out with no particular haste.

"You know who I am," Talus admitted, flashing the inlume wreath around his head in warning, "but who stands watch on a castle that no longer exists?"

HAMIRATE BROTHERS

"Your reputation proceeds you, Talus, but I don't know your two companions. I am the strongest of Vistomus' seven hanyo, and I rather enjoy this spot. It reminds me of my old throne. *King Under the Open Sky*, I was called."

Talus tensed.

Unlucky. We were so close. Why did it have to be him?

"Zeres Teritus...the Harbinger. That's the only man I know who went by such a title."

"Then you know your executioner, King Bellator. Let this be an entertaining duel." Zeres leaped from his Edo Castle perch and landed with cursed energy rippling at his feet. There was no grace to his movement—only deadly, fearsome power that emanated from his body as if it was leaking black smoke.

"Stay back. Grace, keep Glenn safe. Try and get to the tower," Talus bellowed without taking his eyes off the threat.

Zeres didn't let a flicker of emotion twist his face. His glassy brown-beige eyes looked past Talus as he called out, "Artera, make sure they don't interrupt my duel with the Visrex of Wings."

A short girl appeared with a flash of white Soul Step. Her skin was a caramel-ash, and her hair was the darkest night, pulled into a tight bun.

"Don't worry, Zeres. They won't be taking another step towards the Eye," Artera replied.

Soul Energy churned from Zeres, rising in a vaporous cloud from his body. The gold of his jewelry reflected through it in occasional shimmers, but his form became obscured.

A wave of foreboding aura screamed through Talus' senses.

This was no ordinary Soul Energy. His Observation probed and found only thick, palpable wave of toxic decay.

"You must be one of Vistomus' Voro with that concentration of his curse mark upon you." Talus spat, buying himself seconds to analyze as he shifted away from the slow-rolling attack. Yet, he knew his statement wasn't quite right. There had been no visible claim on Zeres' skin.

From behind the cloud of Soul Energy, Zeres growled, "That dread you feel is my own. I reinforce it with as much of the Mark of the Chosen

CHAPTER THIRTY

as I wish, but Vistomus has no sway over me. He is a cunning trickster, but his simple aura cannot possess me."

Talus knew intuitively that he could not so much as risk coming into contact a single time with *the Harbinger's* energy. The King of Anite taunted, "So you say, yet you're not one of his emir…merely a mirza."

Crimson light tested the smoky energy in winged form.

It met the churning mass and cut through it.

However, Talus' light began to crumble like burning parchment as it passed toward Zeres.

There was an electric hum of clashing Soul Energy, but it pitched and whined sharply as crimson dissolved.

Withered away. Zeres' Soul Energy is toxic to other wielders.

Nearly impenetrable, but he's slow.

That's the one weakness that I can leverage.

Zeres called out, hidden from sight, "I desire to test my strength in battle, not lead a group of pompous wielding pups. It's beneath me. I left that tiresome task to Raggan."

Wings of fire unfurled behind Talus as he performed Severance.

The massive, feathered creations beat with a powerful thrust, sending forth a wave of light.

Zeres' wall of cursed energy consumed it—but Talus followed with a flurry of feathers that sprayed behind it the first attack. They tested the disrupted cloud in rapid succession.

The small crimson beams were quickly dissolved, but some found thinness in the smoke.

Two broke through!

The first struck the rocks of the castle foundation.

But the second found flesh. Talus could sense that much.

A dull grunt received the pain.

It may have only caused a small cut, but the feather had proven that the cloud of necrotic energy could be overcome.

How? How can I create something that can overwhelm such defense?

Zeres may be incredibly strong, but he's no tactician, or else Vistomus would have made him an emir.

Talus' thoughts turned to regret.

HAMIRATE BROTHERS

He had spent so much effort analyzing and observing the cloud of darkness between him and his opponent that he had neglected to watch for Zeres' bodily movement.

Existing in a more living vibration, Zeres' physical presence was cloaked by the distraction of his thick aura barrier of death.

It hid him. Made his person forgettable amidst the spectacle.

As if he would never leave its protection.

In the second it took to comprehend the trick, Talus recognized that when Zeres received the minor damage from the feather, he immediately left his barrier.

Zeres was upon Talus.

They were matched in height, and the white mustache and maddened eyes looked from an even level at Talus as Zeres stilled from his Soul Step.

His undamaged arm reached.

Jewels and gold flashed before Talus' face.

Black smoke shot out from his fingertips.

It brushed against him, tickling the end of his beard and eating away at the fibers of his hair as Talus fell away just out of reach.

"I kill you, and it's finished. My duty will be done. Then I can leave this forsaken *ostaka* land," Zeres muttered as his deathly emanation brushed with Talus.

Talus spun, rolling around Zeres' lame arm.

He evaded successfully, but just barely. More necrotic emission was flowing in his direction.

Behind him, Grace was in battle with the short female mirza, Artera.

"Stay back, Glenn," Grace ordered.

"You don't have to tell me twice," Glenn groaned as he backed toward the bamboo grove behind them.

Grace drew two manus daggers, the skulls in their hilts reminding her of the somber reality that death was near at all times in the life of a Necogen assassin.

Caldus...I won't see you on this side, my son...but your daggers will serve me well in dismantling the organization that wronged us.

Starting here in this battle.

CHAPTER THIRTY

As Amon's daggers gleamed with threat, Artera held an open palm out in a halting motion.

Snow white energy pulsed from her palm in an outward beam.

Soul Energy shot past Grace's ear, narrowly missing her.

Stunned by the quick, nearly fatal start to the battle, Grace regripped the hilts of her son's daggers and observed aloud, "An Inner Path user?"

Artera gave the slightest of nods.

"Inner Path Nineteen…" Grace murmured. "You're quick to open the fight."

"You're as knowledgeable as your reputation suggests," Artera responded with a tone of respect.

Caldus, my forever lost son, be with me in this manus stone.

Grace rubbed the hilts tenderly and dove toward Artera with an assassin's agility and finesse.

∞   ∞   ∞

Scavok and Aizo had crossed the southern gate, leaving Saitani's soldiers behind them as they entered the Imperial Castle grounds.

Within a minute, they encountered two mirzas.

A lumbering, one-armed giant and a dark-skinned woman with white-toned anima stones embedded in her cheekbones approached.

"These two again," Aizo grumbled.

Bysis landed from his Soul Step and slung his katana over his shoulder. His voice droned deep and slow with a hint of excitement at what he saw, "Diya, it's those wielders from the warehouse raid."

"Bysis, your powers of observation exceed your intellect," Diya said with disdain. She drew a manus blade katana from her hip.

"Thank you…I think…" The oaf creased his brow as he processed what he suspected might not be a compliment.

Aizo sighed. "Shall we switch the matchup this time?

"*No,*" Scavok rumbled with rage. "The witch is mine. I have questions for her." His haggard beard shadow emphasized the malice in his voice.

HAMIRATE BROTHERS

"Guess I'll take the giant again," Aizo said with a frown. "At least he has one less arm this time."

Bysis scowled back. "Losing it has only made me stronger. You don't stand a chance, Aizo Mudar."

Diya hissed with a twisted eagerness, "And you, dog of the king, will find that your blade has a match. I don't have to stop a weapons heist while fighting you this time."

Scavok drew Safisay, its winged hilt reassuring him that he would get the vengeance and answers he sought. "And we don't have to try and defend one either."

The master assassin took advantage and pressed his offense.

Diya had only seen faster Soul Step from Naith.

Glacial blue projected from Scavok's blade as he swung deftly from Diya's left. She was proficient with her swordwork. The Krog woman deftly countered his blade and neutralized the Soul Energy coming at her.

Scavok spun and struck down at her leg.

She parried.

He brought the short sword around again at her throat.

The katana came between steel and flesh once more.

A devilish grin spread as the Soul Energies clashed in an electric symphony with the ringing of steel. "Surely you won't get answers out of me if you've already removed my head?"

Violet thorny vines crawled from her fingertips and blade. They reflected off the yellow marbling of her irises as their blades became tied together by her luminous tendrils.

"I'll leave just enough attached to get my answers from you," Scavok growled with hatred as he struggled to free his sword. He was stronger than the woman, but their blades were bound together. "Tell me this, *Witch*, when your kind steals innocent women and children," he grunted as he failed to separate his sword, "what becomes of your victims? I've seen the Sisters of Noxim slaughter with no regard, but the young ones?" Scavok's voice cracked as he finished.

There was a flick of Diya's tongue as she savored the suffering.

CHAPTER THIRTY

Ice-blue ropes of Soul Energy formed at Diya's feet, burning her skin and rooting her in place. The short sword flashed—meant only to vaporize immediately around the blade as he yanked it back.

The vines around Safisay turned to glittering dust.

Diya managed to raise a veil around her shoulder and arm so that Scavok's next swing only grazed her hand. Blood flowed down her fingers, but she only smiled, wiped it across her face, and activated the anima stones embedded in her cheeks.

Her thorny roots grew from the ground, shredding Scavok's net of ice at her feet, and she distanced herself away from Talus' Master Assassin.

"Lose someone at Pacem Derex?" Diya provoked.

Scavok did not hide the emotion in his voice. Scars hung in every word, though his eyes and facial muscles were cold and motionless. "My wife and newborn son had been staying there before we knew there would be a revolution. *Visiting me.* I gathered information for my king, yet I didn't know a Bellator boy would open the gates and draw first blood against his father's cause. That Saida, a member of the Council, would betray us!"

Diya cackled. "Saida sure did warp Ares to pull that off. You fools and your compassion. See what it got you?"

"Yes," Scavok said low and viciously. "That's why I'll show you none." He swung in a series of blows that met the katana. Violet and blue exploded. "I watched *you people* kill my wife." His tone trembled while his face remained weathered stone. "But my son—a witch carried him out alive while I was defending my King."

"Ahhh," Diya cooed. "An infant taken alive. They make *the best sacrifices* to Noximor."

At that, Scavok's eyebrows betrayed him with a quiver. Some ember of hope that he usually hid from himself died in the pit of his stomach then. "What do you mean?"

"The Sisterhood gives enemy children as blood offerings for Noximor," Diya said with psychopathic apathy. "Common. Though I wasn't the one who took your child. Would have received a nice reward, I imagine."

HAMIRATE BROTHERS

A furious barrage of swings came down on Diya. The physical strength behind them shook her wrist bones through her katana grip.

The Mirza's face glittered once again with the embedded reservoir of anima stone energy.

Steel became tangled once more.

Scavok snarled with heavy breath, weighed down by more than the exhaustion of battle, "That name keeps coming up these days. You freaks and your imaginary demons!"

Blades ground against each other, edge to edge, glowing hot with Soul Energy. Muscles tensed. Net and thorny vine clashed around them in a war of light as the two vied for dominance.

Grunting, Diya hissed, "That's where you're wrong, Anite dog. Noximor is *more real than anything you could fantasize*. The strongest of the Danaqi. The rightful ruler of our world. King of Bishiwal!"

Strands of his silver mane fell over Scavok's face. The elsu crests on his armor gleamed under ice-blue Soul Energy. His voice was harsh and unforgiving. "Tell me, will you beg for mercy from me or Noximor when I slay you?"

"Noximor shows no mercy. Strength and dominance are the only languages his servants know."

Scavok gave a slight nod.

His fingers slipped from his winged hilt purposefully.

Safisay was left hovering, fused to Diya's katana of thorns.

Twisting with masterful skill, Scavok simultaneously spun around Diya and unsheathed a dagger from a baldric beneath his outer robe.

In one swift motion, Scavok Alter drove the knife between the witch's back ribs, leaving her gasping for air.

Diya fell to her knees.

Two swords clattered to the ground.

Scavok picked up Safisay as a net of blue light bound Diya to the spot. She was helpless.

The short sword kissed her chest with its point.

The corner of her mouth twisted in slight amusement as she murmured, "Does the Order of Soul Wielders not show mercy?"

CHAPTER THIRTY

"*I* will show you the same *mercy* that your Sisterhood gave my family," Scavok said as his emotions returned behind his stone exterior.

Behind Scavok, the Aizo's battle was also drawing to a close.

When it began, Bysis had the advantage.

The giant had seen Aizo's Severance before. Familiar with the implanting of Soul Energy into the air and ground to create a minefield, the Mirza had manifested his silver arm and swatted through the glittering wall of orange light.

The air erupted, but Aizo observed how Bysis survived the direct explosions. *The oaf concentrates all his energy into that arm and his skin. It's like Solido, but instead, he blends the Soul Energy into the surface of his body—like a tough armor hide. He must feel every bit of pain but is able to avoid significant damage—a true brute!*

Bysis gripped the sword with both his arm of flesh and the Soul Energy prosthetic, wound back, and sent a slicing projection of silver glow that split the ground.

Aizo reeled, narrowly avoiding being cut in two.

No sooner had he settled, another crushing blow followed.

The Inlume dodged and slid to avoid the attacks.

"Powerful but slow. There's no tactic to your offense," Aizo critiqued as he avoided waves of katana Soul Energy projections. He wagged a finger chastisingly. "You're like a wild beast."

"That's what Diya calls me. Always insults," Bysis roared. His swings became erratic, more frequent, but weaker.

The ground around them was scarred from a dozen katana blows.

Good, Aizo thought, *even a beast tires.*

"Not an insult. Merely some wisdom to improve your technique," Aizo continued to provoke. "I've taught many children and new wielders. You could learn a thing or two about fundamentals. *Sloppy.*"

It was true, yet Bysis could also kill him in a single blow. Aizo knew he was playing a risky gamble by enraging the Mirza.

A frustrated scream responded as Bysis missed again by inches.

His dull, menacing eyes shook beneath bleached eyebrows. His jaw clenched, striating his muscled cheeks with his wrath.

HAMIRATE BROTHERS

With each successive flurry, Aizo shifted his stance and whirled, drawing him closer to Bysis. The distance was closing. He was almost within reach of the steel.

The katana came down once more.

Aizo could see his reflection in the glowing metal as he slid past it. His wild hair, flowing sideburns, and scraggly beard were captured briefly in the blade.

Bysis struck the air and split the ground again in a fit of rage.

Aizo reached under the luminous, silver arm and ran his fingers across it as he moved behind the giant's body.

Orange twinkled like a sea of stars inside Bysis' arm.

It gurgled and bubbled.

Bwmmm! The Soul Energy limb burst, scattering wisps of wriggling vapor. The katana fell to the grass.

While Bysis clutched his bloodied stump of a shoulder, Aizo dove, grabbed the katana hilt, and somersaulted out of Bysis reach.

Screaming, the Mirza released a beam of Soul Energy from his open mouth that emulsified the torn earth and moved with the turn of his head.

It was enough to pierce through even his Solido, that much Aizo knew for certain. He sensed the dense, heavy aura and Soul Stepped just beyond its pursuit.

The torrent of Soul Energy couldn't continue for long.

It was a rage-induced dump of Bysis' entire Soul Reservoir.

Yet, Aizo was unsure he could stay out of its range long enough to survive.

Silver light melted the ground behind Aizo.

Then, it reached his heels.

He leaped on planes of orange energy, launching himself at Bysis.

Concentrating the strength of a full-bodied Solido into his feet alone, Aizo coasted against the edge of the blast intended for him.

Zmmmm.

The clash of Soul Energy gave an electrical whine as Aizo's orange-coated feet ground against the outer periphery of the silver beam.

Aizo twirled his katana as he propelled himself over Bysis.

CHAPTER THIRTY

The Inlume landed behind his opponent, brought the blade around as he turned, lit the katana until the manus stone shone orange, and drove it into Bysis' back.

In the vision of Observation Wielding, he watched as his Soul Energy imparted through the metal and into Bysis' enormous back muscles. The particles of his Severance channeled through the katana and erupted just beneath the skin.

The armored skin shattered, leaving the Mirza bloodied as he fell to his hands and knees.

Now, Scavok had Diya pinned with a blade to her chest, and Aizo drew the katana from the defeated Bysis.

Victory sang with the whistle of the wind in a moment of calm that allowed both Soul Wielders to lower their heart rate.

Heavy footfall approached from the west with no intention of stealth. It was the sound of struggling armor taking every step with desperation.

Midnight-colored samurai armor approached, sword swinging at the coming warrior's waste. A golden lion-dog bounced atop the kabuto helmet.

Saigo Takayoshi ran as if fleeing a demon.

Holding Diya's katana in his left hand, Scavok drove it through the Mirza's chest as she wheezed on her back. She let out a weak cry but was pinned to the ground, drained of Soul Energy from the battle, breathing through a collapsed lung from the knife, and now had steel that staked her to the ground. Her aura and life force were fading.

"That'll keep you still," Scavok declared coldly.

Aizo kept Bysis' katana at the giant's throat with enough pressure to prick the skin in threat. The Mirza was weakened enough not to struggle. His rage had turned to defeat.

"What news from the battlefront, Saigo?" Aizo called as the samurai leader neared.

The spaulders and gauntlets stilled as Saigo sucked in gasping breaths. "Aizo-sama...Scavok-sama...Saitani is winning...but... nearly all the Emperor's forces in the west...and half...half of my bushi are dead."

HAMIRATE BROTHERS

All four wielders' eyes turned to the samurai with curiosity.

"How is that possible?" Scavok asked with tension in his throat.

Saigo's eyes narrowed as he stared at the kami with guttural fear in his voice. "Akuma…it's coming. IT'S COMING!" He screamed the final words with primal horror.

Aizo tried to ease his panic. "What's coming, Saigo? It's alright."

"A monster. *A demon*! Not something like you kami—or even these hanyo. A true akuma! It slaughtered everyone at the battlefield." Saigo cried out.

The armored bushi drew his katana and turned away from the Soul Wielders.

"It's coming this way. I had to warn someone—I'm fortunate I found you two before…*it did*."

∞   ∞   ∞

Heavy breathing came from beneath the bone helm of Naith Lelantos. He stared down his old Hamirate Brother, Carnus, from behind the shadow sockets of the bleached skull.

Carnus had a hole through his upper chest near the shoulder. It had gushed blood, but the battle-hardened wielder had remembered his training and sealed the wound with Soul energy. He had relied on his Observation Wielding to battle Naith, forgoing his physical sight to keep up with the fastest Soul Step he had ever encountered.

The clash had been a frantic race to finish as the victor. One slip-up meant death from either of the formidable wielders.

Carnus reflected as both men caught their breath.

Have to end this soon. His speed is draining me.

Gotta get to Eos and Durath. I swore to protect them.

I never got to raise you, Koda. I was trapped here…but I hope you've become every bit the talented, determined wielder those two have.

In his mind's eye, he beheld Naith's movement—it was a blurring streak of cursed energy and ruby gauntlet. For a brief instant, he even saw where Naith was moving before the footsteps landed.

CHAPTER THIRTY

The battle was pushing him to new levels despite how long it had been since he had last fought. Though, in his reclusive life, he had lived in a constant state of Observation Wielding, fearing the day the Mitad would discover him.

Indigo bathed a slab of earth as it rose from the ground ahead of Naith's path.

It slammed into his head.

The skull helm fractured and fell.

Naith's uncovered head was left bare.

It was a mutilated stump of burns and lumpy growths.

"*Alru maek*," Carnus whispered in the old tongue as he saw what lay beneath. "What happened to you, Naith?"

"Not a pretty sight, is it?" Naith cooed. "You remember Hariban Gorfa? Of course you do; how could you forget?"

"The Primane Hariban who slaughtered the Hamirate at the Battle of Tacitus...everyone heard what happened to him." Carnus knew the truth now—that Gorfa had acted on behalf of Vistomus after Anzolo was killed. "Gorfa's body was mutilated after the war. Strewn across the kingdom. It fueled the anger of the next war! That was you?"

Naith laughed uncontrollably at Carnus' revelation. "I was young and fueled by vengeance against the persecutors of the Hamirate holocaust. Caught up to Gorfa. Caught up to two other Primane wielders with him. They tortured me a bit...gave me this face...but it was their undoing. I had the taste of Vistomus' gift by then. I let it save me as my face was emulsified by those Primane scum for amusement."

"Naith..." Carnus whispered with sadness.

"Don't pity me. It was the taste I needed to give in fully. Never went back. I learned the power of the Mitad that day and came to understand the folly of the Hamirate Brotherhood."

Carnus sensed the flare of Naith's Soul Energy at his feet.

Naith finished, "Now you know. Now you die. Goodbye, Brother."

Carnus was ready.

I have to use it now. He'll be close enough to kill me.

It's a risk. But it will end this.

HAMIRATE BROTHERS

The scrollwork of the hunting gauntlet got close enough for Carnus to admire the details. It was a beautiful weapon that had pierced above his heart.

In the movement, Naith had done precisely what Carnus expected. His feet touched the ground.

Beneath him, indigo blazed.

The animus-coated finger nearly found his face, but the illusion of his death within reach was required.

A hole appeared beneath Naith, deep enough for his entire body.

As the gauntlet went to claim its mark, gravity took Naith's body.

He fell into the trap at his feet.

The swipe of Naith's index finger nearly caught Carnus on the way down.

It missed by an inch. Cursed energy sparked before his pupils.

Carnus brought his fists together, punching his knuckles against those of the opposite hand. He did so through the hideous throbbing of his wound.

The earth mirrored his hand motion.

The hole closed on itself.

Naith Lelantos was crushed, defeated, and buried simultaneously.

Carnus picked up the fractured bone helm with a tender touch.

"We were brothers...once..."

Sadness overwhelmed him. *How has life taken such a path?*

There were so many chances for it to end a better way. Yet we chose this?

He set the two pieces of corcinth skull over Naith's burial spot.

I have to find Eos and Durath.

∞   ∞   ∞

Durath worried about Eos, but he fulfilled his duty to the mission and trusted his friend to handle the Mirza, Rius. He cut south of the Imperial Castle and soared over a street that led directly to the southwestern wall of Fujima Tower.

Security guards fired bullets from below, but Durath was a blur of speed that their human perception could barely track. He paid them no

CHAPTER THIRTY

mind, confident his trailing wall of emerald light would deflect any rounds that came near him.

When he came upon his final destination, he sprinted up the ten meter, sloped stone fortification, bounding on Soul Energy to the white wall of the ancient guard tower.

Skyscrapers cast a contrasting background against the traditionally tiled swooping roof as he approached the entrance of the time capsule-like building.

A pulsing aura vibrated through the Fujima Tower.

It was not human.

The energy announced itself as far older and more mysterious than even the buildings of the Imperial Castle grounds.

Durath shivered. *The Left Eye.* It was inside, and it was being used...for an end they only knew would bring death and destruction.

The Leorix King's Son leaped over a black iron gate and charged through the front door, preceded by a wave of emerald.

It crumpled inwards and snapped from its hinges.

The scene Durath witnessed was momentary. He took it in for only a few seconds before everything unfolded.

A stone table was at the center of the small, square room.

On it, a young boy no older than fifteen, gangly and unmatured, lay strewn over it. His body was limp. His ashen skin was pale and dotted with perspiration. Dull black hair was matted to his face.

The childish eyes were a magenta that was almost scarlet.

Dacian Shaman. Durath knew the eyes by reputation. Redder than all other Krogs. The shamans of the Dacian continent were mythicized in rumors and tales.

A heavy glow cast over his exposed chest.

The source of the light had a life of its own.

Inorganic. Chilling. Like a piece of nature that became sentient.

It was a ruby stone, but it shuddered and jolted—its form wavering out of its solid, physical state beneath a pair of pallid hands.

The hands belonged to a gaunt face that was sharp like carved wood. The man was focused singularly upon the Left Eye of Izanagi as it blipped in and out of the visible realm, merging into the young boy's chest.

Vistomus observed them intently. His bald head reflected the shimmering ruby hue of the work he oversaw.

"Careful," The Mitad leader warned. "You must match the vibration of the Eye to his lifeforce *exactly*. You're letting it fall below his frequency."

When the doors folded into the room and announced the Leorix intruder, Vistomus looked up with a calm, controlling stare and stated with an unwavering tone, "Don't get distracted, Tessio. We must finish the process at all costs. Cyra!" He shouted to the long pony-tailed Mirza.

Cyra reached into his sleeves and then cast his hands out, spreading whatever he had procured from the pouch at his wrist along with a flood of slate-blue energy. It formed an instantaneous grid that wrapped around the entire surgery-like procedure that was taking place at the center of the tower.

Snarling, Cyra addressed Durath, "You again. I owe you for that cheap trick at the warehouse. Using metus stone," he muttered with bitterness. "You remember how well you did against my impenetrable barrier last time?"

Durath recalled it well. The wall of gray-blue light had more than strength to it. A dozen inlume wielders combined might not have been able to break it. The wielding technique had swallowed up everything he threw at it.

"It had to be done," Durath said with no remorse. "Should have planned better, *Mitad scum*."

Cyra sighed. "I should have known you'd choose the most difficult way. You can still leave now. You're lucky I'm tied up here, otherwise I'd take care of you myself...but Kallag? He's itching for a fight with you."

Marigold Soul Energy slammed into Durath's chest.

It had manifested so swiftly that he hadn't been ready. Nor had he seen its wielder in his blind spot in the corner of the room.

The yellow-orange energy flashed before his eyes with a searing heat and a threatening crackle. A tattooed fist and shirtless body were behind it.

CHAPTER THIRTY

Durath flew out of Fujima Tower through the doors he had destroyed. His chest ached, and his lungs struggled to find air as he landed on his back on the path outside.

Square runes forked into arks up Kallag's arms and shoulders.

An oni mask covered the lower half of his face. Its twisted grin was fanged and terrifying, hiding the boyish face beneath.

Durath sprung to his feet despite the burning in his ribs. He had been in many wielding tournaments and battlefields, and pain was nothing more to him than a taste on the path to victory.

"A Vurangian. Fought one of your kind in a tourney once. Gave me a heck of a time, but broke most of his bones by the end of the match." Durath swept his maroon fur cape back as he shifted into a fighting stance.

"You lie," Kallag accused. "No mountain savage could best a trained warrior of Vurang."

The maroon cape glimmered under the gray sky.

Emerald light manifested all around Durath as he pulled additional reserves from the lining of his cape. It had been a gift from his father for winning against a Leorix hariban for his twentieth birthday duel; lined with a carefully sewn array of anima stones, the cape was beyond price.

"I don't lie, Vurangian. I learned what fearsome opponents your people are. So, I won't hold back!"

A pair of emerald horns charged Kallag.

The attack blazed a trail of light that crashed into the oni-masked Mirza. Marigold energy shattered around his arms as he braced against the attack and was thrown back into the tower wall.

His mask and injured jaw muted and distorted his voice, but Kallag chuckled as he recovered. "You're going to be a fun one, aren't you?"

Behind Kallag, Vistomus ceased his fixation over the boy at the stone table. He turned his cold, emotionless eyes away from the cultish procedure and let a small grin form.

"It seems my favorite Bellator approaches." Vistomus put his fingertips together in a pleased contemplation. "I have business with him. Cyra, guard Khasun well. Tessio, do not fail me."

The screams of a child filled the Fujima Yagura.

HAMIRATE BROTHERS

Drops of sweat fell from Tessio's forehead onto Khasun's splayed, rigid body.

Vistomus stepped through a gap in Cyra's barrier.

The slate light resealed the gap as soon as the Mitad leader passed through to the other side.

CHAPTER THIRTY-ONE

ETHEREAL BOUNDARY

Eos followed Durath's path around the Imperial Castle. He had left Rius alive…though he wasn't sure how much longer the defeated Mirza could hold onto life in his state.

Pings of aura shot into his awareness.

Some he recognized. Aizo and Scavok. *They were near.* Perhaps just through a few trees and down the road. He felt the intensity of their struggles. Durath was engaged in battle atop the hill.

Talus' Soul Energy was distant but so concentrated and similar to his own that Eos recognized his father's aura from across the Imperial Castle grounds.

His Observation was more heightened than it had ever been, but there were traces of other wielders he didn't recognize.

Someone's approaching.

ETHEREAL BOUNDARY

The wielder was different from the others. Something about the way his Soul Energy manifested was unnaturally twisted.

Familiar.

As Eos realized why, he also accepted that he wouldn't make it to the Fujima Tower. The new presence was coming directly for him—far too fast for him to reach his goal.

He had felt the distinct Soul Energy once before.

His head had been covered by a bag…deep underground in the rebel tunnels beneath the North American Sector desert.

Vistomus Fulmen intercepted his path moments later.

A rippling wall of lightning sent Eos to a knee-aching halt. He cut his speed abruptly to avoid being struck by the plasma called down from the sky.

"Eos, there's no rush," Vistomus chided with a smile. "We have all the time in the world. I've been wanting *so very much* to speak with you."

Catching his breath, Eos glared at Vistomus for enough time to communicate his loathing. His golden eyes burned with anger at all the so-called *Raijin* had done to the land of Nippon-Wa.

"Yeah…I got the invitation. Rius was quite *diplomatic* about it."

Gray fingers rubbed his temples as Vistomus laughed with amused regret. "Yes…he was a rather poor choice, I admit. He turned out to be far too strong-willed. I hope you can forgive the rudeness."

Eos was so close, yet the swooping, decorative tiles of the three-tiered tower were still out of reach. From the building, he heard a faint screaming. It was the excruciating agony of a child, but he could get no further. "Oh, I think there's far more you need to apologize for if you want me to humor your offer."

"Bellator, what have I done to offend you?"

Eos rumbled with vitriol, "The sins of the Mitad are all on your shoulders. We can start with you chasing Aizo to Earth and leaving me stranded from my home, and we can end with the untold suffering across more nations than I even know the name of."

Vistomus raised an eyebrow as his calm demeanor cut through Eos' anger. He was unflinching and uninterested in anything other than his own plan. "Our plans are for a greater purpose. Perhaps I should make some tea if you intend to clear *so many* grievances? But I have a better idea. Why don't you take it up with Master M? I only came to extend his invitation."

The bait worked. Eos chewed on the name briefly before asking, "Master M?"

"The man who leads the Mitad. The orchestrator of all our fates."

"And why would he want to speak *to me*?" Eos wondered aloud.

"Why don't you ask him yourself? The terms are quite generous. You can have whatever you'd like in the world if you simply meet him in person."

"Sure," Eos spat. "I'll take the Left Eye of Izanagi for starters."

"Done."

"The catch?"

"The full terms are something like this. Leave behind the Order, the inlumes, Talus, and all the other fools. Come with us and meet Master M. In exchange, you can have it all. More power. The Left Eye of Izanagi. *Control over your curse.*"

Eos nearly laughed with spiteful disbelief—until the final words. Master M could undo his curse if anyone could. All this journeying, searching, struggle, and suffering…and even Carnus had no solution.

We're bearers, Eos. It's a part of us. We're flawed and must remain that way. Always fighting. Always on the edge. That was Carnus' answer.

What if he didn't have to be on the edge of losing himself? He didn't need to join the Mitad, only meet with them.

The temptation was invigorating.

Vistomus recognized that he had hooked Eos. Satisfaction curled his lips. "Oh? You'd like Master M to relieve you of the Mark of the Chosen?"

"He…could do that?" Eos shuddered.

"Master M could teach you to be a far greater wielder than any of those pitiful inlumes could dream. The Mark of the Chosen would be *your slave*. It would pose no threat to you ever again. You could tower above every member of the Order with us."

Eos weighed the temptation in his heart. "And if I refuse?"

ETHEREAL BOUNDARY

"Then, I remove the last fragment of Maxima's Soul Energy from you, break Aizo's seal to pieces, and you can join us as the newest member of the Voro within the hour."

"All or nothing. Leaving me with a lot of choices, Vistomus."

"Rather generous, I'd say." Vistomus smiled wryly.

It was only days ago that Eos had nearly lost himself to the curse. He couldn't let himself get that close again.

Fear gripped him.

Vistomus knows about Maxima's energy.

His secret defense was found out. Then it dawned on him.

"Is that why you had her killed?" Eos' voice grew deeper. His temptations were wiped away by the trauma of watching his sister disappear under the Mircite River.

"Perceptive," Vistomus spread his hands innocently. "I had no part in it, but Saida knew she was a weakness to the Mark of the Chosen. She broke his concentration when performing the technique's invocation all those years ago. *An infant*—can you imagine his shame? All of Master M's plans at risk because an infant bested him."

The bald Mitad leader laughed callously.

"I can imagine," Eos seethed through a clenched jaw. "I don't know a more talented Soul Wielder or purer heart than my sister. You wouldn't have stood a chance against her at any age."

Sighing, Vistomus ended the banter. "So, you choose to become one of the Voro then? You could ask for us to leave the land of Nippon-Wa *and* give you the Eye." His tone became that of condescending tempter, "Think of all the good you could do."

It weighed on Eos' soul.

The idea of being free of his curse.

The prospect of saving Saigo and his samurai from ever having to fear *Raijin* again. A free nation. The Eye safely away from the Mitad.

It would just cost…*him. Talus would understand the choice.*

Right?

Chaos to Order. Pursue the path of light.

It was becoming more difficult to determine which path that was with every passing day.

CHAPTER THIRTY-ONE

"Tempting," Eos decided. "But I'll take my chances."

Static rippled through the sky—the air split with a violent thundering hum of Soul Energy.

"NO!!" a voice called out from behind them.

Carnus had arrived.

Eos recognized that Vistomus was about to strike him, yet he was helpless before the almighty power.

Carnus rotated mid-spring, contorting his body to the ground.

Indigo light shot from his hand and through the earth as he landed with a sweeping stomp and a grand punching gesture to direct his Soul Energy.

White lightning shot horizontally in a pure bolt at Eos.

The heat was enough to burn his skin from a distance.

His heart missed a beat as dread consumed him before the lethal technique struck.

As it came for him, a mound of glowing earth rose from the street, shimmering with Carnus' energy, and deflected the lightning.

Carnus grabbed Eos and pulled him away from his fear-locked stance just in time. Another bolt of lightning landed where Eos had stood.

"Wake up, Eos! You're going to get us both killed!"

Eos' panic eased. He rolled with Carnus around the raised mound of stone that had defended them.

Crackling engulfed the two.

Dozens of streams of electric Soul Energy tore apart the sky.

Bolts struck the ground all around them in a rain of lightning.

The jittering beams of white stabilized, forming a cage.

Eos and Carnus were caught inside it, tortured by the sound of ion-splitting doom. In every direction, lightning struck continuously, just feet away from their bodies.

"So, the traitor makes his appearance!" Vistomus screamed from outside the lightning cage.

"The Traitor came to make things right," Carnus called back solemnly.

"Carnus, *my dear old friend*, it's a bit late for that."

ETHEREAL BOUNDARY

"It's too late for me. But not Eos. I won't let you take him too!"

Vistomus tensed his curled fingers as if maintaining the cage with the hand gesture. "I'll need Eos alive. So, you need not fear about that—"

"You won't consume the boy with your curse!" Carnus interjected, his voice gripped by raw emotion.

"I don't think either of you have much choice in that," Vistomus teased scornfully. His eyeballs turned black like marbles of pure night. The Tide of Noximor spread from his sockets, blackening and dilating his veins. Tongues of black, flame-like ink began spreading over his cheekbones.

The torrent of never-ending lightning morphed into the curse.

The luminous electric streams became marred with darkness.

Then, a bolt came from above, seeking Eos.

The black lightning zipped through space and touched his forehead. Raven hair hovered as if his entire body was charged and levitating.

Eos' head jerked, and his eyes rolled back in his head.

The Mark of the Chosen rippled over his skin, instantly surpassing his capability to resist. Vistomus was possessing him.

This was more overwhelming than the last time he lost control.

His bones were ablaze.

Skin felt like it was melting as the cursed energy beaded at the surface and began to rise, magnetized to the black lightning.

Then, the ink-like substance came from his lips.

His nose.

Eyes.

Finally, Eos' throat spewed the foreign energy.

Carnus watched helplessly. He knew that so much as touching Vistomus' Tide would send him into a similar state.

For a moment, the Viator Hariban reverted to his cowardice.

The scar on his chest ached at the memory of the Fracture *he had caused*. The deaths *he was responsible for*. The spread of evil *he had allowed* in his passive hermit years. And it fed a vicious cycle of inaction.

"Fight it, Eos," was all Carnus could muster.

CHAPTER THIRTY-ONE

Eos was nearly floating off the ground as Vistomus' control became absolute.

Visions of the Soul Void shuddered in and out of his mind.

Zala's form haunted his vision as if an enemy was helping the process of possession from within. The masked man was reaching inside him—stretching his grasp outside of Eos.

The body and mind-shattering experience was so intense that Eos faded between unconsciousness, pain, and visions of the white-masked entity from his Soul Void.

Death fluttered over him, introducing itself with a tempting, warm embrace—a welcomed alternative to his suffering.

Within the lightning cage, Eos was suspended, lifelessly limp.

The curse began to pulse as it left his mouth.

Dying sapphire light fought weakly.

A single droplet of Maxima's energy emerged.

The curse was extracting it.

Both internally and externally from Vistomus' pull.

Immense pain. Eos could barely form a thought as he fought for consciousness.

He stood in his Void, watching as Zala reached through a portal—through the fabric of the ethereal realm and into physical reality as Vistomus heaved out the last of Maxima's light from the other side.

Grasping for a second of willpower, Eos called out in a whisper.

"Narruh...Narruh Risha..."

Golden Soul Energy blazed across the Soul Void sky.

The crimson elsu snapped through the space to the ethereal boundary. It joined Zala's reaching arms. The molten talons dug into Zala's skin and fought.

The war for Maxima's Soul Energy straddled worlds.

Eos saw the elsu reach Maxima's light.

His limit was broken. Eos let the caress of sleep take him.

The Anite King's Son fell away.

In the physical realm, golden light shimmered from Eos' lips.

The sapphire bead hovered on the brink of parting from Eos entirely. It was trapped in opposing tides of crimson-gold and ink-black.

ETHEREAL BOUNDARY

Maxima's energy waivered as opposing forces tore at it.

Carnus watched Eos' torment as he drowned in reflection of his past mistakes. Paralysis had its hold…until he remembered the one thing that had brought him back during his moment of hopelessness.

A kiss from Grace.

Perhaps it was the greatest treasure of his life.

He drew on everything he had experienced at the Fracture.

The way the particles of energy flowed through all of the material world. *Nature's Path.* He imitated the wielding that Izanagi's Left Eye allowed.

The Flow of All Things. He had experienced it once.

A pure vision.

Carnus knew what he must do. He had understood it like a prescient wave of knowledge since being in Saigo's castle with Aizo.

The seal on his curse was masterfully crafted. It allowed him to wield as if the Tide of Noximor did not plague him. Yet…he had asked for it to be imperfect.

He had asked for it to have a loose thread he could pull on.

A weakness to unravel should he need to sacrifice everything.

Carnus pulled that thread of Soul Energy.

In an instant, he wished for death.

The curse possessed him with more control than when he had fractured North America.

The curse owned him. He gave himself to it freely.

Because he was offering only a corpse.

His skin was black with living ink. Carnus plunged his right arm into the torrent of lightning that seized Eos.

It reacted violently, cracking and burning his skin as his heart palpitated erratically.

Through the cramping of every facial muscle and immolation of his flesh, Carnus managed to whisper, "Find Koda for me, Eos. Please."

His lips turned to crumbling ash as the words parted from him.

With his final strength, he swept his foot forward, still clutching Vitstomus' lightning in his burning hand, and pointed a spear-hand strike through their cage.

CHAPTER THIRTY-ONE

The tensed fingers pierced the crackling bolts of their imprisonment and directed Vistomus' hideous technique back upon its owner.

The cursed lightning fragmented Carnus' hand into dust as electricity surged through his heart and organs.

Vistomus received his own attack in the chest.

The lightning bit its owner with a nearly lethal current that Carnus threaded through the flow of Nature's Path as he remembered it.

It was imperfect. Much of the black bolt was scattered into the air, but it freed Eos and crumpled Vistomus into a heap.

Eos came to consciousness standing on his feet.

The pungent odor of scorched flesh was all around him. Vaporized remains hung in the air, and Carnus was at his feet—at least, what was left of the Viator Hariban, former Mitad Emir, and Nippon-Wa hermit-healer.

He had lived so many lives, but Carnus had never lived down his mistakes. In his last moments, he perceived his life as no more than a sacrifice to undo some small piece of the Mitad.

He had lived and died in the shadow of his past.

But it had delivered Eos through the conflict.

I'll never forget your sacrifice, Eos thought as tears formed in his eyes.

Eos' stomach heaved in revulsion as he reached down, focused intensely on the woven pattern of Carnus' kimono so that he did not process the mutilated body. He patted the robes, searching for what Carnus had asked of him.

A leather pouch was tied to Carnus' ribs under the kimono, and Eos removed it as a single tear broke free.

"I'll find your son, Carnus," Eos whispered. "I'll give this to Koda, and he'll know what a great man his father was. That you were a fighter against the Mitad's tyranny…that we shared the same burden…that you saved me…"

Eos' stomach spasmed as he stumbled.

Death. So…much…death.

It followed the Mitad like a calling card. Death was their work and craft. Destruction was their fruit.

ETHEREAL BOUNDARY

Eos looked up to the Fujima Tower, knowing he still had a mission under its tiled roof.

A gurgling, agonized voice broke the silence.

"That was—*aghh*—clever. The traitor had—*aghh*—grit in his final moment. I'll give him that," Vistomus slurred and choked as he stood.

In a blind panic, Eos remembered what his father had ordered of him. *Preservation. Carnus' sacrifice mustn't be in vain.*

Eos sent a crimson elsu into the sky, and it exploded like a firework, shooting golden light in a canopy over the Imperial Palace.

Vistomus' eyes locked onto Eos as he held out the pointed nail of his index finger. Electricity rumbled as the Mitad wielder started the technique again through pure vindictiveness that overcame his pain.

A flicker of white light. Lightning formed.

Screeeeeech!

An elsu's call threatened Eos' attacker.

Feathers, like snow in a blizzard, streaked past.

Vistomus screamed as talons tore flesh from his bald head.

Ahktar. Thank you.

Blood poured over Vistomus' eyes as he fell back.

Ahktar had bought Eos a moment to refocus.

∞   ∞   ∞

Across the Imperial Castle grounds, Talus became distracted from his fight against Mirza Zeres Teritus. An explosion of crimson shimmered overhead. It was a distress signal from his own blood—no other energy was so perfectly matched in color to his own, and he identified the aura immediately.

"Grace, I need you to flee!" Talus screamed in alarm. "That was Eos' signal."

Zeres' dull brown eyes became concerned, and he uttered a throaty rasp. "Surely the Visrex of Wings wouldn't concede so easily?" Gold chains rattled over black cloth as Zeres lunged for Talus.

The Anite King outran the smoke that pursued him with ease.

It was slow, and he was fleeing.

CHAPTER THIRTY-ONE

With an outstretched arm, Talus swept Glenn up in from the edge of the bamboo garden and lifted him into the air.

Like a maddened animal, Zeres pursued.

White hair flowed behind him as his powerful stride tried to keep up with Talus'. In frustration, he opened his arms so they were outstretched as wide as possible.

Then, Zeres brought them into a fearsome clap with straightened arms as he ran.

His necrotic Soul Energy shot out like smoke from a pressurized chamber, rushing at his fleeing enemy. It was a thin trail, but its lack of volume was compensated for with speed.

Talus had analyzed the slowness of the black smoky energy to be Zeres' weakness—he hadn't expected this!

The feeling of approaching decay rushed at Talus' back.

Too fast! It would catch him.

He couldn't even use Solido against it. That much, he was sure.

"Glenn!" he urged.

The non-wielder grumbled as he was being manhandled from the battle scene and ordered simultaneously.

"Yeah, *yeah*. I see it!" Glenn groaned, facing Zeres as he held on to Talus' only arm for dear life. He wrestled awkwardly with his staff, trying not to fall as they sped through the air.

He managed to orient the iron wings that ornamented his staff and hid a metus stone chunk toward the coming rush of cursed energy.

The black smoke met Glenn and diverted as if it found an invisible barrier around its target.

"I've had about enough of this! I'm not one of you wielders," Glenn cried in complaint as he was jerked across the Imperial Castle's park.

Ignoring him, Talus warned, "Another is coming!"

True to his Observation Wielding, another stream of Zeres' energy was clapped at them. The Mirza was falling behind, but his attack was still fast enough to cover the distance one more time.

Necrotic energy rolled, withering leaves and branches in its wake.

The maneuvering of Soul Step jerked Glenn roughly.

He fumbled the staff.

Thin fingers found the amber-marbled wood—but it was too late.

He couldn't orient the metus stone tip in time to block the coming attack from Zeres.

A wave of topaz light sliced through the trees.

The Soul Energy formed a burning curtain between Zeres and Talus.

Looking over his shoulder, Talus saw a short woman swinging a glaive blade. She had a fray of graying chestnut hair, and she let the three broken swords of the inlume bathe her face in a wreath of topaz. Two other women stood by her side.

"Go to your son, Talus! I'll handle this clumsy oaf," Saier Fey called out.

Talus had no time to thank her. He only nodded without breaking his sprint.

Master Saier Fey? Here? You're on the wrong world entirely.

And aren't you supposed to be watching my daughter?

The thought broke a cold wave of new fear over him as he went to Eos' distress call.

Saier Fey stood between Zeres and his quarry.

Her Soul Energy had broken the massive, white-mustached man's attack, but his dark energy had eaten away at her topaz essence in a way she'd never experienced. It was as if his Soul Energy was toxic to other wielders. It ate away at their manifested light. If her technique had not been a projection—if it had been connected to her body still—she sensed that she would have tasted immediate defeat.

"Another inlume dog?" Zeres rasped with murderous rage. "What is this? A Visrex flees and leaves an old woman and two girls to defend him? *Pathetic.*"

Fey smirked as she swung the glaive in a full circle and assumed her fighting stance. Her injured bicep kept one arm barely clinging to the hilt, but she didn't let her pain and weakness show.

"I think this *little old woman* will be more than a match for you. But if you're worried, I can fight with one arm to match yours," Fey taunted Zeres' withered hand.

Shaking her head as if waking from a tormented dream, Jezca let out a worried whisper, "Eos is struggling. He's losing."

CHAPTER THIRTY-ONE

"Shared visions?" Fey murmured.

"Yes. His curse mark is consuming him!" Jezca confirmed.

Fey reasoned with her, knowing Maxima must be ready to explode with anxiety at the words, "We don't know where he is or the reality of his situation. We have a mission *here*."

Behind them, Grace and Artera were caught in a beautiful dance of white and pink energy that clashed in a symphony of electric humming. Neither held malice toward the other, nor intended to lose the battle. The combination created a kind of testing game that bantered with light.

Grace noticed that Artera was becoming increasingly distracted. Her Observation Wielding was not analyzing her opponent; instead she was searching.

There was an aura far off in the distance that concerned her more. The Master of the Inner Paths repeatedly glanced off to the west.

The distraction was so great this time that it held her gaze for a full second. It was almost enough for her to catch a streak of rose-pink Soul Energy in the face.

The heat of Grace's energy snapped her back into the fight.

Artera put her caramel-toned fingers together so that her hands formed an open triangle. In the space between them, she locked on Grace Lapithos.

The beautiful, lean woman was framed perfectly in Artera's gesture—her stern demeanor, toffee-streaked blonde hair pinned with gold and jade, the fine red and white threads with intricately woven petals. The triangle window of Artera's hands beheld Grace.

Snow white Soul Energy cast out.

Inner Path Ten—Inner Containment!

Walls of blinding, bleached aura surrounded Grace like frosted panes of twinkling glass.

She was trapped.

Artera's soft voice spoke through the barrier of her technique after a frustrated sigh, "Have the Eye for all I care. I'm needed elsewhere."

In shock, Grace didn't have time to try and break out of the confinement. No sooner had Artera's words ceased, her Soul Energy faded, and the only thing Grace heard was jumbled in the wind.

ETHEREAL BOUNDARY

It sounded like Artera said, "Rius, you idiot…" as she turned away, her violet-black hair whipping around.

Zeres shouted with a thunderous warning as his fellow mirza passed to his left, "Don't you dare abandon your mission, Artera!"

"Sorry, *King Under the Open Sky*," Artera responded with a short, sarcastic snarl, "This isn't Cavnan, and you're not my emir."

Artera disappeared into the horizon of trees.

A deep, angry growl came from Zeres at the disrespect.

Grace, free of her opponent and without Glenn to defend, called to the nearby Inlume, "Master Fey!" There were tears of joy in her eyes. "I didn't think I'd ever see you again. What are you doing here?"

They all eyed Zeres as he shifted his position, surrounded by the four women. Artera had abandoned him to an inlume and three others. Yet, he showed not one flicker of fear or doubt. His brooding expression only darkened.

Fey's chestnut hair bobbed as she laughed in disbelief. "Grace, I could hug you right now, but I'm a little busy with this fool. What's the mission?"

A look of understanding crossed Grace's face. Her overjoyed expression hardened as her Necogen and Priori instincts were triggered. "They have the Left Eye of Izanagi. Vistomus is finishing some ritual with it that will probably kill us all within the hour."

Fey didn't look at her old friend again nor at the young woman beside her as she eyed Zeres and ordered, "Jezca, go with your mother now. Help with her mission to retrieve the Left Eye. Blue Corcinth, you're with me."

Maxima hesitated, begging lowly, "Eos is in trouble."

"I won't blame you if you go, but you're needed here," Fey responded with the wisdom of a teacher in her tone.

The corcinth mask only nodded.

She didn't know where Eos was or his situation. Fey was right. It cut her through the heart to reconcile it, but she could better serve Eos' cause where she was.

Jezca flashed her rose energy beneath her feet and appeared beside Grace. For the first time, she stood before her mother as an adult.

CHAPTER THIRTY-ONE

"J...Jezca?" Grace stuttered aloud as she looked at a young reflection of herself with the addition of an animus stone eye. Her training instincts battled with those of a mother. Her heart waivered.

Maple eyes met a similar umber brown.

Then, she nodded with the composure of an elite assassin, a Priori senior council member, and Hyperborea's most accomplished archeologist. "Follow me, my daughter."

Grace started for Fujima Tower, and her daughter followed, two sets of platinum blond hair moving in unison.

"Not likely," Zeres bellowed. His necrotic smoke moved in a channeled plume after them.

Topaz Soul Energy cut in a magnificent wall from Fey's twirling glaive. As the light went out, she danced acrobatically around Zeres' thinned defensive wall.

Her onyx blade swung around, making a strike at the huge, white-haired Mirza.

Zeres shifted easily out of the way, but when he slipped his body from the attack, it left his functional arm exactly where Fey had intended.

His body was exposed, and his smoke-like Soul Energy was slow to reorient in defense.

Fey drew her index and middle fingers to a point while she curled the others before her nose.

There was a flicker of topaz that sparked around the gesture.

The Inlume lunged and jabbed her extended fingers.

They pierced into Zeres' shoulder, drawing blood.

Zeres stomped after her, but his arm would not raise. Necrotic energy ceased to emanate as rapidly from that side of his body.

"You hag!" he snarled.

"Perhaps you might consider focusing on your opponent?" Fey remarked, feigning being offended.

The mustached scowl turned into a laugh as Zeres' arms hung uselessly. More energy began to flow from his lower body to compensate for his damaged limb.

ETHEREAL BOUNDARY

His voice was low and gravel-filled, "Your Severance works not unlike mine. I understood it immediately. Physically disabling limbs, but also narrowing Soul Energy channels."

"Perceptive," Fey said with Maxima by her side.

Maxima was the Blue Corcinth in persona. She hid her sapphire light in case Zeres could somehow identify her. The chances were nearly zero, but she awaited Fey's order.

"You inlumes are far too forgiving. A temporary disabling of wielding is for the weak-minded. Never let your enemy have another chance!"

A sharp grunt and exhale of breath preceded a lurch of black energy that curled and churned in an avalanche at Fey.

The agile woman had capitalized on Zeres' distraction, but she had gotten too close.

Smoke gripped her ankle as she recoiled away.

The burning was instant.

Her skin was being eaten away—that was certain.

But her energy channels were afflicted by a soul contagion.

She felt a technique like her own crawl through her lower leg.

However, this was a creeping death!

A gurgling laugh proclaimed victory.

"I don't waste time. My enemies *perish*!"

Soul Energy channels withered.

Fey could sense internal paths collapsing within her leg.

It's spreading.

Fast!

Soul Energy ceased to flow at her calf.

A single plane of her soul's manifestation appeared.

Only her left leg was able to perform Soul Step.

I won't be able to wield at all within the minute.

"I'll need your help," Fey addressed Maxima. "Hold him back for a few minutes. I need time to prepare." There was a gulping dread in the voice, like she knew her life would be forever changed in the next second—like she was about to do something self-destructive and forbidden.

CHAPTER THIRTY-ONE

Her glaive glowed brighter than Maxima had ever seen.

It went from its yellow-orange brilliance to a hot, blinding white that made the metal deform.

The hilt shifted in Fey's hand.

The blade swung.

There was no blood.

The wound was seared the instant the glaive cut.

Fey's leg was cleaved above the knee.

Her charred limb fell beside her.

"A wise but costly decision, Inlume," Zeres observed callously.

Fighting not to pass out with every fiber of her being, Fey clutched her leg and bit her lip until it bled.

She wavered.

Pure will and a lifetime of training the mind kept her standing.

One leg balanced her small, wobbling body.

Great Soul…give me strength!

Maxima audibly gasped.

She knew her master was vulnerable. There was no consolation. No words of care. The slight hesitation in her mind only earned her a sharp reply from Fey.

"It was…spreading! Had…to be done!" Fey spoke in sharp, broken whispers. "Wouldn't have been able to wield at all otherwise."

Maxima nodded, accepting the action without contemplating, lest her emotions delay her further.

Fingertips touched as the necrotic smoke neared.

The Blue Corcinth pulled a sapphire sphere apart into two orbs and cast them out with open hands. As they left her, the energy divided.

It split and multiplied, replicating at an unstoppable rate.

I can do this. Maxima recalled her time in the mirror fragment.

I have to go all the way. She remembered her training with Fey beyond her second and third inner gates.

If this Mitad wielder can do that to Fey in a single touch, I must end this.

Zeres' Soul Energy rolled into Maxima's duplicating army of orbs. The sapphire rotated and spun around her as if they were in a centrifuge.

ETHEREAL BOUNDARY

The darkness met them and spread like ink diffusing through water. The blue energy shrunk on this contact—but as it did, the cursed attack was neutralized and faded.

The torrent of spinning sapphire absorbed the smoke.

As each droplet shrunk to nullify Zere's energy, another was born from a nearby sphere splitting.

Fey stood on one leg, her limb on the ground beside her.

She formed her pointed finger gesture again, but this time with both hands. Each index finger went to her temple, and she closed her eyes.

Maxima had stopped Zeres' advance, but that wasn't enough.

She needed to delay him, to buy a few more seconds for Fey before the Mirza could adjust his strategy to reach one of them.

The furiously spinning orbs was warring against the onslaught of the cursed attack.

Zmmmm!

The clashing lights ground against each other.

It was a calculated risk.

A fleet of orbs broke off from the vortex of sapphire.

She just had to hold for a few seconds without being overcome.

The detachment whipped right of the smoke and pelted Zeres from the side.

His energy was focused on overwhelming the Blue Corcinth's replicating wall. He had left no defense.

The Soul Spheres struck!

Explosions rocked the massive man.

His offense fell at the surprise.

Maxima's light glinted off the Mirza's golden jewelry.

Zeres braced himself and accepted the wounds.

A flurry of orbs followed.

The King Under the Open Sky turned away and huddled for protection as he let his necrotic energy leak from him with no control in an attempt to survive. Every bit of his effort was consumed by the flurry of sapphire that was upon him.

CHAPTER THIRTY-ONE

When Maxima's Soul Energy ran out, she was drenched in sweat. Her clothes were heavy with moisture, and her breathing was a panting search for oxygen.

Zeres stood, burned and bleeding on every inch of his body. Yet his barbarian battle heritage was comfortable continuing on death's door.

Maxima looked back to Fey in a pleading hope that the Inlume was ready with whatever she was preparing.

The Severance had exhausted Maxima's Soul Reservoir.

She was empty.

The Harbinger creaked slowly toward her, moaning in pain.

Fey had a crown of topaz around her head.

Three broken swords lit up her forehead as she struggled to balance her glaive against her hip while keeping her fingertips to the inlume crown.

"You think I merely disabled an arm temporarily when I stuck you? Foolish barbarian king," Fey shot vindictively but with a tint of bitter remorse, "I planted the seed of your end. Take your final breath and make your peace."

"Mmmmm?" Zeres grumbled through the bite of his blistered wounds. He went to stride forward, but his body did not move. His Soul Energy retreated into vapor.

The Harbinger was paralyzed.

Fey brought her left hand out in front of her, keeping her gesture but turning it palm-out toward Zeres. With her other hand, she carefully grasped the hilt of her onyx glaive.

"I hate this technique above all else. It's a cruel and evil thing to do…" She let suspense hang in the air as retribution for her lost leg before she revealed the truth of her ability to the trembling giant.

"I paralyze and immobilize. You were right about that," Fey acknowledged. She brought her blade up to strike. "You kill off Soul Energy channels. That is a wretched thing to do, but it matches your dark and putrid heart."

The glaive shone white hot again, bleeding topaz at the fringes.

Fey finished, "However, I can also spread my technique through your Soul Reservoir. I possessed you. Body and soul. Your movement.

Your wielding. Your narcissistic confidence. They belong to me for a few seconds."

Zeres' limbs were locked out, even his withered hand which had not moved at his command in decades.

His body was controlled like a puppet.

Cursed energy flowed from his fingertips and poured into his open mouth. His necrotic attack filled him from the inside.

He wriggled and squirmed as he was tortured.

Fey's eyes winced, and her lips tightened.

It hurt her soul and drained her energy nearly as much as Zeres to perform such an advanced level of Severance.

It had a cost.

A necessary cost.

Fey swung her blade.

Zeres was hewn from shoulder to hipbone by the glaive's projection.

The King Under the Open Sky fell to the ground in two separate pieces.

He never moved again.

Fey collapsed, exhausted to a point near death.

Soon Jakka. Maxima won't need me for much longer. Maybe...I'll join you now. Fey thought as she closed her eyes. The last thing she saw was Maxima running to her.

CHAPTER THIRTY-TWO

AKUMA

When Aizo attempted to sense this *akuma* that Saigo warned of, he found nothing. Scavok confirmed the same with his Observation Wielding.

"Wait!" Aizo bellowed, "There is...*something* coming. It's not like any aura I've ever seen...like a hole in my sight."

Scavok let out a disturbed grunt. "Mmmmm. What in the Great Soul is that? You're right to call it a demon, Saigo."

It came upon them floating like a ghost. Navy robes trimmed with golden stars fluttered with the foul presence. As it came close enough to discern features, Aizo saw a mask that glistened like the rainbowed sheen of a pearl in the day's sun. The face covering morphed from milky white to metallic pink-silver as the creature moved.

When the wielders tried to observe the creature's aura, they only perceived the blotting out of the flow of life around it—like a photo-negative of Soul Energy.

AKUMA

Saigo charged toward it, filled with bushido courage and the memory of his comrades slain by the beast.

"Saigo, wait!" Aizo pleaded.

Midnight armor met the wraith-like entity head-on.

Claws of Soul Energy, the color of dried blood, sliced through the steel of Saigo's katana and tore into his katchu protection.

The Samurai was thrown across the field as his blade pieces were scattered in the grass.

"Bishiwal..." Bysis whispered weakly. He called out to his companion, "Diya, are you still alive?"

Labored breathing was the only reply.

Bysis petitioned his opponent, "Listen, Inlume, that thing will kill us all." There was pure fear in his previously headstrong voice.

Aizo stroked his beard in contemplation and assumed a fighting stance, leaving Bysis free. "That much, I believe, Mirza."

The two inlumes sent out testing waves of glacial blue and tangerine orange. The Soul Energy was deflected by the foot-long claws that draped from the Bishiwal's sleeves like blades. What wasn't repelled was absorbed into its body.

Scavok and Aizo moved away as the nightmarish Bishiwal hovered over Diya. Pinned to the earth by a katana, she could not move, let alone flee.

A mask of tangled vines like metallic milk loomed over her.

"Diya!" Bysis called.

"P...please..." managed to leave her lips.

Aizo, in an act of mercy and further testing the Bishiwal, sent a Soul Sphere at it as it drew close to the dying Mirza.

The Bishiwal whipped its hooded head around with intuition and struck out, defending with its brownish, murky energy. Then, it turned back like a wild animal feeding.

"What in the...what is that?" Scavok asked, repulsed.

"Bysis here called it a Bishiwal. So, tell us, Mirza, how do we defeat it?" Aizo asked in haste.

"You don't," Bysis uttered as he clambered to his feet and fell forward in a run towards Fujima Tower. "Have to warn Vistomus.

CHAPTER THIRTY-TWO

Diya's groaning pitched and then went silent.

Scarlet liquid bubbled from her skin.

Scanning the scene, Aizo saw the defeated woman's blood was rich with Soul Energy from battle. It surfaced with the red droplets.

Aizo turned away in disgust, but Scavok watched as the liquid gathered and was sucked under the Bishiwal's mask.

A dull, color-drained liquid fell back down a second later, the Soul Energy-rich life force harvested.

It turned its head as if catching the scent of prey.

The Bishiwal floated away from the lifeless body, but Saigo stood in its way, panting and wounded.

He held his wakizashi, the samurai's short sword, as his katana was in pieces behind him.

Another set of armor ran up behind him. It was jade and crowned with a dragon head.

"Father!" the voice implored in Japanese.

Saigo's battle-crazed expression softened, and he spoke to his son in their native language. "Kikujiro? What are you doing here?"

"This akuma is the sworn enemy of the Grand Ise Shrine's priests. It hasn't shown itself in centuries, but we are warned by our elders with every generation of high priest—that it could come when the Eye is activated."

Saigo was pained by his injury as much as his strained relationship. "Then you will fight alongside me to stop this monster?"

"I will."

"Then you will wear that armor proudly and honor both sides of our family."

"Father, if I didn't hand over the Eye, they would have taken it and killed everyone at the shrine—at least I was able to warn you all."

Saigo only nodded with a deep hum of acknowledgment.

Glancing at the ground in shame, Kikujiro admitted, "I also accepted their offer to go to Takamagahara. I want to learn more about my ancestors—but it allowed me to keep track of the Eye. That is my ultimate mission, passed down from my ancestors and actualized when Carnus turned it over to my care."

AKUMA

The Bishiwal rattled its claws and turned its head curiously as the samurai and the priest in bushi armor blocked its way.

Aizo called out to Scavok, "I need to get to the tower and find Eos. Protect Saigo and Kikujiro from that monster."

"You leave me with the easy task," Scavok laughed sarcastically.

"I know how much you like a good hunt. Think of it like that. Do your master-assassin-ing," Aizo teased as he dashed to find his young anatus student and, hopefully, get to the Left Eye of Izanagi before it was too late.

"Demon hunting, eh?" Scavok grumbled to himself.

The Bishiwal swung its murky arm. The blade-like phalanges shattered Saigo's secondary sword, leaving him with none. The inhuman form crashed over him.

An ocean-blue energy string whipped and deflected the Bishiwal away from his father. It wove around in warning to the Bishiwal, casting Kikujiro's Soul Energy glow against its twisting mask.

The creature's arm grew bright and tore through Kikujiro's water-like technique. That was all he knew. His lessons with Himiko-oujo, Grace's Nippon-Wa alias, were rare, and his long-diluted bloodline limited his aptitude.

The Bishiwal swung.

Kikujiro's sword scattered in pieces.

Jade armor was cleaved through.

Just before it fell over him, Scavok intervened, his glacial-blue Soul Energy emanating from his short sword.

Kikujiro was spared for the moment, but he was without a blade and bleeding profusely.

Safisay clashed in a frantic melody of humming Soul Energy until the might of the Bishiwal sent Scavok to his back.

Only Saigo remained standing, and he charged in with his last weapon, a small knife. It sunk into the Bishiwal's side.

Heat melted the blade and seared his flesh.

The monstrosity was made entirely of warped Soul Energy.

Stumbling back, Saigo had no defense for the next strike.

CHAPTER THIRTY-TWO

It came on him like a reaper. He saw the distorted reflection of his lion-dog headpiece in its mask as it went for the kill.

The talons found jade armor instead—Kikujiro fell in front of his father with the last of his strength. Saigo watched the demon's fingers pierce through the other side of his son. He let out a bellowing cry.

Kikujiro fell to the ground and pushed out final words before the Bishiwal pounced, "Better…than seppuku. I'm sorry…Lord Saigo."

"My son!" Saigo heaved in misery. He found his broken katana on the ground, wrapped his fingers around the hilt, and dove for the Bishiwal.

Scavok Soul Stepped to intercept him.

The Bishiwal fell over Kikujiro like a wild, feral animal feeding.

It repeated the evil they had witnessed as it fed on Diya, but Scavok forced Saigo away from the scene.

"The cost of this Eye!" Saigo wept as he pounded Scavok's muscular chest. "The *price* of being part of these kami games!"

Seconds later, the Bishiwal turned.

A wave of Scavok's energy projected from his sword.

The Bishiwal absorbed the entire blow, shuddering and screeching with wild sounds.

As if catching the scent of its prey once more, it hunched away from them and bolted away from the battle.

Scavok was left consoling a silent Saigo over tattered jade armor.

∞　　∞　　∞

Agonizing shrieks filled the air outside the Fujima Tower.

A scent like burnt iron from Tessio's wielding ceremony putrefied the air and mixed with sweat in Durath's nostrils.

Marigold energy glanced off his shoulder as he rolled back with it, letting it make contact but not explode against him. His emerald Solido combined with his body's motion to slip Kallag's attack.

A corcinth mirage formed over his fists.

Durath returned the blows with his own, sending a stream of roaring green corcinths tearing towards the Mirza.

AKUMA

Horned images of Soul Energy collided with their target.

The Varungian brawler absorbed the blows with his Solido. Durath's stronger lion-like forms broke through his defenses, but his hardened body accepted the overflow damage with only a grimace.

"What are you doing to that child in there?" Durath asked as he held his fighting stance like a brawler, squared to his opponent.

Kallag's boyish face smirked, "Not for me to know. I'm only here to guard him."

"Guard him? Sounds like you're killing him," Durath grunted.

The blonde-haired Mirza jabbed twice with his tattooed arm, projecting bursts of yellow-orange light. They caught the Leorix King's Son square in the chest and crackled against his veil of Soul Energy.

"With your reputation, I wouldn't expect you to get distracted by a few screams," Kallag provoked. "They called you the Corcinth of the Arena. Well, that was back when you had a kingdom, wasn't it? Though I suppose your mother is still there. Perhaps I should have the Overseer check in on her?"

Durath struggled to ignore the threat.

"He'll find that I learned my wielding from my mother then!"

Mother. As soon as I get back to Corland...I'll find a way to get you out.

In his heart, Durath knew she would never leave the stone thrones behind. The Leorix were a people of their mountain.

There was a whoosh as two female wielders rushed up the path to the tower on planes of rose Soul Energy.

Durath weighed his opponent's reaction, but there was none. "Not going to stop them?" he asked.

A nonchalant shrug answered. "Cyra will stop them. I can clean them up after you."

"This has been the most fun I've had outside a tournament duel, Varungian," Durath admitted. "But you're Mitad. So, I'm going to have to end this now."

Emerald horns curled above Durath.

Between them, a sphere of light grew into being.

Kallag's eyes grew wide.

This had been a wielder's boxing match up until this point.

CHAPTER THIRTY-TWO

Blow for blow, they had exchanged their punches.

Now, Durath had manifested an advanced form of Severance.

The manifestation between the pointed emerald horns burst!

The sphere became a beam of Soul Energy.

It engulfed Kallag in a blinding wave.

The scream of the child inside the building died down.

Whatever ritual was being performed was coming to an end.

Inside Fujima Tower, Grace and Jezca faced a glowing indigo barrier. Jezca stood beside her mother, eager to say so many things held captive across worlds and decades, yet they first had to recover Izanagi's Left Eye. She felt intensely close to Grace. The Soul Energy of her bloodline, which she had felt across worlds through the constellation stone while in Lenape, was near her.

That was enough for now.

Until the urgent task was complete, their reunion was on hold. So, Jezca's right eye lit up like a crystal ball. Pink vapors drifted from the stone as she honed her Observation.

The man with the black ponytail behind the wall controlled the energy. He defended the child strewn over the center table and the thin-faced man working behind him. The indigo barrier wasn't particularly strong.

Jezca tested it with a manifestation of pink that clawed in three slashes against the blue-gray curtain of light.

Zmmmm! The clash was short-lived.

Her attack was absorbed into the defensive technique and routed like blood through veins that Jezca could see with her wielder's sight.

She tested again.

What she witnessed confirmed it. The rose Soul Energy spread again, diverting to specific points in a network that reinforced the wall.

"There's no point," Cyra announced. "We're nearly done, and my wall is invincible." He held his arms out to reinforce his wielding with the clarity brought by physical gesture.

Grace muttered with annoyance, "He has a point. I've trained to wield as an assassin. Speed. Precision. Stealth. Those are my strengths. I fear we've been matched improperly for our skills. I can't brute force

∞ 504 ∞

through something like that." She cursed to herself in Japanese; the language flowed naturally from her tongue.

"No," Jezca whispered as her stone eye flickered with luminous vision. "There's something more to his ability. The wall is like Solido but not especially strong. He's using something else. There's a trick to it," she explained, still searching for what the trick exactly was.

"Just another minute. It's nearly finished," the man who loomed over the motionless child called out.

The boy was soaked through with sweat that dripped from his limp arm hanging off the table. He was eerily still.

Pink light flashed again and again in probing glances against Cyra's barrier.

A proud smile crossed her lips, "That's it! We're going to need those daggers."

Grace drew Amon's daggers. Their manus stone blades gleamed.

Jezca had a sadness in her umber eye as she explained, "Caldus may have saved us. This guy isn't defending against us with Solido." She directed her next words at the Mirza, "Isn't that right? Pretty expensive ability you have there. I'd say you must carry a king's fortune on you at all times."

Cyra's eyes narrowed, and he released a sharp exhale of defeat. "Tessio!" he urged. "I need you to be done *now*. We gotta get that kid out of here."

"Almost. Just another minute!" Tessio answered through intense concentration. The glow of a vibrant red stone was dying as it became covered by Khasun's flesh. The Left Eye of Izangi vibrated in and out of its physical state as it disappeared into the boy's chest.

In that glimpse through the tint of indigo Soul Energy, fear gripped Grace. Her face went pale as she murmured in realization, "Sahar Alakil...It was never Vistomus or Saida. They planned for another all along!" She nearly dropped her daggers as she was filled with dread. "They're trying to create a Ro-hatam."

"A what?" Jezca asked, confused.

"An entity who has their soul shattered and merges their body with a powerful manus stone. They give up their humanity to merge with pure power, but it was a legend. From a very long time ago. Eras ago. Not real. *It wasn't supposed to be real!*" Grace's head shook as she rationalized what was happening.

"What does that mean?" Jezca asked. The fear was spreading into her mind as her mother's calm was shaken.

Grace spoke her understanding softly. Her words were haunted and horrified, "They weren't trying to cause another Fracture War or use the Eye as a weapon. They were trying to create a human weapon and merge a Tool of Karnak with a human being!"

"Then we must stop them! This wall is full of suspended fragments of purest anima stone. It's a grid," Jezca explained. "He's diverting Soul Energy from his wall into the shards of anima, controlling the flow rate to not break such tiny stones."

Grace looked at her daughter proudly. "But if we strike them directly?"

"Exactly. Mother, hit with Caldus' daggers exactly where I do."

Cyra cursed.

Rose energy clawed at the barrier, directly striking the anima stone shards suspended in the indigo Soul Energy.

Glowing daggers followed immediately behind in a flurry of blows from Necogen-trained hands. The assassin's speed didn't allow Cyra time to rearrange his anima stones network.

Zmmm. The clash crackled, turned to a dying whine, and the fine grains of manus stone crumbled into dust. The dagger strikes were more than Cyra's tiny shards could absorb. They were too small.

Where Cyra had diverted Soul Energy with calculated distribution into the shards, Grace was crushing them with the direct contact of surging animus stone blades.

Grace moved in a swift series of thrusts, targeting where Jezca signaled. *Crack. Crack. Crack.* The wall of indigo Soul Energy began to fall.

"We're out of time!" Cyra screamed. He reached into his sleeve only to confirm what he already knew. The pouch on his wrist was empty.

Tessio appeared behind Cyra as the wall fell entirely.

AKUMA

His straw-colored hair fell over his sunken face as he grinned with satisfaction, "That's fine because I'm already done."

The barrier fell, and Cyra drew his katana.

Tessio held a winged spear and whirled it at Grace and Jezca.

"Then we need to get Khasun out of here," Cyra said with tension in his voice as the two Mitad Mirzas faced down the women.

"I'm exhausted. The ceremony didn't leave much left, so let's end this quickly," Tessio hissed to Cyra.

The spear shone like a manus blade but did not merely project its wielder's energy. The metal vibrated, and the whole spear stretched.

It stabbed across the distance to Jezca.

There was no time to see the human body wind up.

The spear grew to fill the distance instantaneously.

Jezca's stone eye was aglow. She had been analyzing—carefully observing the spear wielder. If she hadn't, she would have been dead, but the intense vibration of Soul Energy in the manus weapon was visible to her priestess eye. She witnessed the blue light fill the metal, spread through its manus-imbued material, curl with the tainting of cursed energy, and begin to transform the matter itself.

The priestess dove to the side, narrowly dodging the blade.

But she had no time to rest. A half-second later, the spear returned to its ordinary state and vibrated in anticipation of the next attack.

Quick reactions from Necogen training and keen Observation Wielding kept her alive, but warm liquid dripped down her arm.

Fear filled the future Monte High Priestess.

She dodged in complete panic. The gold links of her ornate circlet clinked. The priesthood broach bounced against her chest. Her blue dress fluttered behind her as she twirled for her life.

Cyra swung his manus katana at Grace.

Glowing blades clashed as she deflected it with daggers.

There was no lethal intent—*yet.*

Not like the bloodlust that dripped from the spear wielder's aura.

The katana came at her with refined technique, but still only in warning. Her son's daggers lit up, more powerful than any manus blade

CHAPTER THIRTY-TWO

she had ever beheld. Their animus projections deflected the katana entirely before the blades made contact.

"It's over," Cyra explained calmly. "The ritual is done." He grunted as he narrowly dodged a dagger swipe. "Let us take the boy to safety, and no one needs to die here."

Grace scowled. "I know what you've created. I can't let Master M continue with whatever he is planning."

"*Even I* don't know what that boy is!" Cyra exhaled sharply as his barrier wavered before his abdomen and saved his gut from a stab wound. "But he's still a boy. This is my last offer for peace."

"He's not just a child anymore—he's a human weapon. I've feared this legend. *Now it's real,*" Grace said more to herself than to Cyra. In her peripheral vision, she saw Jezca dodging for her life.

The spear stabbed so quickly that it almost teleport to where Jezca was. She couldn't stop moving. One moment of stillness…one flicker of distraction from the Observation of her stone eye, and she would be finished.

Blue fabric tore.

The wing of the spear grazed her ribs through her dress.

The Priestess tripped at the surprise of the pain.

As she fell, a half-bound collection of papers fell out.

Grace watched as Tessio's gangly fingers picked up the broken binding. Despite being many years apart from them, she knew its leather and pages by heart.

Tessio picked up half of Grace's journal.

∞   ∞   ∞

Eos could see Vistomus. His too-rigid lips and sharp features moved, but they made no sound. At least, not for Eos.

"Cyra, take this and Khasun, and get out of here! I can hold off these two," a twisted voice spoke.

In flashes of waking dream, Eos' vision shifted to another place. *Near.*

Usually, he experienced this in his sleep. Usually, it felt distant.

AKUMA

Danger! Fear! Blood!

Emotions and thoughts that were not his own filled his head.

Vistomus was gone—a mirage of smoke blown away in the breeze. A new face was before him as he grasped his bleeding leg. It was a familiar one. Features he had briefly seen but memorized…had learned to hate.

Tessio was before him, grinning sadistically with sweat dripping from his brow over sunken eyes. Straw-colored hair matted to his face from some exhausting work he had completed before pointing his spear in battle.

"I have the journal Saida's been looking for, *and* the ritual's complete. A priestess girl's head will make a fine trophy for this day!" Tessio teemed with delight.

No, not again. Not another life lost to Tessio.

Major Clark was one death too many.

Jezca!

I need to get to Jezca!

Tessio's murderous features waivered.

Vistomus snapped his fingers three times, trying to focus Eos' attention. "I know you're a little worse for wear, Bellator, but try to stay with me here."

Eos knew he needed to get to Fujima tower, but there was no way he could just run past Vistomus Fulmen, even if the Mitad leader was severely wounded from Carnus and Ahktar.

Eos wasn't in peak fighting condition either. Defeating Rius and struggling against the curse had tested his wielding endurance.

Father will be here soon. Just need to buy another few minutes.

Black hair shook in long, wavy strands as Eos returned to the present location.

"Ah, the King's Son is back with us." Vistomus belittled as he shrugged off the ache of his burnt skin and wounds and wiped a stream of blood from over his brow, "Now, Master M would like a word, and he's grown impatient. He happens to be available this—"

Vistomus went still. His body didn't move, and his eyelids closed.

The Mitad leader's voice became deeper and less melodic.

CHAPTER THIRTY-TWO

Someone else spoke then—through Vistomus Fulmen.

"Eos...I've long waited to meet you. I apologize that my attempts have not always been *satisfactory to your disposition*. I didn't want to create so much discord between us before we speak face-to-face."

"Disposition? Discord?" Eos choked on the words. "*Yeah. That's one way to put it.* You sure have a strange way of sending invitations, *Master M*. What do you want with me?"

"Merely to train you." Vistomus' lips moved for Master M.

"I have Aizo for that. I'll have to pass."

Vistomus' possessed tone turned to a laugh. "A washed-up inlume? No, Eos...I offer something much greater. I've seen your full potential in my future sight. I can help you reach it."

"Master M, your charitable nature is far too benevolent," Eos spat. "I'm still going to have to turn you down. I don't need your training."

"You'll come to me on your own in due time, I believe. Or my emirs will drag you kicking. Or my Mark of the Chosen will bring you to me. It matters not the means at this point. I'll see you very soon, Bellator."

Like a ghost had ceased haunting a place, the sober consciousness of Eos and Vistomus were left alone again. No more possessions from Master M. No more flashes to Jezca's experiences.

Just Eos and Vistomus.

Father is close—just a few more seconds.

"Tell me one thing, Vistomus. Your wielding is similar to what Soul Wielders do, but it's not exactly the same, is it?"

"Perceptive, Eos. There's no reason for secrets between us. Master M picked me for my potential and fulfilled it in me as he will with you. He trained me to bend my Severance and manipulate it to something between Soul Wielding and Nature's Path. The shamans of Dacia wield by mixing their Soul Energy into Nature's Path. They have a more holistic way of wielding that cannot be achieved once you are formed as a Soul Wielder."

"So, a wielder must choose between the two styles?" Eos asked.

"Precisely. However, most on Corland are born with their Human Essence formed in a way where Nature's Path is out of reach. Master M trained me to be unique. I'm the closest thing one can become to being a Dacian shaman while still having an Essence formed as a wielder."

"*How special,*" Eos shot sarcastically. "What do you need with the Left Eye if Master M taught you all that?"

A twinge of dissatisfaction crossed Vistomus' brow. "I said *the closest* to a Dacian shaman, but I'm still *not one*," Vistomus snapped as a tender spot was agitated. "Master M took me further than any other wielder. I'm a class unto my own, but for his purposes, my path was not…"

"Not good enough?" Eos stabbed where Vistomus' ego was most apparently fragile.

"You're fortunate that Master M wants you with your tongue intact," Vistomus snarled. "Now, shall we resume where we were when Carnus threw away his pitiable life? Or will you come with me more easily?"

"See, the thing about that…" Eos let his answer hang. There was an approaching aura that he had been waiting for. Only a few more seconds and Talus would arrive. "…is that you're going to have to take that up with my father."

"Clever boy!" Vistomus realized why Eos had been so willing to talk with him after the crimson elsu of Soul Energy had burst in the sky.

Talus emerged into the clearing through the tree line. He bound in with speed and power using Soul Step, wasting no time to analyze the situation.

Without delay, Talus launched an assault of crimson feathers.

Vistomus snapped his head at the attack and countered with a wall of rippling lightning that fended off the Anite King. "Saida already removed one wing, Talus. Do you really have another to spare in a battle with me?"

Ignoring the bait, Talus asked, "Are you okay, Eos?"

Shaken but whole, Eos patted Carnus' letter under his kimono fold to assure himself it was still there. Something else was inside the parchment: solid and rigid but thin. He had no time to examine it, and replied, "Yes, but Carnus is dead."

Talus' lips pressed together, and his braided beard rose as his chest heaved in a distressed sigh. "Vistomus, I won't let you hurt another wielder! Eos, get somewhere safe!"

CHAPTER THIRTY-TWO

"I need to go to Jezca! She's in the tower but losing a battle," Eos explained urgently.

"Go!" Talus agreed.

Vistomus only watched as Eos sped away toward Fujima Tower on planes of shimmering crimson. There was no point in stopping him or holding the King's Son hostage. Master M wanted Eos, and he would have him eventually.

Besides, there was a new danger to contend with. Soul Energy wings grew to a span five times Talus' own—his Severance spread in two plumes of feathers. If Vistomus hadn't prepared for the attack, he'd have been killed in his already weakened state.

The massive avian appendages beat twice as if taking flight, sending out a wave of suffocating aura that made Vistomus nearly choke. Then, they broke away from Talus.

The wings glided with unbelievable speed.

A cage of lightning formed around Vistomus.

Bolts of pure white split and crackled in a constantly morphing form on all sides of him.

When Talus' technique reached Vistomus, he muttered, "Speed like an elsu." His throat rumbled as he closed his eyes, letting Observation Wielding and his perception of Nature's Path take over.

Branches of lightning reach out in wriggling, exploding fingers of electricity in a war against every individual feather that made up the wings.

Light, like lava, enveloped him so that it was red behind his eyelids, even with them closed.

Zmmmmm-crackle-zmmm!

The Severance techniques clashed in an almighty roar that threatened to split the Imperial Castle grounds.

Behind Vistomus, Glenn hid behind a tree, out of sight.

His chest thudded so wildly that he thought he was having a heart attack. His palms were sweating, and the amber-marbled white wood of his staff slipped down until the iron of the wings fixed atop it was touching his skin.

AKUMA

Glenn's shaking fingers gripped the iron as he bit down on his lips until he tasted blood.

The battle on the other side of the tree line was shaking the earth and physically weighing on his shoulders from the aura.

"Wielders! The whole lot can stay aw-w-way from me," he trembled aloud. "I'm not s-s-supposed to be here. T-t-this isn't my task."

Twist.

The metal-cast wings separated from the staff body as he unscrewed the ornamental ferrule.

A pike of sharpened black stone was revealed beneath.

Approach from his blind spot. He won't sense you since you're not a wielder. Talus had explained during their approach. *When I attack, his attention will be entirely on me. Do not fear his lightning. You'll be able to walk right through it.*

Right through it? Glenn thought. *I can't walk through lightning! I can't walk a single step right now!* He shook his head, distracted himself from thinking, pulled out the flask at his waist, and gulped down sake.

The flask hit the grass, empty.

"I better be treated better than the emperor himself for this," Glenn muttered as his hands stabilized.

He gripped the staff firmly and rounded the tree.

His heart was still pounding.

But there was a pleasant buzz in his head that distracted him from the absurdity of his task.

Glenn charged, metus stone spear pointed ahead.

There was a god-like clashing of wielding powers before him.

Lighting was wrapped around a gigantic manifestation of wings.

The earth vibrated.

Crackling stunned his ears.

The air smelled burnt by the energies.

Eos better never complain about anything again.

I'm done with wielders after this insanity!

Glenn plunged his entire body into the lightning cage.

Dwarfed by the veil of feathered lava above, Glenn adjusted the level of his staff so that the spear point would find its mark.

Lightning parted before him.

CHAPTER THIRTY-TWO

I'm not going to die?

Metus stone drove into Vistomus' back ribs.

Glenn wrenched the wooden staff down, breaking off the pointed tip, separating the staff in two, and leaving crumbling pieces of metus stone littering his body.

The circle of white bolts wavered around him.

The vines of lightning that wrestled with crimson wings shrank.

The ostaka who had raised Eos and Maxima had felled Raijin—the terror of Nippon-Wa.

The god of lightning felt his ability to wield wither into a hopeless abyss of emptiness. The metus stone took its effect, embedded in his flesh.

∞   ∞   ∞

Eos Soul Stepped up the wall of the Fujima tower, passed Durath as he enveloped a Mitad wielder in a beam of emerald light, and continued without a moment of hesitation.

As he went to the tower's door, a man with a black ponytail and sheathed katana ran away from the tiled roof. He held a child in his arms with a half of a broken book pressed between his fingers and the young boy's body.

In an instinct from his visions—he knew! This man carried both the Eye of Izanagi, in whatever form it now existed, and Grace Lapithos' journal. He sensed everything their side sought was before him—within his power and reach to affect.

The Eye could be pried away from the Mitad here and now.

The journal that held every piece of knowledge Grace had uncovered about the Lost Era, the Kenat, and so much more could be returned to the brilliant researcher's hands.

Secrets of centuries that could unravel so many mysteries.

Right there.

He could take it all.

Jezca could be killed by Tessio.

Her life or the Eye and the journal?

AKUMA

What would Aizo advise? What is the proper choice for a member of the Order? Which was disciplined? Correct? Moral?

Thoughts overwhelmed Eos as Cyra rushed by in a blur of speed.

He had to decide now before the Mitad Mirza was out of reach.

His heart took over where his logic could not decide.

Jezca is bleeding. She needs me.

It was a choice of compassion—a decision of love.

Eos burst into the tower to find the Monte Priestess pressed against the corner of the wall, bleeding through her robes as Tessio's spear flashed with untraceable speed and stabbed repeatedly at Grace and Jezca.

Cursed energy rose from Tessio like a haunting specter as he used the additional power to overwhelm two talented wielders simultaneously.

A single crimson elsu manifested and flew across the room.

It crashed into the bloodthirsty spear wielder in a burst of fiery Soul Energy.

Tessio was engulfed in the explosion.

His body hurled through the wall.

Through the hole in the plaster, Eos saw the curse mark recede from Major Clark's murder. He knew that feeling. The possession fading created a moment of clarity.

"Eos," Aizo called as he burst through the tower's entrance. His inlume crown wreathed his head in orange as a warning to any Mitad member he might encounter.

Evaluating his options as four wielders now faced him, Tessio had a moment of cold realization and followed Cyra's trail.

"Let him go," Grace uttered through a clenched jaw as she held pressure on a leg cut and began to seal it with pink energy. "We're safe. That's all that matters."

"Eos," Jezca mouthed in surprise.

"You're really here..." Eos whispered in disbelief that his shared vision had been true.

"I found you," Jezca's voice trailed weakly. Blue robes were soaked to a dark navy color by numerous surface slices.

Her brilliant pink stone eye went dim.

CHAPTER THIRTY-TWO

Eos caught her as she fell from blood loss and exhaustion.

"Bring her here," Grace said. "Let me close her wounds."

∞   ∞   ∞

Vistomus Fulmen roared, "Filthy *ostaka* trash!" at Glenn and used the fading remnants of his wielding abilities to distance himself from Talus with Soul Step.

No sooner had he done that, the lumbering Mitad giant, Bysis, came sprinting full tilt to his master. He babbled in panic about a creature called *the Bishiwal*.

Talus loathed the idea of battling Bysis again after having already faced the Cavnan Barbarian King, Zeres, and Vistomus. His focus was now on protecting Glenn.

Crimson wings sheltered the non-wielder as Vistomus cast his last bolt of lightning in a last attempt at vengeance.

"Bysis," Vistomus moaned as his vision faded into blindness. A depressing void of hollowness chilled his body and soul. Metus stone fragments were embedded throughout his flesh. "I can no longer wield. I need you to carry me to Khasun. We must see this through."

The bleached eyebrows rose in shock. "Master Vistomus…"

"No time—if the Bishiwal is here, it's coming for the Left Eye! We must get to Khasun."

Bysis scooped up the bald Mitad leader in his arms and took off, filled with fear of the horrid creature that would pursue him.

"Where, Master?" Bysis panted.

In the fading embers of his Observation Wielding, he saw no trace of his mirzas inside Fujima Tower. Dread filled him. Had he failed—no! Khasun's aura was not there either.

Vistomus coughed weakly, "They must have gone to the safehouse at the docks."

I spent so many years curating this space…the Imperial Palace for the ceremony…manipulating Nature's Path to make this single task possible. Only here. It could only be done here. No other option. Vistomus lamented the end of his efforts being disrupted by Talus' crew of wielders. *Using the Left Eye for so long during the integration ceremony must have drawn the Bishiwal…we'll be lucky to escape alive.*

The Bishiwal was pursuing them, that much he had sensed.

Not far behind.

Closing in.

Vision dimming.

Bysis found Tessio waiting near the East Garden of the Imperial Palace. The lanky Mirza stood with a spear over his shoulder, waiting to see what became of the disastrous Mitad battle.

However, three approached him.

Bysis carried Vistomus in his arms as a cloaked entity flowed over the grass like a ghoul in pursuit. The giant settled before Tessio and panted, "Things went bad, Tessio."

"You don't say?" was the spear wielder's sarcastic reply.

Vistomus was weak and barely conscious, but that didn't stop him from calculating…planning…devising a victory. "Tessio, I need you to carry me to the safehouse until Bellia can evacuate us. Bysis, hold off our pursuer until it loses our trail."

Bysis' mouth hung open, but he quickly composed himself and accepted his duty. He handed their emir master to Tessio as he slung the spear over his back into its holster.

Disobedience would result in death. Tessio would gladly carry it out himself and have a laugh about it later. There was no option, and Bysis was not cunning enough to think of a way out. He was a brute with more raw might than the other hanyo. Battle was the only way he knew.

Then, with a scarred back and mostly empty Soul Reservoir, Bysis, whom the people of Nippon-Wa called one of the *hanyo*, turned to face certain doom against a real demon.

∞　　∞　　∞

Artera fell to her knees over Rius' battered body.

"You fool," she cried over his bloody heap.

The handsome face she so loyally followed was covered with his long brunette hair and blood. His aura was undetectable.

CHAPTER THIRTY-TWO

Why couldn't you resist your ego-driven battle lust? What about that Bellator tempted you badly that you had to prove yourself?

She beat the ground with her caramel hands in frustration.

"How are you going to find him now? How are you going to avenge your little brother? You idiot!"

Her hand touched his chest hesitantly.

There was a faint thump against her palm.

It was almost unnoticeable with how weak the heart was beating.

One last chance. It'll cost me...but I'll give some of my life force...happily.

I want to hear you call me Ara one more time.

Inner Path Four—Healing Veil!

Snow white Soul Energy enveloped Rius as she nursed him with her own life. Regular healing arts wouldn't be enough to save him in his current state.

She felt her heartbeat connect with his.

Warmth spread from her hands.

Rius glowed under her aura.

Time passed. Eyelids flicked open.

"Thank the Great Soul," Artera whispered.

His bright green eyes shimmered like emeralds under her healing light. She shook her head in disbelief and joy. "What are we going to do now?"

"I...made plans...Bellia will...come for us." Rius' words were like catching the extinguishing light of a firefly. Weak and faint, he barely finished the sentence.

"Bellia? Why would she do that?" Artera asked angrily. "You failed. Vistomus will kill you! I abandoned my mission. We're as good as dead! Both of us!"

"Provisions...I made provisions..."

"What could you have possibly done to earn a second chance?"

"Not a second chance...a way out..." Rius said, his words faint.

"What did you do?" Artera wondered anxiously.

"Copied letters...for Ares."

"Oh no. Whose letters?"

AKUMA

Rius managed his last words, "Vistomus…and Raggan's. Ares asked me to. Plans…I…" he slipped away.

White light hummed as Artera filled with dread.

ßCHAPTER THIRTY-THREE

LIGHTNING CATCHER

The Meiji Jingu Shrine had turned into a samurai encampment. In addition to Saigo's remaining warriors, the shrine hosted the combined kami forces of both Saier Fey and Talus Bellator's parties in the morning following what was remembered as the Great Kokyo Kami Siege.

A crested ibis glided overhead as Eos and Aizo walked through the shrine grounds. Its vibrant red face contrasted against white feathers, reminding Eos to check on Ahktar. The noble elsu landed on his arm and accepted an offering of seeds before bursting away with a stream of aura in the sky that could be perceived for miles.

LIGHTING CATCHER

Thank you, Ahktar. You stopped Vistomus' attack and bought me time for Father to arrive. That's twice you've saved my life on Nippon-Wa. I don't have enough seeds to pay you back in full.

Eos had reunited with Maxima, who had been believed dead for months. It had been even more joyous than after the battle with Ares at the Thelon River. He held his beloved sister close, and the two barely slept as they recounted their time apart. She had worn a blue corcinth mask to hide her identity the entire time and now carried a new, confident demeanor.

Shaking his head in joyous amusement that his sister was alive after all, Eos broke the morning silence in nature with his inlume master. A weight suppressed his happiness. Duty gripped his heart.

"Aizo, I've made so many mistakes…and you taught me to take responsibility, to think like the inlume I want to be, to put the group's mission before my own desires…but…"

Stroking his wild gray-bronze hair, Aizo laughed. "Please don't tell me you've done something else foolish that you haven't told me about. There's only so much my heart can take after the battle we had."

"No," Eos reflected, "it's not that. I just…I'm not sure I made the right choice."

"Which choice was that?"

Golden eyes flickered with passionate memory. "When I arrived at the Fujima Tower, I knew that the Mirza passing by carried half of Grace's journal—all the secrets we want to keep out of their hands…that we want to learn ourselves. I *knew* he was also carrying away the Left Eye of Izanagi in that boy. *I knew* everything we were fighting for was getting away…and yet…"

"Yet, you went to save Jezca despite it all?" Aizo finished.

"I weighed it. I didn't know what the right decision was. You told me to act with discipline. To act like an inlume, but that's getting more difficult to discern."

Aizo let out a large sigh and put an arm around Eos. "My boy, if you hadn't rushed in to defend that girl, I would've disowned you as my student."

CHAPTER THIRTY-THREE

Eos' face was blank with shock. "I made the right choice? The Mitad got away with the Left Eye and Grace's notes. I thought maybe that was just my selfish desire that won."

"It may very well be your selfish desire," Aizo said, chuckling deeply again. "You chose a human life over items. It was a difficult decision, but perhaps Jezca is more important to our cause than papers and a rock. We don't know how the Great Soul moves, but your act of love and compassion was not a mistake."

A wave of relief swept over Eos, washing away the guilt he had held onto all night. At that moment, they were joined on the walking path.

Durath's regal fur cape flowed over the grass. "Master Aizo, Eos," he hailed them. "Mind if I join you?"

"Not at all," Aizo beckoned with a hand wave.

Eos felt the bulk of the leather pouch under his kimono. It simultaneously saddened and comforted him. He was still processing Carnus' death and hadn't decided whether to open the bag or keep its contents undisturbed.

"We lost Carnus," Eos said aloud. "He died to spare me from becoming one of the Voro."

"See," Aizo prodded, "that's more proof. Carnus sacrificed most of his years to keep the Left Eye from Vistomus, but in the end, let it go because he believed in your life more than the danger of the Mitad having it."

Reflecting, Eos knew this valuation must have been true for Carnus to act as he did.

Durath's deep voice echoed the Inlume's logic, "My father sacrificed his life and entire kingdom for the Bellators. *His friends*. He always told me that a good king can choose humanity over the calculated good. Carnus would have been a good king." He nodded to himself, proudly remembering Ramath's wisdom.

Aizo hummed his approval. "I miss Ramath. Always reigning in our troublemaking and bailing us out…even to his last day. Now, many tasks are beyond our ability, like the choice you had to make. Carnus was of the Hamirate Clan, and their elder, Zeri the Great, had a saying which I recite often: *The Great Soul hides his fingerprints in our struggles towards the good.*

Reflect on that and let's not talk anymore of it. Maxima is alive, and Nippon-Wa is free!"

"Well, I swore to Carnus that I'd find his son, Koda, in Primane. I intend to do that when we return to Hyperborea." Eos was determined to honor his savior's final request.

Durath's eyes went wide. "Primane territory? Now, that sounds like an adventure I could get behind. That borders Corleo!"

Aizo pinched the bridge of his nose as if overcome by a headache. "No more talk of adventures for you two. You're worse than Talus and I were at your age!"

They turned to lighter conversation as they returned to the shrine, passing through the natural cypress wood grains of the torii gate entrance.

Under the shrine's sweeping Meiji-era roof, Jezca was reconnecting with Grace and learning about her lost Lapithos heritage, Siago and Saitani were having tea and discussing restoration plans, and Maxima tended to Saier Fey with Talus observing.

"Maxima, you're a wonder worker," Fey commended Maxima as she let a soft glow of sapphire fall from her hands to Fey's amputated leg. "No wielder your age is as talented at so many disciplines…but I will still need to get to the Sanofem when we're back in Anondorn. Your efforts are keeping Zeres' remaining poison at bay, but there are still traces trying to spread through my leg."

Talus stroked his braided beard as he sat cross-legged.

"We'll get you the care you need immediately, Master Fey." Talus shook his head, astonished. "I can't believe you ended up here. My daughter was dead, then she crossed worlds to rejoin me under the tutelage of her mother's teacher!"

Grimacing in pain, Fey clarified, "I'm only watching her. Didn't sign up for any new pupils. *I'm retired!*" She gave Maxima a wink.

Talus smirked, "How could I forget? *Retired.* Of course. It seems my daughter picked up enough wielding skill to defeat the Cavnan Barbarian King by your side…as you got some much-needed *retirement exercise.*"

Without drawing the attention of Talus, Fey reached into Maxima's sleeve and tapped the faded stain of her violet ash promise.

CHAPTER THIRTY-THREE

When Aizo returned, Jezca tended to the burns left by Bysis.

After a few minutes of soothing healing, while she chanted a prayer in the old tongue, Aizo brushed her away. "Thank you, Priestess, but I got away with minor injuries. You don't need to be worrying over me." He let a flare of orange erupt from his fingertip to demonstrate his vigor.

"As you wish, Inlume Mudar." Jezca bowed her head.

"Besides," Aizo said teasingly, "there's someone else who I think you should be tending to before me."

Jezca found Eos outside near two camphor trees tied together by a tasseled rope. He was reading a placard that described the *shimenawa* rope made of rice straw that bound the more than one hundred-year-old trees together.

"I guess we're going to share dreams and visions for the rest of our lives, Eos," Jezca mused. She approached with her platinum hair pulled back, proudly displaying her anima stone eye.

She wore a golden belt with the Manus Priesthood's emblem of folded hands before a stone, and a beautiful, chained circlet glimmered on her head.

Eos caught himself staring a few seconds longer than he intended and smiled. "I don't think it's so bad. The visions have saved us both now. I'd say they paid themselves off...mostly."

Jezca laughed with a shy yet genuine happiness she hadn't felt since the Mircite Valley. "I *have* gotten to know you even though we've been worlds apart."

"Oh, you think you know me from a few dreams?" Eos tested playfully.

"Eos Bellator, I've seen you strike military leaders in the face and stand in front of a gun as a child to protect your sister. I've seen you face down the infamous Ares for what you believed in. I was there when you helped us take down the Mircite Valley factories. I think I know plenty well what kind of man you are."

Eos blushed, realizing Jezca had been dreaming just as much as he had, and she had seen into his intimate childhood.

LIGHTING CATCHER

"Oh…all that?" Eos stumbled on his words. "Well, I'd say you're cheating." He stepped closer to meet Jezca between the two united Japanese trees.

Golden eyes stared into Jezca, and for the first time, she felt like she was the one being looked into with supernatural sight.

Distracted by Eos' presence, she managed to let out, "Yeah…maybe I cheated a little bit."

Jezca offered to heal Eos, and they sat under the camphor tree shade, talking as her feminine touch cast a soft pink glow over his wounds.

Not long after, an envoy appeared to announce the arrival of Emperor Antoku, who sought an audience with Saitani Umetaro, Saigo Takayoshi, Talus Bellator, and all the kami involved in liberating Nippon-Wa.

The Emperor was coming to announce unconditional surrender.

The required parties gathered in the central shrine chamber as Emperor Antoku was carried in on a palanquin. The wooden structure, ornamented with golden cranes and red curtains, resembled his throne room.

The curtains were drawn back to reveal a young boy seated on a lacquered throne seat. His child's body was engulfed in the sokutai ceremonial garb of his office. The sleeves of his outer robe draped to the floor in streams of brownish-red. His boyish face was adorned with a kanmuri silk cap crested with the imperial royal family chrysanthemum.

The eleven-person audience consisted of Saigo, Saitani, Glenn, and the Hyperborean wielders, except for Fey who rested from her injuries. They all bowed before the Emperor as he stood to address them.

"It is with joy that I announce my surrender in this battle," Emperor Antoku's adolescent voice echoed in heavily accented English. "My father, Toba, would have shuddered at such words but could not have foreseen the evil kami, Raijin, holding his throne hostage. Thanks to all your efforts, Nippon-Wa is once again free. Let me start by thanking the fearsome Raijin Slayer. Which of you accomplished this feat of god-like battle prowess?"

CHAPTER THIRTY-THREE

Before an answer came, Eos and Maxima simultaneously stifled giggling. They remembered the title of the nobility before them and held back any jokes they would have otherwise made.

"That would be me, Your Majesty," Glenn began hesitantly after shooting both of the children he had helped raise sharp looks.

"Your name, great warrior?" Emperor Antoku asked.

"Glenn Parker."

"You shall be honored in Nippon-Wa forever as the Great Raijin Slayer, Glenn Parker. Perhaps it is no more than a trinket to such a powerful warrior, but I would like to offer you the finest katana from my personal collection. Is there anything else I can offer you to show our gratitude?"

"I'm honored..." Glenn was lost for words. He hadn't expected to see a fraction of the action he had endured, let alone be involved in defeating the Mitad during the battle. "I only came to see Japan...I never intended to—"

"Ah!" Emperor Antoku burst out. "Then, you shall be given the finest tour of Nippon-Wa. All food, drink, and accommodations shall be provided to the hero of our nation."

"He'll drink the country dry," Eos snickered to Maxima.

Glenn once again shot a fearsome look at the siblings.

"No respect," he muttered to himself. "That would be excellent, Your Majesty."

"It is settled then. You will enjoy our hospitality and see our country. Perhaps Saigo or Saitani have a companion in mind for your tour."

Saitani lifted his large body up from his prostration and interjected, "Glenn has friends within our organization that he's worked with. I have just the two men in mind for the trip."

Glenn's face went pale as he realized Saitani intended to send him on a journey with Minoru and Kamatari. Glenn murmured to himself, "On second thought, maybe a nice return to Colonel Kane's bunkers would be nice."

"Next," Emperor Antoku continued, "I would like to welcome Saitani and Saigo back to the Imperial Advisory. Your wisdom has been missed, and your advice has been felt in this battle."

LIGHTING CATCHER

"We are honored to rejoin your council, Emperor Antoku," Saigo returned. "I will serve you as I served your father and advise you as I always have since you were a small boy."

Emperor Antoku continued, "Thank you. Yet, I am deeply saddened by the loss of Kikujiro. I consider it the loss of my own brother since you raised me for many years. We shall honor him with a grand memorial fitting of the High Priest of the Grand Ise Shrine."

This brought some consolation to Saigo's weary soul. His body was beaten down, and his heart was tired from leading a resistance to the kami infiltration for so long. His head was scarred from Ahktar, and his chest wounds barely allowed him to move in the presence of the Emperor, but finally, there was rest in the future.

"Thank you, Emperor Antoku-heika. Let us remember him with the new freedom of Nippon-Wa, which he long sought," Saigo concluded.

"Finally, I must express my eternal gratitude to the kami who defeated all of Raijin's hanyo. For too long, they have terrorized the innocent people of our nation."

Talus answered, "We only regret that someone from our world brought so much suffering here."

"Will you stay in Nippon-Wa for a while?" the Emperor asked.

"No," Talus sighed. "Your people have had enough of kami in their land. Raijin has created problems in our home world. We must get back to help our people, and our injured require special care."

"Then you will return to Takamagahara?" The Emperor referred to Hyperborea by the name of the high plane of the kami.

"Yes," Talus affirmed. "As soon as today, if we're able."

Formalities drew on, but hours later, the Hyperboreans were saying their goodbyes, leaving Glenn in the care of Saigo and Saitani.

Then, the nine stood under the torii gate.

The entire shrine had a magical atmosphere, peaceful and filled with something beyond the physical realm. This effect was concentrated most at the torii gates. The upward-curved kasagi roof on the shrine entrance created a threshold of wonder to pass under. Bounded by the natural wooden pillars, the entryway towered above the wielders.

CHAPTER THIRTY-THREE

Grace had brought them to the gate. She explained, "There are places of concentrated Nature Energy—the kind that can be seen with the Left Eye of Izanagi. Maxima, do you remember where you were when you left Hyperborea?"

Maxima nodded. "We were in the Setudo Castle, overlooking the lake. The portal opened over the lake, and we had to run to it to escape Saida."

Grace hummed as if Maxima had affirmed her explanation. "Setudo Royal Lake is one such place. In Nippon-Wa, these torii gates can be points in the nexus between our worlds...like this one."

"Then it's time to go home." Eos smiled, marveling that he was able to say such a thing when there was a time, not long ago, when he did not know Hyperborea existed.

"Together," Maxima added happily.

"Together," Eos affirmed. "I only wish we could bring the Left Eye back with us."

Talus ended the pessimistic reflection, "The Bellator family is reunited, and you two have accomplished more than any anatus Soul Wielders of your generation already. I'd say freeing Nippon-Wa and finding Grace was enough of an outcome for this *simple information-gathering mission* we started."

Eos' expression perked up at the feedback. "Father, it *sounds like* we're ready to be promoted to errants," he joked, knowing the anxiety it would cause Talus and Aizo.

Quick to jump in, Aizo shot them down. "I can only imagine the mischief you'd cause as an errant! You're not ready for such trials—nor am I!"

Grace sobered the conversation. "The Bellators have saved me and this country. Still, the Mitad have a new human weapon that we don't understand."

"And the Bishiwal have returned," Fey added, leaning on her crutch as she prepared to cross worlds.

Eos looked at Maxima, Jezca, and Durath. His voice was humble and confident. "With all of us working together...I think we can handle anything."

LIGHTING CATCHER

Fey shared a knowing look with Grace. It was a glance of Priori knowledge. They had much to prepare for when they returned to Hyperborea.

Smirking at his reckless optimism, Grace nudged Maxima and asked, "Are you ready to open the portal?"

Maxima held up the Mellizo Glyph taken from Saida's vault.

At the catalyst of Maxima's Soul Energy, the runes on the rectangular vial glowed, and it excited a reaction at the threshold of the torii gate. The space between began to shimmer, waver, and open the fabric of their world.

The nine wielders and Ahktar passed through the gateway, leaving Nippon-Wa and Earth behind.

Walking alone along the path, Saigo saw the dying embers of Soul Energy wisps as the torii gate became a simple wooden structure once more.

"Catching lightning in a troubled land, the white wings fly free like mine..." Saigo recited the poem created from his vision. He reminisced, "You would have made a fine samurai, Eos. You have the heart to catch lightning."

www.ingramcontent.com/pod-product-compliance
Lightning Source LLC
Chambersburg PA
CBHW030537020726
47494CB00005B/1413